The Wizard's Crown

Art of the Adept
Volume 5

By

Michael G. Manning

Cover by Christian Bentulan
Map Artwork by Maxime Plasse
Editing by Keri Karandrakis
© 2022 by Michael G. Manning
All rights reserved.
Printed in the United States of America

ISBN: 978-1-943481-44-6

For more information about the Mageborn series check out the author's
Facebook page:

https://www.facebook.com/MagebornAuthor

or visit the website:

http://www.magebornbooks.com

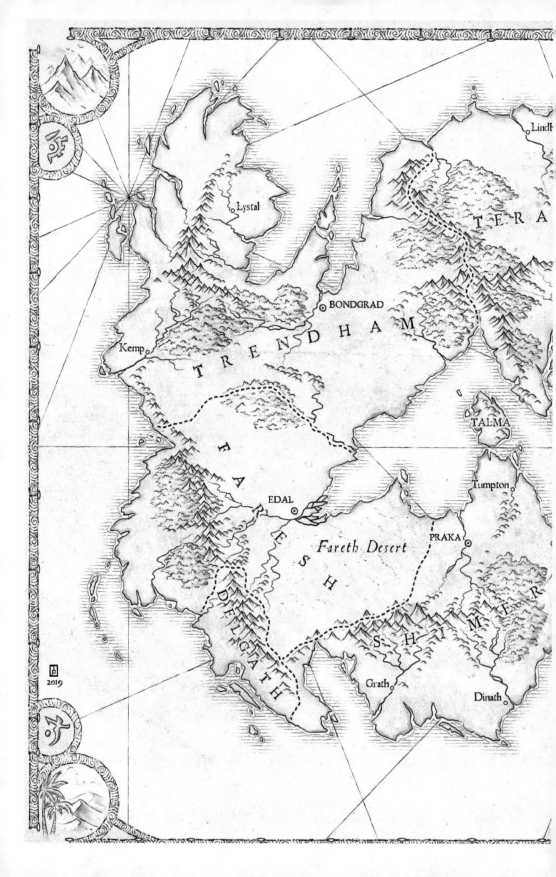

CHAPTER 1

"Try again," Will ordered, his voice firm. Selene began the spell again, but as the construct neared completion, Will spoke up once more. "Stop." Her construct froze in place, the next rune wavering in the air as she tried to slot it into its position. Her brows knitted together as she strove to finish the task.

The tip of her tongue emerged from the side of her mouth, and her face twisted into a strange expression, but nothing happened. "It feels like all the turyn turned to solid stone," she complained. The runes of her construct began to slowly wink out as the spell unmade itself piece by piece. "How are you doing that?" she growled in frustration.

"It's my spell," said Will smugly. "It's only natural—I can do whatever I want with it." Lifting one hand, he beckoned toward the spell construct as though it were a person, and it drifted toward him obediently, as though it were a dog rather than simple energy.

"No," Selene snapped, moving between him and the traitorous spell. Her hands reached out to it and the spell construct shivered.

Will whistled in admiration, then added, "That's it. I can feel you pulling at it." For a moment, the spell paused, and it seemed that Selene might regain control, then it slipped through her fingers and passed completely through her body on its way to Will's open palm. He spun it in place for a second, then dismissed the runes, causing them to scatter into shimmering sparks that soon faded.

She stared at him in frustration for a moment. "That's so unfair. I learned magic before you did."

"But you weren't a third-order wizard."

Her eyes narrowed. "I am now, supposedly."

"I started down this path before you did," Will replied. "It's to be expected that you'll have to play catchup for a while. Whether you'll be stronger or not"—he shrugged—"who knows?"

"What determines that?"

"According to Arrogan, it depends on several factors: the wizard's order, time, practice, and their native talent."

"You mean their stubbornness."

Will grinned. "I said that too, but the old man said that it isn't really the same as the personality trait. It isn't really skill either. While it seems to become stronger as you practice, a wizard can be highly skilled but still not have the same strength of will as someone less skilled."

She nodded. "Like when you took that spell away from Ethelgren."

"He was really strong," said Will, "but it might be that I'm just naturally gifted with a high degree of magical stubbornness." He stared at her for a moment, secretly admiring the shape of her ever so faintly crooked nose. No one would dare mention the tiny flaw in the symmetry of her features, but Will found it endlessly attractive for reasons he couldn't name. He reengaged his brain, hoping she wouldn't notice the lapse. "I know how unfair it feels though, having your magic suppressed. I felt the same way facing the demon-lord, not to mention the lich."

Selene chewed her lip for a moment, thinking. "At least you had your, what did you call it before, resistance?"

Will nodded. "You have it too. They call it resistance, but it's just a function of having a strong will. Control weakens with distance, so even a really powerful wizard has trouble making their turyn directly affect another wizard. Unless they're really close, I suppose."

She raised one brow. "Define close."

He used a simple spell to create a floating ball of fire, then directed it slowly toward her. It burned steadily until it was within a few inches of her skin, then the flames began to falter as the turyn feeding them began to unravel. "I'm a few feet away, but it's right next to you," said Will. "My distance and your proximity make it difficult for me to force it to do something you wouldn't want. Physical harm is something we always strive to avoid at a level far below conscious thought, so your will is even stronger when it comes to being burned."

"Thank goodness for that."

Will moved closer, until their faces were just a few inches apart. "But now I'm just as close and the distance is no longer much of an advantage." He pressed the flame closer, and it burned brighter, causing the hairs on her arm to curl and smoke. Selene refused to flinch, but her nostrils flared as the heat against her skin began to become painful. A faint hiss escaped her lips.

Rather than relent as she had expected, an evil light came into Will's eyes, and his gaze became intense. The fire brushed against her, and Selene felt her skin begin to burn. "Will, stop!"

The fire fizzled and died, but Will merely smiled. "Not bad."

She backed up a step and rubbed her arm. It was red and some of the hair was gone, but the skin wasn't actually seared. She gave him a hard look. "You went too far. You would have burned me for real if you had kept going."

His expression was smooth and even. "I didn't stop. You did that."

She gaped at him. "And if I hadn't?"

"You'd have to do some healing, or get me to practice mine."

"That isn't funny. You know burns aren't easy to heal. Do you want to leave me with scars?"

Will grimaced, and a faint look of apology crossed his features, but it vanished just as quickly. "I'd still love you the same. It's more important to me to know you're safe."

"From everyone but my husband, apparently," she said sourly.

"From me too," he amended. "Just remember, force effects can't be stopped the same way."

"I'm still practicing the point-defense spell, but I don't know when I'll be able to reflex cast it." She gave him an inquisitive look. "How's your own practice going? You haven't said much lately."

He frowned. "Slowly."

"Maybe you should spend more time with our students rather than keep beating your head against the wall practicing."

"And do what? They can't do anything right now but adjust to the compression. I've set their exercises and check on them daily. Aside from that, all I can do is provide a good example and hone my own skills."

There was a subtle sense of approval visible in her gaze, but her words were challenging. "You're seeking more power. Is that really necessary? You can reflex cast more spells than any wizard or sorcerer alive today, and your strength of will is almost too much to believe. Why push for more?"

He was familiar with her devil's advocate conversational style, and he knew her questions were merely meant to reaffirm his choices. In the past, such tricks would have annoyed him, either because of his own naivety or because it showed manipulative intentions on the part of the speaker. From Selene, it actually soothed his nerves, because he trusted her down to his bones. The little debates she sparked served to help him examine himself and ensured the two of them were still in line with each other regarding their plans for the future.

"I do want more power," he said honestly. "What I have isn't enough. It will never be enough, not as long as creatures like Grim Talek exist. If he were to appear now, I could do little to protect anyone, except maybe myself, and even that is questionable."

"You can't protect everyone."

"Without power I can't protect *anyone*. The more I can do, the more options I have, even in the worst situations."

A faint motion beside the open doorway at the far end of the hall they were practicing in might have alerted a wary person to the presence of a possible observer, but neither Will nor Selene seemed to notice. "You won't need any of that for our plan, and once Lognion is dead our greatest threat will be gone."

"I'll need it for our cover plan to be credible."

She paused, then nodded. "You're right."

Will smirked. "You just wanted to hear me say it, but I know you're just the same. You've been working yourself hard every spare moment you get. Together we'll survive this."

Her faced showed pride for a moment, then uncertainty crept back into her expression. "Seeing your confidence makes me feel better."

"Confidence, or ambition?"

"In my world they're practically the same thing," she answered. "I know you don't really want any of this, but I'm not sure of myself."

Will laughed. "You're all of it. My contribution is negligible. Have you made contact with all of them yet?"

She nodded. "It's all under the table, but most of them have given subtle hints that they'll fall in line should the power structure suddenly have a dramatic shift." She saw Will relax, but then hurried to add, "It doesn't mean anything, though. The lords pay attention to the direction of the wind better than any sailor. If there's any hint of weakness, they'll toss me to the wolves."

"Us," he corrected.

Her eyes met his. "That's why you're so important to this. They need a bigger wolf to strike enough fear in them that they don't step out of line."

"We're still aiming for the week before the Winter Ball?"

Selene frowned. "That's the decoy plan. We move a few days before that."

"I misspoke," said Will. "That's what I meant. I'm still nervous, though."

"About what? You don't have to do much."

"The timing. Maybe we should wait."

Her eyes flashed a warning. "We can't wait. It has to happen as soon as possible, and this is the best we can manage. If we delay, you won't be around to see whether it works or not."

"But the information we have indicates the king won't act until the spring…"

"That's *his* decoy plan," hissed Selene. "That's the only reason we learned about it, to lull us into a false sense of security. If we were well informed enough to peel back all the layers, there's a second plan, likely sooner, but even it won't be the main one. It'll just be a backup, and something completely different than the primary plan. The one he intends to kill you with will be much sooner and something so simple you won't expect it."

Will rubbed his temples. "This is all too devious. It makes my head hurt."

"That's why you did so well in the war. Complicated plans fall apart. You kept yours simple and to the point. Father knows that too, which is why the real plan will be the simplest one. Don't try to figure it all out. You'll put yourself at risk of making a mistake. Let me handle the intrigue."

He raised one brow. "You think you're tricky enough to outsmart him? You weren't able to lie to him, just like everyone else."

"I grew up under his thumb. I couldn't lie to him, but don't underestimate me. I hid plenty from him."

A new voice reached them from outside the hall. "What are you doing?" They both recognized it as Tabitha's.

"Bringing them the news," said Laina.

"Then go in, or better yet, I'll tell them myself," said Tabitha. A moment later, she strode through the open archway and began walking toward them. Laina followed a step behind her.

"I didn't want to interrupt," said Laina in a low voice.

"More likely you were eavesdropping," replied Tabitha from the side of her mouth. Her voice was soft, but Will had enhanced his hearing and could easily pick out the words.

"That's your hobby, not mine," growled Laina, but there was a sheepish look on her face when she met Will's gaze.

He glanced at Selene, then back at his two sisters. Selene wouldn't have been able to hear what had been said, but he could tell her later. With a smile, he greeted them. "Some news afoot?"

Laina scowled, and her mouth opened but her younger sister cut her off. "Mother needs me at home. Do you mind?" asked Tabitha.

Laina showed almost nothing outwardly, but Will felt a ripple run through her. Their connection was almost imperceptible most of the time, but standing this close he could almost feel her emotions. Tabitha had surprised her. "You're still adjusting to the second compression," Will stated. "I don't know if this is a good time."

"I already feel close to normal again and it will only be a couple of weeks," said his sister, calmly making her case. "I'll be back long before you're willing to let me try the third compression."

He felt another ripple of disbelief from Laina. Or was it more than that? Will glanced over to look in the older sister's eyes. *Does she think Tabitha is lying?* Laina looked down, but Will addressed her anyway, "What do you think?"

Laina's chin came up, and her fire returned. "If we're being *honest,* this is a terrible time. Tabitha should remain here."

"Why do you need to go home?" asked Selene. "Is Agnes well?"

"She's fine," said Tabitha quickly. "If you don't mind, I'd rather not say. It's a private matter."

Laina's anger was simmering like an overheated pot left on the fire too long. Will imagined he could almost feel heat radiating around her. "We could talk about it," suggested Selene. "I hope you know you can trust us with—"

"It's a family matter," said Tabitha brusquely. Her tone became apologetic almost immediately after, and she hastened to add, "Not that I don't think of you as family, but this isn't mine to share." She cast a hopeful gaze at Will.

"I suppose it will be all right," he said slowly. "As long as you don't overwork yourself and you make sure you return within two weeks."

Tabitha looked relieved, but Laina's agitation rose to new heights. "If you'll excuse me then, I need to go pack," said Tabitha. After Selene nodded, she turned away, but Laina made no move to leave. Tabitha looked back. "Laina if you don't mind, I could use your help."

Will expected a snappy response, but Laina kept her composure. "Of course."

Moments later, the two of them were out of the room. Selene looked at Will. "What did you make of that?"

"Laina's mad, and she knows Tabitha isn't telling the full truth."

"I could tell that much," she responded pertly. "What do you think it could be?"

He shrugged. "I don't have to wonder. Laina will tell me later."

"Or she'll tell me," Selene returned with a smirk.

Will gave her a challenging look. "I'm her brother."

His wife lifted her chin in response. "She's my best friend."

He lifted one brow. "We've shared souls."

"You're also a boy. I suspect this may be something she'd prefer to discuss with her own kind."

"I was a girl for a while," he argued, but Selene rose on her toes and nipped his jawline in a surprise move that startled him—as well as starting a chain reaction of other physiological responses. "Are you trying to win by distracting me?"

"It's only fair. You started it."

That surprised him. "How?"

She eyed him up and down. "Standing there like that, square-shouldered and confident, plus look at what you're wearing." Selene shook her head. "You're obviously trying to distract *me*."

He laughed. "These are my practice clothes—and might I remind you, you're the one who chooses my wardrobe these days."

"But you're the one who wears them like that." She paused, then clucked her tongue at him in mock disapproval. "Such a wanton, and now you remind me you were a girl for a short time. Poor Laina. She's lucky she got her body back so quickly. Who knows what someone like you would have done with it?"

CHAPTER 2

The next day, Will was sitting at his desk, which was situated in an exotic room that seemed to have more in common with a balcony than an office. There was a roof over it, but two walls of the room were taken up by massive double doors that were kept open when the weather was nice. As a result, the room was supplied with a pleasant breeze and plenty of light, plus the scent of the greenery outside.

He didn't actually have much in the way of paperwork. Blake was much better at that, so most of Will's time in the office was spent on other matters, and lately that mainly consisted of him working his way through the secrets of the Wayfarer's Society. As part of the new accord, his grandmother had turned over copies of everything she had learned when she found their hidden vault. Some of that Will had shared with Wurthaven, allowing them to begin constructing a teleport beacon in Cerria as well as another in Myrsta. When finished, the two beacons would enable easy teleportation between the two sister nations that had recently been unified.

The construction of the beacons involved complex theories and advanced artifice that were beyond his current skills, but he was learning. Master Courtney and the researchers at Wurthaven were the ones making the real effort, but Will didn't see any reason he shouldn't at least learn as much as possible. More importantly, there were other facets of transportation magic, which would prove invaluable to any magic user who could master them.

The first and most obviously valuable information gained was regarding the base teleportation spell itself. That spell hadn't been lost, but without the beacons, it had become mostly useless for long distance travel, or so most had believed. The knowledge left behind by the Wayfarer's Society contradicted that common wisdom.

While the teleportation spell was still taught at Wurthaven, to those who bothered to learn it, it was severely limited in its application because the caster could only travel to a location they could see. Add to that the spell wasn't just ninth- or even tenth-order, it was considered twelfth-order, which was really just a short way to state that a spell was too complex for a person to memorize, much less construct and cast in a reasonable length of time.

The few modern wizards who had learned it only memorized sections of it, and they referred to the written text while constructing the spell in order to complete it without mistakes. As a result, it took extensive practice to master and took nearly a quarter of an hour to cast. Combined with the line-of-sight limitation, the spell had become little more than a magical curiosity in modern times.

According to Arrogan, during the days when the beacons had still been active, a few highly accomplished wizards within the Wayfarer's Society had used the spell often enough to actually become able to reflex cast it, but none of them had been third-order wizards. That had seemed strange, so Will had asked, "Why not?"

"The founder was a second-order wizard named Flandry. He was well before my time, but according to most he was highly ambitious and never quite got over the fact that he never got the opportunity to try the third compression during his apprenticeship."

"Why not?"

"His master was second-order. I told you before, most teachers wouldn't train their students beyond their own capability. There were only a few third-order wizards at any given time, so for the most part, only their students were given the chance to try. Anyway, back to Flandry—he was jealous of those who exceeded him in raw power, so he was always driven to prove his superiority. He had a notoriously short temper and gained a reputation for threatening other wizards who argued with him."

Will frowned. "That doesn't seem wise."

His grandfather chuckled. "He had balls, though that's hardly unique. What was unique about him was that Flandry was able to follow up on his threats. He gained fame for challenging a third-order wizard to a duel and killing the man."

"Really? Was his will that strong?"

"For a second-order wizard, it was undoubtedly exceptional, and the wizard he fought was an enchanter, so he probably wasn't the strongest third-order wizard Flandry could have tackled, but Flandry won through skill, not strength."

Will knew from his experience with Ethelgren that his grandfather didn't have a lot of respect for wizards who relied too much on relics and enchantments instead of developing their natural spellcasting abilities.

"Skill? If the other wizard was third-order, wouldn't he just suppress Flandry's spells?"

"You can't suppress force spells. Flandry practiced—obsessively— and his opponent didn't. The end result wasn't just a win, but what the courts decided was effectively a murder. Since it was a duel, the sentence was rather lenient, but Flandry spent twenty years in prison."

"Twenty years is lenient?"

"It is when you might live to be three-hundred," replied Arrogan. "He was second-order, remember? Anyway, it worked out well for everyone. During his incarceration Flandry couldn't do much but he was still obsessed with regaining his freedom and proving his superiority. He spent most of that time working on the foundations of teleportation and travel magic."

"He created the teleport spell to escape?"

Arrogan snorted. "Maybe, but he didn't. He waited until the day he was supposed to be released and teleported out of his cell. He made sure they saw him do it, just as a way of letting the authorities know he could have left whenever he pleased. He really became famous after that, and over the next year he founded the Wayfarer's Society, and they began building beacons in every major city—but he would never let third-order wizards join, nor would he teach them any of his secrets."

"Wow," said Will. "I guess he had the last laugh."

"Not really," said the ring. "The mother of the wizard he killed wasn't too happy about his success after prison. She killed him just a few years after he was released."

"Was she a wizard too?"

"She was, but she didn't use magic to kill him. She just walked straight up to him, and before he knew what was what, she shoved a fillet knife through his chin and into his brain. He died almost instantly, but from what people used to say, she kept at him for a while. People could hardly recognize him by the time they pulled her off of him."

The memory of Selene repeatedly stabbing Bug after his nearly successful assassination attempt flashed into Will's mind, causing him to shiver. "I've seen that sort of fury a few times."

"Then you should also know that a wizard has to keep their cool. A knife is one thing, but if you lose your mind with magic, a lot more people could get hurt."

Will had lost control of himself a few times already. Each time had resulted in spectacular destruction, and he considered it almost a miracle that he hadn't done something so bad he couldn't live with himself. "I'll keep that in mind," he answered.

"Do. That's why she used a knife. Back when wizards were more common, that was one of the big rules. Never use magic when angry."

"You didn't teach me that one."

Arrogan laughed. "Well, it's wise to keep your cool, but we usually get angry for a reason. If I'd followed that rule, a lot more bad things would have happened than did. Try to stay calm and rational, that's my best advice. I wouldn't have taught you to begin with if I thought you were prone to fits of rage."

Will felt uncomfortable thinking about it. During the recent war, he'd lost his temper on several occasions, and he still wasn't certain if the end result was justifiable. He ended the conversation and went back to studying the books in front of him. It was shortly after that when he learned the reason why the wizards of the Wayfarer's Society had been able to reflex cast the teleportation spell.

"It isn't the same spell," he muttered to himself in astonishment. The spell outlined on the page in front of him was less than half the length of the standard teleportation spell he had seen in the library. He didn't have a copy of it in his personal journals, but he was certain that the spell in front of him now was not only shorter, but much simpler. *But why?*

He considered asking Arrogan, but recalling the previous conversation gave him a pretty good guess. *Flandry deliberately made the public version difficult to use,* thought Will. The spell laid out before him now was complex, but not so complex that he couldn't memorize it. It was probably around sixth- or seventh-order in complexity, and Will had already mastered other more difficult magics. There was no reason he couldn't do the same with this one.

Being able to cast it relatively quickly would be handy in certain situations, and if he could eventually reflex cast it, then it would be immensely useful both in combat and when traveling, unless the energy cost was extremely high. He'd have to practice with it to know for sure. The line-of-sight limitation was still a problem, but as he read further, it seemed that some of the members of the Wayfarer's Society could teleport great distances—without having a beacon to target.

Unfortunately, the text didn't explicitly state how that was done. It laid out the necessary qualities for a teleport beacon to operate successfully and then casually mentioned an alternative at the end. *"Of course, those who have mastered the gates of the mind may see places beyond the eye and travel farther than those who have not."*

Will stared at the page in frustration until he realized he was growling at the book. He pushed it away with a sigh and stared at the ceiling. "But how, damn it?" Glancing up, he saw a startling pair of bright viridian eyes staring at him from the open balcony doors. Will froze.

A grey cat was sitting quietly in a bright spot where the sunlight pooled on the floor. It met his gaze calmly for a long minute, then casually began licking one paw to groom its face. Will's heart was pounding in his chest, but after his mind started working again, he felt a wave of disappointment wash over him.

It wasn't the goddamn cat. This cat was similar in appearance, but it had longer hair and a flowing white ruff under its chin as well as white stockinged feet. A few seconds later, he realized it was also probably female, judging by the head. He studied the cat's turyn for a moment, just to be sure, but there was nothing out of the ordinary to be seen.

It's just a regular cat, he told himself. *Or is it?* The goddamn cat had also appeared completely normal most of the time—until it was necessary to be otherwise. "Hello?"

The cat ignored his greeting, seemingly being absorbed in her afternoon bath.

"Have we met before?" asked Will.

His visitor declined to respond.

"Can you talk?" He had to ask, though he felt foolish even as he did.

The cat looked up, and almost as if she was responding deliberately, opened her mouth and trilled at him. Will sat back in his chair and let out his pent-up breath. *Of course, she's just a normal cat,* he thought. Something wet rolled down his face, and he lifted one arm to wipe his cheek with the sleeve.

He took control of himself then and sat up straight again. "I shouldn't be rude, should I?" he said, directing his words at the cat. "Wait right there. I'll be back." He half expected the cat to vanish the moment he stood up, but she stayed put. Heading out the door, he went downstairs and hurried to the kitchen.

There were plenty of things there that one could offer a cat, but Will chose a large piece of ham left over from the previous day's evening meal and cut it into what he thought would be bite-sized bits. Jeremy, the cook that Selene had hired, watched him curiously but said nothing. Will scooped the meat trimmings into one hand and left without explanation, then jogged back upstairs.

"She'll probably be gone when I get there," he told himself. Strange cats were usually rather skittish. He was surprised to see the cat sitting on his desk when he returned. She appeared completely at ease. "Did I leave a mess on your desk?" he asked.

The female cat merely looked at him and trilled once more, sending a warm feeling through his chest. *I've been bewitched,* he decided silently, expecting her to run as soon as he approached. She didn't, though, and after he had regained his seat, he opened his hand and dumped the small pile of meat trimmings onto his desk. Selene would have been horrified to see him put food directly on the lacquered wood, but she wasn't present.

"Don't tell anyone I forgot to bring a bowl," Will cautioned his guest as she began to nibble at the food. He didn't attempt to pet her, fearing it might frighten her away, so he stayed silent and watched her eat.

She seemed in remarkable shape for a stray, well-groomed and slim without seeming underfed or scrawny. "Do you live around here?" he asked. "Has someone been feeding you?"

The cat paused and gave him a look that somehow conveyed annoyance, then resumed her feast.

"Of course not," Will agreed. "You're far too smart and independent for that. I hope you'll forgive my impudence in offering you food. Clearly you aren't a beggar."

The cat finished half of what he had put down, then stopped and gave him a serious look. Will kept still. After a long pause, she first sniffed his hand, then moved closer and stretched her neck so she could bring her nose close to his. Will felt warm air as she snuffled and sniffed, then he jumped when she suddenly sneezed in his face.

The cat bolted, and after he had blinked and regained his composure, she was nowhere to be seen. Will deflated slightly, feeling disappointed, though he wasn't really sure what he had expected. Then, without warning, the door to his study opened and Laina strode in without warning. She closed the door quietly behind her.

Will and his sister stared at one another for half a minute, neither saying a word, until finally she asked, "Don't you have anything to say?"

He covertly drew a handkerchief from a desk drawer and wiped his face, unsure if there was any visible snot on it. He doubted it though. *Laina would have said something.* "You came to see me," he stated, wondering at her meaning.

"I thought you'd start badgering me after yesterday," she declared.

"Is there something you want to tell me?"

"No." Her tone was flat and final.

"Something about Tabitha?"

"No."

Will shrugged. "Then there's no point." He changed the subject, "How are you adjusting to the second compression? You seem to have recovered faster than the others." Because the king already had his magical claws on her soul, Laina was the only one who Will had been unable to use the heart-stone enchantment on to facilitate the first compression. Given the fact that Laina was already an accomplished spellcaster, the task of learning to compress her source should have been virtually impossible, yet she had somehow managed it through sheer stubborn pride.

Laina's eyes flashed with pride for a second, but the expression was quickly replaced by annoyance. "It probably runs in the family," she responded. "Aren't you curious?"

"About what?" Will kept his face studiously blank, knowing it would aggravate her.

"About—" Laina's mouth froze, and she seemed to struggle with something for a moment, then she closed her lips and recomposed herself. "You know what I'm referring to."

He knew she meant her sister's return to the capital, but for some reason Laina didn't want to state it outright. "I can guess," said Will. "But I trust you to tell me if there's something I need to know. I won't pry."

"That's a relief," she answered, her voice stony.

She's really upset, thought Will, wondering at what she really wanted. Because of that, he was already watching Laina carefully when she suddenly sprang at him, hand outstretched. She was trying to catch hold of him, to bring her skin into contact with his.

He reacted instinctively, but somehow still avoided the more violent options that had lately become all too easy for him. Rather than put a shield in front of her hand or face, which might have resulted in a painful injury, he put one beneath her leading foot as she lunged, causing her to trip and pitch forward across his desk. She started to twist, but Will leaned over and put one hand on the middle of her back, pinning her down. When Laina flailed at him with her bare hand, he caught her wrist, keeping his hand above the cuff of her sleeve to avoid direct contact.

"Just let me touch you!" she barked in frustration. "You know you want to!"

"It's too dangerous. *We* agreed on that," he snapped back. "You're stronger than this."

"That's not—!" Laina's voice cut off, replaced by a growl of frustration. "Let me up, I won't do anything." Her body relaxed. "Your desk smells like ham."

Will started to let go, but then a glimmer of metal caught his eye. "What's this?" Forcibly turning her wrist, he saw an unfamiliar ring on her hand. It was remarkable for being cheaply made, probably of tin, but what really shocked him was the oily-looking needle mounted on the inside of the band. It was clearly an assassin's tool. "Where'd you get this ring?"

"What ring?"

Without further ado, Will attached a source-link and paralyzed his sister before recovering his handkerchief and using it to carefully remove the ring from her hand. That accomplished, he released the spell and watched as Laina straightened up. Her eyes grew wide with shock as she saw the ring he held. "No. How? That's not why I came. You know me better than that."

"Why did you come then?" he demanded.

A host of emotions seemed to storm across her face, but fear wasn't one of them. "I need to tell you—" Once again, Laina's words stopped, but this time she refused to give up. Her frame began to shiver and shake, and her jaw worked up and down until Laina's eyes rolled up into her head. Blood trickled from her nose.

"Stop, damn it!" Will shouted. "You're killing yourself. Just stop."

Her only answer was a frightening series of choking noises. Worried for her life, Will paralyzed his sister once more, and then working from within, he forced her throat muscles to relax. Once he was sure she could breathe, he constructed a sleep spell and sent her into unconsciousness.

As gently as he could, he moved Laina to the floor and checked her over, both for injuries—and for more weapons or poison. Using his sleeve, he wiped away the bits of ham and fat that were stuck to her cheek. He should be furious. Will *wanted* to be angry, but all he felt was emptiness and despair.

"You've got a lot to answer for, Lognion," he muttered. "I was going to kill you anyway, but I'll be twice as happy to do so now. Trying to use my own flesh and blood to murder me—that's a bridge too far."

Once he'd had a few moments to think, Will slipped one arm beneath her shoulders and the other under her knees and lifted her into his arms. The door was awkward, since he'd forgotten to open it first, but he managed. He sent the first servant he encountered to find Selene and ask her to meet him, then he carried his sister back to her room.

CHAPTER 3

"We're missing something," said Selene, worry prominent in her features.

"It was obviously your father, there's no doubt about that," Will observed.

She nodded impatiently. "I agree, but that's why I *know* we're missing something. You're still alive."

Will frowned. "It could easily have turned out otherwise."

"Could it?" She chewed her lower lip. "Do you know of a poison that could kill you fast enough to keep you from using a potion?"

"No, but she might have been able to stop me."

"She's still recovering from the second compression—magic would be difficult," argued Selene.

He shook his head. "I think she's completely over it. She's much faster than the others."

"But even so, she didn't try to fight you with magic."

"I don't think she even knew she had the ring on," said Will. "She seemed surprised, and it felt genuine to me."

"Then why did she lunge at you?"

Will looked down, feeling mildly embarrassed. "To touch my skin. She—we—it's been difficult for both of us. I think it's beginning to fade, but there are still moments when the pull becomes very strong."

Selene's face remained smooth, but the tips of her ears shaded ever so slightly toward a brighter pink. She understood Will's problem on a rational level, she trusted him, and she loved Laina, but somewhere deeper down, beyond her control, the situation irritated her. "She's as stubborn as you, and the fact that she managed to get through the first compression without magical compulsion shows just how strong her will is. I doubt she would have a sudden lapse."

"He's playing mind games," suggested Will. "What if he's ordering her to forget things?"

His wife's eyes lit up. "Giving her commands then making her forget them? If he had ordered her to kill you, we would have seen it.

She nearly killed herself trying to communicate with you just a short while ago. She would have resisted an outright order to kill you from the outset."

Will shook his head. "Imagine yourself in her place you can't—"

"I've been in her place," snapped Selene.

"—then you know you can't fight every command. You didn't even know what he was doing until he gave you an order you absolutely wouldn't obey. Suppose he contacts her in the middle of the night, tells her something, or demands information, then tells her to forget the conversation, what would she do? Is she going to fight his control and die, or accept it? It gets even more complicated if he gives her a command that feels natural."

"Or he tells her something she feels you have to know," said Selene, following the argument to its conclusion. "What happens if your skin touches?"

"Nothing if we fight it, but it's difficult. Our souls start to fuse again and our thoughts get mixed up together." Will ground his teeth. "It makes sense now. She was trying to get around his compulsion not to tell me whatever she had learned. Now that I understand, it won't be a problem. You'll just need to keep an eye on me and make sure we don't lose control…"

"No," said Selene brusquely. "Don't fall into the trap."

"Huh?"

"It's layered," she replied. "He knows exactly how the heart-stone enchantment works. He's had who knows how many years to learn all of its intricacies. He used it to make her put that ring on and then forget it. He told her other things and let her remember them, knowing she would be desperate to tell you. My father knew *exactly* what she would do."

Will nodded. "And she failed, so now we can find out what she wanted to tell me."

Selene sighed. "Killing you would have been a happy accident for him, but he expected this to fail. The real trap is in whatever information he's trying to pass to you through her."

Will groaned, putting his face down and grabbing hold of his hair with both hands. "I am so sick of these stupid games."

"Welcome to my entire life," said Selene wryly. A moment later, she moved closer and slid under his arm. The two of them remained that way for a while, quietly drawing comfort from one another. Finally, she spoke again, "Are you starting to regret letting her learn?"

Because of Laina's unique situation as the only person in the household who was directly bound to the king via the heart-stone enchantment, Selene and Will had had a long discussion regarding whether she should be included in the new wizardry training. In the end, it had been Selene's own moment of defiance, when she had resisted her father's command to kill Will, that had been the deciding factor. Neither of them thought the king could successfully give Laina such a command, but as always, reality turned out to be much more nuanced.

"No," said Will after a short pause. "Whatever happens, whether we live or die, I'll feel better knowing she's better equipped for the future."

"Even if she's the one that kills you?"

He squeezed his wife harder. "I had the same thought about you once, remember?"

"Doesn't mean it will work out as well this time."

A rustling came from the direction of Laina's bed, and they both turned to see that she was awake, watching them silently. Laina's eyes were puffy and red, but there were no visible tears. "I'm sorry," she mumbled. Lifting one hand, she rubbed her face, then stared at her palm. "Why didn't you tie me up?"

Before Selene could answer, Will replied, "Because you aren't a threat to me."

His sister coughed. "I think I just disproved that theory."

"You proved the opposite," argued Will. "Not only do you lack the power to harm me directly, but your loyalty is so strong that even the heart-stone enchantment can't compel you to do so."

Laina glared at him for a second before making a face of disgust. "I don't know whether to be angry or nauseated by what you just said."

Selene laughed softly, then looked at Will. "Stop provoking her."

"What do we do now?" asked Laina.

"Nothing," said Will. "This was meant to produce a hasty response. We won't give him one." He glanced at Selene, and she met his eyes with a look of agreement. He could imagine her silent thought, *We stick to the plan.* Then he continued, "Soon we can start the third compression, and then—"

"I want it now," interrupted Laina.

"You need to finish recovering," urged Selene. "It's only been a month and a half. Most of the others are still struggling."

"I was ready two weeks ago," said Laina waspishly. "Don't make me wait just because the others are slow."

It was subtle, but Will saw the trace of annoyance that passed over his wife's face at that remark. She had taken months to recover from the second compression and even longer after the third. Laina's offhand remark cut at her pride. "There's no reason to hurry," said Will.

"Sure there is," argued Laina. "I'll be exhausted, weak, less able to do you harm. I don't know what you have planned, and I know you can't share it with me, but perhaps it will make me less of a useful tool to Lognion in the short term."

"Get some rest," said Will. "We can talk about this tomorrow."

As they started to leave, Laina made one last request, "At least lock me in the room."

Will laughed but didn't give her a response as he closed the door. A few minutes later, when they were down the hall, Selene turned to him. "That was a rather reasonable request. It might be foolish to ignore it."

He raised one brow. "Stop testing me. You would have chosen the same thing."

She smirked. "Why?"

"Because you'll give orders to Darla and a few others to keep an eye on her, both to prevent her from harming us or herself, but also in the hope of finding out what your father would order her to do."

"You're learning fast for someone who says he never wanted to be a royal," she observed.

"I still don't like it," he declared. "If I had my way, we would leave all this behind and start fresh in some out-of-the-way place where no one knows either of us."

"And do what?"

"Make medicine, help people, deliver babies, that sort of thing."

Selene gaped. "You expect a princess to become a midwife?"

"You're overqualified," scoffed Will. "I could be a midwife, though. You can be the town doctor."

She shook her head. "You underestimate yourself."

He puffed up his chest. "Your ignorance is showing. In most small towns, people trust the local midwife a lot more than some fancy doctor."

Selene didn't laugh—her face had become wistful. "You're not the only one who wishes for something like that. Trying to escape the circumstances of my birth probably motivated many of my choices, including the ones that led me to meet you."

"If you were going to marry a hayseed to escape being a princess, you could have chosen better."

She sighed. "True. If only I'd known you were actually the son of a baron…"

They talked a while longer, and even though Selene protested, Will returned to his study. There were quite a few hours left in the day, and he hadn't gotten as far as he had by wasting them. Lately he'd begun practicing his spellcasting twice daily, both in the morning and again in the late afternoon, before supper. In between, he worked on projects, studied, and supervised his students through the misery of their mild exercise routines.

Studying the arcana that Aislinn had given him regarding the Wayfarer's Society was currently one of his top priorities, so he didn't want to waste what little time he had before his second casting session of the day.

The cat was nowhere to be seen when he returned, though it appeared that one of the servants had already come in and cleaned the meat and grease off his desk. Will resummoned the journal and his notes, and since he couldn't seem to get in the mood for reading, he instead decided to try out the new version of the teleport spell.

Over the past couple of years, he'd greatly expanded his ability to construct complex spells, so much so that learning a new one was far easier than it once had been. Memorizing it might take a few days, but following the written diagrams and instructions to build the spell construct took him less than an hour, even though it was his first time with the spell.

He looked it over with eyes that some might consider to be expert, though Will wasn't sure if he would claim such a thing about himself yet. Casting the spell would be foolish, since it might contain an error, so Will employed an advanced technique he had learned during his spell theory classes. He injected a tiny amount of turyn into the construct and then observed the turyn resonance that began to emerge. A second later, he removed the energy and let the spell construct disintegrate.

Keeping the output resonance in mind, he began carefully reconstructing the spell. This time it took less than half an hour, and once it was finished, he repeated the process, pushing a small amount of turyn into the construct and observing the output. He disassembled the spell and started building the spell for a third time.

In his classes, Professor Dulaney had taught them to use a specially prepared crystal to record the output resonance, but Will had abandoned the practice almost as soon as he'd left the classroom. Unlike modern wizards, his ability to reproduce—and more importantly in this case—to precisely *remember* magical resonance patterns was practically flawless. Arrogan had told him that it was something to be expected with third- and even second-order wizards.

Finishing the spell construct for a third time, he tested it again and compared the output resonance it produced to his memory of the first two tries. It matched perfectly. That meant it was unlikely that his spell construct contained an error, unless he had made the same exact error three times in a row.

"Which means I probably won't die if I actually cast it," he mumbled to himself. *Probably.* There was still the fact that no one currently living had ever used the spell before. *Unless one counts the goddess of magic herself,* thought Will. He no longer trusted his grandmother, but he knew she couldn't lie, and as far as he knew, she didn't have any current plans that would benefit from his accidental death.

So the spell would probably do what it was purported to do.

Steeling himself, Will looked through the open balcony doors and fixed his gaze upon a spot beside a stone statue of Temarah. It stood some fifty yards from the house and was flanked by several neatly trimmed bushes. Keeping it firmly in sight and mind, Will began filling the spell construct with power.

That was another aspect of casting a new spell that could be dangerous for a novice—using the correct amount of turyn. Some spells were infinitely variable in their ability to take in small to large amounts of magical energy, but others were binary, meaning they required a certain minimum threshold of power in order to produce the desired effect. Such spells weren't usually dangerous if the minimum turyn requirement wasn't met, but they could potentially be disastrous if the *maximum* turyn was exceeded—explosively disastrous in simple cases and weirdly dangerous in an almost infinite number of ways for more complex magics.

For a teleportation spell, that could mean having his body scattered, torn apart, sent to unanticipated destinations, or any number of other possibilities.

And those were problems associated with purely binary spells. Reality was even more complicated, because some spells didn't fall neatly into the category of binary or variable effect spells. Some had a minimum threshold but didn't necessarily have a maximum and vice versa. Because of this, the wizards at Wurthaven had adopted certain standards for documenting new spells, and they had carefully curated older works to include notes that clarified important things that had been omitted by the author. All modern spell copies included notes regarding turyn requirements and whether the spell was binary, variable, etc...

The journals that Aislinn had given him from the Wayfarer's Society were written before such things were standardized, and new members probably had the benefit of verbal explanations when learning Flandry's original and more efficient teleport spell.

Will had never even used the current overcomplicated version, but he suspected that might be an advantage, since he didn't have to unlearn anything. He was also fairly confident in his skills after the past few years of rapid and intense spell acquisition. He wasn't the same young novice who had once nearly blown himself up with a new spell construct.

Slow and steady wins the race, Will thought as he gingerly fed turyn into the spell construct, being careful to keep his eyes and concentration fixed on the location he had selected. He felt the transition when the spell activated and instinctively stopped the flow of energy. The spell construct he had been holding was gone, and though he hadn't felt anything physically, his eyes were already registering the change in light. He was standing beside the statue.

It was disorienting more for the fact that it *wasn't* disorienting. There had been no sense of motion or change. In his memory it was more as though the world had simply changed around him. Will let his breath out explosively, then followed with a deep inhalation as he collected his thoughts. *That was amazing.*

He immediately started to repeat the spell, but his journal was still open on his desk, and he didn't know it well enough to reconstruct it purely from memory. Instead, he cast an elemental travel disk, which had recently become yet another of his growing repertoire of spells he could cast instinctively. As he floated up on it to hover a few feet above the ground, he noticed the cat he had recently fed was sitting nearby, watching him with apparent interest.

"Want a ride?" His question was more a joke than anything else. Will didn't really expect the strange cat to join him, but he lowered the disk beside her and paused for a moment anyway, just to entertain himself.

The cat hopped aboard and sat down as nonchalantly as though it were something they did together every day. Mildly astonished, Will pretended to be unsurprised and gently took off. The cat never batted an eye, and when he reached the house and lowered the disk, she stepped off as though it was the most natural thing in the world. The cat darted away into the bushes off to one side without so much as a glance back in his direction.

"You're welcome for the ride," remarked Will, smiling faintly.

Rimberlin House was a big place, and there were several back doors. The one Will had chosen was usually called the west garden door, and before he could put his hand to the handle, it flew open. Sammy and Tabitha stepped out with more animation in their steps than he had seen in weeks, though they still showed signs of fatigue in their expressions. In another week or two, they would probably be fully acclimated to the second compression.

"When did you go out?" asked Sammy.

"A minute ago."

Before he could say more, Tabitha asked a fresh question. "Was that a cat with you?"

Will could only surmise that they had seen his approach through one of the windows. He nodded, glancing at Sammy to see her reaction. His heart tightened when he saw the sudden hope in her eyes, and he immediately shook his head. "It was just a stray."

His cousin had been devastated when *her* adopted pet cat, Mister Mittens, had disappeared and failed to return. Sammy had never found out that her cat was actually a demigod, or that he'd sacrificed his life to save Will's. He had been torn on the matter of whether to tell her the truth, but one of the goddamn cat's last requests was that he stay silent and let her think he had merely run off.

Personally, Will thought that leaving Sammy with some hope was worse than giving her the truth, but he abided by his savior's last wish.

"It was pretty," said Tabitha. "I've never seen a stray with such a fluffy tail."

"It was fluffy?" asked Sammy.

Tabitha nodded. "Like a feather duster."

"It's a she," Will informed them. "If you put some food out you might be able to coax her inside."

The girls went looking for the cat while Will returned to his study. Deep down, he would have liked to go with them, but he couldn't justify letting his schedule slip. *Train, study, train, exercise, teach, study, train,* he chanted mentally. These days, he didn't even give himself time to play in the kitchen. His anxiety grew with every day that passed, bringing King Lognion's death closer to him. If things went according to plan, he wouldn't need to lift a finger, but in his heart he didn't believe it.

He needed more: more power, more versatility, more offense, and more defense. He needed more of everything, and it would never be enough, not until his power was great enough to defeat his own nightmares. Despite his recent successes, what dominated his mental landscape was how close he had come to failing. The demon-lord had been too much, his grandmother was too strong for him, and most of all, Grim Talek the lich had perfectly demonstrated how powerless he truly was. The lich had handled him like an adult handles an unruly toddler.

CHAPTER 4

A few days later, Will found himself reflecting on the fact that he disliked physical training even more than he had in the past. Perversely, this made him lean into it. Blake complimented him often these days, but Will knew the truth. What skill he possessed came purely from repetition and hard work. He wasn't naturally talented like his cousin Eric had been, for whatever good it had done him.

The redheaded berserker bearing down on him swung at his torso with a heavy wooden club that moved faster than it should have, for his opponent's strength was beyond human. There was no blocking it, unless he wanted to break his own bones or use a force spell. Will dropped as low as he could and used a minor telekinesis spell to rip a small hole in the ground beneath his rival's descending foot.

Even though the ginger warrior had already committed to the swing, her strength and reflexes were supernatural; she altered the swing in midair and still managed to graze his shoulder—then stumbled as she lost her footing. Will ignored the pain as the club glanced off, and rammed the rounded point of his practice sword into the woman's gut hard enough to lift her feet off the ground. Two sharp, snapping sounds echoed at the same time, the result of his point-defense shield intercepting wooden bolts that had been fired in quick succession.

It took enough of his attention that he was almost caught by his brutish opponent's leg sweep. Since he was already low to the ground, there was no dodging it. Rather than try, Will summoned a travel disk. The hard stone rose from the ground, and though it didn't have time to finish forming, it was already moving in the direction of the oncoming leg. Flesh met stone and the warrior's bone cracked audibly. Will deflected yet another wooden bolt at almost the same time.

Tailtiu swore loudly. "That hurts, damn it!" Rolling away, she dropped the club and her hands began growing long, wickedly sharp claws.

Will didn't pause. He sent the travel disk forward to keep her off balance while springing forward with his wooden sword aimed downward, ready to drive the point into her chest or throat. "Hold!" Blake's voice rang out loudly.

He stopped, though his weapon shook from adrenaline, or perhaps fatigue. Tailtiu snarled and surged upward, until an invisible field of force drove her back into the ground. "That's cheating," she growled. "You're only supposed to use force spells to stop the ranged attacks."

"He called a halt," panted Will.

His aunt's blood was already beginning to cool. "Oh. I didn't notice." She visibly relaxed.

Will dismissed the force-push spell he had used. It was one of his favorites that he'd learned from studying Ethelgren's work. Simple and plain, it was nevertheless an infinitely useful spell. It could be used to push large or small objects, as long as they were within thirty feet or so, and it had originally been used against Will to immobilize him against a wall. It could do a lot more, though, from gently moving small objects to crushing things against one another.

Better still, it was one of his ever-growing collection of spells that could be reflex cast, along with other staples like the force-wall and force-dome. His constant and unforgiving practice regimen had started producing results, and it seemed as though not a week went by that yet another spell became part of his instinctive repertoire.

Tailtiu stood up, towering half a head taller than him, though she was already beginning to shrink. Her height vanished gradually, while at the same time her heavily muscled arms and legs slowly returned to their usual slimmer form. Her chest became smaller as well, reshaping itself to display petite breasts rather than heavy pectoral slabs. Will watched, fascinated as always by the change. "You're insanely strong already—why do you insist on changing?"

Blake Word stepped out of the bushes, bow in hand. "Because I asked her to. You don't need practice against smaller opponents as much as you do against the big ones."

"Either way, she's inhumanly fast and strong," observed Will.

Blake shook his head. "Strength is one thing, but mass is another. You do very well with smaller or medium-sized opponents, but the big ones are still giving you trouble."

"If I wasn't handicapped by our practice rules, I'd just blow a hole through her, and it's easier to hit a big target. Of course, we couldn't practice like that, but you understand what I mean."

"It wouldn't kill me," offered his aunt, her tone thoughtful, "but you'd need to get me back to my realm soon after." As was often the case, she was entirely serious.

Will laughed. "No. Besides, the other reason for me not using force-lances is that I need to remain free to use the point-defense shield, in case there are attacks that my other defenses can't handle."

Blake nodded. "Anyway, for her to use large, massive weapons, she needs to be bigger herself, regardless of her innate strength, otherwise the momentum of the weapon will just throw her off balance."

Tailtiu rolled her eyes. "That's not the real reason. It's because you don't get as sexually aroused when I look like your big friend, Tiny."

Will sputtered, "What?"

She nodded. "That's what Blake told me. He said you'd be able to fight better if you weren't getting erections every few minutes."

"I haven't—" Will protested.

Blake cut him off, "I didn't say that!"

She grinned, and the two men stared at her for a moment before looking at one another, realizing they had been had. "Lying is fun," said the fae woman. "I never knew how much I was missing."

They laughed for a bit before Blake returned to the subject at hand. "This sort of practice is useful, but you're already to the point where it's getting too easy, even with multiple handicaps. It would be nice if we could do something with multiple opponents. Perhaps when your students are ready…"

Will responded immediately, "No."

Blake frowned. "Why not?"

"I'd kill them," Will announced flatly. "The problem with reflex casting is that I often do it before I'm fully aware of what I'm doing. It's easy to say I won't use a lethal spell in practice, but once it's ingrained in me it's hard not to use deadly force. Tailtiu can survive a mistake on my part, but with regular people—I'm just not willing to take the risk."

"Then I guess we'll move on to terrain and environmental tactics tomorrow," said Blake.

"What do you have in mind?" asked Will.

Tailtiu and Blake shared a glance. "It's a secret," said his aunt. "Your wife is full of ideas. With her spells and some preparation, we should be able to test you in ways you haven't anticipated."

"Do you think we'll continue this kind of training with your students once they're ready?" asked Blake.

Will shook his head. "It will be years before any of them have gained the spells and talents necessary, and besides, while I think the world needs proper wizards, I don't think they need to be turned into war assets or assassins. I'll give them some battle training, but I'd rather they develop in a more natural fashion."

"And *you* aren't natural?"

Will grimaced. "Do you think I'm safe to be around? Startle me and I'm liable to blow someone's head off. That's not normal, and this training is only making it worse."

"You're the one who insisted on it," observed Blake. "Even though you said it wouldn't be strictly necessary."

Will glanced around, wondering if Lognion had some hidden observer. Part of the reason for his practice was to lend credence to Plan C, a surprise one-man assault. The only person capable of it would be Will himself, but it was only a decoy plan. The practice sessions were mainly to establish it as an actual possibility that the king couldn't completely discount. Privately, Selene had made it clear that he wasn't to attempt such a thing under any circumstances. Will agreed, but he'd decided to be ready to do it anyway, just in case. "It's necessary, whether it's for tomorrow or next year. It's necessary until—" He stopped there.

"Until what?"

He just flattened his lips into a grim smile without answering the question. *Until there's no one left to be afraid of.* Turning away, he headed back toward the main house. "It's time for me to check on the students."

***

There was still some time left before the midday exercises, but Janice was waiting for him when he returned. She had a serious look on her face. "Can we talk privately?"

Will nodded and pointed upward. "My study?"

"Perfect."

Up the stairs and down the hall to the right was his office. Will opened the door and stepped in, watching Janice as she followed him. She closed the door behind herself, something she rarely felt the need for in the past. "Is it that serious?" he asked.

"Not really," she replied in a tone that said the complete opposite. "I just wanted to tell you in person. I'm not going to try the third compression."

Will frowned. "You've done well so far. Are you worried?"

"We still don't know how dangerous it is."

"That's true, but you recovered from the second compression fairly well. I think you have less to worry about than most of the others."

"I just don't want to do it," she insisted. "I'm scared."

Something rang false in her words, though Will could tell she was genuinely worried about something. Speaking carefully, he made a suggestion. "It's still a week away. Why not sleep on it? You don't have to decide this minute."

Janice shook her head. "Nothing is going to change in a week. Besides, I've decided to return home. I haven't seen my parents in over a year now."

His eyes narrowed. "You didn't have any such plans a few weeks ago."

"I miss them," she replied. "Just because you didn't realize I was homesick doesn't mean it isn't true."

She's defensive, thought Will, *and I didn't accuse her of lying.* He remained silent for a few seconds, studying his friend's face, then asked, "What's happened?"

Janice scowled. "Nothing has happened. I've just made up my mind."

Definitely a lie. "Tiny was just here a month and a half ago. Have you talked about this with him?"

"He knew I was thinking about it. I'll send him a letter."

Another lie, and her expression had faltered for just a second when he mentioned Tiny. Will was certain she hadn't said anything to the man because he and Tiny had already planned a surprise for her. Sir Kyle had agreed to relinquish Tiny into Will's service. The big warrior was due to return in two weeks, and Selene would be knighting him shortly afterward. Tiny didn't know about the knighthood specifically, but he had also told Will that he planned to propose to Janice as soon as he came back.

Will glared at her. "You're a terrible liar, even worse than me." She didn't reply, so the two of them simply stared at each other for a minute. Today was the day he would announce that they'd begin the third compression in a week. It was also the day he had planned to recheck the female students for pregnancy. It was a silly precaution, since he was certain none of them could have become pregnant, but Arrogan had insisted it be done.

His eyes widened slightly, and Janice's cheeks began to flush. "Today's the day for the pregnancy test…"

"No need to worry. I know the spell. I've already checked myself," she replied, her words tumbling out in a rush.

"Why would you check if you knew there was no need?"

Her face was blood red now.

"Did Tiny sneak into your room before he left?"

"No!"

"But you're pregnant?" Will phrased it as a question, but it bordered on being a statement.

Janice started to protest but changed her mind after a single word. "No—yes, damn it, Will! Just let me leave with my dignity! I'd rather not have the others know about this." She covered her face with her hands at the end.

"Dignity? What are you ashamed of? You love him, don't you? Besides, he snuck into your room and—"

"Will," snapped Janice, interrupting him. "He didn't sneak into my room. He was completely against this."

Will gaped at her. "Well, obviously that is not *entirely* true, otherwise we wouldn't be having this conversation."

Janice's hands made tight fists. "I snuck into his room, ambushed him on his last night here."

"Huh?"

"I was sick of waiting. He's so old fashioned. I just didn't expect…"

"To get pregnant? You could have used a spell. Surely you know that?"

"Yes! I know. I wasn't thinking clearly, and at the time, I just don't know. I was out of my mind, and now I've ruined everything!"

Will was confused. "Sped things up a little, maybe, but I wouldn't say ruined. What are you talking about?"

"You know how traditional John is," she replied, as though that explained everything.

"And?"

"We aren't married."

Will frowned. "Did you hit your head or something? You know he'll marry you as soon as you tell him."

"I didn't do this to trap him!" growled Janice. "That's why I want you to keep this a secret. He's never asked me to marry, and I don't intend to force this child on him."

"By the Holy Mother!" swore Will. "Janice, you've never been this stupid before. You should know he wants to marry you, child or no child."

"He's going to be in Darrow for at least a year. When I said good-bye to him that night, he understood it was the end for us."

"The hell he did!" barked Will. "He was planning to surprise you. He'll be back in a couple of weeks. He's planning to propose to you then!"

Now it was Janice's turn to look confused. "But he's sworn to Sir—"

"Sir Kyle released him to me," interrupted Will. "He actually left to settle his affairs before returning here. I need a captain of the guard."

"Oh."

"I need you too, Janice. Surely you realize how valuable you are? I don't have that many friends, especially ones as talented and intelligent as you."

Her mind was still processing everything she had just learned. "But I can't be third-order, not now, and by the time I've had this child…"

"Do you think that's the only value you have?" asked Will. "Sure, I'd rather you live longer, but you're a lot more than just a top-notch wizard. I never had any intention of using you as a soldier anyway. Second- or third-order, it really doesn't matter. Be happy, raise a family, pursue a career at Wurthaven, or work for me—whatever you choose to do, having you as my friend is all I ever wanted. I want you to be happy."

Janice blinked, her eyes growing wet. "John is going to be so embarrassed…"

"He'll be as excited as a puppy, don't be stupid," argued Will, standing up suddenly. "The main thing is that you'd better not ruin the surprise."

Uncertain, Janice leaned back slightly.

"The proposal," Will reminded her. "You aren't supposed to know he's returning, so don't spoil the surprise, and don't tell him you're pregnant until after he proposes."

"That isn't fair—" began Janice.

"No, it wouldn't be fair if you wind up doubting his motivation for years to come. Let him ask you first, then you can surprise him. Either way he'll be happy, but that way you won't have any lingering doubts."

"But…"

"No buts—promise me," insisted Will.

She started to answer, then burst into tears. Will had known Janice for years now and he'd seen her hurt, mauled, and near death, but while she had cried some during those occasions, it had been different. The tears had been muted by shock and fear, or partially suppressed for the sake of whatever had been occurring. This time was different. No one's life was in danger, the world wasn't ending. Janice was simply a woman, one who had been feeling alone and under pressure for quite some time. Her outburst was genuine, heartfelt, and full of raw emotion.

Will was caught entirely off-guard. He stepped forward and embraced his friend. "I didn't mean to make you cry."

Her replies were muffled and distorted. Will failed to grasp most of it, but he caught the last few words clearly. "I was so scared…"

He squeezed her a little tighter. "You're not alone. Not as long as I'm alive, and I'm not the only one in this house who would tell you that. If Tiny were here, he'd be positively offended that you thought so little of him."

She'd been slowly calming down, but his words set off a new storm. It wound down faster than the first, and her words were clearer. "It's not that I think little of him, it's that I think so *much* of him."

Will pushed her out to arm's length, frowning. "You're the last person who should say that, Janice. I didn't kill Dennis Spry over some worthless guttersnipe. You're worth ten times more than that noble prick, so don't ever think you don't deserve love."

Janice was still sniffing, but she smiled faintly and daubed her eyes with one sleeve. "You would have killed him no matter who it was, guttersnipe, whore, or princess. I didn't understand at the time, which upset me. I felt responsible. It wasn't until later that I realized I wasn't even part of the equation. It could have been anyone."

He narrowed his eyes. Janice was eloquent, but he could tell she had stopped just shy of adding, 'I didn't matter.' "It wasn't anyone. It was you, and I'm very grateful for having met you, Dame Shaw."

"What?"

"Assuming you say 'yes,' and you actually marry our oversized friend, then you'll officially be 'Dame,' after Selene knights him."

Janice rubbed her cheeks. "I'm going to need some time to process that thought."

CHAPTER 5

Janice stepped out, and they discovered Seth waiting outside the door. "Can we talk for a minute?"

Will nodded an affirmative while Janice made her way down the hall. Then he ushered his one-time roommate into the study. "It's almost time for the session, so we'll have to be quick. What's on your mind?"

"I want to stop."

It seemed so reminiscent of the start of his previous conversation that Will almost replied with 'Are you pregnant?' He held his tongue, though. After a second, he asked, "You're referring to the third compression?" Seth nodded, so Will asked, "Why?"

"It doesn't feel right."

"What does that mean exactly?"

"It's just a feeling. Getting through the second one was hard, and I still don't feel quite like I should."

"But you're sleeping soundly through the night, and your overall turyn levels have returned to normal," Will reminded him.

Seth nodded. "Yeah, technically that's true, but something feels off."

"You adjusted almost as quickly as the others and well within the time-frame that means it should be safe for you."

"I don't think I have what it takes." Seth stared at the floor. "I'm scared."

"So?"

Seth glanced up. "Didn't you hear me? I'm afraid. I'm a coward Will. I'm not like you. I think I'm fine with just second-order."

Speaking frankly, Will responded, "I'm scared all the time, Seth, every day in fact. Don't let that stop you."

His friend seemed incredulous. "Afraid of what?"

Will shrugged. "For starters, the king wants me dead, but if you look back, there hasn't been a day in years where I didn't have something crazy going on. I've been afraid of a lot of things through it all."

"I don't think there's anyone left that can really threaten you, even the king."

"One on one? Maybe, maybe not, but that's not the point. Being powerful isn't enough to make me safe, much less those around me. And there are a thousand different types of fear. I'm afraid of failing as a teacher, as a husband, as a friend. I'm afraid that the path I'm heading down will bring you and everyone else I care about to a bad end. And I haven't even mentioned the things I'm an outright failure at, like being a duke. Sometimes I'm simply afraid that everyone is laughing at me behind my back, even though I know it's a silly thing to worry about."

Seth seemed shocked. "Who would dare laugh at you?"

Will's lips twisted into a wry smile. "My friends, hopefully."

"You're the most confident person I know. It's hard to believe you're scared of anything."

"Everyone is scared," declared Will, putting his palm on his friend's chest. "What's important is how you deal with it. Don't let it stop you."

Seth stared into his eyes, and Will saw a faint tremor pass over the young man's features, but then his jaw firmed. "You're right."

"You're going to go for it?" asked Will.

Seth nodded. "Yes."

Will smiled. "Good. We're almost late. Let's go."

A few minutes later, they were outside. Seth joined the others while Will and Selene stood together. Selene often skipped the sessions since they usually just involved forcing the students to exercise when they would rather do absolutely anything else. It was always worst when they were fresh off a new compression. At those times their bodies were continually exhausted, starved for the energy needed to function normally.

The first compression had been the worst, when the students had had to learn how to maintain the compression of their source to avoid literally burning themselves alive from the inside out. The second had been easier, but it still made them tired to the point of wanting to sleep almost continually for several weeks. Will hoped the third compression would be similar.

Technically the third compression was the most dangerous, but they hadn't lost anyone yet, and the student wizards had all recovered within the time period that Arrogan had indicated was probably safe for them to continue. Selene was present because she knew that today Will would adjust the spell-cage that limited the amount of internal turyn they could hold.

Will studied the line. His cousin Sammy stood at one end with Emory Tallowen next, casting occasional glances in her direction, a fact that mildly annoyed Will for reasons he barely understood. Next was Seth, his old roommate, followed by Matthew Holmgren and Shawn Campbell. Matthew and Shawn were both from Will's class at

Wurthaven, and though he had never been particularly close to them, he had nothing bad to say either. Both had been solid students, and they had performed well during the recent war with Darrow.

As expected, Janice was absent, along with Tabitha, who had left the previous week. Laina was also missing, which came as a surprise. "Where's Laina?" Will asked, turning to Selene.

"I'll explain after the class," she replied.

Will frowned. "If something happened, you should have told me beforehand."

"I tried, but you were busy with Janice and the door was shut. Anything I should know about?"

He gave her a grumpy look before responding, "I'll explain after class." With that, he started the preliminary spell diagnostic before proceeding. As Sammy was the only girl remaining it only took him a moment to make sure she wasn't pregnant. He'd felt safe in assuming she wouldn't be, but Janice's revelation had shaken him.

Knowing that Emory was smitten with his cousin, Will gave the young nobleman a hard stare as he performed the spell. Emory shrugged innocently while Sammy frowned at Will in annoyance.

Since there weren't any surprises, they proceeded with adjusting the source-cages within each of the students. Will did the first few and Selene did the rest, perfectly replicating what she had seen him do. The effect wasn't instantaneous, but the students were soon looking uncomfortable as they began compressing their sources. The resulting paucity of turyn made their faces pale, and fatigue became apparent in their features.

"Does anyone have any questions before you return to your rooms to rest?" asked Will.

Emory responded, "Where's Janice and Laina?"

"Janice won't be continuing for reasons of her own," said Will. "As to Laina"—he glanced at Selene—"I don't—" His sentence cut off as Seth suddenly vomited onto the grass.

Everyone took a step back, and then Shawn, who had a sensitive stomach, began retching in response to Seth's expulsion. The next few minutes were chaotic. Will sent the others back to their rooms while he and Selene helped the two nauseous men. Seth's stomach quieted down after a few minutes while Shawn's got better as soon as he was away from the noxious sights and smells.

It was almost a full hour before Selene and Will were alone. She looked at him and gave him a rueful grin. "Shawn wouldn't last long if he had to tend patients."

Will chuckled and nodded. "I would have reconsidered including him if I'd known he was so sensitive."

"He's a wizard, though, not a doctor."

"How would he react to seeing someone's brains splattered against a wall?" pondered Will.

"I said wizard, not soldier," corrected Selene. After a brief moment, she added, "Is that what you think of your role these days?"

He winced. It wasn't long since he'd been proclaiming the opposite to Blake. With a sigh he answered, "It seems as though violence has become the foundation of my life. I can't help but think that our students will face the same thing, even though I keep arguing the reverse."

Her features softened. "That's how it should be."

"But it isn't."

"It will be, once you take the crown."

"Once *you* take the crown," Will corrected. "I'll do the bloody part, but I'm not fit to rule."

"You're wrong."

His eyes narrowed in suspicion. "You honestly think I'm better suited than you?"

Selene said nothing for several seconds, then answered, "No, but you don't give yourself enough credit. Together it hardly matters, for I'd be there to advise you, but even if I wasn't around, you would make an admirable monarch. You have good instincts, and you've learned to be ruthless when necessary. Putting all that aside, you have the most important attribute—you care about the citizens more than your own pride or power."

"None of that makes either of us necessarily better than Lognion," he observed. "Your father may be arrogant, but he's an effective ruler."

"He's cruel."

"To you, to us, to those who are his tools and to those who get in his way, but for the kingdom as a whole—has Terabinia ever had a more successful king, or been more prosperous?" asked Will.

"Part of the capital was razed to the ground last year," Selene observed.

"Due to an attack he had nothing to do with, and most of the destruction was caused by Ethelgren. *I'm* responsible for that."

"You were a student, yet you found the power to master an ancient artifact and rescue the city from an undead invasion. In the end, you saved the king himself from that master vampire."

"Which led to a war."

"That you won."

"Because your father appointed me to lead it. Isn't that a king's job, making smart decisions?"

She sighed. "He was hoping you'd die or at the least be discredited."

"In the worst case, the kingdom would have been the same, possibly even stronger. Certainly, it was bad for *us*, but for Terabinia? Our nation was bound to be better for it no matter how things turned out," argued Will, shaking his head.

She frowned. "The war precipitated the demon crisis. That might have been the end of everyone."

"That was a mistake on Grim Talek's part. You can't assign blame for that to Lognion."

"Well then, I suppose we should just sit and wait for him to eliminate you," said Selene sourly. "Is that your argument?"

Will grimaced. "No, I'm just not sure we're any better than him."

"He's a monster." Selene's tone was hard.

"As a person, yes," Will admitted, spreading his hands out. "But as a ruler? Look, I'm not saying we should do anything different. I just don't think we should fool ourselves by pretending we're better for the country than him. What we're doing is personal. It's him or us, and that's as much his fault as anyone's."

The expression on his wife's face was that of barely suppressed anger. She took a breath, and it vanished a second later. Will admired her self-control, the product of a childhood he could barely conceive. "You're wrong," she said finally. "But I'm not going to argue with you when you're obviously just looking for reasons to beat yourself up. Laina went back to Cerria."

He blinked, trying to process the abrupt change of topics. "She snuck away?"

"It was her idea. I helped her pack."

Will's mood went from defeated to angry, but he tried to emulate his wife's previous example. Closing his eyes, he took a slow breath, then tried to object reasonably. "She was supposed to undergo the third compression today. Do you think there's going to be another opportunity later?"

"She'd already done it to herself when she came to me."

"What?" The answer surprised him so much that Will almost shouted. "By herself?"

Selene nodded. "She was able to get through the first two compressions even though she was already a spell caster and without needing the compulsion of the heart-stone enchantment. Is it really that surprising? You know how strong her determination is."

"When it's Laina you call it determination, but when I'm the subject you call it stubbornness," said Will wryly.

She chuckled. "Whatever it's called, it seems to run in the family. You're both mule-headed."

"I just can't believe she managed it. I didn't think it was possible to do alone. I couldn't have done that."

"You were a complete novice. She's been using magic for years," she remarked.

"Which is supposed to be a drawback."

She shook her head. "Not for her, maybe not for you, if you were in the same circumstances. After all, at some point in history there had to have been a first wizard, right? Someone able to use spells, or at the very least wild magic, someone who managed to be the first to compress their own source without help or guidance."

Will went to the side table and retrieved a bottle of wine. "I need a drink. You?" When she nodded, he deftly uncorked the bottle and poured a glass for each of them. After he had handed one over to his wife, he returned to the subject at hand. "You shouldn't have let her go. Even if she managed it by herself, she must still have been exhausted. Traveling could be dangerous."

"If it was you, do you think I could have stopped you?"

"If I was tired and exhausted, definitely."

She sighed. "You always assume everything is about fighting head-to-head. Certainly, I could have locked her up, but she would have escaped one way or another. Besides, she was acting in the best interest of everyone concerned."

He knew what she meant. It went without saying that Laina was acting to help her sister, or perhaps to protect Will and Selene. After a second, he made an addition, "Except her own."

Selene took a slow sip, then responded by lifting her glass as if to toast him. "Pot. Kettle."

CHAPTER 6

Will woke briefly in the middle of the night. His eyes slid open groggily. There was no sense of urgency or alarm, but he wasn't sure what had wakened him. Adjusting his vision to the darkness automatically, he soon spotted a grey lump on the bedcovers close to his feet. It took a moment to realize what it was, but when two green-gold eyes appeared, he was certain. The stray cat had found her way into the bedroom and made herself a comfy spot near the foot of the bed.

He and the cat stared at each other in the dim light for a long moment, then the cat closed her eyes with a sense of finality. "Suit yourself," Will mumbled and did the same.

When he opened them again, Selene was rising and putting on her dressing gown. Rubbing at the matter in his eyes, he glanced around. The cat was nowhere to be seen. "Did you let the cat in last night?"

She raised one brow. "What cat?"

"There's a stray that's been hanging around the house. She snuck in during the night and made herself at home on the bed."

"You were dreaming." Selene pointed at the door, then the window— both were closed. "Unless the cat can manage doors or shutters."

"Huh." It hadn't felt like a dream. Shaking his head, he rose and used the basin on the other side of the room to wash his face before beginning to dress as well. Despite Selene's head start, Will was ready to go downstairs a few minutes before she was, but he was happy to wait, content to watch as she skillfully wove a ribbon in and out of a long braid that artfully decorated her tresses.

They didn't speak. Although some would have been nervous, or simply annoyed by such long, silent stares, Selene was unbothered. Whether it was her upbringing or simply her innate confidence, she accepted his watching gaze as a natural consequence of their relationship. When she finished with her hair, she stood and smirked. "Entertained?"

Will grinned. "Enthralled."

Stretching up on her toes, she kissed him quickly on the cheek. "Let's eat."

A few minutes later, they were downstairs in the dining hall. Breakfast was usually informal, without a firm insistence on punctuality or waiting on everyone to appear, but even so, Jeremy only kept the kitchen open for a short period of time. Lunch was a bigger meal, and he couldn't afford to waste half the morning serving everyone at different times when the noon meal would require hours of preparation. As a consequence, everyone knew when to show up at the right time if they didn't want to wait until noon to eat.

Seth was absent.

Will gestured to the empty seat. "Did he eat already?"

Shawn Campbell shared the room with Seth. Exhausted from the third compression, he looked up with a haggard expression. "I could barely drag myself down the stairs this morning. Seth is still sleeping." He bit into another sausage and chewed without enthusiasm. A second later he added, "I think he made the right choice. I don't have much of an appetite."

One of Jeremy's kitchen assistants, a young woman named Kara, brought two plates out and set them on the table in front of Will and Selene's customary seats. She'd probably been watching for their arrival. Will gave her a grateful smile and took his seat. Before he took his first bite, a thought occurred to him. "Did you talk to him?" he asked Shawn.

Shawn shook his head, answering around yet another mouthful. "No. Didn't want to wake him."

Will frowned. After each compression, it was usually difficult to sleep. While awake it was easy to maintain the control required, but generally it took several weeks for the body to develop the ability to maintain the appropriate turyn production during sleep. Rising from his chair, he stepped back from the table. Touching Selene on the shoulder, he said, "I'm going to go check on him."

She nodded, seeing the worry in his eyes, though she kept her features calm. Shawn piped up again, "It won't hurt him to miss a meal."

Suppressing his irritation at that remark, Will left. His anxiety grew with each step, and by the time he reached the stairs, he was jogging. He took the steps two at a time and didn't slow down until he had reached Seth's door. One deep breath and he went inside.

Seth appeared completely at rest, but Will's senses registered the awful truth immediately. There was no turyn evident around his old roommate, and a faint smell in the air was probably the result of loose bowels. No more than two steps in and he was certain of the awful truth.

Seth was dead.

Moving to the bedside, Will took note of the grimace on Seth's face; the muscles had already tightened. The skin was pale but still soft to the touch, and underneath the body had turned a dark pink as the blood had pooled there under the influence of gravity. His friend had died hours ago, possibly right after going to bed.

"You were right," said Will to the empty room, knowing he was truly alone. "I should have listened." The turmoil inside his heart was such that he couldn't have said what he was feeling, but it robbed him of any desire to move, so instead he sat, leaning his back against the side of Seth's bed. *This could have happened to Selene. It might still happen to Laina, or Sammy.* His face tightened with guilt, not just because it was his fault, but also because he was glad it hadn't been one of them.

"I'm the worst friend anyone could have," he said aloud, wishing Seth could still hear him. He had no desire to get up, so he sat in the room for ten minutes or so, until Emory appeared in the doorway. Like the others, he looked wan and pale. Will studied him with critical eyes. *He could die at any moment.* Then he lowered his head. *Would I care?*

"Selene asked me to check on you."

Will answered in a voice devoid of emotion. "I'm fine."

Emory moved closer, staring at Seth's morbidly twisted expression. "Is he…?" Will didn't bother replying, but after a few seconds Emory realized the truth. "Holy Mother, you told us this could happen, but I didn't think…"

"No. I suppose I didn't either."

"Is there anything I can do?" Emory's voice was tentative.

Today's physical exercises will involve lots of digging, thought Will darkly. It wouldn't, of course. It would be a week before the students would be able to think about doing much of anything. *I'll be burying him alone.* "Get some rest. Keep breathing." He slowly got to his feet. "I'll go tell the others."

"I know you were close. If you want to—"

The young nobleman was just trying to be supportive, but Will wasn't ready for that. "We *were* close. Remember that before you make any overtures. Getting too close to me tends to have unhealthy consequences."

Emory was no shrinking violet. Despite his fatigue, an angry spark appeared in his eyes. "I've already followed you to war and back. I'm well aware of the risks."

Will paused, realizing he was being an ass. "That's true." He still didn't feel like apologizing.

Emory caught his arm before he could leave. "If you don't want comfort from me, just say so, but if you're looking for someone to vent your anger on, look elsewhere."

Will raised a brow, his eyes on the other man's hand.

The young nobleman released him, but his visage was unrepentant. "I know. One word from you and my future would be at an end. I won't live my life in fear. I won't apologize for caring, and if you change your mind later, my door will be open."

My door, thought Will sourly, but he held his tongue. His mood was beyond foul. "You're right, and I appreciate the offer."

Downstairs, Will didn't put off the unpleasant task. He shared the news with everyone at the table and continued sharing it with those who came late to breakfast. Inside, he was a mass of guilt and unwelcome emotions, but surprisingly no one else took the news as hard as he expected. There were gasps and exclamations, perhaps a few tears, but none of the others were wracked with sorrow.

Somehow that made it worse.

Seth had always been a friend, but never a central one to him, and now he was beginning to realize it was the same for the others. Aside from their newly heightened fears of dying, the others were more worried about Will's reaction. *Does that mean I was his best friend? How awful is that?* The realization did nothing to help his guilt. *If I had cared more, would I have listened when he wanted to stop?*

Will didn't share his inner turmoil. He spent the rest of the day handling tasks. They buried Seth in the afternoon, and Selene spent a few minutes saying kind words. It was an unofficial memorial service of sorts. The real funeral would be held later. It would be at least a day before Will's letter reached Seth's family, and days more before he received a reply, but the body wouldn't wait.

That evening, after supper, everyone tried to find time to talk to him alone, but Will avoided them all. Selene watched him throughout, a faint look of disapproval in her eyes, but she didn't try to corner him herself. That would come later. At bedtime she would have her moment.

He shut himself into his office and tried to cry, but tears wouldn't come. He wished they would, if only to give lie to the idea that he hadn't cared enough for his old roommate. Instead he sulked, feeling dark and regretful. Will tried to spend some time working on the materials left behind by the Wayfarer's Society but fell asleep in his chair. He only became aware of the fact that he was sleeping when he woke later, a soothing vibration sinking into his chest.

He opened his eyes, and after struggling to focus for a moment, realized he wasn't alone. A warm, furry, and softly vibrating creature was comfortably curled up on his chest, just below his chin.

Strangely, he wasn't startled. It felt too natural, too soothing for that. It was a magical moment, accompanied by the feeling of wonderment that came so often during childhood but now seemed so rare. Despite being the preeminent wizard of the day, Will found himself entranced by the magic of the present.

Will didn't want to move and disturb the cat, so he remained still, studying his companion. Despite being a stray, she was well groomed and didn't smell. As he studied her, she opened her eyes and looked back at him. He decided to risk scaring her and lifted one hand to gently scratch between her ears. The cat closed her eyes, and the rumbling on his chest grew stronger.

I could get used to this, he thought. Relaxing, he let his mind drift while he stroked the cat. "You need a name," he mused out loud. The feline in question opened her eyes, and he imagined her asking the question, why?

"It's a human thing. It helps us keep track of everything. What do you think of Evelyn?" The cat blinked once, then closed her eyes. "I could call you Evie for short," he added.

She didn't object, so he let his thoughts continue to drift. His mind instinctively avoided the subject of Seth, and instead he found himself mulling over the teleportation spell he had learned and its implications. Practicing it to the point of reflex casting would no doubt be useful, but what he really wanted to know was how the Wayfarer's Society wizards had used it to teleport great distances without a beacon. The book had mentioned 'the gates of the mind' but that phrase meant little to him; however, in his relaxed state, his brain began linking together other bits of knowledge he'd learned in recent years.

In particular, Arrogan's lesson regarding congruent planes came to the foreground of his mind. Two planes of existence were congruent with every part of his native plane, the ethereal and the astral planes. The ethereal was physical, and as far as anyone knew, every plane had its own ethereal plane that copied longstanding features. By contrast, the astral plane was purely mental with no real geography. It connected minds and souls, and the only places to be found within it were those that related to other individuals with whom one had formed a bond of some significance: friends, family, and even enemies.

The realization that came to him was slow and gentle, but nonetheless profound. 'The gates of the mind' had to refer to the astral plane. "If I can teleport to a place I can see nearby, maybe I can also teleport to a place I can see through the astral plane," he muttered quietly. If so, that would mean he could travel anywhere, assuming someone he was connected to was there already.

But how to do it in actual practice. That was the question. Will had gotten much better at slipping into the astral plane. In the beginning, it had taken complete sensory deprivation and sheer terror to enable him to leave his body, but during the recent war he had spent a lot of evenings practicing so he could check on Selene and his friends while he was far from home. Lately he had gotten good enough he no longer had to block off his senses at all.

Will closed his eyes, relaxed in the particular way he had become accustomed to, and thought of his father. The sensation of his body, of the purring cat, the sounds of Rimberlin House, all of it faded away, and after a momentary darkness, the image of Mark Nerrow came to life in front of him.

His father sat in the office he had commandeered in Myrsta, the former capital of Darrow. As the newly installed governor, it would have been customary to take the palace of the former Prophet, but it had been completely destroyed during Will's final battle against the demons invading their world. Will studied the furnishings around the room and decided that his father had probably taken the residence of one of the city's noblemen. The office was appointed with tasteful and expensive decorations, well-made furniture, and glass windows.

He probably looked at all the best houses before picking one that suited his tastes, thought Will. His father had impeccable taste, something that Will would never share. From a nobleman's perspective, he was handicapped by his pauper's upbringing.

Despite their differences, Will had faith that his father was one of the best possible choices for the job of governing the new province.

Mark Nerrow frowned at the letter he was reading, then looked up as a messenger entered the room. "Has the eastern patrol returned?"

"No, milord."

Mark rubbed his forehead, massaging what was probably the beginning of a headache. "They should have returned yesterday."

"Should we send another?"

"Tell Commander Hargast I want to see him. If half a company isn't enough, we need to go out in force. Whatever wiped out that village is obviously a serious threat. I'm going to send Second Division, and I'll ride with them."

The messenger left, and Will's father sat brooding in the dimly lit office. Will desperately wanted to ask him what was going on, but unfortunately Mark Nerrow had never developed a sense of the astral, so it was impossible for him to see or hear Will. *But if I could teleport to him that wouldn't be a problem,* thought Will hopefully.

He spent several minutes trying to cast the spell, but all his efforts were fruitless. Without a body, hands, or any sort of physical form, he simply couldn't manipulate the turyn that floated in the air within his father's office. He was quite literally hundreds of miles away, and his only connection was to Mark Nerrow himself. The objects and energy within the room were completely beyond his ability to touch or influence.

Stubborn as ever, Will continued to try for ten minutes more, before finally giving up and returning to his body. He opened his eyes to find Evie staring seriously at his face. Seeing that he had returned, she relaxed and returned to her nap. He wondered idly whether she had sensed his departure and been waiting for him to return, but quickly dismissed the thought.

Returning his thoughts to teleportation, Will realized he wouldn't have been able to complete the spell even if he had found a way to cast it. He still needed to perfect his memorization of it. Sitting up, he put Evie on the desk and summoned the journal so he could look it over once more.

Anything to avoid thinking about what had happened to Seth.

CHAPTER 7

The next week was a miserable one. Will and Selene were both on edge, worrying over whether any of the other students would succumb to turyn starvation. Seth's father responded to Will's letter with cordial and polite language, but that did little to ease his guilt. No one showed ill will toward the king's daughter or her husband. It was impossible to know whether Seth's family blamed him or not.

Ten days after the third compression, Will began to relax. Sammy was already beginning to recover her normal energy and activity levels, and the other students, while not so quick, also seemed to be recovering.

Matthew Holmgren was found dead the next morning. As before, Will was the first to find the body when the young crafter's son failed to turn up for breakfast. This time he didn't wait. Without pause, he went back downstairs and made an announcement at the table. "Matthew passed away during the night." Everyone fell silent, and it almost felt as though no one dared breathe.

Will continued. "I had thought we were past the danger period, but obviously I was wrong. If any of you feel as though you aren't making progress, I urge you to tell me and I will undo the spell cage. Reaching second-order is accomplishment enough and I'd rather not lose anyone else."

Sammy was the first to respond. "I've come this far. I won't quit now." There was solid determination in her voice.

Will had expected as much from his cousin, especially considering how fast she was recovering. She looked almost normal. Her cheeks held a rosy glow, and her eyes were bright with vitality. Emory Tallowen, watching her as always, followed right along. "I don't intend to stop either."

Will's eyes narrowed as he turned toward the young nobleman. Emory's face was pale, and there was a visible tremor in his fingers when he casually reached for the butter. *If anyone should give up, Emory should.* But Will knew the young man's pride wouldn't allow it, especially now that Sammy had cast her lot. *He's going to die.* Will felt a heavy rock settle at the bottom of his stomach, but he knew he couldn't force Emory to change his mind.

He turned his eyes instead to the last remaining student, Shawn Campbell. "Well, Shawn, how do you feel?"

Shawn answered with a strange look on his face. "I don't feel very well." Opening his mouth once more, he froze for a second, seeming to struggle internally, then vomited onto the table. A second later, his eyes rolled back, and he collapsed to the floor.

Selene was closer, and it was her spell-cage on Shawn's source, which turned out to be fortunate, for it made it easier for her to remove it. If it had been Will's spell, she might have struggled. Within seconds she had released the spell, and by then Will had reached Shawn's other side, where he began channeling a tiny stream of turyn into the unconscious wizard. Foreign turyn would only have made matters worse, so Will matched Shawn's natural turyn resonance as he trickled energy into the young man.

Servants came and went, offering help and cleaning up the mess at the table, but Will refused to move anyone until it was clear that Shawn was regaining consciousness.

The rest of the day passed with agonizing slowness as they waited to see if Shawn would recover. According to Arrogan, it was rare for an apprentice to survive once compression sickness had taken hold, but it was equally rare for the source-cage to be removed so quickly, so they had some hope.

Days passed, and Shawn remained weak before finally beginning to show signs of recovery a week later. As with Seth, Will sent a letter to the Holmgren family, and they had a small service when the body was buried. Rimberlin House was likely to have yet another sad visit in the future when Matthew's family came to see the place their son was interred.

On the brighter side of things, Sammy continued to regain her strength, and while Emory was coming along more slowly, he had definitely passed through the worst of it. Both were almost certain to survive, despite Will's dark worries.

Will finally began to relax, though his feelings of guilt remained strong. He tried to explain to Arrogan one evening the week after Matthew's death. He was sitting in his study, with Evie curled up on the desk in front of him. The cat had become a regular part of his life, though she remained elusively out of sight when others were around.

"It's a miracle any of them survived," said Will, reiterating his thoughts once again.

"Stop whining," snapped Arrogan. "You've successfully gotten three through the third compression, possibly five if both of your sisters succeed. In my day it was rare to hear of a master training more than one or two."

"Now I understand why they were so reluctant."

"It was partly fear, but ego also had a lot to do with it," clarified his grandfather. "Quite a few of my contemporaries felt the rarity increased their own prestige. That turned out to be a poor planning choice when the Shimerans started bringing demons over, and soon after that sorcery seemed like the only answer to the problem."

"Killing half my students with extreme training doesn't feel like a good solution either," said Will.

"You're reviving the art, and these makeshift apprentices are a little older than I'd prefer. Once you're past this, you can relax and be more selective. Insist on early teens who still haven't learned to use spells. The survival rate will be much higher, and you can refuse to let any attempt the third compression unless they're dead set on it."

Will ground his teeth. "I don't think I want to do this again."

"That's just abdicating your responsibility. If you don't do it, one of your students will have to do so. Are you willing to shift the blame to someone else so early? Or would you rather they wait until they're past their first century? Sorcery has to end, and the only way to end it, without putting humanity in danger, is to make certain there are enough capable wizards to keep the world safe. Lots of first-order wizards, lots of second-order, and whether you like it or not, more like you. Second-order wizards are good for most things, but they don't usually acquire the same talents that third-order wizards do."

His scalp itched just thinking about it, but he knew Arrogan was probably correct. "Can we just not talk about it right now? Give me a year to put my head back together after this first batch."

"Fair enough, and William—"

It was rare for the old man to refer to him by his given name. "Yeah?"

"You've done well, don't forget that. I don't think I could have done half as well at your age, with so little support. I know I've been hard on you, but don't take it to heart. You're turning into a better wizard than I ever expected, possibly better than any I ever knew."

Will's chest tightened at the words. Praise from Arrogan was rarer than hen's teeth. "Thanks," he managed to reply.

"Tell anyone I said that, and I'll call you a liar," added the ring in a gruff tone.

He smirked. "No one would believe me. They'd take it as a sure sign that I had become delusional." He felt moderately better, but the conversation had reminded him of other concerns he had neglected for too long. "I'll talk to you later. I need to attend to other duties." With that said, Will deactivated the limnthal and closed his eyes.

Arrogan had mentioned his sisters, and with all the stress and tragedy of the past few weeks, Will realized he had gone far too long without checking on them. Regular practice since the end of the war had made the task of slipping out of his body and into the astral plane almost routine. Sensory deprivation wasn't necessary anymore; closing his eyes and taking a moment to clear his mind was all Will needed.

Forming his intent silently, the image of Laina appeared before him, and the world around her came into focus. She was in her room in the house Mark Nerrow had acquired for the family in Cerria. Their original city home had been burned to the ground, but the new house was just as nice, though it hadn't yet acquired the decades of expensive decorations and artwork that had adorned the former house.

Laina was sprawled across a cushioned chair with one leg resting on a side table. She looked disheveled with her hair in disarray and dark circles beneath her eyes. Her attire was a match for her face, since she wore a linen shift that had seen better days. She wasn't preparing for sleep, though, for she wore heavy leather work shoes on her feet. The dirt on the hem of her shift also indicated she'd been wearing it out and about.

Will couldn't imagine that Laina's mother would have allowed her to leave her bedroom in such a state, but the evidence was clear, which probably meant she and Agnes were currently at war with one another.

Unlike others that Will sometimes spied on, his sister Laina had acquired a sense of the astral after the events related to the vampire attack on the capital. The bond between their souls also made her sensitive to his presence, and though her eyes had been closed, they now opened. She turned her head slowly until her half-lidded eyes could focus on Will's vantage point. "Go away," she said in a hoarse voice that lacked energy or conviction.

"Selene told me you went ahead with the third compression. Are you sick?" Will asked worriedly.

Laina's face gained animation for a moment as she snarled and hurled a firebolt in his direction. It passed harmlessly through him but left a black scorch mark on the stone wall behind his vantage point. "I was over that two weeks ago. Tabitha is almost over it as well. Get out."

He hadn't realized she had done the same for Tabitha. Anger warred with relief, but there was little he could do in his disembodied state. "That was foolish."

"It was her choice. One of the few she can still make for herself," growled Laina.

Will clearly remembered the logic behind allowing Laina to leave, as well as not trying to find out what information Lognion had planted with her to tempt him into disaster, but his anxiety was too much. "What's going on?" he asked. "I can't bear it. You look like hell."

Laina started to curse him, he could see it in her expression, but then her face softened, filling with regret, or perhaps sorrow. "I can't tell you. Please go. Selene was right."

"Tell me anyway."

"I can't!" she shouted briefly, then lowered her voice before adding, "even if I wanted to."

"He wants me to know. You know that."

"Don't try to find out. Do what you were planning. If you succeed, none of this will matter."

That wasn't good enough. "You're suffering. I can't bear that."

"I won't die. Who knows? There might even come a day when we can laugh about this," she responded. The words were clearly meant to reassure him, but she didn't sound as though she believed them. "Please leave me alone."

"This isn't over," Will warned.

Her eyes opened wider, then narrowed in suspicion. "Don't even think about spying on Tabitha."

"Farewell." Then he let her fade from view and changed his focus. Tabitha appeared in his view, seated in a sunny garden. The house they had acquired had an expansive sunroom at its heart, and beneath its glass dome Agnes Nerrow had instructed the caretakers to plant an array of flowering plants. It was still very much a work in progress, and the topiaries still had a long way to go, but the room was already a haven of peace and beauty.

Will's younger half-sister had more charm than he or Laina. With thick, dark hair and bright eyes, her smiles and enthusiasm could light up the darkest of rooms. Today that was obviously not the case, however. Unlike Laina, she was properly dressed, and her hair had been brushed and decorated with braids and ribbons, but the light in her eyes was dimmer than Will had ever seen it. A somber mood seemed to hang over her.

She appeared to have been tatting, as a half-finished piece of lace lay forgotten in her hands while Tabitha stared off into space, lost in thought. He wanted to speak to her, but unlike Laina, Will's younger sister was entirely oblivious to the astral plane. She had no awareness of his presence and thus was entirely unable to see or hear him.

A door opened on one side, and the baroness appeared, followed by a maid carrying a tray laden with tea and biscuits. Agnes' face softened in sympathy as she looked at her youngest child. "Maybe we should visit some of your friends," she suggested. "It isn't good to brood at home."

Tabitha smiled wanly. "Forgive me, Mother. I'm not in a mood to entertain, or be entertained."

"Things aren't so bad…"

"Mother, please. I'd rather not talk about it. Just let me sulk a while without worrying at me. I'll do my duty. Trust me."

Agnes' features lit briefly with anger, but she hid the emotion quickly. It was still apparent in her voice, however. "Is that what you think of me? I care more about *you* than just fretting about duty."

"Then why am I here?" snapped Tabitha, her voice rising. "Father doesn't even know!"

"What would you have me do?" responded Agnes. She started to say more, but the same door flew open once more, causing the maid to stumble and drop her tray. The silver teapot spilled its contents, and the other treats scattered across the ground. Laina stood in the doorway, wide-eyed and breathing heavily. She had obviously been running. "By the Mother!" swore Agnes. "Isn't it enough that you disgrace yourself but now you're terrorizing the maids?"

Laina glared back, uncowed. "Stop talking!" she barked. "You're being watched."

"All the more reason you should bathe and put on proper clothes," said Agnes angrily.

Tabitha's face brightened for a moment. "Is it him?"

Laina's eyes settled on Will, then she nodded. "Don't talk about anything else until I make sure we have some privacy."

Agnes was frowning. "Are you referring to William? I don't understand the fuss. After everything you've done for him, and what he's done for us, you act as though he's a threat. Is he here now? I could tell him the news and save the expense of a letter."

Laina's eyes blazed as she glared at her mother. She was busily constructing a spell, and it was almost done as she replied, "I will explain, but give me a moment!" The spell finished coming together, and then a force dome went up around the women.

Unlike in the physical world, force spells were entirely opaque to those in the astral plane. Will's vision of Tabitha vanished, and without the connection, he quickly found himself back in his own body. Opening his eyes, he uttered a string of colorful epithets that would have made Arrogan proud, likely because he'd learned most of them directly from the old man.

Evie leapt onto his desk, but she seemed to sense his agitation, for she lay down a small distance away, rather than seeking to get closer. Will agreed with her decision and did what he had learned so well. Rather than stewing in his own agitation, he turned that energy to more productive ends and threw himself into practice and study.

If his younger self could see him now, he would probably be startled by some of the changes. Will's anger *seemed* to vanish, replaced by an implacable resolve as he started running through spell casting routines. After half an hour of that, the rough seas within had calmed enough that he could actually think, and at that point he turned his attention to working on a new spell he had been considering.

It was based on the principles of the spell that he had used to defeat the demon-lord, but if it worked the way he hoped, then it would give him a more useful endgame spell that could be used to eliminate even the worst opponents, but hopefully without endangering himself as much, or causing the same degree of collateral damage.

That didn't mean it wasn't insanely dangerous, however, especially during the experimental phase. One bit of misjudgment could be the end of him, so it was important that he think through the spell construct carefully, and then rethink it. This was his third time going over the ideas and the tentative rune structure he had designed, but he would probably wait a few more days and go over it once more before attempting a preliminary test.

After that, he started rereading the journal of the Wayfarer's Society once more, to see if he could find some new clue to how they managed to teleport without using beacons. An hour of that and exhaustion, a welcome friend when he was worried, sent him to seek his bed.

Selene joined him, and while they settled in for the night, he relayed to her what had happened during his astral surveillance. It wasn't that he particularly wanted to revisit the topic, but he suspected his wife would have additional insights that hadn't occurred to him.

Her response was measured, more so than usual. "She's obviously in agreement with our original thought. Whatever is happening is meant to draw you out and spoil our plans, or send you headfirst into my father's latest scheme."

Will narrowed his eyes. "And what about the cost?"

"Cost?"

"Knowing Lognion, he's baited his trap with something important, something I can't ignore. Something I can't afford to lose. By ignoring this, we might avoid the trap, but we also don't know the price either."

She paused, gathering her thoughts, then replied, "That's true, but you're playing against the master manipulator. We won't attain victory without paying for it. You know his methods. He needs to get at your emotions and spoil your judgment. You've picked your goal. The only question is whether there's anything worth more than that. If not, letting him into your head will only ruin your chances, and then you'll probably lose everything."

Will pondered that for a moment. His goal was Lognion's death, while at the same time preserving Selene and his family from harm. His mother was safe, Selene was safe for the moment, and there wasn't much the king could do to the Nerrow family.

Yet it was his sisters he was worried about. "If he's planning on killing Laina or Tabitha, that's a price I'm not willing to pay."

Selene shook her head. "That wouldn't make sense. The political cost would be too high. Not that he couldn't pay it, of course, but it would be too much like losing for him. He wants to win completely, while simultaneously humiliating you. If he can't have that, he might accept a lesser win, but he won't want to lose anything to get it."

He felt as though Selene was circling something, but he wasn't sure what it was. Will suspected she had a notion of what was going on, but she wouldn't reveal her suspicions. "What do you think Tabitha meant by her 'duty?'"

"I'm not sure, but since she's the younger daughter it probably isn't serious. All the pressure falls on the eldest child. Tabitha's main concern should only be to avoid bringing shame to the family."

Something didn't ring true, but before Will could confront her about it, someone knocked on their bedroom door. Annoyed, he opened it while tightening the belt of his robe. "Yes?"

The servant at the door was young and nervous. "Squire John has returned, milord. Master Blake said you would want to be informed."

"Oh!" Will glanced at Selene, who waved him on.

"I'll need a moment to change. Go ahead. Tiny won't care what you're wearing," she told him.

He nodded and was out the door, happy to see his friend once more.

CHAPTER 8

As quick as Will was, Tiny was already sitting comfortably in the parlor when he got there. The big man looked damp, which made perfect sense since it had been raining a short while ago. His boots were off, and someone had brought a stool for him to prop his feet up in front of the hearth.

He still jumped to his feet when Will entered. "My lord!"

Will frowned. "None of that! You haven't sworn to me yet." He stepped in to give his friend a hug.

Tiny tried to dodge him, protesting, "I'm still wet and musty from the road!"

Will caught him anyway. "Like I care."

"Your wife will, if you come back to bed with mud on you," said Tiny, squeezing him with arms that seemed powerful enough to choke a bull. Pushing him back, the damp warrior returned to his seat by the fire.

Will chose a chair close by. "Didn't expect you for a few more days at the earliest."

Tiny grinned. "I was motivated, and Sir Kyle said he couldn't bear to keep me any longer since it was clear my heart was no longer in it. Poor Thunderturnip will need a week to recover from my hasty ride."

"Thunderturnip?" That was Tiny's nickname for Sir Kyle's warhorse, a massive black charger with a fondness for turnips. "He lent you his horse?"

"He gave him to me," said Tiny. His eyes roamed the room, making sure no one had arrived unnoticed, then blushed faintly as he added, "Told me it was a wedding present."

Considering that an animal such as Thunderturnip was worth more than a small farm, Sir Kyle's gift was generous indeed, but Will knew that the squire had saved his master from certain death on more than one occasion, so perhaps it was a reasonable expression of gratitude. Sir Kyle was known for being unstinting in both business and his personal relationships.

They spoke for several minutes before a few others appeared. Emory showed up to chat briefly, and Sammy stepped in shortly thereafter. Neither stayed long, though, since it was already late and most of the house was already abed. Tiny kept eyeing the door, but Janice never appeared.

"She's probably asleep," said Will, reading his friend's mind.

Tiny nodded. "I'm surprised I didn't wake everyone else with my late arrival."

Will shrugged. "That's almost everyone."

"What about your other students?"

Will winced, but didn't shy away from the subject. "Seth died of compression sickness a couple of weeks ago, then Matthew a few days back. Shawn almost died as well, but he seems to be recovering."

Shocked, Tiny hissed as his lungs drew in a quick breath. "Damn. I'm sorry. I remember you telling me how dangerous it was, but I thought maybe you'd gotten them all past it." He lowered his voice. "What about your sisters?"

"They went back to Cerria, but so far they're fine, physically at least."

Tiny frowned. "They left? Why would—" Before he could finish that sentence, another thought interrupted him. "Oh! I passed a courier from Cerria yesterday. He gave me some letters for Rimberlin. I'm assuming they're for you or Selene."

At the mention of her name, the lady of the house stepped in. Though she was garbed only by a simple gown and a housecoat, Selene still seemed to shine. Tiny rose and bowed quickly.

Selene started to move forward for a hug, but she took note of Tiny's state and hesitated. The warrior held up his hands. "Best not to dirty yourself, Your Highness."

Selene frowned. "I've told you not to be so formal. This is my home, not court." Tiny bowed again, and then she turned her eyes on the letters in Will's hands. "I'll take those up and put them on your desk. I'm sure you two would like to catch up before you come to bed."

She seemed relaxed, but there was something odd about her as Will started to pass them over. Before she could take them from his hand, his fingers tightened as he noticed the royal seal on one of the letters. "Hang on. I should probably look at that."

His wife didn't let go. "Tomorrow will be soon enough."

Will carefully pried the letter from her hand, letting her keep the rest. "You don't want me to see this one, do you?"

She pursed her lips, then seemed to relax. "If it's from my father, then no. It may be something intended to provoke you."

She's lying, or at best it's a half truth, he thought. Stepping over to a side table, Will opened a drawer that held a selection of silverware meant for serving food. A small cheese knife served perfectly to cut the seam along the top of the letter, and moments later his eyes began scanning the page. After moving past some ornate decorations and calligraphy, Will got into the meat of the letter. Several words leapt out at him. *"... cordially invited to the union of..."*

The page began to shake in his hands, and Will's face reddened. After a second, his eyes glanced up and he could see that Selene was white knuckled as she gripped the rest of the letters. *She knew.* "When were you planning to tell me?" Will demanded, his voice low and threatening.

Tiny edged back away from the two of them, noticeably uncomfortable, as Selene replied, "Preferably after he was dead."

"That's still over a month away," said Will. "The wedding is ten days from now." The windows began giving off a strange hum, vibrating as though they could feel the tension in the air.

Selene held her ground. "It won't matter if he doesn't survive for long afterward."

"Matter? Tabitha is my sister! I don't want your father to be alone with her for five minutes, much less several weeks!"

"It's a marriage, not a death sentence."

"She's barely reached her majority."

Selene finally snapped. "So what? This was her decision. She knows what she's doing. Are you the only one allowed to make sacrifices?"

The window shattered as Will answered. "Yes! Yes, I'm the only one allowed to make sacrifices. Not you! Not my family, not Tabitha!" He was roaring by the time he reached his sister's name. "Why would you do this?"

"I've done nothing. It was her choice—to help you."

"To help me?" Will sputtered. "And yes, you've done something. This isn't the first letter, is it? You've known for some time, probably since the day she left." Selene's lips compressed into a line as he continued. "How many letters has he sent? If I open your desk drawer, what will I find?"

She raised her chin. "Nothing. I burned them." She glanced at the other windows. "And if you don't calm down, there won't be any glass left in the house."

Will made a conscious effort to still the turyn around him, but then replied, "I'm so mad right now there might not be a house in an hour's time. Did you really think you were helping? This is not a price I'm willing to pay."

"She's willing," stated Selene. "I would do the same in her place. In fact, I'd do worse to protect you. Much worse."

"I don't want you to protect me. I want you to help me. Why?"

Her composure finally broke, and Selene's voice cracked as she answered, "Because he'll kill you, William. Don't you understand? If you go, you'll die. This is what my father does!"

He started to argue, "You don't—"

"You aren't smart enough!" she shouted. "No one is. It doesn't matter how powerful you are either. This is how he wins. It's how he always wins. Whatever he's set up, if you go back to the capital, you won't survive. The only hope you have—we have—is to stick to the plan. Don't let him provoke you."

"I'm not letting him have her."

"Then you'll die, and what then? Do you think he'll call off the wedding for your funeral?"

The words stung so much that in that moment he almost forgot to breathe. "You're saying I'm being selfish—you—when you're willing to let Tabitha suffer for my sake."

She nodded. "We can't win if you let him manipulate you. Defeating my father is risky enough, but without your power to rein in the nobility after his death, the nation will fall into civil war. This is a price you have to accept, for everyone's sake, regardless of your own feelings."

"For everyone's sake, or yours?"

Selene visibly froze. "What does that mean?"

"You're worried about the transition of power, from him to you. I'm worried about the people I love."

"I don't even want the throne," she argued. "You're the one who refuses to accept it."

"We both know you'd be in charge either way. Your priorities here only emphasize the point."

"That's not true."

The disgust he felt was so great that Will looked away. Instead, he turned to Tiny. "Do you still want to enter my service?"

Tiny seemed confused. That was the whole point of him leaving Sir Kyle's service and returning to Rimberlin, after all. He nodded. "Of course, but…"

"Swear now then. We leave in the morning." The oath and his response went quickly, albeit awkwardly. When it was done, Will started for the door, brushing past his wife, who had been doing a passable imitation of a statue.

His leaving startled her into motion again. "Will, you can't do this…"

"This is exactly what I'm doing," he bit back. "I'll sleep in one of the other rooms tonight, so don't wait up for me."

Despite the abrupt ending, Selene didn't lose her temper, much less her composure. She was made of sterner stuff than that. Ordinarily, Will wouldn't have dreamed of deliberately provoking her, as she always found other ways to find retribution, but he was too angry to do anything else. Behind him, he heard her call for Blake to get Tiny settled in for the night.

For his own part, Will did find a bed in one of the spare rooms, but he failed to sleep. Stubborn as ever, he didn't give up, though. He kept still and brooded, turning the fight over and over in his head. Two hours later and he still felt justified, though he regretted some of his harshness. More importantly, his head cooled, and he began to think things through.

His wife was probably correct in her assessment. She usually was. That rankled, but he still had no intention of letting Tabitha go through with her sacrificial gesture. Even so, charging into the palace was almost certainly the worst thing he could do. Will wasn't convinced he would die, but a lot of others almost certainly would, and depending on what Logion had planned, the collateral damage might extend well beyond the palace grounds.

He summoned one of the swords stored in the limnthal and held it up above his head so he could study it. There was nothing special about it, other than the deadly spell he had placed upon the blade. It was the same spell he had dreamed up for his battle with the demon-lord, though Selene had been the one to create the final design. *No matter how desperate things get, I can't use it in Cerria, though.*

When activated, the spell would translate the steel blade into the ethereal plane, where it would remain until the wielder released the hilt. At that point, the wielder would be moved to the ethereal plane while the blade would return to the normal world. If the blade occupied something solid when it rematerialized—like the space within a human body, or a tree, or anything physical—a violent explosion would result. Any given volume of space could only hold so much physical material, and if more appeared within the same volume, a large portion of it would be converted into pure energy.

When he'd used it before, the resulting blast had leveled a large area and he was afraid if he used it inside the palace, it would not only annihilate everyone there, it might also cause significant collateral damage to the building. He sent the sword back into storage and summoned out a handful of steel spikes. Laina's bodyguard called them war darts, and they were meant to be thrown by hand. Each one weighed a couple of pounds, and their points were razor sharp.

They were made such that their balance was close to the point, making it easy to strike a target properly. Will had no intention of using them in a purely mundane fashion, however. The new spell he was working on was meant for them, and if it worked properly, it would give him a trump card that caused less collateral damage than the ethereal sword spell.

But it might be even more dangerous for the user, thought Will. Given the ranged application, he hadn't figured out a way to precisely time the transition from ethereal to material and vice versa. Instead, he was counting on making sure that only a tiny portion of the dart actually translated to the ethereal and back again. If the amount of matter was small enough it should also limit the size of the explosion, but although he had calculated the numbers several times over, he couldn't be sure what they meant in the real world. Smaller, fine—but would it be small enough?

That meant he couldn't really use either of his surefire game-enders. One would kill thousands of innocents, and the other might kill him *and* an uncertain number of bystanders. The real question was whether he was wizard enough to not need such tactics to win. He'd been training for years, and although in the early days it hadn't seemed to matter, he was now starting to reap unexpected benefits almost daily. Constructing spells, even new ones, was easier than ever, and he was continually being surprised when he discovered he was able to reflex cast yet another spell during his practices. His will was strong enough now to suppress the spell casting of anyone near him, with the possible notable exception of Grim Talek, the lich.

Combine those factors with his continually improving battle reflexes, honed through daily practice, and his rapidly expanding repertoire of spells—the conclusion was inevitable. *I should be invincible,* he told himself. But he knew better.

Lognion himself was a partial unknown. Will had a rough gauge of the man's will from previous encounters, plus the monarch's utter defeat by the master vampire Androv showed him that the man was obviously not invulnerable. Will had been the one to defeat the vampire, and worse opponents since. One-on-one, he was fairly confident he could win, but the king wouldn't be alone.

He knows all this too, and I'm letting him pick the battleground. "Selene's right. He's setting me up and he's sure of his own victory." There was only one answer, not to fight. If the king was trying to provoke him publicly, it meant the man wanted Will to start the fight. That would give Lognion the excuse he needed, and whatever happened thereafter would be seen as the justifiable response to treason.

Not only that, but it would resolidify Lognion's power. After the war with Darrow, Will had earned a reputation as a nearly unstoppable force. If he was shown to be a traitor, and then defeated by the king, no one would dare to oppose Lognion.

"But I'm still not letting him have Tabitha," Will muttered. "So, what do I do?" And then he knew.

Jumping up he kicked his way free of the covers and pulled on a robe before rushing out of the room. A minute later, he was outside his own bedroom. Without pausing he opened the door and went in, and for a few seconds he thought Selene was absent. The bed they shared was a wreck, with all the blankets and covers twisted into a tangled mess covering the center of the mattress and exposing the sides.

But the room was redolent with her distinctive turyn, and when he glanced at the bed a second time, he saw a slender foot sticking out of the chaos. "Selene? Are you alright?" he asked tentatively. The foot promptly disappeared, pulled back into the twisted linens. "Too late. You've been spotted," he told her.

Reaching out, he started to untangle the bedsheets and nearly lost some teeth when the foot reappeared, kicking dangerously close to his face. Since she couldn't see, Will assumed she wasn't aiming for his head, but then again, he wasn't entirely certain. "I'm sorry."

"No, you're not."

He sighed. "You're right, and I'm still angry about you hiding this from me, but I think I have a solution."

The amorphous mass in the center of the bed went still, then rose up. A few seconds later, Selene's head appeared. Red, swollen eyes, blotchy cheeks, and hair that looked as though it might house an entire family of rats. His wife was anything but beautiful at the moment, yet despite his residual anger, her appearance tugged at something within his chest. She studied him warily. "You're going to stick to the plan?"

He shook his head. "No, but I'm not going to fight."

Her features froze. "What does that mean?"

"I'm not going to do what he wants. He wants to provoke a fight. A premature fight that allows him all the advantages."

Her expression turned sour. "Obviously, but just saying you're not going to fight doesn't explain anything. What do you actually mean?"

"Your father is trying—"

"Don't call him that," she snapped.

"The king is trying to draw me into a political situation and force me to start hostilities there. That way he can kill me and reap the rewards of reaffirming his power. He's greedy, you see?"

She looked thoughtful. "Explain further."

"He's given away part of his design," said Will. "He wants to strengthen his position. Winning the war with Darrow made me popular. It made me dangerous to him, politically, so he doesn't just want to eliminate me quietly, he wants me to reveal my hostility, to give him the moral high ground."

Selene nodded. "I'm pretty sure I've told you all this before."

"But I didn't realize how it allows us to predict his actions to a certain degree," agreed Will. "He wants me to show up angry and reveal my intentions. That's why he's marrying Tabitha, to provoke me."

She sighed. "I'm going to throttle you if you keep restating the obvious. I've said *all* of this already. That's why you can't take the bait."

Will shook his head. "I'm not letting him have her, but I won't bite either. If he wants me dead, *he* will have to start it, and that spoils his plans."

"So, what? You're going to politely tell him no and walk out with your sister?"

"I'll show up, play nice, and pretend I'm unwilling to fight. I won't declare anything, but the first chance I get, I'll take them and run."

His wife stared at him in confusion. "Huh?"

"I'll take her and run. She's not a prisoner. I'll take Agnes and Laina too. Given how angry she is, I imagine Laina will help."

Selene gaped. "That ruins everything—for us. It will start a civil war. You won't be able to kill him cleanly. Plus, he *controls* Laina. As soon as he finds out they've fled, he can use the enchantment to question her. He'll find you immediately."

Will set his jaw. "That's the best I can offer."

"Civil war?"

"It screws up everyone's plans, his and ours, but I'll be alive. I'm not letting him have my family. Not you, not her, not Laina, Sammy, my mother, not even Agnes Nerrow. If the world has to burn, so be it. I never claimed to be perfect. I'm not taking the blame for Lognion's actions. He's pushing me into a corner, the consequences are on his shoulders, not mine."

Selene inhaled deeply, held it a moment, then exhaled. "Fine. I'll take it, but you have to remain cool-headed."

He hadn't expected that response. "You agree?"

"No. It's terrible and we're going to wind up with a messy, chaotic war, but as long as you're alive that's enough for me. I still think the other option is better."

Will grimaced. "She'd be his wife for weeks, months maybe. It's unthinkable."

"She's tougher than you think. It's just sex, William. Especially for him, I don't think he even has human desires, not as we know them. He's a monster, but he'd just be going through the motions to get the child he wants. Maybe I'm terrible for this, but I think it's much better than what you propose. A lot of people may die in this war you're about to precipitate."

"It's not *just* sex, it's rape. I won't make this a war, though. We won't mobilize. I'll take them and hide them with my mother. After that I'll be an outlaw—until I manage to kill him."

"And Laina? This is insanity."

"You take her somewhere else. He won't be out to kill you or her."

"He'll use her to get you, and you overestimate his fatherly sentiments."

"I won't give him that much time. As soon as they're hidden, I'll switch to Plan C. One way or another it will be over and done within a week or two at most."

Plan C hardly deserved being described as a 'plan.' It was shorthand for a surprise one-man assault. Selene frowned. "Once again, how is this better?"

"It won't be at the time or place of his choosing. That's the best I've got," said Will. "He may have the better plan, but I have the bigger hammer. All I have to do is avoid stepping into the trap. If I fight anywhere or anytime else, I can win."

She stared at him worriedly, chewing her lip. "You sure about that?"

"You designed the most recent training scenarios. Do you think anyone could stop me?"

Her reply was immediate. "No, but a million things could go wrong." She paused. "If you succeed, you're stuck with me. I'll hold onto you until you're sick of the sight of me."

Will smiled faintly. "Never happen. What if I don't succeed?"

"I'll follow you into death, track you down in the underworld and make eternity miserable for you," she replied venomously.

He smirked. "Sounds like I win either way."

CHAPTER 9

Tiny was much relieved when it became apparent that the tension between Will and Selene had dissipated. The rest of the household was thrown into turmoil, however, when Will announced his sudden trip and Selene began issuing orders in preparation for it. She gave the staff little more than an hour from breakfast to pack their things and prepare the carriage for the trip to the capital.

Some energetic discussions occurred over who would be coming and who would not. Sammy was devastated by the news she would be staying home. Emory also seemed mildly disappointed, but he hurried to assure Will he would be ready to protect the house if the need arose.

That set Will to bristling, for he knew the young nobleman was referring mainly to Sammy, and he was loath to leave the two of them alone together. Technically they wouldn't be alone, of course. Janice was staying behind, as well as the staff, but that didn't feel like enough for him.

Tiny also had concerns. "You're going into a risky situation. Is it wise to leave your best wizards behind?"

Will stared back at the big man, measuring his intentions. *He's disappointed that Janice won't be with us.* "They're barely past the compression sickness. Even if they feel mostly normal, I wouldn't risk them in a stressful combat situation."

"Janice told me she elected not to undergo the third compression. She should be fully capable currently. She's been to war before, and although she's still a newly minted second-order wizard, she's already well trained and experienced." Tiny paused, then went on, "I understand that Sammy is still a novice, and Emory, despite his skills, is possibly still compromised by the recent compression, but Janice is fully prepared to support you."

Will raised one brow. "You spoke to her this morning?"

Tiny nodded, disappointment flickering briefly across his face. "Not for long. She said her stomach was bothering her." The massive knight shifted on his heels, seeming uncomfortable. "I'm not sure I believe it, though. It seems as though she's avoiding me."

Morning sickness. Will put a hand on his friend's shoulder. "Trust me. She really isn't feeling her best right now, otherwise I'm sure she would have argued when I told her I wanted her to stay here."

Tiny narrowed his eyes. "A foolish decision."

"I have you to watch my back, not to mention the most powerful wizard in the world."

"I'm just a simple warrior, and you can't count yourself when it comes to guarding your back."

Will smirked. "I meant Selene. Her knowledge is greater than mine, her skills are extraordinary, and she's had the longest amount of time to adjust to the third compression. I wouldn't bet on it just yet, but before long I'd guess she might be more than enough to beat Lognion all by her lonesome."

"Three is still a very small number."

"We aren't going to fight. This will be a social event."

"Followed by a kidnapping."

Will scowled. "She doesn't belong to the king. She'll come willingly."

"And if not?"

He sighed. "Then I suppose it'll be a kidnapping after all. Having second thoughts about swearing to me?"

"Ask me again and I'll knock you down. I'd be there with you, oath or no oath. Janice would be too if you let her," said Tiny gruffly.

Will nodded, but he knew better. Janice had a new priority, one that he fully supported. In fact, he felt terrible that she still hadn't told Tiny yet. What if something happened? Because of her anxiety, she had barely emerged to see Tiny, and thanks to Will's latest crisis, his friend wasn't ready to propose yet. The two of them needed to talk.

More importantly, was it right for him to risk Tiny's life? Janice was simple enough, for she carried the child within her, but what about the unwitting father? It reminded him of Selene. She'd chosen to let Tabitha make a sacrifice to keep him safe, prioritizing him over her friend. *I'm doing the same thing,* Will realized. *I love Tiny, but I'm willing to risk his life for the sake of my sisters, and he doesn't even know what he might lose.*

It aggravated him that he couldn't tell his friend, but Janice had been adamant. "Please, it will only distract him. I need to tell him myself, when we have time together," she had said. He'd agreed, but he didn't like it.

Will looked up, seeing someone advancing toward them quickly. Tiny noticed and turned to face the newcomer. "Who is it?" he asked.

"Tailtiu," said Will simply. She was currently in her burly masculine form, which was why his friend hadn't recognized her. Tiny blanched at the name, clearly uncomfortable. Tailtiu's overt sexual nature had embarrassed him several times in the past.

The fae woman grew even larger as she approached, until she stood a few inches taller than even Tiny. She gave the knight a wink as she addressed Will. "You have a visitor."

"Who?"

"One of the Drak'shar," she replied. "The same one that followed you during parts of the war. I recognize its stink. It seems to want to talk."

Will nodded. "Show me."

She frowned. "The creature is dangerous. Better to destroy it."

Tailtiu still carried mental scars from the time that the vampires had tortured her, scars that should be impossible for one of her kind to have. Nonetheless, she both hated and feared the undead monsters. "Is it dangerous to you?" he asked.

"Of course not," she scoffed.

"Then it's barely a threat to me," said Will. "Which way? I'll meet him privately." He'd already deduced that the vampire must be his old classmate, Rob. Tailtiu growled, but pointed off to the left, toward part of the grounds that contained a lot of large topiaries. Tiny started to protest, but Will waved him off. "It's fine. I know who it is."

He moved confidently, while behind him he heard his fae aunt muttering, "Barely a threat? That makes me so damned horny." Then she asked Tiny, "Still monogamous? I could offer you some interesting exercise."

Will tried not to laugh and kept his mind on the meeting in front of him. Rob he could handle, hostile or not, but if Rob's master, the lich, was present, then he might be entirely helpless. Grim Talek was probably capable of hiding his presence from Tailtiu, which meant that Will might be putting himself in danger, but bringing support wouldn't change anything. The danger was just as great whether he was alone or with an army. The lich was immortal, magically flawless, and entirely amoral. Will could only hope the conversation would be peaceful if the undead paragon was present.

He found Rob standing on the other side of a massive, sculptured bush, unflustered by the morning sun. His old friend smiled, flashing sharp fangs as he approached. "Long time no see."

Will nodded. "You look better." The last time he had seen his friend, Grim Talek had tortured the young vampire by grinding up his internal organs and bones with a nasty spell. "I notice you aren't getting a tan either."

"I'm learning to draw turyn again. The spell is my own," said Rob, obviously proud, then he lowered his eyes. "I want to apologize."

Will didn't trust his old classmate any farther than he could see him. "What for?"

"I behaved badly toward you in the past. I was obsessed. It's— it's hard to describe, but in the early years after the transformation, the thirst, the urges, they tend to make it difficult to think properly. I'm better now. Almost—"

"Human?"

Rob met his gaze with frighteningly inhuman intensity. "No. Never that, but I'm more civilized at least. In time, my master assures me I'll be far better than merely human."

"Is he here?" asked Will.

"No, he sent me with a warning."

Will's hands twitched, then tightened into fists. "I'm getting tired of threats. If you're truly alone, you should be careful with your words."

Rob blanched. "I'm on your side, Will, even if you don't trust me."

"You serve your master."

"Your patron," returned Rob.

"What?" Will's temper flared. "Are you trying to provoke me?"

"He's been helping you, even if you aren't conscious of it," said Rob. "He calls you his 'disciple.'"

"I'll reduce him to dust, given half a chance," spat Will. "Just a few months ago I framed your master for a murder. Isn't he aware?"

Rob smiled. "He knows, and he wanted me to tell you that the opinions of mortals don't concern him at all. If anything, he found your stunt humorous. He favors you greatly, Will. For me, or any of the others, such actions would result in extinction."

"I'm getting tired of this," said Will. "Give me the message. Drag this out any longer and I'll put an end to your suffering."

"I'm only trying to help, but very well. My master warns you to stay at home. You're walking into a trap."

Will sighed. "I know it's a trap."

"You cannot kill Lognion, not yet. No one can."

"Your master's former student, Androv, nearly killed him not too long ago. I can do even better."

Rob shook his head. "You saved the world from what would have been Androv's greatest mistake. Have you read the book?"

"What book?" Will was genuinely confused.

"My master's book, left behind for the generations to come. He told me you should have read it by now. If so, he warns you that Lognion is the beast mentioned in the book."

"I don't have any book written by your decrepit master," growled Will. "You aren't making any sense."

Rob looked genuinely confused, his eyes widening. "But you're Master's chosen. You must have read the book. He teaches that you will save the cattle and bring us a golden age of blood, when every appetite will be sated."

Will lifted a hand, and even though they were separated by more than ten feet of space, he tugged at the spell protecting Rob from the daylight. "You're irritating me beyond my tolerance. Explain yourself or I'll let the sun have its way with you."

Rob held up his hands. "I don't know. I haven't read the book, nor even seen it. Master left it to your kind, in preparation for the day that someone like you would arrive." The vampire backed away. "You shouldn't threaten me. I'm an adept of the fourth order now. Though I'm young now, someday I will surpass you."

"Tell that to Androv," growled Will. "Leave, I'm almost out of patience."

Rob vanished with frightening speed, and Will returned to the others. Tiny was the first to ask, "What did it want?"

Will had spent the last minute as he walked back thinking about what to tell them. Rob's warning wouldn't sit well with Selene. "Threats," he replied simply. "Grim Talek is unhappy with what I've done to his reputation. Today's message was posturing."

Selene was standing by the carriage. "We need to leave. You can explain in more detail while we travel."

Tiny would be riding alongside, on Thunderturnip, so he merely shrugged, then gave Will a look of encouragement. Inside the carriage, Selene waited expectantly, and as they began rolling, he did his best to explain. She wasn't entirely satisfied with his answers.

"Why would he threaten us now?" she asked. "It doesn't feel right. Does the lich know where we're going?"

"Probably," said Will. "I think he wants to shake my confidence. He likely has a grudge over losing Darrow. Overthrowing your father would be yet another feather in our cap."

"From what you've said, he could kill you if he wanted. Why doesn't he?"

Will shrugged. "I think he's somewhat like the king. He likes games. A brute force win doesn't give him any satisfaction."

Selene eyed him suspiciously. "Maybe."

He asked a question to change the focus of the conversation. "Do you really think we should be taking the carriage? We won't be able to use it later." The trip to Cerria took half a day by wagon or carriage while they could make the journey quicker on fast mounts. If Will and Selene used travel spells, they could get there in just a couple of hours.

"Definitely," she replied. "A speedy arrival won't help us. Tonight is the first of several events to introduce Tabitha to the populace. It doesn't start until late afternoon, and you're not planning to abscond with your sister until afterward. By arriving just before, we give the king the least amount of time to react."

"Assuming he isn't already aware of our movements somehow," observed Will.

She nodded. "True. Either way, though, we've limited his time to prepare by some amount. Tonight will be limited to the nobility, so it will also be the smallest crowd and the one he least wants to offend, which should keep him on his best behavior."

"I'm not sure I understand why he's having multiple gatherings to accomplish the same thing."

Selene took a deep breath and began to explain. "It's a bit like how ordinary people publish banns when they are about to get married, but for royalty it's much more involved. As the head of state, Lognion's marriage is a significant event for the entire nation. The parties leading up to the wedding will get larger each day, but only the most important people get to be at all of them. The nobility, those with the most wealth and power will be present tonight—and every other night. Tomorrow, the invitations will include rich merchants, guild masters, and other captains of industry. The next day, those with less wealth and influence will be included, and the final day will be a public event."

She paused, giving him a pensive look, then added, "And you're wrong about the carriage. Laina and I can use it since we're escaping separately."

"You'll be caught sooner," Will cautioned.

"We can ride separately, and when the pursuit gets close, we can split off and let the carriage serve as a decoy for us. A decoy for the decoy, so to speak."

"Unless he uses Laina against you from the beginning."

"She won't be conscious," Selene responded. "Since she's presumably going to be cooperating, I can keep her asleep for at least a full day. He won't be able to issue any orders if she's unconscious. If we get lucky and he misses his chance when I wake her to handle her necessities, we might be able to remain uncaught for several days."

He nodded. "With Tailtiu's help, I can get Tabitha and Agnes safely to Barrowden and be back in Cerria within less than a day. Hopefully this will be over before you're caught."

Mentioning his planned confrontation made Selene visibly nervous, but she hid it well. "Can you travel that quickly with others tagging along?"

"I'll be alone on the return trip."

She froze. "What about Tiny?"

"I'm leaving him with Mom and the others in Barrowden. He'll be more use there, and he would just be a hindrance when I fight the king."

"You don't have eyes in the back of your head, William—"

Will held up a hand to forestall the rest of her argument. "Tailtiu will be with me. He's about to be a father." As he spoke, he noticed her right hand tightening on part of her skirt, though her features remained smooth.

She nodded, then stared out the window for a moment. "As I should have expected."

"Are you upset?"

"Let's not talk about it for a while. I didn't get enough sleep."

CHAPTER 10

"Presenting Her Highness, Princess Selene Cartwright and her husband, William Cartwright, Duke of Arenata. They are accompanied by Sir John Shaw and his companion Denise…" The announcer's voice remained calm, but he stumbled slightly over 'Selene Cartwright.' Will had argued for a more conservative approach, but despite her usual calm, Selene hadn't been willing to compromise on that point. She had insisted that her father was more cautious when angry than otherwise, as he viewed emotion as a weakness.

Despite being the smallest event of the week, the palace ballroom was still full. No one among the nobility had wanted to miss the chance, and having an opportunity to attend the first night was a clear indicator of power and the favor of the king.

Their arrival was unexpected since they hadn't responded to any of the invitations, much less appeared at any social events in the capital recently. Not only had they arrived without forewarning, but they'd also appeared late, two hours after the start. According to Selene, arriving late was a privilege and statement of power. "The later you show up, the more influence and authority you have—presumably. The one rule, though, is one must never arrive after the royal family. The king is always the last to appear. Daring to enter after him is considered an affront."

"I'm not here to fight, remember?" Will had reminded.

Selene had nodded. "Again, the angrier he is, the more cautious he will be. He's at his most aggressive when he's calm."

Descending the steps to the main ballroom floor, Will couldn't help but notice everyone's eyes had fixed upon them. He met each gaze with steady eyes and a haughty smirk, while Selene's response was the opposite. She accepted the attention as her due, returning the curious stares with a charming smile. Those who approached, she met with warmth and familiarity, addressing each and every one, lords, ladies, and even their children, with their names and a polite question regarding their health or similar doings. Her memory for such details was simply colossal, and Will was continually impressed.

He knew some of the names, but in general he paid close attention to Selene's introductions since he recognized only a fraction of the nobles present. It was with a sense of relief that he was able to greet Baron Lambel and Baron Hargast without needing any assistance. They were his own vassals after all, and he knew both men well from the recent war.

"You are a vision of health and vigor, Your Grace," complimented Lord Lambel effusively, "though even you can't stand beside the vision of beauty and grace without seeming plain in comparison." The young baron tipped his head respectfully in Selene's direction. "It's a pleasure to see you here this evening, Your Highness."

After a short exchange, in which Lambel introduced his wife, Evelyn, the baron turned his attention to Tiny and Tailtiu. "Is that you, Squire Shaw?" he asked with a smile.

"Sir John, now," Tiny answered politely with a blush. "I'm honored you remember me."

"Sir Kyle would let none forget your name. To hear him recount it, half of all the enemy casualties were done by your hand." The baron glanced at Tailtiu. "I haven't had the pleasure of meeting your companion, Denise—I didn't catch the rest of your name."

"Mortiferous," replied Tailtiu promptly.

The baron's brows went up. "How unusual. I haven't heard a name quite like it before."

"It isn't really my name," Tailtiu added honestly. "It's more a description of what I do."

Lambel looked uncertainly at Will, who merely shrugged, then the man asked hesitantly, "You'd describe yourself as deadly then?"

Tailtiu nodded agreeably. "Though not always in a violent sense. Sometimes I fuck them to de—"

Will choked on a laugh, but Selene intervened, speaking over the fae woman. "Lady Evelyn, tell me about your journey. When did you arrive in Cerria?" Tiny took the opportunity to warn Tailtiu to silence with a stern shake of his head.

Others approached, such as Baron Hargast and the newly minted Duke Lustral. The greetings and introductions were endless, and through it all Will could feel Lognion's eyes studying them from the balcony above.

The ballroom itself was enclosed by a wide upper balcony that looked over the main floor on all sides. It was there, on the north side of the room, that King Lognion entertained a steady stream of well-wishers while showing off his future bride. If his daughter's rude appearance bothered him, he showed it not at all.

Will's attention was drawn back by Selene's voice. "Lady Nerrow, it has been too long!" Turning, he saw that Agnes Nerrow had finally reached them, accompanied by a younger man with a distinctly martial air to him. Selene continued, "Sir Nelson, this is my first time seeing you since your elevation to knighthood."

Will ticked off the details in his mind. Given that his father was in Darrow, Agnes had elected to bring a younger vassal as her escort. The knight in question seemed capable in ways that some landed gentry did not, which made him think her choice might be grounded in a real need for security. *Mark isn't here, and she's under immense pressure from the king. No number of men-at-arms would be enough, but she must feel better having a strong arm beside her.*

"I am honored you remember me, Your Highness," said the knight in question, then he nodded respectfully in Will's direction. "And I've been wanting to meet you since the war, Your Grace." He offered his hand, which Will then shook.

"Were you with us in Darrow?" he asked.

Sir Nelson nodded. "I was in Fifth Division, serving as squire to Sir Brad Wolver in the Second Battalion. I was merely a sergeant at the time."

Will smiled. "Don't be so humble. The sergeants are the backbone of Terabinia's military. In many ways, they're one of the most important components, more so than the officers, in my own opinion."

Sir Nelson rushed to respond, almost stumbling over his words in his enthusiasm, "But not *you*, Your Grace. You were no mere officer. You were the heart of the army!" He blushed a second later, realizing what he had said. Glancing around at some of the noblemen within earshot, he apologized, "No disrespect meant to the officers who helped guide us to victory, but you were an inspiration to us all, Lord Cartwright."

The young knight's obvious devotion was mildly embarrassing, but Agnes Nerrow stepped in at that point. "Your Grace, it has been too long since we visited." Ordinarily, a lady would have offered him her hand at that point, but she stepped forward instead. Following her example, Will suddenly found her hands on his shoulders as the baroness leaned forward to bestow a kiss on each of his cheeks. It was still a formal greeting, but one that denoted much greater familiarity.

"Your Excellency, you do me too much honor," said Will.

Agnes waved a hand dismissively. "The reverse is true, William. Remember your rank now." She glanced briefly at Selene as though admonishing the princess to train him more thoroughly in etiquette, then winked. "Since you've married the daughter of my heart, you're as good as family to me now."

"Speaking of daughters," interjected Selene, "I haven't seen Laina yet, tonight."

"She was on the balcony with Tabitha a short time ago," answered Agnes. "No doubt she's mingling somewhere now." Her eyes flickered back and forth between the two of them briefly, and she lowered her voice. "Given her remarks over the past week, I didn't expect the two of you to appear in public."

That was probably the most she could say without creating a scandal, should she be overheard. He and Selene had planned specifically for this meeting, so he decided the moment was right to take the initiative. "We didn't expect to be here today either. In our haste to return, we failed to have our house prepared. I don't want to impose but..."

Agnes beamed at them. "Say no more. I'd much rather you stay with us!"

Will thanked Agnes, then gave Selene quick glance and a smile as she took the lead and continued the conversation. Their main goal was now accomplished. All that remained was another hour or so of socializing and then they could withdraw. The next step was simply to meet at the Nerrows' city house before making a late-night escape from Cerria.

All they had to do now was finish their time at the party peacefully.

Sir Nelson's voice interrupted that thought. "Speaking of your daughter, I see her coming over now."

Will looked up and saw his sister Laina was indeed approaching. Though she wasn't the bride, she was the best-known member of the Nerrow family, having become famous during her teenage years as a charity organizer for the Mothers of Terabinia. She had also given a rousing speech to rally the citizens during the vampire attacks and had subsequently garnered even more credit for the city's survival. The crowd parted as she approached, carrying small tray laden with several delicate glass flutes filled with an amber liquid.

She smiled at Will, but the expression didn't quite reach her eyes, which barely hid a simmering anger. The fire in her gaze seemed to accent the burnt orange of her dress as she finally moved into speaking range. "What are you doing here?" she demanded.

"I finally figured it out," said Will simply. "I think we're on the same side."

"What does that mean?"

Selene intervened, "He wouldn't cooperate with my idea, so you will probably approve."

Laina blinked. "I'm not even sure which side I'm on anymore. Besides, it's awfully late for this." As an afterthought, she held the tray out to Will. "Here, have a glass."

He smirked. "You're serving now?" Behind her, he saw people moving quickly aside as Tabitha pushed her way through the crowd to join them in a hurry. Glancing up, he saw Lognion watching with an amused expression while the people nearest him gossiped. Tabitha had apparently left his side in a rush.

Laina grimaced. "I needed an excuse that would get me across the floor sooner."

Will took a glass, and Selene was reaching for another when Tabitha finally got to them. She was red cheeked and holding her dress up to keep it from tangling around her ankles. Her expression was either angry or distraught, and as soon as she had gotten to them, she threw her shoulder into Laina, sending the tray of drinks to the floor. Without pause, she slapped the remaining glass from Will's hand. "It's poisoned!"

Laina blinked at her sister in confusion, but Agnes didn't hesitate. "Tabitha, what are you doing? You've caused a dreadful scene!"

The youngest daughter didn't flinch, or even spare a glance for her mother, instead replying in uncharacteristic fashion. "Mother, shut up." Then she wheeled on Laina. "You saw that man adding something to the tray. What is wrong with you?"

Before the argument could play out, a shout rose from the upper gallery, followed by several high-pitched screams. Will saw a man stumble and fall, a crossbow bolt buried in his chest. Several well-dressed bodyguards moved to surround the king, and four black-clad men appeared from somewhere on the left-hand side of the balcony. They carried more crossbows, which they fired before dropping them and racing toward the king, knives in hand.

Everyone in the room seemed to hold their breath for a moment as the crowd registered what was happening, and then pandemonium broke out. People screamed and men yelled. A particularly loud voice carried from above, "Assassins! Duke Cartwright has tried to murder the king!"

Will looked around in confusion, then realized he already held a blazing sword in hand. Weapons were forbidden at royal events, but he had reflexively summoned his rapier at the first sign of commotion. He didn't even remember putting the silver sword spell on the blade. He stared at the crowd in shock for a strange second, then all hell broke loose.

There was motion behind him, and he heard Tiny grunt before the body of a grown man went flying past. Then the king's voice echoed through the room. "Faithful subjects, William Cartwright has betrayed us. Kill the usurper!" The words were more than theatrics, however; they were a command that resonated in the ears of every nobleman who had graduated from Wurthaven and received the heart-stone enchantment.

Will understood the danger instantly, and his mistake. He should never have come. He'd mistakenly thought the king would rely on him losing his temper, but the monarch had been more than ready to fabricate his own excuse. "Fuck," he muttered, but before he could do more, Tabitha threw herself at him, knocking him from his feet. Something hard struck his skull and the center of his back.

He lost awareness briefly after that, until he found himself blinking and staring at the floor. Someone was lying on top of him, and it took him a moment to realize it was his younger sister. "Tabby-cat, you have to let me up," he groaned, trying to shift out from underneath her, but his hand slipped in the blood pooling around him.

All around them, people were roaring, some in fear and others in rage. Tiny was fighting barehanded, and Tailtiu had transformed into something halfway between a bear and a wolf. Sir Nelson was on the floor a short distance away, part of his skull missing, and Agnes Nerrow was crawling toward Will with blood trickling across her face. The look of horror on her features as she stared in his direction would haunt him for the rest of his life, though it looked as though that might be a very short time indeed. What was she seeing?

Standing over him, Selene fought a solitary battle against what appeared to be every sorcerer in the room. Rather than opt for an all-encompassing force-dome, she was using the point-defense spell, which allowed her the freedom to attack while she blocked the never-ending onslaught of offensive spells aimed at them.

She fought with a single-minded fury Will hadn't seen in her before, and though she was badly outnumbered, for the moment Selene seemed to have the upper hand. Elementals appeared and disappeared as their owners died. The crown princess killed with ruthless efficiency, but it was apparent that she wouldn't last forever. She couldn't stop every attack, so she focused on the force-spells, relying on her resistance to protect her from elemental spells, but she was still a relatively new wizard. Cuts and burns marked the places she had already been wounded.

And then Will realized what had horrified Agnes Nerrow. As he extricated himself from his unconscious sister, he discovered that it was her blood beneath them. Three crossbow bolts had pierced her chest and torso, almost pinning her to his back as they had fallen. The heavy blows had been the points slamming into his brigandine. "No, no, no…" He finally got free and tried to lay her on her side to avoid putting pressure on the shafts that impaled her. *Is she breathing? No!*

At the same time, he heard Laina begin to scream. She'd been motionless for some time, struggling against the king's command, but it seemed as though she might be losing the battle. "Kill me! Selene, please! Kill me quickly!" A spell construct was beginning to form between her hands.

There was no time. Will needed a year to address all the problems around him, and it felt as though he had less time than the blink of an eye. He saw Agnes' terror, Tabitha's limp body, and Laina's bloody tears as she began to craft the spell for a firestorm. Selene saw it too, despite everything else she was dealing with, and she yelled for him. "Will, hurry!"

He moved without wasting time for thought. Summoning a regeneration potion, he tossed it to Agnes, hoping she would understand it was for Tabitha. Then he gathered his feet under him and leapt up from the floor, moving in Laina's direction. He had no plan, but he had to help her. Laina's face held a look of desperation as the spell formed in her hands, but there was hope when she saw him rush close.

Will's hand reached out for hers, and the world vanished as their souls touched.

The view within was worse than the chaos of the ballroom. For the first time, Will could *see* the visible effects of the heart-stone enchantment as Laina fought against its imperative. She was wrapped in a fiery vine covered in thorns which tore at her soul, even as the flames burned her.

Get out, she screamed mentally. *It will kill us both!*

The vine, now a molten chain, kept them apart, but he could feel her pain. It was cutting into Laina from the outside and simultaneously tearing her apart from within. What he could see was merely an illusion, his mind's vain attempt to represent the ineffable reality of her struggle against the king's control.

Pushing forward, Will's reached for her, the skin on his hand blistering and peeling away as he connected with his soul's devastated twin. Pain blasted his consciousness, but strength flowed between them, and Laina began to glow in his mind's eye. She grew brighter and brighter, and while the pain continued to lash them, the ropes binding her turned black and began to wither. It shouldn't have been possible, but it was happening.

Laina stared back at him in triumphant disbelief as the heart-stone enchantment shattered. For a moment she was free, and Will found himself drawn in toward her center, the same pull they always felt since the day they had once merged and nearly lost their individuality.

No. Laina pushed him away, her rejection coming at him like a strong wind. *You've done enough, thank you.* He could feel the sorrow radiating in her thoughts—and then she began to disintegrate.

Will's heart screamed its denial, but the destruction was inevitable. Just as the chains had come apart, so too Laina's soul began to fragment before him. *Let me help you!*

Freedom is enough, she answered. *Tell them I love them. Tell yourself as well.* Reaching out, Laina's hand seemed to pass through him, and he felt some small portion flow into him, and then she was gone. The vision of her in his mind faded like smoke on a windy day.

He was alone.

CHAPTER 11

The world returned, filling Will's ears with a keening note of sadness so great it seemed to swallow everything. Gradually, he realized he was kneeling, with Laina's limp but still living body crumpled in front of him. The note he was hearing was his own mournful wail, and as he cast his eyes to one side, he saw Tabitha's ashen face where she sprawled lifeless on the ground nearby.

Agnes was unconscious, and the fragments of glass near her hand spoke to him of a potion that had been trampled in the fighting. He had lost everything.

Will's keening left his throat to become a tangible force that engulfed the room. For a moment, the fighting stopped as people clutched at their ears. He caught himself then, reining in the power before it could do irreparable harm to Selene and his remaining friends. In the silence that followed, Lognion spoke from the balcony. "Everyone hold for a moment. William, before you die, I want you to—" The sound of his voice died suddenly, and a look of puzzlement came over Lognion's face.

"No." Will's voice came from everywhere and nowhere simultaneously. "You don't get to talk anymore. Your day is done, Lognion. No one will hear your voice again. Ever." Straightening up, he looked around the room.

Selene was still standing, barely. Tiny was obviously wounded, but stood behind her with what appeared to be an improvised club made from a chair leg. Tailtiu writhed on the ground nearby, her body wrapped in a steel net that burned and smoked. The king had planned for everything.

Thunder boomed and rolled in the sky above the palace, sending deep rumbles through the building. The skies had been clear not long before, but the world seemed to echo William's internal rage. No one moved, so Will spoke to Tiny. "Free her and go."

Lognion backed away, then exited the balcony through the central set of double doors on the second floor. Two of the Driven seemed to take his movement as a call to action, but when they stepped forward, their spells died in their hands. Searing bolts of light ripped through their bodies, and seconds later they fell lifeless to the ground. Will barely spared them a thought as he returned his attention to Selene.

Unfazed, she spoke up. "You need our help. This isn't the time. We've lost too much."

Will's eyes were dead as he returned her gaze. "Get them out. Agnes is still alive. Get them out."

"Will—"

"I'll follow after I'm done." He turned his gaze to the balcony above, and when he spoke again, his voice resonated throughout the palace, throughout the city, and even to the farms that lay miles beyond. "Lognion is no longer king. He has surrendered his authority through his vile actions and foul behavior. His rule is at an end, and any man woman or child who dares to gainsay me will be buried alongside him.

"Those within the palace should evacuate now if they wish to survive. Anyone standing between me and the soon-to-be-dead Lognion Maligant will die with him. I will assume anyone who refuses to run has thrown in their lot with the dead king." As he finished speaking, a low rumble in the sky seemed to punctuate his statements.

Selene stared aghast at him. "This is a trap. This is what he wants!"

The words only made him angrier, and lightning struck the palace somewhere nearby, causing a shocking boom followed by plaster dust drifting down from the ceiling above. Will had felt it coming, or brought it down, he wasn't really sure, but he could still feel the energy swirling in the sky above, mirroring his mood. "My sisters are dead. Lognion will follow them, no matter the cost." His gaze drifted down, and he saw Agnes Nerrow was awake again, staring at him with a strange expression. Looking up, he saw that the balcony was deserted, and he realized he needed to hurry.

Will turned away from Selene and the others and started forward. Tiny hurried up behind him, but before the man could put a hand on his shoulder, Will warned him, "Don't."

"I'm coming with you," said Tiny.

Will glanced back. "You took an oath. Right now, I need a soldier, not a friend. Help Selene get them out."

"Will, you're not—"

Will glared at the big man. "I'll kill you. Do you understand? Once I start, I'm going to kill everyone and everything until Lognion is dead. Go home. You're about to be a father. Janice needs you." A travel disk formed beneath his feet, lifting Will up to the balcony, closest to the doors that Lognion had withdrawn through. Tiny watched him, mouth slightly open, then turned back toward the others without a word.

Will lightly stepped off the travel disk and onto the balcony, dismissing his spell gracefully the instant he no longer needed it. His movements, his magic, everything spoke of economy in motion with nothing wasted. His muscles saved their strength, but the efficiency of his spellcasting wasn't to conserve turyn, it was to spare his will.

Turyn was in abundance. It hung thick in the air, remnants from the brief spell battle and the elementals that had been called and dismissed. Turyn wouldn't be a problem. Now that most of the civilians were fleeing, Lognion would fall back upon the Driven, his elite force of military sorcerers.

No, there would be turyn aplenty. He smiled grimly as he walked, for he knew all of it belonged to him.

Throwing open the doors with a quick application of the force-push spell, Will marched onto a wide hall known as the grand terrace. It featured a broad walkway with doors leading into a variety of large rooms on the left side, punctuated by open spaces with railings on the right-hand side that looked down on part of the palace gardens.

He wasn't there for the scenery, though. He created a sloped force-wall in front of himself, catching the immediate volley of force-lances and elemental attacks. Dozens of elementals, earth, water, and fire, blocked his way. The force-spells had come from the sorcerers commanding them, while the earth-spears, water-drills, and fireballs emanated mainly from the elementals.

His force-wall collapsed under the onslaught within seconds, but Will had already erected an elemental stone barrier behind it, using the palace floor to supply most of the stone. It absorbed most of the rest of the barrage, and his second force-wall stopped the remaining force-lances that managed to get through even that.

Will had been doing more than simply defending, however. It had taken him a moment to get a feel for the arrangement of his opponents, but as his defenses crumbled away, his will took hold. Spells failed and elementals grew weak as he took ownership of the majority of the power in the surrounding area. Dropping the remaining force-wall, Will switched to using the point-defense shield to stop force attacks while he simultaneously began releasing waves of searing light-darts.

Ethelgren's light-darts spell could create five missiles at a time and although they could theoretically be targeted at multiple opponents, Will had always found it difficult to target more than two at a time, and then only if they were close together. His months of practice, however, had taught him the real reason for having multiple missiles with each casting.

The Driven were veterans when it came to battle magic. Despite losing most of the benefit of their elementals and finding themselves bereft of any spells other than force-spells, they were well versed in using the same point-defense spell that Will preferred. But that spell only covered a small area, and it could only be in one place at a time.

The light-darts spell was an elemental spell, meaning it could never be quite as fast as a force-spell, but it was still incredibly quick. Will was able to repeat the spell with blazing rapidity, and although the light darts weren't as damaging as most elemental attacks, they did the job. Firing them in a spread that threatened his opponents from top to toe, he moved from one target to the next, taking out feet, legs, arms, and sometimes heads—whatever happened to be uncovered when his missiles arrived.

Even veteran warriors made mistakes when something burned a hole in an arm or leg, and those lapses usually resulted in more holes appearing in other, more vital areas of their bodies. Men died, and Will felt a small jolt of satisfaction and joy as he saw them fall.

This was good. This was right—but he was running out of targets. He needed more to kill.

Marching forward, he blocked a force-lance on his left and turned his skin to iron to stop a volley of crossbow bolts that arrived with unfortunate timing. The iron-body transformation saved his life, but the force of the quarrels still staggered him, causing him to stumble. Regaining his balance, a second later, he saw that the soldiers hadn't retreated. They were reloading with all the speed that months of practice could give them. It wasn't fast enough, though. It couldn't be.

Will took a second to construct a spell that he still couldn't reflex cast, a fireball. There were other ways to kill them, but he wanted to hear their pain. He wasn't disappointed. When the flames blossomed around the soldiers, they screamed beautifully, until their lungs shriveled from the heat. Will moved on, heading for the wide staircase that terminated the grand terrace, leading down to the central hall of the palace.

He caught a glimpse of Lognion below, well beyond the foot of the stairs. The king smiled then continued his retreat as a sudden shiver in the floor warned Will of trouble to come. Then the stairs, the grand terrace, and a significant portion of the ground floor of the palace vanished in an explosion that rocked the city and was felt for miles around. Nothing could be seen of the epicenter, which had been just a short distance below where Will had been standing. Dust and smoke choked the air and eliminated any chance of visibility.

Rubble, masonry, and massive wooden beams rained down over the next minute. The air was still occluded, but once the debris stopped falling, two of Lognion's Driven emerged from one of the still-standing palace wings. They and his other remaining sorcerers and soldiers had been hiding there in a reinforced section prepared just for the explosion. One summoned an air elemental, and a brisk wind soon arose to clear the air.

As the smoke thinned, Will's form could be seen standing atop an elemental travel disk. He had finally used the first of his prepared spells, one that translated the user into the ethereal plane. While there, he had been tempted to move forward, but had decided against it. The last place he would find a trap when he returned would be at the site of such a large explosion. His return to the material plane came just seconds before the elemental had cleared the air, and he gave the two sorcerers a vicious smile when they saw him.

The smell in the air was familiar. *Alchemical blasting powder,* he noted mentally. *Selene was right. Lognion didn't chance using enchanted spellbombs because he couldn't be sure I wouldn't be able to suppress them.* To be honest, he wasn't sure whether he could either, but his contingency plan had been designed to handle either type of explosive.

Will killed the two sorcerers before they could run, then summoned a quick mist to replace the smoke and obscure him visually. Without moving, he spent the next thirty seconds re-preparing the spell he had used and storing it away. Lognion was a thorough man, and he couldn't be sure he wouldn't need it again.

The mist was no obstacle to his sight, and he watched his enemies gather as he finished the spell. They arranged themselves in a wide semi-circle about thirty yards away from where he stood in the middle of his temporary cloud. His will was already upon them, so the sorcerers could only use force spells, and their elementals had been dismissed rather than allowing them to furnish him with yet more power. As they were planning to attack, most of them chose force-walls, half-domes, or other partial-cover, defensive force spells, since being fully enclosed would prevent the use of any type of offense.

They also had a large number of crossbowmen with them, arranged to fire from three positions. They wanted to force him into a hard defense that would keep him from attacking, or kill him if he tried anyway. Will grinned, tasting the iron tang of blood in his mouth.

He released the fog, but before it could begin to disperse, he began feeding a wind-wall spell with all the turyn he could gather. The area it needed to cover was far too large for the spell to function in its usual manner, either as a defense or a deadly-closeup offense, but that didn't worry him. The ground was littered with detritus from the explosion: sharp splinters, jagged stones, and shards of glass from the palace's once expensive glass windows.

The wind didn't need to be powerful enough to destroy instantly, or by itself—it only had to be powerful enough to lift those makeshift missiles into the air. Seconds ticked by as the air rushed around, going from the equivalent of a strong dust devil to something stronger than most storms even if it wasn't quite a tornado. Will's defensive mist disappeared, while his enemies cursed and cried out.

The unlucky ones, or perhaps the lucky ones, depending on perspective, died quickly, lacerated and bludgeoned by glass and stones, but most survived for a while. Armor saved some of the soldiers, and the Driven adjusted their defensive force spells. Being at the center of the chaos, Will didn't need to devote any of his attention to deadly flying objects; he spent it on something better. Killing the king's men.

Light-darts flashed out in rapid succession, killing several men every second. Chaos reigned as some fled and others tried to fight, while at the center of it all Will exulted with each death and every cry of pain. At the end, all that remained were two sorcerers who had surrounded themselves completely with force-domes, and a few soldiers who Will simply hadn't had time to kill yet. Some of them started to beg, but he silenced their voices and killed them anyway.

This was good. This was right.

"I warned them," he muttered, considering the two Driven who were left, watching him with terrified eyes from behind their defensive shields. Killing them would take more time than he liked, if they remained focused purely on defense. Fortunately, there was an easy solution. Smiling maniacally, he walked past them. "Time to kill the king," he pronounced matter-of-factly. He knew they had no choice.

The heart-stone enchantment compelled them. They *had* to stop him from reaching Lognion. The shields went down, and he caught one with a source-link and removed the other's head with a force-lance spell so quickly they never had a chance to react. Will stripped the one that still lived of all turyn and the man collapsed, unconscious. He could've left him alive at that point, but he killed him anyway, smashing the man's skull into mush with a force-lance as the sorcerer lay helpless on the ground.

It was the principle of it.

For a moment, Will wasn't sure which direction to go, but he reasoned that the king would be where the turyn was thickest. *All those elementals, all those defenders and guards—he'll be in the thick of it,* Will thought. Turning to the right, he walked through the rubble and collapsed walls and into the somewhat intact palace garden.

The king's defenders were growing desperate. Will could tell by the attacks that followed. The explosion had probably been their last-chance, no-holds-barred, surefire defense. Those that remained didn't know what to do. His survival at this late point in time wasn't in the plan. Soldiers, sorcerers, and elementals rushed him from a variety of directions, but there was no cohesion or order to their attacks. Their command structure was gone, or too confused to give good orders.

Will ripped the turyn from the air around them and clapped his hands. The sound lasted only a moment, but then it expanded and moved outward, echoing against nothing, held purely by Will's desire. Each time it repeated, it grew louder, until after less than a minute the shock of it was so great it caused men to collapse and ears to bleed. This was his talent, and he had saved it for late in the fight so as to conserve his strength of will.

Soldiers, sorcerers, horses, dogs, and a few remaining guests who hadn't yet gotten off the palace grounds—all fell to their knees, and some died simply from shock. Will surveyed the devastation with eyes that could see in even the darkest of nights. Most of those on the grounds had survived, but none of them would be fighting anytime soon. *I can kill them at my leisure,* he thought pleasantly, *but Lognion comes first.* The adrenaline coursing through his veins knew the truth.

This was good. This was right.

"I'm over here, Willi—"

The king's voice vanished the moment Will focused on the man and silenced his speech. Lognion was over a hundred yards distant, but Will vanished and reappeared just a few feet away from his enemy as he used another of his prepared spells and teleported to the king. "No one said you could speak." His battle-joy was gone, and only icy hate remained as he stared at the monster who had slain both his sisters. "In fact, I distinctly remember saying you would never speak again. Are you trying to make a liar of me?" Light-darts flashed from his hands, accompanied by a rapid sequence of force-lances, but all his attacks were stopped cold by a force-dome that Lognion brought up at the last moment to save himself.

Will spent half a second to scan the area. The king hadn't brought out any of his thousands of elementals, since that would only give Will fuel to use against him. But the man was still drawing on his link to them, using them as an immense reserve to power his defense. Frustration filled him, and then Lognion began trying to speak, mouthing his words slowly to make himself understood since Will would never hear him, force-dome or no force-dome.

Moving up to the force-wall, Will stared at it for a moment. He had seen a spell that could eat through force effects once, but he had never learned it. He'd killed the vampire that had used it against him, but he remembered what it was like. He might not know the spell construct, but he could reproduce the resonance of that strange grey energy. Lifting his hands, he sheathed them in power, but kept it away from his skin, then he shifted it to match the disintegrative turyn he remembered. The energy turned grey, and he sank his new claws into the king's shield, delighting as he felt them begin to slowly penetrate.

The king continued trying to communicate, and despite himself, Will watched the man's mouth. "Meet my gu—"

The last word was impossible to decipher, but Will resisted the urge to shout 'what' back at his silenced opponent. The meaning became clear a moment later as two men appeared and began walking toward him from opposite ends of the yard. They were large, as men went, nearly Tiny's size, and they were clad in a strange, shimmering scale mail that seemed to hug their bodies, as though it was part of them rather than something they had put on. Neither held traditional weapons, relying on strange, clawed gauntlets instead. Will released his improvised weapons and stepped back from the king's defensive wall. It seemed he had a few more to kill first.

He tried not to laugh. "This was your last defense?" His humor vanished when his light-darts fizzled harmlessly against the newcomers, and his expression became grim when they drew close and his force-lances failed to do more than briefly stagger them. *What the hell are they made of?*

CHAPTER 12

Will summoned a travel disk at the last moment and used it to propel himself into the air before he could be sandwiched between his two new opponents. They stopped with amazing alacrity, for such large men. The two looked at each other and seemed to come to a consensus quickly. One circled out, while the other kept his eyes on Will and bent his knees.

The travel disk wasn't a spell meant for flying. It could only keep him fifteen to twenty feet above solid ground, but it was still much too far for a man to attack him without a long weapon or some sort of ranged attack. *Is he planning to jump?* Will couldn't believe it, but even as he thought about it, he realized that his enemy's feet were also clawed.

His armored opponent leapt, soaring through the air with the grace and speed of a giant cat. Will maneuvered to the side, neatly avoiding the man, only to find the other had been watching and waiting while Will's attention was focused on the first enemy. The second one was in the air behind him, mere inches from seizing Will with his deadly clawed gauntlets.

With a thought, Will activated the ethereal spell once again and vanished from the material plane—and then he felt the wind rush out of his lungs as his opponent slammed into him in the ethereal plane. Sharp claws tore through his formal clothes and pierced the brigandine protecting his chest. His skin became iron in the instant before the claws reached his flesh, but they cut into him regardless.

In that moment, Will nearly died. He had misjudged his foes. They weren't human, or anything even remotely close to human. What he had thought was armor was their metallic, scaley hides, and their weapons weren't worn, but natural instead. Time slowed, and Will saw the monster's mouth open, displaying teeth that would have made a crocodile jealous. A fraction of a second longer, and the thing would have bitten his head off.

Fortunately, it hadn't caught him cleanly. The claws that had cut him were from a *glancing* blow. Panic and adrenaline gave him strength, and a force-push spell launched him away from the reptilian beast. From the corner of his eye, he saw the other had also crossed into the ethereal and was charging toward him from the side.

He released the ethereal translation spell, returning to the material plane, where he immediately created another travel disk and shot forward. Despite his speed, it was close, for both the monsters had crossed back into the material plane with him. *Or did they?*

Moving in a wide circle punctuated by quick changes in direction, Will avoided the monsters while he adjusted his vision again to see partly into the ethereal. The truth stunned him. The creatures hadn't shifted at the same time he did; they existed simultaneously on both planes. He'd never heard of such a thing.

Keeping his knees bent, Will raced back and forth around the palace garden, never getting too far from Lognion's defensive position. Even dealing with something like this, he wasn't prepared to surrender his prey. *Lognion dies, no matter what, even if it kills me.*

Luckily, with the travel disk and some familiarity with his enemy, Will was just able to keep out of their claws, but he couldn't devote the time necessary to pry Lognion out of his defensive shell. Frustration built within him, and his cold rage began to heat up into something dangerous, something that would drive him to make mistakes.

Racing across the grounds, Will hit the monsters chasing him with a variety of spells, but nothing worked. Elemental attacks and nearly every other sort of magic he hit them with did nothing. They barely acknowledged the existence of magic. Only two things seemed to have any effect at all, however small. Elemental earth spells that fired razor-sharp shards of stone *did* have a small impact, but it was nothing like what it should have been. With the power Will put into the spells, they should have punched holes through the attackers even if they were made of metal and stone, but they did little more than leave scratches.

Force spells worked better, but it was still like trying to kill a bull with pillows. The spells had a physical effect, but it was weaker than it should have been. At one point, Will tried to stop one with a force-wall, and the thing only seemed to slow down before gradually forcing its way through the spell. It shouldn't have been possible.

He became so engrossed in dealing with the monsters that he almost forgot Lognion. Will nearly missed the shift in the ambient turyn that signaled a change. The king dropped his shield and launched a force-lance at Will as he came within range. Before Will could respond, the king replaced his defensive dome, but that wasn't the real problem.

A quick point-defense shield stopped the force-lance, but the distraction cost him. One of the monsters had shifted direction and caught him off-guard. Its shoulder slammed into his body and sent him flying. Pain shot through him, and an inaudible crack told Will something had broken inside his chest. He hit the ground and rolled, not gracefully, but in the same manner a ragdoll might roll. The pain was blinding, far worse than the initial impact.

Even so, his eyes remained open, staring at Lognion as the creatures closed on him. Tears of pain and rage were streaming down his cheeks, but it seemed as though fate had conspired against him. It wasn't fair. Nothing worked, and the king was laughing at him. When they tore him apart the last thing he would see would be Lognion mocking him.

The closest of the beasts dropped to all fours and brought its savage jaws to bear. It shredded the force-shield he erected and clamped onto his shoulder. The teeth went through his armor and cut into his iron-skin almost instantly. Will screamed, and the world went white.

But he wasn't screaming from the pain. It was anger, the absolute rage of a child denied its desire. Blue-white power erupted from his skin instead of blood, ripping through the monster and climbing into the sky above. It happened in an instant that would have been impossible to measure, except that Will felt it, directed it. The monster spasmed and released him, stunned but not dead. Its twin never paused.

The power returned from the sky in a lightning strike that made the initial surge seem almost insignificant. It slammed into the one that had bitten him and then flowed across the intervening space to strike the second monster. The shock of sound and light was so great it nearly rendered Will insensible, but his rage wouldn't relent.

Rising to his feet, Will staggered toward Lognion, who stared at him with an expression of mild surprise. Lifting his hand, Will pointed at the king. "You're next." White sparks of lightning ran from his fingers, dancing across the ground around him. He realized then that it covered him, flowing across and down his skin like rivulets of water.

"William, you amaze me once a—"

"Silence!" His yell struck the king's defensive shield like a battering ram, but there wasn't enough turyn remaining in Will to break through. He was still able to silence the king's voice, though. "I told you already. You—don't—get—to—speak."

Lognion needed to die. Will felt it more keenly than any desire he'd ever experienced. It was worse than thirst, lust, hunger, or any other emotion he could imagine. But his will was beginning to flag. He could feel it. He still had turyn left, but soon he would begin to lose control.

The electricity racing along his skin was an unconscious product of his anger, but it was wearing him down quickly.

And the king was still as safe as ever behind his unbreakable force-dome powered by the stamina of a thousand elementals. Will pulled at the air around him, searching for the power he needed, but it wasn't nearly enough. It would never be enough.

Then he raised his eyes to the sky. He'd felt the power there, though it was so distant it seemed unreachable. The storm was his doing, somehow, and when the king's beast had almost killed him, he had finally made contact with the part of himself that had created that storm.

Still furious, Will reached into the ground around Lognion's shield and *pulled* at the turyn there, combining it with his own and everything he could draw from his surroundings. It was a more conscious effort than what he had done with the reptilian monsters, but he grew more certain as he worked. Actinic streamers of blue-white power shot up from the ground and flowed around Lognion's shield and into the storm above.

A split-second later, the storm answered.

Will was ready this time, protecting his eyes and ears from the sound and fury that slammed into the earth. He was connected to it, and he couldn't, *wouldn't*, let it go. The vast power of the storm flowed down around him like rain, striking the king's shield repeatedly until it collapsed a second later. It happened so quickly that Lognion likely never registered its impact.

"Yes! That's what you deserve!" Will's heart soared and his eyes lit up with delight. Lifting his arms, he called more lightning, lusting for it like a long-absent lover—and it came. It thundered into existence and smashed into Lognion's already dead body, but Will needed more. The king was dead already. He needed more people to punish.

He sent several more bolts into the monsters that had attacked him, then began considering targets farther away. The palace garden still held a number of living people. Most were the king's sorcerers or defenders, those who had been stunned and deafened by his earlier sonic attack. Some were guests who had failed to flee quickly enough, and a few were probably just unlucky servants who hadn't expected any of this.

It would be difficult to figure out which ones were active supporters of the king. "I warned them, though," he muttered, his rage still unsatisfied. It would probably be safer to eliminate them all, for Selene's sake, when she began to rule. With a manic smile, he brought a lightning bolt down on the head of a man he saw trying to crawl away. It was probably a soldier, but he wasn't very worried about it.

A large man appeared from the direction of the palace. This one was walking normally. Will almost killed him before he recognized the shape. It was Tiny. "I told you to leave," Will whispered, making sure his voice would be plainly audible in his friend's ear. To punctuate his words, he brought two lightning bolts down just thirty feet apart, on either side of his friend. "Stay and I'll kill you, along with the rest of them."

Tiny fell, but rose again, his legs twitching from the proximity of the blasts. "You have to stop. It's over."

"It's over when they're all dead!" Afraid he might kill Tiny, Will turned and walked in a different direction, toward three men who had collapsed. At least two of them were still breathing.

One looked up, fear in his eyes. "Please, milord. I have a family."

"Do you still serve the king?" Will's voice came out sounding strangely hysterical. "Do you?"

"No. Please don't kill me! The king is dead. I'm just a soldier!" The man's face was twisted into an expression of absolute terror.

But Will knew it was just an act. His nostrils flared as his anger rose again. "Liar! Of course you would say that!" The lightning would purge the man's evil.

"Behind you! They're not dead!"

He wanted to ignore the voice, but it was Tiny's, and deep down he trusted him. Whirling, Will saw that both the reptilian creatures were climbing back to their feet. For a moment, he merely goggled at them. *How could anything have survived that?* Tiny was running toward them, and behind the massive knight Will saw a second, smaller figure. In his paranoia, Will almost killed the woman before he realized it was Darla.

The two attacked the closest monster, and the result was almost comical. Tiny was moving at a speed that suggested he had taken a Dragon's Heart potion, but it hardly mattered. He struck at the beast with a sword he had picked up somewhere along the way, and despite his strength and size, it accomplished exactly nothing. The monster's reaction was still slow, but it ignored Tiny, and for reasons of its own chose to strike Darla instead. She deflected the swing with her own weapon, but the claws shattered the blade and ripped straight into her chest, tearing through her ribs. She fell in an awkward heap.

"Get back!" Will screamed. The lightning was still coursing over him, but he didn't dare use it with Tiny so close. Instead, he began pounding the humanoid lizard with force-lances straight to the head.

At forty yards, his turyn dropped quickly, and he began to feel fuzzy. His will was almost at its limit. Even if he had more power, he would soon be helpless. Thankfully, the monster chose to run toward him instead of going after his friends. The second one followed, and as soon as they were far enough from Will's companions, he unleashed the storm once more.

Lighting slammed down, lashing the beasts repeatedly. They kept moving for several seconds before finally going limp once more. Only then did Will relent. Exhausted, he sank to his knees. There was nothing left in him; his turyn was gone and his will utterly used up. The pain in his chest returned, stealing his breath away.

Tiny lifted Darla and gave her what appeared to be a potion. Then he began walking toward Will. He stopped in horror as he passed the closest of the reptilian beasts. It was beginning to twitch. "Will, it's still alive. *They're* still alive!"

Will stared back numbly. "I guess we die then." He didn't have the energy to care, and consciousness was fading fast. In fact, at that moment, death sounded rather attractive. He needed a rest.

Tiny dropped the female assassin and drew his only remaining weapon, a feast dagger. Kneeling down, he tried to cut the monster's throat with little effect. Stabbing the eyes was equally useless, so he opened the thing's mouth and tried stabbing the interior. Will saw him pull the knife back with an incredulous look. The point of the blade had snapped off.

The knight paused, then looked at Will. "I can't kill it, but I don't think I can carry both of you." He was clearly torn, but he climbed to his feet and started toward Will.

"They're after me," Will warned. "You can't run fast enough. Take Darla."

"Use this." The faint voice came from the fallen assassin. With one hand, she offered a long knife with a black blade to Tiny.

The big man took it immediately, while Will stared at her suspiciously, for he recognized the metal. The blade was made of demon-steel, and as far as he knew, the only samples of it were in his possession, primarily in the breastplate he wished he'd been wearing not long ago. Tiny wasted no time, and he thrust the point into the monster's mouth. He met some resistance, but he leaned into it, and after a short pause the point sank in, passing through the back of the throat and into the creature's spine. It shuddered and went still.

The blade, however, burst into black flames, causing Tiny to hiss in pain as he withdrew it. It was obviously burning him, but he held on bravely and turned to the second monster, which was also waking up.

"Wait," Will cautioned. "Bring me the knife."

"I've got to hurry," said Tiny, his voice filled with pain.

"You'll kill us all." Will held out his hand. "The blade is near its limit. It will explode if you do that again." He didn't mention the fact that Tiny himself was already dying, poisoned by the turyn that fueled the dagger's flame. Tiny hesitated, but Will was insistent. "Quickly!"

Tiny handed the weapon to him, and Will drew out the demonic turyn, absorbing it until the metal stopped burning and eventually went from black to silver. He would have liked to use it on the second beast himself, to save Tiny from further injury, but he was too weak to stand. He handed it back. "Here."

Tiny finished the job, though by now the king's guardian monster was aware enough to struggle. The knight tried cutting its throat, but finally settled for pushing it through one of the eyes since the thing wouldn't cooperate and open its mouth. Once again, the knife burst into shadowy flames. Tiny dropped the blade the moment he was certain their last enemy was dead, and it was clear he was in a lot of pain.

Will tried crawling closer, but the pain was too much. "Come here." He could see the dark energy flickering beneath the skin of Tiny's forearm. Demonic turyn was similar to poison for living creatures; it would slowly kill his friend if not removed. Thankfully, Will knew what to do. Years before, he'd done the same for Selene, long before he'd had any understanding of what or why.

When Tiny was close enough, he clasped the warrior's forearm and began drawing out his turyn. His will failed him partway through. He simply couldn't move turyn any longer, not Tiny's, not even his own. "Damn it!"

Having had half his vital energy drained out, Tiny was barely conscious, but there was still fire burning in his veins. "What's wrong?"

"I can't get it all," said Will. "I'm not strong enough."

"It's all right," said Tiny. "You did enough."

Will didn't have the energy for tears, but he wanted to scream with frustration. "No, I didn't. You'll die."

"I was prepared for that," said the big man tiredly. Tiny sagged until he was fully prone. "You warned me. Twice." His eyes closed, then opened again a moment later. "Be sure to take a regeneration potion before you pass out. You look pretty bad."

"Gods damn you, Tiny!" Will swore. "If you aren't dead and I wake up healthy enough to move, I'm going to kill you for real."

Darla finally spoke again. "Death shouldn't be this noisy."

Will could see that the worst of her wounds were already closed. "You aren't dying."

Her eyes were devoid of emotion when she looked at him. "My heart is dead."

Pain stabbed into him as Will realized what she meant. Darla was one of the rare individuals who was astrally sensitive. She was probably the only other person who had seen what happened to Laina's soul. Even if the body was still breathing, she knew her lover was gone. Will's face twisted for a moment and his eyes closed tightly, but when his body started to sob, a shiver of pain stopped him cold. He could barely breathe as it was—crying was out of the question.

Time passed, but unconsciousness wouldn't come. Tiny hadn't spoken in a while, and Will began to wonder if he was awake. Death would take hours, or even a full day, depending on how much of the magical poison was left in the warrior's system. The big man's voice shocked him out of his daze when he asked, "Did you really mean what you said?"

Will knew what he was referring to. "She was supposed to tell you when you came back, but things happened too quickly. You need to ask her to marry before she tells you, otherwise she'll think you are asking for the wrong reasons."

"You said I was dying."

"I'm going to fix that," said Will. "You've probably got at least half a day. There's time."

"Is that why you still haven't taken the potion?"

Will grimaced. "If I do, I might not wake up until tomorrow. Besides, I need to stay awake and keep watch."

Darla snorted. "You couldn't protect yourself if you wanted to. A small child could kill you right now."

"Drink the potion, Will," said Tiny seriously. "You might not last. I can see you're hardly able to draw breath."

"Fuck off."

"One of us needs to survive. You can. Promise me you'll take care of my child."

Darla growled. "I'm going to kill both of you if you don't stop whining."

Tiny turned his head toward her. "He's too stupid to live. You'll take care of my child, won't you?"

"Give me the knife," she rasped. "I need it."

"Do you hear something?" asked Tiny, thinking she'd detected a new threat.

"I'm going to cut your tongue out with it."

Will almost laughed, but it turned into a sharp, gasping whimper. He twisted his head to look away, and it was then that he saw someone coming toward them from the southern end of the palace garden. It was Selene, gliding across the ground at speed, carried by an elemental travel disk. She was alone, and he couldn't decide whether to be relieved or angry that she hadn't abandoned them as he had commanded.

The others spotted her soon after, and they watched in silence as she approached. When she was a few feet away, Selene dismissed her spell and stepped off next to Will. Her face was grave as she studied him. "Can you talk?" He nodded and she continued, "Where are you hurt the worst?"

"Ribs, collarbone too maybe. Help Tiny first. He's got turyn poisoning."

Her glare said it all. She held out a glass vial with the stopper already removed. "Drink it."

He turned his head away. "Tiny first."

Selene wouldn't take no for an answer. With her other hand, she reached down and lightly pressed against his upper chest. Will let out an involuntary scream, and as soon as his mouth opened, she poured the contents of the vial into it. "Idiot," she pronounced as he choked and sputtered.

"Says the woman who is bleeding," he snarled back.

"*Was* bleeding," she corrected. "I had the sense to bind my wound before returning to find the fool I married." Rising to her feet, she went over to Tiny and began draining him of the rest of his turyn. Selene was still pretty fresh, as third-order wizards went, but she was able to convert the demonic turyn into something harmless, and she even returned some energy back to Tiny, taking care to match his natural frequency. The massive warrior passed into unconsciousness long before she finished.

Darla was also out cold, but Selene examined her before returning to Will. "Why are you still awake?"

Will's eyes were swimming in his head. "The bodies, we need them. Help me store them."

"I'd do it for you if I had a limnthal," she groused.

He smiled faintly. "Tomorrow, after I have a nap."

She chuckled sourly at his joke, then kissed his forehead. Something wet landed on his cheeks, but neither of them mentioned it. Standing up, Selene took the easy route and grabbed his ankles, then she dragged him roughly across the ground, until he was in easy reach of the monsters.

Will gave her a disgruntled look but held his tongue. Storing them should have been easy at that point, but for the first time, he came up against the limit of his limnthal's storage space. He was forced to abandon two barrels of ale and all of his jars of fresh water before he could store the heavy bodies.

That done, he relaxed, and the world quickly began to fade. The last thing he heard was Selene asking, "What were those things?" He was out before he could reply that he didn't know.

CHAPTER 13

Will's eyes opened on a rather ordinary scene. He was in bed, and given the furnishings, he thought it was probably the Nerrow family's city house. He was alone, which was rather refreshing. In the past, he had often awakened from traumatic events only to be overwhelmed by either Selene or one of his other loved ones. The silence was welcome.

Besides, he had a lot to think about.

His newfound talent with storms, or lightning, or whatever it was—that merited some consideration, but it wasn't at the top of his list. The strange, nearly unkillable monsters that had been guarding the king, those were also worth serious investigation. Neither of those things held his attention, though.

Tabitha and Laina were dead. His only siblings were gone, and he'd only just begun to get to know them, to build some kind of understanding. He'd been an only child his entire life, and finding that he had two half-sisters had been immensely important to him, despite the complications. With Laina he had fought, but they had already shared much. Tabitha was a different story.

She was so young, so bright, and I hardly had a chance to know her. His vision grew blurry, and he rolled over to bury his face in a pillow. He could only hope it muffled the sounds of his misery.

It had been his fault, too. He often talked about not accepting blame for the actions of others, and it was certainly Lognion's evil that had resulted in the tragedy, but it wouldn't have happened if he hadn't showed up. He'd been arrogant enough to think he could predict the king's choices, and his mistake had cost a lot of people their lives.

He'd killed a lot of those people himself—deliberately. Remembering his psychotic rage made him worry for his own sanity. *Surely that wasn't normal, even for someone who'd just lost family.* He had wanted to kill people, not just Lognion, not just Lognion's guards, but people. Any people.

Will hadn't always been that way. Years ago, he had been nauseous and vomited after killing a soldier just to survive. Yesterday, he had *enjoyed* doing it. The memory was very clear, and deep down, some part of him still reveled in it. The recent war had greatly accelerated the process, but he had hoped that the peace of the last few months might have helped.

Clearly it had not.

For a moment, he wished he had someone to blame. Someone he could punish for how twisted he had become. Someone he could kill.

Will blinked and shook his head. *I'm becoming a monster.*

His misery was interrupted by the sound of someone raising their voice. The sound was muffled; it probably came from a different room some distance down the hall. Unconsciously, Will increased the sensitivity of his hearing.

"You heard me! I want him out of this house! He's your husband, so I understand you won't abandon him, but I won't be bound by your foolishness. You never should have married him!"

Will blinked. The voice belonged to Agnes Nerrow. Up until yesterday, she had treated him very warmly, but obviously things had changed. *She blames me for their deaths,* Will realized. Selene responded, "You're the closest thing to a mother I have ever known. You're better than this, Agnes. I understand your shock, but I have faith that you'll rethink your words once you calm down."

"And I never thought a daughter of mine would hold a snake to my bosom, but I suppose I was wrong. All three of you knew, didn't you? You made quite the fool out of me!"

"It wasn't a conspiracy. Laina figured it out on her own. Tabitha didn't know at—" Selene's voice cut off abruptly with the sound of a slap. Will's eyes went wide. *Surely not,* he thought.

Agnes' voice was dripping venom. "So you used my one innocent child as bait in your murderous plot to usurp the throne?" She waited, and when Selene didn't answer, Agnes continued, "Don't look at me with those eyes. I don't care if you're about to be queen. Hang me if you want. You've already ruined me. This family was all I've ever had, all I cared about."

"You still have a family. We all love you, if you could just understand. *He* loves you as well," said Selene.

Will winced. *Not a good answer, Selene. She just lost both her daughters and you're offering us as a substitute?* He was mildly confused. Normally his wife was better at understanding others. Agnes replied, "He who? My husband, who preferred his bastard son to his legitimate wife and children? Or do you mean the bastard child who snuck into my home and turned my family against me while using my daughters as pawns in his savage political game?"

"I can't talk to you like this," said Selene. "Maybe later, after you've calmed down. I'm out of time, but I'll be back in a few hours."

"Get your house in order and take him out of here. I won't have him under my roof a minute longer than necessary." Will didn't hear anything for almost a minute, but then Agnes added, "Go! He'll still be alive when you return. I wouldn't sink that low, but don't expect me to feed him. Wait." Another pause. "Where is the meeting?"

"The cathedral," answered Selene.

"You don't have a retinue. Even that giant man you brought with you is still in bed. You can't show up alone."

"I don't have much of a choice," said Selene.

"Charles, go with her. Take the house guards," ordered Agnes.

"How many?" asked a male voice.

"All of them."

"Thank you," said Selene.

"This isn't forgiveness," said Agnes. "You've spent my blood to steal this throne. I have nothing left, but you *owe* me a debt."

At that point, Will tried to rise, but the room began to spin. He managed to get his feet on the floor, but when the world started to go black, the best he could manage was to lean back so he would fall onto the bed rather than the floor. Darkness swallowed him.

The touch of a hand on his forehead woke him sometime later. Looking up, he saw a woman sitting on the edge of the bed, and he blinked to clear his eyes. It appeared to be Tabitha. *Am I dreaming?* "Tabby-cat? Is that really you?"

He had never used her nickname before, though he'd heard both Selene and Laina call her that on occasion. It was something he had wanted to do, but he hadn't felt as though he had the right. Fundamentally, he was a stranger. Dreams had different rules, though. She nodded, then replied, "It's me. I'm glad you're alive. I never would have forgiven myself if you died on my account."

"I wish I had died instead of you," Will muttered. "Laina too. I'm a monster, but for some reason the good people always die, and nothing happens to the bad ones."

She squeezed his hand. "Stop it. My brother is a good man—the very best. I won't listen to you speaking ill of him. Besides, we all made it through. Laina is asleep in her room."

Will frowned and sat up. "This is a dream, right?"

"I don't think so," said Tabitha, leaning forward to hug him tightly. "I was scared to death yesterday. I've been scared for weeks."

"You should have told me."

"I wanted to protect you. You ruined everything yesterday, but I was so glad."

Will's chest tightened, and he was grateful that the regeneration potion had done its work, for he felt no physical pain. His heart ached terribly, though. "It's all my fault."

She nodded, and he felt her chin dig into his shoulder as she squeezed him tighter. "It's all your fault, and now everything will be all right." She released him and smiled. "Brother."

"You knew?"

Tabitha nodded again. "Not at first. Everyone always assumes I'm oblivious, and I suppose I prefer it that way."

"When did you find out?" he asked.

"After our house burned down, when we stayed with you and Selene."

"You should have told me you knew."

Tabitha grinned. "It was more fun teasing you."

He stared at the blankets. "It was better before. Your mother hates me now."

"Mother will come around. Laina is stubborn. She'll knock some sense into mother eventually."

The brightness, the confidence in her voice, undid him. Will put his head in his hands and felt the tears begin to spill over. "No, she won't. She's gone. Your mother will truly despise me once she understands that."

"Will, that's not true. Don't even say that. She's just asleep. I checked on her before I came in here. Other than a few bruises, she wasn't hurt at all."

His eyes were swollen when he finally looked up at her and shook his head. "Lognion ordered her to kill me, but she fought the command, and the enchantment killed her. I was there, with her. I thought I was helping, but I only made it worse."

Tabitha could see and hear that he was broken inside, but still she shook her head in denial. "No. You've been asleep for most of the day and I'm sure you've had terrible dreams."

"Where's Darla?"

"She's been keeping vigil beside her ever since she woke up."

"Ask her. She knows the truth. She saw it happen."

Tabitha was on her feet, and while she didn't seem angry, she was obviously agitated. "You need more rest," she advised. "Believe me. Everything is fine." She left on that remark.

Alone again, Will activated the limnthal and asked Arrogan a question. "How long can a body survive without a soul?"

"I don't think anyone's ever done a solid study of the subject. It's a fairly rare state of affairs. What I can tell you for certain, however, is that from watching over you I know for a fact that a body can survive without a brain for well over two decades." The old man snorted at the end, unable to resist laughing at his own joke. Will didn't respond, and after a long, awkward minute, Arrogan gave the question more consideration. "It's probably similar to how long a person survives if they can't wake up. You likely know more than I do about that. Food, water, bodily necessities—the limit probably lies in those things. Assuming they don't just die immediately for whatever reason."

"Her body isn't dead yet," said Will bleakly.

Arrogan was almost tentative when he asked, "Whose?"

"Laina's."

"Ouch. Are you sure she's gone? What happened?"

Once upon a time, such a question might have caused his pulse to quicken with hope, but Will knew very well what he had seen. He explained to the best of his ability before his voice got too thick to continue. "See what I mean?" he said as he finished.

"I'm sorry, boy. I know what those girls meant to you. How is the other one? Tabitha, was that her name?"

Will nodded, wishing for perhaps the hundredth time that the ring could see his gestures. Sometimes speech was too difficult. Taking a deep breath, he managed to get the words out. "She's fine. I thought she died too but they got a potion in her before it was too late. She saved my life." He realized then that he had forgotten to thank her. *She put herself between me and three crossbows.*

"How is everyone else? Selene?"

"She's fine. Everyone's fine, I think. Lognion's dead, though."

Arrogan sounded genuinely surprised. "Really? How?" Will wasn't in a fit state to relive everything, but he gave a brief account of the fight, including his new talent. His grandfather couldn't keep from gloating. "A lightning bolt? The only sad part is it probably happened so fast he didn't even have time to know he was dead. What about the elementals?"

That forced Will to explain about the strange bodyguards. He did that, adding his own speculation as well. "They were in both planes, the material and the ethereal. I don't think they were switching back and forth, they just naturally existed in both, the same way a river does, or a mountain. I think maybe that was why they were so tough. It was almost as though they were *extra* real. As if Tiny, Darla, myself, everything, just wasn't real enough to affect them. It's like we were dreams, or ghosts, and nothing we did mattered."

"They had scales?"

"Yes. Do you know what they were?"

The old man sounded strangely befuddled. "Yes? No? I think I might, if I were alive. It feels like something that should trigger a memory. It feels like I left myself a note, but I can't read it, probably because I'm dead. The magic won't work."

"I'm more confused now than before," said Will.

"You still haven't read the book, have you?"

Will rubbed his face with his hands, more tired than ever. *Just one day— one day without more of this insanity,* he pleaded internally. As usual, fate ignored him. "No. I haven't. The lich said the same thing, by the way."

"Grim Talek? He's in the book!" The ring sounded excited. "You spoke to him again? When? Why?"

"Not directly. He sent Rob to give me a warning. He said that coming to Cerria was a trap."

"Hmph. It was."

"I knew that. He also asked if I had read the book and then spouted off some nonsense calling me Grim Talek's disciple."

Arrogan growled. "He said that about Valemon too. Don't listen to him."

Valemon was one of Arrogan's previous apprentices, one that Arrogan had later killed, who was known to modern historians as the Prophet and the founder of the religion that had been a large part of the civil war between Terabinia and Darrow. Will frowned. "He also mentioned something about being of the 'fourth-order,' but Rob never went through any of the compressions, so I'm not sure what he meant."

"The fourth-order is death," Arrogan clarified. "Any wizard who tried another compression beyond the third died. Some said that the fourth compression was how Grim Talek originally became a lich, though. That it killed him, but he simply refused to die."

"Was that what you did when you were shot and died?" asked Will. "You said you'd been dead for half the fight."

"Maybe," admitted his grandfather. "I just wouldn't let my body stop until it was over. Then again, my current condition is somewhat similar to being undead, except I don't have access to magic, not unless I possess someone."

"What about the master vampire, Androv? Was he similar to a lich as well?"

"Any undead spellcaster would be the same. Dead, without a source, but somehow still absorbing and using turyn like a wizard. Most vampires can't use any magic at all, even if they were trained while alive. It takes a lot of time and training, a lot of will, for them to regain any magical ability. Some claim that over time it makes them stronger, but the evidence is sparse. Only very old, very experienced undead have the strength of will to challenge a living wizard when it comes to magic."

"Grim Talek's will was greater than mine," Will admitted. "When I met him near the end of the war, I couldn't do anything."

"He's well over a thousand years old. In fact, we don't have any idea how old he actually is."

"But he's in the hidden book at your old house?" asked Will.

"I think so. I don't remember."

"Why not?"

"The book has been passed down for generations. It's an heirloom of sorts. Some say it was written by the First Wizard, or that Grim Talek wrote it himself, or that they were the same person, but it's all conjecture. No one remembers what's in the book, just that they made the choice to forget."

"You're getting cryptic again," Will complained.

"It's a spell, a type of contract. Reading the book begins the act of casting it on yourself. At the end, you're left with the choice of finishing the spell and forgetting the contents or cancelling it to remember."

"Why would anyone want to forget what they had just read?"

"I can only tell you what my impression was when I made the choice," said Arrogan. "I remember knowing that I'd never sleep again if I didn't forget, that I would live in fear. There are a lot of secrets in that book, not just from the first writer, but from other wizards that came later. None of it is any good. It's just recorded there in case it's needed later, but I mostly remember a feeling of hopelessness. That none of it mattered."

"Why not burn it then, if it didn't matter?"

"The spell included triggers. Things that would restore some of the memories, if certain conditions were met, so the current lore-master would be prepared when and if the time came."

"If what time came?" Will asked.

"Beats me," said the ring with an almost audible shrug. "I just feel as though those lizard monsters might be one of the triggers. It's pretty unusual to hear about bidimensional creatures like those."

"Bidimensional?"

"You said they existed in both the material and ethereal dimension simultaneously. That's very rare. I've only heard of things like that with demigods, like the Cath Bawlg, or demon-lords."

"They're bidimensional too?"

"The Cath Bawlg was multi-dimensional, that's part of why he was so dangerous. Demon-lords are bidimensional to a degree as well, but with them it's different. They carry a little piece of hell inside them, like a seed. At least that's what I was taught. I'm not sure how accurate any of it is. Not many higher-dimensional beings sit down and let us study them and run tests."

A knock at the door ended the conversation. Will dismissed the limnthal and made sure the blankets were covering his lower body properly, then answered, "I'm awake. Enter." A maid stepped in, carrying a neatly folded envelope.

"This came for you, sir."

Will held out his hand. "Thank you."

The maid bowed. "Since you're awake, would you like tea or something to eat?"

He looked to the window. The sun was hanging above the houses to the west, indicating he had slept most of the day. It was too late for lunch and too early for supper. "No need to make anything special for me. Leftover bread and small beer will do fine."

"There's fresh fruit, sir. It wouldn't be any trouble." She smiled faintly, barely hiding her nervousness.

The maid was pretty in a delicate but awkward way that was probably appealing to many. Will's eyes noted the line of her shoulder and neck. It was the sort of unconscious appreciation that came without thought, but in his mind's eye he momentarily imagined the carnage a force-lance would wreak if it struck her. It was a vivid image. He could see her skin splitting, bones shattering, muscles and tendons torn apart, exposing the vital organs beneath—

"Milord?" The question brought him back to the present with a shudder and the taste of bile in his mouth. His vision was barely a fiction. Less than a day ago he'd committed such violence dozens, perhaps hundreds of times over.

Will looked away, focusing his eyes on the floor. The ornamental rug there was overlain with a memory of a man's skull exploding. *I did that,* he thought, clenching his jaw. "Yes, please. Fruit sounds delightful." His voice sounded far too calm in his own ears. *It should be shaky. I should feel sick, or nervous—something!*

More scenes played through his head while the maid left. He was still replaying the bloody memories when she returned a short while later. He thanked her without giving any sign of his thoughts. The tray in front of him was laden with crisp slices of apple and pear. The crunch when he bit down on the first piece made him think of bones breaking. Will put the tray aside, his appetite gone.

He didn't feel ill, though, which still bothered him. He was just— empty. "I need a distraction," he decided, then remembered the letter the maid had brought. *Perfect.*

Will took the envelope from the nightstand and broke the wax seal with his thumb. The outer page had been neatly folded with care and precision, while the single page within was clean and precisely lettered. It was either from a nobleman or someone who could afford a professional scribe. He opened it, and by the time he had finished scanning the first lines, he was on his feet.

> *Dear William,*
>
> *Your presence at the party yesterday was truly a surprise. I do hope your sister is well. I'd wish the same for Laina, but we both know the true state of affairs there. In any case, congratulations on your victory and good luck replacing me. Fortunately for you, I am not vindictive, otherwise I might do some truly awful things, and considering how rude you were during our battle, I think I would be justified in such behavior.*
>
> *I won't lower myself, though. Instead, I will give you some fatherly advice. Considering how you handled Bradshaw, and the fact that you're still alive today, I can only assume the lich has taken you under his wing. Seeking powerful allies is usually wise, but be careful that you don't rely on those who have too much power. They always expect to be paid. Grim Talek will probably be furious with you for forcing my hand.*
>
> *Tell him not to fret. My defeat hasn't changed anything other than forcing me to abandon the game. I had thought to enjoy it for a few more millennia, but I suppose I should get on with my life and find a new home. You will probably have at least a few years, perhaps even a decade, to enjoy ruling the world.*
>
> *However, in the end it won't matter. One way or another, you'll only serve as food for my offspring. The egg-guardians you fought yesterday were merely a taste. My true children will devour everything, including one another, until just a few remain. Such has always been the destiny of your world.*
>
> *You are cattle.*
>
> *But every rancher has a favorite bull, and so I thank you. To honor you, I will remember you in the tales I tell my cattle in the next world. I cannot leave you completely untouched, though. As you have taken my home, I will take yours, insignificant as it may be.*
>
> *Farewell and good fortune to you!*
>
> *Lognion*

CHAPTER 14

Several violent impulses ran through Will's mind in quick succession, but he discarded all of them. Smashing up the room wouldn't improve his reputation with Agnes, and burning the letter wouldn't do either. Selene needed to see it.

He dressed quickly and efficiently, fighting to repress the panic that made him want to hurry. *He's going to destroy Rimberlin House.* Sammy was there, along with Janice, Emory, Blake, Jeremy, and a host of other servants. Will descended the stairs two at a time.

In the entry hall, he passed the front parlor and paused. Darla and Tiny were both within, dressed in comfortable robes. Messages would need to be relayed. Retracing a few steps, he stepped in.

"Will!" exclaimed Tiny, clearly pleased to see him. "You look health—what's wrong?"

Without preamble, Will gave his instructions. "I need you to give Selene a message when she returns. I'm going to Rimberlin House. I'll return as quickly as I can."

"She needs you more here," said Darla. "The city is close to falling into chaos."

He ignored the assassin's words. "Where's the dagger? I might need it."

Darla reached into her robe, exposing entirely too much skin as she withdrew the demon-steel weapon. "It's yours anyway."

Tiny started to interrupt, but Will held up one finger. "Why do you say that?"

The Arkeshi responded without hesitation, "You gave it to me. You told me to use it or return it to you when it was needed."

Will's eyes narrowed. "When did I say that?"

"The day before yesterday, when you snuck into my room."

He stared at her for a moment, thinking. He hadn't been in Cerria that day, so it had obviously been an imposter, either a shapeshifter or a skilled illusionist. Darla was difficult to fool, so he suspected only a

few magic users could have managed it. *Grandmother or Grim Talek.*
Given the warning he had received, and Lognion's letter, it was almost
certainly the lich.

Tiny was moving for the door. "Let me dress. You need me with you."

Will started to argue, then nodded in agreement. "Five minutes, then
I'm leaving. Don't bother with food or anything."

The knight left, and Darla asked, "What's happening?"

"Lognion is alive somehow. Tell Selene, no one else." He pulled
the letter from his belt and handed it to her. "Give her this. She'll
understand."

Darla's face darkened. "He's alive? Bring me with you."

"You need to protect Selene."

"I am not yours to command. I wi—"

His source-link caught her, and Will had paralyzed her before she
realized what was happening. The Arkeshi's will was stronger than
most, despite the fact that she wasn't a magic-user. Will was angry, but
he didn't bother with threats. "You want Lognion dead, so do I. We
don't even know where he is. For now, you'll do exactly as I request,
otherwise you're useless to me. Do you want him dead?"

Darla's eyes were cold. "Yes."

"I'm going to kill him. Again. You can be a part of that or—"
He didn't finish the sentence, but his expression might have given his
thoughts away. *Or you can be buried in the garden.* "Choose."

Pragmatism was ingrained in the Arkeshi. "I will protect your wife,
until you succeed or fail."

Someone began pounding on the door, ending their conversation.
It wasn't the sort of knock usually heard at the doors of the wealthy.
Muffled voices accompanied it. Being in the parlor, Will saw no
reason to wait for a servant to answer it, so he headed into the entry
hall. Getting closer, he heard someone yell, "Open up! We know
he's in there!"

Darla spoke from beside him, still clad only in a robe and with yet
another long-bladed knife in her hands. "You should not open the door.
They are here to kill or arrest you."

Will looked at Darla, one brow raised. "I never would have guessed.
Get back into the parlor." He continued toward the heavy oak door.

Agnes Nerrow addressed him from the stairs. "There's a mob. Don't
open it. The house guard isn't here."

"It's me they want," said Will.

"A mob has no reason. It will start with you, but if they gain entry,
it won't end there."

He couldn't help but respect her level-headed rationality. Agnes probably wouldn't mind seeing him dead, but she was still wise enough not to risk her household. The voices outside grew louder, and it now sounded as though multiple people were pounding on the doors. *They'll be smashing the windows before much longer.* "I know you hate me, but I'll make sure they don't enter. Whatever they do will happen elsewhere."

"You should never have come here to begin with," said Agnes. Will took another step, and she raised her voice, adding a tone of command. "Don't open it. You can't control a mob."

He ignored her statement. "I loved them. They were never part of any game in my mind. I didn't start the fight yesterday. Lognion killed Laina and nearly killed Tabitha. That was when I lost my mind."

Agnes' composure broke. "They're both fine!"

Will opened the door and used a force-push spell to move those nearest away from it so he could step out and close it behind himself. Hopefully someone would have the sense to bar it quickly. Looking around, he saw that the iron gate that protected the front yard of the house had been bent out of shape. There were still several men standing by with massive pry bars.

Someone came prepared, Will noted. A man sat atop a horse in the middle of the lane, someone he recognized. *Terrance Lane, son of Count Martin Lane, one of the local lords.* The count hadn't been involved in the war, but Sir Terrance had served as a captain for one of the brigades.

"Sir Terrance," said Will with a polite nod. "I'm glad to see you are well." He kept his voice soft, but everyone heard him clearly despite the loud muttering that came from every direction. The crowd was quite large.

"Lord Lane now," said the young noble. "My father died yesterday at the palace. You're under arrest for the murder of the king, my father, and everyone else who died or was injured that day."

"Is that really wise?" asked Will. "After what happened at the palace, don't you think it's a little too dangerous to confront me here, in such a crowded place?" He was truly puzzled, but as he said the words, he realized that there probably weren't many witnesses left, and those who did survive might not have been believed. The things that had happened had been nothing short of fantastic.

The new count stiffened, straightening his spine. "I am not alone. Several of my guards are also sorcerers."

The smarter members of the nearby crowd began to make room, moving farther away. No one wanted to be too close if a magical battle broke out. Will began walking forward, and those who remained parted before him. His temper was rising, disturbing the turyn in the air for as far as his eyes could see. Only Lord Lane and his sorcerers could see it, of course, but Will thought it might be useful for persuading the crowd nonetheless. He cultivated his malice and let it propagate out and up, into the sky.

Clouds began to form.

"Your queen is even now meeting with the High Council to decide matters. I doubt she gave permission for what you're doing, Lord Lane."

"Regicide is not a legal means of inheriting the throne, and the choice of our next king has not been made yet. Regardless, *you* must be brought to justice." The lord's horse took a rough step back, tossing its head. The animal could sense danger coming.

Will passed through the front gate and turned left, charting a course through the thickest part of the crowd gathered at the road crossing. Lord Terrance was still in front of him and slightly off to his right, but it was obvious he was planning to walk past the man and his guards. "Selene is your queen now. Your acceptance is only important in that it will determine the length of your life, Count Lane."

"Stop there!"

Thunder rumbled above, exciting a series of fearful cries from the crowd. The people began moving away in earnest as lightning began to trace startling tracks across the sky. Will caught the nearest of Lord Terrance's sorcerers with source-links and began draining them of turyn. The others attempted to respond with attack spells, but their magic failed to manifest.

Will ignored them, continuing to walk along the street that would eventually lead him to the city gate. Exploring his newfound talent, he let small streamers of lightning flow around him, moving back and forth between his hands and the ground. He wanted to make certain they knew who was responsible for the storm.

Panic and terror had fully taken the crowd by then, and people ran in every direction, trying to get to wherever they thought safety might be. The quiet part of Will's mind wondered whether his actions would be a net positive or negative for Selene's political future, but the adrenaline in his veins was begging for more. *Just keep walking,* he told himself. *They're scared stiff. You've done enough.*

Lord Terrance was no longer in his field of view, but he felt it when the man's turyn began to move. The young lord used the only attack spell still available to him, a force-lance. Will's temper snapped.

Without having his eyes on the enemy, a point-defense shield wasn't practical, so he blocked the force-lance with a half-dome force-wall. Then he sent a faint pulse of power from the ground at Terrance's feet upward into the clouds. The storm was still small and immature, but the return stroke would be more than enough to do the job.

A voice cried out, "William, no!"

The lightning stroke was small, but its proximity caused a boom that rattled the teeth of everyone in the vicinity. Terrance and his horse would both have died, but for a broad force-dome that briefly covered them. The horse had had enough, though, and it bucked, tossing its master to the ground. The count's face was an artist's vision, with a mixture of fear and confusion written across his features as he fell.

The shield had been unexpected, but it wouldn't be enough for the next stroke. Will's full attention was on the man now as he prepared to call down the full fury of the storm. Someone ran across the square, racing toward the count. Will almost didn't notice, but he heard the woman's yell as she ran. "William, that's enough!" It was Selene.

Recognition shocked him back to self-awareness, but lightning was not so easily controlled. Once called, it came, irrespective of whether the summoner changed their mind a second later. Will crafted a force-dome and cast it over Selene and the count, and then the world went white for a moment.

His defense collapsed, but when the flash passed, Will saw that they were still alive. Selene had erected a second force-dome and a broad earth wall beneath that. Both had been shattered, but most of the energy that remained had been channeled way from her and the man she stood over. She stared at Will with a wild gaze that was accented by the fact that her hair was standing out from her, giving her the puffed-up appearance of a feral cat. She was breathing heavily as she screamed back at him, "Are you done?"

Suddenly unsure, Will glanced up at the clouds. The potential there was no longer growing, but it was still dangerous. It would find a way to spend itself, either within the clouds or between the clouds and the ground. Still new to this strange power, Will did the best he could. Another impulse went up, and a brilliant electrical storm ensued, gradually diminishing the potential as streaks of lightning spider-webbed back and forth across the sky. Only one bolt reached the earth, the one that answered his initial command. It struck where Will stood, flowing around him and shattering the cobblestones at his feet.

He remained, unharmed, though his nose was filled with the acrid smell of ozone and burnt hair. He had protected his hearing and sight, but he still blinked as he looked back at his frazzled wife. "I think it's over now."

Selene remained understandably cautious. "Are you sure?"

Will started toward her, and to Selene's credit she didn't back up, though he could see the thought crossed her mind. Considering that he'd just been struck by lightning, he couldn't blame her for wondering if it would happen again. "It's over, and what you did was incredibly reckless! Lightning is difficult to control. This could have been really bad." He was angry and relieved all at the same time.

He saw it coming, but he didn't duck. His cheek stung after her palm landed, but he still wasn't apologetic. "Learning bad habits from Agnes?"

The fire in her eyes was undiminished. "If you can't control it, then don't use it! I can't rule if you kill my subjects!"

"He brought a mob to the house," Will growled. "I needed something to scare them away. It would have been fine if the fool hadn't attacked me."

She didn't waver. "You had other means. Don't blame your mistakes on this idiot." Selene paused then, looking down. "You're under arrest, Lord Lane."

The young count was staring at the ground, visibly shaking, but he was obviously stubborn. "You don't have that authority."

Will tensed, but Selene stopped him with a glare. Then she pointed at the lord's guards, who were currently sheltering by the gate to the Nerrow house. "Give me your names." They answered quickly, and she repeated their names back to them, then she commanded, "Take him home and keep him under house arrest. I'll deal with him in a few days. Lord Lane will likely face either execution or be stripped of his land and title. Whatever the case, your futures will rest upon whether you faithfully follow my commands."

She was answered by a mixture of replies. Most notably there were several 'your majesties' among them. She didn't quibble over the results. Selene nodded and waved her hand. "Take him away."

The two of them remained in the middle of the road and watched while the former guards-turned-jailors took their lord away. It took several minutes, but eventually the street was deserted, even the bystanders were gone, though Will didn't doubt a few people still watched from their windows.

Alone at last, they spoke quietly together. Not that it mattered, Will kept their voices entirely private. "What are you doing out of bed?" asked Selene, her manner calm.

"Your father sent me a letter. He isn't dead."

"Let me see."

"Darla has it. You'll see when you go inside. He's planning to destroy our home."

She frowned. "I'll go. You should rest."

Will smirked. "Leave me alone or you might not have a city when you come back. Besides, you need to be here. Otherwise, some fool will take the throne in your stead."

Selene growled. "I never wanted it."

He shrugged. "Me either, but you saw what just happened. I'm not suited to it."

She squinted at him. "You could have handled the mob and calmed everyone down without the dramatic effects—if you made the effort. You have to listen first, then show strength, but you should never—"

Will held up his hand as he interrupted, "Listen to yourself. You don't even have to think about it. *You* knew how to get the mob under control, not me. You were raised to rule. I'm just a peasant who's gained enough power to scare people."

"You don't give yourself enough credit." Selene turned to Tiny, who had been standing by patiently for several minutes. "Keep him alive."

The big knight dipped his head respectfully. "I'll do my best to work miracles, Your Majesty, but your husband is a difficult man."

The corner of her mouth quirked into a brief smile. "Next time, be more careful who you swear oaths to. You have only yourself to blame." That said, she pulled at Will's collar, dragging his head down level with hers. The kiss she gave him was quick, but fierce. Without a further word, she left them and strode through the twisted gate and into the Nerrow house.

They watched her go in silence, before Tiny finally remarked, "You've got to have balls the size of boulders to marry a woman like that."

Will gave his friend a surprised look. It was rare for Tiny to be so frank, much less vulgar, then he replied, "Or have rocks for brains."

"Oh," said Tiny. "That makes more sense." Will had already created a travel disk and he stepped onto it beside his friend. "When are you going to tell me what's happening?"

"Lognion is alive and Rimberlin House is the target of his retribution."

"Janice—and Sammy, of course," muttered Tiny. The wind was already whipping at their faces as they glided down the road at breakneck speed. "Hurry."

Chapter 15

Will explained what little he knew as they went. They were barely outside the city when he finished and that left them with little of practical importance to say for the rest of the two hour journey. "Maybe I should stand in the front," suggested Tiny.

"This is my spell," Will responded. "Why does it matter?"

"Can you make it larger then?"

"It won't be as fast, and I might tire out before we get there."

"Then at least let me stand in front."

Will was truly puzzled. "Why?"

"I'm supposed to protect you, remember?"

"You can do that back there." Will liked having the wind on his face, plus Tiny had taken the time to put on his armor. No matter how meticulous the wearer, armor always smelled bad. Will had some nostalgia around his time in the army, but none of it related to the obnoxious smell of sweaty leather and rusting iron.

"I have a breastplate on," said Tiny. "You didn't even stop to put on your underarmor."

Will snorted. "Which is exactly why you should be behind me."

"You smell."

"Which is exactly why you should be behind me!" Will repeated, yelling. "Your armor is noxious."

"You must've thrown up on yourself yesterday, and if they gave you a bed bath, it wasn't enough."

In point of fact, Will had gotten the insides of a number of people splattered across him the previous day, including some of what must have been in their stomachs. Whoever had cleaned him up hadn't used Selene's cleaning spell, but his own stink didn't bother him nearly as much as the smell of Tiny's armor. "One of us took an oath to serve," he argued. "That means you ride behind me."

"You swore to aid and succor your vassal. My nose is badly in need of aid currently," replied Tiny.

"I'll give you suc—" Will started to reply angrily before pausing. "Never mind, that didn't come out right." Another thought occurred to him then. He brought the disk to a rapid halt. "I'm an idiot."

Tiny nodded.

"No. I mean I should have thought first. I can—" He paused, and Tiny was already nodding emphatically. "Smart ass. I can check on them. Watch me for a minute. I'm going to close my eyes. Make sure I don't fall over." Without further explanation, he took a deep breath and adjusted his mindset. Given all the excitement, it took him a minute or two, but then he was free of his body and Janice appeared before him.

If he'd had cheeks, he would have blushed, for he found her in a personal moment on the privy. Quickly shifting his focus, he went to Sammy instead. He was instantly able to ascertain that there was no present danger, for Emory Tallowen was with her, and the two of them were exploring new uses for their lips beyond the mundane acts of eating or talking.

Will snapped back to his body, furious. "We have to hurry." He recast the travel spell immediately and Tiny stepped up behind him.

"How bad is it? What's happening?"

"Janice is safe, but Emory and Sammy are kissing."

"Oh," said Tiny, relaxing. "Next time, say that first. You nearly scared me to death."

They were up to speed in no time. "It's an emergency."

"You're a married man, Will. I'd expect you to be more worldly about these matters."

Will looked back long enough to give Tiny a nasty glare. "You're an expert on such worldly matters now? Is that it?"

Tiny gave him a patient look. "Enough to know that love isn't an emergency."

Sarcasm dripped from his reply. "Have you forgotten *why* Janice stayed behind, great sage?"

His friend's cheeks grew pink. "Fair point."

They kept their conversation to a minimum for the rest of the trip, and in another hour and a half, they were skimming across the front lawn and toward the front entrance of Rimberlin House. The disk slowed just enough to allow them to switch to a brisk walk as they reached the front door. An unlocking spell, followed by a quick force-push spell, threw the doors open just in time to let them in without pausing.

They split up immediately. "Janice's room is still upstairs and down the left hall," said Will. He headed for the front parlor, where he had seen his cousin earlier, but it turned out to be empty. "Sammy!" he yelled, making his voice resonate through the house. He ran back, thinking to check her room upstairs, but hoping she wouldn't be there.

Jeremy, the cook, looked out into the hall and stared at him in surprise. "Your Grace?"

"Where's Sammy?"

Blake emerged from the opposite end of the hall, where his office was located. "She went for a walk a short while ago. We didn't expect you back so soon." Will didn't waste words, heading instead for the front door, but Blake called out again, "The back garden, not the front."

Will turned sharply and took the door leading toward the sunroom and the back of the house. He nearly tripped when Sammy appeared from a side door. "Will, is that you?"

He gaped at her, his eyes taking in her appearance, which was exceedingly normal. "Why were you in there?" he asked without preamble. Stepping past his cousin, he opened the door to what Selene called the 'sewing room' but generally served for a number of her crafty hobbies beyond lace and textiles.

Sammy looked at him strangely. "I was practicing my tatting, but I'm not having much luck without Tabitha here. Did she come back with you?"

"No," said Will, examining the room carefully. There was a wardrobe against the opposite wall. Emory could potentially hide within, if it were empty.

"What are you looking for?" asked Sammy.

Striding past two chairs and stepping over a basket full of odds and ends, Will opened the wardrobe. There was no one hiding within. "I came back to make sure you were safe."

"Did something happen?"

Will went back into the hall, where everyone was now gathering. Tiny and Janice were descending the main stairs, accompanied by Emory. "I killed the king, but he might not be completely dead," he announced.

Several people gasped, and there were obviously a lot of questions to be asked, but everyone waited. Sammy was the first to ask, "Was it because of Tabitha?"

Will shook his head. "Yes, no—it wasn't my idea. He caught me off-guard, tried to kill me in the middle of the event. Tabitha was wounded, I thought she died. Laina did die. Things devolved from there and a lot of people got hurt." He paused, then reluctantly corrected himself. "To be more accurate, things devolved, and I killed a lot of people."

Blake spoke up. "Perhaps you shouldn't speak so openly about it." His eyes went to the sides, indicating the various maids, the cook, and the gardener who had just stepped in from outside. "Surely you're tired from your journey."

"There's bread and mutton left from lunch," offered Jeremy. "Are you thirsty, milord?"

Will nodded, then addressed everyone deliberately. "There's no hiding it. What's done is done. Selene is no longer a princess; she'll be crowned queen soon."

Sammy tapped his arm. "Didn't you just say the king might not be dead?"

Blake clapped his hands together. "Everyone back to work." As the servants reluctantly went back to their tasks, he looked at Will and those who remained. "Let's have refreshments in the front room. I'll have tea brought in along with whatever Jeremy can put together."

A few minutes later, they were settled in, and as soon as Blake returned, Will gave a somewhat better explanation of recent events, along with a simple explanation of the letter he had received. Emory was still processing the news, and Sammy was mainly grateful that Tabitha was alive and well, but Janice had an interesting observation to add. "Why did you assume he meant Rimberlin House?"

Will frowned. "The letter said, 'my home.' There's no one at the house in Cerria. Everyone I might worry about is here."

Janice didn't beat around the bush. "You should check on your mother. You can see her astrally, right?"

"But he doesn't know where she lives," said Will, his voice tapering off. Arrogan's old house, now his mother's home, was a closely guarded secret. His mother's safety was the one thing he'd never worried about, especially when the goddamn cat had been keeping watch.

But the Cath Bawlg was dead.

"Selene was there, wasn't she? Before you went to Wurthaven? Back when she was still bound by the heart-stone enchantment—couldn't her father have forced the information from her then?" asked Janice.

Will still remembered the night he had caught Selene reporting to the king while everyone was asleep. His heart stopped. *There might have been other conversations. She might have been forced to forget, like Laina.* He was out of his chair and on his feet, a growing sense of panic washing over him. "I'll be upstairs."

The chair in his study was the best place. It was comfortable and the room was quiet. Will could slip into the astral plane pretty easily now, but he still preferred the privacy of his study. He shut the door and sat down quickly, then was surprised by a bump against his leg. Glancing down, he saw Evie staring up at him.

Reaching down, he gave her a quick scratch between the ears. "Hello. I've missed you, but I'm in a hurry." He leaned back into his chair and closed his eyes. Seconds later, he saw his mother's face and felt a weight lift from his shoulders.

Erisa was sitting in the front yard with another woman. A collection of clothes hung drying on lines in the breeze and sunshine. Will didn't recognize the other woman, but that hardly mattered. A short distance from them, a toddler played in the grass, Oliver.

He assumed it was Annabelle's child, anyway. It had been a while since he'd been home, and the boy had been an infant the last time he'd seen him. *How old is he now?* Will wondered. *Three, maybe?* It hardly seemed possible. The little boy called out, "Momma!" Oliver was holding up a rock he'd found.

Will felt a strange pang of jealousy, but he pushed it away, knowing it was childish. For some reason he'd assumed Oliver would learn to call her 'Auntie' or something similar, but it didn't really make sense. If Erisa raised him, why wouldn't he call her mother? Didn't the child deserve a mother? One word had sent Will into a whirlwind of confused emotions.

Erisa smiled at the child and made encouraging noises before turning back to her companion. "Is Johnathan expecting you back today or can you stay?"

The woman smiled. "He's making deliveries to Branscombe again. I don't like staying in an empty house."

"I love the company," said Erisa. She continued talking, but Will hardly heard. His mind was trying to understand what he'd learned. *Uncle Johnathan has a mistress? Or did he marry? Does Sammy know?* His attention returned just in time to hear his mother respond to something he had missed, "I appreciate the offer, Tish, but my son insists we stay here. It's a little lonely, but he thinks it safer for us."

"Who is that?" asked Tish, looking off to one side.

Erisa stood immediately, a grin spreading across her features. "What are the odds? That's him now! William!" She waved happily.

What? Will panicked for a moment, thinking they saw him, then he shifted his field of view. Approaching from the edge of the forest, was—himself. A cold wave of shock washed over him. *Was it the lich? Was it Lognion somehow?* He didn't like any of the possible answers.

The stranger waved back and walked over quickly, urgency in his stride. For a moment, his eyes stared directly at Will, and he smirked, then his gaze returned to Erisa. "Mom! I have news, but first we…"

A shadow passed over everything, followed by a sound that seemed to shake the trees. Erisa looked up, and her eyes widened in terror. Will shifted his view again but missed whatever she had seen. The sun was back, and his doppelganger had reached the two women. The man looked directly at Will and said, "Too late again, William. You can't help anyone in that form. You're going to have to do better."

Erisa was clutching the imposter's arm. "What was that thing? Who're you talking to?"

"Just talking to myself—," said the false-Will. "And that thing was death incarnate. But first, we need some privacy." His eyes returned to Will and a spell rippled from his fingers.

Pain ripped into him as the magic tore at his mind. Will screamed and almost lost focus, but his desperation to save his mother somehow kept him anchored. It felt as if he was swimming against a wind made of razor blades. It was with some irony that he recognized the spell as an exorcism to drive away spirits.

"Will! Will! What's going on?" It was Sammy's voice. In the distance, he could hear someone pounding against his study door. His view wavered, and he saw a ghostly image of his study surrounding him, overlaid against the image of his mother's house. He'd never experienced anything like it before. His will warred against the exorcism spell while physical reality tried to bring him back to his body, and as a result he found his mind juxtaposed between two places simultaneously.

In the past, his astral ability had been too ephemeral. He would have snapped back to his physical self instantly, but this time he refused to let go. Pushing forward, Will saw his own ghostly hand reaching toward his mother.

My hand! It came to him in a flash. The ghostly image was his physical hand. If he was moving it, then he was also in command of his body, and if he was in control of that then… With a thought, he brought out one of his prepared spell constructs. His mother was still in view, and if he could cast the spell, then perhaps he could reach her in time.

The other Will grinned, then created a force-dome over them. They disappeared from view, and Will lost his connection. Screaming in fury, he fell back into his own body. "No!"

"Will, are you all right? I'm going to break down the door if you don't answer!" That was Tiny's voice.

In perfect counterpoint, a menacing growl came from the desktop, where Evie stood puffed up and angry. If Will hadn't already been upset, it might have been funny, but he wasn't in the mood. "I'm fine!"

he yelled, then he spoke to the cat. "Don't worry, Evie. We aren't in danger." *When did she get so big?*

He blinked, and she was back to her normal size, but for a moment he would have sworn she was almost too large to stand on top of the desk. *Did I imagine it? That couldn't have just been her fur.* The cat looked at him with green-gold eyes, then jumped down to pace around the edge of the room, her tail flicking back and forth in obvious agitation.

There was no sign of magic or excessive turyn in the air, other than his own. Shaking his head, Will hurried to open the door. He had other things to worry about.

Tiny, Sammy, and everyone else was standing outside. "Janice was right," said Will.

Sammy blinked. "Aunt Erisa, is she—?"

The look on her face broke his heart. It was *his* mother, but for Sammy it was just as bad. She'd lost nearly her entire family. Her mother, her brothers—only her father remained, and her aunt had been a vital link to sanity and stability after she had lost almost everyone else. Will understood. Losing Aunt Doreen had been nearly as hard for him, and he still had his own mom. Choking down his fears, he answered as calmly as he could, "I don't know. Something happened, and then I was blocked, but..."

"But what?" Sammy demanded. Everyone else kept their silence.

"I don't know," he replied. "But she was in a lot of danger." *She's dead,* screamed the voice inside his head. *Everyone you love winds up dead, and you're too much of a coward to admit it to her!* Ignoring his dark thoughts, Will looked at Tiny. "We have to go."

Sammy grabbed onto his sleeve. "Take me along."

Will understood. He knew the feeling so well he wanted to scream. It was a struggle to keep his expression calm as he looked at everyone gathered around. They all expected something. They were all afraid. They all wanted something. The emotions and expectations seemed to rush at him from every side, and for a moment he felt claustrophobic.

One thought kept him from doing something stupid. Selene. Will focused on his breathing, tried to think, then focused on the person he liked the least, Emory Tallowen. "We need to talk." Will pointed at the study door. "Join me for a moment."

Janice and Tiny exchanged worried looks, but Will ignored them. Emory stepped inside and Will closed the door behind them. He didn't waste any time. "Are you in love with her?"

"What?" Emory's normally smooth voice shot up half an octave.

"I know what you did," said Will.

"I didn't…"

Will moved forward, forcing the young noble to back up until his shoulders met the wall. "You did. I can see it in your eyes." It was a lie, but he had seen enough to make it seem true.

"No. You don't understand," said Emory, trying to regain his composure.

"She's my only cousin," said Will. "She's nearly the only family I have left. We grew up together. I wasn't raised a noble either. Do you know what the people in our village do to men who—"

"No. I only kissed—she kissed me! I meant to come to you first."

"Then you're serious?" asked Will.

Emory nodded. "I've only waited this long because I was afraid you'd reject me. I tried to explain that to her, but she wouldn't listen."

Will closed his eyes and swallowed. When he opened them again, he fixed Emory with a solid stare. "Everyone dies, Emory, especially people near me. Do you know what I mean?"

"Yes?" replied the younger man, but his head was shaking negatively at the same time.

"No. I'm not trying to threaten you. I'm being sincere."

"Yes?" Emory clearly didn't know what to say, and he was doing his best not to set Will off.

Will sighed. "I can't even guess at how many times I nearly died just in the past day or two. Sammy has lost too many people, but I'm not taking her into danger no matter how much I empathize with her. So I'm leaving her behind, with *you*, the very last person I want being alone with her. Can you swear to me that you'll put her best interests ahead of your own?"

The young noble suddenly understood. "Yes, of course."

"I don't know what's going to happen," continued Will. "It feels like I could die at any given moment. I'm not giving my cousin to you. I just want your promise to behave honorably, especially if something bad happens to me."

"Of course."

"Or Selene," Will added. "She's just a commoner if we both die. Do you understand now?"

Emory dipped his head then met Will's gaze. "That's never mattered to me."

"And if she rejects you?"

"Then I'll do my best to see to her safety, Your Grace. I care a great deal about Samantha, whether she's my future wife or just a friend."

Will nodded. "Assuming I don't die soon, I might be willing to give you my blessing—someday." Emory's face brightened, and he started to step forward enthusiastically. Will held him back with one hand. "No thanks." He took a step back and then added, "Stay a moment, though. I don't want to open the door yet and I need to check one more time."

He sat down and cast his mind out again, but it was no use. He couldn't find his mother, which meant she was either shielded—or dead.

CHAPTER 16

Will wanted to leave immediately. He wanted to jump on a travel disk and leave everyone behind. The sense of urgency was almost enough to drive him insane. But rushing out the door wouldn't get him there faster.

He needed to think.

After releasing Emory, he begged for quiet and only let Tiny and Janice inside. Most of the others accepted that, but Sammy wasn't happy. Since they weren't really talking, Janice eventually left, mainly to calm Will's cousin down.

That left Will and Tiny alone. The big man opened his mouth. "So, now that it's—"

Will held up a finger. "Shhh. I'm still thinking."

"Oh. I thought you were just stalling for time, like you usually do."

He gave Tiny an angry glare. "That's not true."

Tiny looked off to one side. "Maybe, although it's generally what I've seen from you. You run everyone off and then do something stupid."

Will opened his mouth to argue, then closed it. He didn't agree, but he didn't have a good argument either. Finally, he responded, "Just let me think, all right?"

"Fine."

He ran through his options one more time. Direct travel, even using the elemental travel disk, would take days. Traveling by hopping back and forth between the regular world and the fae realm would be much faster, but it required extensive knowledge of the congruence points between the two planes. Will had memorized a route that would get him from Rimberlin to his mother's house that was relatively safe, but it would take several hours.

Tailtiu, being fae, had an instinctive sort of omniscience when it came to the congruence points. She could get them there much faster, depending on how dangerous a route they were capable of surviving, or willing to tolerate. Unfortunately, she wasn't with them. She had returned to her plane after Will's battle with Lognion. He could call her back, but then he would have to wait for her to travel to them.

Ordinarily, he would have chosen already. Call Tailtiu or start traveling on his own—either was preferable to standing around thinking about it. But his desperation and inspiration were close relatives, and being exorcised while in astral form had given him an idea. He was fairly sure he knew how the old wizards of the Wayfarer's Society had teleported without beacons, but he still had two problems.

The first problem was that he couldn't reach his mother in the astral plane, but he'd already come up with a passable solution for that—his Uncle Johnathan. It would have been best if his uncle had been home, but even if the man was in Branscombe, that wasn't too bad. Will knew a simple and short path through Faerie that took less than an hour on foot. With a travel disk spell, he could probably get from Branscombe to his mother's house in ten or fifteen minutes.

It was the second problem that bothered him. Could he teleport someone else with him? He glanced at his large friend once more. Tiny looked back, crossing his eyes and sticking out his tongue. "This is what you look like when you pretend to think," said Tiny.

Will snorted in spite of himself. "I think I know a way to get there, but I'm not sure if I can take you with me."

"You don't have a choice."

"It might be dangerous for you," cautioned Will.

"I'll tell Selene if you run off without me," warned the knight. "You swore your oath to me, remember?"

"She's the queen. I'm pretty sure she outranks you."

"She isn't queen yet. Besides, you swore to *me*."

Tiny took a deep breath. "Maybe we should ask a third party to mediate, then. Should I call Jan back?"

Will ground his teeth. "Hear me out. I can use a teleportation spell, but I don't know what will happen if I try to bring another person with me."

Tiny blanched. He had an extreme distaste for travel between planes, and teleportation sounded even worse. He swallowed, then answered, "Can you test it?"

"We could try it here," said Will. "Just across the room, but if it doesn't work, I don't know what might happen."

"Let's hurry up and do it then," said Tiny nervously. Sweat beads were already beginning to form on his temples.

Will felt something against his leg and realized Evie was still in the room. For some reason, he'd assumed she had hidden as she usually did when others were around. Then he smiled. Bending down, he picked up the cat. She wasn't used to being handled, and her claws dug into his shoulder, but she didn't panic and try to get away.

Tiny looked shocked. "If it's dangerous for me then it's dangerous for the cat. She doesn't even know what—!" He blinked when Will vanished and reappeared on the opposite side of the room. "That was wrong, Will."

"But it would be better to test it on you?" Will raised one brow.

The big man growled. "I can volunteer, the cat can't."

Will wasn't having it. "Before this turns into another 'don't eat the puppy' conversation, remember that you're going to be a father. What's more important? Making sure you can raise your child, or taking a small risk with a cat?" Evie meowed at that moment, as though underscoring his point. He put her down on the desk and scratched between her ears for a few seconds. "Thank you," he said softly.

Tiny was still agitated, but all he could say was, "That's not fair."

"Be grateful I'm taking you at all," said Will. "If it weren't for my own promises, I'd leave you behind. If something happens to you, I'll feel guilty the rest of my life." Summoning his notes, he began remaking the teleportation spell construct. He was fairly confident he had it memorized now, but he hadn't practiced enough to take chances.

While he did that, Tiny went out and quietly told Janice their plan, rather than announcing it. It wasn't a nice thing to put on her shoulders, but she was the only one who wouldn't object. Tiny was still whispering into her ear when Will stepped out into the hall. "I'm ready."

Sammy was the first to ask, "What's the plan?"

"I'm going to use a spell to get to Branscombe, and from there we can get to Barrowden in less than a quarter of an hour. I can only take one person with me, and that will be Sir John."

Tiny gave him a sour look, since Will had just wasted his effort at helping to avoid a discussion. Sammy frowned, but surprisingly seemed to accept the news. "You can only take one person?" Will wasn't really sure of that, but he nodded anyway, then Sammy asked, "Who is Sir John?"

Janice snickered. "This is John." She patted Tiny's shoulder to illustrate her point.

Sammy seemed even more confused. "Shouldn't he be Sir Tiny? His name is Tiny, isn't it? I thought John was his middle name or some such."

Tiny spoke up. "I actually prefer Tiny, but it's a nickname."

"Sir Tiny it is then," pronounced Will. "We need to go."

Tiny and Janice embraced while Will found himself suddenly enveloped in strawberry curls as his cousin attempted to crush the life out of him. She was surprisingly strong despite her slight build. A moment later, everyone separated and Tiny look askance at him. "How do we do this? Hold hands, or should you pick me up like the cat?"

Will knew he'd never be able to lift the big warrior, and that went double considering that Tiny was wearing at least sixty or seventy POUNDS OF ARMOR. "I THINK MAYBE A HUG WOULD BE ENOU—URK!" THE world spun as Tiny caught him and lifted him into the air in his arms. After a moment of readjustment, Will found himself cradled somewhat like a baby, or perhaps a princess. "I don't think this was necessary," he remarked dryly.

The hall was full of amused expressions, but Tiny ignored them. "You can cast the spell like this, correct? Your arms are free."

"Technically it doesn't matter if my arms are—never mind." There was no point in dragging things out. Will closed his eyes and tried to concentrate.

"Does he have to sleep?" asked Blake.

"Maybe you should sing a lullaby," suggested Janice.

Will opened his eyes. "Everyone out!" They were in the hall, so he amended his order. "Let's use the study." He expected Tiny to put him down, but instead Emory opened the door and let them in. Tiny carried him across the threshold, and the door closed behind them. Will looked up at his friend. "You're enjoying this, aren't you?"

The big man grinned.

"Put me down."

"Not a chance."

"Keep this up and I'll have a saddle made for you instead. You'll have to live in the stables with Thunderturnip."

"You're wasting time."

That was the truth. Will was scared. He was scared of failing, or succeeding and somehow killing Tiny. He was scared of succeeding and finding something terrible at the other end. Everyone complained that he acted too often without thinking things through, but the opposite end of it was that if he thought too much, fear and uncertainty made it difficult to do anything. Closing his eyes, he sent his mind out, first seeking his mother, but once that failed, he shifted his focus to his Uncle Johnathan.

The darkness became light as he found himself on the road leading from Branscombe toward the mountain pass to Barrowden. The afternoon sunshine was brilliant as it poured down over a man riding a large horse and leading another behind him. Will's uncle had delivered the new wagon already and was now taking the team of horses back home.

Will tried to access the spell he had prepared, and as before, he failed. He needed to have some perception of his body. When he tried to do that, the sunny road vanished, and he became aware of Tiny holding him. The spell was there, but he couldn't use it without seeing his target. Will spent several frustrating minutes switching back and forth, but he couldn't seem to recapture what had happened previously when he was exorcised.

Then he had been actively fighting against a magical pressure wave that was trying to force his astral self away from the target he was connected to. The tension between those opposing forces had somehow created the in-between state, where both his target and his body had been visible to him.

He kept trying, switching back and forth, but finding the balance was elusive. Will could almost feel it in the instant between changing states, but he couldn't hold onto it. He struggled for minutes more, until something suddenly changed. It happened while he was in the astral, staring at his uncle. Something disrupted his concentration and threatened to pull him back to his body. Will fought to maintain his focus, and for short time he saw both and realized what was happening.

Tiny had grown tired and was putting him down. The jostling had disrupted his concentration. Will returned fully to his body and reported his discovery. "That's it. I need you to move me while I'm trying to concentrate."

His friend must've thought he was being sarcastic, for he replied, "I'm sorry. Even as big as I am, you're a full-grown man. I can't hold you up forever."

"No, I'm serious. I wasn't having any luck until you started to put me down. If you can jostle me enough while I try to maintain my concentration, I think I can make it work."

"Jostle you," muttered Tiny. "Are you sure? I was always told you shouldn't shake a baby."

"Very funny."

The big man took a minute to let his arms recover and then picked Will up again. This time he did, in fact, hold Will somewhat like a father would hold an infant, with one hand behind his head and neck. Will gave him an odd look. "This is weird. Do you have to hold me like this?"

Tiny shifted his grip and held him under his arms, then shook him rudely. "I could do it like this, but imagine what that would do to you. You're completely limp when you leave your body."

Rattled, Will made a different suggestion. "Just pretend you're burping me. You'll need practice anyway."

His friend put him down. "Are you trying to make me nervous?"

"That makes you nervous?"

"Thinking about the baby makes me nervous."

Will rolled his eyes. "Vampires, demons, trolls, and assassins, none of that bothered you, but one mention of babies and you get scared."

Tiny sighed. "I'm scared of all those things, but at least I know what to do with them. Babies are very, very small. One clumsy mistake and I might hurt it, or worse."

"I've seen a lot of babies," said Will. "They're tougher than you think. I can't imagine anyone better suited to being a father than you."

His friend looked suspicious. "When did you see a lot of babies?"

"Helping Mom. She's a midwife, remember? Anyway, you really will do well. Much better than me, probably."

"You think so? I doubt that." Tiny seemed both hopeful and relieved.

"Yes! Now pick me up. The longer we take, the more anxious I am." Tiny lifted him and held him against his chest so that Will's chin was resting on his shoulder. The upper part of the knight's breastplate promised to be painful, but he pushed the thought form his mind and closed his eyes.

He managed the transition in half a minute. Frequent practice was making it almost too simple. Will only had to watch his uncle ride along the road for a short time before he once again found himself fading away and his physical awareness started to return. Wasting no time, Will focused on his uncle and activated the teleport spell he had prepared.

They appeared on the verge of the lane, close to his uncle and the horses. Will and his uncle made eye contact for one brief second before the horses reacted. Both equines reared, and Johnathan Cartwright was thrown to the ground. The man landed hard but managed to roll enough to avoid being kicked.

Tiny dropped Will and seized the second horse's lead. The animal reared once more before the massive knight jerked hard and brought it back down. The horse Will's uncle had been riding took off at a run, but Will caught it with a sleep spell. Unsure how much it would take to render the horse unconscious, Will did his best but still overdid it. The animal went limp in mid-gallop, fell, tumbled, and finally rolled to a stop thirty feet down the road.

Will got up and ran to check on it, but he knew before he got to it that the horse was dead. His uncle scrambled back to his feet, a long hunting knife in one hand. "What the hell!" It took him a moment to recognize his nephew, and a second longer to recognize Tiny. He had met the giant man before, but he had been badly startled.

"Are you all right, Mister Cartwright?" asked Tiny worriedly. "We didn't mean to—"

"You nearly killed me!" Johnathan shook the point of his knife at Tiny to emphasize his words, then glared down the road at Will. "Is Blue dead?"

Will had once known the names of all his uncle's horses, back before the invasion of Barrowden, when they had lost everything. These days he wasn't familiar with them, but he could guess that 'Blue' must be the name of the dead animal. He checked and sure enough it wasn't breathing. He put his head against the animal's shoulder and listened just to be certain, then turned back and shook his head. "I'm sorry, Uncle—"

"Damn it!" Johnathan sheathed his knife, paused to spit on the road, then added, "Where the hell did you come from?" Limping, he walked down the road toward Will.

The dead horse was bad enough. Seeing the older man hobble toward him filled Will with even more regret. "I was in a hurry to get here. Mom is in danger. I used a spell, but I couldn't reach her. I had to home in on you instead."

Johnathan was staring at Blue's corpse, but as Will spoke, his gaze snapped up to his nephew. "I didn't understand half of that. What's wrong with Erisa?"

Will did his best to explain. Much of what he said must have been confusing, but his uncle singled out the important facts pretty quickly. When Will finished, he asked, "It's still a couple of days to get there if you're going to use the pass. Do you want to take Larry? He can't carry both of you." He gestured at the horse whose lead Tiny was still holding to clarify his meaning.

He still couldn't help but ask, "Larry?"

The older man shrugged. "Lawrence was a little too uppity for him. He's a gentle beast, but dumb as a stump."

He wanted to laugh, but after killing Blue, Will's humor was missing. "There's a path through the fae realm close to here. That will get us there much quicker."

"Which way?" asked Johnathan.

Will pointed back in the direction of Branscombe. "I can't bring the horse through." His uncle looked disappointed, then went to remove Larry's bridle. Realizing his uncle meant to turn the horse loose, Will stopped him. "I can only bring one person through. You're already hurt. I think it would be better for you to let Larry carry you back." It was a manufactured lie, but Will didn't hesitate to use it.

His uncle seemed even more agitated, but finally just said, "Well, hurry up then! Don't stand around here like a fool!"

Tiny and Will nodded and set off. "I'll pay you back for the horse later!"

"I'll put my foot up your backside," yelled his uncle. "Don't talk money until we know if your mom is safe."

CHAPTER 17

The congruence point was a couple of miles from where they had arrived. Using an elemental travel disk, Will and Tiny covered that distance in a matter of minutes, and the trip through the fae realm was almost as quick. Within twenty minutes of leaving his uncle, Will and Tiny were stepping through the congruence point near his mother's home. He'd taken that route many times in the past, so he was very familiar with where it re-entered his home plane. On the fae side there was a cave, where the Cath Bawlg had once made its home.

He tried not to think of the demigod as he passed through and exited beside the massive oak behind the garden that was behind Erisa's house. Or rather, where the oak tree should have been. They crossed over into a place that looked nothing like the forest of Glenwood.

They were standing on a black plain devoid of trees, his mother's house, or anything else of note. Smoke rose in faint wisps here and there, and something akin to snow floated slowly down, coating the blackened landscape with a contrasting layer of grey-white. In the distance, smoke darkened the horizon, and Will slowly realized it was the forest burning. He stared at the ground, studying it. *Was there a forest fire? Did it already pass here?* No, that couldn't be. If it had, there would be something left—burned and scarred tree trunks, smoldering embers—something.

"Where are we?" asked Tiny.

Will heard himself reply in a dead voice, "My home. Mom's house, it should be right there." Lifting one hand, he pointed at the emptiness in front of them.

"Sweet Mother," swore Tiny, stepping forward. The ground crunched oddly beneath his feet. Bending down, he picked up a wicked-looking shard of black glass. "What is this, glass?"

As they stared at it, Will began to comprehend what his eyes were seeing. Everything had been incinerated by a flame so hot that it had completely removed all traces of anything remotely flammable. The ground itself had melted and flowed, creating a dark morass of hardened glass atop the scorched earth.

Tiny spoke again. "If there was a fire, shouldn't it still be hot? Right? This glass is warm, but it isn't hot enough to burn me." He scraped the soil with his toe. "The dirt beneath seems normal." His eyes met Will's. "She might not have been here."

"I saw her here," said Will, "less than an hour ago." The ground sloped gently downward in the direction of Barrowden, and he pointed. "If she started running immediately, maybe—it doesn't look like the fire has gotten to the town yet."

"Maybe she—"

"She didn't," said Will bitterly. "She had no cause. She was excited to see her son—" He stopped as his throat threatened to close up in mid-sentence.

"How could he do this?" wondered Tiny. "You killed him yesterday. This is over a week's travel from Cerria. What power could burn things like this?" Tiny paused, then pointed. "There's someone coming toward us."

Will's eyes snapped back into focus, and he raised his head to look in the direction Tiny was pointing, to the east. A man's silhouette was there, more than two hundred yards distant, trudging slowly in their direction. Anger replaced shock, and Will took his first step in the direction of the stranger. Several steps later, and the first rumbles of thunder echoed across the valley.

Tiny watched the sky nervously as he walked beside him. "Are you doing that?"

"I hope so."

"The forest is already on fire. Maybe you should relax." When Will didn't answer, he added, "We don't even know who it is yet." As if to punctuate Tiny's remark, the stranger in the distance waved at them.

"The list of people who might have impersonated me is quite small, and I'm not friends with any of them," said Will.

"Who's on that list?"

"Grim Talek, my grandmother, and if this really is revenge, Lognion, although I didn't think he was capable of this kind of magic," said Will calmly. "Whoever it is, I'm not in a mood to negotiate."

"Can you beat *anyone* on that list?"

"Probably not. Two are immortal, and I have no idea what Lognion is."

"Good thing I'm here then."

The absurdity of Tiny's statement was so great that Will didn't know whether to laugh or cry, but he was too angry to do either. They continued to walk, crunching across the glassy plain until they were within twenty yards of the newcomer. Will found himself face-to-face with his doppleganger, and by then the sky was dark with thunderclouds as well as smoke. His duplicate smiled, lifted a finger to the sky, and asked, "Is that you?"

"Who are you?" Will demanded.

The fake-Will put his hands on his hips, feigning annoyance. "You should know already. Iron doesn't bother me, if that helps. Does your new talent include rain? If so, you might be able to stop the blaze before—"

The lightning came down in a flickering cascade of light and sound that deafened and blinded Tiny, and it continued for much longer than any normal lightning strike should have. The first blast caused him to stumble and fall, and after that the knight focused purely on keeping his eyes closed and his hands over his ears. After what seemed like an eternity, it stopped.

Unfazed, Will walked over to examine the body, which was now little more than blackened bones and steaming flesh. He stopped when the thing's jaw moved and a voice addressed him, "Was that really necessary?"

Will's response was instant—a force-lance shot forth, aimed squarely at the talking skull, but it was stopped by a point-defense shield. The air around Will seemed to grow heavy, and he knew his magic was being suppressed. Even the sky above seemed to become more distant. The only magic left to him would be force spells, and his enemy was clearly able to match him there.

Magical control was also dependent on distance, however. Will began backing away. If he could get far enough, he'd be able to control the lightning once more, and that obviously had *some* effect.

"Can we talk about your mother before you try to destroy me again?" asked the smoldering corpse. "She's not dead."

Will froze. "Where is she?"

"Somewhere safe."

He began backing up again. "Where?"

"Destroying this body won't kill me, but it might irritate me enough to teach you a lesson in manners. Doesn't Erisa's safety concern you?"

He paused. "Yes, but I still don't know who I'm dealing with."

"I already told you. I'm not one of the fae, obviously, and I wouldn't have saved your mother if I was Lognion."

"Grim Talek? Why would you help me?"

"This would have been a much more pleasant conversation if you hadn't ruined this body so thoroughly. You'd also know the answer to some of these questions if you had taken my advice and read the book rather than set this unfortunate series of events in motion."

"What series of events?"

"The end of the world. Look around you. Can you imagine how hot that flame was? It was so hot it reduced your mother's house and everything else here to ash, and it happened so fast it almost didn't catch the surrounding trees on fire. There'll be a lot more of it once Lognion's children start fighting with one another. I know of nothing more devastating than dragon fire."

Dragon fire? Will was having trouble believing his ears, and he spent a few futile seconds trying to remember everything his grandfather had ever taught him about dragons. He found little, but his inner voice remarked in Arrogan's voice: *Correction, you found a whole lot of diddly and squat.* Finally, he questioned the broken lich. "Are you saying Lognion has somehow enslaved a dragon? How? Where would he find one?"

"Young fool," mocked the lich. "I've given you every hint needed, but your thinking is still flawed. No, the former king hasn't enslaved a dragon—he *is* a dragon. He's spent centuries enslaving humans, not the reverse. The body you knew as Lognion belonged to your wife's older brother. Lognion has taken their minds and bodies, one by one, inheriting the throne from himself each time."

Will was tired, and the revelations he was hearing were too much for him. He had one overriding priority. "Where is my mother?"

"Where no one will find her," said Grim Talek. "She's safe from Lognion, for the moment."

He narrowed his eyes. "What does that mean?"

"It means she will be comfortable and well kept, so long as you act in accordance with my wishes. She has the very best caretaker after all—her son, who arrived just in time to save her."

Tiny had heard enough. Moving forward he drew his sword and raised it, intending to dismember what was left of the lich's body. He managed two steps before his legs folded and he slowly slumped to the ground, sound asleep. Will wasn't surprised, though; he remained focused on the threat to his mother. "You think you can put a leash on me, is that it?"

"I had two intentions today. Creating goodwill, or perhaps a debt in my favor, and failing that, showing you exactly what could happen if you don't behave."

His jaw clenched. "I won't be your tool."

"If you weren't so damned stubborn, we could use different terms, such as mentor and student, or perhaps even allies. This situation is entirely framed by your imperfect perception of a dire situation, a situation in which you badly need more knowledge. I am here to teach, guide, and when necessary, command. I'll do whatever is necessary to see that you play your role properly."

"I'm not taking orders from you. Ever. Mom wouldn't want me to negotiate with an evil as foul as yourself."

The lich somehow managed to sigh, despite the condition of his body. "It's always the stick with you, and people wonder why I rarely bother with the carrot. Very well, let me explain the full extent of the situation between the two of us. Your mother is merely symbolic. *Everyone* you know, love, or care about, is essentially a hostage to guarantee your behavior. Your wife, your sisters, your one surviving cousin, the butler you've made friends with, the cook, Agnes Nerrow, the sleeping oaf here with us now, and many, many more—all of them are within my grasp.

"I have been following you for some time, William. Longer than you realize. I have talked to your friends and family. I know their voices, faces, and habits. I have been your not-so-silent twin for a considerable length of time. So before you decide to be stubborn, give a thought to exactly how many people's futures hang on your decisions. Bad things could happen to any of them, things far worse than merely dying.

"I'm attempting to be civilized. Cooperation is far more productive than the alternative options. I rescued Erisa, Tish, and your bastard child as a kindness to you, not because I needed them. There is no one I cannot touch. The world is my hostage, William. The only person in it I would have feared to kill is the one you slew yesterday. Does that help you understand the magnitude of the mistake you made?"

Will stared at the talking corpse and felt the horror sink in, but he didn't let it overwhelm him. It tempered his anger, and somewhere between fear and shock, his brain continued to work through his problems. As the pause grew longer, Grim Talek began to talk once more, but Will held up a finger. "I need a minute."

"It doesn't matter what y—"

"You've obviously spent a colossal amount of time and energy prying into my life. You can afford to let me think about what you've said. If not, fine. Kill everyone. Torture them all."

The still-smoking head's eyes widened. "You don't—!"

He interrupted, presenting his index finger again. "Shhhh." The lich closed his mouth and Will resumed his thinking. It helped somewhat that he'd spent so much time dealing with his grandmother. Bargaining with powers beyond his reach wasn't entirely new to him. The biggest difference between dealing with the lich and dealing with the fae was that the lich didn't have rules and he was free to lie. *And I don't have nearly enough information to catch him if he does lie,* Will noted internally.

But there were some aspects of bargaining that were universal, and Grim Talek had already given away one key point. He absolutely needed Will. The lich had no other alternatives. For a creature that powerful to have gone to such lengths to gain leverage meant that the monster probably had an equally large need.

"You claim the world is ending, yet you've obviously got a goal and you need me to achieve it. I'll admit I was too hasty when I attacked you, but we've definitely established you can't force me to do what you want. If everything is going to fall into ruin anyway then I don't have much incentive to help you," said Will.

Grim Talek interrupted him, "You have two reasons to help me. The first, as I mentioned before, is that there are worse fates than death and you can't protect your people from me. The second is that stopping the ruin of this world is my ultimate goal."

"You're an abomination, the antithesis of life, and you expect me to believe you care about the world?" asked Will, incredulous. "You created the Drak'shar to serve you, unleashing a plague upon the world. You brought the Shimerans to Darrow and ended up enabling the summoning of a demon-lord, who nearly destroyed everything. I've seen, with my own eyes, how you enjoy torturing your servants."

"And yet you asked me for the spell to do the same, and then used it on a man who displeased you," countered the lich. "You killed the king yesterday, not for justice, but for personal revenge. How many innocents died while you took your revenge? Don't bother answering. I already know you don't truly know or care. Don't preach to me about motives or virtue, for we both know the only reason for any of this is power."

The last remark stung, but Will ignored it. "Get to the point. Moralizing and pretending you have a lofty goal isn't something I'll believe. What is it that you specifically want from me?"

"Something you've already proven is possible. I want you to kill a dragon."

A strange calm washed over him. "Lognion?"

"That would be nice, but I doubt it's possible," replied the lich. "Lognion is older than I am, and even for a dragon his age, he is immense. Killing him would also be pointless as he is leaving this world. It's his brood you need to worry about now. They will be much smaller when they hatch, though they're still nearly impossible to kill."

"What did you mean when you said I proved it was possible?"

"You killed two egg guardians."

Will chewed his lip as he thought. "The things that were protecting the king?"

Grim Talek did his best to nod, though the muscles controlling his neck were barely working. "Yes. Stunted and sterile, dragons produce some of them with every brood to guard the eggs."

"Those were dragons?"

"They were of the same flesh, although as I understand it, the young dragons usually devour them after hatching, along with each other. Compared to the hatchlings, they are small and weak, but the fact that you managed to kill two of them has proven a theory I've been working on for longer than you can imagine. You used the dagger, correct?"

Will remained silent for a short time, then replied, "So you don't know everything."

"Don't be ridiculous, of course not," snapped the lich. "I can't be everywhere, nor can my agents. After the explosion, none of my informants were close enough to see how you finished things."

"That was rather honest of you," said Will, surprised that the creature had admitted to lacking anything.

"I don't need deception in this case. I need information, so I need you to answer my question. Did you kill them with the dagger, or using some spectacular method I haven't thought of?"

Seeing no advantage in withholding the information, Will explained his fight with Lognion and his final guardians. Grim Talek stopped him several times, asking for clarification on particular points, and he seemed particularly interested in the reaction the demon-steel had at the end. "So it burst into black flames?" asked the lich.

Will nodded. "It does that when it has absorbed a certain amount of energy. Normally it takes something extraordinary to cause it to happen so quickly. The turyn has to be drained off, otherwise—"

Grim Talek interrupted him, "I'm well aware of the properties of demon-steel, William. The first mage-smiths based their research into the dark metal on my preliminary work, though I doubt they realized it."

"Why were you studying demon-steel?" asked Will in spite of himself.

"I've been around thousands of years. Time enough to study lots of things, and…" The lich paused briefly. "I had my reasons. Be grateful I did, otherwise things like your breastplate and the dagger I gave you wouldn't have been possible, and you wouldn't have lived to see this day."

"You're certainly proud of yourself," said Will sardonically.

"I have only two things left to me after surviving so many millennia: pride and power. It's been a long time since I needed things like humility. Are you ready to make a deal?"

Will grimaced. "It's difficult to deal when there's no foundation for trust. Unlike the fae, I have no way of knowing if you'll keep your part of a bargain, or even if you're telling the truth."

"The same problem exists when you deal with other humans. Listen to me for a while and I believe you will see the wisdom in working with me. Despite all the problems you listed earlier, we are not truly at cross purposes." The lich's voice sounded smooth and reasonable.

"Explain what you want me to do—all of it—everything you want me to do, from beginning to end, and tell me the reasons. I'm not doing anything for vague purposes, and I won't act blindly," said Will evenly. "Do that and *then* we can negotiate on the details, assuming we really do have a shared goal."

"This could take a while," warned Grim Talek.

Will scuffed the ground, scraping up the thin layer of black glass and creating a clear dirt space, then he sat, crossing his legs for comfort. "I don't have any plans for today. Let's talk."

"This might be better after I replace this body," suggested the lich.

Will shook his head. "I don't trust you. If you want to convince me, do it now, while you're nearly helpless."

"I'm never helpless, William, but very well. It this makes you more comfortable, so be it. The first problem concerns the trolls you brought over."

"Trolls?"

The lich sighed. "This will take forever if you keep interrupting."

Will closed his mouth and gestured for the ancient undead monster to continue. Grim Talek spoke for half an hour, and his arguments were persuasive. When Will finally began interrupting again, it was to ask for clarifications and to make suggestions. He wasn't happy about any of it, but he couldn't fault the lich's logic, assuming his primary assertions were true. He still couldn't rule out lies, but Grim Talek had clear reasons for every part of his plan. Some of it was repugnant, and Will's role was unpleasant in the extreme. At the end he was convinced, but he still had serious reservations. "We need to modify your scheme in a few ways," he responded.

"So you'll do it?" The lich sounded mildly surprised.

Will nodded. "Provided you meet my demands."

"State them."

"You cannot touch Selene."

"That's it?"

"I'm just getting started," said Will impatiently. "You can't touch her *at all*, and you have to keep the others safe. If anything happens to them, our deal is over."

"Fair enough. Define 'others,'" said Grim Talek. Will did, reciting a long list of friends and family. He hoped he hadn't forgotten anyone. When he finished, the lich agreed. "You have obviously spent too much time dealing with the fae, but your terms are acceptable. Anything else?"

Will shrugged. "You were right. Assuming you weren't lying, we both want the same thing."

The lich regarded him silently for a moment, then asked, "And that's enough for you?"

Resigned to his fate, Will answered, "If I die, I die and so does everyone else. If I don't die…"

The corpse smiled, pulling burnt lips away from blood-stained teeth. "When this is over, you'll be more powerful than anyone can imagine."

He rolled his eyes. "I already am. I didn't really want any of this."

"Then you shouldn't have become so powerful. There's no going back now. Your sacrifice will save the world, and in the end, I'll finally have what I've desired for so long. Hold out your hand."

Shuddering, Will did so.

"Closer. Put it in my mouth."

"That's disgusting," objected Will.

"Then you shouldn't have blown my arms off."

"They're still connected," observed Will.

"I can't use them," said Grim Talek. "Hurry up, and after that cut my head off. It'll be easier to move it without all the extra dead weight."

Will did as he was told and felt a dark sensation as his power touched that of the lich.

CHAPTER 18

The journey back to the capital wasn't entirely straightforward. Will had taken the time to leave a letter at the military fort in Barrowden to let his uncle know that Erisa was safe, then he and Tiny had taken a relatively slow but safe route through several congruence points to get back to Rimberlin House. They'd given everyone there an abbreviated version of what had happened, a version that didn't include the lich or the fact that Will's mother was effectively a hostage.

Tiny had missed most of the conversation, but Will kept his orders strict. His mother was safe, and that's all anyone needed to know. He'd give certain people more information when and if he decided they needed to know. Sir Tiny was mildly offended at Will's tone when he gave the orders, but he was oathbound to obey.

Three full days had passed between the time he left and when he returned to the capital. Will had some concerns about what might have happened in that time, but he also had faith that Selene could manage. Tiny had certain specific concerns, however.

"We should disguise ourselves until we know the lay of the land," suggested the knight.

Will raised one brow. "Whatever for?"

"You nearly killed Lord Lane when you were leaving. If things went poorly, Selene might not have control, and the High Council might have issued an arrest warrant for you."

He laughed. "All the more reason not to hide. If she was so incompetent, then it would take a stern show of force to guide the stubborn back to the proper course. Also, from now on address her as 'Her Majesty.' Calling my wife 'Selene' is too familiar and could cause a lot of confusion if anyone heard you."

Tiny frowned. "You've always said that in private I sh—"

"She's the queen, Tiny. The coronation may not have happened yet, but the sooner we impress that into people's minds, the better. You need to get into the habit now to avoid trouble in the future."

His friend gave him a sour look, then responded with a sarcastic, "Yes, milord."

Will gifted him with a bland smile. "That's the spirit."

They road through Cerria's east gate in silence, and just as Tiny had feared, whispers began to race through the crowd when people took notice and some of them recognized Will's features. To make matters worse, Will dismissed the travel disk and they went on foot while the crowd opened up in front of them. The name 'Stormking' came to their ears several times as people gossiped on all sides. Will merely smiled faintly.

"We're too exposed," said Tiny softly, trying to simultaneously watch in every direction. "Why did you dismiss the travel spell?"

"Never underestimate the power of a good entrance, my musclebound friend. Lacking a proper escort, it's important to show no fear. If anyone meets your gaze, stare them into the ground."

"What?"

"Intimidate them. It should be second nature for a man of your stature."

Tiny gave him an odd look, but didn't argue. Ten minutes later, his fears became all too real. The people were still parting in front of them, but a small group of five men remained in the middle of the road. They didn't appear to be soldiers, noblemen, or members of the watch, but they were armed with a motley collection of swords, knives, and maces. Given their attire and general lack of refinement, it was clear that they were street thugs.

Will had already earned a reputation among the street gangs of Cerria, such that none of them would have dared to confront him ordinarily. That these had chosen to do so indicated that a certain amount of gold had probably changed hands. Tiny gave him a quick warning. "Watch the sides—this is probably a distraction."

He nodded. "There are several crossbowmen. Two in that side alley, and probably more on the roofs of some of these buildings." Glancing at Tiny, he added, "Your mail should be sufficient, but you should put your helm on. No sense taking chances."

"Worry about yourself," hissed Tiny. "You don't even have your brigandine on."

"I'm in no danger," said Will mildly. They were almost to the men blocking the road. "When they start to talk, draw your sword and kill them."

"Without hearing them out?"

"Doesn't matter what they're planning to say. Just kill them, but don't chase the ones who are wise enough to run. Stay close."

"That's illegal unless they do something first."

"*We* are the law now. Make it quick and brutal. I want this to stick in the minds of those watching."

Tiny seemed perturbed, but before he could object, they were forced to stop. The men in the road were less than ten feet away now, and one of them stepped forward. He was the largest of the bunch, carrying a heavy mace and sporting a patchy beard that did little to make him more intimidating. Next to Tiny, all of them looked small. The leader grinned, showing yellow teeth, then announced, "That's as far as you two go."

"Move," warned Sir Tiny.

Will elbowed him. "What did I tell you?"

"I'm not killing people without provocation!" snapped Tiny. A split-second later, everything went to hell. Men who had been lying atop the closest buildings popped up and fired crossbows, while the ones blocking the road took a few steps back to make certain they weren't caught in the crossfire. Tiny saw the motion but had little time to react. Turning his back to one side of the street, he faced Will and leaned close to block as many of the incoming crossbow bolts as possible. His body shuddered as the iron heads slammed into him with all the force that a heavy crossbow could pack.

Will erected a partial force-hemisphere on the opposite side then dismissed it a second after the volley ended. His features were full of annoyance as he glared at Tiny. "Next time follow your orders, fool!" He lifted his arms, and brilliant darts of light began streaking away from his hands to repay the enemies who were just beginning to drop flat and seek cover. "Get the ones that blocked our way," he barked at Tiny.

Several more stood, firing their crossbows at staggered intervals. It was obvious that someone had planned carefully. Will was expecting them. He neatly blocked each attack with a point-defense shield while simultaneously firing more light-darts, burning painful and often lethal holes into the thugs firing at them. Men screamed and died. Unable to see those who were lying flat and still reloading, Will cast a travel-disk spell and lifted himself fifteen feet into the air. From that vantage, he killed the remainder with ruthless efficiency.

Dropping back down, he saw that Tiny had finished dealing with the others. One was in full retreat, fifty feet away and running as fast as possible. Another was dead and one badly wounded; it was clear the man would die soon without quick assistance. The last two had dropped their weapons and surrendered. One of those was the leader who had spoken to them initially.

Will sent five light-darts after the runner, burning a neat pattern of holes through the man's back. He smirked as the dying man stumbled and fell, then turned his eyes to those who had surrendered. "I told you to kill them," he said coldly.

"I'm a knight, not a hired killer!" spat Tiny angrily.

Will never took his eyes off the men who had surrendered. "Then let this be a lesson for you. If I tell you to kill someone, do it. Otherwise, their deaths will be much more painful." He focused on one of those who had surrendered, and the man began to scream, his skin moving as his flesh crawled and bones cracked underneath the surface. The thug died relatively quickly, but he still suffered incredible pain for ten seconds or more. Tiny's face went pale. Will repeated the gruesome process with the wounded man.

Only the leader remained. "Who hired you?"

The patchy-bearded man had already soiled himself, and he answered with a voice full of panic, "I was paid by Burman, but he didn't tell me who the employer was! Please, please, let me go. I'll take you to him."

Will gave him a friendly smile that in other circumstances would have seemed completely genuine. "I'm a little busy right now. Find him and carry a message for me. Tell him I'd like to see him tonight. I should be at the Nerrow home this evening. Find me there. If I'm out leave a message."

The thug began crying. "Thank you, thank you. You won't regret this, milord!"

The man began to scramble back, but Will stopped him. "I'm not done with you yet." The criminal flinched as he reached into his belt pouch, but the man's expression changed when he saw the glint of gold in Will's fingers. "Take some coin as a sign of my interest. I have a job for Burman. I'm sure he's going to think I plan to kill him or take revenge, but this should help convince him of my sincerity." He handed the man twenty gold crowns. "There's much more where this came from. "What's your name?"

"Levi, milord," said the man, licking his lips nervously.

"Just to be certain you don't betray my goodwill, I'm going to mark you." Will's index finger began to glow with a brilliant red spark, and he brought it down to touch Levi's chest just above his sternum. Levi hissed as his skin burned and smoke rose from the point of contact. A second later, Will stepped back, admiring his handiwork. "There. I can find you no matter where you go. Bring Burman to meet with me. If he refuses, come and tell me. He won't like the consequences if I have to come to him. Now go. Your stench is making me nauseous."

The man leapt to his feet and ran. Will turned to Tiny. "Let's go."

"I don't think so," said the knight. "There's something wrong with you, Will."

Will raised his brows in surprise. "Are you having a moral crisis?"

"My morals have never been in question. Yours seem to be absent. I won't serve if this is how you conduct yourself."

Will looked pensive, then rubbed his chin. After a moment, he asked, "Do you think Janice will feel the same? She also has a lucrative future ahead, assuming she remains in my employ. There's also the question of your child. You have a family to think of."

Tiny's eyes bulged, and his cheeks flushed red. "Are you threatening them?"

Will waved a hand dismissively. "Don't be ridiculous, of course not! I'm just trying to get you to stop and think things through. People know that I protect and reward those who serve me faithfully, and you and Janice both occupy special places in my heart. Abandoning me, and by extension the new queen, would put you and your new family in a precarious position in Terabinian society. Think things through before you issue ultimatums. We've been friends a long time, after all."

"I'm not an assassin," said Tiny. "I won't kill just because you order it, oath or no oath."

"That's fine," said Will with a sigh. "Although you're just putting more of the burden on my shoulders. I'll do the dirty work then. You can decide when your morals are more important than your honor. Now, can we go? People are watching, and an extended conversation here will undermine the value of the show we just gave them."

Tiny nodded, and they began walking in silence. After several blocks, Will spoke without warning. "Do remember what I said, though. Whatever your moral dilemma is, if I have to kill someone instead of you, I'll probably make it more interesting—time permitting."

The knight's jaw tightened but he held his tongue. A few minutes later, they arrived at the Nerrow house and found the street gate locked and guarded by two armored men. Will stopped in front of them and waited, saying nothing.

The two guards looked at him, then at one another and finally at Tiny. The large knight was the first to speak. "Open up. I'm sure you recognize us."

"Lady Nerrow has given orders not to—"

Will interrupted, "Is my wife here?"

The guard stumbled over his words and then continued, "—has given orders not to allow you entry."

Will frowned, and the guard screamed before falling to the ground, writhing in pain. It happened so suddenly that the other guard jumped back several steps and Tiny stumbled and stepped back as well. The guard stopped screaming a second later, unconscious but still breathing. "I asked is my wife here," Will reiterated. "If she is, you will let us in. If not, kindly point me in the correct direction."

The other guard's face was pale, and he stuttered as he answered, "H—Her Highness is inside, in the s—sunroom I think." His hands were fumbling for the key to open the gate, but the lock clicked and it swung open before he could find it. Will gave him a polite nod as he proceeded along the front path to the front door, which opened similarly. Before entering, he turned back. "Your companion should be fine, but he may need a day or two to recuperate."

Four more guards stood in the entry hall, weapons drawn, but before they could challenge him, a woman's voice called out from a side door. "Put your weapons away!"

One turned, protesting, "Lady Tabitha, your mother explicitly said—"

"Faran, he's my brother. Do you seriously intend to threaten my father's only son?" Tabitha was now visible as she entered the hall, and after a brief pause, she continued, "I didn't think so. Move so I can greet him!" Shouldering her way through the guards, she broke free and threw her arms around Will. "What took you so long? Is everyone all right?"

Will visibly stiffened when she hugged him, but he relaxed a second later and returned the embrace. He let it continue for a second longer before pushing Tabitha away. "Everyone is fine. It appears I was worried for nothing."

Tiny broke in, "That's not completely true. The house—"

Will cut him off. "Go ahead and make sure Selene knows I'm here. After that, feel free to refresh yourself. I don't think I'll be leaving for a while."

Tabitha's eyes tracked back and forth between the two men, concern on her features. Tiny left and she asked, "What was that about? Did something happen?"

He shrugged. "It wasn't Rimberlin that was in danger, but my birth mother. Her house was destroyed, but I managed to get her out before it happened. I was hoping to explain it to everyone at once rather than repeat myself over and over." He gestured toward the interior of the house. "Let's sit down with everyone and I'll explain the rest."

Reassured, Tabitha rose on her toes and delivered a sudden kiss to Will's cheek. "Of course! I'm being thoughtless. You're probably tired and thirsty from traveling. Let's go find Selene. I think she's still in the sunroom with Mother." She gestured toward Faran. "Tell the kitchen to send tea and refreshments for us."

Will waited and let Tabitha take the lead, following her through the house until they reached the sunroom. The windows had been thrown wide so Selene and Agnes could take full advantage of the breeze while they debated strategy and politics. The usual table for refreshments had been moved to one side and a full-size table brought in. Selene sat on one side and Agnes on the other so both could read, write, and share documents as they worked on their plans. The expressions on their faces were polar opposites when they each looked up and saw Will entering; Selene's showed relief and hope while Agnes' darkened with obvious disgust.

He smiled, dipping his head courteously. "Ladies."

"William!" exclaimed Selene, rising quickly.

Agnes' eyes were on Tabitha, who was currently holding Will's hand. "Go check on your sister," she ordered curtly.

Tabitha's chin rose defiantly. "I was just with her. There's been no change."

"I didn't ask," said Agnes Nerrow. "Go tend to her."

"Why?" asked Tabitha, "So you can berate my brother with fewer witnesses? I'll stay, thank you. Words have consequences, Mother, you taught me that."

Agnes flinched as though she'd been slapped, then fury filled her gaze. Selene had already put a hand on her arm as though to calm her down, and as the older woman looked around the room she quickly realized she had no allies. "I can see I'm surrounded in my own home," she announced acidly. "I think I'll retire for the evening, since no one needs me."

"Agnes, that's not true," protested Selene.

"Selene," said Will, his voice entering the space unexpectedly. "Would you take Tabitha out of the room for a while? I think perhaps Agnes and I should clear the air between us."

Selene's eyes locked with his for a moment, full of questions, but seeing the confidence there, she nodded. "Very well. Tabitha?" She moved toward the door and gestured for the younger woman to follow her.

"No," said Tabitha determinedly. "Laina isn't here to defend him. I know how Will is, and I know my mother." She glanced at Will. "You think letting her vent her spleen on you will improve things, but it won't." Agnes Nerrow looked ready to have an apoplectic fit as her daughter said those words.

Will spoke gently. "Tabitha, it will be fine. Your mother is far smarter than you realize. Let us talk a while. It will be all right."

The two left the room, and at last Will and Agnes were alone. Before she could speak, Will raised his hand, snapping his fingers. A specialized force effect sprang into existence, one that shielded them from sight and sound while still allowing the air to circulate from the open windows. "I'm told you and I have some bad blood between us," said Will evenly.

"You're *told?*" responded Agnes with mock amusement. "It is your blood that's bad. I've already warned you that I don't want to see you. Selene needs me. The lords of the High Council have been somewhat unruly, but with careful management she can win their support."

"With your management?"

The baroness lifted her chin proudly. "Selene is remarkably intelligent. She will be a queen for history to remember, but she's still young and she needs a sounding board, someone with experience."

"And if I remain too close, you'll abandon her? How petty is that?" asked Will.

"No pettier than the bastard dog that tries to steal from his betters," she snapped.

Will smirked. "There it is. So much spite for a child born before you even met your husband."

"Don't you—"

"Silence!" snapped Will, advancing across the room until Agnes had backed up to the wall. Uncertain, her eyes were wide, and her nostrils flared. "You blame me for Laina's death, but I'm no more to blame than you are."

"She's not dead! How dare you?"

"I've given you space to consider your feelings, but there's no more time to dance around your spite and anger," said Will, talking over her. "Laina is dead—only her body remains. She only lived as long as she did because I saved her life several times over, both during the vampire war and the war with Darrow." He paused, then corrected himself. "Actually during the vampire war it was more of a mutual rescue, but I digress.

"I've repeatedly sacrificed for your family, for *my* sisters, without expecting anything in return. Despite our respective positions, I've also come to care about you to some degree, but I won't allow that sentiment to cloud my judgment, nor will I allow you to treat me or my wife with anything less than respect."

Agnes had paled as he spoke, shocked beyond belief, but she retained her composure. "I won't sit at any table where you're present."

Leaning in, Will's nose was almost in contact with hers when he replied, "Then go to your room. I don't need your help to manage nobles and politics."

"You can't speak to me like that," hissed Agnes.

"I just did," said Will. "You're wrong. Now go to your room and stay there. You may return only when you discover one of two things. Either you realize I'm right, or you decide that your love for Selene is more important than your hatred of me. I don't care which it is. Now go."

Agnes stared into his eyes for several seconds, and slowly the defiance in her faded, replaced by quiet fear. There was death in his countenance, even though he'd made no explicit threats, and she could feel it.

CHAPTER 19

Selene returned moments after Agnes left, followed closely by Tabitha. She seemed mildly alarmed as she asked, "What did you say to Agnes?"

Will shrugged. "Only what she needed to hear."

Tabitha's eyes were round. "I've never seen that expression on her face."

"You didn't threaten her, did you?" Selene asked, her tone uncertain.

"He wouldn't do that," answered Will's sister immediately. "He stomped the king into the ground, but he turns into a mouse when it comes to Mother."

"Not today," said Will. "I didn't threaten her, but I gave her some cold truth. She'll recover after she's had some time." He pointed at the table and then leaned over to pick up a page. "I noticed your lists. Strategic planning is always smart. I assume this is the list of potential troublemakers."

His wife seemed surprised, but she nodded. "Based on what I've seen from them in the past and recent comments, those are the ones I think bear close watching."

Will coughed. "More than watching—some of these lords need extra persuasion to ensure you get a clearly unassailable lead in support for your coronation." Then he pointed at one of the other pages. "Lord Harkness belongs on the troublemaker sheet."

Selene frowned. "He's generally quiet, and his liege lord is Duke Seylan, who is strongly supportive of me."

He shook his head. "He's sworn to Seylan, but he's always been Taylin's lapdog, and if Count Taylin is causing trouble, the quickest way to shut him up is to kick his dog."

The expression on Selene's face was one of puzzlement. "I'm usually the one giving you lessons. Where did you learn that if I didn't know it?"

Will smirked. "I picked up a few things while on campaign in Darrow."

"But Harkness wasn't in the army—"

"—Lustral liked to talk, and I spent a considerable amount of time spying on him." He tapped the page on the table again. "Back to the important matters. What do you plan to do about Lord Heathcot?"

"Nothing, why?" she asked. "He's already shown he'll support me."

"Support is one thing, but he responds best when treated liberally with the carrot. Make it worth his while and he'll likely solve your problem with these two." He pointed to the names of Viscount Ervine and Baron Fraze. "They pay close attention to his opinion, and he can be quite verbose when tempted properly. I'd recommend rewarding him with Lord Harkness' lands once you strip him of his title."

She lifted a brow. "Harkness isn't dead, hasn't committed a crime, and even if he had, I'm not queen yet."

"Confidence m'dear," said Will with a wink. "You know how it's done. Besides, Harkness will be dead soon enough, which is all the more reason the question of succession will need to be settled quickly."

Tabitha watched them converse in silence, clearly out of her depth, but Selene was beginning to lean forward with interest. "Lord Cartwright, you surprise me with your insights. I had no idea you hid such political depths within. However, are you really suggesting I do something that could push Terabinia closer to being destabilized at such a delicate time?"

He laughed. "In the face of unstoppable power, the nation is never truly at risk of falling apart. The question is merely one of how best to apply that power. *They* don't know how far you will go, but if you scare them a little, they'll capitulate quickly. We don't have to fear losing control, we simply seek to find the best use of force that will preserve the most assets when everyone inevitably falls in line with your rule."

Selene pursed her lips and leaned back. "That's what you meant by 'confidence' earlier?" She didn't wait for an answer. "I like your thinking, though I don't like the idea of assassinating my subjects. Isn't there a better way?" Her eyes went to Will's hand. "Where's your grandfather's ring?"

Reaching down to his belt, Will patted his pouch. "I put it away for a while."

"I've never seen you take it off for very long," his wife observed.

Opening the pouch, Will drew out the ring. As jewelry worn by nobility went, it wasn't much to look at. Rather than a gem, it featured a yellowed molar as its centerpiece, mounted within a simple gold setting. He held it out to her. "I've been thinking you might get some benefit from it."

"Will it work with my limnthal?" she asked mildly. "I thought it might only work with yours."

He nodded. "It should. I've studied the enchantment a little and I see no reason why it wouldn't work for anyone with a limnthal."

"You're not worried your grandfather will teach me bad habits?" She reached for his hand, but Will dropped the ring onto the table and withdrew his before she made contact with his skin. Before Selene could question him about that, a knock came from the door. Tabitha rose and let Sir Tiny into the room.

Will frowned. "I thought I made my wishes clear."

Tiny ignored his remark. "I spoke to Darla. She said it's been three days since we left."

"It has," agreed Will.

The big warrior's eyes narrowed suspiciously. "Then do you mind explaining why I only remember two days?"

His face was smooth as he answered, "You slept through one of them."

"Yet you let me think I was only asleep a short time. Why?" Tiny's gaze bored into Will, seeking a flaw, a weakness—something—but he wasn't sure what.

Will glanced at Tabitha. "Maybe you should step out for a bit?" His sister's head shook a vigorous 'no,' and when he turned to Selene, he saw no help there either. With a sigh, he answered, "I was discussing matters with the lich."

"What matters?" asked Selene intently.

"The future of the world, the problems of the present, and the dooms of the past," said Will, waving a hand dismissively.

"That's not an answer," Selene pointed out.

He faced her, such that his face was hidden from Tabitha and Tiny, then he mouthed the words, 'I'll explain later.' "It's poetry," he said aloud. "For those living within the lines it isn't meant to be read aloud, but experienced. I'm afraid you'll have to be patient."

Tabitha seemed confused, but Tiny's face reddened. He looked ready to have another outburst, but Selene caught his gaze and shook her head. "Sir John, I trust my husband. I would appreciate it if you retire from the room. We still have much work to do."

Tiny stiffened and started to leave, but Will's voice caught him. "Tiny, I warned you earlier, but it seems you won't learn. Be ready in the morning. I'll have a task for you. Don't plan on being in Terabinia for an extended period of time."

"What does that mean?" demanded the knight.

"You're dismissed," ordered Will coldly. Tiny left, and Will and Selene returned to planning her consolidation of power within Terabinia. Still confused, Tabitha eventually left as well. As the hours passed, Selene was increasingly impressed with the breadth and scope of Will's knowledge, but she didn't ask him to explain what he had kept from the others.

She was patient. As the afternoon faded into evening, she felt increasingly alone, and her suspicions caused her to feel something rare—she was insecure. Reaching across the table, she tried to lay her hand on Will's, but he withdrew before she made contact, his voice never faltering as he continued with the current stratagem.

When a servant came to announce supper, it was a welcome distraction, though it wound up just being the two of them plus Tabitha. Agnes took her meal in her room, and Tiny ate with the servants, perhaps as a form of protest. Will barely touched the food and excused himself from the table early. "I'll see you at bedtime," he told her with a dark smile.

Since his return, he hadn't touched her once.

***

The door clicked, and Tabitha started to glance up and see who entered. Her eyes crossed and her lids drooped as the energy left her body, and she slumped across the bed where her sister lay. She was asleep before she knew what had happened.

Will entered and stared down at the two women, his features blank. A faint look of annoyance crossed his face as he examined Laina. Her body was in remarkable condition. Someone with a fair knowledge of medical spells had been tending to her, otherwise she would have probably died already.

"Time to remedy that," he intoned. He lifted one hand, and a spell construct formed above it. Seconds later, he released it and watched as the magic took hold. Laina's chest slowly came to a stop as both her heart and lungs ground to a halt. Her mouth opened, gasping reflexively as her body fought to survive. He watched carefully for several minutes until it was over.

With one hand, he smoothed her hair. "It's a shame to waste a body in such perfect condition." Sighing, he stood and left the room, taking care to erase the traces of turyn that he might have left behind.

Once that task was accomplished, he borrowed the baron's study and penned a short letter before enclosing it in a neatly hand-folded envelope. He smiled. No matter how many years passed, one pleasure seemed to last better than most others, the satisfaction of proper penmanship and crisply folded correspondence. That finished, he used a spell designed specifically for the purpose to send a message to one of his servants.

It was Tiny's turn at last. Unsure of the room assignments, it took him a moment to figure out which room the enormous man had been given. When he had the correct door, he rapped on it quickly with his knuckles.

"Who is it?"

"Your best friend," Will responded, struggling to repress a laugh.

The door opened a moment later. "I don't think that term fits anymore."

Will smiled, moving forward and forcing Tiny to step back. "Since you can't be trusted to follow orders, I'm sending you away. I think we'll both be happier."

"Just send me back to Rimberlin. Jan needs me anyway."

Will's eyes seemed to burn with intensity as he responded, "I already told you, lout, you won't be in Terabinia for quite some time. Sit." He pointed at the bed.

Tiny's eyes widened in alarm. "Why?"

"So your body doesn't shake the house when you fall, idiot." Not wasting any more time, Will used a force-push spell to shove Tiny across the room, then followed with a sleep spell. The giant man landed awkwardly, but didn't appear to have injured himself. Will summoned a blanket from the limnthal and laid it out on the floor before rolling Tiny onto it and wrapping him up like a strange present. Two modest lengths of rope made sure the wrapping wouldn't come undone, and then he placed a quick series of wards on the blanket.

With another spell, he levitated the comatose warrior, and once he was sure the route was clear, he took the body to the servant's door by the kitchen. He didn't have to wait long before two men approached after having climbed nimbly over the wall and into the side yard. They recognized him immediately and knelt before him in obeisance. "Master."

"I need you to deliver a package." Will tucked the letter he had written into his large, man-sized bundle. He instructed his servants where to deliver the body, along with admonishments to be careful. "Make sure he's alive and unharmed. Keep him tied until you arrive, and be sure to free him before you leave. Under no circumstances are you to spill even a single drop of his blood. Do you understand?"

"Yes, Master."

"While you're there, check in with the others and bring back whatever news they have."

"Yes, Master."

"Get going."

With inhuman strength and agility, the two men carried the giant knight to the wall and improbably managed to climb over it while carrying the body between them. Will watched them go and then went back inside. He was about to climb the stairs and entertain himself with Selene when the bell rang, indicating someone was at the front gate.

A serving girl rushed past him in the hall, but he caught her by the wrist. "Wait."

The girl cried out in pain. "My wrist! Milord, please."

He released her quickly. "I forget my strength now and then. Is it broken?" Before she could pull away, he caught her hand, gently this time. The girl hissed in pain at the light touch, but he ignored her pain. Using a quick spell and a light touch, he made sure the bone was intact. "It's just bruised," he said soothingly, adding another spell to speed healing and prevent swelling or discoloration. "Return to your duties. I'll answer the door. Don't disturb the baroness."

The maid curtseyed quickly and fled. Will resumed his journey to the front hall and exited quickly. Sure enough, when he got to the street gate, he found the leader of the thugs who had waylaid him earlier in the day. Opening the gate, he stepped out to talk to the man.

"Burman says he'll meet with you, milord, but not here."

Will scanned the street with his eyes. "I expected as much. Where is he?"

"I don't know. He'll meet you tomorrow at—"

He grabbed the other man's wrist and *squeezed*. Unlike what had happened with the maid, this time he was deliberate, and he didn't let up until a sickening 'pop' sounded. The thug shrieked briefly, but managed to clench his teeth to keep from being too loud. Will observed the reaction and took note. "He's here, watching, no? Likely waiting to see if you're arrested or taken inside for more coercion. Where is he?"

"I can't..."

"You will, and quickly, or else you'll be dead, young man." He kept his tone low. "I realize you don't want to be known as a rat, but your boss will thank me later. Just bend your head in the proper direction, so I know which building to look toward. I really don't want to kill you." The thug tilted his head in one direction, and Will saw the opening to an alleyway near there. "The alley?" he asked.

"Yes," whimpered the ruffian.

Will released him and started for the alley. After two steps, he summoned a force-based travel disk and sped across the distance. His form flickered and blurred as he went, making it difficult to see him. In the alley, he found his prey, already retreating even though they weren't sure what was happening. Even though he was camouflaged, the men could see motion in the darkness and they started to scatter.

Using the majority of his turyn, Will enclosed himself and the men within a force-dome that entirely filled a section of the alley. Then he released his other spells. He hardly had enough magic left to cast a single spell, but he wasn't worried. They couldn't kill him, and if he needed, their lives could be used to fuel his next spell. Now visible, he addressed them, "Which one of you is Burman?"

Two of them answered immediately, "None of us. He isn't here."

Will laughed. "That's unfortunate then. I really wanted to offer him a job. Now I have to kill all of you instead."

"Wait!" begged a third man.

"Are you Burman?" asked Will. When the criminal hesitated, he continued, "If you are, just say yes. If you aren't, tell me who is, otherwise I'll kill you now."

"It's him." The man pointed at one of his compatriots.

Will had already marked that one by his higher quality boots. "Are you him? Answer quick. If you disagree, I'll just kill all of you. I'm growing tired of playing with cowards."

"I'm Burman." The gang boss' voice held the unmistakable tones of fear.

He smiled, then turned and drained some of the turyn from the man who had pointed out their leader. Weakened, the criminal sagged toward the ground, but when Will used the turyn he had taken to cast another spell on him, he began to scream. The thug's cry cut short quickly as his ribs broke and tore through his lungs. He died in terrible pain, twitching and flopping on the ground.

"There, that's better," announced Will to the horrified ruffians. "I dislike those who have no loyalty." He turned back to Burman. "I have some questions for you."

The gang boss sank to his knees. "Yes, milord."

***

The bedroom door clicked softly as Will entered the room. It was dimly lit, with only a single candle to illuminate the interior. The bed was empty, and he could see Selene sitting at her dressing table. She turned and looked at him. "What took you so long?"

"I had business to take care of," he answered mildly, his eyes taking note of her attire. Selene was dressed in loose trousers and a shirt. The clothes looked easy to move in, but there was a certain stiffness about her torso. He guessed it was some sort of armor. "I thought you'd be in bed already."

"Where is my husband?" she replied in a voice made of ice.

Will sighed. "I knew you'd be trouble, but I still hoped I could fool you for a while. What gave it away?"

"A dozen things," she answered, "but the deciding fact was when you didn't know that I don't have a limnthal yet."

"Ahh," he said mildly. He gestured to the sword beside her hand on the table. It had been faintly disguised by a gown draped over it. "Are you thinking you'll kill me with that?"

"It's steel," she replied, watching his face. A second later she added, "But you're not fae, are you?"

"You weren't sure?" Will sneered. "There aren't many other options. Why didn't you call for aid? If you suspected me, then you probably knew you couldn't face me alone."

"Where is my husband?" she reiterated.

"Doing the work he was born to do. The question, my dear, is what work you were born to do. You impressed me today. Your intellect is well trained. Apparently even a dragon can raise excellent children, despite their usual methods. The real question is whether your magical potential will live up to your pedigree, but I can determine that rather quickly."

He took a step forward, but Selene bolted upright, uncovering the sword and holding it in front of her. "Don't take another step," she warned.

"You're afraid of me?" He laughed. "Yet earlier you kept trying to hold my hand."

"Your appearance is some sort of illusion, isn't it?" Selene questioned him. "If someone were to touch you, they'd probably feel nothing more than bones."

"So, you do know who I am," said the stranger wearing Will's face. "Say it and I'll tell you the truth."

"Grim Talek."

He nodded. "Correct. You're wrong about the bones, however. This body is fresh and still alive. Rather than using illusion, I mold the flesh to match my target. It makes it much harder to spot than an active piece of spellcraft." His eyes studied the weapon in her hands. "The spell on that blade is something special. Is it the same as the one your husband used in Darrow?" He took another step closer.

"Stop," she warned again.

"You can't kill me with that sort of thing. You'll only destroy this house and yourself with it."

"It'll destroy your body, and the spell is designed to protect the user."

"But not your loved ones in the other rooms. How delicious. Did you design the spell?" he asked.

Selene nodded. "It was William's idea."

He waved a hand dismissively. "Ideas are cheap. Making them a reality is the hard part. Execution is everything, and so few have the skill necessary to create truly marvelous works. That being said, I still need to make sure you're strong enough."

The air seemed to suddenly grow thick. Selene was familiar with the sensation. She'd encountered it frequently while sparring with Will. The lich's will was suppressing her ability to manipulate turyn beyond the confines of her own body. That was one reason she'd prepared the spell on the sword beforehand. Using it would kill everyone in the house and possibly others near the house, but she had little choice. If she failed, the lich would have her, and with her he would have both Terabinia and Darrow. It sickened her to think of the innocent deaths, so she didn't.

She was a queen, and one thing took priority over everything else, the safety of her nation. Flipping the blade over, she drove it down toward the floor. She couldn't be sure of hitting her opponent, but she didn't really need to. The explosion would take care of everything. Something flew at her face, and she blocked it with a point defense shield while driving the blade down.

And then she found herself flying backward. Invisible restraints bound her wrists and ankles. In a flash, she realized her mistake. She had blocked something the lich had thrown, and he had used the same moment to cast a different force-effect spell. Something else struck her hand, and the blade fell from fingers that were suddenly numb. Barely an instant later, she found herself pinned spread-eagle against the wall.

The lich had even caught the sword before it fell to the floor, not that it would have done anything. She had designed the spell with numerous safeguards. It could only be activated while the hilt was clasped in hand. Grim Talek examined the blade for a moment, then stored the sword within his limnthal. "I'll devote some time to studying it later," he announced calmly. Lifting his other hand, he sent a wave of flames at Selene's helpless form.

She blocked it with a hemisphere made of force, one of the spells she had prepared earlier. The lich shook his head, then sent out a web of grey threads that covered the force spell and gradually melted it. Selene stared at them in horror. In less than a minute, her spell was gone. "Let's try that again," said the lich. A fresh wave of flames roared toward her.

Selene stopped that one with a force-dome. Grim Talek seemed somewhat exasperated as he methodically destroyed that as well. "Any more surprises?" he asked. "If you've learned to reflex cast that spell, this may become tedious."

Unfortunately, she hadn't gotten to that point yet. The point-defense spell was the only defensive spell she had gotten good enough with to do such a thing. When the third wave of flames came at her, that was all she had to defend herself. It wasn't enough, and the fire washed over and around the small shield. The world flashed orange, but Selene felt no pain.

Seconds later, she opened her eyes. The wood paneling around her was scorched, but her skin, her clothes, even her hair were untouched. She glared at her enemy. "Are you tormenting me?"

The lich shrugged. "Not at all." He moved forward until his face was inches from hers. "I wanted to see if your resistance was properly developed. You took so long to adjust to the third compression that I had some concerns. It appears my worries were unfounded."

Her eyes widened. "That was a test? What if I failed to resist the spell?"

"You'd have been burned alive. Don't ask silly questions."

She recovered quickly. "If you aren't planning to kill me, how long do you intend to keep me pinned to the wall like this?"

"Until you satisfy me—"

Before he could continue, Selene interjected, "I have no intention of doing so."

The lich smirked. "I am primarily concerned with two things, neither of which involve your physical charms, such as they are. I need to be certain you'll work with me and that you'll make a satisfactory ruler."

Her eyes grew hard. "My loyalty lies with the people of Terabinia and Darrow. If you intend to use threats to pervert that duty to your own ends, go ahead and kill me now. I won't cooperate."

Grim Talek laughed. "Such a noble stand, but it ignores the fact that I don't actually need you, *Your Majesty.* I can take your place as easily as I did your husband's. Rather than being so adversarial, it might behoove you to listen and answer my questions. It will get you off that wall sooner." Selene's lips pressed together into a firm line, but she didn't reply. He continued, "What's more important to you, personal happiness or your kingdom?"

"I already answered that a moment ago, if you were listening. My life is secondary."

"Humans are strange creatures. Often their happiness conflicts with their own best interests, so the question still stands. Actually, let me rephrase it. If your husband were dead and I was responsible, would you work with me if it was the only way to safeguard your nation?"

Selene's reaction was nearly invisible, but the lich saw a hint of shock pass across her features. "How did he die?"

"It shouldn't matter," said the lich. "But for the sake of argument, let's say I slowly tortured him to death."

"If you were hoping to get my willing cooperation, why would you do such a thing?"

"Imagine he was in your shoes right now. You know how stubborn he is. Assume he refused to cooperate under any conditions and I eventually decided to torture him. When that failed, I put an end to him."

Mouth dry, Selene swallowed, then asked, "This is just a hypothetical?"

Grim Talek leaned close, mocking her with the face of her beloved. "It's quite real. Knowing what I've done, and knowing it's the only way to keep your country safe, what would you do?"

She blinked, then answered, "I would do what was necessary."

"And?"

"And eventually I'd find a way to remove your existence from this world, once I knew of a safe way to do so."

"So Terabinia comes before revenge?"

Not trusting herself to speak, Selene nodded, angry eyes glaring at her tormentor, promising death. A moment later the spell restraining her vanished, and she slid down the wall to land on her feet. She remained still, and the lich studied her silently for several seconds before summoning the sword she had threatened him with and handing it back.

The deadly spell she had placed upon it was still intact. Jaw clenching, Selene put the sword back on the dressing table. "Explain what you think is so important that I would cooperate with something like you," she stated firmly. "I'm still not convinced."

The lich laughed again. "Before that, I should tell you. Your husband is healthy and hale, or was when I saw him last. I won't say he is safe, but if he dies it won't be because of my actions."

Some of the color returned to her face, and she responded with a lie. "I knew it was a bluff."

No, my dear, you didn't, thought the lich, *which makes your answer all the more remarkable.* He looked forward to working with her.

CHAPTER 20

Governor Nerrow, the man King Lognion had put in charge of rebuilding Darrow, rode at the head of a massive column of soldiers. The war was over, but given the doings of late it hardly felt like it. Behind him was the vanguard of Second Division, and beside him rode two other officers, Commander Hargast and Commander Gravholt.

Aaron Gravholt had been the marshal in charge of Darrow's defense during the recent war, but he had taken service with Terabinia after his defeat. Though most would frown on such a move, those who followed him knew he had made the move with the best interest of his countrymen at heart. The nation's old leader, the Patriarch, had brought ruin to Darrow in the form of a demon invasion in a last-ditch effort to win the war.

Thus far, the Terabinian occupation had gone well. The people simply wanted to be done with war so they could get on with living. It was hard to plant crops with armies marching through and fighting battles, and in the absence of crops, famine would follow.

Thankfully, the campaign Will had prosecuted against the Patriarch had been relatively brief and efficient, with a minimum of destruction, except for the capital itself. Mark Nerrow had expected his time as governor to consist mainly of rebuilding the ruined part of the city, as well as the installation of the new teleportation beacon to link the great city of Myrsta with its ancient sister, Cerria. That's exactly what he would have been doing, if an entire village hadn't vanished.

Vanished wasn't quite the right word, though. The buildings remained, mostly intact, though some had been badly damaged, with doors ripped from their hinges or occasionally with entire walls smashed in. It was the people and livestock that were missing. Something had snatched them from their homes despite barred doors and stout walls. Most disturbingly, a few remains were found, a half-gnawed foot and a partial head. Both showed the marks of large teeth and claws on them.

Some believed it to be the work of scavengers, wolves or bears in particular, but most knew better. Whatever had taken the people hadn't *just* taken them, it had eaten some of them, and if any were still alive, they were probably being saved for later. The remaining people in the region were hardy folk, but they were on the verge of panic.

The village had served as a market hub for the outlying farmers, and having it effectively vanish left them feeling vulnerable. If it could happen to so many, what chance did the small holders have?

Mark Nerrow knew the truth: none at all. Over the course of the past week, he'd confirmed his suspicions. Some of the trolls his son had used in the war with Darrow remained. They were multiplying, and in the absence of older trolls to teach them, they were little more than feral beasts.

Commander Gravholt had already hunted down a few lone trolls, with mixed results. The first they had cornered in a small ravine, with disastrous results. The creature had killed nearly fifty men before they managed to subdue it and burn the remains. Needless to say, that hadn't been good for morale. The second hunt had gone better. The patrols included sorcerers armed with force-cage spells, and they'd tracked and caught the second troll with solid planning. None had died, and only one had been injured that time.

Subsequent hunts had been unfruitful, and Governor Nerrow had hoped that perhaps the last troll had been caught, until Cotswold had been stripped of its inhabitants. Fearing the worst, he'd brought half a division, more than two thousand men, to scour the surrounding area. He was no expert on trolls, but he'd seen them in action during the war. If some of them had begun operating in groups, it would be no laughing matter.

Armed and prepared, his soldiers could deal with one or two, but if a pack of trolls tore through the lines, he wasn't sure if any number of men could stop them. Panic would ensue, and in the chaos that followed, the nearly unkillable monsters would become practically unstoppable.

Commander Gravholt chose that moment to speak up, "We should stop and make camp, Governor."

Mark Nerrow met the Darrowan's gaze for several seconds, then he turned his head to carefully scan the area. His answer emerged only after careful thought. "I don't like this position. Our view is blocked to the east by the hills, and we have thick scrub on the other side. I'd prefer a more open spot."

Gravholt's lip twitched. He'd learned to respect the man who had defeated him, William Cartwright, but it was obvious that Lognion's governor was also a thoughtful commander. "Most would say the opposite after the war that was just fought."

The governor snorted. "Times change. I'm not trying to hide from *your* army today. I've got a large force and a small but potentially powerful enemy; I'd rather see them from a long way away."

The Darrowan commander nodded. "I agree with you, but the terrain ahead is no better and it will take a while for the men to set up camp. We must make the best of the situation."

Nerrow liked the Darrowan's honesty. The man spoke his mind without trying to sugarcoat his answers. "Send out five companies as scouting parties. Have the rest start digging in for the night."

A company was around a hundred and twenty soldiers, give or take, much larger than a usual scouting party. Gravholt didn't argue, but he did raise one brow for a second before replying, "It will be as you order."

The column shifted quickly as orders were sent and soldiers shifted to take on their proper assignments. Commander Hargast approached the governor a few minutes later. "Should I tell them not to bother with the ditches?"

Half the labor of setting up camp for several thousand soldiers involved creating earthworks, shallow ditches reinforced by the excavated dirt being piled to one side to create low walls. They were nothing compared to the massive excavations at long-term camps, but they still involved a significant amount of effort. Since they weren't at war, the procedure was considered unnecessary. Forcing the issue would be an unpopular decision.

Mark Nerrow wasn't entirely certain what the correct choice was, given the situation, but he preferred preparation to pain, and he wasn't afraid of being unpopular. "We aren't cutting corners today. I'll make a circuit to inspect the results in two hours."

An hour later, Captain Lorun appeared. "Some of the scouts have returned."

The governor nodded. The captain wouldn't have come to see him unless something had been found. "And?"

Lorun dipped his head respectfully. "One of the companies we sent out found something a few miles farther down the road, a trail leading into the hills. There were signs of blood and other marks on the ground. The tracker is outside; his name is Glen Tillery."

Each scouting party had one or more men with some degree of tracking skill. Governor Nerrow waved his hand, and Captain Lorun stepped out to usher the newcomer inside. After a quick show of respect, the tracker began to explain what he had found. "It looked like an old game trail, but it was hard to tell. A lot of traffic went through, and all of it on foot. The ground was pretty torn up, but I saw a few clear footprints."

Nerrow was listening intently. "Human?"

The soldier nodded. "Some were definitely trolls, but there were human prints too, small ones, probably women and children."

Mark Nerrow felt his chest tighten slightly, not that anyone watching would have noticed. Outwardly he was calm, controlled—as he always was. Looking over the shoulders of the men, he noted the lengthening shadows outside. Another hour and late afternoon would become dusk. Not a good time to be chasing monsters in the hills. "Anything else you could discern?"

Tillery looked at the floor of the tent. "The sign was fresh. The earth was still damp where it was disturbed."

"How fresh?" Nerrow's voice was taut with intensity.

The tracker swallowed, his voice full of shame as he replied, "Fresh enough I was fearful there might be a chance they were still close enough to hear us and turn back on us. Forgive me, sir. If we'd gone forward, we might have caught up to them, but I ain't never been so scared in my whole life."

"You had your comrades with you and a sorcerer to back you up. If it was just one—"

Tillery interrupted him, "It wasn't, sir. It was more than that."

The governor's eyes narrowed. "How many?"

"I dunno, sir, at least seven or eight, but it could be a lot more. They're moving in a column, so their tracks are on top of each other. Could be seven, could be seventy. All I know is more than one is too many for our patrol."

"I agree," responded Governor Nerrow. Silence reigned as he considered his options. The wise course of action would be to wait until morning, but his son William came to mind suddenly. He knew what Will would think of such a cold-blooded decision.

Will had accused him of caring little for the lives of those in his care, managing the people who lived on his lands with no more concern than a man might have for his cattle. Mark Nerrow knew it wasn't true, but the thought still bothered him. He made his decisions based on reason, and he always tried to do what was best for the majority. Being a lord, it was largely coincidental that such choices almost always favored his own wellbeing as well. Mark pushed the thought away.

He had a choice to make, and he wouldn't let personal matters cloud his judgment. Closing his eyes, he let his mind go quiet for a moment, and the decision solidified within him. Opening them once more, he looked at Captain Lorun. "Step outside and send a runner for Commanders Gravholt and Hargast. We'll continue preparing the camp, but I'll send a full battalion to rescue the villagers. With the blessing of the Mother, perhaps we can save some of them."

The governor had already removed his armor, but he glanced to one side where his manservant was already hard at work. "Put the rags and oil away. I'm leading First Battalion from Second Regiment personally." He turned back to Captain Lorun and the tracker. "If I'm going to send good men on a risky fool's errand, I'll at least be there with them."

***

Will sat in what remained of Arrogan's basement, the old lab that had been built under the house that until recently had been his mother's home—until it had been erased by dragon's fire. He was alone, without light, holding a small but solid leatherbound tome. On the outside it didn't seem very special, aside from the fact that books were expensive and this one was obviously well made. The cover and spine bore no markings and there was little sign of wear.

It was not a book that had been frequently used.

In fact, if Will wasn't mistaken, it had only been opened on occasions when a new wizard took the head seat as leader of the Council of Wizards. Twice if you counted those who also decided they had contributions or additions to make to the book by the end of their careers. According to Arrogan, it had been handed down from one head of the council to the next for centuries upon centuries. According to Grim Talek, he was the first head of the council, the first author, the originator of the book.

Arrogan wouldn't have been happy to hear that, and Will wished desperately that he could talk to the old man and seek his advice, but he no longer had the ring. The ring was with Grim Talek, and perhaps, if the lich hadn't lied, with Selene. Will had been replaced.

His old life, his old responsibilities, those were gone. Selene, Tiny, Janice, and everyone else—they were no longer his problem. Deep down, Will hated his choice, but he knew it was the right one. With the Grim Talek as an enemy, he couldn't keep them safe, but with the lich as an ally, there was no better guardian. Alone, Will was free to do what needed to be done, and if he succeeded, he would win on all fronts. If he failed, well—they wouldn't even know he had died.

There was a third possibility, too. He might succeed and then die anyway. The price Grim Talek wanted for his assistance was potentially more difficult than defeating a dragon, and if Will failed to deliver, he would be forced to pay in flesh and blood. Will rubbed the space between his eyes. *Let's not think about that right now.*

As he opened the book, Will's eyes adjusted until they found a type of light that would let him easily discern the letters on the page even in the darkness. It was as easy as breathing now, one of a hundred ways his body had adjusted to magic, both wild and structured. Arrogan's only remaining student, the first true wizard of his age, began to read.

The introduction was, in itself, a spell, one that had to be cast to continue. Failing to do so meant the reader couldn't continue, and casting it was essentially an acceptance of terms, the terms of a wizard who had died thousands of years ago—Grim Talek's terms. Without hesitation, Will created the spell construct described in the text and allowed it to sink into his body and mind.

Sometime later, he closed the book, still only a third of the way through. Will blinked and stared at the blank cover. He had no memory of what he had just read, but he could still feel the spell of the book lingering in his mind, and he knew how it operated. He would remember nothing until the end, when he had made his choice, and maybe not even then. Only while he was reading would the contents be visible to his conscious mind.

Currently, the only thing remaining to him was a sense of awe, coupled with a dark foreboding. The contents of the book had been both astonishing and frightful, that much he knew. When he reached the final entry, he would be given the choice of deciding whether to remember or forget. From what Grim Talek had said, most chose to forget. The ability to sleep soundly at night was invaluable, especially when the horrors that lay beneath the foundations of reality were completely beyond the ability of the reader to do anything meaningful about them.

Those that chose to forget would only remember things if certain conditions were met, conditions that predictably necessitated the need for such terrible knowledge. But Will doubted he would be able to make such a comfortable choice. Lognion's brood represented the end of human civilization, unless he could find a way to destroy the hatchlings.

For now, he just wanted to pee. Rising to his feet, Will climbed up and went outside to relieve himself and stretch his legs.

It was dark outside, which meant more time had passed than he realized. Will wasn't sleepy yet, so he figured he would read for a while longer. The book's spell would allow him to take as many breaks as necessary, for sleep or bodily functions. He just wouldn't remember anything until he had finished and made the final choice. Going back down, he made himself comfortable, but before he picked up the book, he decided to check on Selene.

A brief moment of meditation and he was able to cast his mind free. The act of leaving his body had become almost commonplace for him now, which was why he now had to use spells to anchor himself when he slept. Selene's image appeared before him, and he saw that she was sleeping alone. The alone part was important to him. Grim Talek had pledged to maintain certain boundaries during his impersonation.

Whatever lie he used, I bet she's mad as hell at me right now, thought Will. *Unless he told her the truth, in which case she's probably even madder.* Moving closer, he wished he could kiss her cheek. *I love you.*

Selene stirred, and for a moment her eyes blinked open, and she murmured, "Will?"

He watched her intently, but a second later her eyes closed, and Selene drifted back to sleep. Had she heard him, or had it been coincidence? He wasn't sure. Laina was the only person he knew of who had developed astral sensitivity, and that had been after their souls had comingled. Will hoped it was true. If Selene developed the ability, they would be able to communicate more easily while separated. He was tempted to try again, but she needed her sleep.

Will looked in on a few others in quick succession. Janice, Tabitha, and then, before he could stop himself, his thoughts turned to Laina. The empty grey darkness that engulfed his awareness was harmless, but the pain it brought him was immense. He had known it already. He'd *witnessed* it, but the harsh emptiness drove the fact home. His sister was gone.

Hurting, he forced his attention to one last person, his father, and Mark Nerrow gradually came into focus. What Will saw came as a surprise. His father was riding a horse, despite the fact that night had already set in, and he wasn't alone. Mark Nerrow was armed and armored, looking as fit and hardy as ever. Will shook his head imperceptibly. His father looked every inch the nobleman, as though the man had been drawn from the pages of some old romance.

Around his father rode numerous soldiers. A few carried lanterns, but the overall radiance made it clear that there were sorcerers using either spells or their elementals to create light above them. *How many are with him?* Will wondered. He knew his father was supposed to be in Myrsta, so he hadn't expected the man to be out riding with a military contingent. The immediate conclusion was obvious: Grim Talek hadn't lied. There were trolls causing problems in Darrow, and Mark Nerrow had decided to take a personal hand in the matter.

Will wasn't particularly close to his father, but he felt a faint sense of pride seeing him riding with the soldiers. The nobleman took his responsibilities seriously, despite some of the cutting remarks Will had made to him in the past. Will had other things to worry about, though.

Trolls didn't see much better than humans at night, but they had keen noses, and anything that limited visibility and increased confusion would favor them greatly over the soldiers of Terabinia. *So why aren't they camped?* Something urgent must have arisen for his normally cool-headed father to take such risks.

Snapping back to his body, Will began preparing spells that he couldn't yet reflex cast: teleport, earth-wall, fire-wall, and a large offensive fire spell. His repertoire of instinctive spells was so large now that he doubted he would need any of them other than the teleport, but it was nice to have options.

Returning to his trance, he focused on Mark Nerrow once again. The next part would be tricky without Tiny or someone else disturbing his body to divide his attention, but it was something he needed to master anyway.

The Governor of Darrow was still astride his horse, but he was no longer moving forward. He appeared to be near the head of the column, staring at something dim ahead of them. "They have to hear us," he muttered to the officer beside him. "We're only sixty or seventy yards away, and that's not even considering the torches and spells."

"Could they be asleep?" asked the captain.

Mark Nerrow shrugged. "Who knows with trolls? But there's nearly six hundred men with us. It's hard to believe they haven't noticed us."

"A trap then," said the captain. *Yes!* agreed Will wholeheartedly.

"We haven't seen more than one of them at a time. Are they capable of that kind of thinking?" asked a lieutenant from the other side. As the officer stopped talking, the sound of a child sobbing carried to their ears through the still night air.

Governor Nerrow grimaced. "We have eighteen sorcerers with force-cages ready and almost six hundred soldiers to support them. As long as we know what to expect, we have the upper hand."

"Unless there's more than eighteen of them," observed the captain.

Mark had already used spells to enhance his night vision so he could confirm what one of the sorcerers had reported. "There's only six trolls visible, along with fourteen captives. If there's more, they'd have to have dug pits to hide in, or be positioned some distance away for an ambush. Even so, we can handle twelve more even if that's the case."

Subcommander Dranner, the battalion's senior officer, spoke at last. "If any of that's true it's trouble. We haven't seen that sort of thinking and planning from them. Just seeing them in a small group like this bothers me." The sky rumbled as if to punctuate the officer's remark.

Governor Nerrow grimaced at the thunder. "We're here, and now that we are it's best to act quickly before it rains." Incinerating a body to ash took considerably more power than simply burning someone to death. Six troll bodies represented a large amount of flesh and blood, and if it started raining, it would be that much harder to completely destroy their remains. The other officers met his eyes and silently conveyed their determination. Nerrow gave the order. "Let's move. Sorcerers to the fore, and let's get them contained before they can do anything."

Meanwhile, Will was still attempting to withdraw his attention just enough to access the teleport spell he had prepared. The situation had him worried, which made it more difficult. He agreed with his father's decision, but he feared the worst. *Taking captives, camping in groups—that means one of the troll leftovers had enough brain to retain language,* he observed silently. If one of them had retained some memories and language, it might have taught the others and organized them.

Will's perspective followed along, close beside his father as the battalion marched forward in double time. The trolls leapt to their feet as soon as the humans started toward them, making clear the fact that they'd been well aware of the army's presence, but they didn't charge to meet them, seemingly content to wait.

Seeing the uncharacteristic patience on the trolls' part, Nerrow slowed the marching speed and the ever-perceptive sergeants along the front line began exhorting the men to watch the ground ahead for traps or pitfalls, even before the governor added his own caution. The distance between soldiers and trolls gradually dwindled while the monsters waited, stretching long arms and grinning with filthy teeth.

Closer and closer, the soldiers advanced until they were scarcely ten yards away, and still the trolls had not moved, though they had reached down to claim large clubs that had been hidden at their feet. With so little distance between them, the trolls finally leapt fearlessly at the shield-wall, but by then it was too late. The sorcerers hidden amongst the second line raised their hands and used the force-cage spell each had been holding. In less than a second, it was over and all six trolls were safely contained. All that remained was to secure the captured villagers and burn the trolls to dust.

Well disciplined, several companies moved to surround each caged troll while others moved to free the captives and establish a perimeter. All in all, the fight was over without excitement, and some of the men began to chatter as their nervous anxiety started to fade. Other than that, the only sound was that of the trolls bellowing impotently within their magical prisons.

Mark Nerrow remained alert, and intangibly Will continued to observe as he floated along beside his father. His mood couldn't be described as alert, however; a better description would have been *frantic*. None of the men in the army understood troll, but he did. What sounded like incoherent rage to the soldiers was crude but effective speech. The captive trolls were calling out to allies in the distance, describing and gesturing toward the humans they thought were controlling the spells that held them.

None of it made it easier for Will to relax his attention and cast a teleport spell. Quite the opposite. He found himself yelling soundlessly at his father. *A perimeter won't help! They need to put up defensive walls! Now!*

"Listen to 'em yap! They're no better than animals," jeered one of the soldiers standing guard by a force-cage. Others agreed with him, but the sentiment died quickly as a massive rock sailed into their midst, crushing the first man it hit and badly wounding several others as its momentum carried it through the group of soldiers. A second of stunned surprise followed, but it ended quickly as cries of pain and confusion went up from several places at once. More rocks were landing, tearing through the men around each force-cage.

Two of those struck were sorcerers, and their spells died the moment they went down, leaving two trolls free in the midst of the clustered soldiers. Rocks continued to fly, and the freed trolls went to work with their clubs, sweeping men into broken piles while they ignored the spears of their foes.

The battalion had more than six sorcerers, of course, and replacements quickly moved up to recapture the rampaging trolls, but the rocks were still flying. Another sorcerer died while they were still attempting to restore order, and the third free troll managed to kill yet another.

Mark Nerrow could see the battalion teetering on the precipice of chaos and disaster as replacements attempted to restrain the trolls while others tried to get defensive walls in place to stop the hail of stones. Using one of his earth elementals, he managed to erect a fifty-foot earthen wall along one side, and he sent a steady stream of commands to the others.

The commands themselves weren't as important as the sound of his voice. His presence and unwavering confidence held back the panic that had threatened to undo their discipline. More walls went up, protecting the sorcerers keeping the trolls caged. Nerrow tried to get a count of his remaining sorcerers. They'd lost five so far, leaving them with thirteen, fourteen counting himself. With six maintaining the cages, they had eight holding walls around the others.

A roar cut through his train of thought as the source of the thrown stones finally reached them. Trolls were running at them from several different directions, and most of the men were outside the defensive walls. Although the soldiers formed lines, their lines meant nothing as the massive trolls smashed through, heedless of their weapons.

How many? thought Will. He couldn't tell, but it was more than ten. Three of the sorcerers dropped their defensive spells to cage the newcomers, before realizing there were too many. More men died, and panic ensued. Giant clubs rose and fell while the soldiers realized the futility of their plight.

CHAPTER 21

As the battalion teetered on the brink of a rout, Mark Nerrow understood that firm orders and calm determination wouldn't be enough to keep the men's morale from breaking. Worse, even if they didn't panic, it was quite possible they'd just be delaying their defeat. That didn't mean he had to die, however. Being an accomplished spellcaster and possessing six elementals, four greater and two lesser, Mark could easily escape and preserve himself.

He felt shame for merely having the thought, but he took that shame and used it to fuel his anger and determination. A disaster now might mean an even worse loss in the future, and if the trolls had more time to multiply, and worse, organize, it might mean an unending series of ever more desperate battles. It might eventually lead to their own extinction.

Mark's jaw tightened, and he sent mental commands to his elementals. His son might look down on sorcery, but it gave him access to far more turyn than any individual could hope to produce, plus his elementals could act semi-independently. His two fire elementals, both greater, moved out to his left and right until they were just beyond the shield-wall, which was mostly hypothetical at this point. A circle of flame flickered into existence, encircling the soldiers and a few of the trolls already among them. At the same time, his two earth elementals buried two of the trolls in their midst, and his water elemental channeled its turyn into Nerrow himself.

His air elemental waited.

Betwixt them all, Nerrow coordinated their actions and began funneling turyn to both the fire elementals and the air elemental. The circle of flame grew brighter and hotter, the flames changing from dull orange to an intense yellow-white that put off so much heat it burned anyone unlucky enough to be within ten feet of it. The trolls on the outside shied away from it while the men and trolls within did similarly.

"Men of Terabinia and Darrow, take heart! This is not our day to die! Show these dogs that we do not bleed for naught!" The words came to Mark Nerrow without effort, and later he would not remember saying them, but many heard him nonetheless. Punctuating the end of his cry, the governor sent a final pulse of turyn and a command to his elementals. The air elemental exploded outward, sending a gale-force wind over the heads of the battling men, sorcerers, and trolls. It struck the flame-wall which was simultaneously swelling with latent heat and power.

A searing wind of intense heat and flames roared outward twenty, thirty—forty feet. It caught many of the trolls that had withdrawn to safety just beyond the reach of the flame-wall. Had they been human they would have died then, for the heat burned their skins to ash while roasting eyes and the lungs of those who happened to take breath at the wrong moment. Blind and burning, those that could wailed in pain.

Had he had an infinite source of power, Mark Nerrow might have been able to end it there, but even a man with six elementals had limits. The fire elementals rapidly depleted their power, and the air elemental was done even sooner. He'd accomplished his goal, however. Most of the trolls were temporarily disabled. The sorcerers within their position re-caged the free trolls and the soldiers holding the line were able to restore order and discipline. Mark shouted a new order: "Burn the ones we have before the others recover! We can win this if we reduce their numbers quickly enough."

The few trolls that hadn't been burned seemed to realize this as well, and they pushed past their burned brethren to assault the line again, seeming desperate to disrupt the humans before things turned against them. The battalion had firmed up though, and frightening as the three trolls that threw themselves at the line were, the veterans managed to keep them at bay with a multitude of spears. At the same time, the two or three sorcerers not already engaged in managing a force-cage began employing their spells to burn the imprisoned trolls.

It seemed they might just pull through, barely.

Mark Nerrow employed his water elemental to assist the soldiers holding the shield-wall, while his mind calculated their odds. It would take the sorcerers several minutes to completely destroy the captive trolls, and it would likely exhaust their turyn temporarily, but if they could manage it then the caging sorcerers could capture the unburned trolls. If they could find the time and energy to destroy those before the ones burned by his fire-wall recovered, they would win, simple as that.

The sky rumbled again, and Mark glanced upward. A fat drop of rain landed on his cheek, and he had to force himself to suppress the howl of helpless rage that welled within his heart. *Not now!* As if in reply, lightning lit the sky briefly, and more drops fell, becoming a steady downpour. Furious, the governor glared at the black cloudy skies. "Damn the Mother! Why?" It was blasphemous language, but it was obvious that fate had abandoned him already.

Everyone understood the implications, trolls and men alike. One group took heart, and the other struggled to hide their despair, but the conclusion was foregone now. The once-valiant defenders would soon become nothing more than food, helpless prey to be devoured.

"Father." Will put a hand on the governor's shoulder to bring the man back from his dark thoughts.

Nerrow jumped, then stared at the man standing beside him. "What the devil? How?"

Will smiled. "I'll explain afterward."

"That's a big assumption," said Mark darkly, but there was fresh hope in his eyes. "Can you blast them all back, the way you did the Darrowans during the war?"

Will knew what he was referring to. He'd once turned a massive magical assault by the Darrowan spellcasters back against them, using his talent to convert their turyn into a shockwave that killed or incapacitated thousands in the blink of an eye. That wasn't an option here. "It wouldn't stop the trolls for long," he pointed out. "Besides, I'd need a source of power. There's nothing here but you and your subordinates." He didn't bother mentioning that both were already mostly tapped out.

His father looked at him from the corner of his eye. "Do you have some other miracle then?" The remark was half joke, half wish.

To be honest, Will was uncertain. He'd devoted all his efforts to getting there, without thought to what he would do once he arrived. "What do you need most?"

"Either an end to the rain, or enough power to burn those trolls to dust in spite of it," said the older man immediately.

He wasn't sure if he could do it, but the words gave him an idea. Will reached for the storm clouds above, but he found them tantalizingly out of reach. The distance from ground to sky was too great to bridge with the meager amount of power available to him. Frustrated, he looked around, gazing at the depleted elementals and fatigued sorcerers scattered among the soldiers. He could use them, but they'd be helpless for a period of time afterward.

Then his eye settled on a dying man nearby. The soldier's leg was missing, and without a quick tourniquet and serious medical attention he'd be dead within minutes—if he lived that long. Will could save the man, if he devoted himself to that task alone. Or he could have given out regeneration potions worth a thousand crowns apiece and saved most of the wounded. He had more than a hundred safely stored within the limnthal.

To use them all would be to spend a fortune in healing magic, and it would still be a fruitless gesture. That type of regenerative magic drew on the strength of the patient to restore the body. Most of the wounded would be left unconscious for hours, and those who remained wouldn't be able to move them—not while they were busy being torn apart by trolls.

He couldn't save everyone. Some would have to be sacrificed. *And the logical choice is to use those already dying.* He made his decision without hesitation, feeling the familiar sensation of something hardening in his chest. A dull pain that probably represented the slow death of his conscience. Source-links shot out from his body and connected to three wounded men. Two were obviously dying, but the third would probably have recovered.

He didn't have time to pick and choose.

His father watched him curiously. "What are you doing?"

Taking turyn from others rendered sorcerers and other spellcasters nauseous, but that wasn't the case for a properly trained wizard, and with Will's level of practice, he could draw upon almost any quantity of foreign turyn without being sickened. He ripped the energy from the wounded men so quickly that had they been awake they would have fallen unconscious immediately. Taking a few steps, Will found more injured men and repeated the process.

Those in the worst shape died quickly, while those with minor injuries were rendered insensible. What Will was doing couldn't kill a healthy person, but it was a hard thing to deal with for someone already badly wounded. Ten, fifteen, twenty, Will couldn't contain the quantity of turyn he harvested, so he let it flow into the air around him, creating a dense area of ambient energy around himself.

It didn't matter if it was within or without, it belonged to him, and when he sensed that it was enough, he looked back to the sky with eyes that were filled with actinic sparks. The turyn around him raced upward, forming a tenuous line that reached for the firmament, stretching until it contacted the swelling thunderheads above. It carried his *will* with it, acting as a medium, and when he finally made contact, the turyn locked within the storm became his as well. Power raced back and forth between the storm and the ground as Will consolidated his command.

A feeling of intense euphoria filled him, and Will knew he had done the right thing. The deaths meant nothing. His choice was all that mattered, and the decision of a god was innately right. His lips pulled back to reveal white teeth that seemed to shine with the reflected illumination of the electric arcs that crawled back and forth across his skin.

Trolls and men alike froze at the spectacle, and a strange quiet arose, as everyone seemed to wait expectantly on him. Will's eyes roamed as he took stock of the scene. Four trolls were actively fighting, but there were many more who would be able to reenter the fray within a minute or two. The few that the sorcerers had caged were in the worst shape, but the constant downpour made it nearly impossible to finish burning them.

Will turned in a slow circle, and then without warning, he unleashed hell on earth. Thick waves of lightning flowed down to the earth like a waterfall of light. It struck the trolls with frightening accuracy, and if any were missed in the first thunderous onslaught, Will paid them special attention in the second assault. The sound and flash that accompanied the lightning rendered everyone deaf and blind. Men screamed, horses bucked, and some soldiers who happened to be a little too close to the trolls died.

Realizing the damage the cacophony was doing to his allies, Will silenced the following waves of lightning, using some of the ambient energy to dampen the thunder. The result was a horrifying lightshow as trolls sizzled, flopped, and exploded under repeated and strangely muffled lightning strikes. Will let it continue for a full minute, until he was certain that the trolls were so badly wounded they wouldn't be able to rise for some time.

As devastating as the lightning was, its damage was limited, burning thin lines through the bodies of those it contacted. It was great at destroying things or starting fires, but it wasn't a good tool for completely incinerating flesh. With a thought, Will stopped the rain, calming the opposing forces that were causing the clouds to drop their moisture. The same action lessened the potential remaining for him to tap, but he'd already gotten what he needed. It was time to clean up the mess.

He had all the turyn he needed, so long as he remained connected to the storm, but his will wouldn't allow him to play storm god forever. It was hard to judge, but he still had some time. If he could reflex cast the right fire spells, he could get rid of the trolls on his own, but even then he might not have enough time to finish the job. Fortunately there was a more efficient way to do the job, one that would spare some of the strain on his will.

Mark Nerrow had put a force-dome around himself and was standing close by, his jaw ever so slightly agape as he surveyed the destruction. Will waved at him to lower his shield. His father hesitated, an odd look in his eyes, but after a few seconds dismissed his protection. Without preamble or permission, Will attached a source-link and began channeling energy into his father, carefully tuning the frequency to keep from making the older man sick.

"What are you doing?" asked Mark.

"You're better suited for roasting them," said Will, the bitter taste of ozone on his tongue as he spoke. There were still arcs of electricity crawling over his face and body.

His father nodded, directing the fresh power to his fire elementals. "This won't be enough, you realize. Everything is damp, and I'll tire long before—"

Will cut him off. "There's turyn aplenty. I'll keep feeding you power until its done."

"Very well." Mark Nerrow began using spells of his own while dividing the extra energy between his fire elementals. Even so, he knew he couldn't finish all the trolls in time. Continuing to work, he asked, "Can you do this with the other sorcerers as well?"

He could, but there were problems. "Only if you want them all vomiting. Matching turyn frequencies with more than one person at a time would be difficult."

"Will you be able to do—" the governor paused, looking for words. Finally, he waved at the sky. "—can you call the lightning down again? This is going to take too long." Black, greasy smoke was filling the air as the sorcerer and his elementals carefully reduced three separate trolls to ash. The stench was nauseating.

There were at least twelve more, and most of them were already twitching. Will could probably do it again, but something else bothered him. Summoning a book from his limnthal, he began thumbing his way to the index while simultaneously asking, "Do you think this is all of them?"

"All the ones that attacked us," said Mark. "None have escaped as far as I know."

Will found the page number he wanted and began thumbing back toward the middle of the book. "No, do you think this is all of them in Darrow?"

"I didn't think there were this many until a few minutes ago. I have no idea now," answered his father.

The spell he found was fourth order in terms of complexity and Will had never cast it before, much less practiced it. Two or three years ago he wouldn't even have dared to attempt such a spell for the first time without at least a few days of practice, but despite his youth, he was a long way from his time as a novice. His constant and unrelenting practice, both with spells he knew and learning new spells he thought he would need, had given him a degree of expertise far in excess of what most would expect. Running his eyes down the page, he spent two minutes looking over the rune structure, and then while he silently read it a second time, he crafted the construct above his left hand.

Throughout the entire process, he continued to feed turyn to his father. The first three trolls were gone, and Mark was now starting on another three, but the other nine were beginning to climb to their feet, despite the soldiers steadily hacking and stabbing at them with swords, spears, and axes. The monsters' regenerative capacity in the face of ordinary wounds was nothing short of amazing. It was enough to make even a vampire jealous.

The men moved aside as Will walked forward, fearful of the lightning that still crawled back and forth across his skin like deadly snakes. "Move back from the trolls and form a tight perimeter," he ordered. His voice was soft, but it rang clear in the ears of every warrior. They obeyed, and as they withdrew, he stepped out, approaching the nearest troll.

The creature was probably nine feet tall, or would have been if it had been standing. It was also clever, for it had been hiding its recovery. Once Will was within six feet of it, the giant sprang forward, uncoiling its long limbs and sweeping deadly claws at his hips, just below the waist. The attack was perfect, too fast for him to leap back, too high to jump over—there was no avoiding it.

Will stopped the attack at the last second, interposing a point-defense shield. The troll's arm rebounded, but Will had already dismissed the force spell and switched to the force-push he had learned from Ethelgren, flattening the massive monster against the ground. A few of the other trolls were moving as well, jumping up to converge on him.

Calling down lightning would take seconds he didn't have, so instead Will lifted his hands and discharged most of the power he currently held within himself. Blue lines spiderwebbed out from him in every direction, catching his attackers and sending them twitching to the ground. For a moment, the sparks that had been crawling over him vanished, but seconds later they started reappearing as more turyn flowed into him from the sky above.

At the same time, his call to the heavens had been heard, and lightning flashed down, doing a far more thorough job on the trolls and buying him more time. Only the one he held pinned to the ground remained untouched. Will looked down at it and asked in trollish, "Who leads?"

The creature's eyes widened, surprised to hear its own tongue coming from the mouth of a human. "What?"

"Who is chief?"

The troll responded in heavily accented Darrowan, "Stupid."

Will's expression didn't change, but he applied Grim Talek's bonebreaker spell to the troll and watched its body twist and crack for several seconds while it tried to scream with torn lungs. Eventually he relented, and the troll's body began healing immediately. Using one arm, he waved his hand at the other incapacitated trolls. "Which one?"

"Not here!" barked the monster in trollish. "Stupid is chief." The only notable exception was that the word 'stupid' was again repeated in thick Darrowan. Will finally understood. Opening one hand, he cast and released the spell he had prepared just minutes ago. Nothing visible happened, but to those with turyn-sensitive eyes, a complex spell structure crossed the space between them and disappeared into the trapped troll's skin.

Glancing back, Will could see that his father was now working on his third set of trolls. That would make nine eradicated. He wanted to get rid of more, but there was a growing tension in his head, neck, and shoulders. It was a sensation akin to that of an incipient headache, but Will knew the true meaning. There was no lack of turyn to be had, but his will was beginning to feel the strain. Directing so much energy, controlling the storm, sustaining his father's efforts, it was beginning to wear him down.

For the moment he was in control, but he'd learned his lesson the hard way once before. If his will broke, he'd be powerless for weeks, months, or possibly forever. He released the spell pinning the troll to the ground, then warned, "Take the others and give Stupid a message. Grak Murra will speak to him."

Grak Murra was William's troll name, 'Troll Mother.' The troll gave no sign whether he recognized it, but he edged away carefully, to avoid provoking a defensive attack from the wizard. "Stupid is not stupid," said the monster without a trace of irony. The first Stupid was spoken in Darrowan while the rest of the sentence was in trollish. "He will not come."

"I will find him, when I am ready. Go." Swiveling his head slowly, Will warned the other trolls, "Go now, or I will burn you all." Turning back to the soldiers, he switched to the language of his birth. "Hold fast. Don't engage. They will retreat." He kept walking until he reached Mark Nerrow. His father was just finishing the cremation of his current set of trolls when Will severed the source-link.

Mark looked at him. "I can finish these, but I will need more if we are going to fight."

Will was still holding onto the storm, but he was beginning to have trouble maintaining his focus. As soon as he saw the remaining trolls were backing away, he released the connection. "The fighting is over for today."

His father seemed unconvinced. "I couldn't understand that growling jibber-jabber. You may have cowed them for now, but I don't believe for a minute that those things are done with us."

Annoyed, Will let his irritation show in his voice. "Then set guards, rest your sorcerers, this is your command." Stepping closer, Will put a hand on his father's shoulder. He tried not to notice how the man flinched at the touch. Ignoring that, he put some of his weight on the older man to stop himself from swaying. His next words were a whisper. "I need a place to sit with some dignity. I think that would be best for morale." His eyes moved to scan the soldiers around them.

Frowning, the governor eased closer, supporting his son in a manner that spoke more of friendliness than desperation. With practiced ease, he began giving orders. "We'll camp here. We need to treat the wounded and see to the captives we recovered before we move. Set up the command tent. We can return to the main force at dawn."

CHAPTER 22

By the time the tent was up, Will was already feeling steadier. It wasn't his body that was tired after all, nor did he lack energy; it was a fatigue that rose from the core of his being, from his soul itself. The feeling was hard to describe. The most obvious sign was an increasing difficulty shaping turyn, but at the extreme, when his will was in danger of breaking, it would become a debilitating sensation of not being able to do anything. The mind and body might be willing, but the heart would fail to deliver.

Because of that, the only times he had managed to break his will involved moments of extreme emotion or stress, generally after he'd already pushed himself. Today he hadn't gone nearly that far, but given the desperation of the situation, it could have happened. Trying to finish all the trolls off might have been enough to do it. *Maybe I'm getting wiser,* he thought with a silent chuckle.

The memory of his euphoric madness came to mind then, disabusing him of that notion. It made him uncomfortable to think about, but he couldn't avoid the reality. Years of violence, stress, and anxiety had left their mark on him, causing him to train with a single-minded focus that went beyond discipline and firmly into obsessive neuroticism. With each passing year, he felt more powerless, less safe, and less able to protect himself or those important to him. As a result, when forced to actually use his power, it seemed to result in a perverse flip in his personality. Fear turned to rage, anxiety to euphoria, and worst of all, his conscience was replaced by a swelling egotism.

"That's not who I am," he whispered to himself, but he had trouble believing it. Even now, as he regained his sensibility, he didn't feel truly guilty. He'd killed some of the soldiers to save the others, and it bothered him a little, but not as much as it should have. *It was necessary.* That's what he really believed.

Mark Nerrow entered the tent, carrying a metal flask. Producing a small wooden cup, he poured a small drink and handed it to Will. "Sorry

I don't have anything better, but we didn't bring much with us. This was supposed to be a quick rescue, not an overnight camp."

Will nodded and drank the contents in a single gulp, grimacing at the burn which followed. He'd been staring at the ground between his feet, but he looked up and met his father's eyes when he returned the cup, unsure how to respond. "Did any of the villagers you were rescuing survive?"

"A few, but more importantly, you don't look like a man who just saved an army," said Mark, his tone light.

Will looked away. "You're a terrible liar."

Mark frowned. "I wasn't lying, I was trying to lift your spirit."

"You're no good at it. I saw the way you looked at me out there. I don't blame you either, but don't pretend—"

His father interrupted, "You scared me witless, there's no denying that. But that was then, this is now. You caught me by surprise. I've never seen—that. I don't even have words for whatever you did, but it worked and most of us survived. That's enough to make me grateful— son. I thought it might be a year before I got to see you again."

Will blinked, trying to process what he'd heard. Mark Nerrow only acknowledged their relationship when they were alone, but Will couldn't remember being called 'son' before, not during a conversation. "She knows," he replied darkly.

"Knows what? You lost me." said the governor.

"Agnes," said Will. "She knows I'm your bastard."

His father remained quiet, his face stoic. "It was only a matter of time. I'd planned to tell her once the king recalls me from this post."

"It's worse than that. Laina's dead. Tabitha nearly died. Agnes blames me, and in some part, I agree with her. I have a lot to tell."

Silence fell over the room, and his father remained completely still, a blank expression on his features. Eventually, he moved again, first saying, "Let me find a seat. I don't think I heard you right." Taking two steps, the normally graceful lord bumped into a camp table and nearly fell before steadying himself and settling on a stool.

"Laina's dead," repeated Will. "Lognion ordered her to kill me, and she fought the enchantment until it destroyed her soul. I watched it happen."

"W—why would the k-king order that?" asked Mark, stammering slightly, his voice faintly tremulous.

"I was planning to kill him. Not then, but another day. He was going to kill me anyway. He moved first and laid a trap for me at Tabitha's engagement—"

The older man broke in, "Tabitha's what?"

"The king was going to marry her," said Will.

"I wasn't consulted," said Mark, as though that made the very idea impossible.

"Agnes agreed to it, but it was just a trap to lure me in—and it worked."

The governor put his face in his hands. "Laina's dead, and you're what, a fugitive? What of my family? Has the wedding already happened?" Despair rang thick in his voice.

Will answered immediately, "No. I killed him, or rather I tried to— he wasn't human. Selene will be queen now."

The beginnings of a grief he had not yet begun to deal with brought the older man's frustration to the fore. "Wait, what? Selene is queen but Lognion isn't dead? You're not making any sense!"

Taking a deep breath, Will started over, beginning with the news of Tabitha's engagement and running through the events that followed with mechanical efficiency. Over the past few years, his relationship with his father had gradually changed. While he couldn't really call it paternal, he had developed trust in his father, along with respect for the nobleman's integrity. When he reached the explanation for how Tabitha had nearly been slain while shielding him with her body, his voice cracked.

He hadn't really had a chance to grieve. He'd come close when Tabitha had tried to convince him that Laina was still alive, but events had kept prodding him forward, preventing him from dealing with his emotions. Glancing up, he saw his father waiting patiently, though surely the man must have been dying to know the rest of it. Will blinked to clear his eyes, and after a second, his throat loosened up so that he could continue.

It was less than a minute later, as he tried to describe Laina's inner battle and inevitable death, that he was seized by a wracking sob that strangled his words and destroyed his composure. He fought to control himself for some time, but when he felt Mark's arms around him, it undid all his efforts.

Eventually he recovered, though he still felt embarrassed. Mark Nerrow was the last person he would feel comfortable exposing his emotions to. The man still didn't feel like a father to him, not that he had any idea what such a thing would feel like. Will dared a look into the older man's eyes then looked away. His father's eyes were still dry.

Mark seemed to read his mind. "It doesn't feel real yet. Later, tomorrow, next week, whenever it truly sinks in—I don't know what it will do to me. I've never lost a child before."

Will nodded. "Sorry for that. I know you need to hear the rest." He opened his mouth to continue, but Mark stopped him for a moment, putting a hand on his head as if he was still a child.

"Don't be sorry. I'm honored you care enough about my daughters to weep for them, to feel so deeply about a family that's brought you nothing but misery. Don't apologize for that." The older man pulled Will's head down and against his chest, ignoring the fact that Will was taller. "For accepting them, for doing what you have—thank you. I don't have the right, but I'm proud of you." Mark Nerrow's eyes were no longer dry when he finally released Will. Wiping his cheeks with a sleeve, he motioned for Will to continue. "Maybe you should finish quickly, though. I think it's starting to sink in."

He did his best. The rest was easier to communicate, although some of it was shameful to admit. Will left nothing out, dispassionately including his lethal responses to cries for mercy. He finished with a simple description. "It was like today, except I was angry."

His father lifted his brows, then lowered them and let out a long sigh. "I'm glad I wasn't there. Today was terrifying enough." When Will didn't respond to that, he added, "So, you're human."

Will gave him a questioning glance.

Mark explained, "During the war you seemed almost inhuman. You did lose your composure a few times, and you took risks that seemed suicidal, but overall I was a little worried about your excessive self-control, especially when it came to mercy toward our enemies."

"I murdered people who had already surrendered."

"You were *alone*," countered the governor. "Mercy is a luxury, one you couldn't afford without an army behind you. Many of those you fought were bound to Lognion in ways that made it impossible for them to truly surrender. They might say one thing, but the enchantment would make that irrelevant. You had no way of knowing who you could safely ignore, and being alone, it would only take one mistake to make you a dead man."

"That's just a rationalization for—"

"The hell it is!" interrupted Mark. "It's the truth. You're just feeling guilty because you enjoyed it. Am I wrong?" Will stared back at his father for a moment, then closed his mouth, unable to argue. Mark continued, "So, I'll repeat what I said earlier—you're human. You were mad as hell. You thought Laina and Tabitha were dead, and you were out for blood. People died who didn't deserve to, and you feel bad about it, that's fine, but the blame lies with Lognion."

After a moment, Mark added, "From what you just described, Lognion was dead, but you said he wasn't human earlier. Maybe you should explain that."

Will nodded. "He sent me a letter the next day, then a dragon appeared and burned my mother's home to the ground. That's how—"

Mark interrupted, "Is Erisa—?"

"She's fine," answered Will, "and Lognion is the dragon."

"Lognion is the dragon," repeated Mark Nerrow in a voice that was devoid of understanding. "You mean that in a figurative sense, don't you?"

Will shook his head. "I didn't see him, but his flame was hot enough to turn soil to glass. There was nothing left of the house."

Mark gaped at him for a moment, then asked, "Erisa wasn't there?"

"The lich saved her."

"Pardon?"

That led to another extensive conversation. Will explained what had happened, as well as the bargain he had made. Ordinarily, he wouldn't have shared so much, but for some reason he felt the need to confess, to tell someone everything. It was likely the fact that he wasn't overly close with his father that made it easier to share. Selene, Sammy, Erisa, none of them would have understood. They cared too much to accept the price he would pay. "So, Grim Talek is impersonating me in Cerria, lending his political skills to Selene's cause, while I'm here to clean up the trolls."

Mark seemed calm, but his voice was tight with anger. "Trolls be damned—he expects you to kill a dragon? That's ridiculous! Selene is savvy enough to handle the succession, especially with you beside her. Which one of you is immortal? It isn't you! The damned lich should deal with his own problems. Let one monster fight the other. What do you get out of this? Nothing! But you agreed to such a ridiculous price? I never took my son for a fool!"

"The price wasn't negotiable," said Will quietly.

"You had him helpless!"

"I beat him, but I couldn't kill him," corrected Will. "It was agree or let him kill Mother."

"A devil's bargain! Don't you have any care for yourself? What of those who depend on you? Erisa certainly wouldn't agree with this."

"That's not the point, Father," responded Will, almost stumbling over the last word. "Grim Talek's been around for at least a thousand years, possibly two or three thousand, and he couldn't do it. He's been trying for ages. If he could manage it, none of this would be necessary."

Mark narrowed his eyes suspiciously. "Isn't the lich more powerful than you?"

Will shook his head. "It isn't that simple. His condition creates both advantages and disadvantages. He can't be killed, not without destroying the phylactery that houses his soul, but he also can't do some of the things he could do when he was alive."

"What do you mean?"

"Like what I did outside just a while ago," explained Will. "Or the things I did during the war, destroying gates and turning magic into pure sound. Those are considered 'talents.' Special abilities that high-order wizards develop."

"Grim Talek could control storms?" asked Mark.

"I don't know what his talents were," said Will. "Apparently they vary. But when he gave up his mortality, it took a toll on his abilities. His will is as strong as ever, but somehow the strain of maintaining his existence robbed him of his natural talents. I think the same is true of his vampire wizards too."

"I thought you killed the vampire wizard—what was his name?"

"Androv," Will supplied. "But there are a few others. I'll know more when I meet them."

"What?"

Will sighed. "That's what I meant earlier. Grim Talek's taken my place, but I've also taken *his*. He's given me control of all his resources to accomplish the goal, including his servants and underlings."

The governor sat back down and rubbed his face with both hands. "This is too much. Do you think they'll really obey you?"

He nodded. "I can handle them. More importantly, I'll be taking notes. I'll make sure you have a copy for after this is all over." His father stared at him blankly, so Will continued, "No one knows how many there are, or where they are. This is an opportunity to find out. I'll learn as much as I can, and after I slay the dragon, you'll be able to organize a long overdue cleansing."

"You can do it yourself," snapped Mark. "If you can kill a dragon, that should be simple."

Will shook his head. "The price comes due once I slay Lognion. I won't be able to. You and Selene can organize the operation while Grim Talek is preoccupied with me. Even if you don't get them all, it will still be a significant victory."

Mark's words grated out slowly as he replied, "You can't pay that price. It's impossible. You already know that."

"Probably," admitted Will.

"Then let me take your place," said his father earnestly.

Will sighed. "You can't. You don't have the power needed."

"No one does! It might as well be me trying and failing. I can pay the penalty in blood just as easily as you."

"He won't accept you. The only reason he's forcing this on me is that he thinks I might actually be able to give him what he most desires."

"Temarah's tits!" swore his father. "How many impossible things should any one person be expected to do? I'm not helping you in this. It's ridiculous and I won't be party to it."

"I only have to do one impossible thing," stated Will. "Kill the dragon. That alone will ensure everyone's safety. Grim Talek's promise will protect everyone else, even if I fail to satisfy his expectations."

"Even if we massacre his underlings?"

Will grinned. "As long as I make an effort in good faith, he'll keep his word. He won't touch you or any of the others I've named— ever. No matter what you do. I was very explicit in the wording of our arrangement."

"You think he'll honor it? He's not one of the fae."

He laughed. "Grim Talek complained that I've spent too much time dealing with them, but he'll keep his word. It's all he has left. He gave up everything else, good, evil, lust, love, pleasure, pain—honor is all that remains."

Mark scowled. "He's a monster. Don't try to pretend he's a hero of some sort."

Will shrugged. "Maybe he is. Considering his sacrifices, he's probably more deserving than me. I can't begrudge him his reward."

"Are you that tired of living?" asked his father sadly.

Maybe, thought Will morbidly, but his words were lighthearted. "I'm not giving up. If an ancient lich thinks I might have the power to do these things, then at the very least I should have as much faith in myself."

The conversation died at that point and an extended silence took its place. Eventually, Mark rose to his feet. "You should get some sleep."

"I'm leaving in the morning," Will announced.

His father nodded. "I'll handle the troll problem."

He shook his head. "Take your men back to Myrsta. I've marked the trolls. I'll find them and clean up the rest of my mess."

Mark frowned. "That was a tracking spell you looked up earlier? How long will it last?"

The timing was precisely the reason Will had needed a better spell than the simple one he had learned previously. "A week," he answered.

"You'll still need help."

Will nodded. "I've got new allies. Better to let them share the load rather than risk more lives."

Once he was alone, Will took out a flat square of silver metal engraved with runes. It was a gift of sorts, from Grim Talek. Focusing on one particular collection of runes at the top, he channeled a trickle of turyn into the device. The surfaced shimmered and went from reflective metal to a dull, bottomless black. "Mahak," he murmured.

A full minute passed before a male face appeared in the blackness. There was a strange angularity to the features, which combined with a heavy black beard to make Will wonder where Mahak was originally from. "What?" asked the man with obvious irritation.

"I expect a prompt answer from now on."

Mahak glared back with obvious contempt. "You haven't even identified yourself."

Will's response was calm and measured. "You know who I am. Grim Talek has placed you at my disposal. I suggest you make a good impression on me."

"He told me to help you. That doesn't mean you deserve courtesy or respect."

Will stared back silently for several seconds. Allowing himself to be drawn into a verbal argument would only undermine his position. Threats only worked when the receiver believed them to be credible, and in this case, they would only make Mahak more adversarial. "You're somewhere in Darrow, correct?"

Mahak nodded silently.

He continued, "I have a troll problem in the hills north of Myrsta. I need you to meet me with a contingent of warriors and however many spellcasters you can muster on short notice."

The vampire frowned. "Muster? You are mistaken if you think of us as an army."

"Deflection isn't helping me," returned Will. "I don't care what you think of yourselves as. I know quite well the sort of things you're capable of, as well as the assignments your master used you for. How many wizards do you have?"

"A few."

"What does that mean? I need numbers."

"Myself and Theraven are the only ones in Darrow. Currently, we are near Maldon."

Will made a mental note of the information, feeling both hopeful and disappointed simultaneously. Two wizards weren't enough, but at the same time he was glad to know how limited the undead were when it came to magical resources. "I need the two of you, along with as many reliable fighters as you can assemble, to meet me in Cotswold in two days."

"Two days? That's not enough time."

With a sigh, Will replied, "You don't need rest."

"We don't travel during the day."

"Are you saying you're too weak to protect yourself and your underlings from the sun?"

Mahak hissed in anger, giving away his inhuman nature. "Fine, if that is what you wish, *human*, we will make haste. However, your present may suffer from such rough travel."

"Present?"

The vampire moved aside and adjusted the view to show something large bound up in canvas in the shadows behind him. It appeared to be vaguely man-shaped, though it was too large to be a person. A head was exposed on the far end, but Will couldn't see the face. If it was a man, he was extraordinarily large. "Who is that?" asked Will.

"A present from our master," said Mahak with a sneer. "I will do my best to make sure it's still alive when we reach Cotswold." The vampire severed the link without another word.

Angry, Will tried to reach him again, but Mahak refused to respond. It took several minutes afterward for Will to get over his irritation. It was obvious that their first meeting would be a bad one. Mahak would do everything in his power to undermine him, without being guilty of disobedience to his true master, Grim Talek.

No, Will corrected himself silently, *that's not necessarily true. He might go further than that.* Grim Talek had described Androv, the vampire wizard that Will had slain, as a problem too difficult to deal with directly. Will had inadvertently solved the problem for him. A wizard as old as Mahak might very well be just as powerful as the lich. The lich's advantages were primarily age, experience, and the fact that he had created the vampires originally. Physically, Grim Talek's only advantage was being impossible to kill, while the vampires had two weaknesses, their need to feed and their fatal allergy to sunlight.

Mahak's loyalty to the lich might not be much more than lip service to avoid a direct conflict.

"That's fine," muttered Will. "I know a thing or two about *direct* conflict."

CHAPTER 23

The next morning, Will slept until one of the officers was brave enough to wake him so they could take down the tent. Dressing quickly, Will grabbed one of the folding camp chairs and carried it outside to sit in while the battalion readied itself to begin marching again.

"Want something to eat?" asked his father when he returned from the morning inspection.

"No thanks," said Will politely. He was all too familiar with camp food, and he had far better stored in the limnthal. He wasn't hungry yet, but it would be there when he wanted it later. "I'll be leaving soon, but I need this chair for a little while. Mind if I keep it?" The ground was muddy, and he was glad for something that would allow him to meditate without sitting in the muck.

The governor lifted one brow, then nodded. "Go ahead. How long will you be sitting? We need to move soon."

"No need to wait. I won't be traveling with you. I'll find my own way," said Will, earning an odd glance from his father once more.

"Suit yourself."

Will did. Taking a deep breath, he enjoyed the feeling of sunshine on his face for a minute before closing his eyes and adjusting his relationship with the physical world. In the past, it had been a matter of sensory deprivation, but with time he had developed a finer touch with regard to his soul and body. Slipping his earthly bonds, Will floated free and looked back at his body sitting quietly in the camp chair.

He hadn't slept well, even though he'd been thoroughly tired. He kept remembering the form on the ground behind Mahak. Will only knew one person that large, but it simply couldn't be Tiny. He'd sent his friend back to Cerria with his doppelganger. Tiny would be safe in Cerria.

It didn't matter how big his friend was, how strong, how tough—Tiny was human. Human meant vulnerable, mortal, frail—dead. Sammy had once accused Will of trying to keep her home because she was a girl, but it wasn't just her. *I don't want any of them with me,* thought Will. His friends and family were a weakness. Grim Talek's recent example, taking Erisa hostage to protect her, was a perfect lesson.

Not only did they make Will more vulnerable, none of them had the power to reasonably fight the things he had to face. Tiny was only a match for vampires when he took a dragon-heart potion and that wasn't a viable solution to be used on a regular basis. Trolls were even worse, and the egg guardians were impossibly hard to fight.

No, from Will's perspective it didn't matter whether it was Tiny, Janice, Tabitha, Sammy—none of them had the power to help, only the ability to create vulnerabilities that he couldn't afford. The lich's deal was perfect. His friends and family would be guarded by his most dangerous foe, the most powerful spellcaster in existence. That left Will free to find a solution to the trolls and Lognion. If he died, he would do it alone.

Disciplining his mind, Will sent his thoughts toward Selene, and seconds later she materialized in front of him. She was sitting at a table he recognized, a favorite spot for quiet breakfasts at the Nerrow house. It was located in the sunroom, and Tabitha sat across from his wife. Both women had stern expressions, but Will didn't hold it against them. Mornings were tough for everyone.

Selene looked up from a sip of hot tea, and her eyes flickered toward Will's viewpoint. She stared at him for a moment, squinting to try and improve her vision. In a panic, Will withdrew, returning to his body. Opening his eyes, he blinked at the bright sun. "She's definitely sensitive," he told himself. Overall, it was good news. With a small bit of practice, they'd be able to communicate over any distance without needing the assistance of magical devices.

In the past, they'd been able to do so using the heart-stone enchantment, but Will had released Selene from that a while back, despite her resistance. "I should have talked to her," he muttered, while silently cursing himself as a coward. He didn't want to have that conversation.

She'd be furious with him for the choices he'd made. If he somehow survived, he would eventually have hell to pay, and he wasn't sure what scared him the most, paying Grim Talek's price, or facing his wife. A clean death at the hands of a troll or via dragon-fire might be preferable to either of those options.

Refocusing, Will stopped delaying and turned his attention to Tiny. Grim Talek had promised. The big man would be in Cerria. He would be safe. Seconds later, sunshine surrounded him, falling warmly on and through his astral form. Looking around, Will saw he was on a cart that was primarily loaded with large clay jars. In the center was a massive bundle that looked exactly like the one he'd seen behind Mahak the night before.

Shifting his perspective slightly, Will found himself staring directly at Tiny's unconscious face. Given the sunlight, the big man had to be unconscious, for if he had been dead, Will wouldn't have found him at all.

Will's heart sped up, and his former uncertainty transformed into anger.

He already had a teleport spell prepared, and for the first time, he found the perfect balance as soon as he attempted it. His perception slid halfway to his physical body and stayed halfway with Tiny. Activating the spell he appeared in the back of the cart, sitting now on a wine jar rather than the camp chair. For a split second, Will was annoyed that he'd forgotten to bring the chair.

The cart had only two wheels, but it still had a wide wooden board at the front for the driver. Two broad-shouldered individuals sat there, cloaked and hooded, while the rough country road jostled them up and down. Will stared at the back of their hoods for several seconds, fighting the urge to kill them before saying a single word.

The road noise gave Will a chance to collect himself and decide what to do. The two driving the cart were probably vampires, but even their superior hearing didn't help when it came to such a noisy environment. *They may react violently if I startle them,* thought Will. If it hadn't been for the wind against their faces, their noses would have already alerted them to his presence, even though their ears had not.

Tiny seemed whole, but Will could feel the heavy aura of sleep magic keeping the big man unconscious. He could remove the spell, but that might result in even more chaos if Tiny started thrashing about. Will felt reasonably sure that Mahak had thought to use his friend as some sort of leverage, and even if not, he had no intention of leaving Tiny alone with such predators for even a minute longer.

The solution was simple, and it arrived on Will's face with a grin. Taking care not to alert the drivers, he lifted one hand and prepared a fresh teleport spell. That task took him a minute, and then he immediately slipped free of his body again, seeking a safe place to take himself and his friend. Finding the balance between here and there, Will put his hand on Tiny's chest, and they were gone.

***

Janice was reading a book in the parlor when Will and Tiny arrived at Rimberlin House. Their appearance displaced a considerable amount of air, creating an odd whooshing sound, which combined with the sound of Tiny's body settling onto the parquetry of the floor. Surprised, Janice let out a sudden squeak. Her arms flew out, sending the book perilously close to the hearth while her involuntary attempt to stand and simultaneously back away caused her comfy chair to tip backwards.

Will got his bearings in time to see the chair tilt and teeter, Janice's legs flailing as she tried ineffectively to right herself. Reflex casting, he created a tiny force-dome beneath the back of the chair and the floor, stabilizing it, which left Janice awkwardly lying back with her feet in the air. The hem of her dress followed the dictates of gravity, creating an awkward confusion of fabric around her hips that didn't quite expose her, but was enough to make Will turn his head in sympathetic embarrassment.

"Will!"

"Yes?" he answered.

"In the name of the Mother, why? No, save that, how? How are you here? No, save that too. Why am I stuck like this?" Janice demanded. Her initial shock had passed, and now she sounded merely annoyed.

"There's a force-dome bracing the back of your chair," Will replied. "Just lean forward."

"I can't. I'm too far back, stuck like a pig in a wallow. Can you pull the chair back down?"

"You aren't wearing any undergarments—are you?"

"If you've seen enough to ask that, it's an academic question, isn't it?" snapped Janice. "Just fix this. No, wait." Will could hear her shifting in the chair, then she continued, "All right, now help me."

Risking a look, Will saw that she had tucked her skirts in around herself enough to cover up all the interesting bits. He rose to his feet and quickly grabbed the front of the heavily cushioned armchair and pulled it back down, taking care not to jostle Janice any more than was necessary. "Sorry about that," he told her.

The long stare she fixed him with communicated a wealth of information, mostly regarding his failings as a person, but she said nothing. When she did speak, it was to inform him, "My bladder seems to be about the size of a walnut these days."

"Pardon?"

She sighed. "I have to run to the privy every fifteen minutes. It's a lot simpler if I don't have to bother with necessaries."

"Necessaries? Oh!" She had meant her underclothes.

Janice was up and kneeling beside Tiny a moment later. "Holy Mother! What happened? John?" Her face turned back to Will. "Is he hurt? Why is he enspelled?"

Will shrugged. "I'm not sure. I found him in the back of a cart with some vampires. This was the most obvious place to come."

"Vampires?" Janice blanched at the term. When Will had first met her, she'd been brunette and had had two brown eyes. During an ill-advised rescue, which had saved Will's life, she'd had half her face torn off, including one eye and part of her scalp. He had gotten a regeneration potion to her the next day, but because of the delay, she hadn't healed exactly as she had been. The missing eye grew back blue, and a portion of her hair was white.

The mismatched coloration gave her an exotic look, and she was rather self-conscious about it. More importantly, she still suffered night terrors from the experience. Will felt bad for even bringing up the topic. "I sent him to Cerria, but somehow he wound up in Darrow."

"Darrow? What?" Baffled, she asked, "What were *you* doing in Darrow? I thought you were in Cerria?"

"Let's wake him up before I explain. He's probably even more confused," suggested Will. Kneeling down beside Janice, he worked with her to untie Tiny's bonds. If either of them had been born to money, they probably would have simply cut the rope, but the thought was foreign to them, like smashing a door rather than opening it. Rope was expensive.

Frustrated, Janice worried at the knots near Tiny's wrists, slowly loosening them. "I should have learned that spell for knots."

Will raised one brow. "There's a spell for undoing knots?"

She nodded. "It was in one of the primers I read during General Studies. Never thought I'd need it, but then again, I had other problems in those days."

Eventually Tiny was free of the ropes and canvas. Janice grunted as she stood up again, and Will noticed that her abdomen had developed a faint swell since he had seen her last. "Maybe you should sit back down. I wasn't thinking straight when you were crawling around untying him."

Janice gave him a sour look. "I'm pregnant, not ill."

Will shrugged. "Don't expect me to stop being more careful of your health, whether it's silly or not."

She rolled her eyes, then made a request. "Before you wake John, use a cleaning spell on him." After a pause, she added, "It's more so for him than me."

It was a good idea. Tiny fairly reeked of sweat and urine. The big man likely hadn't been conscious for at least a day or two, and his bladder had failed him at some point. Janice was right too. Tiny would be mortified if he thought Janice had seen (or smelled) him in such a state of disrepair. With a thought, Will cast Selene's Solution and remedied the situation. The spell not only cleaned Tiny and his clothes, it even smoothed out most of the wrinkles in his tunic. Satisfied by the results, Will took hold of the magic keeping Tiny unconscious and gently unraveled it.

The warrior's lids fluttered and opened, his eyes focusing slowly on Will. Through dry lips, he croaked, "Go fuck yourself."

"He definitely recognizes you," remarked Janice dryly.

Hearing her voice, Tiny craned his neck back to look at her. "Jan? Huh? How did I get here?" Pushing himself up on his elbows, he edged back toward her and away from Will. "Are you all right?" His eyes were full of accusations, and they never left Will as he moved, but the question was obviously for her.

Leaning forward in her chair, Janice put her arms around Tiny's shoulders and hugged him. "I'm fine. What happened to you?"

Reaching up, Tiny touched her cheek with one hand, keeping his gaze on Will. "Ask him."

"I found you tied up and being transported like a load of turnips," replied Will. "I'm not sure how that happened. You were supposed to be in Cerria."

Tiny's eyes quickly scanned the room. "Is this Rimberlin?"

"Yes," answered Janice. "I'm glad to see you, but you seem upset."

"Damn right I am," swore Tiny, bitterness plain in his voice. He fixed on Janice then. "We need to talk."

Her hand went to her belly unconsciously. "I know, but maybe we should discuss how you came to be a prisoner of vampires first."

Tiny glared at Will for a second. "I don't have anything to say to him. We should talk in private. This is about our future."

Janice frowned. "What's wrong, John?"

Will put a hand on his friend's shoulder, offering a sympathetic expression. "I need to know what—" he paused as Tiny flinched, pulling away from the contact.

"I want to be released from my oath of service," spat Tiny, then he turned back to Janice. "That's why we need to talk. This concerns you too."

"What?" Will was flabbergasted. "Why would you—"

Tiny moved to stand in front of Janice. "Don't bother with more threats. Jan can make up her own mind, once I explain what's been going on."

"John, what's happened?" demanded Janice urgently.

Will had a sinking feeling in his stomach. "What did he do?"

"Who?" asked Janice, looking back at him, even more confused.

The conversation quickly began to spiral out of control, and Will could only see one way to make Tiny and Janice stand still long enough for him to explain, so he blurted out the only thing that would get them to listen. "I sent Tiny back to the capital with a doppelganger."

Red-faced, Tiny stared at him angrily. "A what?"

"A copy of himself," explained Janice. "What kind of doppelganger?"

"Grim Talek, the lich, disguised as me." They both stared at him for thirty seconds, until finally Will added, "I didn't tell Tiny. He thought it was me."

Tiny's expression grew even darker, if such was possible. Janice watched the big warrior's face and then looked back at Will. Her question was a single word: "Why?"

Feeling defeated, Will shrugged, then pointed at Tiny. "He's a terrible actor. If I'd told him the truth, everyone would have figured it out."

Tiny's voice was heavy as he responded, "Do you know what that *thing* tried to make me do?"

Janice's hand went up, silencing Tiny temporarily, then she turned at the waist. Her other hand came up, and although Will saw it coming, he did nothing to avoid the stinging slap that followed. She glared at him for a moment, then said, "That's for John." Will started to say something but she cut him off. "Apologize."

Will halted, then did so. "I'm sorry, Tiny. I know it wasn't fair of me to send you blindly into that situation."

Janice spoke again. "That was for lying to him. You can apologize again after John explains what happened to him. He'll probably forgive you. Depending on how bad it is, I might not."

"He swore he wouldn't hurt any of you. That you'd be protected. That was the bargain," said Will.

Tiny's eyes narrowed. "I suppose ordering me to murder helpless men doesn't count then, or insinuating that Janice might suffer if I didn't follow orders."

Ouch! Will had no idea what to say.

"Did Selene know?" asked Janice.

"No," answered Will quietly. Tiny continued, giving a brief explanation of what had happened. When he finished, they both stared at Will silently, and he knew he had little hope of redeeming himself. "I'm sorry," said Will simply, then he turned away.

"That's it? No explanation?" demanded Tiny.

"Why bother?"

Tiny growled while Janice demanded, "Because we deserve answers."

"I never expected I'd even have an opportunity to explain," said Will. "I just wanted to keep both of you safe."

"Even if we wind up hating you?" asked Janice.

He nodded. "Better that than being friends with a lich."

Janice's sharp intake of air signaled a loud response, but this time it was Tiny who stopped her. "Wait," he said softly, before addressing Will, "You're planning a suicide. Aren't you?"

Will turned back. "No!"

"Yes, you are, you selfish bastard," accused Tiny. "Now it makes sense."

"That's not it," Will protested weakly.

"Yeah, yeah it is," pronounced Tiny. "I don't know what this bargain of yours entails, but I know you. What the hell did you agree to?"

"I agreed to the only thing that offered a chance of making the world safe for you and your child. The details don't matter."

"I'd still like to know," said Tiny.

"You can't help," Will replied tonelessly.

"Tell us anyway," said Janice. "At least then we'll know whether to pour a drink on your grave or piss on it." The venom in her voice was strong enough that Tiny looked at her in surprise.

Tired, Will stared at them for a moment, then nodded. He walked over to an empty chair and sat down. "Fine." Then he proceeded to explain his bargain and the reasons for it.

CHAPTER 24

Throughout Will's explanation, Tiny remained silent, leaving Janice to occasionally ask questions, which she did whenever Will's story didn't satisfy her curiosity. At the end, she made a summarizing statement to ensure she had heard him correctly. "So, you believe this guarantees our safety?"

"Physically, at least," agreed Will with a nod.

"But only if you can kill the dragon?" she added.

"And the dragon brood," clarified Will. "Otherwise, everyone dies eventually, whether it's next year or twenty years from now. Once they hatch, our world becomes a battleground, and we're just spoils of war. Lognion really isn't a threat, but I need to kill him first, both to get him out of the way and to prove it's actually possible to kill them."

Janice pursed her lips. "Noble as it sounds, why do you feel the need to guarantee our safety? None of us asked to be treated like children."

"It's what he always does," growled Tiny angrily.

Will closed his eyes. "You're right, but it's more than that. Before this, my biggest worry was the lich. He's stronger than me. I don't understand him well. He can be almost anywhere, impersonate anyone, and he's demonstrated no personal boundaries that I can trust. Being immortal, he can kill anyone and anything I care about, and I can't do a thing about it."

"You beat him when we met him the other day," argued Tiny.

He shook his head. "And it meant nothing. I destroyed a vessel. After he abandons one body, he has countless others to use. I have no way of knowing where he might go or what he might do."

"Just because he could do something doesn't mean he will," said Janice. "Why are you worried about that?"

"I'm not worried about it anymore," answered Will. "Before, I didn't know anything about his motivations; now I do, and they're actually closely aligned with my own. Kill the dragon, save the world, et cetera."

"Why does he care about the world?" demanded Tiny. "He's undead."

Will wasn't entirely sure, but he had a possible theory. "I think Lognion is the reason he became a lich." Both of his friends gave him blank stares, so Will held up a hand. "Hear me out. It happened a long time ago, and from what I can gather, he may have been the first leader of the Council of Wizards. The dragon appears, no one can stop it, and eventually they learn it's creating a clutch of dragon eggs somewhere, with the inevitable consequences we've already talked about."

"How does this make him into a lich?" asked Tiny skeptically.

Will continued, "Suppose he tries his best for however long he can, but he can't find a way to stop Lognion. Suppose Grim Talek is getting close to the end of his life, and he knows none of his successors have a chance. Or maybe he is killed while trying—but somehow thwarts death. I don't know how it happened, but I can see why it might be his last chance. He couldn't do it while alive, so he becomes undead to carry the fight on indefinitely."

Tiny snorted. "If he's such a tragic hero, why is he so evil? He created the vampires, Will! You told me you've seen him torture your friend, Rob, and while I was stuck with him, he tried to get me to murder men without even offering them a chance to surrender."

"I'm no better," stated Will, staring at his feet. "I've killed innocents, by accident, in anger, and simply because it was necessary. I've tortured monsters and men. I've made excuses along the way, felt guilty quite often, but the farther into this I get, the less I care. What would I be like after a thousand years? Grim Talek isn't good, but he certainly isn't *just* evil. He has a goal, and that's all that matters to him."

Janice spoke up. "What's his goal?"

"I've already told you," said Will. "Destroying Lognion and his brood."

"That's what he said, but there's no good reason to believe him," argued Tiny.

Will straightened. "I believe him. His final price wouldn't make any sense if he had any other motives beyond that."

"Price? What price?" asked Tiny.

He shook his head. "I'm not sharing, but it's almost as bad as the dragon. The only good thing is that even if I fail at it, you and your family will be safe."

"What if you don't pay this price?"

Will sighed. "The world will go on without me, but if I don't try, Grim Talek will eliminate anyone I've ever known. So it's either die trying or live while he kills everyone else."

"That's horrible!" exclaimed Janice.

Tiny agreed. "Definitely not a tragic hero, if that's how he operates."

"I never said he was," stated Will. "He just doesn't care anymore. If he doesn't get what he wants, he'll vent his frustration on those I love. It's the best way he knows to motivate me. In any case, it hardly matters—even if I can't pay it, he'll still honor the agreement to watch over those I care about."

"Except you'll be dead," concluded Janice.

Is that so bad? thought Will. *Both of you are starting to get sick of me, and I'm beginning to hate the person I've become.* He couldn't say any of that, however, so he simply shrugged, but his face must have given some of it away.

Janice stared at him for several seconds without blinking as her eyes grew damp. Tiny's expression darkened, and when he saw the tears welling in her eyes, he grew even angrier. His voice came out as a growl. "Go fuck yourself Will."

He was already constructing a new teleport spell. It was time to leave. Before he could finish, Janice put a hand on Tiny to stop him from saying anything else. Then she asked, "At least eat before you leave. Jeremy's cooking is probably better than whatever they have where you're going."

Will pursed his lips. She was right. "I don't want anyone to know I'm here. If anyone else sees me, it could spoil the plan."

"The plan to let Grim Talek ruin the country while he lives with your unsuspecting wife?" snapped Tiny.

That sparked his temper. "She's figured it out already. She's smarter than—" he stopped himself there, because he knew he was about to start a fight, then amended his remark. "She's smart."

Janice intervened. "Go up to the study. I'll bring food for you. I've been eating enough for three people lately. Besides, I'll tell Jeremy that John just arrived. Eat and rest. I'll make sure no one goes in or finds out you're here." She turned to give Tiny a disapproving glance. "You should wait in my room. We still have a lot to talk about."

Will was tempted to make a face at Tiny while Janice's eyes were elsewhere, but he refrained. With two quick spells for silence and camouflage, plus the technique he had learned from Darla, he became nearly undetectable and left the room, making his way up to the study. Good food was more compelling than his need to escape their judgment. Plus, he still had a book to finish, and Rimberlin was much more comfortable than the cold basement he had been reading in before.

As he went up the stairs, he heard a cat's slow yowl echo through the house, and from a nearby room, Blake cursed, "There it is again! It's making me insane. Where is the damned animal?" One of the maids responded to him, "The house is haunted, I'm sure of it."

Will frowned. It was just a cat. There wasn't anything mysterious about the sound. Shaking his head, he went to his study, but before he could open the door, he heard a loud and enthusiastic mew. Evie was standing a short distance down the hall, and she had spotted him. She fairly pranced as he went into the study and held the door to let her follow him in. Pleased with his manners, she leapt to the top of his desk and allowed him the honor of scratching her head, ears, and chin.

Despite himself, Will smiled. "At least someone is glad to see me." Sitting down in his chair, he leaned back and put his feet on the desk, turning his chest into a gently sloping surface that was ideal for the happy cat to curl up on. Evie's contented purring vibrated through him, and Will felt some of the tension he'd been holding for the past week gradually fade away. *Maybe life isn't all bad,* he decided.

He couldn't start reading, since he wanted to eat and the book might keep him enthralled for hours, so he waited, enjoying Evie's company and giving her the attention she had lacked for the last week or two. When the door opened half an hour later, it was without the customary knock. Janice entered, carrying a large plate laden with an overlarge meat pastry and a small berry tart.

Will doubted he could eat so much, and his raised brow communicated his disbelief, then he asked, "Jeremy made this for Tiny, didn't he?"

Janice nodded. "Imagine his surprise when I go back down in half an hour and tell him John is still hungry." That made him grin, but Janice didn't reciprocate. "I still haven't forgiven you," she informed him. "I'm insulted you think so little of our help that all you consider is how to keep us in the dark, or how to protect us."

He had no reply, so he merely nodded.

"Since you seem to be able to travel almost anywhere now, consider this. You don't have to sleep on the road, or wherever it is. We can keep your presence a secret. Come back whenever you get the chance. You can eat and rest in safety." Apologetic, Will wanted to say something, but she was already at the door. "I'll check on you this evening. If you're still here, I'll bring you more food." Quickly stepping out, Janice was gone.

He stared at the door after she had left for a minute or more. *I'm definitely an asshole. I don't deserve such friends.* His self-reproach was interrupted, however, when he heard Evie greedily gnawing at the edge of his meat pie. "Hey!" He shooed her away before cutting into the pastry and extracting a piece of meat to offer the hungry cat. "You can have this piece. I can't eat the whole thing anyway."

Evie accepted his offering and took it to the far corner of the desk to eat it in relative peace while he began filling his own belly. She accepted a few more pieces before he was done and moved on to try the berry tart. As usual, he wasn't disappointed, for Jeremy had outdone himself once more. He took the plate and put it down on the floor beside the door, both to clear his desk and to make it easier for the cat to pick through his leftovers, then he sat down and summoned the book.

The world vanished as soon as he opened the cover while he simultaneously remembered everything he had read up until that point. It wasn't all unpleasant, but most of it was. No one had used the journal to hide good news or benign magical revelations. The first wizard had spent centuries studying Lognion, and trying to learn as much as possible about dragonkind. The dragon had arrived from elsewhere, and it seemed that dragons belonged to no dimension and all of them at the same time. They were solitary in nature, and although a single clutch of eggs could number several dozen, it was rare for more than one of a given brood to survive.

The hatchlings deserted the nest immediately after hatching, to avoid predation from their siblings, but over the course of a few years, they grew rapidly to a significant fraction of their final size. Since their magical and mental faculties lagged far behind the development of their savage nature, the new dragonlings generally destroyed one another while running rampant in their new homeland. Eventually, they would develop the ability to travel to other planes and leave, but by that time there were usually only one or two survivors.

Most of that information had been gleaned from conversations with the elves, who, as it turned out, had already lost their original home to dragons. Hercynia had been their second home, but once Lognion had arrived, they had promptly relocated to yet another plane of existence, returning only occasionally to trade with the humans who remained.

They hadn't even tried to fight. Still remembering their first encounter, the elder race had chosen to move as soon as they learned a new nest had been established in Hercynia.

The term 'first wizard' was something of a misnomer as well. Though the original author of the journal didn't name himself, it was apparent that he had been the last member of a larger magical society which had collapsed after Lognion's arrival, along with the civilizations of the time. The dragon had systematically destroyed every city, every place of learning, every cultural center, and every government that had existed before it came, reducing mankind to a new dark age of ignorance.

With that accomplished, the dragon had vanished, leaving humanity to rebuild itself over the centuries that followed. The first wizard had survived, consulting with the elves, searching for a means to destroy the dragon, and trying to locate the nest that he knew existed in secret somewhere. As far as Will could tell from what he had written, the first wizard had failed on all fronts, aside from the general knowledge he gained from the elves. Obviously, the book couldn't include the man's death, but his final centuries were bitter and fruitless.

Except that he refused to die, thought Will, *assuming he was the one who became Grim Talek.*

The fact that the first wizard's studies had yielded not a single clue on how to kill a dragon, or even wound one, was singularly depressing, and those who followed after him hadn't even attempted to find answers. Lognion had vanished, supposedly, and if a nest truly existed, it wouldn't hatch for centuries or even millennia. It was a problem for another day.

Now it's my problem.

The writers who followed had their own problems—and devastating solutions. They dealt with rogue necromancers, magical plagues, and invasive monsters, such as the trolls. Some had created rituals too risky to ever attempt, or explored horrifying magics that warped the soul and mind.

Most disturbing was the work recorded by the tenth writer, who hadn't had many real problems during her time and so had spent her life studying the nature of reality itself. During her investigations, she had devised a ritual to grant her a special type of perception that she hoped would allow her to see the foundations of reality, the essence of the universe that underlay magic itself. After convincing her contemporaries to assist, she had claimed success, though most of her colleagues denounced her as insane. The second half of her portion of the book consisted entirely of chaotic ramblings and descriptions of what she saw. Most of it sounded like a living nightmare.

Every shadow was alive, and nature itself was merely a thin veneer that barely hid an ocean of empty darkness—well, mostly empty. She had been convinced that the void contained evil intellects too terrible to consider. Consumed by paranoia the tenth writer had spent decades researching spells and barriers to block out the shadowy alien horrors that haunted her. She had eventually killed those who assisted her with the original ritual, to prevent the knowledge from being widely known. Will got the sense that she had probably committed suicide afterward, though he couldn't be sure.

Naturally, the ritual was recorded in the book, and just seeing the rune construct made Will's skin crawl. He couldn't see any use for it, but it disturbed him that to retain the rest of the book's knowledge he would have to remember it as well. The writer had also recorded the most successful barrier spells she had created. The earliest ones were supposedly able to block the passage of all manner or spirits, demons, or intangible entities, but that hadn't been good enough. The final version created a barrier similar to a force effect but with far deeper metaphysical ramifications. If the description was accurate, it actually created an artificial division in the astral plane, isolating the interior completely from all influences or contact with other minds.

It was interesting in the academic sense, because force effects were already essentially a type of magic based on the astral plane. That was why they could block spirits (or Will when he was projecting) from contacting or teleporting to someone he had a bond with. The tenth writer hadn't thought that was good enough and her spell created an effect that somehow *physically* divided an essentially non-physical dimension into two separate parts. Unlike a force dome which could exclude spirits, or a banishing spell that could forcibly reject them, the tenth writer claimed her spell had actually been able to trap one of the void intellects that was tormenting her. Afterward she had tried using the spell on herself, but the psychic isolation that resulted only drove her deeper into insanity.

Another peculiar writer, the fourteenth, had also had a relatively peaceful life. Combining lots of free time with a strong curiosity and a keen intellect, the fourteenth writer had devised a ritual that theoretically would unravel whatever plane of existence it was used in. It had never been tested of course, since the author had suspected that the unravelling might not be limited to just one plane. It might potentially spread like fire, consuming and destroying every dimension until nothing was left.

Except the endless void that the tenth believed in—that would probably survive, thought Will darkly. So far, he hadn't found anything useful in the book, other than material to fuel his nightmares for decades to come. Feeling tired, he closed the book.

It was a relief to have the memories fade into obscurity, though he still felt vaguely uneasy. Checking the window, he saw that the day was almost done, and he'd spent most of it in the study. He couldn't remember how far he had gotten, but he had the feeling of nearly being finished. It was tempting to stay for dinner and then read into the night, but he needed to talk to his father and find the meeting place with Mahak.

The vampires probably wouldn't arrive until the next night, certainly not while driving a cart, but if they abandoned it and were motivated, they could conceivably cover the entire distance in a day. Will scratched Evie between her ears and then stepped back and constructed a fresh teleport spell. Her green eyes watched him with silent intensity as he slipped from his body and found his father in the astral plane. Less than a minute later, he found the right balance so he could activate the spell and he was gone.

Mark Nerrow was resting in the command tent when Will arrived. The governor hadn't slept much the night before, and it had been a long day once he rejoined the main force. The sudden appearance of his son made him flinch involuntarily, but he controlled himself quickly. Lieutenant Stadler, who was attending him, was not as well prepared. The startled officer jumped, took a step back, tried to draw a sword he wasn't currently wearing, and then fell over a small stool.

Will held out his hands in a peaceful gesture that probably alarmed the officer even more, but fortunately the governor regained his voice quickly so he could calm the man down. "It's Duke Cartwright, Stadler, relax." Then his eyes turned to his son. "Surely there's some way you could warn people? Every time you do this, it leads to an accident or a near heart attack."

It was a good thought, and Will paused to consider it for a moment. Currently, the only people who he could warn in advance were Laina and probably Selene... His mind stuck there. *Laina. Laina's dead.* His chest tightened, and his stomach turned sour. Mark was waiting for a response, but seeing none forthcoming, he asked, "Did you have an idea?"

Will shook his head. "No, but there are three possibilities. If you were astrally sensitive I could tell you directly, but I have no idea how to teach that skill. There's also a device that can be used to communicate across vast distances, but it would take time to construct and I haven't learned how yet."

"And the third?"

"The heart-stone enchantment, but you're still bound to Lognion, aren't you?"

Mark Nerrow's face darkened. "I haven't felt a change, but I'm not sure if I would. Unless he contacts me to give new orders, I'm not sure if I can even know." It wasn't news that Will enjoyed hearing, but as he listened to the words, a fresh insight struck him, and he began to pace. His father gave him a curious stare. "You've definitely had an idea this time."

Will nodded, silently running through his thoughts. Given the fact that his father was still bound to Lognion, it wasn't safe to discuss the subject. *But there's a strong possibility I have a connection to the dragon as well, even without the enchantment.* In the astral plane, he could find anyone with whom he had built a significant relationship, and that didn't just mean family and loved ones. It could be anyone who evoked strong emotions and with whom he had spent sufficient time.

It would be the simplest of things to test his theory. He merely had to step outside of himself and think of Selene's father. If the connection between them was strong enough, he'd know immediately. The only thing stopping him was fear, fear that the dragon would be able to sense him as well. He had no way of knowing, but if Lognion was astrally sensitive as well, then Will would have given away the secret. Not only would the dragon then expect him to try and use the knowledge, but Lognion would probably also use the same information to spy on him instead.

The best thing he could do was file the idea away. Meeting his father's eyes, he changed the subject. "Regarding the trolls—I think I will need some help after all."

The governor's eyes lit with interest. "I was hoping you'd say that. What do you need?"

"Fire elementals," announced Will. "I can find the trolls, and I think I'll have warriors that can keep them under control while we work, but it will still take a lot of fire to make a clean job of it. Five or six elementals should be enough, along with the sorcerers who control them."

Mark frowned in puzzlement. "Warriors? Where did you find more soldiers?"

Taking a deep breath, Will told him, "Not soldiers, vampires."

His father let out a tense breath. "I was afraid you'd say that. How can you trust them? How can you fight trolls while at the same time worrying that your *allies* might try and turn you into food the moment they smell blood?"

"These aren't like the wild ones we saw in Cerria," said Will. "Those were newly made, consumed by hunger and unable to control themselves. These will be much older and wiser, decades at least, if not centuries. Their instincts won't be a problem."

"So instead, you'll have to worry about their pride," returned Mark. "I've dealt with old men before. They may be wiser, but they won't take kindly to being ordered around by someone they consider a child."

Will smiled. "I've learned a bit of diplomacy."

Mark snorted. "And when diplomacy fails?"

"I've learned a lot more about destroying dignity and crushing ego."

The governor nodded, then replied, "That's a dangerous way to lead. Many a commander has found a knife between his ribs trying to operate in that fashion."

"I don't need them forever," said Will, "just until the job is done."

His father rubbed his chin thoughtfully, then responded, "How am I supposed to explain this to my men? Authority only goes so far, especially when it bumps up against primal fear. The vampires are going to scare the piss out of my sorcerers, and I can't just lie to them either. They're skilled and experienced enough to figure out what they are, even if we try to hide it. Most of them were in Cerria during the vampire plague; they remember."

Will didn't really have an answer for that. "Tell them the truth and ask for volunteers. Make sure they know I'm personally going with them, if that counts for anything. I don't know how many we need, but seven or eight fire elementals will probably be enough, depending on how many trolls are left."

They talked for a while longer, and after he had gotten some directions and advice concerning the local geography, Will said his goodbyes and crafted a force-travel disk. He ordinarily used an elemental version of the spell, to keep his defensive options open, but since the enemies he was currently worried about couldn't use spells, he opted for the force-effect spell instead. It had several advantages, namely greater speed and responsiveness, as well as being able to carry him higher above the ground.

Taking it up to its maximum height of fifty feet, he was above all but the taller trees and was able to maximize his speed. Even so, traveling at night would have been too dangerous, but Will could see clearly by starlight alone, so there was no danger of running into the occasional tree that was tall enough to threaten him.

Being so high gave him an advantage in picking out landmarks as well, which was useful given that the area was largely new to him aside from what he'd seen on maps. He carefully noted the terrain around the governor's encampment and then set out to find the hiding trolls.

Skimming above the trees, Will followed the beacon that had haunted him since he had cast the tracking spell on the troll. It was a directional signal that presented itself to his senses like a blinking light in the distance, and while the target was currently too far away for him to gauge the distance, once he was within five or six hundred yards, the light should grow in size to indicate the target's nearness.

North and east he went, covering something close to ten miles as he passed over several small valleys between the hills. He fully expected the troll camp to be in one of the valleys, where it was warmer. Trolls didn't have a problem with cold, but they preferred warmer temperatures, so it was a surprise when the signal indicated that his target was located two-thirds of the way up one of the larger hills.

Will used a camouflage spell and zoomed quietly over the spot. He might have gotten closer on foot, but he had no easy way to fool their noses, and he figured a quick overhead pass on the windy hillside might be less noticeable.

Once he was close enough, he spotted the cave entrance. It was partly obscured by a rock outcrop and several scraggly bushes, but the troll sitting beside it, presumably on guard duty, brought the secret to his attention. That and the fact that his signal was pulsing somewhere within the hillside.

It was a clever place for them to hide their camp, and once again Will found himself surprised by their intelligence. They'd chosen a colder but better hidden location that made it impossible to know their numbers without going inside. If they had a fire, it would probably be comfortable too, but he didn't see or smell any sign of smoke. *So they're either too dumb to make fire, or too smart to risk giving themselves away.* From what he'd seen so far, he was betting on the latter.

How in the hell had they developed so much over the span of half a year? If their originator actually was Stupid, the troll who had grown from a portion of one of the trolls he had used against the demons, it shouldn't have been possible. Stupid had only known one word; he'd clearly grown from a small, non-brain-containing portion of one of the other trolls. These trolls had language and planning skills. From what Will had been told, that took years, assuming there were older, smarter trolls around to teach the young ones.

Could Stupid have actually been a troll prodigy? Clegg had told him that the trolls produced from his flesh were smarter, or least Gan had been, but none of the trolls he had made were brought along for the fight against the demons. Well, except for Gan himself. *My firstborn,* he thought wryly, before shuddering.

Maybe Stupid had been a piece of Gan? Maybe he'd been a bigger, smarter piece than Will had assumed. He had no way of knowing, and he now wished he had checked on the trolls after the battle. He'd been unconscious for several days, and Selene had been the one to return the troll mercenaries to Muskeglun. *What if she missed one?*

In the end, it didn't matter. He had to eliminate them. Leaning to one side, Will took a route that curved slowly around, and he headed back the way he had come, retracing his steps and making a conscious effort to pick out more landmarks to guide him on his return. The tracking spell should last five or six days, but he'd never used it before. *Better safe than sorry.*

Once he was close to his father's camp, Will changed course and followed the small road that led west toward Cotswold. He didn't really expect the vampires to arrive early, but he wanted a chance to scout the area beforehand. The village was a quicker trip, and when he got there, Will couldn't help but imagine horror that had befallen it.

The buildings were all there, and unlike a village attacked by other humans, nothing had been burned. Instead, the buildings had been physically violated; in some, the doors were ripped from their hinges, while in others a wall had simply been smashed apart. The evidence of violence seemed almost casual, as though it had cost the invaders nothing to perform, and in fact it hadn't. Will could easily imagine a troll tearing its way through barred doors, or using a club to stave in an entire wall. For the occupants, it must have been absolutely terrifying, and it had only gotten worse when the invaders began eating some of them right in front of the others.

Will had been chased by trolls once, during one of his early visits to Muskeglun, but his experience paled in comparison to what had happened to the villagers—and as usual, it was ultimately his fault. It was an uncomfortable realization, but as with other things, it bothered him less than it would have in the past. *I did what I had to do; now I'll fix the mistakes that inevitably resulted,* he told himself. It was small comfort for the dead and the survivors, but it was all he could do.

He brought the force-travel disk to rest in the center of the empty market that had once been the town's main feature. Stepping off the disk, he dismissed it and turned in a slow circle to survey the area. Despite his power and training, he still had to suppress a shiver. Standing alone in the dark, abandoned space, feeling the cold wind on his neck, and knowing there might be vampires waiting in the shadows for him—it was enough to make even the most stalwart feel uncertain.

Will automatically smoothed his turyn and wrapped a camouflage spell around himself without even thinking about it, becoming nearly impossible to detect. He rarely bothered with the silence spell these days; it was easier to use his natural talent with sound. If he didn't want to be heard, he wasn't. Vampires did have good noses, but not good enough to pinpoint him.

Feeling more secure, he began a slow walk around the empty town to familiarize himself with the area. He was probably alone, but tomorrow he wouldn't be, so it wouldn't hurt to get the lay of the land. As he walked, he ran through various scenarios in his mind, putting himself in Mahak's shoes as he examined the buildings. The vampire wizard could take a multitude of different courses, ranging from an honest meeting to a simple ambush or ever more complicated plans. Will had never met the vampire before, so he couldn't guess. Instead, he considered how he would react to each possibility.

After an hour he was convinced the vampires weren't going to show up a day early, and he'd done as much planning as he could, so he found a quiet corner in one of the buildings and cast his mind free, turning his attention toward Tiny.

And immediately regretted it. Will returned to his body without hesitation, his cheeks flushing. He wouldn't seek Janice either, as she had been with Tiny. Examining the shed he was sitting in, he remarked quietly, "I guess I live here now."

A few short seconds later, he regained his composure, and several thoughts ran through his mind. Tiny and Janice hadn't been in her room, or any other bedroom at Rimberlin. They were at some other house, though it was also well appointed. He wondered where they had gone, and his curiosity was almost—but not quite—enough to make him return for a broader look at their surroundings. There had been something familiar about the room, though he couldn't put his finger on what it was.

Returning to his meditation, he checked on his other loved ones. His mother was still unreachable, hidden behind a powerful force effect. Selene was sleeping, and he couldn't help but think she looked terribly alone. In person, her personality and confidence always made her seem larger than she was, but asleep she seemed small and vulnerable. A pang of guilt struck him for a moment.

Pushing that aside, he checked on his cousin, Sammy. *Please don't let me see something like I did with Janice and Tiny.* It hadn't occurred to him before, but if he caught Emory in her bed chamber, he wasn't entirely certain what he would—or wouldn't—do. It was a relief to find her alone in her room, sitting at the desk and practicing a spell construct.

Will knew that Emory had been teaching her the runes and familiarizing her with the basics, but he hadn't expected her to be quite so far along. It was only a few weeks since she had finished the third compression, and Sammy had never been taught to express turyn before that, so even drawing a single rune in the air was a significant leap. *Is that her Cartwright determination, or the power of love?* He decided he didn't want to know. *Just be proud of her.*

Glancing around the room, he saw a simple board leaning against the wall across from the doorway. Written in charcoal across the visible face was a message: *My room is safe. Please come in.*

Will glared at it. *What does that mean?* Was it something Sammy would put out for Emory to see? Was it for someone else? He didn't like any of the possibilities that his imagination was conjuring up for him to see. If Janice and Tiny were both away from Rimberlin, there was no one to look out for Sammy, or keep her from making a bad mistake.

He was tempted to teleport to his cousin and ask her directly, but he decided against it. *She's safe; that's what's important.* As for the rest, he'd have to trust her. Returning to his body he got up and went for another walk. The ravaged town was empty of people, and although most of the doors were ruined, the homes were still in good condition.

He searched out the largest home, which still only had one sleeping room with a large family bed. Most importantly, the bed was relatively clean, and the bloodstains were in the main room, not the bedroom. Will summoned an embroidered roll of cloth and went back outside. Using a small tack, he fastened one end of the rune-covered cloth to the corner of the building and then walked his way around the building.

Of course, the perimeter of the home didn't quite match the length of the fabric, but he used a couple of sticks to extend the perimeter farther out until the two ends of the roll could be brought neatly together. With a thought and mild effort of will, he infused the ward with turyn, and once it was complete, he removed the cloth and rolled it back up. The runes remained, glowing faintly in the air where the cloth had been.

Will silently thanked Tabitha, for though he and Selene had designed the ward, it had been her talented hands that had embroidered the long stretch of cloth with the complex rune structure. Unlike the simple wards he had used in the past, which were usually limited by the time it took him to manually inscribe them, this ward was vastly more sophisticated. It included three layers to make it difficult for even a wizard to sneak through (though it was still possible). It also had triggers for humans, demons, and the undead. Non-human animals were ignored to prevent false positives from mice, cats, or other creatures.

The ward's only function was to alert him, even if he was asleep. Traps or other magical effects were difficult to include since unless one knew exactly what would trigger the ward, the results could be ineffective or even disastrous. Demons and undead were immune to many dangers, while small children were not.

With an overabundance of caution, Will then built a fire in the main fireplace before leaving and going to the smaller house next door. The bed there wasn't as nice, but it was also clean. He created a second ward, similar to the first, but smaller and entirely enclosed within the walls of the bedroom itself. It would be difficult to spot without entering the dwelling, so his thought was that if the vampires showed up early, they'd assume he was in the building with the fire and visible ward.

He was sacrificing a bit of comfort for extra safety, but with the use of the floor-warming spell Selene had taught him years ago, the small bedroom wasn't really a hardship to sleep in. Will settled in, removing his boots and brigandine so he could rest. He cast an anti-possession spell that Arrogan had recommended to him long ago, its purpose to keep him from traveling astrally while unconscious. Slumber found him quickly, transporting him to a world of dreams in which he watched Laina die in front of him once more. Unable to wake, he found no relief as the dream moved on to feature Tabitha and Sammy being murdered by vampires. Selene came to help him, but to his horror he found she had become a lich, and where he expected warmth from her, he found only a cruel coldness radiating from her eyes.

At the end, he escaped and somehow found his mother, but she had no words to comfort him. Instead, she looked at him with pity. "What did you expect? You left the fox to guard the hens," she told him.

Opening his eyes, Will found himself still lying in the bed in Cotswold, feeling disturbed and simultaneously well rested—a bizarre dichotomy. It took him a few minutes to put his boots on, put his brigandine back on, rearrange his clothes, and most importantly, get his mind in order. He considered what to do with the day, as he had no plans other than meeting Mahak that evening.

He could simply wait in Cotswold, but that seemed like a waste of time. He also wanted to finish the book, but it was too dangerous to do that in such a vulnerable location. The simple solution would be to return to Rimberlin and read there, assuming Janice and Tiny had gone back. Removing the anti-possession spell, Will settled into a cross-legged pose and set his spirit free to check on his friends again.

Alarmingly, he was unable to find Janice or Tiny, though not because they were dead. Searching for Laina had taught him what it was like to seek a soul that had passed on, for it would lead him to a raw emptiness. No, Tiny and Janice were hidden behind a shield. It was exactly what he had come to expect when trying to see his mother. *Has the lich betrayed our agreement?* Had Grim Talek captured them and put them in the same place as his mother, or somewhere similarly shielded?

He returned to his body and took several slow breaths. *Janice could just as easily have put a force-dome around Tiny and herself for privacy. Don't jump to conclusions,* he cautioned himself. Returning to his meditation, Will sought out Selene instead. She appeared before him, elegantly dressed and seated at the head of a long table. A delicate crown of silver and diamonds sat atop her brow as she gazed serenely at the collection of peers arrayed along both sides of the table. It appeared to be a meeting of the greater peers of the realm.

Will's perspective was located a few feet in front of her, just above the middle of the table, and while he wanted to study the room, the first thing that caught his eye was himself. Standing just behind Selene and slightly to the right was his stand-in, Grim Talek. Seeing his own face staring back at him would have startled him, if he'd been in his body. Being intangible, it just sent a cold shock through his spirit.

The false-Will was also dressed in court attire, with a dark grey doublet, black woolen hose, and a simple gold circlet on his head. Although the lich had taken a relaxed posture, he radiated danger in the same way a stove might radiate heat. Grim Talek's eyes studied the men seated in front of Selene with same attitude he might use if he were looking at a collection of bugs, and electric blue sparks appeared at random intervals around his eyes and in his hair, as though he had leashed the power of a storm and only barely held it in check.

Will took all that in within a second of appearing, but as he stared at the lich, he realized that Grim Talek was now looking directly back at him, a smile curling the corner of his lips. Selene was staring at him as well, and her lips parted as though she might question him, but then she looked away, turning her gaze back toward the council she was currently addressing.

They can both see me, realized Will, *and I just distracted her in the middle of what looks to be an important meeting.* With a thought, he returned to his body again.

He studied the wall for a few minutes, letting his emotions subside. Seeing Selene and knowing she was seeing him had stirred up his heart again. *Damn, this isn't going to be easy.*

He had no reasonable expectation of living until the end, so any conversation they had would just be a goodbye disguised with a lie. He wanted to explain, but it was even worse than with Janice and Tiny. Selene would see through his plan as easily as they had, and she wouldn't react any better. Avoiding her was cowardly, but Will wasn't certain that talking would accomplish anything other than hurting her more. *And I might lose my nerve.*

Aside from seeing Selene, Grim Talek bothered him almost as much. He now knew for certain that the lich was astrally sensitive, which made him feel incredibly vulnerable. What would happen if he was attacked while spying on someone? Arrogan had told him a few things about such occurrences in the past, but he wasn't sure he remembered all the details. Will knew a banishment spell would cause incredible pain and send him back to his body, but there might be even worse possibilities. What if someone tried to put a force spell around him? Would it trap him and sever his connection to his body? Would he die?

Pushing all that aside, he decided to try Sammy once more.

CHAPTER 26

He waited until Sammy returned to her room and he was certain that she was alone. It appeared as though his cousin was determined to do some more practicing, so he waited until she was back at the desk and facing away before teleporting to her bed. He'd been sitting in a chair in Cotswold, so he was able to arrange his physical arrival so that there was a minimum of difference between his position there and his position in Rimberlin. The bed was slightly lower, so he only dropped an inch before settling into the mattress.

There was still enough sound for Sammy to notice, causing her to turn and look at the bed. She startled visibly, but somehow managed not to yell. Swallowing, she smoothed her features quickly and then remarked, "You saw my sign, right?"

"That was for me?"

She rolled her eyes. "Who else would it be for?" A second later, she held up her hand. "No. Don't say it."

Will shrugged.

Sammy's cheeks colored. "Picklehead! I can't believe you'd think that. It wouldn't make sense anyway."

"Pickle-what?"

"If I had such intentions, a sign would just tell everyone in the house what we were planning! Grow a brain! You're supposed to be my smart cousin," she snapped, but there was a faint smile on her lips.

Relaxing into their familiar banter, Will replied, "I thought I was the handsome cousin."

Sammy laughed, causing the curls that framed her face to bounce. "Maybe if you took care of yourself. How many days have you been wearing those clothes?"

Will sniffed, glancing down at himself. "I used a cleaning spell yesterday."

"You smell fine, but you're so rumpled you look like someone crumpled you into a ball and then tried to flatten you out again."

He frowned, then protested, "It's not that bad. The spell took most of the wrinkles out."

Sammy nodded. "Sure, the wrinkles in your clothes, but not your hair—or your face. Maybe you're getting old? Do you think this is how it happens?" Contorting her features and scrunching up her nose, Sammy affected a twisted expression. "It looks like you've been doing this with your face for the past week. You probably need to relax. The queen might seek an annulment if you get too ugly." She covered her mouth in a parody of shock and surprise. "What would happen to me then, if Selene replaced you? Would I be banished too?"

He laughed, but her joke landed uncomfortably close to his recent thoughts, and something must have shown on his face. Sammy started to question him, but he interrupted her, "If you were banished, I suppose I'd be forced to bring you along on my adventures then, wouldn't I?"

"As long as I can bring Emory with me," she returned with a determined stare.

"Emory? You'd bring your beau along while I was suffering from such rejection?"

"Just because you're a picklehead doesn't mean I have to suffer too." Sammy became more serious then. "Janice and Tiny went to the capital. They didn't tell me all the details, but I got the distinct impression they were less than pleased with you. And at the same time, I'm supposed to keep your presence a secret. Who are you hiding from?"

"Lognion."

Sammy frowned. "He isn't here. Besides, he's in hiding from you, remember? You blew up his house, walked all over his elementals and sorcerers, and then you burned his fake human body to a crisp."

Something about Sammy's blasé demeanor put Will at ease. It made it feel as if they were just joking about something back in Barrowden, back before he knew anything about wizards, vampires, or dragons. "He's not hiding, he just doesn't care. I'm insignificant to him."

"You're underestimating yourself," said Sammy confidently. "You always overestimate others, and you can't see yourself clearly. Maybe the dragon isn't shaking in fear, but he's being careful so you don't find the things he wants to protect."

"I already—" Will stopped, realizing he was about to reveal a secret that could end his small chance of success. *And potentially put a massive target on Sammy*, he added mentally. He shifted directions. "You're probably right, but you're also missing an important piece of information. Dragons are incredibly resistant to magic, and not just magic, everything in our world. I'm not even sure how to explain it, but they're essentially more *real* than we are."

His cousin eyed him up and down for a second, then replied, "That's not what you were about to say, but fine, I won't press you for details on what's obviously yet another secret." With a sigh, she continued, "And I bet you've already found a solution to killing them, haven't you?"

That surprised him. Will had always loved his cousin for her silliness, even though she could be annoying at times, but he'd never thought of her as perceptive. "What makes you think that?"

She grinned. "I knew it." Then she lowered her voice to a whisper. "You're not hiding—you don't want him to see you coming."

His eyes went wide with alarm. "Stop. Not another word."

"Trust me. Have I ever given your secrets away?" she asked.

Will nodded. "You told Mom I was in love with Selene before I was ready."

"That doesn't count, and besides, I was guessing. She already knew anyway."

Will pointed at the chair, which was just far enough away from the desk that he could put a force-dome around it and the two of them after she had sat in it. "You've guessed a lot, but you have to stop now. I can't help what you think inside your own head, but you can't say any of it out loud. Not here, not elsewhere, not to anyone, not even to me, do you understand?"

"Fine. Why though?"

"Lognion still has his hooks in thousands of people. Most of the nobility, all the past graduates of Wurthaven, and who knows who else? And that's not even counting the people who report to those people. There's also the fact that you don't always know who you're talking to. I know of at least two who can imitate me to such a degree I can't even tell they aren't me. If either of those two even imagined you knew the things you were guessing at just now, they'd kill you on the spot."

Sammy's expression grew serious as the gravity of his words sank in. "Who?"

"Does it matter?"

She nodded. "If something goes wrong and they kill you, I need to know where to start when I avenge you."

Will laughed, until she kicked him in the shin. His boot saved him from most of the pain, but the look on his cousin's face said she wasn't joking around as she warned him, "I'll accept that I'm just a novice for now, but that won't last forever. I'm going to be dangerous someday. So at least tell me who you're worried about. I'll keep it in my head with all the other stuff you don't want me talking about, but don't leave me blind. Please?"

To Will, the premise seemed unbelievable, but he couldn't argue with Sammy's logic. She was dead serious. It would be a terrible insult to ignore her request. *Could she defeat Aislinn, Grim Talek, or Lognion?* The answer was obvious—of course not—but the determination in his cousin's eyes said something different to his heart. *Maybe she could, given time to learn and grow.* She was a third-order wizard now, though she was only just beginning to learn spells. He couldn't begin to judge her future potential.

Something shifted in his heart, and a crack opened, letting light shine into the darkness and despair that had somehow made its home there. It was a tiny thing, and hope couldn't instantly replace his apathy, but it made itself known. *If she could do it someday, there's no reason I couldn't do it sometime in the near future, as long as I keep my head clear.* Green eyes bored into him as the gears in his mind gradually began to move toward the possibility of a future.

"Laina wasn't the only one who cared," said Sammy, leaving the rest unsaid.

His fear had made him foolish. He could see it clearly now. Some of his precautions were warranted, but he was limiting his chances of success by trying too hard to keep his friends and family perfectly safe. It was disrespectful to them, and it eliminated the possible contributions they might have to offer. The empty smile left his features, and his eyes turned down. "You're right. Grim Talek, Aislinn, and Lognion, those are the three I'm worried most about. The first two can impersonate me so well I probably couldn't spot the difference, and Lognion still has ears in every noble house and lowly tavern across Terabinia and far beyond. The lich has a large informant network as well, possibly better than the dragon's. As for Grandmother, I have no idea what her resources are, or even if she's involved in this, but it's hard to believe she is simply a bystander." He paused, then stared into his cousin's eyes. "If anything *does* happen to me, you'll need to play a long game if you really want revenge. It would be the work of a lifetime."

"Apparently I'm going to live a very long time," she replied. "Thanks to your torture."

"Training," Will corrected. "You still have a lot more of it to do, but the painful part is over at least." They talked for some time after that, and Will shared most of the rough details he had given Janice and Tiny. He finished with a request. "Tell Tiny and Janice I want their help. I'm not sure what they can do, but I'm willing to trust that they might think of something I'm missing."

"I think that's why they're in Cerria," said Sammy. "They wouldn't tell me anything, but I'm sure they've probably consulted Selene, which by the way, is probably bad news for you if you haven't told her any of this yet." Will visibly winced, and Sammy grinned. "I guess even the Stormking is afraid of the Queen of Terabinia."

Will scowled in confusion. "The what?"

"You haven't heard?" said Sammy enthusiastically. "That's what they're calling you in the capital now—the Stormking."

"But I'm not taking the throne, Selene is."

She shrugged. "The Stormking probably isn't concerned with the petty matters of we mere mortals. He rules the skies and punishes the wicked with javelins of lightning."

"Stop. That isn't funny."

"Then maybe you should stop parading around the capital with sparks hovering around you all the time."

"That isn't me."

She nodded. "But the people don't know that, and from the stories the deliverymen have been bringing, it seems like whoever is pretending to be you is making the most of the rumors." Sammy paused, then added, "Can you show me?"

"Show you what?"

"You know." Sammy wiggled her eyebrows and made odd crashing noises while waving her hands up and down. "Just a little. I'm dying to see it."

Will sighed. "It's dangerous. Besides, I don't even know what my copycat is showing people."

"Liar. You could show me if you wanted to."

Remembering what he had seen of Grim Talek at the council meeting, Will had to admit he probably could. He didn't know the spell that the lich was using to mimic the visual effects of his talent, but he could certainly produce real sparks. His talents, both with sound and storms, were essentially a form of wild magic, and his use of them was innate rather than structured. Pursing his lips seriously, Will pushed Sammy away and then withdrew his hand before producing a long ribbon of brilliant electricity that ran from his fingertips up to his shoulder and then down the other arm. It was over in less than a second. "There. Satisfied?"

She clapped her hands together in obvious delight. "That looks wicked! Can you teach me to do that?"

"Probably not, at least not the same way. I'm sure there are spells that can create similar effects, but you'll have to learn them individually. What I did was part of a natural talent."

"Can I learn the talent?" she asked.

Will shrugged. "From what I've learned, third-order wizards, and sometimes even second-order wizards, develop talents like this, but there's no way of choosing. It depends on your unique nature."

Sammy scowled at him. "Thunder and lightning, loud and flashy—not to argue with you, but neither of those things are remotely like your personality. Before you left home, you were mostly quiet and deliberate in your doings. Even now, you're nothing like what the rumors claim."

"That's a relief. I doubt the talents relate to personality per se, but if so, maybe they're opposites."

"What do you think mine would be then?"

Will gave his cousin a sly look. "I'm not sure. Probably something subtle and elegant."

Her mouth dropped open for a split second, then Sammy jumped forward to flick his ear painfully. "That was rude!"

He winked at her while rubbing his ear. "But true." Something bumped into his leg, and he looked down to discover Evie had come out to reintroduce herself. He addressed the cat amiably. "Hello little lady."

"Whoa!" Sammy stepped back, raising her arms in surprise. "Where did she come from?"

"Under the bed?"

She shook her head. "No. I've been looking everywhere for her. No one's seen her since you were here last, but we've been hearing her yowling all over the house. I was starting to think she's a ghost."

"Yowling?"

"Looking for you, I suppose," Sammy answered. She watched somewhat jealously while Will scratched the grey cat's head, but when she crouched down to do the same, Evie hissed and backed away. "Why do you like him but not me?"

"She just has good taste," offered Will. The cat turned her head and licked the back of his hand. The word 'taste' echoed once more in the air.

"Did you say taste twice?" asked Sammy.

He hadn't, but he nodded anyway. "Not sure why I did that." Will watched the cat as he spoke, silently wondering if it was somehow responsible for the sound. *Surely not.*

They talked a while longer, and then Sammy left to give him peace and quiet so he could finish reading the ancient journal. As before, from the moment he opened the cover it was as if a hidden part of himself suddenly revealed itself. The memories of his previous sessions came back to him, and it amazed him that he could have ever forgotten what he had read, as so much of it was disturbing. The insane paranoia of the tenth writer bothered him the most with her ramblings of unseen evils and hidden entities watching from every shadow.

The ritual for unlocking what she had called 'null sight' kept nagging at the back of his mind. The idea that secretive beings could be watching him at every moment, completely unseen and unheard, bothered him more than he wanted to admit. The ritual would grant him the ability to sense them, or give him permanent hallucinations, depending on how one viewed the subject. He wanted to try it just to reassure himself, but then he wouldn't be able to turn it off.

Some things are better left unseen, he told himself. He pushed forward with his reading and was somewhat disappointed when he reached the end with no entry from his grandfather. The old man had been so devout in his quest to eliminate the heart-stone enchantment that he hadn't even recorded it in the journal. It probably wouldn't have been the worst thing written in the book, but then again, Arrogan would probably have felt that the previous writers might have done better not to record their dangerous knowledge.

None of it was the least bit useful, thought Will, *except for ruining your sleep or giving you waking nightmares.* The least useless bit of knowledge in the book was the fourteenth author's ritual for unraveling or destroying an entire plane of existence. It might be useful as a tool of extortion, or as a deterrent, but Will could see no way to use it against the dragon. Dragons had no home plane, they roamed through the dimensions nesting and destroying as they saw fit. He certainly couldn't use it to threaten the destruction of Lognion's nest. Doing so would eliminate his entire world, negating the goal entirely.

Reading the book had been a waste of time. It was full of nothing but madness and uselessly dangerous spells that had no practical use. Choosing to forget the contents would be the obvious choice, for remembering would likely leave him with impractical fears and strange nightmares.

The spell that had begun when he opened the first page now made itself known again, offering him the choice of memory or peace of mind. The runes hovered in his mind's eye, offering blissful forgetfulness or uncomfortable remembrance. Beneath them was a short acknowledgment that should he choose to forget, there would still be triggers to remind him if one of the ancient threats covered by the text presented itself to him.

That's why Arrogan thought he felt he should remember something. The egg guardians would have triggered the knowledge written down regarding the dragon, Will realized. It wouldn't help him, though. There was no practical remedy, just a depressing history of Grim Talek's failure—assuming that Grim Talek was indeed the first writer.

A shock ran through him. There was something he might be able to use, though it wouldn't help him against the dragon. But would it be worth it? Assuming he found some other way to avert the dragon apocalypse, would one spell be worth remembering the rest of the horrors contained in the book? *It might save my life, though.*

Was that reason enough? Grim Talek had pledged to devote his existence to protecting those that Will had named, so long as he didn't break faith with their agreement. Will's survival might run counter to that goal.

"To hell with that, and to hell with the lich. Your life is worth living." It was Laina's voice, and it seemed so real that it almost jolted him from his trance. He knew it was his imagination, but it firmed up his conviction. He made his choice: remembrance.

Will opened his eyes, and almost fell over backward when he saw Sammy's face directly in front of his own, studying him with great interest. "What the hell?"

"You've been sitting there mumbling to yourself for at least an hour, but the pages are blank," she told him. "Tell me the truth. You've lost it, haven't you?"

Glancing down, he saw the pages did indeed look blank, but then again, the physical book was merely a key. The true knowledge was encoded in the spell that was anchored to the tome. No casual onlooker would see anything while he was reading it. Will explained as much to her, closing the book as he did.

"When do I get to read it then?" she asked.

"Hopefully, never. It's meant for whoever the senior living wizard is. At the moment that's me. If it ever falls to you, then you're probably in for a bad time."

Her eyes narrowed. "You're just making me more curious."

Will glared at his cousin. "It will give you nightmares. Promise me you'll never read it unless you're the proper person."

"Or what?"

"Or I won't tell you where I'm going to hide it."

She seemed confused. "You don't trust me not to read it, but you'll tell me where it's kept?"

"I'll be sharing the secret with you and no one else—well, except Selene. Isn't that worth keeping my trust?"

Sammy's shoulders sagged. "You know me too well, but why tell me at all then?"

"Someone should know where to find it, in case something happens to me."

CHAPTER 27

Will teleported back to his father and used an elemental travel disk to quickly make his way back to Cotswold. The sun was just about to set when he arrived, which made everything seem more ominous. The sun wouldn't really matter to Mahak and his subordinates, since the ancient wizard would be easily able to protect them from the ill effects, but the darkness was still an additional weight on Will's psyche. He still had nightmares about what had happened in Cerria with the master vampire Androv.

But I'm not the same as I was then, he reminded himself.

He stopped well before entering the outskirts of the town and dismissed his travel spell. Then he applied a camouflage spell and smoothed his turyn. Even without the camouflage spell, he would be difficult to spot, since the assassin's technique made it hard for anyone to notice him, even if he was fully visible.

At this point, he doubted that the vampires were in the town. For most, it would make sense to arrive early and get the lay of the land, as he had done, but vampires tended to lean heavily on their superior senses. They could see quite well at night, so waiting until the cover of darkness was a given for them in most circumstances.

Of course, Will could see just as well, and far better in a multitude of other situations, so that advantage was effectively null, but Mahak probably didn't know that. Smiling to himself, Will walked slowly toward the center of the town where the market square was and settled himself into an abandoned stall that stood like an island in the middle of the open area. The location was a tactical choice on his part, since he knew the vampires would expect him to choose a less conspicuous place, but he was confident in his concealment. It would be the last place they looked.

Not that he planned to hide; it was just that he wanted to choose his moment. He didn't even stand inside the stall, he stood against one of the exterior walls. *They aren't going to see me anyway, so I might as well be somewhere I can move freely,* he thought to himself.

As a matter of habit, he checked the new force spell he had prepared for the occasion. It wasn't one he could reflex cast, but he thought it would be ideal, and it amused him that the original inspiration for its use had come from his original meeting with the vampire Androv. It *wasn't* the same spell Androv had used, but the form and function were similar to a spell the vampire had used against Lognion's sorcerers.

Will applied an iron-body spell and prepared for a long wait. He didn't know if Mahak's will would be as powerful as Androv's had been, but if it was, he might find himself unable to cast anything but force spells within a certain range of proximity to the vampire wizard. Making sure he couldn't be scratched or bitten was worth the inconvenience of using the defensive spell now, even though he would have to keep it active for however long he was forced to wait.

Leaning against the wall, Will let his mind go blank and slipped into a wakeful trance he had learned during his early days in the Terabinian army when he had to stand watch. Standing guard was boring, and many a soldier suffered the stroke of the lash if they were caught napping, so most learned to adapt. He wasn't asleep, but neither was he quite awake; his eyes were open and his mind was idling, waiting for a fresh sound or motion to bring him back to full awareness. How long he stayed thus he wasn't quite sure, but when something alerted him, the sun was down and darkness had settled across the empty town.

His shoulder was sore, and his legs felt stiff, but he ignored that as he adjusted his vision to suit the current lighting conditions. Will wasn't even certain what had alerted him, but as his view improved, he saw grey figures moving around the market square. The vampires were spreading out, and it was evident from their faces that their attention was on the building he had warded the day before.

Watching them, he noted that some were sniffing at the brisk evening air. No doubt they smelled him, though they still weren't aware of his location. One of them stood just twenty feet away, still staring at the place they thought he was hiding within. *Which one is Mahak?* He still didn't see the wizard, but with different lighting conditions and his relative unfamiliarity with the individual, it was entirely possible he'd overlooked the leader.

The vampires he could see looked ordinary enough, clad in plain tunics and loose trousers, though they carried a variety of two-handed weapons, mostly swords and axes. Will approved of the weapons, but he'd hoped for armor. Most of them were male and of fairly average size, another disappointment.

"Human! Come out! Don't expect me to walk into your traps. Show some trust and meet me in the open!"

The one that spoke was thirty yards distant, closest to the warded home, and Will was certain from the sound of the voice that it was Mahak. The vampire was exceptionally tall, possibly tall enough to have an inch on Tiny, but where Will's friend was wide, Mahak was painfully slender. The blood drinker wore a respectable but not ostentatious wool coat that helped compensate for his thin frame, but if the vampire hadn't called out, Will wasn't sure he would have identified him.

It was time to gamble.

Focusing his attention on Mahak, Will performed a multitude of actions in quick succession. He summoned his falchion and put a silver-sword spell on it within half a second, then teleported directly behind the master vampire. He would have preferred to teleport first, for a better dramatic effect, but he wasn't sure if his will would be strong enough to use the spell at such close range. *Better safe than sorry.*

The creature felt the shift in turyn even though Will kept his arrival completely silent. Mahak was already turning, his face taking on an involuntary expression of surprise as he lifted a hand that was tipped with long claws to defend himself. As Will had expected, the vampire's speed was nothing to laugh at. Without proper preparation, he wouldn't have a chance against the fiend's lightning reactions.

The other Drak'shar were reacting similarly, turning to him, ready to spring to their master's defense, but Will's next spell had already appeared, a force-wall that formed a ring closely around him—and Mahak, with nothing separating the two of them. "I'm right here," said Will evenly. "I have no need for traps. Unless you intend to test me."

Mahak regained control of his reflexes just in time to avoid raking his claws across Will's face, but one of his subordinates failed the test, crashing nose-first into the force-wall. Schooling his expression, Mahak raised one brow and replied, "Most mortals wouldn't risk such proximity to one of my kind. Are you brave or foolish?" The vampire's eyes noted the burning sword, but his visage remained calm.

He was already in the process of determining the answer to the vampire's question as his will contested that of the ancient wizard. Will wasn't trying to cast a new spell; instead, he was trying to take possession of Mahak's protective spell against sunlight. If he failed both, he and the vampire would know it, and at that point his only option would be to kill the Drak'shar before Mahak returned the favor and stripped him of his iron-body spell.

Assuming he won, he would then have the somewhat difficult job of getting control of the blood drinkers after killing their leader, but to his surprise, it didn't come to that. The struggle lasted a brief second, and then Mahak's will crumbled. The spell protecting the vampire tore free and faded away. Will and his opponent both knew immediately, though none of the turyn-blind regulars outside the force-wall were aware that anything had happened.

This was Will's preferred outcome, assuming Mahak was reasonable. Smiling, he kept his voice smooth. "Now that we've said our hellos, can I expect your cooperation?"

Mahak struggled for a second longer, then answered in a voice that suggested he was chewing nails. "Do you expect me to kneel?"

"They can't hear us," said Will reassuringly. "So no need to worry about losing respect. A small bow will suffice. After that we can pretend to be friends, and once this is all over you can go back to whatever you were doing before and tell them I was lucky you were feeling generous. No one has to know you came within a heartbeat of being burned to ash." Sparks played over his fingertips as he spoke.

The vampire wizard said nothing for several tense seconds, then bowed slightly at the waist, tipping his head toward the ground as he did. As he straightened up again, he said, "You are not what I expected."

"You thought Androv's end was a fluke."

Mahak lifted one brow and pressed his lips together in an expression of irony, lifting one hand expressively as he answered, "Let us say I was skeptical—even the best swordsman can trip and die on the blade of a novice. In light of new information, I must reassess my doubts."

Will tried not to let his relief show. Androv's death hadn't been luck, but it had depended on a stroke of inspiration that had struck him at the very end. If Androv hadn't wasted time toying with him, he was certain he never would have survived, much less found victory. Today, he had no idea how it would turn out, though he was certain it wouldn't be such a lopsided battle anymore. "I'll drop the force-wall and allow them to hear us again. When I do, call your people together and have them kneel so there's no mistake in the future."

Mahak nodded, and Will released the spell. Half a minute later, the vampires had gathered in front of him, and after their leader's curt command, they knelt respectfully. None of them were as large as Will had hoped. Singling out one with an unusual stir of turyn around him, Will commanded, "Theravan, join us inside while I discuss my plans with Mahak."

The wizard stood and nodded, hiding his surprise. Theravan hadn't been using any active spells, so he probably hadn't expected to be identified. Will led them to the ward boundary around the house, then reassured them, "It's a simple alarm ward. It won't harm you."

Mahak snorted. "A clever use. I was convinced you were within."

"The simplest things make the best tricks," said Will.

Theravan spoke then, his voice dry and raspy. "Few have such an understanding at your age."

"My teacher was a very irritable old man. I had to be creative to get through his training," Will replied. Once they were inside, he led the two Drak'shar to what must have been the main family room and gestured toward the chairs arranged around the hearth. "Have a seat." From the limnthal, he summoned a bottle of wine and a glass. "I would offer you something to drink, but I'm not willing to part with anything that would suit your taste."

Theravan studied Will's limnthal with interest during the brief moment it was visible, then produced his own and summoned an unmarked bottle, which he offered to Mahak. Before Will could say anything, he asked, "So it's true. Arrogan was your teacher."

Will nodded, and Mahak chimed in, "You and Theravan have something in common. One might describe you as cousins, of a wizardly sort."

"Cousins?" Will was confused. Looking at Theravan, he asked, "Did you know Arrogan?"

Theravan shook his head, causing the wispy white hair that lay against his temple to drift about. "Only in passing. Aislinn was my teacher a decade before she met him. May I see your limnthal again?"

Will reactivated it, and the soft-spoken vampire did the same with his own, holding his hand out so they could compare the two. "They're almost identical," said Theravan before pointing to the final set of runes. "Yours is only different here, in the place where Arrogan added his own signature. Before that, we have the same wizardly ancestry, up to the point where mine ends."

"So Theravan is your uncle, so to speak, in a wizardly sense," clarified Mahak.

"Arrogan was my grandfather, many times removed," said Will.

Mahak laughed. "Not in the true sense. In Theravan's time, wizards put some store in the pedigree of their teachers. He and Arrogan were brothers of a sort, since they shared the same teacher. As Arrogan's 'son,' you would be his nephew."

Theravan waved his hand dismissively. "It wasn't anything official, just a custom of the time."

Will turned to Mahak. "You said 'Theravan's time'—does that mean your time is significantly different?"

"I'm a thousand years his senior," said Mahak. "You would not even recognize the world I was raised in."

Will did a quick bit of mental math. If Theravan was slightly older than Arrogan, he might be seven hundred and that meant Mahak had been around for the majority of two millennia. Without thinking, he asked the first question that occurred to him. "And Androv?"

The ancient vampire answered without hesitation. "He was older than Theravan but younger than me, though I'm not sure if he had a full millennium behind him or not. He wasn't the most sociable, if you understand."

"He was a prick," said Theravan without reservation. "Most of us become somewhat antisocial, but he was exceptional, even for a vampire."

To clarify, Will asked, "Exceptional in...?"

"Being an asshole," said Theravan. "If you want to measure fangs, Mahak was stronger." Mahak gave the younger vampire a disapproving glare, but Theravan didn't seem to care. "Why do you care? He already has your measure, Mahak. There's no use in trying to hide things. You don't want to live forever, do you?"

The confession surprised Will, but he still struggled with part of it. "Fangs?"

Mahak sighed. "A more human expression would be dicks. If we were measuring dicks, I was stronger than Androv."

Still tense, Will couldn't help but chuckle. For vastly older wizards, the two of them were almost likable. *Arrogan has ruined me,* Will realized. *The old man was so irritable that these fiends seem more genial than he was.* He wished he could speak to the ring just to relay that tidbit. As so often happened, he regretted the thought, for it made him feel even more alone. He was unlikely to ever see the ring again. Pushing his dark thoughts aside, he observed, "Your candor is remarkable."

The senior vampire nodded. "Much as I hate to admit it, Theravan is right. Neither of us cares much about survival. This existence is a burden."

Will frowned. "Not to spoil the mood, but I'm fairly certain you were planning to kill me when you arrived. Help me reconcile the disparity here."

Theravan started laughing, which earned him another dark look from Mahak. The senior vampire stared him into silence, then responded, "I intended to establish control. I wouldn't have killed you unless you seemed too weak to be helpful. In truth, I thought our master had tricked you into presenting yourself for easy recruitment."

"And now?" asked Will.

"Now I am not so sure. As badly as we need new wizards, it would be a shame to spoil you if you're truly on our side."

"Spoil?"

Theravan interrupted to clarify, "Turning you would destroy your talents."

Will spoke up. "It's a mistake to think I'm on your side. Let me be clear on that."

Mahak studied him intently for several seconds. "What do you think of when you think of 'our side?'"

That set Will back in his thoughts, but after a brief pause, he gave the simplest answer he could think of. "Death, or rather undeath. Parasitism. You survive in the darkness by virtue of stealing blood from humankind. Am I wrong?"

Theravan's face darkened at Will's response, but Mahak merely nodded with a sense of resignation. "That's the heart of it, I suppose. The ugly reality we cannot deny, but your answer ignores our purpose."

Will broke in before Mahak could begin his self-righteous rant. "You say 'our' purpose, but are you referring to all vampires, or merely yourself?"

Mahak stopped, then answered, "Fair point. I meant Theravan and myself, and once upon a time, Androv too perhaps, before he lost himself to madness. Now, may I finish?"

Will gestured for him to continue.

"The reason we are here, the reason we are *still* here, after all this time, is because of the dragon and its nest. That alone was why we agreed to be transformed into the abominations we now persist as. Why do you think this world hasn't been overrun with vampires? It isn't because we can't increase our numbers—we don't *want* to make more of us," said Mahak.

"What happened in Cerria would seem to contradict that statement."

"That was Androv," hissed Theravan from one side.

Mahak nodded. "Our master chose Androv for a reason, and he might just have foreseen that Androv would lose control or worse, might actively seek to spread our disease."

"Again, you argue against your so-called noble-cause," stated Will.

"Don't be so naïve," returned Mahak. "You already know our master wanted an easy solution for Androv. He hoped Lognion—or you, the dragon's pawn—would remove the madman from the game, but even if you didn't, he had a larger purpose for what happened in Cerria."

Theravan interrupted, raising one hand. "I'd like the record to show that I was against the entire thing. The end does not always justify the means."

Mahak gave the younger vampire a dark glare, then continued, "You know the reason our master chose to survive beyond his own normal span, why he created us, but have you considered what he has been doing for these many centuries?"

Will leaned back in his chair. "From what he told me, it's mostly been a failure, aside from some of the small tidbits of information he's gleaned from the elves and other sources."

"Do you really think he would spend an eternity without finding some way to make use of it? He's been looking for the nest," explained Mahak.

Impatient, Will nodded. "Which he hasn't yet found. Instead, he's spent uncounted centuries fighting wars and treating the nations of Hercynia as playing pieces on a gameboard." Other than finding a method for killing dragons, it was the greatest problem hanging over his head, although Grim Talek had assured him that an answer would soon be revealed—hopefully.

"We're close," said Theravan softly. "So, so close."

Mahak shushed his subordinate. "He's been winning, which is remarkable enough, considering his opponent. Our master is the greatest political genius in history, and over the long centuries he's driven the dragon out of every nation, one by one—except Terabinia. Do you understand?"

Will frowned. "Are you implying what I think?"

Mahak nodded.

"But Terabinia is still a large nation…"

"Consider how large our world is! Finding the nest was an impossible task without narrowing the search down somehow. In the beginning, after the dragon's arrival and initial destruction, Lognion controlled everything through proxies and puppets. The first tribes, the resurgence of small kingdoms, the early empires—they all belonged to the dragon. Our master has had to work his way through all of them, overthrowing good and bad rulers alike, forcing the dragon to surrender control. Darrow was only the latest and probably the final example of this."

Will interrupted, "By Darrow, you mean…?"

The ancient wizard smiled, showing disconcerting fangs. "The Shimerans were one of Grim Talek's more recent conquests, and he used them to create the threat that led to the modern political situation. The Terabinian War for Independence, the Prophet, all of it was orchestrated by our master as a response to the demon threat. Sorcery, the civil war that split Darrow, your teacher's betrayal to rid the world of the heart-stone enchantment—all these things were byproducts of our master's war with the dragon.

"Across the centuries and continents, through the rise and fall of empires, our master has driven the dragon from every nation, until all that remained was Terabinia, the half of Darrow that Lognion *chose* to retain when it was clear he couldn't maintain control of both," concluded Mahak.

"Because the nest is there," muttered Will, his mind reeling at the implications.

Theravan spoke up. "The game of nations was never a game, not for our master. It was the only method he could use to narrow down the location of the nest."

Considering all the wars, suffering, and ensuing chaos, Will could barely comprehend what he had heard. "Surely there was another way?"

Mahak shook his head. "The elves abandoned Hercynia when the dragon came. In fact, they traded with the fae for their new world, in exchange for allowing the fae to access this plane, and when demonkind threatened their new home, they traded knowledge of this world to them to guarantee safety for their new dimension."

Will's mouth fell slightly agape. He had always understood why the goddamn cat hated demons, and even the fae seemed understandable, but the elves had seemed blameless.

"In their defense, it seemed logical, since they knew this world was already doomed," added Theravan.

"If you hadn't stopped Androv, we might already have the final puzzle piece in our hands," said the older vampire.

"A pyrrhic victory," commented Theravan. "Allowing Androv to run amok in Cerria never sat well with me. Even to find the nest, destroying an entire city was just too much."

"That's monstrous," declared Will.

Mahak nodded. "Enough time and we all become villains. Our master is the finest example, but I am no different. Even gentle Theravan, barely past the normal span of a wizard, is half numb to the wellbeing of mortals and the moral concerns of good and evil." Looking up from his hands, Mahak's eyes bored into Will. "But some things are necessary, and only a greater monster can defeat a dragon. We chose to join Grim Talek for that purpose."

Will let out a long exhalation. "And everything I've done has gotten in your way—stopping Androv, liberating Darrow."

"I prefer this outcome," said Theravan. "We lost the war, but you've driven Lognion into the open and given Terabinia into our master's hands. Soon enough we will know the exact location of the nest, *and* your city was spared a genocide."

Something else was clear to him as well. Grim Talek had asked him not to deal with the fae, even for simple matters. Will had thought it might be to isolate him, or restrict his access to certain information, but in light of the past he realized it was because of their ties to the elves. Old promises might force them to betray him. Closing his eyes, Will rubbed at the bridge of his nose, fighting back an incipient headache. When he opened them again, he addressed the two vampires. "And we still have a more pressing troll problem to deal with."

Theravan smirked, then nodded at Mahak. "You have an expert to help with that. Mahak lived through the first troll outbreak. I'm sure he has a few tricks that can help."

Mahak snorted. "No tricks, but I know a spell that will interest you."

Will leaned forward. "Oh?"

"As I'm sure you've realized, burning bodies is a pain in the ass, requiring far more turyn than is often practical. In my time, we developed an efficient cremation spell to make the chore easier," explained Mahak.

"How much easier?"

The vampire shrugged. "It's still work, but for rendering flesh into ash, it takes roughly half the turyn."

Will's eyes widened. "That's significant. Much better than the battle spells I've seen."

"That's the difference. This produces a slow burn that efficiently uses fats and certain other tissues to support the incineration. The initial cast is too slow and requires too much turyn to be practical in battle, but for getting rid of bodies it is perfect and only needs to be cast once, hence the savings in time and energy," said the ancient wizard.

"So it isn't usable in combat?" asked Will.

Mahak shook his head. "It's too slow. It's only useful for corpses, or trolls that have been rendered insensible, otherwise they might cut or tear off the burning locus. A troll could cut itself completely in half if necessary to escape the part of its body that was burning."

Will nodded. "The warriors you brought, will they be of any use?"

"You were hoping they'd be bigger, weren't you?" snickered Theravan.

"Well, now that you mention it..."

"You've seen enough trolls in combat to know that there's no matching them physically," said Mahak. "Even as strong as the Drak'shar are, we would have to be the size of a troll to even approach parity, and even then, our healing..."

Will interrupted, "I've studied the differences. Your bodies can heal almost any wound, but they don't replace lost parts. Tear a troll in two and you will eventually have two trolls, but cut a vampire in half and you wind up with two crippled vampires."

Theravan rubbed his chin before interjecting, "It's been a long time since I met a mortal with enough experience, much less wit, to observe and draw those conclusions."

Mahak rolled his eyes. "If you're done with the compliments, can we get back to the topic?" Theravan shrugged, and his senior continued, "As I was saying, pound for pound, trolls are slightly stronger, they're much larger, and for creatures their size they are impressively fast. The young ones are as cunning as wolves, and some of the old ones may be smarter than some humans. Our only advantage is magic and usually, intelligence. Using Drak'shar as your fighters solves a few problems, but they won't be able to simply overpower the trolls. What we do have, given our smaller size, is better speed and mobility. That is why I didn't bother limiting my choices to the biggest Drak'shar I could find."

"So how did you choose?" asked Will.

Mahak looked at his subordinate, then answered, "I didn't. I brought them all."

"All?" Will gaped at him. "You want me to believe there are only ten or twenty vampires in Darrow?"

"Twenty-two," corrected Theravan. "Twenty-four if you count Mahak and myself. There are others scattered across various nations, but not many."

Will couldn't reconcile the new information. "I don't understand. How does Grim Talek accomplish anything with so few?"

Mahak snorted. "Most of his servants are human, obviously. The Drak'shar are kept few to minimize the risk of what happened in Cerria with Androv. Generally, our master uses the Drak'shar for special tasks that require great stealth, and Theravan and I are reserved for only the most critical of matters."

"Then let's discuss how best to clear out this troll den," said Will.

CHAPTER 28

Two days later, Will and his father stood on the hillside just below the entrance to the troll cave. The morning sunlight was just beginning to crest the hill to the east of them, and it illuminated the two men, the sorcerers they had brought with them, and the vampire contingent gathered around them.

The vampires looked mildly uncomfortable, for although they were protected by Mahak and Theravan's spells, the sun was a constant reminder that death was close by. Will's father didn't look any happier, however, and he nervously eyed the fanged warriors around them.

A solitary troll stood guard outside the cave entrance, and though the wind favored them, the troll had obviously smelled something, for it kept looking from side to side as though searching for something. Mahak turned to Will and mouthed, 'Ready?'

Will nodded, then answered clearly, "Go ahead. They won't hear anything unless I allow it."

The vampire glanced at his subordinates, and together they raced from the cover of the trees toward the wary troll. It saw them coming, and although they were faster, the distance gave the troll plenty of time to react. Lifting a heavy club that seemed slender in the troll's hands, it batted the first vampire into the air, sending the hapless Drak'shar tumbling down the hillside. The troll released the club then, favoring the speed of its clawed hands to catch the next two warriors around their waists.

Will was damping the sound of the fight, but in his mind, he could imagine the sickening crunch as the troll squeezed, breaking two spines and nearly bisecting the undead assailants. The vampires spasmed, their mouths open in silent screams as they clawed and bit at the thick, greyish green skin of the troll's arms.

The rest of the vampires fared much better, striking at the troll's legs with short, heavy blades to cripple it. Theravan circled around and used a force-wall to block the cave entrance while Mahak darted in at an opportune moment to drive his slender smallsword directly into the troll's weak spot, its groin.

Few knew that trolls' brains were located directly behind their genitals, rather than inside their skulls. Fewer still survived meeting a troll long enough to communicate that knowledge to anyone else. The troll began thrashing senselessly, smashing the two vampires it had in its fists against the rocky ground. Mark Nerrow had been waiting for this, and he moved up quickly, casting the cremation spell that Mahak had shared with them the day before.

Meanwhile, the other vampire warriors severed the troll's arms at the elbow and wrist to free their broken companions. They tossed the separate troll pieces back onto the smoldering torso while everyone waited—waited for the vampires to heal, and waited for the troll to finish burning away. Once those two things were complete, Mahak started to dismiss his force-wall, but Will bade him to wait.

Turning to his father and the two human sorcerers that had come with him, he told them, "Time for the breathing spell." They used the spell immediately, for they'd all had it prepared beforehand.

The spell he was referring to actually was technically named 'water breathing.' It had been given the name simply because of its original purpose. The spell created a concentrated pocket of air within the caster's chest that allowed them to go for thirty minutes or more without needing to breathe, which was likely to be necessary once they started burning bodies underground. Will had actually never used it in water, but it had served him well on several occasions when breathing was unwise. The main downside was that it also made it impossible to speak, but they had planned out their roles and tasks carefully with that in mind.

The troll's remains finished turning to ash, and it was time to move. Mahak removed the force-wall from the entrance, and the vampire squad charged into the dim interior. Screams followed, and two of the undead warriors were thrown bodily back outside, their bones crushed by the impact of massive clubs. Will started to move forward, wanting to assist, but his father put a hand on his shoulder, silently shaking his head no.

None of the other Drak'shar were hurled out, and after a few seconds Mahak entered the cave to erect a new force-wall farther in, preventing any other trolls from emerging to help their fallen brothers. Mahak signalled for the humans to follow a second later, and when Will went in, he saw three trolls on the ground, their bodies in various states of dismemberment. Although they had won, the vampires looked even worse; of the nearly two dozen Drak'shar who had charged in, only a handful appeared uninjured. The rest were busy reattaching various body parts or simply resting while their bodies recovered from shattered bones and torn flesh.

Will wondered how many times they could repeat that trick before they began to get dangerously thirsty, but almost as soon as he had that thought, Theravan began moving among them, passing out small clay jars of blood summoned from his limnthal.

The sorcerers did their part, beginning the cremation of the three trolls while Will studied the force-wall blocking the tunnel that led farther into the hill. On the other side were more trolls. Two beat at the invisible wall with clubs while another dug at the ground, trying to get around the barrier. Will could see at least two or three more behind them. The timing for their next advance would be tricky. If Mahak wasn't careful, they might wind up with all five trolls among them, and given what had happened with just three, that would be a losing fight for them.

Of course, Will and the sorcerers could probably turn the situation around, but that would cost them extra turyn, not to mention the risk of losing one of the sorcerers. For their plan to work, they needed to move forward in economical steps, taking the trolls down in small groups while they conserved their strength. Depending on how many trolls were down there, it might take a considerable amount of energy to burn them all, even using Mahak's more efficient cremation spell. *It might be just a few more, but then again, it could be dozens,* thought Will.

The cave was filled with choking smoke that burned Will's eyes, making him grateful that he didn't have to inhale. The smoke made it difficult for even the vampires to see, while for the humans it was even worse. Only Will was unaffected, thanks to his ability to continually tune his vision to types of light that ignored the smoke. Currently, that meant his view was a mixture of strange colors and contrasts. He'd long since learned to ignore the odd colors as he adjusted his vision—the most important thing was contrast and visibility.

The vampires could see heart-light, which meant for them the humans and trolls were glowing in the darkness, while their colder bodies were merely a slightly different shade of grey against the nearly black of the cave walls. The smoke did interfere with heart-light, though, so Will had adjusted his vision such that everything had become lighter and darker shades of black, purple, and grey, with a high degree of variance between the different shades. The smoke was entirely invisible to him, allowing him a perfect view of everyone and everything.

Mahak and Theravan moved close to the force-wall, and after signaling to one another, they dropped the barrier. Theravan would raise the next a split second later, presumably in the midst of the trolls so that only one or two could contest with the vampires. A large stone flew through the smoke as soon as the force-wall was lowered, however, and it would have smashed into Theravan, who failed to see it.

Will stopped it with a point-defense shield, giving Theravan a second to place the next force-wall properly. They wound up with two trolls among them. The humans had already retreated, but even so, the violence was so extreme that it threatened to escape the control of the Drak'shar. One of the trolls was fairly skillful and managed to evade the crippling cuts the vampires directed at its legs. That meant it remained free to act for a minute longer than the previous trolls.

A minute was a long time in battle. Half the vampires were down, broken, crushed, and torn. Mahak, being free from shield duty, tried to aid the warriors with a well-placed force-lance but only succeeded in taking out one of his own defenders. The battle was simply too chaotic and fast moving.

Watching it all, Will took note of several things: One, the vampires were incredibly fast, but there were still limits to how quickly a physical body could move, and the trolls were nearly as quick despite their bulk. Two, Will's training had given him the experience needed to follow the fight. In the past, he had often been overwhelmed by the rapidity and chaos of battle, especially when vampires were involved. Apparently, his years of training, combined with his time at war, had taught him more than he realized. *Enough to see that Mahak is relatively inexperienced in battle,* he observed. *I guess being ancient doesn't necessarily mean one has been in a lot of fights.*

Fifteen warriors were down now, and a thrown leg nearly struck Theravan, which might have been a disaster if the wizard had lost concentration on the force-wall keeping the rest of the trolls at bay. Will couldn't bear watching any longer. The plan was for the humans to stay out of the conflict, but he was beginning to think the conflict might come to him.

Will stepped forward, putting a momentary shield in front of Theravan to stop the leg attack while using a light-darts spell to tip the fight in favor of the Drak'shar. The five light missiles slipped through the mass of whirling fighters, neatly finding their targets on the troll's body—two in each knee and one in the groin-brain. The damage to the knees wasn't enough to drop the troll, but it would slow the troll considerably. The single missile to the groin did even better, causing the monster to spasm and freeze momentarily.

The vampire warriors cut it into pieces before it could recover.

More of the same, the sorcerers burned the trolls' bodies while the Drak'shar recovered. The one difference this time, however, was that the trolls on the other side of the force-wall had disappeared, retreating farther back into the hill. That made Will wonder, were there simply too few left, or were they regrouping? Perhaps there was a larger chamber deeper down, a place where it would be harder to separate them.

A glance at Mahak's face told him the ancient wizard was wondering the same thing, and Will could see his father was similarly worried. Not being able to speak was becoming a nuisance. Even the vampires didn't want to inhale the smoke, though it wouldn't kill them.

A rumble shook the ground, and Will saw the cave beyond Theravan's force-wall collapse. The cave-in was far enough back that none of the others could see it, although they felt it well enough. *Are they so desperate they're entombing themselves?* Will wondered. *Or...?*

Understanding hit him suddenly. It was a trap. There must be another exit, which meant... Will checked his tracking spell, something he'd ignored since they entered. The marker was no longer deeper in, it was above and behind them, in the direction of the entrance they had come through. *Shit!*

Something heavy rolled down the sloping, rocky floor and although Will wasn't the closest, he was probably the only one able to clearly see what it was—a barrel, leaking fluid as it came. The humans were the closest, being on the end of the tunnel closest to the original entrance. Curious and alarmed, one of the sorcerers created a light to try and see better.

Unable to speak, Will grabbed the back of his father's shirt and pulled him away. He was about to try and do the same with one of the sorcerers when the liquid caught fire. It happened so quickly Will wasn't sure if it was a flame from the sorcerers that lit it, or a flame tossed in from outside—either way, the result was the same.

Will sealed the tunnel with a second force-wall as the space behind them turned into an inferno. The sorcerers died badly, leaving Will and his father as the only remaining humans. They were now trapped between two force-walls, and their only way out was a burning cavern. As they watched, Will saw more barrels roll down into the fire, followed by large pieces of wood and dead tree limbs.

Even safe behind the force-wall, they would eventually run out of air, assuming the heat didn't cook them first. He had to admire the simplicity and effectiveness of the trap. Will considered their situation

again. Most of the vampires were recovering, and the troll bodies
were still burning, adding to their growing heat problem. Mahak and
Theravan were staring up at the cave ceiling, obviously giving thought
to how much stone lay between them and the surface.

With the right spells and enough turyn, escape was definitely
possible. Will's grave-digging spell would do the trick, assuming
they had enough time, but it wasn't ideal. Moving into the ethereal
plane wouldn't work, since geologic features were usually old
enough to be duplicated in both planes, so they'd simply be trapped
underground in the ethereal. It wouldn't be on fire, though, which
was a significant improvement.

Mark Nerrow had a greater earth elemental, which would easily be
enough to allow them to tunnel quickly out, but they might face a troll
ambush on the surface. Will could teleport himself and a few others, but
he didn't fancy surprising any of his friends and loved ones by arriving
with a pack of vampires. He also didn't know what the limits were.
Could he take just one or two people with him, or more? How many
trips would be required? His father would have to be last so he could
return each time.

Moving to the ethereal and exiting through a non-burning cave
seemed to be the safest route, but Will didn't know a spell that would
allow him to take everyone with him. Then he noticed Mahak pointing
at his father, then motioning to the ceiling. Mark nodded, and the two of
them worked out a non-verbal plan. They would be using the elemental
to escape.

That still put them at risk of an ambush when they emerged. Will
caught his father's eye and conjured a small light so the other man could
see him clearly, then he pointed at Mahak and nodded agreement before
pointing at himself and then at the burning entrance.

Mark Nerrow frowned, but Will patted himself over his heart,
hoping his father would understand he meant for him to trust his son.
That done, he began constructing an ethereal-jaunt spell. Mahak and
Theravan recognized the spell structure and nodded approvingly, while
Mark's earth elemental began creating a sloping tunnel that would lead
them up to the surface.

Will finished the spell, but waited until his father and vampires
were partway up their new tunnel before dismissing his force-wall
and transferring himself to the ethereal plane. His world immediately
became much calmer. Gone were the flames and smoldering troll bodies,
replaced by an empty grey cave that was virtually identical, except for a
large boulder that occupied one side of the chamber.

That seemed odd. The ground, earth, rivers, and similarly old things were generally identical between the two planes. The only things that varied were man-made structures and similar things. Oh, and the fact that the ethereal plane was nearly uninhabited, except for rare interdimensional hunters like...

Phase spiders! Will's realization came just as the giant arachnid unfolded with deceptively slow grace, then lunged at him with blinding speed. In appearance, it looked somewhat like a wolf spider, though he couldn't be sure what color it was with his altered vision. Fangs and two razor-tipped legs stabbed at him, making a simple point-defense shield inadequate. Will used a force-wall instead, then followed with an iron-body spell. His heart was pounding so loudly it threatened to deafen him.

The spider's fangs struck the force effect and began to glow with a strange grey turyn that Will recognized. It was similar to the spell Androv had once used to destroy his force spells. *Did they get the idea from studying these creatures?* Will's mind provided a wealth of questions, but his body was warning him that he needed to stay focused on the present. The phase spider's entire body was now sheathed in the strange turyn, and he knew he could only hide behind his rapidly dissolving force-wall for a few seconds longer.

As the first hole opened Will fired off a light-darts spell. The result was worse than ineffective; the spider's carapace deflected the light missiles, sending them off in random directions. One even bounced back to strike part of the force wall.

He had a teleport spell prepared, so he used it to move himself to the opposite side of the chamber then launched a fire-bolt. It wasn't deflected, but it had no observable effect. A force-lance seemed to shake the creature slightly, but not much more—there was definitely no damage. The flowing grey power that sheathed the spider seemed to have some of the same properties as a force spell, with the exception that it was corrosive and flexible.

The spider was already on him again.

This time, Will opted for a more martial defense, with a heavy falchion in one hand and a steel buckler in the other. He used the buckler and a rapid-fire succession of point-defense shields to block the spider's sharp, probing legs while he chopped at it with the sharp edge of the sword. The monster's speed and power put his skills to the test, and the sheer mass of its body made him regret it whenever he was forced to use the buckler to block one of the attacks. He was being rapidly driven back toward the cave wall, and he didn't have another teleport spell prepared.

He didn't have to be prescient to know what would happen once he was cornered. With a thought, he summoned a silver coin and used it to cast the silver-sword spell. Argent flames raced along the length of his falchion, enhancing its cutting power and lighting up the darkness of the cave. The effect on the spider was negligible.

Desperate, Will unleashed a wind-wall, though he didn't expect the area effect spell to do much against his heavily armored opponent. He was right, but one thing caught his eye. The spider's grey turyn was ripped away briefly by the fierce wind, exposing matte black chitin. The edge of his falchion cut into the spider's body slightly, marking the hard exoskeleton, though it still didn't penetrate.

The fluid grey turyn flowed back over the spider's body, protecting it once more, and at the same time, Will felt hard stone against his back. He was out of time.

Drawing strongly on his reserves, Will released a second wind-wall. He infused it with power for only a second, then dropped the spell and launched a force-lance straight into the arachnid's hissing face—right between the fangs. The monster's head crumpled inward, but Will didn't pause to examine the effect of his strike. He followed it with another, and another—five, six, seven force-lances slammed into the vulnerable spider's carapace.

The creature was dead and nearly unrecognizable when Will finally reined himself in, his body shaking with adrenaline. In his mind, all he could see were the dripping fangs inches from his face. *That close, I was that close to dying,* he told himself, trying to shake off the fear that washed over him now that the fight was over. He didn't have time to waste, though.

He started moving back toward the cave entrance, drawing turyn in rapidly to replenish his spent reserves; depending on what he found outside, he might need to respond quickly. Less than a minute later, he was outside, blinking against the weak glare of the ethereal sun. His eyes adjusted quickly, but Will took an active hand in the process, adjusting them to see into the spectrum that crossed between the material and ethereal planes.

Four trolls were gathered around the cave entrance, which now appeared to be partially blocked with large stones and small tree trunks. Smoke was billowing out through the gaps, testifying to the powerful blaze burning deeper in. As Will watched, the trolls seemed to take note of something, lifting their heads and scanning the area before moving uphill. At different points, they would stop and put a clawed hand against the rocky soil, feeling for something that couldn't be seen. It wasn't hard to guess what they were searching for. *They can feel or hear the ground shifting as Mark and his elemental tunnel upward.*

The trolls spread out, arming themselves with broken saplings that made effective clubs. One went back to the cave entrance for a moment, only to return with a great sword that despite its size would only serve the troll as a one-handed weapon. Will guessed that the one with the stolen sword must be the leader.

Having four trolls swinging at them with clubs when they emerged from the earth wasn't an ideal way to make an exit. Will trusted that his father and the two ancient vampire wizards would be expecting something of the sort, but he didn't want to risk the outcome. Instead, he formed an impromptu plan and immediately moved to implement it, before caution and reason could instill the fear that would keep him from acting.

He moved to place himself directly behind the leader, made sure he had enough turyn, then released his ethereal-jaunt spell, allowing himself to rematerialize. In the past, he might have used a wind-wall, but he wasn't sure the destructive force would be enough to incapacitate the trolls even briefly. Cutting them wasn't enough; their limbs would need to be sheared through to stop them, and trolls had very thick arms and legs—plus there was the nightmare scenario of trying to locate all the troll bits afterward to make sure they were burned.

Rather than deal with that, Will chose a wild magic solution. Using his talent with lightning, he sent arcing bolts of power through all four of the nearby trolls before they could react to his sudden appearance. This was unlike when he drew down lightning from the sky—that would have taken time and a massive amount of turyn to form the connection to the clouds above. In this case, he was attacking directly and paying the cost directly from his own turyn reserves as he would with regular spells.

It was quick and dirty, and for most opponents it would have been fatal, but Will was under no delusions about how long it would keep the trolls twitching and helpless. Summoning his falchion, he began stabbing the now prone trolls in the groin, moving quickly from one to the next and then back again. A direct attack against the brain could keep one helpless for a minute, sometimes longer. He simply had to keep it up until his father and the vampires could safely exit and get to the business of burning the bodies.

The next five minutes played out as a strange, macabre dance, and Will was beginning to worry that the others would never arrive, but eventually they did. Once things had calmed down and the underwater breathing spells had been dismissed, his father made an observation. "You did so well with these four by yourself, I'm wondering if you really needed us at all."

"I wanted you to feel useful," countered Will with a lopsided grin. "Besides, there were more than four in the cave, not to mention it's hard to burn them while running back and forth stabbing them over and over." He didn't even bother bringing up the phase spider he had encountered.

Will checked his tracking spell, and sure enough it had ended, meaning he had killed the troll with the mark. If there were any more, they'd have to find them with other methods. The vampire warriors spread out and searched the hillside until the other exit was found. It was only partly traversable, however, since the trolls had collapsed it some distance inside the hill to trap them. They found no trace of other trolls, aside from the ones they had already killed and burned.

A discussion ensued, during which it was agreed that the vampires would spend a few nights searching the area to see if any traces of other trolls could be found. The governor would return to his troops and patrol the surrounding region for a week before returning to Myrsta, assuming no more trolls were found. Will, on the other hand, would leave. He had a larger task to attend to.

"Will."

He froze, feeling an overwhelming sense of Selene's presence around him. The voice had been hers, although it hadn't truly been her actual voice. It was a spirit voice, heard only by him, thanks to their connection in the astral plane. Turning slowly, Will saw her ghostly form hovering close beside him. Somehow, she had left her body and traveled to him, just as he had done with her in the past.

Several terrible thoughts passed through his head in quick succession. Was she dead? If so, she might cling to their world long enough to visit him. Alternatively, she might have been dispossessed of her body as he had once been. She didn't appear distressed, though. If anything, the feeling he got from her was one of extreme irritation, which meant she had probably learned to project herself.

He had some explaining to do. *Shit.*

"Are you all right? Did you learn to leave your body, or...?"

Will felt a flash of anger from her as she replied, "Someone else taught me, no thanks to you. I tried to reach you last night, but something blocked me."

"I use an anti-possession spell when I sleep. It keeps me from wandering accidentally, but it also prevents these connections, similar to the barrier of a force spell," he explained hurriedly. A second later, he asked, "Wait. He's teaching you?"

"Yes. He's an excellent teacher, compared to a certain husband I won't bother to name." Will didn't answer. He didn't know what to say, and eventually she continued, "You need to start talking, *husband.*" The last word was emphasized in a way that made him think perhaps the phase spider hadn't been as frightening as he had originally thought.

A hand fell on his shoulder. "William? Who are you talking to?" It was his father.

"Selene," he replied instantly, not taking his eyes off of her. "I think I'd better go. Will you be all right here?"

The governor was probably nervous about being left alone with so many vampires, especially since the sorcerers he had brought with him were gone. Will glanced at Theravan, who for some reason he felt especially able to trust. The vampire wizard nodded, and Will knew he understood. Mark Nerrow answered then, his pride refusing to admit to any anxiousness. "Do as you will. I can get back to my command without assistance."

"Thanks, Father." He still wasn't used to saying it, but he wanted to. He had always wanted to, despite his former grievances. Then he focused on Selene. "Are you alone? We should talk in person."

Her reply was acidic. "I wouldn't leave my body unless it was secure."

"Return to your body. I'll be there as soon as I can construct a teleport."

She frowned. "How? Did you figure out the spell?"

He nodded.

Her features registered a fresh pain. "You didn't tell me you found a solution. More secrets?"

Frustration ate into him. "It's not a secret. It was recent. Just wait, I'll be there in a few minutes." She was gone before he finished the sentence. If the mountain air hadn't been so brisk, he might have started sweating.

Wasting no time, he began preparing a fresh teleport spell.

CHAPTER 29

As soon as Will arrived, he stepped toward Selene. It was a natural reaction after their separation; despite everything that had passed, he needed to hold her. Even angry, she would understand that.

Selene took two rapid steps backward, maintaining the distance between them. She raised her hands as a barrier. "Not so fast."

Will felt a stab of pain at her denial. "I'll explain everything in a moment. I've just missed you t—"

Her eyes narrowed. "First let's make certain you are who you appear to be."

He frowned. "*You* found me. The astral connection can't be faked. Then I teleported here, which also requires an astral connection. Who else could I be?"

Selene replied in a calm voice that nevertheless held an edge of suppressed fury. "That's an assumption that I doubt you have evidence to support. I've already been deceived in ways that I didn't think possible. I won't assume anything. Hold out your hand, palm up."

With an air of resignation, he did so while his wife reached into a small pouch and removed something small. Her hand flashed forward so quickly that if it had been anyone else, he might have shielded himself, or at least flinched back. Since it was her, he kept his hand steady. A new pain, this one entirely physical, shot through his hand. Selene pulled her hand away, revealing a tiny knife blade—no, it was a scalpel, he realized. Blood welled and began to drip from a wound on his palm.

She had stabbed the steel implement deep into the meat of his palm. As he watched, she rubbed some of his blood between her fingertips, sniffed it, and then even dared to taste it with her tongue. That done, she crafted a quick spell and used it on the blood. A wisp of turyn floated above her hand, and though Will couldn't see the image it showed her he guessed it was a picture of himself. The spell was reminiscent of a tracking and identification spell she had used years before to catch him leaving an anonymous message.

"Given the truth of what you said, I should probably learn that spell as well," he observed.

Looking up at him with damp yet angry eyes, she agreed, "You should."

"You didn't need that much blood, did you?" His hand was dripping steadily onto the floor.

"A pin prick would have been sufficient. It only takes a drop."

Will nodded. "I probably deserved it." Taking a moment, he constructed a minor healing spell, then started to use it on his bleeding palm.

Selene waved a finger through his spell construct. Rather than resist, he let her disrupt the spell. "That will only seal the skin. It was a deep cut."

"It's not worth a regeneration potion."

She tsked at him. "There's a lot of medical magic between a simple suture spell and regeneration." A complex spell construct formed rapidly over her palm as she spoke. When it was ready, she closed her eyes and pressed it into his cut.

Will tried not to hiss as the turyn wove in and out, drawing together not just the skin, but the fat, fascia, and the damaged muscle beneath. He'd seen similar spells demonstrated during his one class covering healing magic, and he knew that such spells required more than simply memorizing a rune structure. The caster had to have intimate knowledge of anatomy and physiology in order to apply the spell properly. Specialized spell versions took into account a variety of factors, including the type of tissue, the orientation of the muscle, the number of different muscles, which body part was being worked on—the list of variables was nearly endless. Magic used to heal physical trauma was exceedingly complex, and that was just in the case of wounds to relatively healthy individuals. The treatment of longstanding diseases and illnesses was an entirely different matter.

He had once shown some unusual success adapting wild magic and herbs to treat septic wounds, but that was a small thing compared to the techniques used by wizardly specialists, like Doctor Morris at Wurthaven, who coincidentally was the only person he had seen demonstrate such magic. Glancing at the room around them, Will asked, "Are we in the Healing and Psyche building?"

Selene nodded. "I stepped into one of the private consult rooms before I tried to contact you."

Will rubbed at his palm, trying to rub away the dull ache that remained. "Isn't there supposed to be an anesthetic component to those spells?"

Her eyes glinted maliciously. "I took it out." Then she opened her arms. "You get one embrace, then you have a lot of talking to do."

He hesitated. "Promise you won't stab me again? Are you hiding a weapon?"

"No promises."

Wrapping her in his arms, Will pulled her tightly against his chest. Her arms wound around his waist, and he felt her hands curl into fists as she gripped the back of his tunic. It was the sort of hug that spoke of fear, loneliness, and quiet desperation, and it made his heart ache to think of what her recent weeks had been like. It probably would have been hard regardless, but the fact that he had left her to face it alone had made it much harder. "I'm sorry," he whispered.

"I don't forgive you," she growled into his chest before pushing him away and wrinkling her nose. "By the Mother! You stink! You smell like Myrsta, after we burned the bodies."

"You smell like ammonia and—is that phenol?" he returned.

She nodded. "We've started using it to clean the treatment areas. It seems to reduce the rate of infection after surgeries. Stop deflecting. Why do you smell like a badly managed crematorium?"

"Because I've been burning bodies." He gave her an abbreviated explanation of dealing with the trolls that was so short it was practically criminal. The only reason he got away with it was because he had to move on to explaining a lot more of what had occurred before he had started burning trolls.

He had barely gotten through a description of his conversation with Grim Talek in Barrowden before she stopped him. "Close your eyes," she ordered. When he gave her a curious look, she added, "Do it."

Will did, though he questioned his choice when he heard the slow, distinctive sound of steel being drawn, as of a sword from a sheath. "Umm, if you're planning to do something permanent, warn me first."

"Worried?"

Yes! he thought, but he answered with more consideration, "Mildly, but I trust you, and if I can't then it doesn't matter what happens to me."

Something sharp and cold pressed against his throat. "I felt the same way, until I found out the person holding the blade wasn't even the man I loved. Even that, I could have endured, but soon after I discovered that the viper pressed to my bosom was there because *you* sent it. That made it so much worse. Do you know why I asked you to close your eyes?"

He swallowed. "No."

"Because it makes you blind, like I was. It makes you helpless. How does it feel?"

Will made the mistake of trying to answer logically. "You wouldn't have healed my hand if you were going to do something worse. I believe—"

The edge pressed harder against his neck, digging into his skin. "Stop, or I'll cut your damn head off and then we'll see if a regeneration potion will fix terminal stupidity." After a moment of silence, Selene continued, "Answer the question. How does it feel?"

Oh. "It feels bad."

"Elaborate, William."

"It hurts, but not just here." Will lifted a hand to touch his neck, careful not to appear as though he might try to grab the blade. He lowered his hand to touch his chest over his heart, "It hurts here the most."

"Why? Is it because you feel helpless?"

"Yes, but not only that. The worst part is knowing you might not forgive me. Thinking you might hate me is infinitely more painful."

"Go to hell!" The cold metal disappeared from his neck, and something crashed loudly into the wall. Opening his eyes, Will saw that it was an instrument tray. Selene's face was red, and her eyes were wet with tears.

"I'm sorry."

Selene's eyes locked onto his, accusing him. "You have no idea. You felt that for a minute. It's been weeks! I could barely sleep, or eat! I felt sick the entire time, not knowing if you were alive or dead. Whether you were angry or whether you missed me, or worse, maybe I just didn't matter at all—that's how I grew up, William. Do you realize that? The monster that raised me didn't care at all. I was less than nothing. You never made me feel like that, until now."

He blinked, trying to assimilate her words. He'd known it would hurt her, but he hadn't considered the depth of her reaction, or how it related to her past. "I don't know what to say," he told her. "Sorry isn't good enough, but—"

"Then shut up," she replied huskily, her voice thick with emotion. "But don't you dare turn away." Coming back, she seized the front of his tunic and held onto him. "I may or may not forgive you, but don't ever turn away. Stay with me, do you understand? Even if I never get over this, you have to stay and suffer through it with me."

Holding onto her, he couldn't imagine ever letting go, but her last words sparked a dark thought. "You've talked to Janice, right?"

"Trying to do everything alone is stupid," growled Selene against his shoulder. "We've been working on a better plan."

"You're right."

"When did you come to that moment of enlightenment?" she asked. Her arms were around him now, squeezing him with a strength that hardly seemed possible from such a slender frame.

"After Janice berated me."

"Are you deliberately trying to make me jealous?"

Will chuckled quietly, which Selene could easily feel, earning him a louder growl. "It's just because I talked to her first." His wife began to twist, but he held her tightly to keep her from escaping. "It was easier. Facing her pain and anger was easier than seeing it in you, because you're the one who has my heart. Hurting you is twice as hard, because I feel your pain and my own at the same time."

Selene's face was still hidden from view, and her voice was muffled by his clothing. "Better, though you're lucky I still don't have a limnthal or I might have summoned a dagger before you finished your answer."

"Let's fix that. Right now."

"You have it memorized?"

"Yes, but I have it written out as well, for reference," he told her. They separated, and he summoned his journal. The exam table served adequately as a desk while he created the complex rune structure and double checked it against his notes. It took a solid fifteen minutes, even though he finished putting it together in ten; double-checking it was of paramount importance since Selene would carry the magic with her for life.

She didn't remain idle, however. Selene observed everything carefully and verified his work from the written page as well. "You added something extra at the end."

"It's a signature."

"What?"

"Every teacher adds a symbol at the end, as a signature. You can trace the runes above back to the very first wizard. It's a lineage of teachers and pupils. The one above mine represents Arrogan and the one just above that is Aislinn's," he explained. "Fortunately, I met an ancient vampire who explained it to me before I did yours, otherwise you would have been missing a proper ending, though I'm sure it would have still worked."

"I have your ring," said Selene. "You could have saved yourself some trouble if you had kept it with you."

Will froze for a moment, then relaxed. "So, he stuck you with it. I'm not sure how I feel about that."

"You'd rather Grim Talek carry it? It's your heirloom."

He shook his head. "I'll want it back eventually, but it would be a millstone around my neck as things are currently."

"Why?"

"Shhh." Satisfied with his work, Will lifted the new limnthal into the air and held his hand out to the Queen of Terabinia. Selene's hand touched his, and he passed ownership of the magic to her. "Press it against your chest just over your heart. It could be anywhere, but that's the traditional place to keep it, where your heart-stone enchantment used to be linked." She did, and afterward they spent a quarter hour going over the practical aspects of the enchantment, how to store and summon specific items and how to empty the entire pocket dimension when necessary. "It will get to the point where you don't even think about it consciously."

She nodded, then returned to the previous topic. "Why is the ring a burden?"

He answered with a single word. "Grandmother."

"You're avoiding her name?" speculated Selene.

Nodding, he continued, "Among other things, yes. I have to avoid repeating it or I'll make contact. The fae were involved in several ancient agreements with the elves, the demons, and possibly even the dragon. I don't know the specific arrangements, but we should assume they would oppose what we're trying to do."

"But she wasn't one of them back then."

Will took a deep breath. "From what I've learned, the fae, the people, the plane, everything within it, they're like a single organism. When she became part of it, she was bound by the rules of their existence, including their prior agreements. Doubly so now that she's their leader."

Selene grimaced. "And she made the ring."

"She doesn't have a soul like we do, or if she does, it's a part of her realm. So making astral connections like we do is difficult."

Selene's eyes lit with understanding. "It's a beacon then, like the ones we're building here and in Myrsta. That's how she was always able to find you, and how she made gates to reach you when there wasn't a congruence point nearby."

He nodded. "Tailtiu could only find me when I said her name, although I think that's changed now that she's split apart from the fae realm. We definitely have a direct connection now."

"Split?"

"The change that was created when I connected to her astrally back when the vampires were torturing her. Somehow, her body is still part of the fae realm, but her soul is separate. It's probably something that could use a lot of study, but I'm guessing she might form the nucleus of a new fae realm." *Or she might eventually wither and die,* he thought darkly to himself, but he kept that to himself.

Selene had been sitting, but she was suddenly filled with energy, so much so that she rose and began to pace back and forth—her brain was clearly in overdrive. "Could you do the same thing with your grandmother?"

Will gave it some thought, frowning and rubbing his chin. "I was desperate and highly emotional last time, plus Tailtiu was being tortured within an inch of ending her immortal life, and it was still nearly impossible. I doubt I could replicate it with Grandmother; besides, I've already made plans."

"Go on…"

He held up two fingers. "She owes me two unbound favors. You know what those are worth. I'm going to use them to solve one problem and simultaneously give her exactly what she wants."

His wife looked skeptical. "How?"

"It's still rather vague and it's contingent on defeating Lognion first. Has Grim Talek explained the dragon nest to you?"

A sly look came over her visage. "You mean the one we found the other day?"

Adrenaline shot through him. "*We?* What were you doing with him? He promised to keep you safe."

Selene went to a drawer and opened it; inside were a many different metal instruments. Removing a wicked-looking scalpel, she made direct eye contact with Will before storing it in the limnthal, then she sat down beside her husband. "I'm getting tired of hearing you obsess over my safety. Choose your words more carefully in the future. Would you like to hear the rest of my story, or should I experiment with my new limnthal?"

"Point taken."

She gave him a saccharine smile. "You know about the lich's wars and his long game with the dragon?"

"His vampire lieutenants gave me an interesting lecture on the topic. Terabinia is the only place left." Will scowled. "How close have you gotten with the lich?"

Her eyes narrowed. "Not as close as you are to Janice."

"She's human."

"And the lich is not. You should worry less; he's been an indispensable source of knowledge." Selene gestured at the room around them. "Case in point, there's a good reason I've been spending my free time here with Doctor Morris." When Will didn't comment, she continued, "Necromancy and healing are two sides of the same coin. I've learned a lot from the tutor you sent me, and since he can't admit his identity directly, I have been coming here to explore some of it with the physicians who can make the most of it."

Chapter 29

Feeling uncomfortable, Will shifted in his chair, then got up to stretch his legs. "I know he's not what we thought originally, but he isn't someone we should trust either."

The look in Selene's eyes was intense. "I'm not talking about trust—I'm talking about knowledge. The ban on necromancy was put in place by Lognion back when Terabinia first became independent. Surely you can see what motivated him to do so."

"Nevertheless, it's a dangerous topic."

"Says the man who used a forbidden spell to bring himself back from the dead after stopping my first wedding. Don't get self-righteous with me before even hearing about what I'm working on." She paused, fixing him with a hard stare, then asked, "Ready to listen?"

He exhaled slowly. "I'm not trying to pick a fight. I'll listen, but I reserve the right to my own opinions afterward."

"Fair enough. I'll keep it short. You know that necromancy concerns two different things, one being the manipulation and binding of souls while the other is mostly involved in physical flesh. Grim Talek's existence is primarily a result of the first, as was the spell you used to bring yourself back from death, or even the spell you use to keep from accidentally leaving your body when you sleep."

Will nodded. "It's still a slippery slope."

Ignoring him, she went on, "Even the ring you used to wear is an example of necromancy. Your grandfather has been made into something very similar to a disembodied lich."

"And I would argue it should never have been done—"

Selene interrupted, "—And yet you've carried it and gained a lot of useful information from it, despite the fact that making it was technically evil." Will's lips pressed into a thin line, but he didn't respond. His wife waited a moment, then continued, "But I'm not even trying to get into ambiguous areas like that. *Your* lich comes from a time when the necromantic and healing arts were much more advanced. He knows spells that can heal bruises and mend bones."

Will knew from his studies that generalized tissue trauma, bruising being the most common example, was nearly impossible to deal with magically, short of regeneration potions. Instead, he focused on the other part of her statement. "We have spells that can fix bones."

She pursed her lips. "You're trying to be obtuse. These spells work using different principles. They can revitalize dead tissue and restore internal organs using the body's own vitality. In many ways it's like natural healing, just many times faster, and unlike some of our crude methods for joining cut muscle or fusing broken bones, it does so with very little scarring."

Irritated, Will replied, "Natural healing doesn't bring dead flesh back to life."

"It won't stop cancer either."

"What?"

Selene took a breath, then answered with a tone that was mildly condescending, "I think consumption is what the country doctors and midwives call it."

Irritated by the condescension, he snapped, "I know what it is."

"Then you should also know that those regeneration potions you're so fond of greatly increase the risk that you'll develop malignant tumors. Every time you use one there's a chance something could go wrong, and you wouldn't even know it for years to come, and medicine, as it stands now, can't do a damn thing about it. The spells I've learned from Grim Talek have the potential to fix that, if used by a skilled healer. Doctor Morris has been positively ecstatic about the possibilities. It's unfortunate that he can't use some of the spells, though."

She stopped there, and Will mulled over her words before making a guess. "It takes void turyn, doesn't it?"

Selene nodded. "Some types of tumors have to be killed in place, including the tissue around them. But people who've been trained in the old wizardry can use those kinds of turyn. Even a first-order wizard would be able to use these spells. When this is all over, we can train a new generation of wizards here at Wurthaven. Healers who could eliminate untold amounts of human suffering and disease. This could be the beginning of a new golden age, and it will start right here! And it's not just necromantic techniques, Will. Remember what you did for that dying soldier back when we first met? Wizards who reach the second- and third-order may be able to use wild magic to treat infectious diseases in similar ways. Think about how many children die from similar things." She stopped, staring at him with obvious passion in her eyes.

He still had concerns, but he felt bad for being overly critical. "You've put a lot of time and thought into this. I trust you. You aren't working alone, though?"

"Of course not."

That made him feel better. What he worried about most were the rabbit holes that some wizards fell down while researching such dangerous topics alone. His recent experience reading the journal passed down by generations of head wizards had provided a plethora of examples showing just how dangerous such solitary habits could be. "If anyone can revolutionize medicine, it would be you. Getting back to the here and now, you were about to tell me where the nest is…"

"Oh!" Selene smiled genuinely for the first time since he had arrived, warming his heart. "You've been there already."

"I have?"

"The ley line intersection beneath Cerria."

He immediately knew she meant the chamber where he and the goddamn cat had fought the demon-lord Leykachak, beneath the house that belonged to the Duke of Arenata—his current home. Will was stunned. Lognion clearly enjoyed a strong sense of dramatic irony. "He set us there as unwitting guardians of the nest."

Selene nodded. "He gave us the key as well." Will looked at her in confusion as she pointed to herself. "There's a blood ward."

A chill ran down Will's spine as he remembered the stone table that lay in the chamber. It was designed to catch and channel the blood of a human sacrifice into grooves that fed into a ritual diagram. Will was intimately familiar with it, as he had used it against the Duchess of Arenata, forcing her to become the sacrifice that he had used to summon a demon-lord. The memory of her life slowly draining away while she pled with him for mercy remained as a scar on his soul. At the time, he had assumed the table and blood channels were additions the insane noblewoman had added herself, but now he realized they must have been far older.

He frowned. "But the blood was just a component, and the ritual diagram was designed to summon from the demon realm. That doesn't make sense."

"Ward, William, a blood *ward*—it's a barrier, not a part of the ritual design," Selene replied patiently. "It's keyed to me, or rather, it's keyed to Lognion and his children."

Of course, the body of the man Selene had known as her father was actually that of her older brother, possessed by the dragon known as Lognion, but the principle was clear. The dragon had taken his first human body millennia before and had designed the protections for his nest to respond only to those descended from that human. The dragon probably didn't need the blood to enter, but while continuing his human charade, he needed it if he wanted to check on the eggs. Will's eyes widened as the realizations hit him one after another. *That was why he was obsessed with Selene providing an heir. He probably could have used anyone's body to maintain his fiction, but he wanted to have easy access to the nest,* thought Will.

Then he remembered Androv overpowering the king in that same chamber. The master vampire had opened a vein on the king's wrist and used the blood to heal himself, but if Will hadn't interfered, the lich's servant would have probably done much more. *He wanted to see if Lognion was the dragon's host, and if so, whether he could find an entrance to the nest there,* Will realized. "I stopped Androv from using your father's blood in the chamber," he muttered.

"He's not my father," snapped Selene. "And yes, you got in his way, but you also saved the city."

Another terrible thought occurred to him. "How much blood does it take?"

Selene smiled softly at his concern. "We don't know, but I don't think you need to worry. It's probably very little, maybe just a drop. It would be pretty inconvenient if Lognion had to bleed his host to death every time he wanted to check on the nest."

"Have you tested it?"

She shook her head. "Grim Talek is worried that a test will alert the dragon. He wants to wait until we're prepared to finish the task all at once."

"So you don't know." Will could easily imagine that a creature with a lifespan measured in millennia might have a different concept of what was inconvenient. "What if he only checks the nest when switching bodies? Maybe he sacrifices one host and takes another at the same time? Bleeding a human to death might not be a problem—it could be a security measure." Frustrated, he continued, "What if the nest *isn't* there? Since you haven't tested it, we don't know for certain."

"When Androv was there, they still weren't certain that the king was the dragon's pawn. Grim Talek worried that the dragon might be working through an underling or servant, someone hidden behind the king. Confirming that Lognion was actually the host removed most of their uncertainty. Since then, your lich has gone down and inspected the chamber. He doesn't know the full details, but he was able to detect the entrance to a hidden pocket dimension," she explained. "He's pretty certain."

Without warning, the door opened, and a man's head popped around the doorframe. Will recognized him as Doctor Morris, the physician who had saved his life in the past. "Your Majesty, we're ready to begin the procedure. Oh!" His eyes fixed on Will. "My apologies, Your Highness, I didn't realize you were here." The doctor made a quick bow, then asked, "Will you be observing the operation?"

Confused, Will started to respond, but Selene intervened. "No. My husband has other duties to attend to. Give us a moment. I'll be with you shortly, then we can start."

The doctor bowed again. "Very good. I'll let Dame Shaw know. She said her husband is starting to fidget." With that the physician backed out and closed the door.

Will turned the name over in his mind. *Dame Shaw?* As much as he had studied the nobility under Selene's direction, the name wasn't familiar, and yet somehow it was. He stared at Selene quizzically for a moment before his mouth asked the question that his brain hadn't quite formulated. "Shaw is Tiny's last name, but he isn't married yet, is he?"

Selene stood again, smoothing the plain wool dress she wore. The same dress she had worn when working in the field hospital, years ago. Her face gave away nothing as she answered, "It's amazing how quickly things can happen when people communicate properly and all the facts are out in the open." The sting of knowing his best friend had married in his absence was only barely beginning to sink in when she added, "It was a small ceremony. The other students served as groomsmen and bridesmaids."

Other students—Will took that to mean Sammy and Emory, along with Tabitha and Shawn—in essence everyone at Rimberlin House, except for Will. It was a bitter pill to swallow, but there were other, more important questions. "What operation are you performing? Is the baby all right?" It was still far too early for the baby to be born, but he couldn't help but worry.

Selene waved a hand dismissively as she headed for the door. "Janice and the baby are fine. This is unrelated. I need to go."

"What secret are you keeping from me?" he demanded.

His wife gave him a pitying smile as she opened the door. "Secrets are terrible, aren't they? It's much nicer when we all work together. Never fear, this is for your benefit. I'm sure Grim Talek will explain it to you in due course, so we can coordinate our plans at the end." She stepped out, started to close the door, then opened it again briefly. "You should teleport out, so no one sees you. Prince William will be cross if he sees you here interfering in his end of things." The door clicked shut and she was gone.

CHAPTER 30

Will stared at the door for a solid minute while quietly rehearsing every lesson in bad language he had ever learned. Given that his teacher had been Arrogan, and that he had spent time in the army, it took a considerable amount of time to run through all the creative phrases he had heard. Then he considered following her in spite of her snide warning. It was a testimony to his advancing maturity that he remained in place.

After regaining his composure, he considered his teleportation options. Sitting down, he meditated briefly and slipped out of his body with relative ease, then he began testing various astral connections. He didn't want to return to Myrsta, so he skipped his father and checked his other friends and family first.

Interestingly, he was unable to find Selene, Janice, or Tiny, which meant they had probably shielded the room they were in. Will swore silently before continuing his search. Tabitha was with her mother, whom he definitely didn't want to see presently. Sammy was studying with Emory, and while they were sitting shoulder-to-shoulder, there didn't appear to be anything happening he could complain about.

None of those were good options, so he tried Jeremy the cook, but had no luck. Apparently his relationship with the chef wasn't strong enough. Finally, he tried Blake Word, his butler and sometimes arms-trainer, and was rewarded with a solid connection. The older man appeared to be outside doing some solitary sword practice. Without waiting to reconsider, Will shifted partway back to his body and activated his teleport spell, appearing beside his friend.

Blake reacted as Will should have expected. "Mother's tits!" the old soldier swore, jumping to one side and bringing his blade up into a guard position between them.

Will would have laughed, but at the same time, he stepped back to create more room and stepped on a large rock, which cost him his footing. Stumbling, he fell onto his backside and found himself staring up at his astonished butler, who had his sword pointed firmly at Will's face.

A rumbling growl came from behind Will, causing him to turn his head while simultaneously apologizing. "Sorry about that, Blake..." The words died in his throat as he saw a massive panther stepping around him, its eyes fixed firmly on the sword-wielding butler.

Eyes wide, Blake backed slowly away. "What in Temarah's name is that?"

For a moment, Will's heart seized in his throat, for the only cat of such size he had ever seen was the Cath Bawlg, but as he took in what he was seeing, he realized the cat beside him didn't look the same. It had white fur on its chest and legs, giving the impression of socks. The tail was a thick, bushy grey while the ears were tipped with white curls, similar to a lynx. All in all, despite being the size of a small pony, it bore identical markings to another cat he knew.

"Evie?"

Her tail swished over him like a cloud, but the cat never took her eyes from Blake.

"It's all right, Evie. We weren't fighting. I just scared him," said Will in a soothing tone. Then he addressed Blake. "I think you should put the sword away, so she knows you're not threatening me."

The old veteran glanced nervously at him. "You sure about that?"

Will nodded. "I don't think the blade would do you much good anyway."

Blake kept his eyes on the cat while slowly bending his knees to place the sword on the ground. "Good kitty. See? I'm not going to hurt him." The growling faded, and he gingerly stepped back.

With that, the enormous cat turned her head to Will, completely dismissing the butler's existence. She nudged him with a massive forehead, ruining his attempt at standing as a rumbling purr began to emanate from her chest.

"Dare I ask where you came from, or what kind of cat this is?" Blake's expression had shifted from outright alarm to wary anxiousness.

Sitting now, Will scratched between Evie's ears with one hand and under her chin with the other. In the space of an eye blink, her size had gone from that of a pony to something close to that of a large dog. "I teleported here from Cerria, and I think this isn't really a cat at all." A torrent of emotions ran through him as he added, "I think it's a demigod, or the child of one, or maybe a rebirth. It's confusing."

The butler slowly recovered his sword and sheathed it, being careful not to make any sudden moves. "The cat-god that helped you with the demon-lords?"

Will nodded. "The goddamn cat was immortal, possibly more immortal than I understood."

"That doesn't make much sense."

Will laughed. "It does when you've dealt with as many different immortals as I have. They're all undying, but that doesn't mean some of them can't be killed. Vampires, the fae, demon-lords—they're hard to kill and they have different strengths, but I've managed to kill all of them one way or another. I think the Cath Bawlg is different."

Blake snorted. "I've never had a cat make me nearly piss myself until now, that's for sure. Didn't you say the cat-god died, though?"

His throat was thick as he answered, "I thought he did. No, I'm sure he did. This isn't him, but yet it is. I don't think Evie has his memories, and she seems female. I'm guessing his spirit reincarnates somehow."

Blake rubbed his chin. "Like the legend of the phoenix, reborn from its ashes?"

"Something like that, but real, rather than myth."

"From what you said before, it was capable of killing demon-lords. That kind of power could be really handy—"

"No," snapped Will harshly, cutting the older man off. "My friends aren't tools or assets to be counted. Besides, she's still essentially a kitten."

"An immortal being that's existed for uncountable eons," said Will's friend quietly.

"A child spirit that's only known a year in the world. A friend that somehow found me again after losing everything." Will wiped his face with one sleeve. "I don't want to talk about it."

Blake looked down. "Sorry. I didn't mean to imply anything. Are you hungry?" He gestured toward the house. "I've worked up an appetite, and I think Jeremy has something good almost ready to serve. Maybe with Sir John absent, there will be enough for seconds."

Getting to his feet, Will followed Blake toward the main house. "I need to keep my presence here fairly quiet."

"The queen said as much when she was here."

"Selene was here?"

His old friend looked slightly embarrassed. "For the wedding. Sir John and Miss Edelman decided to—"

"I heard," interrupted Will. "How are they doing?"

The butler shrugged. "Dame Shaw is positively glowing, and your big friend is bigger than ever, although he seems to have lost a little weight."

The last Will had seen him, Tiny was already fairly trim, so that surprised him. "Is he eating enough?"

Blake laughed. "More than enough, enough for an entire garrison. It's the exercise. I honestly don't think it's healthy to train that much. He's going to hurt himself. Despite eating a wagonload at every meal, he looks gaunt."

"Is he sick?"

The older man tapped his temple. "Up here perhaps. There's just not much fat left on him. While he was here, he spent all day either at the pells or practicing with spears." After a brief pause, the butler added, "He asked me not to tell you about it. Said you'd worry."

Will was worried. "True enough, but I'm glad you did." Taking a moment to study Blake's face, he could see that there was still more to tell. "What haven't you told me yet?"

"It really isn't my place," said Blake reluctantly.

"Consider it an order then."

The old soldier stopped walking and turned to face him. "He's abusing the potions you gave him."

That was entirely unexpected. "What do you mean?"

"Those dragon potions, I forget what you call them. The ones that make you stronger, faster—every day he was here, he would take one during the last hour of practice. After that, he was unbelievable. I watched him and I still couldn't fathom it. Someone that big shouldn't move that fast! By the end of it, he'd collapse, half-dead. I'm pretty sure he had broken bones as well. He'd take another potion then before collapsing, and we'd have to get a palette and every man with a strong back on the property to help cart him back to bed."

Alarmed, Will asked, "And Janice allowed that? What about Selene?"

Blake scowled. "Told me to mind my own damn business, thank you very much. Not in those words, of course, but you get what I mean. Sir John was more willing to talk than they were."

"What did he say?"

"Just that if you wanted to fight properly with that kind of speed you had to train with it, which is just a lame excuse for self-torture if you ask me."

They resumed walking toward the garden gate that would lead them into the back side of Rimberlin House while Will mentally tried to tally up how many dragon-heart potions he had given Tiny. He was certain it was no more than fifteen and the rest were safely stored in his limnthal, along with the desiccated and mostly dead vampire that provided the blood to make them. Unless Selene and Janice had captured another vampire, they couldn't possibly be making more of the potions. That set a hard limit on how often Tiny could abuse himself for the sake of this so-called 'training.' It also made the expenditure of such a valuable and limited resource even stranger.

Once they reached the house, Will used a camouflage spell and cautioned his friend once more, "Don't mention my presence to anyone other than Sammy. Just tell her to check my room. She'll understand."

"You really are paranoid."

"I trust you, but there's every chance Lognion has a spy among the servants. I don't want him to know of my comings and goings." *Or to notice that I'm in two places at once,* he added mentally. Smoothing his turyn and silencing his movements, Will effectively vanished as he followed the other man through the door and into the house.

Going upstairs, he went to his study, closed the door, and locked it. Then he summoned the enchanted silver plate he had used to contact the vampires a few days previously. This time, he had someone else he needed to talk to.

With the proper investment of focus and turyn, a face appeared on the mirror-like surface, his own. "I thought you might contact me. Fortunately, I'm alone. I was going to talk to you tonight anyway."

"What have you been teaching my wife?" demanded Will, letting his anger show.

"Anything she asks, within reason," answered the lich. "Nothing that would endanger her, naturally, since that would go against our agreement."

A non-answer if Will had ever heard one, and he'd heard plenty of them from Arrogan over the years. "Knowledge is a tool. You could argue either way regarding virtually anything, including *necromancy.*"

"Most knowledge is neutral, you're right," agreed his doppelganger, "but some knowledge is dangerous simply in the knowing. You've read my book—you should understand that now. I haven't taught her anything that might drive her mad, like Erica's spell to pierce the veil."

"Erica?"

His face was so smug as it answered that Will wanted to punch himself. "I forget they didn't include their names in the book. Erica was the tenth writer in my old journal. I'm assuming you chose to retain the knowledge when you finished."

Will understood immediately. The tenth writer had been the one to study the outsiders, and also the one who had gone insane. It was her barrier spell he intended to adapt to his own purposes, which made him feel vaguely guilty of some unnamed crime. He pushed that thought aside. "Point taken, but I still don't want you teaching Selene necromancy."

"Too bad," said Grim Talek. "The spells are useful, and she's doing something important with the knowledge. Do you *want* children to die, William? Do you want people to suffer needlessly? Your wife has a noble purpose and the intelligence to improve the human condition on a scale not seen since the forgotten age when I was a child."

"Then why didn't you do it, if you're so concerned about humankind?"

The lich hadn't blinked for an unnatural span of time, and his face was completely expressionless when he replied, "Because I thoroughly despise you. Intellectual integrity and hatred for the dragon are the only two reasons I've continued this charade called existence. Once this is over, I expect full payment from you, otherwise…"

Will broke in, "Otherwise you'll have to pretend to be me for decades to come."

"Assuming you don't take the coward's way out, but you know what I'll do to them if you do," sneered the lich.

Closing his eyes, Will took a deep breath. Losing his temper wouldn't help matters. "Do you know what Selene and Janice are up to?"

The monster staring back at him smiled coldly. "Your wife didn't tell you when you snuck in here earlier? Do I sense division in paradise?" When Will didn't respond, he continued, "Of course I know, just like I knew you came sniffing around. Be careful you don't destroy our ruse. If the dragon gets wind of it and spoils our plans…"

"I know," snapped Will. "What is she doing?"

His evil twin laughed. "Something helpful, and no, before you ask, I had nothing to do with it. Most of the theory behind it comes from that clever old man at your school, Master Courtney, but I have no doubt she would have succeeded even without his help. Your wife is brilliant beyond what a cretin such as yourself could ever appreciate. If I'd had a disciple with her wit and intelligence back when I was alive, we might have found a way to stop the dragon from the very beginning."

Will ignored the insult. "Thousands of years and you still talk endlessly without communicating anything. *What* is she doing? I need to know if we're to coordinate properly."

"Making a weapon to help you against the dragon." Grim Talek laughed. "She'll explain in due time. You still have to succeed in your next task, otherwise none of this will matter."

He still wasn't ready to let go of the subject. "Is there necromancy involved in her project?"

The lich held up his thumb and index finger, pinching them until they almost touched. "Only the tiniest bit of necromancy. Nothing nefarious, I assure you. Your wife is very clever. Trust me, you'll like this."

Will growled.

"You need to hurry, William. The forges are ready, and we're running out of time."

"I'm ready," said Will, "but from what Selene said it might be dangerous to do it in Cerria with the nest there. Myrsta might be the only location I can use, but then we have to consider overland transport."

The lich shook his head. "There's a ley line nexus in the mountains between your old village and Branscombe. Use it."

He lifted his brows. That was new information. "I don't know where it is. It would be easier to ask my grandmother. I'm certain she doesn't need a ley line to create a gate."

"We can't risk her involvement, William. We've been over this. The nexus is near the mountain pass—you've been there. As advanced as your talents have become, you'll have no trouble finding it now."

Bile rose in his throat as he thought about the agreement the lich wanted him to broker. "I don't know if I can do this. Surely there's something else we can barter with."

The lich sneered. "Demons don't give a damn about your soft heart, and they care even less about gold or other temptations, but they love souls. You ruined my plans in Myrsta, but you gained enough notoriety with them that you can probably sell this. Channel your inner villain, or just pretend you're me. Surely if I can pretend to be a disgustingly kind idiot for this long, *you* can manage being evil for a day."

Will wanted to throw up, but he hid his disgust. "Are you sure you can deliver? If I make promises and you don't have the—" he stopped, unable to say the word.

"Livestock, William," supplied the lich. "Just think of them as livestock. It makes everything easier. Trust me, the Shimerans are barely smarter than animals anyway. I still have full control over Shimera. The priests are already whipping the crowds into a frenzy for a new holy revelation. Just open the gate at the correct time and place, and the demons will do the rest. You don't even have to watch. Close it up when they're done, and bring their payment back to Wurthaven afterward."

He stared blankly at his own face, not trusting himself to speak.

Grim Talek smiled. "Don't think too hard on it. It's only a few million people. Shimera's never been that populous." As though the sacrifice of millions meant nothing, the lich held up a page containing a short rune sequence, pressing it closely to the enchanted silver so that Will could read it easily. "Copy this down. It's the optimal turyn polarity and frequency for hurting dragons and dragonkin, such as the egg guardians. You can substitute it into most elemental spells without much difficulty. You'll need it when the time comes to fight."

With disquieting ease, Will's brain switched from moral disgust over his ethical dilemma to interest in the magic being presented. Using the scribe spell that he had once learned from the lich, he quickly made a copy of the sequence shown, then he asked, "This will kill them? If so, I don't need to make this deal."

"No, William. It will make a firebolt or similar spells inflict a little more damage to them, but ultimately, it's still just a nuisance. Once, when I still had a living heart, I hung my hopes on discovering this spell sequence, only to be driven into deeper despair when it ultimately failed. Give up on hope. The demons have what we need—get it."

The connection ended, and the lich's face vanished. Groaning, Will put his face on his desk. The sound of purring and a gentle touch on his leg came as Evie tried to comfort him, but it only made him feel worse. Looking down into her green eyes, he muttered, "If you knew what I'm involved with, you wouldn't be so supportive. You used to hate demons, remember?"

The cat tilted her head to one side, then meowed softly.

"I wish you could talk. How long does it take to learn?" he asked, but the cat didn't respond.

CHAPTER 31

He spent the next day in Rimberlin, staying out of sight in the bedroom and his study while working to incorporate the new type of turyn into some of his spells. Ethelgren's light-darts spell was the easiest substitution, and while he couldn't reflex cast it with the change, he felt relatively certain it wouldn't take too long before it was once again instantaneous.

The wind-wall was more difficult and given its more distributed form of damage, he didn't know if it would work well, especially since reducing the elemental air turyn notably reduced the spell's physical efficacy. In the end, he opted for a fifty-fifty mix, though he still wasn't happy with the result. Again, it would take some practice before he could reflex cast it, but since he still spent an hour a day practicing various spells, that didn't seem like much of a barrier. The final battle wouldn't come for weeks yet.

Sammy visited him several times over the course of the day, surreptitiously bringing him meals, as well as ham for Evie. She was visibly jealous of the cat's attachment to him, but since the feline did allow some petting after the proper meat tribute had been paid, Sammy didn't complain.

His cousin probably would have spent more time with him, but since Will's presence was a secret from everyone but her and Blake, she had to account for her time. Emory was passionate about his study and practice sessions with her. Will appreciated the dedication, though he still had mixed feelings about the nobleman's motivation. It wasn't entirely rational, but he couldn't help himself.

After a solid night's sleep, Will woke the next morning to find Evie curled up on his pillow, just above and behind his head. It was comforting and strange at the same time. While he was sure she was either a reincarnation or perhaps a child of the goddamn cat, the behavior was yet more proof that she was different. The ancient cat he had known would never have been so social with him, though he had allowed

Sammy to take an unlimited number of liberties with his dignity. Evie clearly had her own preferences.

Rubbing between and around her ears, Will tried not to think too hard about the grumpy old cat, lest tears ruin the start of another day. He spent some time running through his new training regimen until Blake showed up with breakfast and stayed to eat with him. After an amiable chat and filling his belly, Will was loathe to leave, but he knew nothing good would come from delaying. He started to take advantage of Blake's presence to help him dress, since his under-tunic brigandine could be a pain to don by himself.

Blake didn't seem to approve, however. "Is there some reason not to use the breastplate?"

Will stared back at him but said nothing.

The butler began counting on his fingers. "It's more comfortable, it's easier to move in since it isn't tight against your skin, it's lighter, *and* it's damn near impenetrable. Unless you're going to a ball and want to appear unarmored, there's no reason not to use it instead of the brigandine."

Looking up and to one side, Will admitted, "To be honest, lately I haven't been wearing either of them very much."

The old soldier clucked disapprovingly. "Feeling suicidal, eh?"

"No," said Will, denying the truth. "Just foolish." He stored the brigandine and summoned the demon-steel breastplate. The metal had a black tint to it, like silver that had begun to tarnish, an indication that it held some amount of demonic turyn, even though Will had 'cleaned' it before storing it the last time he had taken it out. Since Blake was about to help him buckle it on, he removed the poisonous energy again, causing the armor to regain its grey metallic sheen.

Blake waited, then asked before touching the metal, "It's safe now?" After Will nodded, the other man helped him put it on and buckled it into place. "What happens if you don't remove the evil every now and then?"

He smiled. "It isn't evil, technically. It's just a type of energy antithetical to our own."

The butler waved his hand. "Evil, death magic, whatever you call it—what happens if you don't clean it out?"

Will shrugged. "Eventually, it will begin to burn with black flames, though I'm not sure if you could see them or not. At that point, it will kill or sicken anyone who gets too close. It will keep that up until it radiates enough energy away to become stable again, somewhere around the midpoint of how much energy it can contain."

"Contain? You make it sound like a cup holding wine."

"That's a good analogy," said Will. "When it's empty, it looks like ordinary steel. As it absorbs energy, it becomes black, and after a certain point it starts to burn or radiate energy. You can keep putting energy into it beyond that, which will increase the time it takes to burn away the excess, but if you put too much in, it will eventually explode. Of course, I prefer to keep it completely drained so it won't hurt anyone near me."

"So, it absorbs good magic?" asked Blake.

Will smiled again, shaking his head. "No, and the word you're looking for is turyn, which is what wizards call magical energy. It doesn't absorb turyn. Demon-steel absorbs kinetic energy and stores it. When it goes beyond a certain point, it radiates that energy as demonic turyn, so the net effect is a conversion of physical energy into a deadly type of magic. As long as it is kept perfectly still, it remains empty, but any motion will gradually increase the turyn stored within it."

Blake rubbed his chin. "Walking?"

He nodded. "It isn't much, but yes. Once it gets to the point that the metal starts burning, it's difficult to force more in without hitting it with something really powerful, like a heavy hammer. In fact, that's how the demons were using this stuff to generate their turyn in Myrsta. They built a device that had something similar to a gong or maybe a bell and then they had a machine that continually pounded on it with a massive striker, continually increasing the turyn stored in it."

"Wouldn't it explode, then? Assuming they kept hitting it?"

Will shook his head, then clarified, "Yes and no. It would if you kept hitting it hard enough and if you did so faster than it could radiate the energy as flames. In the case of their demonic generator, they used a secondary enchantment with a link to drain and radiate the turyn into the wider environment—until I broke the link. That's what destroyed so much of Myrsta."

Blake wrinkled his nose. "Maybe you should wear the brigandine after all."

He clapped his friend on the shoulder. "No, you were right. It's safe while I'm wearing it. My body naturally absorbs and converts turyn around me, even when I'm unconscious. Unless I'm hit really hard, it won't even turn black. Honestly, I've been stupid not to use it more. Heavy blows barely stagger me with it on, since it absorbs the shock, and I can always use the energy against my enemies afterward."

"I've heard enough to be glad I'm not a wizard," said Blake. "Where are you going today, if I'm allowed to ask?"

He probably shouldn't have said it, but Will had been alone too long and couldn't help being slightly dramatic. "To meet some demons."

The older man covered his ears, then made a gesture to ward away evil. "Never mind. Wait a second before you leave. I'll have Jeremy pack you a lunch." Before Will could protest that he already had enough food stored away, Blake was out of the room.

Not long after that, Will was skimming across the land on a force-travel disk. Using a force-effect limited his defensive options while in the air, but it was faster and less tiring than the elemental version. Since everyone believed him to be in Cerria assisting the new queen consolidate her rule, he could be somewhat more carefree than he usually was when he knew his enemies were all carefully tracking his movements.

Using congruence points to travel back and forth to the fae realm would have been faster, but his personal knowledge of their locations was limited, and using a favor would give away his location. Will didn't know exactly what arrangements the fae had with demonkind, the elves, or even Lognion himself, but information was currency to them. Even if his grandmother wasn't personally against him, she might very well barter the information with his enemies—as she had probably done multiple times in the past while he carried Arrogan's ring.

Arrogan had taught him the first lesson: Never owe the fae *anything*. Pay for what you received when you received it and accept no debts. Aislinn had continued his education in her own cruel way, punishing his mistakes and inculcating in him the rules for dealing with her kind. Precise language was a must, and every reward was a bittersweet pill, as the fae *always* had multiple goals. Win or lose, Aislinn would gain more than she lost in any transaction.

Now, with the lich's help, he had learned the only way to get ahead in dealing with the fickle fae immortals, which was not to play the game. As much as losing Arrogan's advice had hurt him, it had finally freed him from his grandmother's surveillance, limiting how much she could profit from following his movements and selling the information—or using it herself.

Will continued traveling after the sun went down, only stopping when fatigue and hunger made it apparent that he needed a respite. Jeremy's packed lunch became supper, since he had just eaten bread and cheese at midday without bothering to stop moving. The food was a delight, for when he unwrapped the cloth tied around the basket, Will found two meat pastries inside. Such food would last a day or two under ordinary conditions, but since he'd stored them in the limnthal, they were almost as good as they'd been fresh out of the oven. Will smiled when he felt the warmth still radiating from them.

A thick crust surrounded minced lamb and a gravy seasoned with pepper, nutmeg, and coriander. Will considered saving one pie for the next day, but he ate the first so quickly that he discarded that option and ate the second without regret. Afterward, reclining against a tree with a full belly, he addressed the empty air. "Jeremy, you were the best decision I never made."

Selene had been the one who forced a hired cook on him despite his objections, and over time, he had gradually come to accept the wisdom of her choice. As if summoned by his reminiscence, his wife appeared before him in ghostly form, reclining sideways as though she were laying on a bed. "Are you camping?" she asked, observing the tree behind him.

Still feeling the glow of a good meal, Will answered lightly, "I am taking my leisure in the wilderness."

She smirked. "I'm glad you're in good spirits, and that I caught you before sleep. Last night I tried, but you must have had that anti-possession spell on."

"I prefer not to go wandering accidentally at night," he replied. "Most of the time I can't reach you during the *daytime*, or Janice, or Tiny for that matter."

"Worried?"

Letting his heart show on his face, Will answered, "Lonely."

Her features hardened. "I'm not sure you appreciate the meaning of that word. Try being queen with a lich disguised as your husband beside you."

"I'm sorry," said Will, being sincere, then added, "Is it safe for us to talk like this?" He pointed to his empty ring finger. There was also the fact that being able to astrally connect meant by definition that neither of them was shielded.

"I've stored it safely away," Selene answered, "and my room is protected in every conceivable way short of putting an actual shield around it. As for *you*—you barely exist since you started this ruse. I feel privileged to know you, much less to be able to speak to you." There was heavy sarcasm in her voice.

She was right, of course. Without the ring, and assuming there were no other beacons or marks on him, no one would be able to find him except the same people he could contact astrally—all of whom he trusted. *Except Lognion,* he noted mentally. So far as he knew, the dragon hadn't used that connection to spy on him. He would have noticed if it had happened while he was awake, and as Selene had remarked, he protected himself while sleeping.

"I love you," he said suddenly.

"I still love you too, but don't think you're forgiven," she replied, and after a short pause she added, "yet." Glancing around, she asked, "A powerful wizard who has mastered the ability to teleport without beacons, and you're sleeping in the forest. While I don't mind the thought of you waking up with a sore back, I have to wonder why?"

"I can only teleport to people I'm connected to," he reminded her. "And this is the only way I can travel without attracting notice."

"Where are you going then?"

Will grimaced. "It's probably safer if I don't tell you. The lich knows."

The look on her face told him he'd pushed the day of his forgiveness even further back, but she didn't argue. Selene had grown up under the strict guidance of a psychopathic dragon, and even the humans around her had all been driven by political expediency and harsh pragmatism. Pushing away her irritation came as second nature. "Speaking of whom, Grim says the engineers and mage-smiths are ready, but we lack the materials."

Grim? Will raised one brow.

"It's tiresome saying his full name each time. Would you rather I call him husband?"

He growled. "Just don't get too familiar. The materials are coming. What about the engineers and artificers? They aren't true wizards. This is going to cost them dearly."

She lifted her chin slightly. "I've given them elementals. They're sorcerers now."

Will had compromised his principles on multiple levels, but her answer begged the question of where the elementals had come from. Since Lognion's disappearance, it had become apparent that he had kept the links to all of his thousands of elementals. No secret trove of unbonded elementals had been found, and as far as Will knew, no one else knew how to create more. The only elementals that remained were those previously gifted to the nobility, who usually only had a few each. While Selene could technically compel her vassals to redistribute their magical assets, it was hard to imagine her doing so while still consolidating her rule. An immediate revolt was the only possible result of such a command.

To the best of his knowledge, the only remaining *human* who knew how to construct the heart-stone enchantment was himself. Arrogan knew, though he'd rather be melted down before he gave the secret away. Will had only learned by making a deal with the dragon, back when he'd still thought that Lognion was human. There was a strong possibility that Aislinn knew it, but given her tragic history and how she'd originally become one of the fae, he doubted she would trade the knowledge unless someone was willing to pay a steep price.

The secret wasn't even written down in Grim Talek's journal of wizards. After a long pause, Will asked, "Where'd you get the elementals?"

His wife, now Queen of Terabinia, didn't answer immediately, but instead returned a steady gaze while she formulated her thoughts. Without remorse, she finally said, "I created them."

The fact that she didn't make excuses or prevaricate perfectly communicated her reasoning. She didn't have to say it, nor did he want to hear it. It would be the same argument he gave whenever he committed an evil act. *It was necessary. There was no better option.* This instance could also be followed by the usual mitigating statements: *We'll free them later, when it's no longer necessary.* Keeping his tone even, Will asked, "Who taught you the enchantment?"

"Does it matter?"

With cold eyes, he responded, "You know I've sworn an oath to eradicate the secret. That was part of the original reason I wanted to eliminate your father. Aside from him and the ring, I didn't have solid evidence of anyone else knowing how it was done, so I'd like to know who it was that taught you."

"I told you not to refer to that creature as my father." Selene rarely played verbal games, but something about his tone brought out her spite. "Who do you think?"

Having dealt with the fae for so long, he couldn't accept the deflection. "I need to hear it from your lips."

"Grim Talek." Selene's chin lifted ever so slightly. "Going to be hard to cross that one off your list if you decide to add it."

Will relaxed slightly. "He's already on my list, so it won't be an extra burden."

"So what Janice told me is true. I didn't want to believe you were that big a fool." She made no effort to hide her anger.

He shrugged. "You haven't forgotten how we started, have you? Remember when I deserted the army to burn down Barrowden? I haven't really changed; I just have a bigger torch now." That fact that Grim Talek hadn't given him a choice didn't matter much either, since Will knew he'd probably have taken up the gauntlet to eliminate the lich after destroying the dragon anyway.

Selene's expression shifted to one of resignation, and she lifted her hands to encircle an imaginary throat. "Sometimes I just want to shake you—or throttle you." She rubbed her face, then added, "I'm in, though. All the way, even if I think you're a fool. What if we succeed, though?"

"What do you mean?"

"Assume we kill the dragon and then somehow kill a lich. I'll be the last one on your list. Will regicide be your final crime?"

"That would be rather hypocritical of me, don't you think?" said Will. "Unless I made it a murder-suicide and removed myself immediately after. I'm thinking supervised parole would be better."

"You'd have to keep an eye on me for centuries then. Are you sure you're up to the task?"

He offered a mischievous grin. "I like challenges, and I would have to keep a very close eye on you."

"How close?" Selene's eyes seemed larger, and her breathing had changed subtly.

Will went from tired, overfull, and moderately irritated with his partner, to desperately hungry in the span of half a second. They'd been apart far too long. "Damn it!" he swore without explanation.

She already understood. "You could teleport."

He wanted to pull his hair out. "How would I get back?" Desperate inspiration hit him. "Can you teleport here?" Selene was probably close enough to their other friends to teleport back to Cerria.

Selene rolled her eyes. "I've just barely learned to contact you like this, and I haven't studied the teleport spell at all, not to mention you haven't given me the specifics of how you make it work without a beacon."

Will growled with frustration, then asked, "Why haven't you learned the spell yet? I gave you a copy. It's not like you to wait on something like that. You usually devour new spells." He was on his feet without realizing it, pacing around the tree he'd been leaning against to try and get rid of some of his unwanted energy. It didn't help, so he changed the subject. "Where did you get the bodies?"

Selene blinked as the mood evaporated. "Pardon?"

"For the elementals," he clarified. The sexual tension disappeared as quickly as it had appeared, replaced by a different tension.

"Do you really want to ask me that?"

"None of this is easy. I just want to know."

"Criminals," answered his wife, but there was a hint of hesitation.

Will frowned. "And?"

"Some of my critics had unfortunate accidents."

"What?" he demanded.

"I didn't like it either!"

"Then why did you do it?"

She threw her hands up. "No one can trace it back to me anyway. They're too scared to even try."

As much as he struggled with his own descent into apathy and rationalizing his deeds, it sounded to him as though Selene had given up entirely. "Was it really necessary? I know you better than that. You wouldn't take the easy way out of a political problem."

The ghostly queen glared at him. "You did it. I just made the best of a bad situation."

"*I* did it?" Will was confused, but then understood. "Oh."

Selene nodded her head slowly. "He stays out of the spotlight most of the time, but everyone's terrified of the Stormking."

"That's what they call him?"

"It's what they call *you*, William. He's just expanding on the part you created when you tore the palace apart and killed the king."

Will huffed. "That's stupid, and I'm only a prince."

"I can't control rumors, William. Do you think I could solve this by issuing a proclamation? Don't be naïve."

He ran his hands through his hair, feeling tempted to pull it out. "I never wanted to be called a king—of any kind—and I certainly didn't want to be turned into a villain used to frighten children at night. You're the queen—don't they understand that?"

She nodded, then answered in a frank tone, "Certainly. I'm queen because they're terrified you'll take the throne. You already removed one monarch, though, and the people are convinced you could easily do it again. You're a child if you cling to hoping the people will love you. You aren't Laina. You cast yourself in this role, so don't whine to me about it. You refuse to take the throne? Fine. I'll do the hard work as queen! Whether you like it or not, you being a villain makes them love me, and that makes my job easier. Would you begrudge me that?"

"I'm not a villain," he said stubbornly.

A cruel edge entered her voice. "Where are you going now, then?"

"What?"

"Demons don't give gifts, William. You know what a mage who trades souls for power is called—a warlock, and just a minute ago you were judging me for creating elementals. What's worse, sorcery or warlockry?"

The accusation left him flabbergasted, and he didn't know how to answer, since she was technically right. Selene didn't wait for a reply, though. "How many people will it take to buy that much demon-steel?"

Ungrateful bitch! You want to kick him while he's down? He's doing the best he can, same as you!

Laina's voice rang out in his mind so vividly Will could almost believe she was there, though he knew it was a hallucination. He was surprised to see Selene flinch as though she had heard it too. She stared at him with a strange expression for a moment, then seemed taken by remorse. "I shouldn't have said that, Will. I'm sorry. I'm tired and not thinking clearly."

Looking down, he muttered, "Don't be sorry for the truth."

"I didn't mean it like that. We don't have any options, either of us. You know I don't think you're a villain. I'm just frustrated and I'm not communicating properly."

Will nodded in agreement, though he still felt wounded, as though she'd driven a stake into his heart. "I'm tired too. We should rest."

"Will—" Her voice was cut off as he reflex cast the anti-possession spell, sealing himself off from the astral plane and severing their connection.

He didn't bother with a fire, or even using the ground-warming spell Selene had taught him years ago. Will summoned his bedroll and stretched out, too upset to even bother to set wards as he had planned to do. Their conversation played back and forth in his mind, looping endlessly while he tried to sleep. At some time close to dawn, he finally drifted into a dream. Laina was there waiting for him, her expression more sympathetic than he remembered in real life.

"She didn't mean it," said his sister in a consoling tone. "She just doesn't like being called out on her own bullshit. She's always been like that."

Will turned away. Seeing Laina was too painful, even in dreams. Blinking to stop the tears, he watched the landscape shift and flow like a river beneath the vivid colors of an imaginary sunset. Not trusting himself to speak, he kept his thoughts to himself. *It was the truth, though. She couldn't help but mean it.*

A gentle hand came to rest on his shoulder. "There's more than one kind of truth. The truth that's important to her is the one that's in here."

Glancing down, Will saw Laina's other hand pat his chest, just over his heart. Unable to stop himself, he met her gaze before his vision became too blurry to see. "You're dead."

Chapter 32

He woke with an ache in his chest and tears in his eyes. Sitting up, Will regretted not taking the time to level the ground better. A terrible catch in his back stole his breath as he tried to stretch out the kinks that the uneven ground had gifted him with. He nearly jumped when something bumped his hand.

A small grey cat looked up at him, her impossibly bushy tail waving gently behind her in the morning air.

"Evie? How did you get here?" he asked, not really hoping for an answer.

A strange meow issued forth as the cat opened her mouth, sounding suspiciously like the word *followed.*

Knowing what she was, he decided to believe it was an answer. "You can't come with me. It's too dangerous. You need to go back to the house."

The cat stared at him with unblinking eyes, then turned to other matters, ignoring his words and his existence as she began to diligently clean places that he preferred not to think about.

"You're not listening to me, are you?" he asked.

If the cat heard him, she gave no sign of it.

"I know you're not just a cat now, so don't pretend you can't hear me." There was no response. "I also know you're starting to understand me, at least a little."

Will was forced to admit defeat. The goddamn cat had never been a conversationalist, and he had fully mastered language. Whatever skill level Evie had with Darrowan, she obviously didn't feel much need to express herself. Will rolled up his bedroll and stored it in the limnthal before using a quick cast of Selene's Solution to freshen up and clean himself. Evie watched it all, and if she wondered why he didn't just use his tongue, she didn't feel bothered enough to ask.

He created a force-travel disk and rose several feet above the forest floor. "Go home, Evie. I can't take you with me."

The cat stared up at him with green eyes, then meowed in a way that tugged at his heart. Words weren't necessary for him to know she didn't want to be abandoned. Steeling his resolve, Will set off, using as much speed as he dared. The trees were too tall for him to get above them, so he had to be careful to dodge between the trunks.

A minute later, a thought occurred to him. *What if she doesn't know how to get back to Rimberlin House?* He pushed on. It wasn't his problem. Evie was immortal anyway, and too powerful to be hurt by almost anything she might encounter in the woods. *I don't even know how she found me this time. She'll be fine.*

But if she *was* the Cath Bawlg reborn, she was effectively only a year old. Alone. A child lost in a strange world she hardly understood.

The travel disk came to a stop. "Damn it!" Will reversed course, moving more slowly so he could scan the area in case the cat had been following him.

Finding her took half an hour, for the cat wasn't where he had camped or in between, but instead had gone hunting. He found her neck-deep in a pile of feathers that dwarfed the little cat's size, and when he approached, she looked up at him and meowed again, her muzzle and cheeks covered in blood.

"Is that an owl?" Will goggled at the size of the predatory bird. Its belly had been torn open, and Evie was currently working her way through what appeared to be the liver. Looking up, she gave him a cute but sanguine 'meep' before returning to her meal. "How in the hell did you catch that? It's bigger than you are."

He reached down to unfold one wing but quickly withdrew his hand as a warning growl rumbled from the cat's throat. "I wasn't trying to steal. I just wanted to look." He couldn't believe he had wasted so much time searching for her. "Clearly you're doing just fine on your own."

The cat stopped eating and sat back on her haunches, satisfied. Another meow informed him he could have a turn with the carcass, and then Evie began cleaning her paws.

Will shook his head in disbelief. "No, thank you." He created another travel disk and lifted off from the ground. "Go home now."

Fifteen feet up, he started to resume his journey only to be startled by the most impressive leap he'd ever seen from a cat so small. Evie landed on the platform beside him, unconcerned by the height, the wind, or his surprise. Unsure what to do, Will increased his speed, heading for his previous destination. Despite the fierce air blowing over her, the cat resumed cleaning her paws and face.

Resigned to his fate, Will focused on traveling and by the end of the day, he realized that although it had been a boring trip, he'd enjoyed it much more than the day before. Evie wasn't capable of conversation, but she was company, nonetheless. He'd spent so much time alone lately that he hadn't realized it was beginning to wear on him.

That night, he made camp and lit a fire for a warm meal, a simple soup of ham and beans. He cut off a generous piece of ham and offered it to Evie before putting the rest in the pot. She graciously accepted, taking it as her due.

He put the anti-possession spell on before doing the wards. He didn't consciously consider it, but he didn't really want another conversation before sleeping. Once the wards were done, Will extinguished the fire and carefully smoothed the ground before putting down both an underlayment and his bedroll. With those preparations and a long lasting ground-warming spell, he would sleep much more comfortably than he had the night before.

Will was still staring up at the stars when a small body walked up and nestled against his neck and cheek, tickling his nose with her fur. He slept without dreams.

He woke before dawn, but he felt thoroughly rested, so he went ahead and put everything away. Based on where he'd landed the day before, he guessed he would get to Branscombe sometime in early afternoon. He removed the anti-possession spell to make sure Selene could contact him if needed. Will already felt vaguely guilty for putting it on so early the night before.

Seconds later, he felt a contact, but not from Selene, or anyone else he cared for. A surge of adrenaline shot through him, causing his heart to race and his pupils to dilate. An enormous eye was visible in front of him, not because it was single, but because the skull that housed it blocked his view. The ghostly dragon vanished an instant later, to be replaced by a tear in the sky.

Will had seen a gate before. Aislinn had used one to betray him during his fight against the demon-lord, Madrok. Reality split as a hole formed, allowing the dragon to fly through and hover above him. Its wings kicked up a windstorm as a monster the size of two haybarns landed in front of him.

He'd chosen a small clearing to camp in, but it wasn't *that* big. Small saplings were scattered here and there, but Lognion ignored them. They bent and snapped as he settled to the ground, forming no more nuisance than would tall grass to a bull.

Fear greater than any he'd ever known filled Will's heart as the massive slitted eyes focused entirely on him. He'd missed seeing Lognion's true form when he'd attempted to save his mother, only arriving after his home had been reduced to ash and glass. Seeing the dragon in the flesh nearly unmanned him. Evie hissed beside him, growing in size.

"I've missed you, William." The voice was entirely human and completely recognizable, for it was the same voice that had once issued from the king's human lips, but the dragon's mouth remained perfectly still. Nothing moved on the monster except its nostrils as hot air moved in and out with each breath.

His mouth opened, closed, then opened again. "You sound the same," was all he could manage.

"Magic," said Lognion. "My body isn't capable of human speech, and my natural voice would likely cause you to void your bowels. I'm glad you've decided to allow me to speak this time."

Will's body was so tense he could barely move as he debated between attempting a retreat or beginning a probably suicidal attack. Evie had already grown to the size of a horse and was still swelling. The sound coming from her throat and the shiver in her flank gave notice she was preparing to leap. Will had seen the Cath Bawlg overpower not one but two demon-lords, but only when they were weakened, or when he was attacking from an ambush. The demi-god had known his limitations— Evie didn't.

Based on what he had seen while fighting the egg guardians, Lognion's size, and the fact that every known power in existence— living and unliving—feared to face dragons, any dragons, much less one of such advanced age, Will didn't expect a positive outcome if she attacked. The desire to protect her overwhelmed his paralysis.

Without taking his eyes off the existential threat in front of him, Will's right hand reached out to touch the fierce cat's shoulder. "Easy, Evie. We aren't fighting today. Relax." As his hand met her fur, he realized it wasn't her shoulder, but mid-leg. His feline ally had nearly surpassed the size of any earthly creature he'd previously observed. He wondered if she would continue to grow until she attained the same colossal proportions of their enemy.

"Surprising wisdom, William, considering how you treated me the last time we met in person. Has something changed?" The former king's voice was tinged with humor.

"You smelled better then. If we fight now, I'll have to take a bath to wash your stench off. That spoils the mood." The words fell from his lips before his brain had a chance to edit them.

Thankfully, the dragon ignored his insult. "I've been looking for you, William. It's been terribly boring since you murdered me and kicked over my game board. Watching a nest full of eggs is hideously dull. If you're going to hatch secret plans to destroy my eggs and save the world, you could at least have the decency to let me watch."

"You have enough advantages already."

"Do I?" The dragon sniffed, inhaling so much air it almost pulled Will toward the enormous snout. "You've got the stench of necromancy around you, William. You've been consorting with my old playmate. It's bad enough you gave him Selene. Have you become his servant as well? I thought better of you."

How much does he know? Will had trained his mind and body for battle, but the fear and adrenaline coursing through him were too much for careful deliberation. *Calm down,* he told himself, taking a deep breath. "Facing you, I'll take whatever help I can find, but I'm no servant to the lich."

"Is that so? Why would you abandon your resources among the fae then? The one that leads them is just as mighty, yet you've limited yourself to allying with the failed wizard I defeated long ago. Trust me, he'll poison everything you've built," warned Lognion.

Raising his chin, Will responded, "I'll deal with him as well."

Lognion's voice rang out loudly in laughter, an eerie and unnatural thing as it was juxtaposed against the dragon's body, which remained still and unreadable. "That's the spirit! You should have been born a dragon, William. I am as proud of you as I am of my own daughter. Neither of you were ever willing to submit. You should destroy the walking corpse first, though."

Will's body was finally beginning to relax as it realized the danger wasn't immediate, and with the change, his thoughts began to clear. An idea percolated somewhere below the surface of his consciousness. "I'll need his help to kill you. Removing him early would be counterproductive."

Lifting his head, the dragon blew a small gout of flame into the sky, then replied, "Dragons eat the weakest first. That's why I plan to save you for the very last. If you bring that dusty skeleton to face me, it won't help. I can crush him in an instant. *You* are the better opponent. I imagine it will take several minutes before I can taste your flesh, assuming you don't flee. I was quite shocked to realize you had killed my egg guardians."

"You say you can crush him, but you can't kill the lich. Otherwise, he wouldn't still be here, taunting you after all these centuries."

"Trickery doesn't suit you, William," announced the dragon. "I am a paragon of chaos and creation, the power that underlies the foundation of the universe. If you want my advice on destroying the unlife that sustains that *gnat*, simply ask."

Cautious, Will declared, "I won't bargain or offer anything of value for your advice."

Massive lips pulled back to display enormous teeth as the dragon smiled, nearly causing Evie to attack. Will had to put his hand against her leg once more as Lognion responded, "Dragons rarely bargain, William, for we have no equals. We take what we desire. I will give you my advice freely, as a parent to the surviving whelp of a nest."

The metaphor disgusted him, but Will was too interested in the possibilities to spoil the conversation. "You know how to kill him?" He already had a plan for Grim Talek, but the dragon's answer might provide vital clues as to whether it would work, or whether there was a better option.

"Two ideas come to mind," said the dragon. "Starving him of the magic you wizards are so dependent on is the first. Vampires are anchored by blood, but the lich is merely a debased and inferior wizard. Without some source of power, his will must inevitably lose its grip on this world, causing his spirit to drift back to the primal source where all souls go to be reforged for the next life."

The dragon's description of death was fascinating, for Will had never heard it described in such a fashion before. Coming as it did from a self-professed paragon of chaos and creation, he filed it away as useful information. "Would Muskeglun work?" he asked, since the plane the trolls came from was famously meagre when it came to ambient turyn.

"I doubt it would be enough. You would need complete isolation, and then you'd need to exhaust whatever reserve he has."

Will knew of no spells that would completely isolate an area to enable such a turyn vacuum, but there were others who could help him investigate the idea. "What's the other idea?"

"The lich has anchored his soul to an enchanted object hidden away somewhere, a phylactery. Destroy it first, then destroy whatever body he is currently inhabiting, and he'll die like any mortal," answered the dragon.

"Do you know where his phylactery is?"

The dragon snorted. "The vermin still lives. That should be answer enough."

Will doubted he could find in the span of a few weeks what Lognion had missed in a millennia-long war. "Do you know what it looks like?"

"It could be anything, large or small, though within some limits, I'm sure. Hiding it is easy. The only hint at its location would be the fact that Grim Talek probably keeps it somewhere close to a source of new bodies so he can replace whatever body he has abandoned or lost."

Will's shoulders slumped slightly. The dragon's first idea was new, though it was similar in some ways to his own. The second idea was basic knowledge that he already knew, offering no real hope. "I don't think your ideas will help."

Before he could say anything, Lognion spoke again. "Not in a span of weeks, William. The greatest flaw of mortals, and youth in particular, is impatience. My eggs won't hatch for years yet, possibly even a decade—there's plenty of time for you to consider a different proposal."

He lifted one brow, surprised. "You aren't seriously trying to make a deal with me, are you?"

Lognion's disembodied voice chuckled realistically, even though the dragon's body remained still. "Why not?"

Will answered plainly, "I've killed you once, and I plan to do so again, hopefully with more final results. Why would you want to work with me?"

"I'm *bored*, William. That's my strongest motivation, alongside the fact that your current benefactor has been a thorn in my side for thousands of years. The game was interesting, but now that I've lost, there's nothing to occupy my mind."

The dragon's complaint seemed childish, but Will played along. "You're confident I'll lose when I come to square accounts with you. You can simply start another game after I'm dead. Leave me out of this."

The dragon growled faintly, sending a shiver through Will's chest and nearly sending Evie over the edge once more. "Without a human power base, my network of spies is deteriorating, not to mention I've already lost once. That's never happened before. If I'm to outmaneuver your moldering corpse-lover, I need to try something new. You are the ideal piece for this game."

"You want a double agent," said Will.

The massive eyes gazed at him with fierce intensity. "You already have his trust."

Shaking his head, Will confessed, "Selene would be a better choice for intrigue."

"She wouldn't cooperate, and her head is already swimming with the promise of Grim Talek's forbidden magics, but if *you* help me, she will have no choice. Without even telling her of my involvement, she can be brought to heel. If your focus is discovering the lich's secret, she will work tirelessly on your behalf."

From his own perspective, it all seemed silly. The game of nations that Lognion had lost did nothing to alter the ending. The dragon eggs would hatch, engulfing Hercynia in a titanic struggle for primacy and nourishment, destroying civilization and most life. Lognion would move on to a new home, and none of these distractions would matter, but the dragon was more concerned with his present boredom and evening his score with an opponent that couldn't hurt him. Under other circumstances, Will might have been tempted. The dragon would probably be an effective ally while trying to find a way to put Grim Talek to rest, but it was a selfish goal, for while it would prolong Will's life and possibly even succeed, he'd be lowering his chance of success against the ultimate enemy.

The lich had to die for Will to live, but the world would continue just fine either way. The dragon had to die no matter what. "No," he answered quietly.

"No?" Lognion's voice was full of menace.

Denying the drake was a mistake. Will knew the proper response would be to simply pretend and play along for the sake of keeping things quiet until they were ready to tackle the nest, but the fear generated by the dragon's massive presence had faded, and something more important had taken its place. In his mind's eye, he could still see Tabitha's body lying on the ballroom floor, studded with crossbow bolts. Worse yet, he had felt Laina's soul being shredded by the heart-stone enchantment. A fire was building in his belly, spreading to his heart and mind. "No."

Lognion's voice was full of puzzled resignation. "Help me understand. For as long as I have dealt with your kind, I have never understood the urge to suicide."

"You killed my sister."

"And your mother, but one sister remains. Are you willing to risk her life for your pride?"

Even angry, Will filed the information away. Lognion's sources were close enough to know that Grim Talek was tutoring Selene, but they didn't know that Erisa had survived. That reinforced the fact that the lich could indeed hide Will's friends and family successfully. "Pride has nothing to do with it," said Will evenly. "If it turns out I can only end one of you, you're the one that has to go in order to save my people. Using the lich to increase my chance of success is worth it, even if it means I'm less likely to survive in the end."

Will and Evie were once again treated to the sight of the dragon's deadly smile. Lognion's voice was accompanied by a deep rumble from the dragon's throat. "Unless I put an end to you here and now."

Widening his stance, Will opened his hands, holding them out slightly on either side of his body. An ominous rumble rolled across the forest, the threat of a storm despite the blue sky and sparse clouds. He'd been drawing power steadily for several minutes already, and without even consciously trying, Will knew the heavens were ready to answer his call. Sparks began to dance in the air around him, and the giant cat moved to one side, preparing to circle around the dragon. "You can try." Will's voice thrummed with latent power, filling the air with tension.

Time seemed to stop while the world held its breath, until finally the dragon laughed. "Not today. As much as I look forward to this fight, it would spell the end of my entertainment." Spreading his wings, Lognion took to the air. The downdraft blasted around Will but didn't move him, as a low-power wind-wall kept the air close to him steady.

As the dragon rose steadily, a new gate appeared, and the dragon flew toward it. Lognion's voice echoed. "I know your plan, William. You should have accepted my offer. Rejection comes at a price." The gate closed as the long tail passed through, leaving Will with nothing but adrenaline and unspent energy.

Will stared at Evie, marveling at her size while his heart gradually returned to its usual pace. The sudden ending of their crisis left him feeling as though he'd run a marathon. His head was swimming as fatigue washed over him. The cat standing across from him was nearly as large as the dragon had been, though she was already beginning to shrink. Evie's fur was already flattening as she relaxed.

"You don't want to fight that thing," said Will, sitting down and feeling the cool earth beneath his hands. "Next time, leave it to me." The great cat yawned as if dismissing his remark, then began to groom herself. He took it as a sign of her lingering tension, but Will still wanted his point to be clear, so he changed tactics. "Dragons taste bad."

Evie's green eyes locked onto him for a second, then drifted away. Lifting a massive paw, she began cleaning between her toe pads, flexing claws that were the size of swords and sharp enough to cut demon-steel. The breastplate Will wore still bore their marks.

"I'm serious. You'll never get the taste out of your mouth."

The giant feline finished with her paw, then stretched out, closing her eyes against the brightness of the rising sun. Despite having recently risen, Will had to admit that a nap sounded wonderful, but he couldn't afford to rest.

CHAPTER 33

Grim Talek answered immediately, though his face appearing in the silver metal only made it seem more like a mirror, since it was identical to his own. "I didn't expect you so soon. Have you already made contact?"

"No. The dragon just visited me."

The lich straightened in his seat, his attention fully focused. "How did he find you?"

Will sighed. "There's an astral connection between us. I'd suspected it previously, but I didn't want to believe it was true."

"You were that close? You should have warned me. This changes everything." Grim Talek ran his hand over his face in a gesture that seemed genuinely human. "Since you don't have any singe marks, I must presume your meeting was peaceful. Did you accept his offer?"

Will frowned. "How did you know?"

"It's only logical, and since you decided to inform me immediately after, I can also guess you were smart enough to accept."

He shook his head. "You need to get everyone to wherever your safe place is. He told me there would be a price to pay."

Grim Talek's eyes widened with surprise. "You told him no?" His mouth opened to say something more, then closed again, speechless.

"That's why you need to hide them. I don't know where he'll choose to strike."

The lich closed his eyes, becoming preternaturally still. "I've already made arrangements. Theravan and Mahak are in place. Moving people around in the absence of an actual threat will only increase the danger of *your* vengeful dragon finding the sanctuary."

Will still remembered finding his home replaced by a field of glass. "He can create gates! He could be anywhere. There might not be time for them to do anything if they don't have any warning."

With a sigh, the lich kept his words slow and clear. "I am not a fool, William. Everything I do is carefully considered. There was no warning with your mother either. Trust me, they'll be safe—my plans are thorough to a degree you obviously don't understand. Unlike your head, they are not full of holes." The long-dead wizard waited for several seconds to let his words sink in, then added, "Also, if you'll take a moment to think, you will remember that gates also need a beacon or an astral link, much as your teleport does. Lognion does have some limitations on his movement."

"He's still got thousands of people scattered across Terabinia tied to him with the heart-stone enchantment. I'm pretty sure he can use any one of those for a destination."

Anger began creeping into Grim Talek's voice. "I am well aware of that, and my statement stands. Are you ready to continue having a conversation, or have you decided to end our agreement because you don't trust me to handle my end of it?"

Realizing the danger, Will ground his teeth together while he struggled to get his emotions under control, then replied, "You guaranteed their safety."

The lich nodded. "Tell me the rest. I'm sure there was a longer conversation, and there are bound to be clues hidden within it."

Will related what had happened, sharing his words with the dragon to the best of his memory, though he left out the parts regarding the lich's potential vulnerabilities. When he finished, Grim Talek considered for a moment, then asked, "You didn't talk to him about ways to kill me?"

Their eyes locked, and Will considered lying. As intelligent as the ancient wizard was, the lich wasn't a nearly infallible lie detector the way Lognion had been. He discarded the thought as pointless. "There was nothing new in what he told me."

Grim Talek smiled slowly. "You're a bundle of contradictions, William. One minute I am convinced you're too naïve to be of any use, then you turn around and show a cleverness I didn't think you capable of. Why couldn't you have shown this wisdom when you were answering the dragon?"

Will's eyes were clear, and he answered with complete honesty, "I don't like games, and I find deception is often a waste of energy. At least you always know where you stand with me."

The lich's lip curled into a cynical half-smile. "Do I? I'm very old, William. Time has taught me many lessons, and one of the most important is that honest men are the most dangerous. They lull you into a sense of false security, and when you think them incapable of deceit, they fool you when none of the world's best liars could have managed it. Sincerity is the best veil for mendacity."

He shrugged. "That's for you to worry about, not me. I'm more concerned about our plan. Lognion said he knows what we're doing."

The lich nodded. "It's fairly obvious what we have to do, so I'm not surprised he knows the *what* of our plan, but learning the *how* of it is more difficult, nor do I think he suspects the scale of it. I can make a few changes on this end, so that once you deliver the materials, he will only see what he expects. I've already anticipated the fact that he has plenty of eyes among us."

Will still felt unsure. "How can you be so certain?"

"No one knows those things which I keep hidden, William, else I would have been extinguished long ago. That your mother is alive and he had no awareness of it should convince you of that. Nation by nation and war by war, I have driven my enemy from one fortress after another, until now he has no place left to hide. It's clear which of us is superior at this game; I have only lacked the power to drive my blade into his heart." Lifting an empty hand, the lich curled it around an invisible hilt. "With my guidance, your power will drive our retribution home and avenge the desecration of our world."

There was such passion in Grim Talek's voice, and despite himself Will shivered as he saw a cold, hateful light appear in eyes that looked exactly like his own.

***

Will finally encountered the road that led from Cerria to Branscombe, and skimming over it was simpler and consequently faster than being forced to regularly dodge trees and other mundane obstacles. Evie perched on the force disk in front of his feet, letting the wind flow over and around the lines of her now much smaller form. He felt better knowing she was there, though he still hadn't decided how he would keep her out of things when he met with the demons. The Cath Bawlg had had a longstanding enmity with the creatures of hell, for they had destroyed the demigod's home plane. Evie might not be aware of that, but Will worried that the goddamn cat's grievance might be etched in her bones.

Violence would be a surefire disaster if it ruined his proposal, but he wasn't certain he didn't welcome it. Sacrificing a nation for the metal they needed was evil yet pragmatic. If the only other option was letting the world burn, could he really refuse to do it? The Shimerans were demon-worshippers anyway, so if anyone deserved such a fate it had to be them.

Thinking about it filled his stomach with acid. Not everyone was complicit, and even those who were had been raised into their beliefs by those who came before them. *And what about the children? They're innocent regardless of what their parents do.* Will's mind worried at the problem ceaselessly.

Until a few days ago, he had quietly dreamed of sharing the awful secret with Selene. Knowing how smart she was, he'd secretly thought that if anyone could find an answer to his quandary, it would be her. Now he knew different. She had already guessed at his part in the plan. If she'd had a suggestion, she would have given it, but she had obviously resigned herself to him committing the lesser evil.

Looking up at the sky, Will swore, "How the fuck can sacrificing millions be the lesser of anything?"

The sound of distant thunder served as a reminder to keep his emotions under control. Will was still getting accustomed to his talents, and while he usually had to make a conscious effort to use them, his abilities were so natural that it was becoming obvious that a lot more was happening below the level of his conscious awareness. Deliberately harnessing the power of a storm seemed to require a substantial amount of turyn in order for him to bridge the gap and create a link to the turyn currents that drove the weather, and yet at moments like this, he somehow produced disturbances and lightning without an obvious link or intentional action.

Doing so deliberately involved transmitting his will, exercising control over his personal turyn to affect the turyn around him— creating a chain of causality far beyond the limit of the energy he could manipulate directly. Using the talent intentionally took a toll on the ultimate resource of a wizard—his will—while unconscious effects seemed practically effortless. He supposed that made sense, as Arrogan's training had focused mainly on giving him control of his body's turyn, limiting what was produced at the source and replacing it with turyn from the environment. Will's talents were a natural progression of that, extending his control far beyond traditional limits.

In the distance, Will could see hints of smoke over the tree line. Branscombe was close. He brought the travel disk to a stop and stared blankly ahead; his mind filled with memories of his time in the army there, back when Darrow had just invaded Barrowden. He hadn't had much power then, but he'd accomplished a lot anyway.

Janice and Tiny had convinced him that isolating himself and discounting his friends' help was a mistake, but a growing realization of potential made him aware that depression and sorrow had clouded his vision even further. "I'm a hell of a lot more powerful than I was back then," he announced to no one in particular.

Things began to click into place within his mind. There was a congruence point with the fae realm near Branscombe, and the trip to the mountain pass and the ley line intersection there would be a much shorter trip using the travel disk than it was back when he'd first walked it as a half-frozen refugee trying to reach the Terabinian army. He looked down at the cat sitting in front of his feet. "We have options." He was seeing much more than the cat, though. In his head, Will saw Rimberlin House and his cousin Sammy, and beyond them he saw Tailtiu. More figures raced through his thoughts as he considered friends and family, allies and enemies.

Evie looked up, meeting his distracted gaze. Sensing the change in mood, she meowed.

Will agreed. "You're right, fuck the demons." A brisk wind sprang up, rushing over the land and chilling his cheeks and nose. It felt like hope.

Demons, dragons, the fae, and even the elves, they'd all treated Hercynia as a passive resource, a plane to be exploited or abandoned—a place to be sold or discarded. Grim Talek had done his best, but failure had tainted the lich's worldview. Will wouldn't make the same error. He smiled, tasting the fresh air. "This is my home."

Pushing fresh turyn into the travel disk, he sped forward. There was much to do.

CHAPTER 34

The anti-possession spell was no longer something just for sleeping. Now that Will had confirmation that the dragon not only had an astral link with him, but also the ability to create gates, it was a requirement. He couldn't afford to allow anyone the chance to track his movements.

He stopped briefly in Branscombe to make arrangements for wagons and men to drive them. In the past, it might have taken much longer, both to get what he wanted and to convince others he could afford what he wanted, but those days were long gone. People in Branscombe knew him, and his station in Terabinian society was vastly improved. Those with the resources he needed took him at his word.

Moving on, he stopped at the congruence point with the fae realm before seeking his final destination. Crossing over, he called the names of those he wanted and then sat down to wait.

He didn't wait long. Against his expectations, Aislinn appeared first, riding toward him on the back of a beast he had never seen before. Initially, Will thought it a horse, then changed his view to thinking it must be a buck, given the large horns, but as it drew close, he could see it was neither. The mount she rode was distinctly equine in form and proportions, though it had cloven hooves. Magnificent antlers adorned the animal's head, but despite all his expectations when the creature opened its mouth, Will saw pointed incisors and long canines.

His grandmother climbed down from the heights, for her mount was taller than most destriers, and stared at him with unreadable eyes. "William."

He returned the greeting. "Grandmother."

Her gaze lingered on his unadorned fingers. "Given your recent secretiveness, I didn't expect to hear from you."

Will nodded, then looked down to inspect his nails. "You've taught me much, Grandmother, including that fact that it isn't wise to overly indulge in sentiment and nostalgia."

She smiled. "My gift has fallen out of favor then?"

"A question before terms have been given and agreed upon? Don't expect me to give away answers for free, Grandmother."

Her laughter rang out with a pleasant musicality almost impossible for mortals to aspire to. "One hour, question for question, no hostilities until the time is done?"

He shook his head in denial. "Not this time. I propose a test of wills, with the loser answering questions freely for one hour."

The ruler of the fae paused, one brow lifting in surprise, then replied, "No guarantee of neutrality after?"

"Why bother? You came alone. If you can best me, it would be foolish for you to bargain away that advantage before we deal with other matters," he answered.

Aislinn's lips parted, showing the tip of her tongue for a moment. "This is a significant risk, William. If you lose, I could take everything, including your life."

Holding up two fingers, he responded, "You owe me two unbound favors. One would be sufficient to save myself from you. I consider it a small risk."

She laughed again. "*You're* trying to tempt *me?* Is this bravado, or do you actually expect to win? Are you trying to add to your wealth by wrangling more favors from me if you prove yourself the victor?"

That surprised him. Will hadn't intended to fight her with the goal of winning another favor, but he could see why she would assume so. His goal was more subtle. *And she should have already guessed what I'm doing,* he realized. Grim Talek's words came back to him. *"Honest men are the most dangerous."* He suppressed a laugh. Aislinn was underestimating him based on what she'd seen in the past, assuming his goals were straightforward.

He answered with a truth that belied his greater reasons. "I just want to see who's stronger."

"How would you like to perform this test?" she asked. "A magical brawl between us could have far-reaching effects without rules."

Will was learning more with each statement she made. *She's actually worried about the outcome.* There was a practical element too, since either of them could potentially call in other resources to win the fight. Such things could prove costly or even waste resources that couldn't be replaced.

He had no intention of fighting her without rules or limitations, though. Even if things were held to just their personal abilities, a normal spell duel against the fae queen—also known as the goddess of magic—would be unwise. Aislinn possessed centuries of experience and an arsenal of spell knowledge that dwarfed his own. Such a battle would inevitably end in his defeat, and worse, it might not give him the information he wanted.

"Your power in this place is unparalleled. I propose a simple test rather than a contest of resources. One of us creates a small spell, perhaps a ball of flame, and we compete for control. Whoever can fully claim ownership and press the flame against the other will be the winner," he explained.

As one of the fae, Aislinn's soul wasn't human—that part of her had died long ago. What had replaced it was a fake; her spirit was a fragment of the plane they were in. That was what made the fae immortal. Their bodies drew upon the energies of their realm to sustain and repair them. Unlike Will, who only possessed the turyn his body created and the turyn around him, Aislinn could draw upon practically limitless amounts of turyn while she was in the fae realm.

His test would sidestep that, as well as the vast difference in their levels of skill and knowledge. It would focus purely on the strength of their respective wills, which was ultimately what he needed to know. That singular piece of data would tell him whether his plan for the demons was doomed to failure.

Aislinn studied him for a moment. "You were strong the last time we met, but not strong enough. Do you think a year has transformed you? You only escaped last time because of the intervention of others." She was referring to his battle against Madrok, when the fae had appeared unexpectedly, thanks to her gate and the secret beacon Aislinn had put in the ring she had given him. The current queen of the fae had crushed his will and trapped him with spell chains while the demon-lord had recovered.

"That was a bitter betrayal," he admitted, "but I've changed. Care to find out?"

"Allow me to choose the spell and we have a deal. Your little flame sounds tedious and boring." Lifting one hand, she created a tiny black orb above her palm. "This will make the contest more interesting."

Will hesitated, looking at the ominous sphere, which was roughly an inch in diameter. "I'm not familiar with that spell."

She flashed a wicked smile. "The spell was inspired by one of your grandfather's students who unleashed a spell anomaly when first learning to express turyn."

He vaguely remembered Arrogan telling him a story about Valemon's spell anomaly. The student who would later go on to found a religion and divide Darrow in a civil war had accidentally created a piece of uncontrolled magic that fed on whatever it touched, growing larger and more dangerous the more it destroyed. His grandfather had stopped the incipient disaster in its tracks, but he'd sounded uncertain about what might have happened if the chaotic magic had escaped his supervision. "What does it do?"

"It's similar to spells you've seen before that can disintegrate matter and eat through force effects, but far more precise and controlled. Anything that touches the sphere is destroyed, and unlike most magic, your personal resistance won't serve as effective protection. If it touches your skin, wizard or not, it will destroy flesh," she explained, her eyes lighting up with anticipation. "Unlike a simple flame, if you allow me to maintain control of this, I could burn a hole right through your chest."

Feeling his mouth go dry, Will answered, "That's acceptable, so long as the contest stops when one of us admits defeat."

"Or dies," she amended. "If you want to tempt me into this little wager, I need something significant to hope for."

He knew what she was implying. If her will proved insurmountable there was a chance he might crumble, giving her the ability to drive the deadly sphere through his heart before he could cry for mercy. Will's death would nullify the two unbound favors she owed him, a much greater gain than simply forcing him to use up one favor to save himself from her if he lost in a less fatal manner. "You have a deal."

Aislinn held out the sphere, then took two steps back, leaving the deadly orb hovering in the air. "I've released my hold on the spell, so there shouldn't be an unfair advantage. Let's see if you can force me to yield."

"I'm ready." He was standing roughly four feet away from the spell, and as he answered he stretched out with his will. There was no resistance at first, but the moment he started to claim the magic hovering in front of him another force took hold, and the formerly yielding turyn seemed to become hard and unrelenting like iron.

The deadly magic began drifting toward him while Aislinn gave him some cautionary advice. "Be sure to admit defeat early, Grandson. Wait too long, and your words might not reach my ears before the orb pierces your heart." The sphere inched closer, seeming to move faster with each passing second.

Momentum and inertia had no actual meaning in a contest such as theirs, but it did have a psychological impact that could definitely influence a mage's will. Seeing the sphere advance threatened to create cracks in Will's psyche, places where the seeds of doubt could take root and grow. Will was no stranger to such things, however. Arrogan had derided him constantly, and since the day he had struck out on his own, he'd faced a never-ending series of opponents who sought to instill fear within him.

Such an environment could only do one of two things to the person living in it. The recipient of such treatment either broke or emerged from the flames stronger than ever. Will didn't like living in fear, and he'd long ago decided that the day he broke would be the day he died. The present moment was a perfect and very real example of that very thing.

Curling his lip, Will twisted his body involuntarily as he reversed his efforts, pulling the orb toward himself. As it surged closer, his influence grew stronger, while Aislinn's waned slightly. Shifting the orb's course to one side, Will sent the orb spinning around him, then drove it back toward the queen of the fae.

Aislinn's eyes widened as the tactic caused her to falter, and the orb flew straight at her breast. Her brow furrowed faintly as she increased her concentration and eventually arrested the approaching sphere. It stopped half a foot from her skin, then began moving back toward the midpoint between them.

Will pushed harder. Beyond the midpoint he was at a disadvantage, since distance from the caster was a factor in how effective their will was. That was the reason wizards could generally rely on spell resistance. Once turyn was close enough to come into physical contact, it was nearly impossible for another practitioner to have more influence than the one being contacted. Of course, if Aislinn was to be believed, this spell would ignore that sort of resistance.

And she can't lie, Will reminded himself. Lifting his eyes from the deadly magic, he observed his grandmother's face. What he saw gave him renewed confidence.

In spite of her eternal beauty and grace, her reputation for unflappability, the so-called goddess of magic was struggling. The fae queen was so enraptured by their battle that her tongue had crept from her lips and she was biting down on it as she strove to best him. It was an expression he'd seen many times on his cousin Sammy's face, and it was so thoroughly human that Will couldn't help but be encouraged. Somewhere deep down, one final illusion within Will's mind was dispelled. His grandmother wasn't invincible—she had limits, just like everyone else.

The orb moved back toward Aislinn, and she began to growl in frustration, but the magic wouldn't stop. Will fought for every inch, and though the battle became tougher the farther the orb got from him, he didn't relent. The ebon sphere reached his grandmother's chest, eating effortlessly through the fabric.

Blood soaked the fae queen's dress as a circular section of skin disappeared a moment later. She hissed in pain as fat and muscle followed, exposing the bone of her sternum. Soon, the deadly magic would reach her heart, and yet she stubbornly continued to fight. Will could understand why.

It wasn't that she cared so much about winning and losing; it was the simple fact that deep down, Aislinn was a prisoner. Born human, her mind rebelled against the endless suffering of her inhuman existence. Being fae, she couldn't die, couldn't even attempt to die, but at her core, she wanted a way out, though she wasn't even capable of saying the words—secretly she hoped he would finish her.

But her nature wouldn't allow suicide any more than it would allow lies. As the magic ate through bone, her voice finally rang out, "I admit defeat."

Will pulled the deadly magic back, then unraveled the spell. Seeing his grandmother's ruined flesh, he couldn't help but feel guilty, but he knew better than to allow sympathy to soften his words. "One hour, then. You'll answer all questions freely without recompense."

She nodded.

In the past, there had always been limitations, a question for a question, or some other price. Today was the first time he could ask for it all. One of his two unbound favors could have accomplished the same thing, but the contest had been his first question, and one that couldn't have been answered otherwise. "Whose will is stronger, yours or Grim Talek's?"

Aislinn smiled. "It has been over a century since we fought directly. When Arrogan and I faced the lich together, he was stronger, but between us, we overcame him. If not for his undead allies and hidden phylactery, we might have put an end to him."

Will frowned. He'd hoped for a different answer.

"But my strength has grown since then," she added, "while his has changed little."

"He's much older. Age is an advantage, isn't it?"

His grandmother nodded. "But not as much as you might think. Your will increases the most in the early years and less as time goes by. After existing for several millennia, I doubt the lich's will grows by more than the tiniest drop with each year. By comparison, I am a youngster of less than a thousand years, and you, sweet child, are but a babe. You have grown strong beyond all expectation, and while you may have achieved the majority of your strength now, you still have some to gain, certainly more than I do and much more than that struggling corpse. If I am not stronger than that fiend, I would be surprised." She smiled. "You played a deadly game to judge yourself against your ally indirectly?"

"Not only him," said Will. "Even if there's diminishing gains with age, I don't understand how either of us could be close to him in strength if he's as old as you say."

"Those without a source suffer from a serious disadvantage, William. That's why undead wizards lose their greater talents. The lich was probably stronger when he was alive, and if he's managed to reach parity with his former self, it is only because of his vast age."

"One of them described himself as 'fourth-order' to me," said Will.

Aislinn smirked. "A euphemism to make themselves feel better about what they have lost. While freedom from death grants time to perfect one's spellcraft, it's a bitter consolation and poor replacement for the glorious sensation of subverting the currents of the world to one's own purpose."

"Do you miss it?"

"I am not dead, Grandson, merely changed."

"But your human self is gone. You are Aislinn only in name and memories, correct? Doesn't that mean you've lost your source, and thus your talents?"

She smiled. "You plumb secrets never revealed to mortal ears. You are right in the essence of it, but while my humanity and the source I was born with are gone, they have been replaced by something else."

"A piece of this place," said Will, gesturing vaguely to the verdant forest around them.

She nodded. "It is very much like a source, but it provides near limitless turyn whilst I abide within this realm. In your world, ley lines are required to power the greatest magics, things I can do here on little more than a whim. My old talents are not so much gone as transformed."

"And yet Arrogan was able to best Elthas whenever they fought."

"Elthas was a fool, and no wizard," said his grandmother with obvious derision. "I was bound to him only by my oath. Never make the mistake of attempting to challenge me here as your grandfather did with the forest lord."

Will smiled.

"Your strength of will is hard to credit, but I feel sure you're wise enough to realize what would happen if we engaged in a broader conflict," she warned.

He agreed with her, but it wasn't a statement to be acknowledged while he stood within her realm, especially without an agreement of a truce in place. He had negotiated only for answers, not safety. An open admission of weakness might force Aislinn to capitalize upon it. He moved on to his next topic instead. "I have questions regarding the gate magics you provided me with. I've succeeded with teleportation, including without beacons, but gates are proving more difficult." He summoned the notes he had made from the limnthal along with a small camp table to lay them on.

Over the course of the next half hour, Aislinn tutored him as she might have done Arrogan once, centuries past, answering questions and pointing out mistakes in his thinking. Will had made several errors in his interpretation of the journals, but one problem still remained. "Assuming I didn't screw things up in some different way, I still should have had a partial success previously, or at the very least a catastrophic failure. Instead, there was nothing."

"Were you using a ley line?"

He shook his head. "I was at Rimberlin House, but it was just a tiny gate I was experimenting with."

"Then you didn't have the power necessary."

"It was tiny," he insisted.

"Since you've teleported yourself, you think you have an idea of the power required?" she asked rhetorically. "Trust me. You do not. To create even a temporary tear in reality and join two disparate places or planes is no trivial task."

"You do it," he said flatly.

"From this plane. Here, I am a goddess in more than name or rumor. In this place, I command nearly limitless energies. Think to yourself, have you ever seen me create a gate from your world that did not touch this realm? In Hercynia I can still create gates, but only if they connect to this plane. I could not create one that went elsewhere, for that I would have to come here first—or use a ley line."

Her words made sense, but he still had questions. "The dragon did it while flying, and I'm sure there was no ley line there. Care to explain that?"

"My knowledge of dragons is limited. Your lich likely knows more, but if what you say is true, I can say this. The dragon is possessed of power at least as great as a ley line, or greater still, like mine while within this realm. Keep that in mind during your calculus for the battle to come."

That was sobering, but Will had little time to waste. "Do you know of a way to kill the dragon?"

"No."

"Do you have any hints regarding the whereabouts of Grim Talek's phylactery?"

"None, other than that he does not carry it with him," she answered.

"Do you know anything about what Selene is working on?"

"My information is limited since you warned her about the ring. Before she put it away, I observed many things. Your wife is versatile and intelligent. Her claim to being able to advance the state of the medical arts is no idle boast. You should admire her but remain wary, for she's taken to necromancy like a duck to water."

Frowning, he asked, "What does that mean?"

Aislinn shrugged. "Little to me, but my old self would have had opinions. Would you care to hear them?"

It had only happened once before, in the early days after he had first met his so-called grandmother. He'd asked her to speak as the woman she once was, and now he was tempted to do so again, though he feared the emotions she might evoke with her roleplay. After a moment's consideration, he nodded. "Speak as your former self."

The transformation was immediate and frightening, as Aislinn's features, demeanor, and posture somehow communicated a complete shift, from heartless cruelty to tragic sorrow. "Your wife is at a crossroads with her art. Her path will be driven by the motivations of her heart, which is always dangerous. Your love may save or damn her, and fond as I am of her, I worry more about what she might do to you."

He watched her face, but from the corner of his eye, Will could see his grandmother's hands had opened, reaching toward him almost involuntarily. He took a small step back. "That's too vague."

Aislinn nodded. "Hold her close and you might keep her from dark temptations; spurn her and she may delve into darker arts. The key to either choice is love, but there's no way to be sure what will happen. Despair is your enemy."

"Again, too vague."

His grandmother shook her head. "I don't have anything concrete. I've seen her working with patients, and what she's doing is nothing short of miraculous. My words are nebulous because I can only share my intuition based on centuries of experience. Every form of power offers temptations, but necromancy offers unique corruptions for body and spirit. If she falls into despair, she will see that there are many ways to turn her new knowledge against the enemy, but necromancy turned to war leads only to evil.

"Look at me, William. Am I not a perfect warning? Look at what I have become." A solitary tear rolled down one cheek. "If she falls into darkness, you will reject her, of that I have no doubt, and then she will become an enemy you have no hope of overcoming. Your heart will become your weakness, for no matter how great your strength is, I fear you could never turn it against the one you love."

The emotion radiating from Aislinn was overwhelming, and despite knowing it was merely an act, Will couldn't help but be moved. "Enough," he declared. "I understand your meaning, but you still haven't given me any details regarding her current work."

Like a light extinguished, the compassion illuminating his grandmother's features vanished in the blink of an eye, leaving only inhuman dispassion. "Other than her efforts with the sick, the main project I observed involves your overlarge friend, but in my opinion, it is a harmless endeavor with only tangential influences from the lich's techniques. You should applaud her, for she has found a way to nullify your worst tendencies when it comes to receiving aid from a friend."

"My worst tendencies?"

"Your refusal to allow them to share your risk. Selene is working on something similar to a golem but with more refinement. The golems of old were always limited by their lack of true intelligence."

Will was unfamiliar with the term. "This is the first I've heard of them."

Aislinn smirked. "Imagine a doll that moves under its own power. Your wife is crafting something similar to enable your friend to fight beside you without endangering himself. Are you not pleased?"

He felt vaguely uneasy and mildly irritated. "I never asked for that. How is she doing it?"

The queen of the fae shrugged. "This is new magic, and I was only able to observe briefly. She has kept the finer details of her work concealed even from me."

Rubbing his chin, Will asked, "But you're sure it isn't dangerous to her, or Tiny?"

"I am sure of nothing, Grandson, but her accomplice in this is your friend Janice. Given her intelligence, not to mention her vested interest in your knight's personal wellbeing, I think it unlikely that they will harm him."

Will's eyes narrowed. Even with a guarantee of truth and unlimited questions, he didn't trust his grandmother. "It took you long enough to tell me what Selene was doing, despite our agreement. Why?"

"I have an internal motivation that goes against some of the oaths I am bound by, preventing me from communicating without at least attempting to divert your attention away from some matters," she admitted.

Realizing they were dancing around matters that could quickly turn dangerous, Will probed carefully. "By internal motivation you mean a desire that is independent of your condition?"

"Define condition."

"Your nature as one of the fae."

She nodded. "That is an accurate way of expressing it."

"What's the subject of that motivation?"

Aislinn's lips parted, then closed. Briefly, Will could see frustration flicker across her features as she struggled to find words that would convey her meaning without violating some other limit set upon her. A second later, she answered, "Your success."

Will had long thought that his grandmother secretly hoped he would win, perhaps almost as strongly as she secretly wished for her own extinction, but it wasn't something he could trust, for no matter what she truly wanted, Aislinn was bound by the rules of the fae. Sentimentality would only make him more vulnerable if he allowed his emotions to color his dealings with her. In this case, the rules forced her to answer him, but Aislinn feared her answers would undermine his chances.

"You're worried I'll try to stop Selene from making this golem?"

She bowed her head slightly. "In matters regarding your friends and family, you invariably make poor choices if you think it will help them."

Fair enough, Will thought. *I deserve that.* As much as he wanted to examine that issue, he was running out of time, though. "Tell me about your agreements with the other powers involved in all of this."

"Are you attempting to bring about my death?" asked the fae queen.

Oops. He needed to be more specific. If the current requirement that she answer any question ran directly counter to one of her other immutable entanglements, it would kill her, for whether she answered or refused, it would violate one of them. "Answer only when possible, but if a conflict exists, merely tell me that instead. Do you have an agreement with the dragon?"

"Yes."

A rapid-fire succession of questions followed, during which Will was able to ascertain that the fae had agreements to share information regarding him with both the dragon and the elves, though in the case of the latter it seemed mostly to be a case of staying informed. The elves had no intention of entering the fray unless their own realm was threatened. As expected, there were no arrangements with the lich, but the demons were a more interesting question. "Do you have a deal with the demons?"

Aislinn's teeth showed as she flashed a predatory grin. "Not since you eliminated Madrok."

"So you're free to act against them without restriction?"

She licked her lips in anticipation. "I am free to accept a bargain to their detriment. My people never act without reason. Favors must be exchanged."

"It's a good thing I happen to have a couple of favors waiting to be redeemed then," Will replied, showing a dangerous smile.

CHAPTER 35

Their hour had come to an end, but Will was now ready to make a deal. "I would like to use one of the favors you owe me. To discuss it, I propose another half hour, no hostilities allowed."

"With the usual restrictions on information," added his grandmother.

He nodded. "Of course. Nothing free unless I specify it as a condition of satisfying the favor once it is defined."

"Agreed."

"I want you to create a gate for me at a certain time and place," said Will, jumping straight to it.

"Where and when?" she asked. When he told her, she immediately shook her head. "That's impossible for me."

Will assumed it was because the gate didn't connect with the fae realm on either side, so he clarified, "There's an intersection of ley lines there. Power won't be an obstacle; I simply need someone with your skill."

"Still impossible. It conflicts with a prior agreement."

"With whom?"

His grandmother smiled. "That isn't pertinent to this deal. Will you answer a question in return?" When he nodded, she answered, "The agreement that would be violated is the accord you made with me after the old one was broken. You didn't trust yourself to negotiate an entirely new accord, so you stipulated it would be the same as the old one, with only the minor changes you specified. The old accord specifically forbade the fae from creating any portal or gateway connecting your realm to any other."

Will groaned. It was a reasonable precaution, as it would prevent the fae from making a deal with someone else to allow an invasion from hell or some other equally antagonistic plane. He'd never expected the accord would prevent him from doing exactly the same thing.

Aislinn claimed her question and asked, "How will you kill Grim Talek?" He hadn't expected something so far from their current topic, but Will knew better than to refuse. He answered, but kept the details as limited as possible without violating the spirit of the exchange. Aislinn nodded in appreciation before commenting, "Clever, though it will be difficult to execute."

He hadn't intended on approaching her on that topic, but now that it was out, he decided to risk another question. "Do you know of anything that would improve the odds of it working?"

"Question for question," she replied, then after his agreement, she continued, "I am not sure your method will work, but I know a spell that would vastly speed up the attempt. My turn. Do you know the nature of the cat following you?"

Will nodded. "I believe it to be a rebirth of the Cath Bawlg, but I don't have incontrovertible evidence." Returning to the subject of his favor, Will tried a different direction. "You can't open the gate yourself, but you could act as a mentor for my agent, correct?"

"I have often been a teacher," said Aislinn.

"Perfect," said Will, rubbing his hands together. "Then in addition to teaching me the spell you just alluded to, I will have you teach the person or persons of my choosing to open a gate such as I previously described. I will also—"

"Providing they have the necessary capability," interrupted the fae queen. "Some time will also be required, depending on their current level of skill." It was a fair amendment, otherwise Will could demand she teach someone incapable and force her into failure. Will agreed, then finished describing what he wanted. When he finished, Aislinn commented, "Your requested favor is rather expansive."

Will shrugged. "It's an unbound favor. I could ask you to mobilize the entirety of your forces and engage in a hopeless war. I think my request is fair. It involves a few disparate tasks and some effort, but it is far more limited than it has to be. Can you refuse me?" He worded the final question to force her hand. If his demands were within reason, she had to admit it.

"No. If that is what you want, then state it fully and I will respond, sealing our agreement."

He did.

A short time later, he was back in his own world again, riding the travel disk once more with Evie at his feet. His head was occupied by his recent meeting with Aislinn and what he would need to do over the next hours and days to maximize the potential benefits of her favor. With as much haste as possible, he skimmed along the mountain road, following the rising terrain until he was up above the snowline.

It wasn't far from there that he'd killed his first man, and though it had only been a few years, it seemed to Will as though it had happened in a different life. He'd killed many more since then, directly, indirectly, and in all manner of circumstances. The minority he had slain in self-defense, and a much larger proportion simply because it was necessary, but most bothersome was the not inconsequential number he had killed for vengeance or while caught up in bloodlust.

Keeping his eyes and senses focused on the currents of turyn that flowed over and through the mountains, Will pushed such dark thoughts aside. Unseen beneath him, the bones of his first victim went by unnoticed, hidden under a blanket of snow. Gradually, Will became aware of a difference in the turyn to the north of the mountain pass. It seemed thicker there, with better defined patterns in the air, as though some more powerful current was creating turbulence. It was a subtle effect that he probably wouldn't have noticed if he hadn't been searching for it.

Ascending through rough and rocky terrain, Will eventually reached a point where the effect seemed roughly similar in every direction, so he dispelled his travel disk and put his feet on the ground. Concentrating, he took hold of the energy around him and used it to touch the power beneath him, questing half blind until he felt something powerful below. *That's it.*

Excited, he hoped it would be a quick task to find the intersection between the one ley line and the other, but his optimism proved to be unfounded. The line he found turned out to be running north and south, rather than east and west as he had originally assumed. Ascertaining that took nearly an hour, and then he spent another three hours following it to the north before deciding he had gone the wrong way.

Heading south again, he followed the north-south ley line back to the pass and then farther south. Night fell, and the moon was high in the sky when he finally reached the intersection. It was located in a deep cut between two massive stone outcroppings. The bottom was deep with snow and packed ice, but Will could see carved stones marking an old path that led from the direction of the pass. At some point in the past, people had been there, probably for the same reason he had come.

Weary from a long day, Will made a cold camp on the ice. Without solid ground beneath him, he couldn't use the ground warming spell, so he had to rely on an army cot and multiple layers of blankets to keep him warm. Will was grateful he was no longer a private contract soldier, for back in those days he'd had only a bedroll and ground pad. He'd acquired the cot after serving as royal marshal in the war with Darrow.

Only high-ranking officers had the luxury of having cots carried in the baggage train, but after experiencing one, Will had seen the wisdom of keeping one stored in his limnthal.

Sleeping directly atop the ice would have been lethal with nothing more than a regular bedroll.

Evie seemed to find his choice of camping spots offensive and disappeared soon after it was apparent that Will intended to sleep there, not to reappear again until morning as he packed away his things. Her green eyes seemed to mock him as he stretched to get the stiffness out of his back and shoulders. "I'm sure you slept somewhere better," said Will wryly.

The little cat answered with a mew that sounded very much like a yes, though he might have been imagining it.

"Well, I'm glad you were comfortable." Creating another travel disk, he and the cat descended into the wide crevasse, which was some thirty yards wide at the top and perhaps only ten at the bottom. Old ice and snow obscured everything, hiding the true bottom, so Will was forced to use a succession of fire spells to melt some of it away until at last he found a flat stone surface. Several grooves and cut lines made him suspect he had found a floor enhanced by deliberate masonry, so he worked from there to clear away more ice.

Not possessing a fire elemental or any special talent with fire, Will had to use the spells he knew and a small amount of wild magic to slowly clear the area. It turned out to be a herculean task, and by the time noon arrived he still had barely made a dent in it. The floor was indeed artificial, but he'd only excavated a circle with a diameter of twenty feet around himself. "This is stupid," he told himself.

Inspiration struck, and Will moved over to the eastern side of the cleared area. On that side the ice was thickest, forming what could almost be called a glacier that covered everything on that side and beyond, eventually sloping away down the side of the mountain once it emerged from the stone crevasse. Putting his hands against the ice, Will used the turyn around him to induce a slow vibration, pushing more and more energy into it until he found the correct frequency. He knew when he found it because the energy of the vibration stopped fading without constant input and began increasing instead.

Grinning foolishly to himself, Will nursed the resonant vibration until the ice began to quiver and crack. It happened slowly at first, and he withdrew his power early to be cautious, but Will soon learned that his preconceptions about how ice fractured were highly inaccurate. Things started as he expected, but the ice collapse propagated far beyond where he had started. Popping and snapping, lines raced up the ice along the sides of the crevasse, and the air quickly filled with fragments and falling snow from above.

The sound grew to a level that filled his ears with a solid roar as Evie nervously backed into his legs. She was growing rapidly in response to the danger, but while Will could see her mouth moving, it was impossible to hear her cries. *Well, shit,* he thought. *We're about to be buried.*

He erected a quick force-dome, and because the frightened cat had grown larger than a horse, he was forced to make it bigger than he would have liked. To minimize the size and maximize its strength, he ducked beneath Evie's belly and made the dome just large enough to cover her. The world went completely white and then dimmed to black as the sky vanished. Several large shocks impacted Will's shield, strong enough to have shattered it under normal circumstances, but he was already drawing on the enormous potential of the ley line just below his feet.

Minutes passed, and silence returned to the furry darkness. It was broken only by a loud and uncertain mew from the large cat whose belly was resting on top of his head. "It's going to be all right, Evie," he assured her, though he didn't feel quite as sure as he tried to sound. The weight on his force-dome indicated they were under a significant amount of snow and ice, and he knew from previous experiences being buried alive that there wasn't enough air to survive for an extended period of time. *How much air does a giant cat demigod require?* he wondered. *Does it change according to her size, or does she really need to breathe at all?*

The cat's voice changed from uncertain to angry or perhaps fearful as an angry hiss issued from Evie's throat.

"Don't do anything crazy," warned Will. "I think you can probably dig your way out once I remove the dome, but if you aren't careful, the ice could easily crush me." As if in response, Evie went silent, but he could only hope she understood. "In a few seconds, I'm going to remove the shield, and the weight of all this is going to drop onto your shoulders. I'll put a fresh shield over myself at almost the same time so you can try to climb out. Just don't panic and kick it. Your claws might wreck my defense, and then I would be in serious trouble. If it turns out that you can't move, just wait and I'll switch tactics. I have another spell that might be able to dig us out, but it takes time." *Please understand me, please.*

The cat uttered a single sound, which despite its distortion sounded suspiciously like 'yes.'

"Get ready. I'm doing it now." Will dropped the force-dome and created another smaller one an instant later, encasing just himself. Everything shifted, but the giant cat remained steady as the ice and snow settled in around her. She gave out a slow rumble that rose rapidly in volume, warning him as she prepared to move.

He heard the mass around him shift, but nothing happened. After a moment, Evie began rumbling again, her body growing once more. Adjusting his vision, Will could see a paw the size of an ale barrel beside his defensive dome. The cat was nearly the size she had been when they had faced Lognion. Claws the size of scimitars dug into the stone, and Will could only hope the cat wouldn't hit his shield. The force of such a blow he might be able to handle, given the massive flows of turyn currently available to him, but the claws themselves might be a different matter. Anything that could cut demon-steel was nothing to be trifled with.

The stone beneath his feet thrummed like a giant drum, and a flash of light appeared overhead as the Cath Bawlg reborn leapt upward, exploding out of the ice like a rabbit hidden by fresh snow. Then darkness returned, and the full weight of the frozen materials resumed pressing down on Will's shield. *Now I just have to get myself out.*

Unfortunately, that was easier said than done. Unlike the time he and Selene had been buried, he had no one to alternate shields with him, and it was already quite clear that the material pressing down wasn't sufficiently packed to hold its place. The moment he released his shield, the air pocket around him would vanish. The grave digging spell he had used before needed an empty space to move earth into.

A darker thought occurred to him then. *Will the grave digging spell work on ice?* It was designed for dirt and gravel. Mentally, he ran through the rune structure to see the specifics and was disheartened to find that it had been designed with efficiency in mind. Broadening the spell's purpose to handle other solid materials would have made it more expensive to cast. Given time, Will could create an adaptation for snow and ice, but doing so while working entirely within his own head would probably lead to a fatal mistake. A few hours at a desk followed by some careful experimentation would be his preferred environment for creating a modified spell.

Teleportation was his other option, and Will already had the spell prepared. The force-dome didn't fully enclose him, as it was just a hemisphere ending at the stone floor. If it had been a sphere or a force-cage, teleportation would have been impossible, but there were other factors to consider. *Can I maintain the shield while slipping into the astral plane to find someone to teleport to?* He could last without air for a minute or two, but the weight of the ice might be too much for his body. Whatever he chose, he needed to do it soon.

Everything began to shake, and a strange chittering cry filtered through the ice. Light appeared and then vanished as the weight on his force-dome alternately eased and then returned again. Hope lifted his heart as Will realized what was happening. *She's digging me out!*

Again, he worried about the Cath Bawlg's deadly weapons, but as the minutes passed, he could tell the demigod was working carefully, pawing around his position to clear the sides nearby before slowly removing the ice directly over his head. The sky reappeared several times before remaining for good, but Will waited until he was sure that Evie had stopped before dropping his shield and clambering out of the modest pit of ice still around him.

"Thank you, Evie. You saved my ass," said Will gratefully.

A giant pink tongue replied, painfully scraping the side of his face. At her usual size, Evie's tongue was raspy, but currently it felt like having his head shoved into a gravel road. Touching his cheek, Will saw blood on his fingertips. He dodged the cat's second attempt. "Maybe you should shrink down first," he cautioned, then changed his mind. "Wait! Can you clear some of this away before you return to normal?"

Green irises the size of dinner plates stared down at him, then slowly vanished as the cat blinked. Rising on all fours, Evie began kicking with her hind legs, sending large chunks of ice and snow sailing away to fall down the mountainside. Adjusting her position and aiming her kicks, the large cat cleared an area some thirty feet across before stopping. She was panting now and obviously tired. Her size gradually decreased, and when she was close to Will in overall weight, she paused and let out a strangely garbled 'meow.'

Will watched her curiously, wondering what the cat was trying to communicate, and after a moment, she tried again, but he still couldn't understand her. Back before his demise, the goddamn cat had spoken only rarely, but when he did, his voice had been perfectly human. Much like the dragon had done, the Cath Bawlg had used magic to create a voice since his throat hadn't been capable of it. Whatever Evie was trying to say, it was obvious she didn't know the same trick.

Frustrated, Evie's body began to shift in unusual ways. A minute later, she stood in front of him on two legs in an odd humanoid form that would be sure to induce nightmares in children if they saw it. She was still mostly covered in fur, but her torso was covered with what appeared to be a dress, if one didn't look too closely. A careful inspection revealed it to be a bizarre and wholly unnatural extension of her skin attempting to mimic clothing. Her forelegs became arms, and Evie's paws were now shaped into something similar to hands, though the curved claws remained.

Worst of all was her head. It had transformed into a terrifying mixture of feline and human shapes and features. The back was partially covered by a fur ruff that poorly mimicked human tresses. The overall effect was something reminiscent of what a drunken cat might think of a woman's shape and form. Grossly, it was correct in size and proportion while completely missing the finer details real human brains expected to find.

Will fought hard to suppress his urge to recoil in disgust. Evie spoke again, and this time her voice was intelligible, though still distorted. "Hungry. Hunt time."

He nodded quickly. "Of course. Take your time. I will be fine."

Alien eyes studied him, then she reached out with one of her grotesquely clawed hands to touch his hand. "No fur." Evie's hand-paws began changing, losing their fur and assuming a shape almost identical to Will's. The claws became black nails that stretched only slightly beyond the fingers. It was an impressive feat ruined only by the fact that they didn't match her body, being overlarge and too masculine for the feminine frame Evie had assumed.

Will had never had much success at shapeshifting with wild magic, despite Tailtiu's attempt at lessons, and he had never dared any formalized spells to reshape his flesh, so he decided it was best not to judge. "I'm not cold," he answered, pulling his hand back and touching his sleeve and then his cloak. "These keep me warm enough."

Evie cocked her head slightly to one side then put her hand on his neck. Will suppressed a nervous swallow as she pulled at the neck of his tunic and slipped her hand beneath it to feel his shoulders and upper chest. As she released him, Will attempted to demonstrate, lifting the bottom edge of his tunic to show her that it was separate from his trousers. "See? My clothes are separate from my body. They don't grow out of me."

Before he could stop her, the inhuman hybrid thrust one hand into the waist of his trousers, exploring the boundary between skin and cloth. Will jumped and nearly fell backward as Evie's rough fingers passed too close to areas he would rather avoid. "That's enough," he told her as he stepped away and restored his dignity.

His companion ignored his discomfort, looking at the sky. "Hunt. Dark." She finished by pointing at the stone beneath his feet.

"I'll be fine," Will replied. "I'll see you tonight when you return. Right?"

Without any expression to confirm his guess, the demigod transformed back into a cat, this time adjusting her size to something approaching that of large hunting cat. Never looking back, she made her way up the now mostly uncovered path that led to the top edge of the crevasse and was gone.

Exhausted, Will sat down on the cold stone and surveyed his surroundings. A significant portion of the outer edges was still covered by ice, but he could tell from the outlines that he sat on a broad stone floor cut and leveled from what had originally been a natural break in a massive stone outcrop embedded in the side of the mountain. The area measured roughly fifty feet wide and stretched more than a hundred feet in length, with one end tapering to an abrupt end partly within the mountain while the other end led to an abrupt drop down a rocky slope more than a hundred feet below.

A lot more ice would need to be melted and cleared away, but Will could see the outline of a large ritual circle composed of two lines that were each roughly an inch deep. They formed a perfect circle over twenty feet in diameter, with one circle a few inches within the other. Between the two was a smooth, empty area where runes or other symbols could presumably be drawn. He was glad the original creators of the circle hadn't engraved their choice of symbols so he didn't need to remove them. The design was highly flexible since one could redraw the runes for different purposes.

The amount of work remaining made him feel even more tired, but it also inspired a fresh thought. *Since I'm planning to bring in a few allies, I might as well let them help with the labor,* he thought with a faint smile. Will closed his eyes and started to slip from his body, but at the last moment a shift in the turyn made him look around.

Given the intense flows of energy just under him, it was a testimony to his sensitivity that he noticed the change amid the relative magical 'noise.' Lifting his gaze, he finally spotted the visitor: Tailtiu was making her way down the steep stone stair path. She had taken the form of a mountain goat with a woman's torso and arms where the head should have been. As a result, she had the appearance of a weird and somewhat small centaur, if such creatures really existed. As far as Will knew, they were only an invention of some of the fanciful romance writers Janice favored.

The choice of form was apropos since it allowed her to nimbly make her way down the parts of the stair that were still occluded. When Tailtiu reached the bottom, she resumed her usual form, that of a slender and aggressively naked woman with red hair. The fae woman retained her catlike eyes with slits for pupils, but unlike Evie, she managed to do so in a way that enhanced her visual appeal rather than sending shivers of terror up Will's spine.

"Took you long enough," declared Will as a greeting.

His fae aunt lifted her chin proudly. "I am a free woman now. I come and go as I please." After a brief pause, she added, "Master." As always, she couldn't help but say the word in a way that intimated a plethora of carnal pleasures awaited him if he would only give her the command.

Will sighed, rolling his eyes. Age, experience, and wisdom made it easier for him to ignore her allure, though he had to admit that his recent solitude caused him to feel more frustration than usual. "Can you turn it down a bit?" he asked.

Tailtiu gave him a coy glance as she replied, "Is something bothering you?"

"I thought we agreed you'd start wearing clothes."

"Around other humans," she corrected, playfully running her hands across her chest. "We are alone here, and the wind feels good on my—skin."

Will didn't bother looking away. He'd learned long ago that showing embarrassment would only increase the teasing. His wife was better endowed anyway, though Tailtiu's inhuman perfection still gave her an unfair advantage somehow. Realizing his thoughts were becoming undisciplined, Will shifted tactics. "You were afraid to come, weren't you?"

His aunt froze, then bit her lip uncertainly, showing a sliver of fear that would have been impossible for her when she had been a true creature of the fae realm. Now that she had a soul of her own, such frail emotions often tormented her. "The beast was here. I can smell it everywhere. You told me it was dead."

The fae had always been cautious and had tried to avoid the Cath Bawlg at all costs, since the goddamn cat had made a practice of eating them whenever possible. Unlike most injuries, being eaten by him had been permanently fatal for the immortals, leaving only bones that would not regenerate. Aislinn had shown no fear, since she was incapable of it, and being who she was, she probably had the least to worry about. The somewhat human-like Tailtiu was a different matter.

Evie had shown no sign of her progenitor's malice toward Aislinn, but Tailtiu didn't know that. "It's safe," Will assured. "The Cath Bawlg has been reborn, but in her current form she is just a friend. She bears no ill will toward your kind."

"She?" Tailtiu lifted one brow in interest. "I hadn't heard of this, but either way I'm not sure I trust my life to your sometimes questionable judgment."

He shrugged. "Join the club. No one else seems to trust my decisions either."

His aunt walked closer, until she was no more than an arm's length away, her eyes moving up and down as she inspected him. "I'm relieved to see you are still whole." Tailtiu looked away. Despite her age and immortality, Tailtiu was a child emotionally. Only recently had she begun to learn to deal with feelings like concern, fear, or affection. "After we parted last time, I wanted to check on you, but…" Somehow his aunt also looked tired.

Tailtiu had fought valiantly when Lognion had betrayed them, but she had been badly injured by a multitude of iron barbs when the king's men had trapped her with a steel net. Selene and the others had freed her while Will had faced Lognion, but he hadn't seen her since. Will nodded. "You were afraid of being hurt again, weren't you?"

She nodded. "I hate this fear you have given me. Every time you call me, it seems I gain a new fear. First the blood-drinkers, now iron, and this cat demon that follows you everywhere—what will be next? Before you changed me, I never felt afraid. I wouldn't have come today except…"

Her words trailed off, but Will understood. "You were worried about me. That's the other side of the coin."

"You feel these things as well?"

He nodded. "All humans do, all the time."

"How do you function?"

"We do the best we can. You get used to it, and some emotions help you get past others. Like your need to make sure I was all right overriding your need for safety. That's the basis for what we call bravery."

"It's foolishness!" she declared angrily.

"That too," Will agreed. "Do you still want to help me? I won't blame you if you go back home now that you've seen I'm healthy and in one piece."

"I am here already," said Tailtiu. "I will work for a price." She opened her arms.

Since her change, they hadn't bartered in the ways required by the fae, so Will wondered about her intentions for a moment. "A hug?" he asked.

She nodded.

"Just a hug, though," Will clarified, well aware of how strong she was. Once within her grasp, he would be at her mercy, and Tailtiu was no longer bound by the old rules. She nodded again, and he stepped forward, opening his arms for the embrace.

As always, her scent was intoxicating, and she held him firmly, but unlike times past she did nothing more. Her hands didn't stray, and her hips remained still. Other than Tailtiu's nudity, the hug was much like one Will might have received from Sammy or Tabitha. Half a minute passed before she released him, but since she was behaving, Will didn't mind. His shirt was damp when she stepped back, and the remains of wet tracks stained Tailtiu's cheeks. "What do you want me to do?" she asked.

She really was worried about me, thought Will, but he felt it wiser to stay on topic. "I just need you to stay here until I return. I need you here as a beacon so I can teleport back."

"How long will you be gone?"

"An hour or two. I should be back before nightfall."

His aunt looked around nervously. "Will the beast come back?"

"Evie is hunting and probably won't be back until nightfall. She won't hurt you even if I'm not here."

"Evie?"

Will nodded. "That's what I call the Cath Bawlg now."

"Please return before it gets back."

"I'll be as quick as I can," he reassured her.

CHAPTER 36

Emory and Sammy were deeply engaged in a practical magic session when Will arrived. They were standing outdoors in the garden while his cousin slowly assembled the rune structure for a point-defense shield. Being careful not to disturb them, Will located himself behind their backs when he teleported so he would be out of view. His arrival still caused a sudden turbulence in the turyn currents around them, but they were both so engrossed in Sammy's progress that neither seemed to notice.

Will stayed quiet to avoid ruining her concentration, and he smiled when he saw Sammy complete the spell. With Emory's help, she was making rapid progress with turyn expression.

Aiming carefully, Sammy released the spell, creating a small barrier in front of herself. "It worked!" she declared. "Pay up!" She cocked her hip and motioned toward Emory with one hand.

Without delay, Emory leaned over and met her lips with his own, bestowing a kiss that was anything but chaste. A second later, he pulled away. "That's all you get."

Sammy groaned in protest, but her complaint turned to surprise when Will's voice found their ears. "I'm glad to see you are progressing quickly."

His cousin jumped slightly, then stared at him with an expression which was at first guilty but soon became angry. Emory seemed frightened, but immediately hid his expression entirely. The young nobleman faced Will with the calm resignation of a man ready to accept punishment for his crime. "Your Grace, I apologize for that. I understand you may wish—"

Sammy interrupted, stepping in front of her tutor defensively, "Don't you dare do anything to Em! He only did that because I insisted, not that it's any of your business anyway!"

Will had been somewhat irritated, but their responses left him feeling suddenly bemused. He lifted his hands and closed his eyes briefly, signaling his peaceful intentions. "I didn't mean to startle you."

"Then why were you spying on us?" demanded Sammy.

"I came to make a request," said Will simply. "After that, I just didn't want to break your concentration."

Emory's face was flushed as he hurried to speak up once more. "Your Grace, I want you to know that wasn't something ordinary for us. It was just—" He struggled to finish.

"A moment of joy?" Will supplied.

"Yes! Wait, no. Er…" The young noble was completely flustered.

After his previous conversations with both of them, as well as time to reflect on himself, Will felt a strong sense of sympathy. "Sammy, how many spells do you know now?"

"I just learned the shield you saw, but I can also cast source-link, force-lance, and fire-bolt." She paused, then admitted, "I'm still really slow, though."

Will's brows went up. "Honestly, that's pretty amazing for someone who only recently began expressing turyn." His eyes went to Emory. "She must have worked very hard to get this far in such a short time."

Emory nodded. "She's ambitious to say the least."

Unabashed, Sammy stood beside her teacher, and after being rejected several times managed to capture his hand within her own. "I was motivated."

Will met her gaze and allowed the silence to drag out for several seconds before relaxing his shoulders and replying, "I have no objections."

Emory blinked, and Will saw a shift in his shoulders as his inner tension eased. Sammy's reaction was the opposite, as her cheeks colored with embarrassment. Will couldn't help but be amazed by the contradictions within her. *Being caught in a kiss hardly fazed her, but being told I'm fine if they court openly turns her into a blushing maid,* thought Will wryly.

Seeing Samantha at a loss for words, Emory stepped in to restore the conversation. "You said you needed help with something, Your Grace?"

"I do. It's something unusual and potentially dangerous."

Before he could add more, Sammy piped up, "I'm in." Emory glanced at her worriedly, then nodded in agreement.

Will gave them a rough explanation, then sorted out some practical details. Sammy returned to the house to let Blake know they'd be gone until evening, and to apprise him of their method of return. Blake assured her that he'd stay in his room after sundown, to allow for a private return.

While she was gone, Emory chose to ask a private question. "Since it seems you're not going to murder me, were you giving us your blessing?"

"She deserves to be happy. I'm giving *her* my blessing, and she seems to like you. You still need to talk to Sammy's father, so don't go overboard." Will's response was terse, but after a moment, he added, "For what it's worth, I like you too, but that could change in an instant."

The young noble nodded. "Thank you, and I understand. I'd be the same if our roles were reversed and it was one of my sisters."

Surprised, Will glanced over. "I didn't know you had sisters. You never said anything. How many?"

Emory shrugged. "Five. It's not the sort of thing to bring up during training sessions when we were preparing for war. We've never really talked much in a personal sense." After a second, he hurried to add, "Not that I blame you."

"Wow. Five," said Will, trying to imagine it. "I grew up with none, then gained two so suddenly it hardly seemed real." He tried not to think about what had happened to Laina.

Sammy returned then, carrying a sack containing heavy cloaks, winter boots, gloves, and several thick scarves. In her other hand was a basket full of bread, cheese, and apples. She lifted it up for display. "Jeremy sends his love as well."

Smiling, Will directed them, "Keep your things in hand and stand on either side of me. Make sure you have a firm grip on my arm, and since I'm doing this standing up, don't let me fall over."

"Are you going to lose consciousness?" asked Emory.

"No, but I'll leave my body briefly to find our destination. I'm getting better at staying partly in contact, but I usually sit or lie down just to be safe," explained Will. Once he was sure they understood and everyone was in place, he began.

He'd already re-prepared the spell while waiting, so he slipped into the astral plane and quickly found Tailtiu, but rather than teleport immediately, he indulged a whim and turned his thoughts to the Cath Bawlg. He hadn't been entirely sure it would work, but sure enough, she appeared before him. Without having his own body for comparison, it took him a moment to get a sense of scale as he watched her tear into a fresh kill, but after a second, he realized the animal was a bull moose.

Will had never seen one up close during his own time in the mountains, but he'd seen a cow moose or two, and those were big enough to frighten him when he was younger. Seeing an enormous bull being casually torn apart was eye-opening, as the animal was significantly smaller than the cat's current size.

Between bites, she looked up and stared at him, confirming that she was definitely astrally sensitive. "I just wanted to see what you were doing," said Will. Though he had no voice, the act of vocalizing would create thoughts that were clearly audible if the recipient was able to perceive them.

Her response caught him off-guard, as the astral connection enabled him to hear a reply that wasn't dependent on the Cath Bawlg's still limited language skills. *I am almost full. The rest of the meat is yours.*

Mildly startled, he replied, "Thanks," then returned to Tailtiu. Adjusting his focus somewhere between her and his physical body, he triggered the teleport spell.

Everyone remained still while Sammy and Emory got their bearings and took in the new environment. Emory jerked for a moment when his eyes discovered Tailtiu standing nearby. "Oh, excuse me!"

The blush that came to his cheeks was a prey signal to Will's aunt. Her visage became predatory as she regarded the young man. "Hello, my sweetling," she replied. "I was just getting hungry."

Sammy gently bopped the side of Emory's head to snap him out of his reverie while Will hurriedly warned his aunt, "Emory is one of us, remember? He's not food." Then he turned to the young nobleman. "You've met Tailtiu before, when she was helping me train at Rimberlin."

Emory had already put his back to the naked fae woman. "Yes, of course. I was just surprised, she, uh, she had, she wasn't…"

"Naked," supplied Will, glaring at his aunt. "This is why I wish you'd practice some modesty."

With a smirk, Tailtiu transformed again, flawlessly creating a thin dress from her flesh that looked entirely natural compared to what Evie had done earlier. The only strangeness about it was the fact that it was summer attire that no mortal would dare use in such cold conditions. The fae woman's smug expression vanished as she looked nervously upward to the lip of the crevasse. Before the others could follow her gaze, something large and dark fell from above, landing near the edge of the cleared area.

Emory jumped, and Sammy let out a startled yelp which stopped a moment later as the object before them came into focus. It was the torn carcass of a disemboweled moose. A small amount of blood seeped from beneath it onto the stone. Realizing it was just the Cath Bawlg returning, Will tried to reassure them, "It's just Evie," but his words went unnoticed as an enormous cat landed next to the dead moose. Having just carried the large animal in her mouth, Evie had taken a size appropriate to the task, and she loomed over them, partially blocking out the sky.

Stunned, Sammy expanded her verbal repertoire with a strange 'eep' while Emory fell onto his backside. The young nobleman raised a force-dome over himself and Sammy a second later, though his face had gone white as a sheet. Tailtiu managed to keep her feet and most of her dignity, but she was now standing close behind Will, one hand gripping the back of his tunic tightly.

Tailtiu's position caused the cat's interest to focus on her with an air of quiet menace. The Cath Bawlg knew the others well, but she could easily sense the danger represented by the fae woman.

"Evie, this is Tailtiu. She's a friend—family, actually." Seeing the shield around Emory and Sammy, he waved at them to dismiss it. "You both know Evie already. She's just bigger at the moment."

Emory dropped the shield, his eyes never leaving the feline. Meanwhile Sammy's initial reaction had already vanished, replaced by fascination as she stared up at the giant cat. "Evie? *This* is Evie?"

Slowly shrinking, Evie was already down to the size of a brown bear, which simplified the introductions. It took several minutes for everyone to fully relax, except for Sammy, who had already begun making overtures toward the cat. As before, Evie allowed her a brief contact, but once Sammy started attempting to pet her, she moved away, circling to stand on the other side of Will.

Will could see the disappointment in his cousin's face, and he felt sad for her. She had been the goddamn cat's favorite before his death, but she was now merely tolerated. Evie was not Mr. Mittens. He was grateful that Sammy didn't know the relationship between Evie and her prior incarnation.

Once things had settled down, Emory asked, "So, what do you want us to do?"

"First, I'd like you to help me clear away the snow and ice. Evie and I started, but some help would be appreciated," said Will. The cat, now her usual size, looked up at him and Will could almost imagine her thoughts: *I did most of the work.*

Evie sat in the center, quietly observing them as they worked, and Tailtiu stood somewhat apart, also doing nothing. Will's aunt knew little of human magic, and her wild talents were ill suited to melting ice. That left the bulk of the work up to the three wizards.

Emory showed Sammy a simple spell for starting fires, one that converted turyn into flame that could be directed and sized according to the user's input, and the three of them got to work. With the boundless energy of the ley line intersection beneath their feet, they didn't lack for power; the job was merely an application of will, time, and attention to detail.

Two hours later, the rest of the old platform was clear, and Sammy had already begun making her way up the stairs. Will noticed that at some point she had stopped using the spell she had learned and was now working with the available turyn in a more intuitive manner, converting it directly to heat and shaping the energy to just the places that needed it.

Wild magic, thought Will. He'd done similar things during some of his early fights with sorcerers, but that had been mostly just redirection, taking offensive fire spells and returning them as an unfocused blast. As far as he knew, his cousin had never attempted wild magic before, and she was currently converting an entirely different type of turyn into the sort needed for heat and fire, then applying it where she wanted it to go.

Emory had also noticed Sammy's success and was attempting to emulate her. As a graduate of Wurthaven, the noble already had extensive experience with spells and spell theory, but wild magic was something that had never been encouraged. He managed to do something similar, but his efforts were much cruder. He saw Will looking at him and shrugged.

Will wondered if Sammy's prowess indicated a predilection for fire. It was far too soon to expect a greater talent to appear, but she clearly showed more control over the flames than her fellow student. Imitating her, Will found himself capable enough, but it took a lot of concentration and required more will than just using a spell. He could see that Sammy's face was relaxed, her attention entirely on the stone steps in front of her as she slowly ascended. *It's definitely easier for her,* thought Will.

The sun was down, and the light was rapidly failing by the time they finished, so Will asked his students to take note of the circles before suggesting they retire for the day. "It will be more comfortable at Rimberlin. We can go over the plan and return in the morning to start setting up. It will be good practice for you."

"Practice for?" asked Sammy drowsily; the lids of her eyes were beginning to droop with fatigue. The work had taken more out of her than she realized.

"I'll explain at home," said Will. "One of us needs to remain here so I can teleport us back tomorrow." He looked at Tailtiu.

"Me?" she asked. "I'm not spending the night here."

"The cold doesn't bother you," Will remarked.

"What about the cat?" suggested his aunt. "She's got plenty of fur." Evie glared at the fae woman, and a growl rumbled from her tiny body. Rolling her eyes, Tailtiu quickly acquiesced. "Fine. Leave me behind. I won't stay here, though. I'll return at dawn. Look for me then."

With that settled, Will took them back to Rimberlin, making two trips: one for his passengers, and a second one for the moose. Although the sweetmeats were gone, and part of the body had been torn away, there were still at least a couple hundred pounds of good flesh that could be harvested. The cat hadn't touched the head, forelegs, or shoulders.

That necessitated some discussion with Jeremy, who had understandable questions. "Did a bear do this?" asked the cook.

"Not exactly," answered Will vaguely.

They ate the meal Jeremy had already prepared while the puzzled chef butchered the moose and prepared some of it for use at breakfast. Then Will retired to his study with Sammy and Emory in tow.

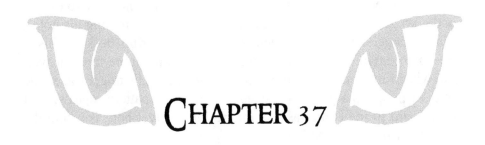

CHAPTER 37

"Everyone in the house knows you're here," commented Sammy.

"My whereabouts aren't as important to hide anymore," said Will. "I don't want to confuse people in the city, of course, but as for the main enemy, he's already caught on."

"What's changed?" she asked, glancing over to see if Emory was paying attention. She wasn't the only one who was sleepy.

The young nobleman straightened up in his chair, then Will began to explain. The story of his meeting with Lognion brought them both to full wakefulness, though it could only hold their attention for so long. As he started getting into the details of what he had discussed with Aislinn, they were beginning to wilt once more.

"Go to bed," he told them.

The next morning, he awoke feeling refreshed, though he had to remove Evie's entirely too bushy tail from his face. After rinsing the hair out of his mouth and eating a quick breakfast, he met with Sammy and Emory again to finish explaining his plan.

His cousin was enthusiastic in her support, but Emory had reservations. "Are you serious?"

Will's expression remained flat. "You've known me long enough already. You should expect such things."

The young nobleman shook his head, then ran his fingers through unruly brown hair. He hadn't had time to use a comb, much less tie it back. "I'm not objecting, but it seems unreasonable to expect Samantha to participate."

Green eyes focused on Emory. "Why?" she asked calmly.

Turning to her, Emory tried to sound reasonable. "He's talking about magic on an entirely different level from what you've dealt with before. The complexity alone—I don't even know if *I* can learn this in the time allowed, and the power involved—one mistake could burn you to ash."

Sammy tipped her head up in a gesture of confidence, then nodded toward Will. "*He* thinks I can do it."

Will hurried to correct Sammy's statement. "I think the two of you can do it together." Mentally, he added, *I hope.* Summoning his notes, he laid a large sheet of parchment across the top of his desk. "This is the primary layout for the runes, and you'll become more familiar with them when I mark them out today for you to see." His finger traced the circle, then tapped a point to one side. "The main pattern repeats, so it isn't as hard to remember as you might think. Over here is where the blood key will be scribed."

Sammy nodded. "Simple enough."

The man sitting beside her seemed baffled by her confidence. "No, Samantha, it most decidedly is *not* simple. He's talking about a *gate.* Such magic hasn't been seen since—I don't know when. No one has used magic like this since the Wayfarer Society went extinct. It requires a damned ley line just for the power needed to activate it, for Mother's sake!"

"Don't swear at me," she growled.

Will intervened. "He isn't wrong." Emory looked at him with relief, while Sammy started to open her mouth in protest. "Wait!" Will held up one hand. "Listen to me, both of you. I don't want you to do it as a simple spell invocation. With the circles and a tiny bit of extra preparation, you can do it as a ritual. That will make handling the power easier."

Emory glared at him. "I never studied ritual magic, aside from the brief explanations they gave us in Spell Theory, and that's enough for me to know you can't just wave your hand and make this a ritual. Are you suddenly an expert?" Seeing the two of them argue, Sammy's own irritation faded, and she turned curious eyes toward her cousin to see what his response would be.

"I'm not working alone," Will responded. "We have an expert to make the changes *and* teach us how to perform the ritual."

"But you won't be the one doing it," reiterated Emory. "We will."

"That's right."

"I'd rather just do it myself and avoid making risky changes," exclaimed the young noble. "I don't know if I'm capable of it, but at least we can avoid risking Samantha."

The lady in question bristled at the remark. "I can help."

"As much as I love you, Samantha, you're still a novice. I have confidence in your intelligence and future skills, but you aren't ready for this, and I won't see you hurt for no good reason!" declared the young wizard next to her.

Will blinked, and Sammy went still for a moment, then asked, "What did you say?"

"It's the truth. You are still a novice. I won't apologize for the truth when a lie could kill you," said Emory earnestly.

His cousin was still processing what she'd heard, so Will intervened. "A ritual, properly designed, will be easier and Sammy can play her part perfectly well without advanced knowledge. She can serve as a conduit while you manipulate the currents. Besides, we need her or it won't work."

"Why?" demanded Emory.

Pointing at the parchment, Will answered, "The blood key; without her blood, the gate won't have a destination."

"Your teleport spell doesn't need blood," argued Emory, "and you're planning to do the same thing as a spell *without* blood. Why do you need it for this, and why hers?"

Sighing, Will tried to explain, "I'm astrally sensitive. Most people require a beacon or line of sight to teleport. I've been using my connection to those who are closest to me."

Unfazed, Emory asked, "You're telling me you have a bond with a demon?"

"No, but I'll have a beacon to use; you won't. Sammy's blood will serve that purpose."

"How?" The young noble was clearly exasperated.

Will pointed at himself. "Neither of you are astrally sensitive, so Sammy can't use our connection, but we do share blood in common. You're going to open the gate for me. If you don't, I'll be trapped."

"You'll be in hell?" asked Emory.

Will nodded.

Sammy lifted one hand. "Are we done debating this?" Emory stared at her, but Will simply nodded. She turned to her cousin. "Can we have a moment alone?" Emory started to rise, but Sammy took his hand. "Not you."

Will was already making his way toward the door, though he paused a moment to smirk at Emory, who clearly believed he was in trouble. As he shut the door Will could hear Emory's defense beginning. "I wasn't trying to insult you—"

"Shhh," Sammy cut Emory's protest short with a gentle finger against his lips. "We need to talk about what you said a minute ago. You said something I wasn't expecting, so a little clarification is required to avoid any misunderstandings."

Will spent some time with Blake and Jeremy, letting them know when they would likely return as well as packing a filling lunch for everyone. When Emory and Sammy reappeared half an hour later, they both seemed calm for the most part, though the young nobleman had obviously received a shock of some sort.

"Are we ready?" asked Sammy, trying slightly too hard to sound relaxed.

"Almost," said Will. "I forgot one thing." He led them back up to the study and spent another half an hour giving each of them the limnthal they had earned, apologizing as he did so. "I should have done this weeks ago, once I was sure you'd completed the third compression, but..." Will held his hands out to either side.

"You've been a little busy," agreed Sammy.

He had already finished his explanation of the spell, so he handed over copies of the rune construct for them to keep. "Add these to your journals so you can do the same for your students someday." When he saw the expression of dismay on Sammy's face, he added, "No one expects you to be able to cast something like this today, but you will, years from now. Of that I have no doubt. Before we leave, you should both go find your books and journals and store them. The same goes for anything else you want to make sure you never lose."

"How much can it hold?" asked Emory.

Will shrugged. "I'm not entirely sure. I've reached the limit before, but I never got around to doing any rigorous testing. It's somewhere close to the size of this study or perhaps a little larger. I keep all sorts of things in mine: spare clothes, weapons, armor, water jars, food, potion vials, blankets—you get the idea." *Alchemical fire, a desiccated vampire, barrels of wine and troll piss, he added mentally. Not to mention enough raw meat, butter, herbs, and other food stuffs to prepare a dozen feasts.* He reminded himself he needed to reexamine the foods he had stored since he no longer had the need for so much. Jeremy would be delighted by some of the cuts of lamb and beef Will could offer him.

Another half hour passed before the two returned and signaled their readiness. Without further ado, Will teleported them, along with Evie, back to where Tailtiu waited. Will's aunt seemed mildly irritated.

"Dawn was hours ago," she groused.

Emory responded, "Our preparations took longer than expected."

Cocking her hip to one side, the fae woman replied, "Perhaps you could make it up to me."

At that point Will expected something different, but Emory gave Sammy a strange look without saying anything, to which she responded by gesturing toward Tailtiu. "By all means. No one is stopping you."

Tailtiu licked her lips and took a step forward before Will intervened. "That was a jest. Remember, friends, not food."

His aunt looked up at him, then winked. "I knew that. I was only going to tease them." Tailtiu's eyes conveyed a sense of weariness. "I'm not the same as I once was, but I am hungry."

Will took a moment to look at his aunt, to *really* look at her, and realized he'd let his old assumptions cloud his vision. Being fae, she had always been perfect and without fault, physically unchanged despite anything that might have happened to her previously. Beneath her eyes were dark circles, and on her shoulders were unusual marks. If she had been human, he would have thought them to be signs of tissue damage, slow-healing bruises. "What's this?" he asked, pressing one hand against her shoulder blade.

Tailtiu winced slightly. "Nothing. A sore place."

"When did you get it?" When she didn't answer he repeated the question. "When?"

"At the party, the day you went wild and killed all those people." She grinned as though he would find her remark funny.

He ignored the terrible attempt at humor. "Why haven't you finished healing?" In the past, only a day or two had been required, even for the most grievous of wounds.

"It takes longer now," his aunt replied.

Will nodded. "A lot longer, apparently. You've been home, in the fae realm?"

"Yes. It just doesn't help much anymore. Feeding would probably help, but…" Her words trailed off.

"You aren't part of the accord. You were excluded since it wouldn't bind you anyway. You know that." Will hadn't wanted to think about it too closely, since he'd feared Tailtiu might be secretly murdering people as she had previously done.

She shook her head. "Remember Dinner?"

It took him a second, but then he did. She'd adopted a puppy and named it Dinner to annoy Tiny. Elthas, her late step-father, had crushed the animal in front of her during his final confrontation with Will at the end of the war. Frowning, Will asked, "I'm confused. You never really fed on animals anyway."

Tailtiu rubbed at her eyes. "Dinner was mortal. Human or dog, it never really mattered to me before. I tried really hard to make sure he stayed mortal after your warnings. I didn't keep him in my world. After—after what happened, I just didn't want to do it anymore."

He thought he understood, but he had to ask to be sure. "Do what?"

"Eat people."

Her head was down now, hiding her face beneath the cascade of her hair. Will looked around to see everyone watching them and felt a sudden urge to protect her from their eyes. Tailtiu had never learned embarrassment, but he felt it for her. Without a word, he raised a force-dome, using a variation that was opaque to give them privacy.

His aunt seemed surprised. "What are you doing?"

The fae didn't need food; their plane supplied them with everything they needed to survive, vitality, energy, and healing when they were injured. If trapped in the human world, they would slowly starve, unless they fed on the vital energies of mortals. They weren't equipped to absorb turyn from any other sources. If Tailtiu was no longer receiving the usual blessings of her home, she had only one alternative, one she had been refusing to partake in.

Opening his arms, Will invited her in. "Come here."

Eyes wide, she didn't move. "No. You don't understand how hungry I am. I won't be able to stop."

"I've fed you before. Remember?" As a wizard, he was one of the few humans who could replace his own energies by drawing from the environment.

She shook her head. "That was nothing. I'll kill you."

Ignoring her resistance, he stepped into her and enfolded her with his arms. Tailtiu tried to push him away, but her body was already rebelling, refusing to apply the force necessary to oppose his relatively feeble mortal strength. Instead, her hands opened and circled his back, tightening to keep him from trying to escape. Unable to stop herself, she began drawing energy from his body, pulling it directly from every point of contact between them.

A predatory growl rumbled in her throat as his vitality flowed into her, but it was just a trickle compared to what she needed. Lifting her chin, she nuzzled Will's throat, opening her mouth to suckle at his neck as though she was a vampire, though her teeth never broke his skin. What she needed wasn't blood.

Will had steeled himself for her hunger, drawing from the ley line before he hugged her, but the greedy pull of her emptiness was more than he expected. Even worse was the pleasure that accompanied it, a natural part of her feeding mechanism that ensured her prey wouldn't fight for long. His legs folded, unable to support his weight as she bore him to the cold stone platform.

He'd intended to control the flow of energies, to replace what she took as she fed, to regulate the speed of it all, but her voracious appetite wouldn't be denied, and the pleasure she radiated overwhelmed his conscious mind. Electric shivers ran through his skin wherever she touched, causing his body to spasm involuntarily.

His breastplate might have stopped her briefly, but it had somehow been unbuckled and cast aside. The clothing beneath it suffered a more violent fate as Tailtiu's hands tore it apart like gossamer so she could get at his bare skin. The world was obliterated in a flash of whiteness as her body finally lay against him, skin to skin.

Awareness returned briefly as she pulled back to choose the richest targets. Her lips and tongue roamed his chest, neck, and finally locked onto his mouth. Will found himself moaning as she drew the life out of him, and in his ears he could hear his heart pounding like a drum, fast at first, but gradually slowing. He was drowning in a river of delight, but he hardly cared. Everything was fading into black, but he felt warm and euphoric.

An empty husk with nothing left, his heart stopped.

From unconsciousness, Will emerged into an all-encompassing light. It was a place he was familiar with, though he struggled to remember why. The words came to him before his mind fully registered the thought. "This is where I came last time I died."

He'd died at Selene's first wedding, deliberately using a necromantic spell that would anchor his soul and hopefully allow him to return if his body was healed within a short span of time, but he had never been able to remember the time in between, while he was dead. Now he did.

"We have to stop meeting like this. Once is enough for most people."

The voice was rich, with a deep but vibrant timbre. Turning around, Will saw a tall, slender man with dark hair and a sharp, well-trimmed beard. Piercing blue eyes complemented an exotic outfit of black leather with aggressive red accents that made it seem the man had been deliberately painted with blood. Will recognized him immediately from some of the iconography in the Mother's Cathedral. It was Temarah's husband, Lord of the Underworld and enemy of the light. Will named him. "You're Marduke."

"That's what they call me now," admitted his visitor. "But I have other names, mostly forgotten, like this one." He gestured to highlight the ominous hunting leathers he wore. "This outfit was to commemorate one of them, when people called me the Blood Count."

Will wasn't familiar with the title, but he was no student of religious lore. "You seem proud of them."

The dark god nodded. "At the time, I was being painted with a black brush by my enemies. They settled all the blood that had been spilled on my shoulders and made me the focus of their blame."

Unwilling to sympathize with the god of evil, Will responded in a sardonic tone, "You don't think you deserved blame?"

"Some of it, certainly, but not the bulk, not by far." The god's eyes seemed to cut through Will, as though they might flay the flesh from his imaginary body. "I let it weigh me down until my wife made these clothes for me." Marduke patted the leather affectionately. "She made me realize their opinions meant little, and instead of accepting shame, I should take the spite directed at me and turn it into a symbol of honor. These clothes represent the monster they saw me as, but I took that image and wore it with pride."

Will shook his head. "Temarah made them?" After the god nodded, he asked a new question. "I've never understood that. Why would the Mother marry her opposite? If she's truly the source of goodness, love, and compassion, why would she even tolerate your existence? Doesn't that mean she isn't good either?" He felt bad saying the words, especially since Temarah had saved him personally once, but he couldn't hide his feelings.

The paragon of corruption laughed. "You're brave to say such things to me."

"I'm going to hell anyway."

The god's face took on a curious expression. "You mean before you *were* going to hell, before you died a minute ago, right?"

"I mean now. That's why you're here, isn't it? To take me to the real one, where the souls of the damned go," said Will.

Marduke waved his hand dismissively. "That place is just make-believe. Unless you create it for yourself, it doesn't exist. If you do wind up in such a place, don't blame me. I'm just here to chat."

The god's smile was so genuine and warm that Will wanted to believe him. "You're a liar."

"So are you," returned Marduke, "though I have to admit I'm a lot better at it than you are. The number of times you've gotten into trouble just because you couldn't lie convincingly—it boggles the mind. In that sense, you and your wife are the opposite of me and mine. Selene is full of intrigue, while you struggle. Penny was likewise much more honest than I was."

"Penny?"

"Temarah," the god clarified. "Her real name was Penelope, back when we were just ordinary people." Marduke rubbed his chin for a moment, seeming to think, then offered his hand. "Nice to meet you. My name is Mordecai Illeniel."

Will took the hand reflexively. It felt warm and human. "You're saying you really were just a man once? How did you become...like this?"

"I destroyed the universe and took on the curse of existence, replacing the old creator and dreaming up a universe of my own." Mordecai's expression was wry as he added, "Somehow, I hoped it would be better than the last, but I have little conscious control. The dream has a mind of its own, and it populates every life with equal parts tragedy and comedy, whether I wish it or not."

Frowning, Will considered what he had heard, then responded, "I find it hard to believe you. If you're the source of everything, what is Temarah? You're known as the king of lies, but if she were here to vouch for you, I might find you more creditable. I've met her before, so I know she'd tell me the truth."

Mordecai's expression grew wistful. "You met her, did you? How did she seem?"

"Sad," he admitted. "I was being whipped. She helped me endure the pain."

The god nodded, then turned his back. "That sounds like Penny. Your predicament would have had special meaning to her." He said nothing for a while, then turned back to face Will once more. "Unfortunately, she cannot appear to give you reassurance while I am here."

Undeterred, Will asked, "Why not?"

"We were two people, but we joined our souls when she died. Since then, we both exist as a single entity. When I am here, she is not and vice versa. Sound familiar?"

"Not particularly," said Will.

Mordecai studied him carefully for several seconds, then announced, "I sometimes forget the differences in magic between this dream and the old one. Your sister is unable to appear the way Penny did. Nevertheless, she is there inside you."

"What?" Alarm filled Will's heart. "What does that mean?" A host of thoughts ran through his mind immediately thereafter. "Can she be saved? Could she possess another body?"

Mordecai put his hands on Will's shoulders. "I did not mean to give you false hope. She's not a separate person anymore. What's left is merely a facet of your soul. Think of a coin with two faces. It's something like that."

"Then she could live if I died?" asked Will.

"No, William. Souls do not have a quantity you can count or measure, like sand or rocks. You could merge with every person you ever loved and there would still only be one soul within you. You cannot bring her back, but flashes of her may appear in your thoughts now and then. When you die, it will be over, until you are reborn in the dream."

The god turned his gaze to one side and gestured. "Besides, in case you've forgotten, you've already died—again." The platform came into view, and Will saw his mostly naked body lying still on the cold stone.

It was an embarrassing sight by any measure of decency. The demon-steel breastplate lay discarded to one side while his clothes had been ripped apart from neck to groin, exposing his bare flesh. Strangely, despite knowing he had died, Will was more concerned by the stains on what remained of his trousers. His end had been bewildering, and there were gaps in his memory, but he hadn't thought things had gone quite *that* far.

Turning back to the god, Will asked, "Did I...?" He couldn't quite finish the sentence. Dead or not, he didn't want to think he'd betrayed Selene. "I only wanted to save her."

Mordecai put a hand on his shoulder. "You should have expected that, given her nature, but no, what you're thinking didn't actually happen. The fae girl stopped herself—and you—but it was too late, and your heart stopped beating anyway."

Will felt a sense of relief, until he became aware of Tailtiu sitting beside his body, openly weeping. In all the time he had known her, from the cruel innocence she possessed when he first met her, to the day Elthas had crushed her first pet into the dirt, Will had never seen his aunt in a more pitiful state. When he had rescued her from the vampires, she had been torn and battered, but although her body now glowed with health, she seemed stricken by a far greater pain.

As he studied the scene Will noticed that his force-dome still remained. Confused, he turned to Mordecai. "Why is the spell still up? Force effects don't linger like other magics. It should be gone if I'm dead."

"This is the moment of your death," said the god. "Time doesn't exist here. Nothing will happen until you pass on to find your next life."

"But she's crying," said Will. "How can she cry if time is frozen?"

"You're seeing with your mind. This is similar to when you travel in the astral plane. Her body isn't actually moving, but you are seeing the reality inside the fae woman's heart. Without time, your perception would be incomprehensible, so your mind renders it as a moving scene." The god gave him a sympathetic look. "We should go. Staying here isn't a kindness."

Feeling suddenly stubborn, Will dug in his heels. "Then why am I seeing it?"

Mordecai seemed sad. "Because I'm not always strong. Sometimes I'm lonely, and you remind me of myself, so I selfishly allowed this so we could talk. Come, the pain will be gone once you let go, along with all the painful memories."

"I don't have to let go," argued Will, remembering his grandfather's end. Arrogan had lingered beyond his physical death. "My will is strong enough to keep me here if I refuse."

"You aren't a lich, William," said the god. "You can delay, but without a lot of frankly disturbing preparation, you can't remain forever without a living body."

Will glared at the Lord of the Underworld. "Your words are right, but you're lying too. I've dealt with the fae long enough to recognize a lie hidden in truth." Pointing at his corpse, he declared, "There's nothing wrong with me physically. If she's stopped feeding, I can restore my turyn—my heart just needs to start beating again. There's no reason I should die here."

The god held his hands out in a gesture of uncertainty. "If you're that stubborn, maybe."

"Why did you try to trick me?"

Mordecai shook his head. "Wrong question. A better one would be why did I try to spare you from the pain of what is to come? The answer is simple mercy. I told you before that you remind me of myself."

Will's eyes narrowed suspiciously. "Do you know the future?"

"No, but I've seen every tragic play you could possibly imagine." Mordecai pointed at Will's chest. "And *you*, William Cartwright, are firmly caught in this one. What will happen to you? I can only guess, though I bet I could come close. No matter the exact details, what comes next will harrow your heart and soul until you wish you were dead. Press your luck far enough, and you might discover a fate even worse than the one I'm already predicting. Trust me, death is a kindness."

As frightening as the god's words were, Will still had reservations. "What happens to everyone else if I die here?"

"They all live happily ever after. It's a win-win," answered Mordecai, making no effort to sound truthful.

"No, they don't."

Mordecai sighed. "Most of them will die, but as I've been trying to get through to you, that's not such a bad thing. Everyone gets a new life, even if this world fails to survive. Get out while you can. Next time around, you may get a quiet life with a fat belly and ten children to tease you while you grow old."

"Screw that," said Will. "I'm staying."

The god vanished, and the sky turned dark. Thunder rolled and clouds raced across the sky while an ominous voice shook Will's heart.

"Defy me and my curse will scour the flesh from your bones and torment you with the pain of a thousand…" The voice stopped there, and after a long pause, finished, "rusty nails."

Confused, Will wrinkled up his nose in disbelief. "That doesn't make sense."

An instant later, the world returned to normal, and Mordecai reappeared. "I never was creative enough with threats. You're determined to do this?"

Will nodded.

"Very well, then I will give you two pieces of advice. One, dragon-fire can burn through anything. Walls, barriers, force effects, almost any magic you can imagine, all things are devoured by the flame, except flame itself—or something very similar to flame. Pay attention." The god brought his two open palms together in a resounding clap, sending a tremendous shockwave of sound shivering through the air, then he smiled. "That wouldn't suffice, but given your talents, you might come up with something that would. Two, don't attempt to kill the lich."

"But I have to," argued Will. "I made a promise."

"You aren't fae. Break it."

"Are you saying it won't work?" Will demanded.

Mordecai pursed his lips, then let out a sigh. "It will work, but the spell you intend to use is a bad idea. It will mark your existence as something separate and draw the attention of things that shouldn't exist. Be patient and you may find another way later."

Growling, Will swore, "I am so sick of vague bullshit answers! Even if I understood, would it really help me win?"

"Winning isn't the best answer. My advice is an attempt to help you lose less miserably." The god faded from view.

"Fuck that," howled Will, suddenly furious. "I'm going to win. Do you hear me?" he yelled into what had become an empty void.

CHAPTER 38

The darkness changed, and with it his perception of self. The world slowly returned, and Will found himself back inside his old shell, a body of flesh and bone that was still warm, though the heart had ceased to beat. His energy was gone, but his will remained, and a savage torrent of turyn was close at hand, roaring through the stone beneath him. Seizing it, he flooded his flesh with energy but failed to attune it properly. Without the seed of his natural turyn to serve as a template, the foreign power tore through him, damaging and revitalizing his tissues in equal amounts. Will's consciousness rode the chaos like a toy boat thrown into rapids.

Searing pain turned every nerve into molten agony, and for a brief instant his resolve faltered.

No! Show them the truth. Show them what I know. Laina's voice echoed around him.

On the edge of despair, he responded, *What truth?*

You're invincible!

He knew she was wrong. Wrong to a degree that bordered on pure stupidity, but he had to live to finish the argument. With crude and intangible hands, Will tamped down the flow from the ley lines and tried to filter out the frequencies that were causing the greatest pain. An eternity of struggle ensued, but gradually the fires within died down and his torment faded. Somewhere in the center of it all, he found a tiny mote of light, a speck of turyn different than what came from outside— his source. It had been absent before, but the raging river of turyn had relit the candle even as it threatened to immediately snuff it out again.

On familiar ground, Will rebuilt his boundaries, walling his source away and controlling its output, sheltering it within a tightly controlled space. Outside that was a larger space, the place where his body and the turyn that sustained it would reside. Purging it of foreign energy, Will slowly refilled it with power filtered and converted to match the tiny example set by his source.

Will's eyes opened, and violent nausea gripped him. Rolling onto his side, he vomited until his stomach was empty, and after that he continued to retch and heave. Everything hurt, as though he had awakened from a near-fatal drinking binge.

As the convulsive movements of his stomach started to slow, Will became aware of a silence around him, punctuated only by an ominous rumbling. Looking around, he saw that his shield had disappeared and everyone was staring at him with various expressions of worry and concern. Sammy was moving forward despite the stench, anxious to help him somehow, while Tailtiu knelt close by, staring at him as though she was unable to believe her eyes.

The rumbling came from Evie, whose gaze was firmly on his aunt. She'd grown to the size of a tiger, and her body was quivering with tension as she prepared to mete out violent retribution. "Evie, don't," said Will weakly. "It wasn't her fault."

Emory stared at Tailtiu in horror. "What did you do to him?"

Will's nose was reporting a variety of disgusting smells, for his body had voided itself from both ends, emptying his stomach and bowels. His only consolation was that the excess of revolting solids and liquids probably helped to conceal the smaller evidence of his orgasmic death. Sammy was already lifting his head, wiping away bits of his breakfast that stubbornly clung to his cheeks and lips. She'd made use of her new limnthal to summon something to use as a towel, and to his horror, Will realized it was one of her dresses.

"Sammy, stop," he protested, trying to push her hands away. "You'll ruin your clothes."

His cousin ignored him, continuing to clean his face. After a minute, she turned to the others. "Does anyone have water? We need to rinse him off."

"We should move him first," suggested Emory. "No point in trying to clean him until we do that." He moved to stand just behind Will's head and shoulders. "Get his feet, Samantha. This end is heavier." They lifted him and took him to the other side of the platform, where Emory summoned a blanket to lay him on.

"Do you know that cleaning spell he always uses?" asked Sammy.

Emory shook his head. "That's an eighth-order spell."

Sammy had only been exposed to first- and second-order spells thus far. "You can't do it? I thought you graduated from Wurthaven? Did you learn anything useful, besides battle spells?"

"I just haven't devoted the time for it yet," said Emory defensively. "It wasn't my main priority during the war. I spent my time mastering the spells *he* wanted us to know."

Sammy's gaze was unforgiving. "So, you're useless. Just say that next time, it's quicker."

"You have no idea how difficult an eighth-order spell is. There aren't many who develop enough skill to use a spell like that, and most of them spend their time learning other things instead. There's lots of simpler spells people use to clean things instead," argued the young noble.

Will's cousin looked up at him again. "Yeah? Know any of them?"

"A few." Emory summoned a second blanket and used it to cover Will's hips.

She gave the nobleman a look of disbelief. "Don't just drop it over him. Wipe him off. It's a little late to worry about me seeing his twig and berries—I'm already scarred for life. Besides, this is family."

"But..."

Will was so weak he could hardly keep his eyes open, but he felt a degree of empathy for Emory's dilemma. Sammy's mood brooked no delay, and the young nobleman's hesitation earned him only scorn. Will would have preferred to be left alone entirely, but no one seemed to care about his opinion.

"What cleaning spells do you know?" asked Sammy.

"One for cleaning and shining boots, another for removing dust from clothes, but it won't handle this. Neither is safe to use on a person. I have one spell for shaving, but that's all it does."

Sammy left her position by his head and grabbed the blanket, granting Will a small amount of modesty. "Useless," she repeated, using the fabric to clean something from his thigh.

Emory let out a decidedly unmanly grunt of dismay as Will was uncovered. "Stop. I'll do it."

"Shut up. You missed your chance," snapped Sammy. "Do you have water? No? How about a container? Go melt some snow."

The noble disappeared from view, and Will's eyes closed despite his best efforts. As he drifted away, he could still hear his cousin swearing quietly to herself, "Prissy fucking dandy-fop, the last thing I need right now is some primping little popinjay... Will, can you hear me? Will?"

Will drifted away, his last thought being, *Poor Emory.*

***

A fire was crackling nearby when he awoke, lending a cheerful sound to the air. The pillow under Will's head was soft and warm but didn't feel right. Sitting up, he realized it was Evie. Roughly the size of a large dog, she'd lain crosswise, and it was her belly he'd been resting on. Sensing his movement, she lifted her head to gaze at him, then put it down again, returning to sleep. Not far away, Sammy sat by the fire with her knees pulled up to her chin. Tailtiu and Emory were nowhere to be seen.

The sky was grey, so Will asked, "What time is it?"

Sammy's head popped up from her knees, relief on her face. "Dusk, but at least you're alive. Are you hungry? Thirsty? Let me get you some water." She climbed quickly to her feet and moved to the other side of the fire where a clay jar sat with melted snow. Apparently, no one had thought to bring cups, since she cupped the liquid in her hands and held them out to him.

Will summoned a wooden cup and gave it to her. "This will be easier."

Looking sheepish, she accepted the cup and filled it from the jar, then returned. Will drank the entire thing and then a second before pausing to say, "Sorry about earlier."

His cousin blinked, then rubbed her face with one sleeve, smearing a dark streak of unnoticed ash across her cheek. "Don't apologize. We're family. Remember when you carried me out of Barrowden?"

That had been a dark day. The day most of her family had died. Will remembered getting her out, but he didn't recall carrying her. "No."

"I do," she replied, "so shut up."

Looking under the blanket, Will saw that what remained of his ruined clothes had been taken away. The smell that wafted up wasn't great, but it was obvious that someone had taken a damp cloth to most of his body. He'd helped his mother do the same with her patients many times, so he had a fair idea of what his cousin had done. "Thank you. Where's your dress?"

She pointed to a pile of red fabric that had been cut into towel-sized sections. "That's the clean half, in case we need more rags. The rest went into the fire."

"Tabitha gave you that one, didn't she? I'll replace it."

"It's just a dress. You can buy me a dozen more—it doesn't matter. You scared me half to death today."

"Can I apologize for that?" he asked.

"Yes."

"I'm sorry."

Wiping her face again, she unwittingly created more charcoal streaks across her nose and down the other cheek. "What happened?"

"Tailtiu was dying. I didn't realize it, but she doesn't gain energy from her home anymore and she hasn't been hunting either. I was trying to feed her."

His cousin's face was a picture of disbelief. "With your dick?"

"No! Hell no! I was giving her turyn, adapting it so she could absorb it. Why would you think that?"

She rolled her eyes. "I cleaned you up, remember? Not only did she rip your clothes off but you had pickle juice all over yourself."

"Pickle-what?" He couldn't believe his ears.

"You heard me. Liquid silk, peter pudding, badger milk..."

Mouth agape, Will exclaimed, "By the Mother, stop!"

"...cum," added his cousin with a malicious grin. "Personally, I prefer pickle juice. It seems more civilized than the other terms."

He'd heard a lot of terms for it while in the army, but badger milk was new, even for him. Shocked beyond belief, he asked, "Where did you learn all that?"

She shook her head at his naivete. "I'm grown now, Will. Girls talk. Tabitha's been an indispensable source of information too, not to mention having Emory around."

His face flushed. "Emory? Did he—?"

Sammy laughed. "No. He's too proper. Did I? Yes. There were a few times when he was getting a little tense, so I gave him a hand, as it were." The look on his face gave away Will's murderous thoughts, so Sammy quickly continued, "It was my idea. He argued a little, but not much. Don't blame him."

Will sighed, then rubbed his face. He was learning things he'd never wanted to know, and his idealized image of his innocent younger cousin was gone forever. Letting out a slow breath, he responded, "I won't do anything to him. He's going to be family anyway, I suppose, so I should get used to the idea."

Sammy cocked her head to one side, puzzled. "Family?"

"I couldn't help but notice his accidental confession this morning. I assumed that's what you talked to him about after I left."

She nodded. "I did, but not because I want to marry him. I was trying to keep him from breaking his heart."

Will scowled. "He's already in love with you. I knew that months ago—didn't you?"

"No," she answered sincerely. "This morning was the first I'd heard of it, so I figured I'd put my foot on the fire before it got any worse."

"Sammy, you were kissing him the other day, and that's not the first time."

"I jerked him off too," she replied baldly. "Doesn't mean I want to marry him. Did you try to marry every girl who played friendly games with your little soldier? Be serious."

Dismayed, Will was almost speechless. "No. I didn't! And no, no one's played games with... by the Mother, what are you making me say? It's only been Selene."

Sammy gave him a sly look. "You've been on campaign with the army, twice. Tabitha told me about the things that go on, the things the camp followers do for the soldiers." She held up her hands. "I'm not judging you, though! It's just life, and soldiers are under a lot of stress. What the camp ladies do is patriotic, to be honest, heroic even."

"Who are you, and what have you done with my Sammy?" asked Will.

She frowned. "So you never...?" He shook his head vigorously. Switching tactics, Sammy asked, "What about Oliver?"

She was referring to Annabelle's child, the one she had claimed was Will's and whom his mother was now raising as her own. "No! By all that's holy, I already told you that. She was abused and forced into prostitution. I only rescued her. Have you been doubting me all this time?"

"Not really," said Sammy, shrugging. "But I figured I'd make sure since we were on the subject. So, Selene's the only one you've been with?" He nodded. "Ever?" When he nodded again, she added, "Wow."

"Isn't that how it's supposed to be?"

"You're going to live to be almost eight hundred, Will, assuming you don't let one of the fae fuck you to death," snapped his cousin. When he started protesting again, she waved her hands dismissively. "I know, I know. You're a saint. You get the point, though."

Feeling thoroughly uncomfortable, Will replied, "What about you? Was Emory your first? What happens to him now?"

She sighed. "No, dunce, I'm still a virgin, technically. I don't want to wind up like Janice. I'm planning to wait until I can use the prophylaxis spell."

"And then?"

Sammy snickered. "I'm not getting married, if that's what you're wondering. Thanks to you, I'll live a very long time. If I do decide to have a family later, I'll probably pick a non-wizard, someone who won't be around to haunt me for centuries after we get sick of one another."

"That's so—so cynical," said Will.

"I'm not a village girl anymore, Will. I've lived in Cerria. The queen is my cousin-in-law. I've been to parties and balls and seen how the well-to-do spend their days. I'm learning magic and I'll live to be positively ancient. I'm not ruling out the possibility someone will sweep me off my feet someday, but right now? I just don't see it happening, certainly not with Emory Tallowen."

Will found himself wanting to defend his other student. "He's a decent man."

She nodded in agreement. "I wouldn't have kissed him if I thought he was an ass. He's better than most of the noblemen. Tabitha's taught me a lot about them. Most of them think nothing of dalliances and secret rendezvous. I knew Emory was nicer than most, but I assumed he knew our little games were just—well, games."

"He's dead serious about you, Sam, completely in love."

His cousin shook her head. "I know him better than you do, and we talked about it. He admitted he didn't mean it seriously when I confronted him. He's a little put out right now, but we both know where we stand."

You mean he was too afraid to admit to it after you crushed his hopes, thought Will. It was hard for him to fathom that his little cousin was now so worldly she was effectively blind to the young man's devotion. Knowing he couldn't convince her, he changed the subject. "You were pretty hard on him earlier."

"I feel bad about that," she admitted. "I was scared to death you were about to die, and after we had just had that other conversation just an hour before—I let my annoyance go too far. I'll apologize later." She paused, then added, "Besides, you saw how he was. Even if he really was serious, I couldn't marry someone like that. He's too soft."

"He survived a war with me. He's seen a lot of blood and death for his age."

"And he still turned squeamish when you needed help," she countered.

That was partly because you were there, thought Will. "Not everyone reacts as quickly, or grows up with an aunt who tends to the sick. I think you're being too harsh."

She shrugged. "Maybe."

"Where is he anyway? And Tailtiu?"

"Your fairy peter-pleaser disappeared while I was cleaning you up. Emory went off to collect firewood, although that was really just an excuse to get away from me."

Will gave her a hard stare.

"I told you I feel bad. I'm going to apologize when he gets back, honestly."

Neither of them said anything for a while after that. Will retrieved the food Jeremy had planned for them to eat for lunch, and they filled their bellies. Studying Sammy's tangled hair and stained face across the fire, he found himself smothering a smile. She noticed his expression and asked, "What?"

"I love you, Sams."

She smirked. "After what I saw today, don't try to hug me."

"I don't even want to be in my own skin," he admitted. Lifting his hand, he effortlessly constructed the runes for Selene's Solution and held them in place so Sammy could see the spell's full complexity.

Fascinated, she studied the intricate globe of runes for a few seconds before asking, "What spell is that? It's incredible."

"The spell you were bitching at Emory for not knowing." Releasing it, he pushed enough turyn into the spell to cause it to expand around both of them, as well as the soiled blankets. The magic swirled around them, pulling dirt and filth from their clothes, hair, and skin. Even the tangles in Sammy's hair were undone, leaving her tresses smooth and wavy. The spell wouldn't style hair, but it did remove frizz.

While she ran her fingers admiringly through her hair, Will added, "I spent a year working on it, among all the other spells I was practicing. I think I mainly kept at it because Selene created it. Not many bother to spend that kind of effort on a cleaning spell, but we grew up poor, so cleaning has an entirely different importance for us, since we had to do so much of it. Emory grew up in a different world."

"Are you still lecturing me about him?" she asked.

"Probably." A different question popped into his mind, though. "Earlier, when you said Tabitha taught you a lot about noblemen, what did you mean exactly?"

A wicked grin spread across his cousin's face. "Your sister is very wise in the ways of men."

Will groaned. "Do I want to know what that means?"

"No. I don't think you do."

"Should I be worried?"

Sammy studied the sky, observing the first stars that had appeared. "A little." She held up two fingers, pinching them close together with a small gap remaining. "This much? I told you she's wise. If anything crazy happens, I'll let you know who needs killing. Deal?"

Summoning a spare set of clothes, Will began dressing so he could stop hiding under the blanket. Reluctantly, he agreed, "Deal."

CHAPTER 39

Emory returned soon after dark, and Sammy did indeed apologize. Will tactfully chose that time to excuse himself and handle urgent biological matters. That didn't take long, but he waited until their conversation tapered off before returning. When he came back, his two human companions seemed calm, so he took that as a sign all was well.

Since the day was gone, there was little point in camping when they could sleep in warm beds, but Will wanted to check on Tailtiu before returning. He explained his intention to the others, and after listening to their inevitable warnings, he prepared to leave his body.

Sammy leaned in at the last moment, whispering in his ear, "Keep it in your pants this time."

Emory was standing on the other side of him and couldn't quite hear. "What was that?"

"Nothing," growled Will. "Just make sure I don't fall over. I usually sit down when I teleport, but I think I can keep my balance now."

Still standing, he slipped partly out of his body and focused his attention on thoughts of Tailtiu. As he had hoped, he was able to find her without completely losing contact with his body. His surroundings had changed to reflect where his aunt was, but his physical self remained as a semi-transparent ghost within his perception, as though there were two of him. It was the same thing he had done before, but in the past, he had left completely and then had to find a balancing point between being away and present simultaneously.

His aunt was in a tree, looking down over a gentle slope near the bottom of the mountain. Will was glad she was still in his world, for if she had been in the fae realm, he wouldn't have been able to teleport to her. He would have had to travel in a more ordinary fashion, through a congruence point and then on foot. A gate would work as well, but that was a complex undertaking for him still.

Changing his perspective, Will waited until he was looking up from the base of the tree, then teleported. Since it was a tall pine with few branches, he cast a climb spell on himself and then started up.

"Don't come up here," warned his aunt.

"Too bad," he returned. "I'm halfway there."

"I'm dangerous."

Will stopped just below her feet. "So am I."

Something wet fell on his arm, but it wasn't raining. "You thought it was safe, but I nearly killed you. I couldn't control it."

You did kill me, thought Will, but that seemed unhelpful. "You were starving, and I was overconfident, but everything turned out all right. I'm still here. Next time will be better."

"Next time you'll be dead!"

He climbed up a few feet more, bringing his head level with her waist. "The important thing is that we don't let you get that desperate. As long as you aren't at the edge of expiring from hunger, it will be fine."

"No it won't," she responded, sounding petulant.

Reaching around the trunk, Will put his hand on her stomach. Tailtiu scrambled away, climbing farther up, but he grabbed her ankle before she could escape. "Don't kick," he warned as she tried to pull free. "I might fall." That was a lie, given the climbing spell he was using, but it served his purpose. His aunt went still, and he kept his hold on her leg. "I'm not dead," he observed.

She glared down at him. "I'm not feeding on you."

"Because you can control it."

"Right now, because I'm still full."

Will shimmied higher, until they were nearly face-to-face with the tapering treetop between them. Reaching across, he put his hand on her cheek. "Take some."

"I don't want to. I'd rather die."

He studied her for a moment, considering his options. Throughout their history, since the day they'd first met, he had continually had to guard himself against her, but now their roles had reversed. To make his point, he had to force her to feed. There were several options that might work to trigger her instincts, at least briefly, but all of them were untenable given his loyalty to Selene. He wouldn't kiss her, or attempt anything worse.

Instead, he tried to tickle her, which failed, but she did open her mouth to protest. "What are you doing?" As she was protesting, he poked his finger into her mouth. A shiver of pleasure shot through him as his fae aunt reflexively drew on his vitality. An instant later, she jerked away, spitting and sputtering. "Fool! What was that?"

"Proof," he replied smugly. "You started and stopped, on your own."

"You did that," she argued.

"But you stopped it. As long as you aren't starving to death, you can limit what happens. You don't have to kill people." When she didn't respond, he continued, "I understand feeling bad because of what happened, but that's just a sign of how far you've come. You're practically human now."

"Humans don't eat humans."

"You can live your own life. It's probably better if you feed from wizards who can replenish what you take, but even if you didn't have that option, you could just take tiny bits from strangers in passing, right?"

Her visage became pensive. "I've never done that before."

"You were a simple predator then, and people were just food. You can live differently now." Will waited while she thought it over, and after a little more wheedling and begging, he finally convinced her to come down. They teleported back to the others, and after an awkward reunion, they settled their plans for the night.

"We'll be back in the morning, as long as you're here for us," said Will.

Tailtiu's eyes narrowed. "That's why you came after me, isn't it?"

Will was ready for that suggestion. "No. Evie could stay here if necessary. Besides, even if it's an imposition, I think you probably owe me at least this much."

Tailtiu gave him a look from under half-lidded eyes. "If you insist, Master."

Sammy's expression was one of disapproval, but Will touched her arm and put his other hand on Emory. Evie leapt gracefully onto his shoulder, and after a few seconds of orienting himself astrally, Will teleported them to Rimberlin House.

With friends everywhere he needed to be, Will decided to make another jump after that. The dragon already knew about their ruse, so he wasn't worried about giving that away. Selene sensed his contact right before he teleported, so she wasn't startled when he appeared behind her.

She was sitting in front of the dressing table in their bedroom, brushing out her hair. She paused and stared at him in the mirror without turning around.

"I'm sorry," he said without explanation.

Selene shook her head. "No, you're not. You said what you meant and so did I." She stared at the brush in her hand. "But I'm sorry for how I said it. I was frustrated and angry, so I made my words as cruel as possible."

"They were still true," said Will. "And we're still on the same side."

Selene wasn't given to sudden action. She normally considered her every thought and word carefully. Without warning, she dropped the brush and stood, turning to face him. The kiss she gave him was rough and fast. A minute passed before she relaxed enough to shift to a more tender approach.

Will's heart leapt at the unexpected turn of events, but he still had more to say. Pulling away, he tried to continue the conversation. "Something weird happened today. I need to tell you about it."

His wife had already maneuvered him back several feet, making sure the bed was there to break his fall before she gave him a strong shove. "Tell me in a little while." She landed on top of him, then buried her head against his neck.

"I nearly died."

The announcement didn't faze her. "You'll die again if you don't sort out your priorities," she told him.

He protested a few more times, but Selene was insistent, and her hands were supernaturally skillful when it came to undoing the laces on his clothing. Soon enough, Will devoted himself to the task at hand. Given the extreme events earlier in the day, he didn't feel the same desperate urgency she did, so after a few minutes, he rolled, flipping Selene onto her back.

Then he gave her his undivided attention.

An hour later, panting for air, they called a truce. After a few minutes, Selene regained some composure and rolled onto her side, propping her head up with one arm. "That was a pleasant surprise," she announced.

Will was beyond exhausted. Still on his back, he responded, "Why?"

"After all this time, I assumed things would be quick the first time," she replied.

After the day he'd had, Will knew there wouldn't be an encore—he no longer had the energy to talk, much less do anything else—but Selene's quick insight was already prompting her to ask a new question. "Is there something you want to tell me?"

His heart sped up slightly. "I wanted to explain an hour ago, but…"

Leaning over, Selene kissed his forehead. "I can see how tired you are, but you said you nearly died. At least give me a quick explanation."

Dreading her reaction, Will caught her up. The older portions of his tale went quickly; she'd already heard about his meeting with Lognion from the lich. Once he reached the events of the day, he slowed down, choosing his words carefully but not hiding the truth. Her response, as usual, was not what he expected.

His wife's face was smooth, showing little emotion. "You're unharmed?" she asked.

"I'm tired, but I don't have any wounds," he answered, trying to read her expression.

"And she's fine?"

Will nodded. "She hid herself in shame, but I convinced her to come back. As long as we don't let her get that far along again, she should be safe."

"So, who is going to feed her?"

Her question sounded perfectly reasonable, but Will sensed hidden danger. "It needs to be wizards, to prevent shortening people's lifespans. Until the others gain more experience, I guess it should be me."

Selene's brows lowered like storm clouds on the horizon. "I don't think that's a good idea." She held up a hand before he could argue. "I know, I know. I truly believe you and I know your intentions were honest. You don't have to waste time convincing me ad nauseum. That's not the issue. It's the sexual nature of it, the pleasure. You might get addicted to it—to her."

"I died today, almost." He hadn't explained the events between dying and returning since his memory was fuzzy. Will thought he'd spoken to someone, but it had faded from his waking mind like a dream at dawn.

"You had an orgasm that nearly killed you," she clarified calmly.

"I spent the rest of the day recovering after I woke up vomiting. It's not something I want to repeat. It won't be like that in the future."

"The safety makes it worse, from my standpoint."

He had to admit her points were solid. "So, what do we do? At worst, she could feed from strangers, but even if she doesn't kill them, she'll still be shortening their lives. I don't think that's a moral choice, except when necessary."

"Let everyone have a turn. Sammy and Emory for now. When possible, I could take a turn and so could Tabitha. That's without even considering the sorcerers we have at Wurthaven working on our projects."

Will wanted to object. Imagining his cousin, his sister, or even Selene experiencing even a mild version of Tailtiu's feeding bothered him. He imagined telling his wife that and could already hear her response, though. *That's exactly why I don't want you doing it either."* After a minute, he decided she was right. "You make a lot of sense," he admitted, then added, "I'm still not happy about the new elementals."

"What we want them to do would drastically shorten their lives without elementals. Is it fair to ask that of them? We can't afford to fail. You know that," she reiterated.

"It's still slavery."

"They were criminals who were going to be executed anyway."

"And a few political rivals," added Will sourly.

She gave him a steady look. "Traitors to the crown. Greedy men grasping for something not theirs to claim."

"I'm not going to change my mind," said Will. "It would be better to let those helping us make sacrifices, or not, according to their own abilities. Offering them stolen power at the expense of someone else's soul, it isn't right. It will never be right."

"I'm going to release them as soon as this is done," she reminded.

"You promise?"

"Of course. Why do you keep doubting me? I don't like it either. Would you like it if I keep bringing up what you have to do soon?"

She was referring to the planned sacrifice of the Shimerans. Will was tempted to share his alternate plan, but he worried that Grim Talek might hear of it and disagree. *Actually, I'm more worried she will disagree.* Selene had a heart, but if it came down to sacrificing a foreign nation or endangering his life, Will knew she would choose to sacrifice the Shimerans. "Let's talk about something else, something happy."

"Exactly my point," she agreed. "Want to hear about what I did today?"

He nodded. "Yes, please."

"I healed a burned child."

"Was there a fire in the city?" he asked.

Selene shook her head. "This was a boy from the village of Reylik. The fire was years ago, when he was eight. He's eleven now."

Frowning, Will was confused. "Huh?"

"The fire took part of one of his hands and badly scarred one side of his face. I couldn't replace the lost fingers, but I was able to restore his face. He looks like any other boy now. His mother cried when she saw him afterward." Selene's face was practically glowing with happiness.

Will had only had one class at Wurthaven on medical magic, but it was enough that he knew old scars couldn't be healed. Burns in particular were difficult to treat, even if they were seen immediately after they occurred. Even the miracle of his regeneration potions couldn't restore severe burns, and other wounds couldn't be fully recovered from if they were more than one or two days old. "You got rid of his scars?"

"Grim has shown me a number of spells based on necromantic techniques that can be used to permanently reshape flesh. More importantly, he's been patient enough to explain the principles underlying them."

"Is this like shapeshifting?"

"Some of it is the same," she agreed. "But this can go further. By utilizing specialized spells, dead tissue can be revived or replaced, if it's no longer present. With more work, I believe I can give that child his fingers back too. I just need to do some more research."

Will paused, then finally said, "That's incredible. Honestly."

Selene focused on him, studying his eyes. "You don't sound like you mean that. What are you thinking?"

He tried to shake her off, waving his hand. "Nothing. I'm just tired. I'm proud of what you're doing."

With a mischievous grin, she asked, "Are you worried I'm going to make myself into a lich?"

That thought had been the farthest thing from his mind, but her jest sent a shiver down his back. "No. Why would you say that? Did he teach you how it's done?"

She laughed. "He might, if I asked. Grim has been very open." Watching the dismay on Will's face, she quickly tried to reassure him, "I'm not going to ask."

He exhaled slowly, feeling relieved. "Thank goodness."

"I think I've almost figured it out anyway."

A feeling of trepidation washed over him. "You wouldn't..."

"Obviously not," she replied. "Yet again, you keep assuming the worst of me."

Feeling slightly guilty, Will nodded. "Sorry. Do you know how he can be killed? Or where his phylactery might be?"

Shrugging, she answered, "No. If he's done it the way I think, then he's nigh unkillable. The magic is perfect. The phylactery is the key, but even if he trusted me, he wouldn't give that secret away." She paused a moment, then asked, "Do you really have to kill him? I don't think it can be done, and it's only going to cause trouble for both of us."

"I don't have any other option," said Will. "If I don't do it or die trying, he'll destroy everyone I love."

"He's bluffing. He just wants to motivate you."

Will shook his head. "He meant it. I won't take the chance anyway, even if I thought he was lying." A dark silence descended on the conversation, and neither of them said anything for a while. Then Will asked, "You really can't think of anything? If you've figured it out, then you understand the mechanism better than anyone else, living or dead. There has to be something."

Scratching her nose, Selene thought about it for a minute, then said, "He can't leave this plane, but I don't think that will help."

"What do you mean?"

"The link between the body he occupies and his phylactery follows the same astral principles you use when you teleport. His current body and the object that binds him here have to be on the same plane."

"So he can't use a gate, or pass through a congruence point?" asked Will.

"Not unless he carries the phylactery with him, which would be pretty foolish."

His mind raced through possibilities. "What if someone shoved him through an open gate?"

Selene shook her head. "That would sever the link, and his soul would instantly return to the phylactery. You'd kill his current body, but he would still be able to come back."

Will growled in frustration.

"You don't sound tired," she remarked, sliding her hand under the covers.

He gave her a wan smile. "Don't bother. I'm a lost cause today. The first time was a miracle, considering…" A thrill ran up his spine at her touch.

"What was that?" he demanded, thoroughly shocked.

Selene's lips curved into a wicked smirk. "I told you I could raise the dead."

Lifting the covers, he saw the truth of her words. "That was wild magic. How?"

"I mentioned it to you after I returned last year. Aislinn showed me some of her tricks. What do you think? Who's better, me or your aunt?"

"That isn't funny," said Will. "You never did this before. Why now?"

Hands on his shoulders, she pressed him down. "I never needed to. Today you need some help, and I need to teach you a lesson."

"Darling, please. I'm exhausted, truly. I need rest," he pled, hoping to bargain with her.

"Darling? I don't hear that often. You really must feel guilty." Another surge of energy from her sent a wave of pleasure from his head to his toes. "I'm not going to steal your energy, though. I'm a giver, not a taker."

Will growled again, but this time it wasn't from frustration. "You've a devil in your heart, temptress."

"Your resistance would have stopped me, if that's what you really wanted," she countered, nibbling on his earlobe. "By all means, milord, exorcise my devil."

CHAPTER 40

He overslept the next day. When his eyes finally opened, the angle of the light filtering through the curtains indicated it was close to noon. Bolting upright, Will found himself alone, though his movement sent a folded note sliding from Selene's pillow onto the floor. Retrieving it, he read:

> *No rest for the wicked. You didn't wake for breakfast, so I left a plate on the dressing table. I won't be back until late, so don't wait. If we don't see each other soon, remember this: I'll love you regardless of any evil you do. I know your heart. Do what you must.*
> *You'll do the same for me, won't you?*
> *Love always, Selene.*

Will rubbed the moisture from his eyes, then tried to smooth out his emotions. He understood what she meant, and he loved the support, but somehow her letter made him feel as though an unseen doom hung over them. Despite her reassurance, he wasn't worried about the demons; it was some unknown intangible dread that cast a shadow over his heart.

He rose and splashed some water on his face to wake up and clean the sleep out of his eyes. The food she had left was cold but delicious, soft bread with butter and honey to complement grilled slices of salted ham. Once he was dressed and armored, Will teleported to Rimberlin House, and after apologizing for his tardiness, he took them back to the ley-line intersection in the mountains where Tailtiu awaited.

His aunt wasn't any more pleased about having been forced to wait, but Will deflected her ire by shifting the topic to her feeding. Tailtiu insisted it wasn't necessary yet, but he wanted to stay ahead of the problem. When he explained to Sammy and Emory that they'd be taking turns, an entirely different conversation ensued.

Both of them wanted to be first, but Emory insisted, then looked distinctly hurt when Sammy didn't seem even faintly jealous. Will was beyond caring—he just wanted to get on with the day. "Can we just get this over with? There's a lot to do."

Tailtiu laid her hand on Emory's cheek and kept it there for a solid minute, while the young wizard made an effort to appear stoic. In spite of his efforts, there was one obvious sign he couldn't hide. After another round of snippy remarks between him and Sammy, Will lost his patience.

"I'm calling your tutor now. Please don't joke around in front of her; she's incredibly dangerous. One wrong word and you could end up on a leash for eternity."

That got their attention. Will repeated his grandmother's name three times, then began lecturing them on the rules. "Accept no gifts, unless she names it a gift. Anything you accept without an agreed payment could be considered a debt. If you ever meet one of the fae without me, always negotiate a duration for a peaceful truce while you settle the terms for your interaction. As long as you're in Hercynia, they can't hurt you, unless you violate the terms of the Accord, or incur a debt that can be paid for in blood. Never travel to the fae realm unless you have the power to compel respect—you don't have the same protection there that you do here."

Emory raised a hand. "Can you clarify that last part?"

"In their realm, we are prey. It's handy to use congruence points to travel back and forth, but if you get caught, you'd better be stronger than whoever catches you. If not, they'll do what they please, or force you into a bargain you won't like. They can't lie, but they don't need to. They can deceive with the truth, and you'll never know their true motives."

"I'm starting to think this is a bad idea," observed Will's cousin.

Will agreed. "Dealing with them is always a bad idea. No matter what bargain you make, they always come out ahead. The best you can do is to know what you're willing to lose before you make a deal and stick to that."

Sammy lifted one brow, giving him a dubious look. "And you're leaving us *alone* with her?"

"I've already made the deal. While she's here, she will teach you just as if she's human. If you ask for anything she hasn't already agreed to, she will warn you—I specified that with her already. Follow her instructions and tell her when you don't understand. So long as it relates to her agreement with me, she'll behave as any other teacher. She will also protect you while she is here."

"If there's nothing to worry about, why are you giving us so many warnings?" asked Emory.

"The fae are always something to worry about. I've tried to think of everything, but she has probably already thought of loopholes I missed.

She has to warn you before you get caught by one, though. Pay attention and don't take her lightly," warned Will.

"Lightly?" huffed the young nobleman. "After what happened to you yesterday, I'm already on the verge of pissing myself."

Will didn't really want to remember that, but he rolled with it. "That was nothing. Let me tell you the story of how my grandmother came to be who she is now and you'll see how much worse it can be."

Floating down from the ledge above, Aislinn landed as though she weighed less than a feather. "Telling bedtime stories to scare the children, William?"

He shrugged. "I had to fill the time."

After a short series of introductions, he let Aislinn get to work. As promised, she behaved just as any human teacher would have. She explained the theory and demonstrated the details while remaining patient. She had no expectation that her students would understand immediately.

The first day was too short to get past the preliminaries, but after the second, Will asked her, "What do you think? Can they do it?"

Aislinn responded with confidence, "I must confess to being worried before I met them, but your apprentices have a solid foundation. Either of them could do it alone, given time to mature. The aristocrat already has the knowledge needed—he just hasn't developed the stability to control such large flows. With your cousin acting as a ritual conduit, he should succeed."

"My life is forfeit if they fail," Will reminded her.

His grandmother smiled. "As is mine. If my teaching is unsuccessful, I will have violated our bargain."

"That's not a motivation for you."

The fae queen clucked her tongue at him. "My nature demands that I do my best. Fear not. I simply made certain the outcome was a win for me either way."

On the fourth day, Sammy was given a break. Aislinn declared she was already fit for her part, and since Will's cousin was becoming frustrated trying to follow along with spellcraft that was years too soon for her to attempt, she was told to find something else to occupy her time.

Will had been elsewhere for most of each day, working on a new idea of his own, so when he came back for lunch, Sammy immediately latched onto him. "I'm sick of this," she announced.

"Aislinn said you were doing well," said Will encouragingly.

Sammy twisted her face into a scowl, wrinkling her nose dramatically. "The stuff they're doing now is just too much. I don't know if I'll ever be good enough for it. It's like that cleaning spell you showed me. I *want* to be that good, I'm just not."

"You'll get there," said Will. "It took me years. Just keep practicing. I have something else you can do if you want to help me instead."

Her spirits lifted immediately. "Really? What?"

Insisting it was a secret, he waited until after lunch, then took her with him when he left, using a travel disk to get down the mountain to a gentler clime. In a small clearing he'd been using, he showed her what he'd been trying to do.

Will took a wide stance, then brought his hands together in an exaggerated clapping motion. The sound that resulted was far greater than that of a normal clap, but it faded an instant later, becoming a strange hum that continued long after. Standing a few feet away, Sammy noticed that Will's outline was blurry. She circled him slowly to see if he looked the same from all sides. He did. "What is that?"

"I'm not sure," he responded with a grin. "I think of it as a wall of sound, but that's not really accurate. I haven't come up with a name for it."

She continued studying the effect. It was sort of like what she might have expected from heat waves in the distance on a summer day, but not nearly as irregular. Her cousin was still easily identifiable, just slightly blurred in a highly uniform fashion. The turyn around him was even more interesting. "That's not a spell," she observed.

Will nodded. "It's wild magic. More specifically, I'm using my talent with sound."

"Could I do that?" she asked.

"Maybe, if you have the same talent. Or maybe even without it. I'm not sure how hard it is for someone else. Talents are weird. I'm just feeling my way around it. Remember what you did with fire last week while clearing the platform?" When she nodded, he continued, "I tried it too. As simple as it seemed, it was a lot more difficult for me."

"But you were able to do it."

"Yes, but that was a fairly basic application of turyn. You just had a knack for it. Later on, you might develop a talent related to it," he explained.

Sammy clapped her hands, her brows knitting together in concentration. She made several more attempts before giving up. "I don't get how you're doing it. There's nothing there. How are you *grabbing* sound and holding it?"

"It's like air, but it isn't," said Will. "It's not turyn, but it is energy. I don't know how to explain it. The clap is just to give me a starting point. Once the sound starts, I keep it bound to one place and feed turyn in to amplify it. The vibrations bounce back and forth over a span of a few inches until I let them escape."

Sammy's shoulders drooped. "That makes absolutely no sense. You expect me to learn this?"

He waved his hand at her. "Oh, no! I want you to help me test it."

"Oh. How?"

"Throw some fire at me."

His cousin seemed dubious. "That doesn't seem very safe."

"You can't burn me, even if it doesn't work," said Will. When she rolled her eyes, he demonstrated by using some unskilled wild magic, sending an unfocused wave of flame rolling over her.

Sammy deflected it without thinking, parting the wall of fire like a curtain so that it passed around her. "Are you trying to kill me?" Panic was written in her eyes.

"I'm trying to demonstrate a point," said Will. "Most magic won't hurt you, unless the other caster is vastly stronger. By the time it reaches your skin your control will be too strong for them to maintain it. I've told you about this before. It's called resistance."

"What if they fling a boulder at me?" she asked.

Will grinned. "You better move. Earth, air, water, fire, they all have different levels of physicality. Fire is almost entirely magic, at least when we create it out of nothing, so your resistance can completely nullify it. Air and water have more physical matter involved, so while you might weaken the attack, it could still do serious damage. Solid earth is way worse, unless you steal the power propelling it while it's still at a distance."

She narrowed her eyes, thinking. "What if there's no magic? What if someone tossed burning oil at me?"

"You'd best block it with a shield," said Will. "Most fire magic, like a fire-bolt, uses turyn as the fuel that feeds the flame. No magic, no flame. If something ordinary like oil is burning then no turyn is required, so be sure to block it." He sent another massive wave of fire at her, but once again, Sammy opened a hole in the fire so that it passed around her. After it passed, she seized the flames and sent them back in his direction.

A split second later, they vanished as his will flooded the area, smothering hers. Sammy gave him a sour look. "That's hardly fair."

Will relaxed. "Sorry, force of habit. Try again."

"You're sure it's safe?"

"Definitely." He was intentionally forcing himself to relax so she could do as he asked, but he didn't expect the blaze that appeared.

As she extended her hands, an intense gout of orange-white fire blasted into him. As expected, his resistance kept him from burning, but the heat in the air all around him was such that it singed the tips of his hair. "Damn," he swore, impressed.

"Are you all right? Will? I'm so sorry!" In a state of alarm his cousin ran over to him. "I didn't mean to do that. Can you see?"

He smiled. "That was great, but I have to wonder, are you secretly angry at me about something? You really gave it everything, didn't you?"

"No! No, no, no, definitely not." She was patting his clothes and hair, searching for burned places. "You're sure you're fine?" When he nodded, she remarked, "I didn't expect it to be like that. I wasn't trying that hard."

Will filed that away as something to remember. "That's exactly what I need, although maybe don't try any harder than that until I tell you to. Let me make another sound barrier, and we can see if it does anything to the fire."

The first test was disappointing, and Will almost lost his eyebrows. Sammy's flames came straight through, and the only real change was that she claimed the sound barrier remixed them as they passed through.

The second, third, and fourth tests were similar failures, although Sammy did get better at limiting herself to a more reasonable amount of fire. They took a short break to rest since they weren't near the ley lines and his cousin needed more time to recover her turyn after so many attacks.

When they resumed, Will tried changing frequencies and increasing the amount of power he used, but none of it seemed to help. Finally, he asked Sammy to use a steady stream rather than intermittent blasts.

"I don't think I can sustain it. I'll run out of turyn."

"Keep it small," Will replied. "Just a small line, something the size of your arm, maybe. If you can keep it going, that will give me a chance to experiment with my barrier and see what works."

"Why do you think this will work?" she asked suddenly. "Sound isn't solid. It can't block anything."

He shrugged, feeling unsure. Will had a vague memory of someone suggesting it, but he couldn't remember when or where. "Sound can shatter gates and bring down castle walls. I have a feeling it can do this too. I don't know why. I might be crazy."

"In for a penny, in for a pound," said Sammy. "If you're mad, I'll be crazy with you." She sent a stream of fire toward him, a ribbon five inches across that flowed through the air like a burning river of water.

For five minutes, Will shifted and changed everything he could, and though he failed, he sensed that success was possible. His efforts did alter the flame, sometimes causing it to widen or bend slightly in one direction or the other. By the end of the day, he was glad to take a rest.

After they returned to Rimberlin, Will discovered he couldn't contact Selene, which probably meant she was working late. He spent the night there, and they got an early start the next day. Since Sammy had been excused, he went over her morning spell exercises with her and let her watch him run through his.

She marveled at what she saw. "How many spells was that?"

He shrugged. "I'm not sure. I haven't counted them. I just run through every spell I've learned at least once a day. The newer spells I'll repeat over and over for the remaining time to help me get better with them."

"You didn't even cast most of them. The spell constructs were just appearing and disappearing, one after another. They were gone before my eyes could even get a good look at most of them."

Will nodded. "I slow down for my practice."

She scoffed. "Now I know you're bragging."

"No. Most of them I can reflex cast now. You wouldn't even see the construct form. I just think it, and it happens instantly. When I practice like this I deliberately slow down so I can be sure I really remember how each one is done. Arrogan once told me he'd forgotten how some of the spells he used were actually constructed, which made it hard for him to teach them. Plus, I think doing this makes it easier to learn new spells that I have to perform the normal way."

"Show me one you're still mastering, then," suggested his cousin.

Holding out one hand, Will crafted the construct for a teleport spell. Due to its complexity, it took him more than a minute, but he was pleased with his progress. Every day, he was faster.

Sammy was amazed. "The runes are flowing together so quickly, it's just a blur. This is slow? I'm doomed. I'll never be able to do that!"

"You will," he insisted. "It may be a few years, a decade, or longer. I've been told I'm far ahead of what most wizards achieve at this age. Arrogan even let slip that he thought I might be close to what he usually expected from someone after a century."

She nodded. "So you're a prodigy. That figures."

"No." Will caught her eyes and spoke slowly to emphasize his words. "I am just stubborn. I have also been put through a long series of life-or-death events. I practice every day, without fail. There have been times in the past when I practiced a lot more than an hour a day. Sometimes I would spend eight or ten hours, when I had the luxury. I've deliberately cultivated this skill, because I can't afford to wait a century."

"You always say Selene is better than you, though."

"*She* really is a prodigy," Will agreed. "She's smart, and she understands spell theory more deeply than most of the professors at Wurthaven. She also started a lot younger than I did, but when I say she's better, I don't mean at everything. She knows more, and she is a genius at spell design, but she doesn't have this kind of speed, not with most of her spells, anyway. My will is also stronger than hers, but that's probably just because I've been a real wizard longer than she has. She's moving at a different pace, but I bet in a century she'll be far beyond me, and she'll probably wonder why she married a dunce."

Sammy stared at him intently, then said, "Don't do that."

"Do what?" He was genuinely confused.

"You build others up and then run yourself down. Yes, you're dumb in some ways, but if you could see yourself the way the rest of us do, you wouldn't say things like that."

Will squinted at her, then said, "Most of Terabinia is scared to death of the Stormking."

"Not them," she said, shaking her head. "I mean those of us who know you."

He studied his feet for a moment. "Well, thank you." Then he looked around. "Let's not start the day being overly sentimental. Are you ready to help me with my new idea?"

Sleeping had done him some good, because within an hour of practicing, he was able to redirect her flame ribbon far enough to avoid his body. By noon, he'd managed to keep it from penetrating the boundary of his sound barrier at all, forcing it to slide away and disperse along one edge or the other. After lunch, they tried using different shapes and volumes of flame, and Will found that his barrier didn't work well for many of them. Yet.

The next day, he was able to divert them all and then Sammy tried increasing her intensity, which led to new problems for him. The sound barrier seemed able to divert almost any flame, but he had to adjust it appropriately. Over time, he found that even if an attack started to come through, he could retune the barrier and divert the rest.

"What do you think it would do to other things?" asked his cousin.

"Like what?"

She picked up a fist-sized stone and threw it at him without warning. Parts of the exterior flaked away, showering him with dust, while more than half stayed together, striking him solidly in the breastplate. Stubborn as ever, he took up the challenge, immediately telling her, "Try again." He changed the frequency and increased the intensity of his barrier, causing the second stone to shatter into pea-sized fragments that peppered him all over.

Half an hour later, he was able to reduce most of the stones to a cloud of dust. He'd also discovered they required more energy to stop than simple flames. As they were finishing for the day, Sammy walked up to the edge of his barrier and pointed at it with one finger. "What would it do to a person, I wonder?"

Will had a good idea already. He decreased the frequency and lowered the intensity. "It won't hurt you now. Try it."

"You sure?" she asked, but before he could answer, she poked the tip of her index finger into the shield. "Ooh!" Sammy jerked her hand back, then tried again. "It feels really weird, and it makes your hand go numb, but it's almost like there's something physical there that you have to push through."

He nodded. "I'm getting better at anticipating how it will affect different things, but I'm certain if I tune it correctly, it would do the same thing to your hand that it did to the rocks."

"Perhaps we shouldn't test it then," she suggested. The day was ending, so they started back up the mountain to meet the others. As they rode the travel disk, Sammy asked, "You never told me exactly why you're trying this new shield. Won't a force spell stop anything your sound barrier does, only better?"

"Anything I've had thrown at me before, yes."

"Then what's this new shield for?"

"It's for something that nothing else will stop, hopefully," he replied.

Chapter 41

The next day, Aislinn informed him that they were almost ready. "What does *almost* mean?" asked Will. "I can't risk this until I'm sure they can open that gate."

Serene as always, the fae queen responded, "They can do it. I'll have them open test gates starting tomorrow. Samantha will be necessary for that, of course, so you'll have to occupy yourself."

Will scratched his beard. He'd neglected it for too long and was now becoming unruly. "Tomorrow, eh? I assume you're suggesting I make the deal today."

"Even if they agree, they will need time to make arrangements. Given your time requirements, it would be best to have them start while we finish here."

"I've been anxious to start anyway," said Will. "Waiting just makes me doubt myself more. May I ask you a question?"

His grandmother answered immediately, "So long as it relates to this task, certainly. If not, there will be a price."

"I'm curious about your opinion regarding Grim Talek's reaction to what we're doing," he explained.

She nodded. "That's acceptable."

Will waited, but she said nothing. Feeling foolish he realized he still had to explicitly state the question. "What do you think the lich will do when he discovers my change to the plan?"

"In my experience, both while I was human and—in the years since—he is rational and unemotional. Although he has a reputation for cruelty, I've observed that it stems mainly from his complete disregard for pain and suffering rather than any actual enjoyment from inflicting torment. From that, I surmise he has few emotions left. Grim Talek is driven purely by reason. Given that your plan might jeopardize the end result, he will not like it. Assuming you succeed, he will accept it without spite, but I am certain his trust in your future actions will be lessened. If you fail, he will make good on his threats against your loved ones."

That was essentially what Will had thought as well. Glancing up at the sky, he could see that it would soon be midmorning. *No point in delaying,* he thought. He took Sammy and Emory back to Rimberlin House, telling them they could have a day to rest. He also made a point of leaving Evie there, fearful she might react badly if she saw the demon he planned to summon.

He teleported back, using Tailtiu as his beacon, but after arriving, he discovered the Cath Bawlg was there as well. Studying the cat, he asked, "How did you get here?"

As she so often did, Evie ignored the question. "I know you can understand me," he insisted. "How did you get here?" When she continued to ignore him, Will tried a different tactic. When he was in the astral plane, she could respond directly to him, mind to mind, so he left his body.

Standing intangibly beside his now empty body, he demanded, "Answer me, Evie."

I go where I please, she replied.

"You don't know how to teleport, though."

I've seen you travel often enough. I merely followed. I can always find what is mine.

Will chuckled. "I belong to you? I don't recall agreeing to that."

From the day I first opened my eyes. Before I learned any of your words. I knew what belonged to me. That is how I found you.

"You mean today, or when you first came to Rimberlin House?"

Yes.

The imprecision of her answer was frustrating, but he figured she meant both occasions, so he let it pass. "I'm going to talk to an enemy today, a dangerous foe. I don't want you to interfere."

I do as I please.

"This is important. You may recognize them and want to attack, but it's important that you don't. Not today anyway," he told her.

I have no enemies, although I did not like the dragon. I have met no others who I despise.

Will didn't think he could get any better reassurances, so he simply reiterated his point. "If you suddenly get angry today, control yourself. I need this in order to kill the dragon." She didn't respond, so he returned to his body. It was a second later that he realized he'd left it standing without support and yet still managed to keep his balance.

"Every day brings small improvements," he muttered, hoping the summoning would also lead to success.

Aislinn and Tailtiu left, to avoid being seen during the summoning, lest the presence of the fae affect his negotiation. Things had gone badly for the demons after their last deal with the fae, though that wasn't his grandmother's fault. Her people had fulfilled their part of the bargain.

Alone except for his cat, Will swept his hand in a wide arc, using a simple spell to clean away the runes that his grandmother and Emory had inscribed for their ritual practices. That done, he used a complementary spell to begin putting down a new set.

The spell was similar to the coloring spell he'd learned at Wurthaven, except it only imbued color to places his fingertip directly touched. It was excellent for the task, since he could write on any surface with it and the writing could only be removed with similar magic. Tracing thick lines of red on the stone between the two circles, Will began placing his runes.

The ritual he was using was barely a ritual, since he was performing it alone, but it did require similar preparation. Unlike the runes used in Arlen Arenata's summoning circle, Will's were far simpler, since he was omitting most of the functions included in hers. There was no punishment function, no defensive barrier, no binding—his circle had only one purpose, to call the entity he named.

Most people would say that attempting to summon a demon with such a complete lack of safeguards was reckless. Even the demon priests of Shimera wouldn't take those kinds of risks, but Will wasn't most people. According to Grim Talek's sources, the demons would be hesitant to answer his call, given that he'd already slain two demon-lords, including Madrok himself, who had ruled Hell for uncounted millennia. Leaving out the normal protections, summoners used was a deliberate attempt to entice Will's target.

Thirty minutes of work saw his runes laid out, a simple sequence repeated many times until both ends met. With but a single drop of blood, which would identify him as the summoner, Will completed the circle. Then he seized hold of the energies hidden beneath him and drove his power into the runes, uttering the name of the one he sought. "Nalarin, hear my call."

Will knew little of the various demon-lords, but Grim Talek's Shimeran servants possessed great volumes of information, much of it historical, and they had current knowledge as well. According to them, Nalarin was the closest demon-lord to gaining ascendance over the others, though she still hadn't fully consolidated her power.

He waited, keeping the turyn flowing through the circle, but no response came. Keeping the circle active was a chore, for though it was only a summoning, the magic provided a path for the recipient to follow when answering the call. In essence, a summoning spell served as a type of temporary interplanar teleport. Hell was a difficult place to reach from Hercynia, so the turyn of the ley lines was needed to create a link to cross the distance between planes.

An hour passed, and Will repeated Nalarin's name several times, but never felt a response. The effort of maintaining the summoning was beginning to wear on his nerves. "Nalarin, answer me. I can do this all day. If you don't answer today, I will do this again tomorrow, and the next day." Fifteen minutes more passed without answer. "Nalarin, ignore me at your peril. I have an offer that will profit you, but annoy me and I will pursue you, even if I must enter Hell itself."

Will felt something then, a nibble at the end of his line, like a fish tasting the bait. Seconds later, something seized hold, and a squat ugly figure materialized within the circle.

He had expected more. The demon in front of him was barely four feet tall, roughly humanoid with mottled grey skin and bulbous, distorted limbs. Unlike Leykachak with his dark armor and imposing figure, or Madrok with his unearthly grace, this demon seemed coarse and vulgar. The miasma of demonic turyn wafted around it like smoke, but the presence of the demon was hardly impressive. As his eyes drifted over it, he noticed a small sign tied around the demon's neck with a single word written in demon blood.

Will didn't recognize the letters. "Who are you?"

"I am Keteg," said the demon. "Sent to answer in Nalarin's place." He pointed at the sign, reading it aloud, "Nalarin."

Confused for a moment, realization finally dawned on him. Rather than come herself, the demon-lord had made a sign with her name, written in her own blood, and hung it on one of her subordinates so he could answer in her stead. He stared at the unfortunate lackey, surprised by Nalarin's childish solution. *She's really scared to meet me.*

Will laughed. "Tell your mistress I have no hostile intentions, so long as she treats with me in a civilized manner. Those who died before her were extinguished for different reasons. Leykachak because he failed to respect my wishes and bargain properly, and Madrok because he came at someone else's behest. If he had not accepted the wrong deal and brought the fight to me, I would never have had to slay him."

Keteg watched him suspiciously, then examined his surroundings. "There's no barrier, no binding—did you intend to summon an imp?"

"Such things are necessary only when facing a greater power." He looked the demon up and down derisively. "I need no protection from one such as you."

"My mistress is no lesser demon. She is first among the great powers of Hell."

Will sneered, "First among the *remaining* powers of Hell, and I've heard that even that is in doubt. If she is bold enough to make a deal with me, her primacy will be assured."

Keteg's eyes narrowed to slits. "Tell me your offer. I will relay it to her."

"I offer nothing," snapped Will. "Tell her if she wishes to pay a fair price for a great victory, then she will speak with me directly."

The demon lackey considered his words briefly, then asked, "You will summon her with this circle, as it is?"

Will nodded. "Unless she prefers I come down and visit her personally, though I doubt she would find that conversation as pleasant as the one I would like to have at the moment."

"You're bluffing."

"Try me. If she finds the lack of barrier or binding to be such a temptation, I invite her to try and exploit my lack of protection. She's welcome to try, but only once. My goodwill and patience will only go that far." Before Keteg could answer, Will commanded, "Go, tell her." Then he cut the power to the summoning and watched the demon fade away, unable to muster the strength to keep himself in Hercynia without Will's aid.

A demon-lord would be a different matter. Nalarin would likely have the strength to keep the summoning active, for a while at least, so Will couldn't count on being able to dismiss her so simply if she came. Will took advantage of the brief reprieve to sit down and close his eyes. Maintaining the circle for so long had fatigued him.

Let her think I'm making her wait, he thought with a smile. A quarter of an hour passed while he recuperated. He was still tired when he stood up again, but he was confident he would be capable enough for the task ahead. Reactivating the circle, he made the invitation again. "Nalarin, come treat with me. Riches await the bold."

The ley lines thrummed beneath his feet, seeming to shake the mountain as the demand for turyn increased a hundred-fold. The greater the demon crossing over, the more energy the summoning demanded. Will channeled the power without trouble, though he was reminded of yet another reason for barriers and bindings: While he channeled the necessary power to sustain the circle, it would be a drain on his will should Nalarin decide to challenge him. Maintaining such a vast flow from the ley lines would handicap him, like a fighter with one hand tied behind his back.

Madrok had been insanely strong, and though Will knew he'd grown since then, he still wasn't sure he was as capable as he wanted Nalarin to believe. He pushed that thought aside as a demonic form slowly took shape before him. She was shrouded by a strange smoke that obscured everything but two glowing red eyes, or rather that was probably her intention.

Will's vision adjusted almost reflexively, piercing the haze and revealing the sinister woman within. He'd imagined she would come as a seductive temptress, something like Tailtiu but with horns and an attitude, but instead Nalarin was clad in heavy demon-steel plate.

The armor wasn't for show, either. The breastplate was smooth and rounded for optimum protection, forgoing the ridiculous artistic breasts that some armorers included for female wearers. If he hadn't known beforehand that Nalarin was female, he wouldn't have been able to guess from seeing the armor. The black armor was dark and deadly, with aggressive spikes on the elbows and knees.

He started with a backhanded compliment. "Nice armor. I'm flattered you felt the need for it."

Realizing her smoke was useless, the demon-lord released it, coming fully into view. "Do not waste my time. What is your offer?" Nalarin's voice echoed hollowly from the nightmarishly sculpted helm that concealed her face. It gave her head the appearance of a grotesquely fanged ape.

"I *offer* nothing for free," Will reiterated. "I desire an exchange of goods. Souls for driktenspal." Driktenspal was the name used for the black metal mined and refined in Hell's forges.

"Driktenspal is too rare. We will not trade," she answered. It was then that she flexed her will, attempting to seize the turyn of the ley lines.

Will clamped down, smothering her effort before realizing her intent. He understood it a moment later; she'd intended to sever the connection, returning herself to Hell. Holding onto the flows with the tenacity of a steel vise, he smiled at the armored demoness. "I will count that as your one attempt on me. The next will be taken as a sign you've chosen death."

In his mind's eye, Will imagined the panic that Nalarin must be feeling, for she couldn't leave while he kept a grip on the magic around them. Without a binding circle, she wouldn't have expected to be trapped thus. The obvious answer would be to attack him then, while he was vulnerable and preoccupied with maintaining the circle. Tense seconds passed before she eventually asked, "How much do you seek?"

"A full ton."

Her voice was incredulous. "So much cannot be found without plundering the weapons and armor caches of half of Hell's lords. Even if you could pay enough for such a fortune."

"How much can you get, then? Since your resources are so limited." Will's tone openly derided the paucity of her wealth.

A shiver ran through the turyn around them, a subtle sign that Nalarin was considering another attempt, but it resolved and then she answered, "Half that. But the price will be more than you can pay."

"I'm willing to open a gate from Hercynia to Hell and keep it open for a full day, during which time you can pillage freely, taking as many souls as you have demons to haul them back."

Nalarin straightened slightly, then replied, "A gate into a barren desert is no prize."

"The gate will open from the place of your choice in Hell to the city of Spela in Shimera. Hundreds of thousands live there, and thousands upon thousands more in the surrounding region. With efficient use of your time, you might manage to take a million humans back with you."

"You lie. You can't compel the Shimerans to allow such a thing."

Will gave her a malignant grin. "You admit that my proposal is generous, then."

"It is, if it is real," she agreed.

"I'll stake my life on it with a blood-oath if you make the pact with me," he announced. Unlike the fae, who were incapable of breaking their word, and who could travel freely to the human realm, demons were quite capable of deceit and betrayal. Humans were deceitful as well, and since the denizens of Hell couldn't reach Hercynia without aid, they had often had no easy recourse if a promise was broken. Blood-oaths were the necessary result, a magic created by warlocks to ensure the integrity of their agreements.

Will had never used one, but he had made sure to learn the technique, borrowing from the journals of Grim Talek's Shimeran priests. A blood pact was simple enough, being similar to a regular spell, with a double rune construct, one for each participant. Blood from both of them would seal the deal, and if either violated the wording of the oath, the perpetrator would find their soul cut loose from their body, an instant death.

Given Nalarin's power and authority, it was rare for her to be asked to enter into such an agreement. "I should not need to lower mys—"

Will cut her off, "You agree that my proposal is fair. If you won't accept and take an oath with me, I can assure you that you will like my counteroffer even less." His words dripped with venom. "I will allow you a minute to reconsider."

Nalarin's hand made a fist, tightening over the hilt of a heavy flanged mace hanging at her side. Will's shoulders tightened, and he wondered if he had pushed her too far. If so he would soon be in a life-or-death struggle he wasn't certain he could win. The demon-lord's hand relaxed. "Let us discuss the terms of this oath."

"How soon can you have the driktenspal?"

"Four days."

"Then let us make the exchange five days hence. I will call again, but when you respond, instead of summoning, I will open a gate between us. Have the driktenspal with you, and my servants will bring it through to Hercynia."

"On nothing but an oath? How can I know you'll fulfill your side of the bargain?" she complained.

"I will remain with you in Hell," explained Will. "In order for you to make the best use of this opportunity, I'm sure you will want to open the gate to Spela in a part of Hell that is convenient for your army. After my servants take the driktenspal, I will accompany you to that location. Once you are ready, I will signal the priests in Shimera." Will summoned a vial of blood from his limnthal and held it up for Nalarin to see. "They already have a sample like this so they can find me."

The demoness considered it for a moment, then nodded. "I agree to the spirit of your idea, but now we must specify the words that will bind us."

They both spoke clearly, stating what their oath would be, and after a few minor changes, they agreed on the final wording. Each of them opened a cut and wrote out their part, using their own blood for ink, then they clasped hands and said the words while forming the rune constructs that would bind them.

"I, William Cartwright, will open a portal to you, Nalarin, five days from now," Will began.

The demon-lord continued, "I, Nalarin, scion of Madrok, will be waiting when you open your gate to me. A full thousand pounds of driktenspal will be ready for your servants to take."

He nodded, then resumed his part, "Once your servants have brought the thousand pounds of driktenspal through to Hercynia, my subordinates will close the gate and I will remain with you, while you convey me to the place of your choosing." Will paused.

Nalarin, spoke again. "I will take you to the place where I desire the gate to be within one day of your entry to Hell."

Will finished, "Once there, my subordinates will open a gate from Hercynia to where I stand in Hell. I so swear."

The demoness responded, "I so swear." The magic took hold, sinking into their skin while the paper that they had written their oath on turned to smoke and ash. It was done. Exhaling loudly, Nalarin unbuckled her helmet and removed it, revealing a startlingly attractive face. Her skin was an exotic mauve shade, and from her dark curls sprouted two small horns. Ebon orbs with golden irises stared at Will hungrily. "Well met, warlock. The excitement you provided has whetted my appetite. Will you dally with me before I go?"

He answered with a cold stare. "That was not part of our agreement."

"Your seed would surely create a remarkable cambion. A second agreement could be made," she suggested. "A far more pleasant one."

Will laughed, releasing the power that sustained the summoning. "You can't afford me."

Nalarin maintained the link on her own for several seconds. "Think about it. In five days, you'll have another chance, and we'll have a full day to enjoy ourselves." Blowing a kiss at him, she faded from view.

Will remained on his feet for a short time, making certain the summoning had completely dissipated before sinking down to the stone platform and stretching out. As the adrenaline faded, he found himself completely exhausted. Staring up at the sky, he tried to absorb its clean purity, but he still felt dirty. "I really am a warlock now."

His many bargains with the fae had led him close to crossing the line many times, but the thing that defined a real warlock wasn't the blood-oath or lack thereof—it was the things bartered for. *A warlock bargains with things he has no right to give, his soul or the souls of others being the worst possibility.*

After an hour's rest, his back started to hurt, and he still felt tired, so he got on his feet to resume his work for the day. The weariness he felt wasn't so much from effort as from the weight on his heart. Evie rejoined him, and he created a travel disk to carry them into Branscombe so he could notify the teamsters when and where they needed to be with their wagons in five days.

Gloomy as a winter storm, Will and the silver-haired cat glided down the mountain.

CHAPTER 42

The next five days were busy ones. Aislinn spent hours each day working with Emory and Sammy to ensure they could create a stable gate. Their first tests involved the easiest type, a gate that didn't cross planes. Will would teleport to his father in Myrsta and find a quiet spot, then they'd use a drop of his cousin's blood and his name to target him before activating the specialized gate ritual that Aislinn had devised.

It was nothing to sneeze at. The technical aspect was identical to what they would have to do later when connecting to Hell; the main difference lay in how much power would be required. Of all the planes Will had traveled to, Hell was notorious for being the hardest to reach. That was a good thing for the most part, since it was the main reason the human realm had never been subsumed by the demons. Apparently, the power requirement was even greater if one tried to create a gate *from within* Hell to reach Hercynia. In his introductory classes at Wurthaven, they'd simply said it was impossible, but once he had reached the more advanced classes, there were additional explanations.

Will didn't fully understand why, but there was a gradient, similar to pulling a cart up a hill. Hell was metaphysically located beneath every other plane of existence, and because of that, it was easier to create a path there than to create a path from there. The second reason was that Hell didn't have ley lines, or any other naturally occurring concentrations of turyn that could be used. The plane itself was described as parasitic, since the demons subsisted on the sacrifices of souls and turyn from other places. In the worst case, other planes, like the one the Cath Bawlg came from, were caught and anchored, like a ship being boarded at sea. Forcible connections were made, and Hell would then poison and suck the turyn right out of the other plane.

That was what had almost happened to the human world the previous year, when the Shimeran priests in Darrow had run amok and gone too far in their summoning. What Grim Talek had planned this time was a slim degree better than that. This time, a nation would be desecrated, but hopefully the rest of the world would be spared.

That wasn't good enough for Will, though, and he was preparing to risk his life and soul to achieve a better outcome.

Their next tests created gates to the fae realm and to Muskeglun. The fae realm was easiest, since it was almost as close as the ethereal, and Muskeglun was slightly harder. Each time, they succeeded without trouble, although Emory and Sammy definitely noticed the strain when they created the gate to Muskeglun.

That worried Will, since he knew from personal experience with summoning circles just how difficult piercing the veil between Hercynia and Hell could be. A gate would require an order of magnitude more turyn than a summoning. He kept his fears to himself, however, since confidence was crucial to will. Doubt would weaken them faster than anything else, which was probably why Aislinn made them practice with easy locations. She told them Hell would be a little more difficult, but definitely understated her warnings.

When he wasn't needed, Will spent his spare time working on three things. One was his normal daily spell practice, which probably went without saying. The second was his new sound barrier, and the third was the two spells he'd adapted using Grim Talek's turyn frequency for dragons: wind-wall and light-darts.

It didn't take long to get to the point of reflex casting those two spells with the changes, so with his extra time, Will explored the use of his sound barrier against a wide variety of attacks and materials. The results he got varied, but followed a discernable pattern.

The amount of effort required to block something depended greatly on the density and solidity of the physical matter involved. Fire was the easiest, followed by air. Water was often denser than earth, but its fluidity made it somewhat easier, except that Will often got sprayed by droplets when he first adjusted the shield for an aqueous attack. That was fine ordinarily, but it was something to seriously consider if acid was thrown at him. Solids were the hardest, but it varied a lot depending on the rigidity of the material. Some things shattered and disintegrated much more easily, while metals had a lot of ductile strength that made them incredibly hard to divert or break up.

Essentially, if someone threw an iron ball at him, Will was likely to get hit, unless he prepared for it well in advance and had a lot of turyn to spare. Similarly, an unexpected crossbow bolt might see the wooden shaft destroyed while the point continued onward to strike him, albeit with less forward momentum.

For many things, an elemental-shield or a force-shield made a lot more sense from the perspective of both efficiency and effectiveness. The more an attack relied on pure energy, like flame, the better the sound barrier worked, although perversely, for anything that was *entirely* energy, it did exactly nothing. Lightning passed through it without any impedance, no matter how much turyn Will used.

The light-darts he used so often were similarly capable of piercing the barrier, but there was some effect. If Will cast them, his acoustic barrier caused them to diffuse over distance, so that they became useless after ten feet or more, which ruined their main use case. If they were fired *at* him, the shield helped little, because the blurring effect wasn't enough to decrease their effectiveness over the two or three feet between his body and the shield.

Force attacks and energy beams like a disintegration spell completely ignored the shield.

Other than its effectiveness against fire and some elemental attacks, the sound barrier did have one considerable advantage, though. It wasn't purely defensive. The acoustic shield was devastating against flesh and bone. Any opponent who tried to run through it would find that out the hard way, not that a bloody pile of goo distributed across ten or twenty feet had any chance of remembering such a lesson. Will could also see through the shield, and unlike a force effect, it didn't block his use of turyn.

When using a full force-dome, the caster usually couldn't do much, even if the ground at their feet wasn't blocked. It was difficult to work around such an obstacle. Inside a complete force-cage or sphere, any magic beyond the boundary was impossible. The new sound barrier had no such problems.

There were many more possibilities beyond just creating a shield around himself, but it would probably be years before he could master all the potential uses. Will nearly lost a hand trying to make a sonic fist attack, which showed him the wisdom of going slowly. Only his ready access to a regeneration potion kept him from being permanently maimed.

Aislinn came to observe him during a brief lull in which he was able to get Sammy's help. His cousin was using the boundless energy provided by the ley lines to blast him with flames of incredible intensity, and when they stopped, Will was covered in sweat. His barrier could neatly and perfectly divert the fire, but the heat radiating around him still caused him to perspire.

"Are you planning to use that in Hell?" asked his grandmother.

His actual purpose had nothing to do with Hell, but it was a trick question, and both of them understood the reason. "Yes," he lied, providing her with the cause she needed to give him free advice under their current bargain.

She responded with a twinkle in her eye, "If you were facing an even hotter flame, something so powerful it could melt stone and steel, for example, the radiant heat around you still might be enough to cook you alive. A cooling spell to provide thermal insulation would be helpful at times like those."

Aislinn had definitely divined his intention, and the hotter flame she referred to was almost certainly dragon-fire. Will nodded. "I've been through Hell once before, and while I never saw a fire that hot, it is unseasonably warm. I've given some thought to learning a spell like that. Do you have one to teach?"

"Many demons prefer fire attacks, so your request is reasonable. Pay attention." The spell she taught him was around third-order in difficulty and would keep the air around him cool and pleasant under all but the most extreme circumstances. He recorded it in one of his journals. Once upon a time, it would have taken him a week just to cast a new spell of that difficulty, but his expertise had come a long way since then. He succeeded on the first try.

Will would have it memorized within a day, though it would probably be months before he could reflex cast the spell.

"Thank you," he told her.

Aislinn tutted at him, wagging a finger. "Thanks implies gratitude, and gratitude implies a debt. Careful with your words, child."

After days of working with her, it was hard not to feel some affection toward his grandmother, but Will remembered her betrayal the year before. Whatever kindness existed between them was purely fictional, a product of his human heart seeking reassurance where there was none to be had.

The fifth day came, and Emory and Sammy prepared the circle for their gate ritual while Aislinn watched. Once she saw that they had made no mistake in the rune layout, she left. It wouldn't do for the demons to get wind of any fae involvement. After the disastrous ending of the last agreement between the two factions, the demons would be unlikely to react well to such a thing. Evie also withdrew, though only under protest. The current incarnation of the Cath Bawlg didn't know anything about demons, but she definitely didn't like them.

Sammy didn't need to prick her finger on this occasion. She called out the demon-lord's name, and that notable's positive response was enough to set the ending location. Emory invoked the circle, and Sammy funneled turyn from the ley lines toward him.

They almost succeeded, but the intense flows of power required became too much for Will's cousin. Just as the gate started to open, she began to wilt under the strain. Sammy's knees went weak, but before they could fold, Will moved instinctively forward to offer a hand, taking some of the load. The gate opened and stabilized.

Beside him, Will could see that Sammy had recovered, so he withdrew slowly. The power needed was less now that the gate was fully open, and she was able to take over smoothly. What bothered him more was the fear in her eyes. *She knows she failed, and now she's wondering if she'll be able to do it without me.* The seeds of doubt could easily create a self-fulfilling prophecy, leaving Will stranded when the time came for them to make a way out for him.

Nalarin was waiting on the other side, still clad in her heavy armor, though she trusted him enough now to leave her visor up so he could see her eyes this time. Directly behind her was a flat stone block, on which rested neatly stacked billets of black metal. Driktenspal was similar to iron in density, so the thousand-pound pile was smaller than most would expect, measuring only two and a half feet on each side and perhaps a foot and a half high.

The demon-lord was surrounded on all sides by hulking subordinates. At her command, they began moving the bar stock from the pile in Hell and restacking it on the stone platform not too far from Sammy and Emory. Will watched with an arrogant, satisfied expression, and once the transfer was complete, he stepped close to his cousin, whispering in her ear, "You're stronger than you realize. Everything will be fine. Love you."

The distress in her eyes when he looked back after crossing over the threshold of the gate said something entirely different, but Sammy kept her silence. Emory slowly removed the power sustaining the gate, giving Sammy time to readjust. Since they were working together, neither could make sudden shifts without endangering the other. She scaled back her draw from the ley lines, and the gate slowly shrank.

Smiling, Will winked as the gate closed. He hoped she took his final words to heart, for he had no idea if she was actually strong enough, but confidence was key. Without it, there was no hope at all, since the amount of power she could channel was unlikely to improve in just twenty-four hours.

In the worst case, he could actually do what Grim Talek expected and use the token he'd received that would signal the Shimeran priests, but Will couldn't stomach that thought. His life wasn't worth the multitudes who would die if he completed the deal in that fashion. The demon-steel was in the hands of his allies now. Once it reached Cerria, Grim Talek and the mage-smiths there would create the weapons needed to kill the dragon.

At this point, Will was expendable.

Not that he had any intention of giving up that easily. Alone and without allies, Will walked beside his enemies, knowing they would kill him given the tiniest of excuses, and yet for once, he had no fear. After the stress and anxiety of the preceding weeks, it was a relief to know there was no going back. The stone was cast.

The turyn in the air was relatively abundant, but oppressive and toxic. When he had first traveled through Hell on the back of the Cath Bawlg, he'd had to use the demon-armor spell to protect himself from the negative energies infusing the plane. Now his innate turyn conversion was sufficient for the task.

He glanced over at Nalarin and saw her looking back at him with a hungry gaze. "How far away is our destination?" he asked. They were halfway through the required actions to satisfy the blood-oath. She still had to take him to her designated spot, and Will needed a subordinate to open a gate to him. Once that happened, he was free to do as he pleased. But if his students failed, and he didn't signal the Shimerans, then he would be in violation of the oath and subsequently die.

"Less than an hour," she responded. "There's no need to rush."

Will had told his friends to open the gate at hour twenty, just to be sure it was within a day and that he would have time to get there. "I'd prefer to get there sooner rather than later," he answered. "Your portion of the oath is fulfilled when we arrive, so I'd think you would prefer to get there quickly."

He could only see Nalarin's eyes, but he saw a hint of something flicker across them as she answered—was she preparing some deceit? "Despite what you may have heard about Hell, there are many pleasant entertainments you would enjoy. We have food, wine, and soft beds, along with a variety of companions your mortal eyes would find unfathomable."

Will scanned their surroundings, noting the barren, rocky plain. Aside from a few boulders with interesting shapes, there was nothing worth seeing. "Really? It doesn't look like much."

Nalarin held out one hand, palm down, and a wide disk of black stone formed, similar to the travel disks Will often used. She stepped onto it and offered him a hand up. "Allow me to show you the sights." He hesitated, but she added, "I am bound by my oath to get you to the designated place. Do you doubt me now?"

"I'm not interested in a tour."

"Should we fail to reach the place where my army waits, there's no reason I cannot name wherever we stand instead. It wouldn't be ideal for me, but our oath could be fulfilled. It's in your best interest to stay with me, wherever I wish to go."

Sighing, Will relented, stepping onto the disk. Nalarin was right, and it was his own fault for not making their oath more specific. She could take him any place she wanted, and he had no right to protest. The disk took off, accelerating to a blistering speed while he studied the demoness from the side of one eye. *Fortunately, I was not the only one to make a mistake, since you failed to clarify that my gate be from Spela rather than simply from my subordinates.*

Nalarin saw him looking and removed her helm, smiling as they raced through the hot air. "Would you like to see my bedroom first?"

"I'm a lover of the great outdoors," said Will. "I'd prefer to see the wilderness here."

Pouting, she agreed with some reluctance and took them on a long route that led to scenes Will never expected. The rate of speed her travel disk was capable of was simply incredible, and the spell also seemed to include a subtle protection that limited the wind speed that struck them as they went. No matter how fast they traveled, the wind in their faces was never too much. Barren plains flashed by to be replaced by badlands decorated by steppes and canyons. Beyond those, she took him to mountains that sported bizarre, spiky trees and fauna so hideous that some of the creatures went past ugly and back to lethal beauty.

There were dark forests that reminded him of the densest woods of Faerie, populated by numerous demons of all descriptions, some furred and others covered in scales. Everywhere they traveled, a red sun bore down on them with oppressive heat and poisonous turyn. Will fully intended to remain awake until he returned home, but as time passed, he began to wonder if he would have the endurance.

Settling to the ground on a grassy plain dotted by small groups of trees, Will saw they had come to a stone fortress. Nalarin pointed toward the heavy wooden gates. "This is my home. You must be thirsty after all this time."

Tired, Will shook his head. "I'm not interested in your bedroom." They'd spent many hours exploring the terrain, and he wondered if the time for his escape was close. "Surely the time must be near."

The demoness gave him a dark smile. "Your destination is here. Look no further." The gates opened, and she led him through the bailey and into a courtyard that almost looked pleasant. "Ware the grass," she told him. "The blades will draw blood if they touch bare skin."

So much for running barefoot, he thought wryly.

Inside the main keep, she showed him to what appeared to be a throne room. The central space had been cleared and a table laid out with various foods. Pitchers holding wine and water taunted his dry lips. Taking up a crystal goblet, Nalarin filled it with wine and offered it to him. When he refused, she shrugged and lifted it to her own mouth. "It's your loss," she told him. Then she tore a strip of meat from what looked like a roast bird and slowly chewed, showing obvious delight. "The food is perfectly harmless, I assure you."

The constant dry heat had left Will feeling weak and somewhat woozy. Ignoring her entreaties, he summoned a small jar of water from his limnthal and splashed a little on his face and collar before drinking most of it. Feeling better, he realized he should have used the new spell Aislinn had taught him, so he summoned his notes and refreshed his memory before casting it on himself. The cool air was a welcome relief, waking him up and making him feel sharper almost immediately.

He studied the food, and although it did indeed look good, Will doubted it would hold up to his own cooking. "If we were in my land, I would cook a meal that would send you into despair at having to return here."

Nalarin snorted. "Given your distrust of my provender, I would not give you the satisfaction of tasting yours."

"Fair enough," he admitted. Then he asked, "Is this the designated place?"

She gave him an odd glance. "So eager to see the end…" she paused, then added, "…of our journey. It is close to us now."

"Show me."

"Very well." Nalarin took him down a long hall to a set of stairs that descended into what was surely the foundation of her fortress.

Remembering his dark days in Lognion's dungeon, Will hesitated. "We haven't seen many of your servants. I thought you'd have an army of demons gathering to exploit the gate I'm providing."

"Never fear, my sweetling, the important ones are here. We have no intention of wasting the gift you've given us." She gestured toward the stairs, but when he didn't move, she took the lead. "The place I want the gate is down here. If you don't follow, you'll violate our oath."

"If you betray me," he warned.

She looked back. "If I betrayed you now, I would die. It's in my best interest to show you the desired location for your gate."

Will was already well aware of the small loophole that remained for her—he'd left it in to entice Nalarin into accepting. "After you name the place, your part is done." She could kill him then and face no repercussions. It was on his shoulders to make sure the gate was opened.

The demon-lord laughed. "You think I will stop you? If your gate isn't opened, I'll have given away a fortune in driktenspal for nothing. Or perhaps you fear I will turn on you after your gate is created? You were not so timid when we made our bargain. The merciless strength you showed then was so great I would not *dare* to risk such a confrontation." Her tone was mocking as she added, "Has something changed? Is it my betrayal you fear, or have you plotted your own? Despite your fury against my kind, you are not known for sacrificing your own. Is there some seed of compassion that has weakened your resolve?"

As her words hammered home, Will knew he was teetering on the brink of ruin. Whatever lay at the bottom was obviously a trap, but if he refused to go, he would die regardless. He'd expected something of the sort, but what confused him was Nalarin's willingness to taunt him beforehand. Was she that certain of victory?

Will took the first step, following her down. "I fully intend to complete our bargain."

The stairs went down roughly fifty feet before the first flight was finished and they reached a short platform. From there, they turned ninety degrees and continued for another fifty feet before turning again. Nalarin took him down a dozen or more such flights before they reached the bottom of the stairs, hundreds and hundreds of feet below her fortress, deep within the bowels of Hell. There, they came to a small room with a single stone door. Infernal runes covered the stones around them, glowing ominously.

The demoness touched the stone door and it slid away, disappearing into the wall. A hallway stretched before them on the other side, illuminated by yet more nefarious symbols. She waited until he had entered before touching the door casing, whereupon the entrance sealed itself. A warding seal appeared on the interior side of the door, though once again Will knew none of the symbols or language used. "What's this?"

"A precaution," said Nalarin. "It's occurred to me that you might want to open your gate somewhere other than where we discussed, since it wasn't specified in the oath. If so, you might bring an army of allies through to assault my home. This door will ensure that nothing on the other side of your gate will go any farther than this."

He no longer had to wonder if she'd noticed the loophole in his half of the oath. *Shit.* Still, he had no intention of returning the way they had come. Once the gate home was open, he'd be taking it to escape. With a nod, he followed her down the long hall. At the end, they passed through another door, and behind them massive slabs of stone slammed down one by one, sealing the path they'd taken with thousands of tons of dark basalt. "You really take your security seriously," he remarked, trying to hide his nervousness.

"You have no idea, *wizard,*" said the demon-lord, opening the next door. Beyond it was a vast, open space. From the echoes that he could already hear, it seemed to be cathedral-like in volume, but when they stepped inside, Will saw that he was wrong. The smooth stone floor extended at least two hundred yards into the distance before meeting the opposite wall. Glancing to either side, he saw that the walls circled the area, and far above them, open sky reflected a dim red light down to the bottom of the pit.

Pit. Will didn't like the word, but that was the best description of the massive hole she'd brought him to. It was made all the worse by the presence of eleven figures waiting on his arrival. From the ponderous weight of power in the air, he had no doubt that all of them were demon-lords.

He'd been expecting an army of minions ready to exploit a vulnerable Shimera, not Nalarin's rivals. A heavy stone in Will's stomach confirmed what he already knew. *I'm fucked.* Whatever trap she had planned, he wasn't going to be able to fight his way out of it. Fighting back the urge to vomit, he smiled recklessly and asked, "To whom do I owe the pleasure of this auspicious meeting?"

"William Cartwright, these notables, including myself, are currently the twelve reigning Lords of Hell, though we've recently had two changes in membership. Thanks to your efforts, we've had to allow more new blood into this august membership than in many millennia prior to your birth, and because of that, everyone here is enthusiastic about making your acquaintance." She smiled, showing sharp canines that verged on being fangs.

As sometimes happened, Will's stress and anxiety reached levels so great that his brain shut off and years of Arrogan's bad influence came spilling out of his mouth in nonsensical fashion. "Well, color me impressed! I'm so happy to meet all of you, I feel like a sailor who's just had his balls and backside shaved and licked clean by a two-penny prostitute."

He had no memory of the words the second they left his lips, but the pause that followed his pronouncement told him he'd probably said something ridiculous. Will hoped he'd been humorous at least, but no laughter resulted.

Eventually Nalarin continued, ignoring his statement. "This is Lord Novok, known as the Terror of the Abyss. This is Basen, also called the Evil That Walks. This is…" The names went on, along with a litany of ridiculous titles.

Will remembered none of it, and when she finished, he asked the question that was at the top of his list of priorities. "What's that over there?"

"Very observant of you," said Nalarin pleasantly, as though complimenting a child. "The center of that circle is where I want you to open your gate."

He stared back at her. "We're still doing that? I was so overwhelmed by the greetings, I almost forgot."

She nodded. "Of course. Did you think we all met here to kill you?"

Her statement brought a chorus of laughs. *Of course, everyone laughs at her stupid jokes,* thought Will sourly. "You want me to stand in the middle, I suppose?"

"If you don't, the gate will open in the wrong place. That would be unfortunate for you. Thankfully, I've completed my part now that I've told you where it should be," said Nalarin. "Don't worry, though, you still have a few scant hours remaining before the time limit is reached."

Will swallowed. That meant it might be close to the time when Emory and Sammy would open their gate to him. If it opened in the wrong place, he was dead. "I should get in position now."

"If that's what you want, go ahead. None of us will complain," she replied, sparking another round of laughter.

"What's the circle designed to do?" he asked. It was ringed with intricate designs and infernal symbols he was completely ignorant of.

"It's purely defensive," she replied. "Yet another preparation to protect us from the wizard who slew two of our kindred. It won't hurt you." A second later, she added, "I'll be happy to make another blood-oath to that effect if you doubt my words."

Their eyes met, and Will saw death and anticipation in her gaze.

Dead if I do, dead if I don't. "Maybe you should show me your bedroom after all," he suggested.

She laughed. "Take your place, mortal. The way back is closed now. If you're too afraid to enter, I will gladly make that oath to convince you of my veracity. If even that is not enough, then all that's left is to watch and wait for you to die here."

Steeling himself, Will turned and walked to the center of the room, crossing over the elaborate circle that spanned a diameter of more than twenty feet. The Lords of Hell followed behind him, fanning out and stepping onto positions marked out around the circle. The instant the first one found his place, a force-dome sprang into existence around him.

He could tell at a glance that the barrier was formidable, but he could probably break it if necessary. A second later the power doubled as the second demon-lord found his position. It increased again as each of the others took their places. When Nalarin stepped into the final spot, the power had reached a level beyond anything Will had seen before.

Studying the edges of the dome, Will realized it wasn't a dome at all, and then their ploy became evident. The force effect went through the floor, creating a perfect sphere. He was sealed in. Nalarin had showed him the place, but there was no possibility of opening a gate there. The sphere caging him would prevent any contact, astral or otherwise. No magic would penetrate the shield, and no beacon would overcome it. Even an ordinary force-sphere would have done the same, but this one he had no hope of breaking.

There were no ley lines in Hell, and he would have needed to use them to create a similar trap if they were back in his world. In Hell, the greatest concentrations of power were found in the demon-lords themselves, so they'd created a circle to combine their strength. Whether or not his will was greater than any one of theirs no longer mattered. Force effects couldn't be manipulated or suppressed with will alone. His influence no longer reached beyond the twenty-foot diameter of his prison.

In a few hours, the time limit of his oath would have passed, and since no gate could be opened to reach him, he would die. They didn't have to fight him—they simply had to wait. "Well, this is stupid," he announced, but they couldn't hear him.

A rune on the floor inside the circle lit up, and Nalarin's voice reached his ears. "You didn't think I was unaware of your plan to betray our bargain, do you?" She was standing on the other side of the circle, in the position that aligned with the rune. Eleven other marked spots aligned with the other demon-lords, in case they wanted to talk as well.

"I'm shocked you think so poorly of me, Nalarin. If you check Spela, you'll see that the priests there are earnestly preparing to open the gate. I promise."

"Dead men don't open gates, William. Your underlings, if that's what they really were, died more than a week ago. Nothing remains of Spela but ashes, glass, and melted stone. Did you really think we wouldn't check? That we would take you at your word?"

If he hadn't already been at the pinnacle of fear, her words would have sent a cold shiver down his spine. Nalarin's description had only one plausible explanation. Lognion had figured out their plan and had moved to make sure they would have nothing to bargain with. The thrill of incipient hysteria clawed its way through Will's heart and mind. He nearly laughed. *We got the demon-steel anyway, asshole!* That thought gave rise to a different question.

"If you knew Spela was gone, why'd you make the deal?"

Nalarin began to laugh with a voice so musical and dread-inspiring, it probably would have made his grandmother jealous. Then she answered, "What did you say to me a few days ago? I can't afford you? You were wrong, William. I paid a thousand pounds of driktenspal for you, and I think it was a bargain. My companions and I now can enjoy watching you fret away your last hours, until your inevitable demise."

The glowing rune that transmitted her voice went out before he could reply, but Will's panic wouldn't let him remain silent. He yelled at the impervious barrier to vent his fear, "I meant sex! You can't afford me for *sex!* Death is cheap, you demonic hag! I'm human—anyone can kill me! All it takes is a sharp stick when I'm not paying attention!" He continued swearing for several minutes, taking time to address each one of his onlookers and pointing to make sure they knew who he was addressing. They couldn't hear him, and their faces told him he was making a fool of himself, but he didn't care.

Eventually, he wound down, and his mind cleared. It was time to think. Half a second into thinking, he tried to summon a weapon from his limnthal—and failed. Contrary to what some believed, the limnthal wasn't a pocket dimension. If it had been, it might have worked. The enchantment was actually a sophisticated link to another full dimension. Whoever had designed it had found a way to link to a place that required virtually no power to connect to. Unfortunately, that link was blocked just the same as teleportation and gates. "Fuck!"

Internally, he debated fruitlessly attacking the magical walls of his cage, but decided against it. There was no point in wasting his strength. He despaired his lost access to the limnthal. It contained hundreds of useless things, from potions to weapons to food, but there were two things inside that might have saved him: two swords he had kept with the spell he and Selene had come up with. The same spell that had saved him against Madrok.

He hadn't come to Hell without planning for a lot of contingencies, but those two bespelled blades had been his trump cards. He might or might not have been enough to take on any one demon-lord by himself, but the spell of mass destruction on those swords could take out any number of powerful foes if they were in the wrong place when it went off.

It had been his idea and Selene's impeccable design, and it had been created for a similar purpose, when he'd thought he was facing an unbeatable demon-lord the year before. Will knew the spell, so he didn't even necessarily need the two swords in his limnthal. He could cast it anew—if he had a sword to put it on.

"But no, my balls were so goddamn big I had to walk down here without a single weapon on my belt. A badass wizard too powerful to need a sword. I can get anything I need from the magical hole in my head!"

The spell had an interesting design, for it exploited the danger involved in moving solid matter back and forth between the ethereal plane. The user had to have a hand on the hilt for it to work. When activated, the final foot of the sword's blade would be shifted into the ethereal, whereupon it would then be shoved into something. That could be your opponent, ideally, but anything in their general vicinity was nearly as good, so long as that thing wasn't also present in the ethereal plane. The blade had to pass into empty space on the ethereal side of things. The second activation occurred when the user released the hilt and the magic reversed.

The wielder would be transferred to the ethereal plane, and the ethereal piece of the sword returned to the plane it had been on previously, where it would appear inside of whatever it had been thrust into. Two physical objects couldn't occupy the same place. For reasons no one completely understood, the result was an explosion beyond all expectations. When Will had used it against Madrok, it had turned the demon-lord into a flat layer of jelly at the bottom of a small crater. The fae and trolls nearby had had their bones shattered from the concussive force of the explosion.

Looking around, Will wondered if it would be enough to break the unbelievably powerful force-sphere. He doubted it, but the circle that defined the magic holding him was engraved on the stone floor. The force effect itself passed through the stone below and it was just as strong there as everywhere else, but if something sent a considerable shockwave through the stone inside the sphere, it might be enough to cause damage to the circle and its magical symbols.

Will knew the spell, but he hadn't designed it. Selene and Janice had done the technical work. He only knew the specifications for its use, and they'd been very clear, it was meant to be cast on a sword or hammer. He'd memorized the rune construct, but he had no idea how to modify it to be used on something else without a considerable amount of study. For a moment, he thought about taking off his belt and laying it flat on the floor. *If I pretend it's a sword, would that work?*

He knew better. His wife was a damned perfectionist as well as a genius. She'd been the one who put in the safeguards he hadn't thought of, and he knew for a fact she would have also been precise in her specification of what it could be placed upon. Frustrated and angry, he almost wanted to cry. Selene's well-meaning caution was going to be the death of him.

Around him, the Lords of Hell watched and talked idly to one another, laughing at his predicament.

CHAPTER 43

It was probably too late. The twenty-four-hour mark had to be close, and with it Will's expiration. Emory and Sammy had almost certainly tried to create the gate already, and assuming his cousin had found the inner resolve to succeed, they'd failed anyway. They might have tried several more times after, only to lose hope as each failure compounded on the prior ones. Will had almost resigned himself to his own death, but imagining the guilt Sammy would feel drove him half mad with frustration. She'd spend the rest of her life blaming herself.

Emory probably would too, but that didn't bother him nearly as much.

Nalarin took a moment to share some delightful information. "In case you don't already know, the death from a blood-oath is exquisitely painful. The blood in your veins slowly begins to boil, but not everywhere. It starts in the extremities and spreads slowly, bringing unbelievable pain as you burn to death from the inside out."

"Thank you," said Will, before adding a supremely clever insult. "Bitch." *I'm going to die, and that's the best I can come up with. Arrogan would be so disappointed in me.*

Think! That thought came with Laina's distinctive voice attached. Will rolled his eyes. As if it was that easy, but even as he thought it, something came to him. *I might not know the spell well enough to figure out where to modify it for the object it can be used on, but I know how it's specified,* he realized.

Actually, that was a little optimistic. He knew the methods that could be used. It could be based on size and shape, or materials the object was made of, or both. Will thought Selene would have probably just used size and shape. If she had included materials, it would make the spell unnecessarily complicated. Sure, the blade was almost certainly steel, but what if the hilt had an ivory handle, or was leather wrapped? What if it was wooden? The quillons might be brass, bronze, or steel. A hammer presented even more possibilities. To be fair, the shape could be similarly complicated, but Will already had plenty of examples of shapes that worked, because he and Selene had used it on swords and war hammers in the past.

It had to be shape. And he knew the exact shape of several swords and hammers that definitely worked, such as the swords stored in his limnthal currently. "All I need is something shaped like one of them," he muttered. Glancing at the intensely powerful shield around him, he changed his mind. The power of the blast was directly related to the amount of mass that wound up coexisting in the same place. A sword was the safest version, since the blast was smaller. That's why they'd used a war hammer against Madrok. "I need a hammer," said Will. "A big one."

Sadly, he had nothing to work with, other than the stone beneath his feet. Most of his attack spells would do little to stone. Light-darts and fire-bolts would do next to nothing to smooth stone. Similarly, his wind-wall would do little. He could probably set up a resonance and shatter the whole thing, but that seemed too extreme. Plus, he had no idea if there was anything below. It was possible the floor might fall away, and he could discover himself still trapped in a rubble-filled force-sphere hanging over an abyss.

The obvious choice was his old favorite, a force-lance. Will began blasting the floor repeatedly, sending cracks in every direction and filling the air with sharp shards whenever a portion shattered and broke. He needed a big piece, something as large the hammer he envisioned. He needed a stone at least three feet in length. The other dimensions didn't matter as much.

A male voice accosted him, laughing. "Go deep enough and you'll just find the bottom half of the spell imprisoning you."

Will ignored the speaker. He'd found his rock. It was much too large, but he had an idea for whittling it down. If he'd had an earth elemental, it would have been simple, of course. Or if he'd had a talent for shaping stone, or if he just knew some stonecutting or stone-shaping spells. Will had none of that.

Clapping his hands together. he created a sound barrier, but not around himself. He kept it small and located it over a smooth, unbroken portion of the floor, then he decreased the size until it was no larger than an ale mug. He tuned the frequency and intensity until he felt it would be perfect for its job—as a stone grinder.

Then he tried to lift his chosen rock and nearly ruined his back. "Shit, that's heavy!" Working more carefully, he straddled it and lifted more slowly, trying to use his legs more and his back less. After several minutes of work, he managed to get it out of the ruined section and onto the smooth stone floor. Then he slid it over to his makeshift magical grinder.

Things went well after that, though as he got close to the end, he had a frightening moment when a large piece of stone cracked and flaked away from the part meant to become the handle. If his weapon broke before it was ready, he'd have to start over. It was likely far too late for Emory and Sammy to save him, but he at least wanted a chance to teach the smug bastards watching him one final lesson.

Taking care, he made his grinder smaller and ratcheted up the frequency so that it could remove smaller more delicate pieces of stone. His hammer came roughly into shape, and when he finished, he felt a faint sense of pride. The head was almost a foot across, much larger than a war hammer. If it had had a longer haft, it would have been considered a war maul, and an oversized one at that. Will hoped it would fit within the spell's requirements, but if not, he could trim it down to a more modest size. Lifting his crude maul by the stone haft, he showed it to the demon-lords observing him. "I'm going to kill you with this, you sons of bitches."

It was a fair warning, and if they'd been brave enough, they might have stopped him. But they had little to fear behind their flawless wall of force. Holding out his left hand, Will crafted the spell once again, then placed it on the weapon. Satisfaction filled him as the spell settled into place without trouble. Smiling maniacally, he reversed his grip, activated the spell, and drove the massive stone head into the ground.

"Eat shit, hellspawn!" Will released the haft and was transported into Hell's ethereal plane. He was still surrounded by a force-sphere, of course, since force spells always existed in both the plane they were cast in and the parallel ethereal plane, but it winked out a moment later while he was still adjusting his vision to see into the plane he had left.

The result was far greater than he had hoped, and he felt sad he hadn't been able to watch. Most of the pit's floor was gone—just gone. The circle, the runes, the demon-lords, everything had been blown away, creating a vast, sloping wall of rubble, rocks, and powdered stone against the walls. Will laughed until he was sick.

Eventually, the spell ran its course, and Will returned to Hell's main plane. He'd already used the underwater breathing spell to save himself from the dust-choked air. It would take some time for everything to settle. On his return, he fell a significant distance; the crater was over fifty feet deep, but he was prepared for that. A force-travel-disk caught him midfall, and though it was too high to operate properly, it slowed his descent until it could maintain its position ten feet above the new 'floor.'

Will took a moment to consider what he saw. Even considering the larger weapon he'd used, the extent of the damage didn't make sense. It was almost as impressive as what had happened in Myrsta when he'd sabotaged the demon-steel turyn converter and caused it to explode.

He made a quick pass around the interior of the blast crater, then skimmed up the sloping sides until he reached the piles of detritus that circled his masterpiece of destruction. Demon-lords had regenerative powers that exceeded even those of trolls, although they operated in a fashion similar to vampires, meaning they didn't duplicate themselves if split into pieces. They also couldn't replace parts that were completely annihilated.

Will wanted to make sure he had done a good job. "Attention to detail, that's what leads to success," he muttered to himself. He searched for pieces and parts, taking time to thoroughly incinerate anything that looked remotely like flesh, blood, or bone. There wasn't much to find. The vast energy released by the explosion had done a very thorough job, but he did find a few pieces of demons here and there.

One exception was Nalarin herself. He found a large portion of her head, but her body was gone.

Understanding came to him then. His spell had broken the floor and ruined the circle. Once the force-sphere had vanished the explosion had slammed into the demon-lords with all the force he'd hoped for, and it had been enough to overwhelm her armor. Rather than retain its shape, becoming ever stronger, the demon-steel had gone straight to complete destruction.

Nalarin had been the one to escort him, and the paranoid fiend had worn a complete suit of demon-steel armor. She'd been covered from head to toe, but she had removed the helm while they were gloating at him. The end result was interesting, and not what he might have expected. The demon-steel explosion had been even greater than the one produced by his spell, and although it had thoroughly annihilated her body, it had also shielded her head partially from the first explosion. Her head had probably come off a split second before the armor detonated, and it had been thrown far enough that it partially survived the larger blast.

Her head was against one wall, partially buried. One side was missing, but the part that remained had partially healed, restoring a single eye, which swiveled to stare hatefully at him. He picked it up and whispered in her one good ear, "I told you you couldn't afford me, but I was flattered nonetheless." Dropping it to the floor, he used the same spell he'd used to clear away ice and snow to slowly roast it until nothing remained but ash and the vile smell of burned flesh.

Surveying the destruction, Will felt a sense of pride. He might be about to die, but he'd done a good day's work, and he'd hardly even had to exert himself. "Usually by this point I'm broken and mangled all to hell," he snickered. "This time, I got twelve demon-lords at once with hardly a scratch on me." It was a shame he had to die, but at least he'd gotten something worth the price.

The twenty-four-hour mark had to be nearly upon him, but he still had time to say goodbye. Finding a clear spot, he settled down cross-legged and slipped out of his body. He couldn't teleport from Hell, but he could see his loved ones. Selene would be upset, but he was too selfish to give up a last chance to see her.

She was behind a barrier, as usual. Biting back his disappointment, Will went to check on Sammy before the others. She would be the one most affected, blaming herself. He hoped Evie would be with her. The Cath Bawlg could see him, and might share his last message so she wouldn't blame herself.

His cousin appeared before him, still on the stone platform where the ley-line nexus was. She was kneeling with her head down, red hair concealing her face while her body shook. Broken by the sight of her grief, Will tried to comfort her, but as always, his hand passed through her shoulder. Sammy cried on, forlorn, while Emory stood close by, distressed at his inability to help.

Both of them looked exhausted. *How many times did they try?* he wondered.

I've lost count, said Evie, walking up to stare at the empty place where his spirit was. *It's a wonder they didn't kill themselves. They would still be trying if the man hadn't finally made her stop.*

Sorry I didn't make it back, he told the cat, but she was already changing, shifting into her grotesque and nightmarish humanoid form.

I will tell them to try again, she responded.

They're too tired! But it was too late. Evie first terrified them, then managed to explain what she had seen, using rough words and crude grammar. Will couldn't help but notice her form was no longer quite as ugly as the last time. The Cath Bawlg had apparently been studying humans over the intervening days.

Sammy stared at an empty spot close to where he was. She had red, swollen eyes, and her cheeks were marred by red, blotchy patches. She was not the sort who became more beautiful when crying. Far from it. "Just wait, we're going to get you," she said firmly.

He wanted to watch, but if he stayed, the gate would open only a few feet from its starting point, so Will returned to his body. Then he cast another travel disk spell and went to the center of the room. The crater made it impossible for him to get high enough to be exactly where Nalarin had designated, but there was no time to do anything else. He hoped it would be close enough.

Minutes passed, until he was sure they had failed, and then the air began to shimmer in front of him. Slowly, it grew, until he could see them through an opening barely large enough for his body to pass. The edges wavered, a sign of instability. Will leapt from his travel disk before it could collapse in on itself and landed on the stone platform inside the ritual circle.

Seeing him emerge, Emory collapsed. The massive flows of turyn snapped back as he lost consciousness, slamming into Sammy before she could release her own grasp of the ley line's power. For a moment, she looked like a blazing fire, her fiery hair standing on end while she stared back at her cousin. Smoke rose from her shoulders, and then her knees began to fold as blood began dripping from eyes, ears, and nose. She fell almost silently, the only sound that of her skull when it bounded solidly against the stone platform.

A hoarse scream tore free from Will's throat as he scrambled across the stone to get to her side. "No! No, no, no! Please, Mother, help me!" He called for the goddess, knowing she was real. He'd seen her once before, but no one answered his cry. Checking Sammy's throat, he found no pulse, so he put his head against her chest. Still nothing.

There were no visible wounds, other than the blood and the smell of burned hair, but Will retrieved a regeneration potion and poured it down her throat anyway. He doubted it would do anything for injuries caused by turyn feedback, but he didn't know what else to do. It might heal some superficial damage, until the magic decided her tissues were dead, then it would stop.

Her heart remained still.

With tears running down his cheeks, Will laid, her down and put his hands on top of her chest. Unsure what else to do, he tried to match her turyn, as best as he could remember it, for currently her flesh was little more than a husk. Pressing the energy inward, he infused her with it and focused on her heart, praying it would help.

Wild magic, especially when used on living flesh, could easily result in more harm than good. Will had done similar things many years before, saving two lives from the illness brought on by festering wounds, but he hadn't had any real idea what he was doing. He still didn't. The healing class at Wurthaven had only taught him enough to know he probably wasn't going to do any good.

But his cousin's heart had already stopped. Lacking better knowledge, Will did the only thing that might help. Seconds passed while he cried over Sammy's unstirring flesh. He begged the gods to help her, but somehow, he knew they wouldn't, or couldn't. They'd told him that once before, though he wasn't sure when.

"Please wake up, Sammy. What am I going to tell your dad?" his voice croaked awkwardly while he cried and pled with her. "Please. Eric's already gone. I don't have much left. You're all I have. Please, Sammy, please wake up."

Still hunched over her, he felt the first beat, and he froze, not daring to believe. An eternity later, her heart beat again. Her mouth opened to draw air, and she choked on the potion still in her throat. Will rolled her onto her side so she could spit the rest out.

Time passed, and her heart continued to keep its pace. The coughing stopped, and her breathing became shallow but steady.

Emory stirred, then sat up. The nobleman blinked several times as he looked over at Will and Sammy, obviously confused. "You made it. What happened?" His expression gradually changed as he realized Sammy was unconscious.

Will struggled to contain his anger. Emory was fine. It was *his* fault Sammy had nearly died. *Nobody passes out on purpose,* he reminded himself. "You overexerted yourself to open the gate. I got through, but you collapsed right after."

Emory crawled over to sit on the other side of Sammy. "Is she all right?"

"No," said Will, his anger showing in his voice. "You passed out first, and she was left holding the bag. The feedback stopped her heart."

Emory's voice broke as he responded, "What? No!" Then he saw the blood on her face. Reaching out, he tried to wipe some of it away.

"Stop that," snapped Will harshly. "She's alive, but I don't know how bad the damage is. Do you have a blanket?"

Emory nodded.

"Fold it and make a spot for us to lay her."

Will used a spell to warm the ground beneath the blanket, then lifted Sammy gently. Emory helped, holding her legs so Will could support her head and shoulders. Once they had her in place, Will summoned a blanket of his own to put over her. From his limnthal, he produced a jar of water and several towels, then he started cleaning away the blood around Sammy's face and ears.

"Mind if I do that?" asked Emory quietly.

Will studied the other man's face for a moment. Emory's eyes were red, and Will could see he was on the verge of tears. *He couldn't help what happened,* he told himself, but his anger persisted. Mastering himself, Will handed over the damp cloth. "Here."

Silent tears began to fall as Emory dabbed gently at the corners of her eyes. "She looks whole, but you said there might be damage? What kind of damage?"

His response was deliberately harsh. "She probably suffered a break in her will, along with a serious shock to her system from the feedback. Beyond that, I don't know. There could be all kinds of internal damage. I gave her a regeneration potion before her heart started beating again, so any physical damage is likely healed, but I don't know about the rest."

"A break in her will?"

Wurthaven had been teaching generations of wizards who weren't wizards, according to Arrogan's definition. Without learning to compress their source, they never developed their will to the extremes that true wizards did. Consequently, injuries to the will were almost unheard of. Only specialists in healing would even be taught about the possibility. Will had talked about the subject briefly with his students, but Emory didn't seem to remember that discussion. Closing his eyes, he focused on patience.

"It's a metaphysical concept, but the best analogy is that of a muscle. As a wizard matures, their will becomes stronger over time. That's what I was told, though I would add I think that pushing your limits probably helps too. That might explain why I'm such an outlier. Anyway, like a muscle, it can be damaged if you overexert yourself. It happened to me once when I was an apprentice."

Emory nodded. "So, she'll get better then?"

"Maybe," said Will. "If you strain a muscle, you can recover in a few days or weeks. Tear it and it might take months. Rip a tendon loose or completely tear the muscle and you will be crippled for life. There's no way to know how bad it is, but for now that's the least of our worries. We don't know if she will wake up. There could be more serious problems with her brain, and I'm not sure if regeneration potions can fix such things."

"You think something like that happened to her?"

Will glared at the other man. "You woke up. She hasn't. People don't lose consciousness for no reason. If this was a simple faint, she'd already be awake."

"She could just be tired. We're both exhausted."

Conjuring a brilliant mote of light with one hand, Will opened one of Sammy's eyes. The pupil was dilated to the fullest and didn't respond to the light. Repeating the process, he found the other eye also failed to respond. "See that?"

"What does it mean?"

"Stroke, concussion, some kind of brain damage. I'm not sure. We'll know better when she wakes up, if she wakes up." As he studied her face, Will noticed Sammy had a ribbon in her hair. She'd braided it in beneath the rest of her hair, so it wasn't immediately obvious. He recognized it, though. Will had bought several ribbons two years ago, and he'd given one to Sammy and one to Selene. *Has she been wearing it like this all this time?* He didn't know. She might have put it in just for today, perhaps as a good luck charm.

Will found the end of the braid and untied it, then worked it loose. He'd return it when she was better. His vision grew blurry, and the braid unwound, and the ribbon slid through his fingers. A strange bump at the end made him focus his attention. A brass button had been attached there, but it hadn't been there when Will had first bought it. Turning it over, Will saw a tiny script engraved in the metal, and with closer inspection he saw the symbols were runes rather than regular script.

Increasing his visual sensitivity, Will saw the faintest trace of turyn, and his suspicion went from one to ten in an instant. Turyn traces faded with time, unless the item was permanently enchanted, and most enchantments had a far stronger turyn signature. Whatever this was meant to do, it was deliberately designed to be nearly undetectable.

He had no idea what its intended function was. It wasn't strong enough to do anything practical, but it could be a type of beacon, or it might be designed to aid scrying. It could even be meant for listening. Such subtle artifice was miles beyond his ken. All he could guess was that it was probably passive, given the tiny amount of power. Tightening his grip, Will ripped it from the end of the ribbon.

The lich? Lognion? Aislinn? It could have been from any of them. Yet more evidence of the constant scrutiny Will was under. Tracking his loved ones had only a few limited purposes, protection or leverage. Pulling back the blanket, Will searched her clothing to see if he could find anything else. He found a second example cleverly hidden in a copper rivet that attached the buckle of her belt. A third was hidden in the sole of her shoe. Unsure if he could find them all, Will produced a knife and began cutting away her clothing.

"What are you doing?" asked Emory.

"Shut up."

Sammy had been dressed as a boy for the day's work. Will cut her tunic up the center and then down both sleeves before pulling it free and tossing it into a pile. He added the belt and her shoes. Then he began cutting up her trousers.

Emory found himself staring at Sammy's bare chest, and his cheeks colored. "You can't do that. Have you lost your mind?"

At that point, Will's anger had combined with his newfound paranoia, so his patience had grown thin. Still unsure what the enchantment did, he couldn't be sure someone wasn't listening to them, even if he thought it doubtful. *It's probably just to locate her,* he told himself. He pulled his cousin's trousers off and added them to the pile, then started cutting her undergarments.

"Stop!" yelled Emory, grabbing Will's knife hand.

Will's fury spilled over as his eyes locked onto Emory's. "Listen, you prissy little peacock! She's family, so take your disgusting thoughts and shove them up your ass. I don't have time to coddle a spoiled rich brat right now. Do you hear me?" Emory's eyes went wide with shock, then Will added, "Take off your clothes."

"What?"

His anger made him move violently with sudden jerks and stops. Will seized the pile of clothing and pulled out the belt before turning it over to show Emory the suspicious rivet. Then he put a finger over his lips to indicate the need for silence. Emory was even more confused, but Will wrote a message in the air, using his turyn to construct normal letters in the same fashion he ordinarily created rune constructs.

From Emory's point of view, it was reversed, so he stepped around to look from Will's perspective, then read the glowing letters: *enchanted buttons, rivets, beacons, spying devices.*

The nobleman began undressing, and Will did the same. Then he summoned all his spare clothes from his limnthal. He didn't see evidence of any suspicious rivets or buttons, but he threw them into the pile as well, reserving only one tunic, trousers, and an old pair of boots. They were from his early time at Wurthaven, and he hadn't used them in at least two years. They were probably safe, so he'd wear them for now, but he'd destroy them as soon as he could find more clothes.

Seeing what he was doing, Emory emptied out his own spare clothing from his limnthal. The nobleman was now completely naked and held nothing but a leather purse in one hand. "What's that?" asked Will.

"Coin."

Will nodded at the pile of clothes.

"There's twenty gold crowns in here. You suspect our coins too?" He didn't wait for an answer before tossing the purse onto the pile.

Coins would be an easy way to sneak such a tracker onto them, but they'd also be a chaotic mess if the recipient used them to pay for things. Whoever was doing the spying probably wouldn't want to try and deal with that, but Will wasn't feeling very trusting at the moment. He had over five hundred crowns along with other coinage in his limnthal. A lot of it he could trace back to his time selling potions at Wurthaven, but the small change was more recent. Will decided he'd just leave it alone. As long as it remained in the limnthal, it couldn't be used to trace them, if it was part of the problem. He considered telling Emory to pick up his purse, but he was feeling spiteful.

They incinerated the pile until nothing remained but ash and half-melted metal bits. Then Will employed his talent to create another sonic grinder and pushed the remains into it. It took a bit of work to render the metal into dust, but there was no lack of turyn where they were. The wind scattered the metal flakes across the stone platform.

The two naked men stood in the cold air, shivering, then Will summoned the last set of clothes he'd held back and started dressing. Emory's face was the picture of shock and indignation. "What the hell?" he demanded, waving his hands in Will's general direction.

Will was unapologetic. "They're old, so likely safe, but I'll get rid of them shortly." He glanced around at their surroundings. "Aislinn or Tailtiu are liable to return soon. I want to be gone before then." He glanced at Evie, who had been watching silently for some time. "Stay here and guard them."

"You suspect the fae?" asked Emory.

He shrugged. "Maybe. Doesn't matter, though. I intend to make sure no one can find her." He pointed at Sammy. "I'll be back soon." Without any other warning, he slipped halfway from his body and located his father, then teleported to Myrsta.

Mark Nerrow was meeting with what appeared to be a delegation of Darrowan citizens, but after he got over his initial surprise at Will's appearance, he made a quick apology and excused himself to talk with Will privately. "What's happening?"

"I need money and clothes," said Will without preamble. "Don't ask why." He pointed at his ear, then leaned in to whisper in Mark's, "Someone is tracking me, or listening. I'm not sure."

His father stepped over to an ironbound chest and unlocked it with a key he carried on his belt. A large number of small pouches were inside, tied and labeled with ribbons to denote what they contained.

Will recognized it from his own time in the military; it was a pay chest. The pouches represented the weekly pay for various soldiers, neatly organized and divided according to rank. The pouches weren't given out, of course, but the paymaster organized them ahead of time, so that on payday he could hand them out. The soldiers would then check the amount and return the pouch for use the next week.

Mark tossed him a heavy pouch with a ribbon indicating it was meant for a captain. There would be two crowns inside, but likely not in gold. The feel and heft confirmed that there were twenty silver clima within. Will started to untie it, but he waved his hand. "Keep the pouch. I'll replace it later. Need more?"

"That's enough for now."

"What else do you need?" asked his father.

The concern on Mark's face touched him, but Will didn't have time to feel sentimental. He gave the question a moment's thought. He'd planned to steal clothes, but there were better solutions considering where he was. "Clothes for three."

"Give me a minute." His father left and didn't return for nearly half an hour. When he did, he had his batman with him, carrying several bundles. The governor left the servant outside and carried the bundles in himself so no one would see Will. "Uniforms," he said simply. "Darrowan, unfortunately, but that's all I could find on short notice. There's blankets, heavy cloaks, boots, bedrolls, field kits—I didn't know what else you might need, so I just threw in everything I could think of."

Will opened one of the sacks and saw a brass candlestick on top, complete with a partly burned candle. He could imagine his father frantically searching his quarters, tossing in anything that seemed useful. He stored the bundles in his limnthal and gave his father a firm hug. "Thanks, Dad." He'd said "father" a few times in the past, but it was the first time he'd said something so familiar.

Mark Nerrow squeezed him harder, then pushed him away. "What else can I do? It would help if you tell me what you're planning."

Will shook his head. "I don't want to be seen. If I return soon, where will you be?"

They were currently in Myrsta, the ruined capital of Darrow, so his father asked, "I could take a walk to examine the repairs. Do you prefer inside or outside the city?"

"Outside."

"How soon? Fifteen minutes?"

Will nodded. "I'll be back in fifteen, then." Constructing a fresh teleport spell, he returned to Emory and Sammy.

He found the nobleman huddled into a tight ball beside Sammy's warm pallet. Given the freezing mountain weather and his nakedness, he should have joined her under the blanket, but instead he sat on the corner with only his feet covered. His arms were wrapped around his knees while he squeezed himself into a tight ball to try and conserve his body heat against the cold wind. Will respected the man's propriety, but under the circumstances, it was beyond foolish. *What if I was gone for an hour or two?*

"You're freezing to death. Why didn't you get under the blanket?"

Emory's teeth chattered violently as he answered, "She's naked."

"So are you!" argued Will. "You could die, exposed like that."

"I didn't want to shame—"

Striding forward, Will pulled the blanket up, then seized his mentally deficient student by the hair. "Get under there, you idiot! What's wrong with you?"

Shaking and shivering, Emory did.

"She's warm. Hold her."

"But…"

Will's eyes communicated his disgust. "Shut up. Is that all you ever think about? I know you're not going to molest her. Is your brain working?" Emory obeyed, saying nothing, though his teeth still chattered behind closed lips. Will sorted through the things his father had given him and laid out three uniforms on the cold stone.

Emory started to climb out and retrieve one, but Will barked at him, "Warm up first, fool!" Swearing and muttering, he changed his own clothes for one of the uniforms, then burned what he'd removed. The boots were slightly too large, but that was common in the army. Several strips of cloth had been included. Will wrapped his feet and used the excess to pad the boots until they were snug. *I've gotten used to tailored clothes and hand-fitted footwear.* Glancing over, he gave Emory some advice. "Pay attention to what I'm doing, otherwise you'll get blisters. I'm sure you've never had to wear anything a cobbler didn't make to fit before."

"Is that why you hate me?" asked Emory a few minutes later, once his jaw stopped shaking.

"Excuse me?"

"I've always wondered, but you finally said it a little while ago."

Will was almost finished dressing. "Said what?"

"You called me a peacock, a spoiled rich brat. I never really thought about the fact that you were a commoner originally."

Will sighed. "Listen, I was overwrought. I'd just been to Hell and back, quite literally. I didn't mean that."

Emory was facing away, and he shook his head. "No. You meant it. It might only be because you were tired, but you meant what you said."

He couldn't argue with the truth. "I don't hate you, Emory. I chose you as a team leader right before the war, remember?"

"But you didn't like me. You liked Bug. I never understood why, but it makes sense now. He grew up like you," said the nobleman.

Bug had been Will's other team leader when he'd trained his sorcerer corps for the war with Darrow. Will had counted him as a friend, but Bug had kept a secret. His family had been held hostage, and he had been forced to assassinate Will. He'd nearly succeeded. "I did like Bug," said Will, "but I liked you too."

"No. That's why you objected to me courting Samantha too." After a pause, he added, "Now that I understand, it's probably why she rejected me."

Will stood and pointed to the clothes. "You're warm enough. Put these on." He separated one uniform and carried it over to dress his cousin. Emory obeyed, and neither of them spoke while they worked on their tasks. Will got the loose clothes onto Sammy's small frame, then cinched them as tight as he could around her waist and wrists. He wrapped her feet and slipped the ridiculously large boots over them primarily to keep the cloth from coming loose. As he finished, he said, "She didn't reject you because you were born noble."

"Why then?"

"I barely understand it myself," admitted Will. "I thought she would be happy about it, but she told me she has no plans to settle down."

"I love her," said Emory emphatically.

Will nodded. "She doesn't believe it, but I don't think it would matter. Sammy's a lot more cynical than I realized. She might be a friend or a lover, but you've got a long row to hoe if you want to convince her to marry you."

"Row to hoe?"

Will chuckled. "A peasant saying. It means a lot of work."

"I've never thought of you as a peasant, nor her," said Emory. "I've never really cared about class and station. It's not how I think."

"That's because you were born to it. You didn't have to," said Will. Emory opened his mouth to protest, but Will held up his hand. "Let me finish. I married the queen, so I've thought about this a few times. I know there's a lot of decent noblemen, but even though the ones like you might not think about it, *we* have to. Commoners face it every day. If they don't show proper respect to the right people, they could be whipped or worse, and that's just the beginning of all the differences we have drummed into us. I may be a duke now—"

"Prince consort is your highest title currently, I believe," corrected Emory.

Will rolled his eyes. "You make my point for me. Even without thinking about it, you subconsciously keep track of everyone's rank and station."

"So we can't be friends?"

He shook his head. "Let me apologize. I've been too hard on you, but that's not what I mean. I'm prejudiced against noblemen, I'll admit that, but I still married a princess." Will held out his hand. "I think you're a good man, Emory. I've thought so for quite a while, though I've been a real ass because you were interested in Sammy. I'd like to be your friend, if you're willing."

The young nobleman looked at his hand and started to reach for it, then stopped. "I don't intend to give up on her. Even if she's a long hoe to row, I can wait, centuries if need be."

Will fought hard to stifle a laugh at Emory's mixed-up idiom. "I'm fine with that." The two men clasped hands. They let go several seconds later, and Will added somberly, "Your determination is admirable, but you'll only have centuries if she's still a wizard."

He regretted saying it when he saw the misery and self-recrimination in Emory's eyes. *I didn't need to say that,* he told himself.

CHAPTER 44

Will teleported them to the outskirts of Myrsta and then restored his anti-possession spell. He intended to use it continuously from that point, except for brief periods when he needed to teleport again. He didn't want to be found, observed, or otherwise tracked.

After a quick introductions with Mark Nerrow, Will and Emory prepared to leave with Sammy. They needed a stretcher to carry his cousin, which he hadn't thought of, but his father saved them the trouble of trying to make one. The governor left and returned a short time later with one he'd taken from the army hospital.

Mark Nerrow strongly suggested they leave Sammy there to be tended, but Will refused. Emory almost took sides against him, until he demonstrated his reasoning. "Notice anything different about her turyn?"

"It seems low," noted Emory.

Will nodded. "I told you I went through something like this once. It was different for me. I still had a spell enforcing the compression of my source, but she doesn't. Nevertheless, she's still a third-order wizard, at least in the sense that her source is still restricted. It isn't producing enough turyn to sustain her, but since her will is broken, her body can't absorb and convert turyn."

Mark frowned. "I thought will to be a conscious aspect of magical ability."

"For you, that's all it is," he agreed. "For Emory, Sammy, and myself, it's more than that. Not only have we trained ourselves to restrict our sources even when sleeping, or unconscious, but we've trained our bodies to supplement the missing energy with turyn we absorb from around us. To do that while sleeping or comatose means our wills are functioning even when we aren't aware of it, manipulating turyn to keep us alive." Will took a moment to brush the hair away from Sammy's face. "Given what happened, her will has broken. She can't do anything with turyn, whether she's awake or asleep, but her source is still compressed. Without regular infusions, she'll probably die."

Matching her turyn, Will slowly pressed more energy into Sammy's body. Watching him work, Emory asked, "If her source is still compressed, does that mean she's still a wizard? That she'll recover?"

"I don't know," admitted Will. "If and when she wakes up, we will have to warn her not to try anything. After a few weeks, if she seems well, we can ask her to try a little magic. If that hurts, she can wait months before trying again."

"If she starts absorbing turyn again, that will mean she's getting better," suggested Emory.

"Maybe," said Will. "I'm doing a lot of guessing. For the present, though, we will have to keep a close watch and keep her turyn levels stable."

They said their goodbyes and left, two wizards on force travel disks, carrying a stretcher between them. The Cath Bawlg rode with Sammy, curled up against her neck. When night fell, Will refused to stop. Darkness was preferable since it meant they were unlikely to be observed. He could see in the dark anyway, so he led and Emory followed, maintaining a constant distance between them. By the time dawn found them, it had been nearly two full days since Will had slept, so they made camp in a secluded copse of trees.

Sammy woke during the day, but she didn't speak. She tried to move, but she seemed too weak to do much. Emory helped her drink and eat some bread before waking Will.

Will was gratified to see Sammy's pupils were responding normally, but she wouldn't answer his questions and grew increasingly agitated the more he talked. She also seemed quite confused by her surroundings, but although she clearly wasn't happy, Sammy was too weak to fight or even sit up. At Will's suggestion, they removed her trousers and helped her into a position so that she could pee.

That made his cousin furious, but nothing emerged from her lips but incoherent grunts. Will refused to relent until she peed, though, then they dressed her once more and put her back on the stretcher. When night returned, they resumed their journey, and by the second day, they reached the place Will had chosen—the abandoned town of Cotswold.

He'd picked out the best house during his previous visits, so he took them directly to it, and they started settling in. Emory started a fire, and Will unpacked some of the sundries he had stored in his limnthal. He cooked a simple porridge using dried peas and salted ham.

Sammy had regained enough strength to sit up on her own, and she had the coordination necessary to feed herself, but she still wouldn't speak. If they talked too much in front of her, she became agitated, so the two men learned to stay quiet. She understood gestures though, so they quickly adapted to communicating with their hands as much as possible. Emory tried writing messages on parchment, but that upset Sammy as well.

Sitting outside on the third day after Will's return from Hell, Emory asked again, "What do you think is wrong with her?"

Will tapped his temple. "Something's not working. Mom told me once that people who hit their heads sometimes forget how to talk or speak. In her case, it might be both, as well as written language. She gets frustrated because she hears the words but can't understand what we're saying."

"She hit her head?"

He nodded. "When she fell, but it could've been the turyn feedback, or a stroke afterward. Only someone like Doctor Morris would be able to suss out the exact reason. I don't know enough." Will was glum already, so he changed the subject. "After I went to Hell, how did things go?"

"We took the demon-steel up to where the wagons were, and they hauled it away," said the other man. "All according to plan. It should be halfway to Cerria by now."

"You gave them the message pouch, too?"

Emory nodded. "We didn't forget. I saw Samantha hand it to the lead driver."

Although he'd been shaky the first day, Emory had been solid and dependable over the past few days. Living without others to cook, clean, or fetch things for him, he'd had to learn a number of simple tasks from Will. Emory had probably been embarrassed by his ignorance, but he'd kept his chin up and hadn't complained. Once Sammy had started walking, she'd taught the nobleman how to make tea using a kettle from the kitchen. Though she couldn't speak, her other faculties seemed to be intact.

Will remained with them in Cotswold for almost a full month, and during that time, he only removed the anti-possession spell four times, to try and contact Selene. Each time, she was shielded, and Janice was apparently with her. Tiny was also blocked. Will supposed the three of them must be in the middle of preparations for the golem or whatever Selene was building.

He considered contacting Blake, since he knew the man must have been worried, but he would have to teleport physically to do that. Rimberlin was probably full of similar enchantments to spy on him, though, so even if he trusted Blake, he couldn't tell the man anything. Only Mark Nerrow knew they were in Darrow, and only Emory, Sammy, and Evie knew they were in the abandoned town of Cotswold.

The lich was supposedly protecting his loved ones, but Will didn't fully trust the undead wizard. Not when it was probably the lich who had been spying on him. Grim Talek must have known what had happened in Spela. Unless the entire nation had been razed, one of the lich's underlings would have contacted their master. *He knew I was walking into a hopeless situation with no way to escape,* thought Will. *If I hadn't been planning to double-cross the demons, I would still be there, and probably dead.*

Maybe the lich would keep his promises, but at least Will knew Sammy was safe. His mother, his wife, and his other friends and family, they were still at Grim Talek's mercy. Will intended to go back for them, but he'd given up his foolish hope of saving everyone. *First the dragon, then the lich,* he told himself. He had to kill those two for his family, his friends, for anyone to be safe. He'd given up on trying to make sure he was the only one to suffer, and if Grim Talek tried to use his mother, Selene, or anyone else as leverage against him, that would be on the lich's head, not his own. *I'm only responsible for my own sins and fuck ups.*

He practiced relentlessly during that time, an hour a day for his usual spell practice, then four hours for the newer spells he wanted to become instinctive. That list included the new cooling spell, teleportation, an ethereal transition spell, and a spell he named 'Erica's Abyssal Barrier.' Erica was the name of the tenth writer, and while she hadn't named the spell in the ancient journal, it seemed appropriate. The spell was meant to protect the caster from unknown entities that somehow existed outside reality.

Unfortunately, the spell was far too complex for him to have any hope of reflex casting it in that period of time. The teleport spell was, too, but he'd been using that one for long enough already that he could tell he was on the cusp of making it instinctive.

But Will had bargained with Aislinn not just for her help teaching his students to open gates; he'd insisted on a spell she suggested would help him with his plan for the lich. Will held up a one-inch cube he'd whittled from a cow bone. Technically, it wasn't as much a spell as an enchantment, and it was called a ward-cube. Similar to the way he used embroidered cloth strips to quickly layout and empower wards, the ward-cube could be used to set up much more complicated wards, including wards with three dimensions.

The Abyssal Barrier was similar to a ward, though it was meant to be cast like a spell. Will took some risks and managed to modify it in such a way that he could use it as a ward, then he made a ward-cube to deploy it. With the cube in hand, Will could deploy the spell/ward repeatedly with the same ease as if he had prepared and stored the spell in advance, but without using up any of his prepared spell slots.

Being able to use the spell at a moment's notice was important if he wanted to catch the lich, and he needed to be able to repeat it if he failed to catch his foe the first, second, or even the third time. Will wasn't about to underestimate the ancient wizard.

The spell practice took up five hours a day, but with the rest of his time, Will experimented with his greater talents. Mainly, that meant learning to better use the sonic barrier he'd devised, but Will didn't limit himself. In the past, he'd never spent time developing them, since they seemed like a natural and inevitable outgrowth of his wizardly growth.

That was the old Will, though. He wasn't taking anything for granted now. He explored his control over simple sounds and complex auditory illusions. He played with empty buildings, trees, and stones, learning the frequencies that they resonated with and how they could be destroyed. At other times, he practiced with Emory, who also sought to improve his skills and was always happy to assist Will with unusual requests.

Beyond all that, Will touched the power that hid beyond the clouds, the distant fury hidden within even the calmest sky. After his battle with the king, the people had taken to calling him the Stormking. Will hadn't liked it, but after a conversation with someone he couldn't quite recall, he decided to claim the title for his own. The common folk might call him that in fear, but he would make sure he deserved the name.

The final battle would probably take place far underground, in a pocket dimension where Lognion's nest was hidden, but according to Grim Talek, the pocket dimension was sustained by the ley-line nexus. If they fought next to that, Will would have access to as much turyn as he could want, even if the sky was far beyond his reach.

Sammy came out to watch him practice some days, her expression wistful as she saw him using magic now denied to her, but she always smiled when he came over to rest beside her. She cried at night sometimes, when she thought she was alone, and Will wondered if that was why, but he couldn't ask her. Even after a month, she couldn't understand speech, couldn't talk, and couldn't write. Will and Emory took turns keeping her turyn levels stable, otherwise she would have surely died.

A week before he thought he might need to leave, Emory asked him, "Where's your cat? I haven't seen her since we came here."

"She's keeping an eye on things for me," said Will.

"A spy?"

"More than that, but essentially, yes. I have to know when the time is right."

Emory had gained even more humility of late, and he asked, "Are you going to let me help?"

Will honestly would have liked to say yes, but his eyes traveled to where Sammy was sitting and peeling onions they'd found in a nearby garden. "I'm not that selfish," he answered. "She needs you more."

Emory let out a slow sigh, running his fingers through his hair. "I wish it was different, but I'm also relieved. I couldn't abandon her, nor do I envy you what lies ahead." The nobleman picked at his fingernails. "You shouldn't go either."

"You love me that much?" teased Will, hitting the other man with his shoulder.

His student didn't take the bait. Instead, he answered seriously, "Yes. I don't want you to die. You don't even have a weapon to use."

By that, Emory meant the demon-steel they'd gotten from Hell. As far as they knew it was the only thing capable of killing a dragon. "Selene and the lich have it. I trust them to make good use of it."

"Then let them kill the dragon! You don't need to do this."

Will gave his friend a curious look. "Are you counseling me to abandon my wife, *your queen*, and leave her to kill a dragon by herself?"

"Yes," said Emory emphatically. He looked around at the empty town for a second. "I'm nobody here. Neither are you. You didn't like me because I grew up with privilege, but these past days here have been some of the best I can remember. Just the three of us."

Will snorted. "I'm going to ignore your open treason and point out that you're enjoying it mainly because *she's* here."

"So? What's your point? I'll stay here forever if it makes her happy, whether it's as her husband or simply as a fool who doesn't know when to give up."

Despite himself, Will felt his eyes grow damp. "Damn it, Emory. You keep that up and I'm going to fall in love with you, even if she doesn't!" He seized the other man's neck and pulled him close, kissing him fiercely on the cheek. "I'll call you my brother, whether you marry her or not."

Emory wiped his cheek, then replied, "I don't see how you are going to survive this. I'm serious."

"Listen up, my apprentice," said Will, adopting a gruff tone that he hoped would make him sound older.

"I'm almost the same age as you—you realize that, don't you?"

"Shut up. You're still my student, so I'm going to impart some damned wisdom. Are you listening? This is something my teacher taught me, so listen carefully." Once he was sure his friend wouldn't interrupt, Will began. "You've watched me for weeks now, and you studied with me before that. The main thing you need to have learned, above all else, is that a wizard's greatest strength is preparation.

"Preparation means having the right magic at the right time, because when you don't, you're fucked. You have to pay attention to what's coming and do your best to have what's needed when disaster starts pissing on your doorstep. Part of that is practice, like we've been doing, and part of that is improving your other skills, whatever they may be. But the most important thing is to always keep thinking ahead."

Emory broke in, "Says the man who doesn't have a single demon-steel weapon."

Will summoned the dagger that had killed the egg guardians. "Like this one?"

His friend whistled, then returned, "That's nice, but I don't think it's going to be enough for a monster the size of a barn."

"Two barns," corrected Will. "You're probably right, but I think I have everything I need. When I leave here, I'm going to kill a dragon *and* a lich, and probably a lot of whatever else gets in between me and those two things."

"You're crazy, and I don't like thinking you're going to walk away from here without any real plan to survive. If you believe you can pull off two such preposterously insane goals, why not add coming home alive and in one piece as well?"

Will's response was dry, "I try to keep my goals reasonable. I can guarantee you I'm going to kill that goddamn dragon and that fucking lich, but that's all I'm sure of." Sammy was done peeling the onions, so Will stood up. "Come on. I want to see if you can dice onions properly today. I'm getting hungry."

"Is that all you care about?"

Will laughed. "I have to make sure at least one of you can cook well enough to keep you both from starving when I leave." Together, they got up and joined Sammy to prepare the evening meal.

CHAPTER 45

Four days later, Evie returned, and it was time to go. Will already had everything he needed stored in his limnthal, but he took out his breastplate and buckled it on over the ill-fitting uniform. Compared to the dashing figure he cut in his former clothing he looked like an army deserter now, or perhaps a battlefield scavenger.

Emory hugged him goodbye. They'd already said everything they could say. Will had no way to explain to Sammy what was happening, but there was nothing wrong with her memory. Words or no words, she had figured out where he must be going. She latched onto him with a strength he hadn't expected, and for several minutes she refused to let go.

Will waited, not minding at all. He tried not to see the look on her face when she finally released him, afraid it would make it impossible to move forward. Turning his back on them, he spoke to the cat. "Lead the way."

Evie vanished, and after a few seconds Will slipped partway out of his body to find her. She had returned to the ley-line nexus in the mountains, so he teleported to her there. "Is this as close as you could get?"

The Cath Bawlg transformed, shaping herself into a woman's form in order to speak. Thankfully, she had improved. Aside from cat-like pupils and razor-sharp claws, she looked almost human, and she bore a suspicious resemblance to Tailtiu. She'd given up on clothes, however. "I can only seek certain places or people."

By *seek,* she meant her strange, spell-less form of teleportation, and by *people,* Will was pretty sure she only meant him, though he wasn't certain on that topic. "Places?" he asked.

"Here, the chamber where the dragon's nest lies, a place in the fae realm where nothing grows, and the house I found you at," she explained.

"Places you have some special connection to," said Will. "Places where something important happened for you."

She shrugged, a gesture she'd learned to emulate at some point. "I have no special connection to the place where the dragon's nest lies, nor do I have any reason to think the dead place in the fae realm is special."

"You helped me kill a demon-lord where the nest is," said Will. "That was in your previous life. The empty place in Faerie used to have a tree with a cave under it. You lived there for a long time before I met your predecessor."

Evie frowned. "Your words mean nothing to me."

"Your soul remembers, though," said Will. "It's interesting to me that you can connect to places, though. I can only teleport to people I'm close to." *Or beacons,* he reminded himself, although there were none currently in existence. The ones in Cerria and Myrsta still weren't ready. He wondered if the Cath Bawlg had some special sense that allowed her to home in on particular places as though they had a beacon, but it was a question for another day.

He cast a travel disk spell and they got on it together, Evie transitioning back down to her usual housecat form. Together they traveled down the mountain pass toward Branscombe. They diverted just before they reached the city and went to the congruence point that led to the fae realm. Crossing over, Will called his grandmother for the first time since the day he had gone to Hell.

She appeared sooner than he expected, within a minute of the third time he said her name. That was unusual, but Will didn't mind. *Maybe she was worried?* He knew that wasn't possible, but it was a pleasant fiction.

"You survived. I thought you dead," she announced flatly.

Her remark was free information, so Will added it to the special file he kept in the back of his mind. "Question for question, truce for an hour, then I intend to invoke the final unbound favor."

Aislinn nodded. "Deal."

"I found some sort of hidden enchantments on Sammy and Emory's clothes. Were you responsible?"

"No." She smiled, then asked her own question, "Did you know the lich betrayed you?"

That was a gift in the form of a question. Aislinn was following the rules, but she was feeding him information at the same time. Once more, Will wondered if she truly cared, somewhere beneath her inhuman exterior. "No. Why didn't you tell me if you knew beforehand? It should have been free, since it was related to the favor you were fulfilling at the time."

"You never asked, and your plan was sufficient already. You are here, are you not?"

Another giveaway question, thought Will. *Is she honestly trying to help me?* He answered her question to even the score. "I am here. I'm prepared to use the final unbound favor you owe me." He waited, rather than asking a question.

His grandmother smiled, then accepted his obvious ploy, asking the next question herself. "Are there any changes to what you have planned for me?"

Will smiled. "Yes." He spent the next few minutes explaining his plans and contingencies. When he finished, he asked, "You understand your part?"

She nodded. "Although I have agreed to the outline, where will the second gate lead?"

"I will tell you at that time, assuming we get that far. I have a question for you, though." His grandmother nodded, so he asked, "If you die suddenly, what will your people do?"

Her laugh was bright and cheerful. "You worry they will seek vengeance. I'm sure you know better. Elthas' subjects never cared after you slew him. We care little for retribution and outrage; our hearts are concerned only with our deals and bargains."

"You took over when Elthas died, and you owed me two big favors," Will reminded her. "Answer the question."

"Very well. If I die while fulfilling your favor, that is between you and me only. No onus will fall upon you. My people will return home and find a new leader. The accord will remain in place. My existence means nothing in the larger scheme of things."

Will nodded. "Then we're done. Wait for my call."

His grandmother's hand touched his arm. "William, do you have the ring still?"

"No. Do I need it?"

"I have no soul of my own. We have no connection. When you call, I will need a beacon to find you quickly," she explained.

The ring might be at the scene, but Will had to be sure. "Blood, then?" He took out a small knife and a glass vial. After she nodded, he made a small cut and let several drops of blood fall into the container before stoppering it and handing it to her. "That should do the trick."

They left then, returning to Hercynia through the congruence point. Will hoped they had enough time. Evie resumed her humanoid form so she could speak. "They were preparing when I left, but the time may be close. I will go ahead." She vanished without waiting for his answer.

He knew where she had gone, and he was trusting her to return and let him know when it was time for him to appear. Will still had a rough outline of the lich's plan, and he intended to wait until they had opened the pocket dimension containing the nest. It was at that point that Grim Talek and his specially prepared forces would rush in to destroy the egg guardians and the eggs.

None of them knew how or when Lognion would appear. The dragon might be inside waiting, in which case the lich would rearrange the schedule, and killing Lognion would become their first priority. Will knew Grim Talek had a plan for it, but he didn't know the details.

Since he was planning to help them anyway, Will could just as easily have showed up early, but after pretending to be dead for a month, it seemed a shame to spoil the surprise too soon. *Liar. You're afraid of what Selene will do to you.* Laina's voice taunted him with the truth as she sometimes liked to do.

"I made an honest effort to contact her several times during the first two weeks," he said out loud. It felt like he was talking to himself, and maybe he was. Laina's occasional remarks felt like his own thoughts, and he couldn't tell if she heard his responses, or if he was simply playing a game with his own imagination. "But after that, it seemed wiser to keep it a secret," he added.

There was no answer, so he said it himself. "You're right, though. I'm not looking forward to the lecture after this." By showing up at the last moment, there wouldn't be time for blame or recrimination, and if he died during the battle, at least he'd miss the punishment and forgiveness phase.

"Always a silver lining," he told himself, thinking of Aislinn, who often included similar rewards in her own plans. With nothing to do and an unknown wait ahead of him, Will left the forest and rejoined the road that led to Branscombe. It was a short walk to the town from where the congruence point was located, one he'd made many times in the past.

There was a large market in the town as well as numerous traders and craftsmen. There was no time to get anything tailored or have properly fitting boots made, but he could at least buy some clothes that were closer to his proper size. If he had enough time, he might be able to show up looking the part of a hero rather than a shambling homeless man.

***

Selene sat at her dressing table, staring at her hands, silently willing them to be still. She'd never suffered from nerves in the past, but since Will's death, nothing had been right, not within, not without. Her life was crumbling, and she could only scramble to catch some of the pieces. A dark depression had swept over her since the day Grim had given her the news.

"Lognion got wind of our plan. Spela was destroyed before the bargain could be completed." The lich hadn't said much more, but Selene understood what must have happened after that. There'd been no sign of Will since, and Emory and Sammy, who he had somehow dragged into the scheme, had never returned to Rimberlin House.

She didn't know what their part had been, but it must have been important since Will had been so adamantly against anyone else endangering themselves on his behalf. Selene had cursed him for his foolishness every night since the news, but the anger didn't help. Night after night, she wept in the empty dark as soon as the lights went out. She must have slept as well, for every morning, she found the strength to return to her work, but she didn't feel rested.

Tiny and Janice worried over her, but it only caused her to withdraw more. Tabitha visited several times, but although Selene still made small talk with her, nothing changed. The world had become a black hell with no meaning.

Selene's only respite was her work. Not the work with Janice and Tiny—that was simple and settled. The work that interested her was her research. She spent increasingly longer hours at the Psyche and Healing building on Wurthaven's campus. Much of it had involved improving the lives of people who had suffered terrible injuries, but now Selene found herself thinking of what she could have done to save her husband.

Death didn't have to be the end.

That was the bitter pill that ate into her gut. Will had been powerful, but even he couldn't face a demon-lord and her army alone and by himself—but with some of the things she knew now, he could have survived.

Grim Talek watched her as the days passed, and his observant gaze didn't miss the fatalism that was starting to consume her. But he didn't mind. She knew that from the lich's perspective, her suicidal thoughts were a boon. She hated his lack of concern, while at the same time appreciating his pragmatism.

They both knew he'd lied about the ritual to open the pocket dimension to the dragon's nest. Lognion could easily have made it so that no more than a drop was required, but that was not the dragon's way. The key to the lock was much more secure if the key had to die to open it. She would be bled to death, until finally the way opened.

Her urge to suicide was a blessing in disguise. Selene stared into the mirror, not caring that her hair was tangled and messy. For the first time in her life, she didn't give a damn about keeping up appearances for her role. The woman staring back at her looked as though she was already dead.

But death didn't have to be the end.

A polite knock came at the door, and Selene stood up to answer it. Her hands were steady now. She opened the door to see her husband standing outside. He was impeccably groomed, as he always was these days, but rather than elegant clothes, he now wore more utilitarian garb. A leather hauberk covered most of his body, and a broad belt girded his waist. Endless leather pockets were sewn into the belt, holding a myriad of small items. His boots were soft soled to give him better footing. Grim Talek looked like a strange cross between a forester and a traveling alchemist. "Are you ready?" he asked.

She wasn't wearing the clothes he'd recommended, which were similar to his own. Instead, she'd chosen a plain grey wool dress. It *was* utilitarian, though not intended for battle. She'd worn similar clothes many times while tending the sick. She'd met Will while wearing a dress that was probably identical, back when she'd been going by the name Isabel.

The imposter arched one brow. "That's not ideal clothing for where we're going."

"Does it matter? That absurd leather conglomeration you're wearing won't stop dragon-fire either. These are my work clothes. They make me feel comfortable." Her tone indicated she was unlikely to negotiate.

Ever pragmatic, the lich skipped over her minor rebellion. "You remember the plan?"

He ran through the details, even though she knew most of them didn't apply to her. Selene wondered if he was nervous and guessed that if anything could get through his unflappable exterior, the events ahead of them today would be the most likely things to do so.

"After the way opens into the nest, my men will enter, followed by your enormous friend. I'll follow, and we'll engage in the order discussed…"

Blah, blah… she annotated his plan mentally. *None of that concerns me. I'm the one dead on the sacrificial stone, remember?*

He paused. "Are you listening?"

"Certainly," she lied.

"Good. This is important, since I may need your help inside. The presence of another third-order wizard could be crucial if anything goes wrong, so I'll be expecting you to follow as soon as you've recovered," he told her. The lich's tone was simple and matter-of-fact, without any hint of deception.

"Of course," she replied, her voice sounding equally sincere. "I know you couldn't possibly succeed without me."

Grim Talek paused, and Will's beautiful blue eyes stared through her. She'd loved those eyes, but now they made her feel cold and barren. "I wouldn't say that," he replied. "After the countless ages I've endured, I like to think my preparations are solid enough to survive even if one of us falls."

"If I fall," she corrected. "You cannot die."

He waved her remark aside. "You know what I mean. If this body gets hit with dragon-fire, it will be days before I can return to fight. I might survive, but the main point is whether we win or lose this fight. It isn't about my life—or yours."

Selene smiled up at him. "I agree completely." She reached out to rest one hand across the inside of his arm. In all the time the lich had been playing as her husband, she'd never touched him directly, nor had he attempted to touch her. A spark leapt from her skin just before she made contact, and he jerked slightly.

He studied his arm for a moment, as though something beyond the pale had just occurred, and then his lips curled into a sardonic smile. "I did not expect that."

She didn't meet his eyes, nor had she expected the strange discharge of turyn. *There must be some kind of resonance.* "Let's go," she responded.

Grim Talek didn't move. "Are you sure about this?"

"You've repeated your plan endlessly. If I had an objection, you would have heard it from me before this."

His gaze never left her. "You know exactly what I'm referring to. It isn't too late to change your mind." His other hand moved with surprising speed and landed just above her left breast. Selene tried to pull away, but he simply followed her, catching her other arm to shift her momentum and press her firmly against the wall. She struggled a moment, but he wouldn't relent. "Hold still!"

Selene stopped resisting, but she stared back at him with hateful eyes until he stepped back. "Satisfied?" she asked.

The lich nodded. "I repeat what I said. I'm not sure if you are fully aware of the consequences, but you still have a choice."

Selene sneered at him. "You said you need me after my blood opens the way, didn't you? I'm sure you weren't *lying*. I've given it careful thought. I *will* be there to make sure Lognion dies. Do you object to that?"

A hungry light came into his eyes. It was an expression she'd never seen on Grim Talek's normally dispassionate features. He licked his lips, then replied, "No. I have none, none at all." He moved back to the doorway and this time bent his arm and offered it to her. "This way, my dear."

She'd initiated the gesture only moments before, but Selene was too irritated for the charade now. "Move. I know the way."

CHAPTER 46

Will was wearing much better clothes when Evie returned. The tunic was mostly obscured by his mail and gambeson, and the demon-steel breastplate didn't help. But *he* knew his tunic was of a better cut of material. More importantly for his outward appearance, he'd gotten a trim from the local barber. His neck was smooth shaven, and his beard had been manicured and styled. For the first time in over a month he felt somewhat like the civilized man that Selene had always insisted he emulate. He'd even replaced his awkwardly sized military boots with a secondhand pair from the local cobbler. They weren't a perfect fit, but they were close.

The armor still made him stink, but that was ever the case. When the choice was between stench or blood, military men always chose the stench of armor, and they wore as much as they could afford.

Evie wrinkled her nose, refusing to approach, but she didn't need to. They both knew why she was there. "Lead the way," said Will. She vanished, and he slipped partway into the astral; he teleported to her location only seconds later.

He found himself pretty much where he had expected, in the ley-line chamber beneath his house in Cerria. Will's memories of the place weren't pretty, and what he saw today did nothing to improve them. The circle was still there, though the runes had been changed. The blood grooves also remained, and they were full of dark fluid. A wide stone archway, twenty feet in width, stood opposite him, in a place where there had been nothing but stone before. The turyn flowing from the ley nexus illuminated its borders, maintaining the link between the human world and the dragon's pocket dimension. They had succeeded in opening it.

Beyond the archway, all hell had broken loose. Flashes of fire and furious screams echoed to his ears, but Will's eyes refused to follow—they had room for only one thing. Not far from where he stood was the source of the blood, a broad stone pedestal with a rectangular shape and a human-sized depression carved into the top. The first time Will had seen it used had been when he had forced Arlen Arenata onto it and used her own ritual against her, draining the blood from her veins while ignoring her begging and pleas for mercy.

Today, it held the woman he loved most in the world.

Selene lay on her back, with her arms resting on either side. Ugly cuts had opened her wrists to fill the stone depressions beneath them. From there, the blood had followed channels to activate the circle.

A sound came from Will's throat, a pitiful and incoherent noise, a mix between a half-choked cry and a yelp of dismay and disbelief. Grim Talek had lied, and he should have known it. The ritual had taken much more than a token amount of blood from her. It had taken it all.

It had taken her life.

Selene's eyes were still open, staring blankly up at the ceiling as he rushed to her side. Something flickered in them, and Will saw her gaze shift, trying to focus on his face. Looking down, he saw that there was still blood coming from her wrists, pumping sluggishly in time with a heart that was hardly beating at all. "Wait. Hold on," he cried, summoning a regeneration potion within the same breath.

She's still alive. That was the only thought in his mind. He poured the potion into her mouth and dripped the dregs over her wrists. If there was life in her still, it would work. It had to. Putting his hands over her heart, he matched the frequency of her vital turyn and pressed energy into her body, which was almost devoid of life. It had worked for Sammy, whose heart had already stopped—all Selene's had to do was keep beating long enough for the potion to work.

Her wrists closed, and her heart sped up, finding fresh strength. It was beating a feverish tempo, straining to make up for the lack of blood. Selene's lips moved. "Is this a dream?"

"More like a nightmare," snapped Will. He summoned a jar and cup from his limnthal and lifted water to her lips. "Drink. You're healing, but you need fluid to replace your blood."

She nodded, then sipped. After a few more sips, she began to gulp, and Will had to refill the cup. "So thirsty," she murmured. "Is he dead?"

Will assumed she meant the dragon. "It doesn't sound like it. I haven't gone in to see yet."

Selene frowned faintly, then focused on his face. "You're crying. Do liches cry?"

Understanding struck him then. "I'm not Grim Talek. It's me. William."

"Don't taunt me," she replied. Her voice was airy and tired but managed to gain some venom. "I'm so weary. I didn't think I would be this tired."

"Of course you're tired, you nearly bled to death!" Leaning forward, he tried to kiss her forehead, but she jerked her head back.

"What are you doing?"

"Damn it, Selene. It's me. Snap out of it."

Her face twisted into an expression of confusion. "You can't be you. You're dead. You went to Hell."

"I came back for you," he replied. He wanted to soothe the pain she was feeling. Will glanced over her body once more, noting the bloody condition of her dress. "You look a lot like you did when we first met, though you were the healer, rather than the patient then."

"What was my name?"

"Isabel."

Tears began to well in her eyes. "How is this possible?"

His expression was guilty as he answered, "There's a lot to explain. Sammy was hurt and we had to hide. I'll tell you the rest after we get home."

"Home," she murmured wistfully. "I haven't had one of those, not since you died." Lifting one arm, she placed her right hand carefully over her heart. "Is it beating?"

Will nodded, then had to wipe his face again. "You're still alive."

"I'm supposed to be dead. I was planning to die," she confessed.

She knew what would happen, but she did it anyway. A surge of anger shot through him, but it wasn't the time. "I'll take you to Rimberlin. You can rest there."

"No! I'm not leaving. I came to fight." She sat up, then nearly lost her balance.

Will caught her before she could roll off the pedestal. Bending his knees, he got an arm under her legs and put the other behind her shoulders, then moved her gently to the wall farthest from the opening to the nest.

Once she was propped up, Selene asked, "Why am I so tired?"

"I gave you a regeneration potion."

"That's going to make me sleep. I'm supposed to fight. Are you stupid?"

It was obvious that she was confused, but Will merely nodded. "Probably. You'd be dead if I hadn't, so you wouldn't have been able to fight anyway."

"You'd be surprised," she mumbled, struggling to keep the lids of her eyes from closing.

"I'm taking you to Rimberlin."

Her eyes jerked open, and a fierce look filled her gaze. "Try and I'll bite your ears off. I'm staying." She studied him a moment, then said, "I'm going to be mad at you later, aren't I?"

"I have no doubt of that," he admitted.

"I love you anyway," she told him. "Even when I hated you for dying, I still loved you. You still love me, don't you?"

"What a silly question," he replied. "Of course I do."

She smiled weakly. "I'm glad you didn't sacrifice those people, but it wouldn't have changed my heart."

"You're crazy like that," said Will. "I don't know how you do it. You might have forgiven me, but I wouldn't have been able to live with myself." He crouched down beside her, and when he saw her chin lift, he leaned in for a gentle kiss. The warmth of her lips drove away the fear in his heart, though he noticed a strange energy around her as he pulled away.

She watched him carefully, then said tentatively, "If I did something like that, you'd forgive me, though, wouldn't you?" When she saw his frown, she changed her question, "Or maybe if you didn't forgive, you'd still love me, right?"

"I don't think I could ever stop loving you. I know you're forced to make hard choices as queen, but you do it for your people." A loud boom drew his attention. Smoke obscured the archway, but while he was looking, a hulking shape flew through to land in the chamber. It wasn't a graceful landing, either.

As it rolled to a stop, he saw that it was dragonkin, another of the egg guardians, like the ones he had met the day he had fought the king. It was missing its right arm, but it rose anyway, pushing off from the floor with its left—until a thousand pounds worth of cat slammed into it. The creature never stood a chance. Already wounded and with only one arm, it couldn't keep the Cath Bawlg's jaws at bay. Evie savaged it, seizing one leg and whipping her head until the dragonkin fell onto its belly. Then, she leapt onto its back and her teeth found the back of its neck. With a sickening crunch, she bit through scales, muscle, and spine.

Unlike most injuries, which seemed only to serve as a mild warning to the dragonkin, the flesh torn free by the Cath Bawlg showed no signs of regenerating. Evie smiled at him, showing a muzzle soaked in blood and fangs happy to have found their purpose. Will turned back to Selene. "I need to get in there."

She grabbed his arm. "He said he doesn't need help. He's prepared for everything. Stay here. There's more of those things, and any one of them could end your life."

"If it's as sure as you say, I'll stay out of it. They won't even know I'm there, but I have to make sure." The silhouette of an armored figure passed in front of the archway, a giant man clad in demon-steel plate.

The warrior vanished from view a moment later, carrying a vicious poleaxe sized to match. "Who was that?"

"Tiny," said Selene with a grim smile. "He's the point of our spear. Nothing will stop him."

Alarmed, Will pulled away and got to his feet. Demon-steel armor or not, Will knew what kind of wounds a man could receive, even if his armor was unbreakable. "He needs my help, then." He camouflaged himself and smoothed out his turyn as he walked.

Behind him, he heard Selene say something, but the din of battle from the nest obscured her words. Evie was nowhere to be seen, so he went through the entrance to the nest by himself, staying to the left and following the wall.

Within, he found a chamber far beyond the size he had imagined. A better term was cavern. The opposite wall was so far away it was hard to judge the distance, and the ceiling was at least a hundred feet above. It wasn't enough for the enormous dragon he had seen to fly, at least not comfortably, but the dragon wasn't in view. Across the uneven stone floor, there was nothing to see but giant eggs in every direction, each one large enough to hold a grown man, or possibly even two. They were widely spread, with twenty or thirty feet between each one, but the nest was so large Will couldn't guess at how many were there. The shells were beautiful to behold, and every one a different color: sapphire, crimson, ebon, and gold.

Will almost felt bad about the fact that they were there to destroy them. Lognion had said that once they hatched, the dragonlings would fight one another to the death, until only one, or perhaps two at most, survived, but much of that fighting would occur after they left. Scattering across the world, the dragons would feed and grow strong, challenging one another while decimating the world.

Will had different plans, but first he needed to make certain that Grim Talek was victorious in the battle presently before him.

Between the eggs, a chaotic melee was being fought. Hundreds of egg guardians were there, fighting tooth and nail against men carrying spears. No, not men. Will studied the lich's allies until he was sure. They were vampires, and they numbered in the thousands. None of them wore armor, but they each carried a single spear tipped in black metal.

It was obvious that the lich had lied again, and Theravan and Mahak, his wizardly lieutenants, had been complicit. Grim Talek had built an army of the undead, and unlike the chaos of Androv's mob, the lich had kept his soldiers hidden and unnoticed, possibly for centuries. Will wondered how he had fed them. Had they been disciplined enough to use animals, or had there been more sinister methods used? He could easily imagine hidden pits, with men and women kept like cattle.

There was no time for speculation, though. Will first needed to see the war won. Afterward, he could think about a new campaign of extermination, if it was necessary. Despite their numbers, the Drak'shar were outmatched. The dragonkin were bigger, stronger, faster, and they recovered from almost any injury, except those made by the demon-steel spearheads.

Even worse, the egg guardians weren't stupid. Many wore steel breastplates, and even those that didn't understood the threat posed by the black metal weapons. They weren't lining up to be stabbed in the heart. Fireballs flashed overhead, incinerating small groups, and at first Will thought it was the lich's work, until he saw the ones being burned were vampires. Some of the egg guardians were using spells.

Grim Talek floated in the air, roughly centered in the vast space, his will stretching out to smother the magic of the dragonkin, but he couldn't contain them all. The casters farthest away were still able to use their spells, and they were the ones roasting the vampires that fought near the walls of the cavern. Will wondered what spell the lich was using to fly like that, feeling envious, but another thought rose in his mind that took precedence. *Where are Mahak and Theravan?*

The two wizards were nearly Grim Talek's equals and if they were involved, most of the dragonkin magic-users could easily have been neutralized. As things were, the vampires were suffering unacceptable losses. Some egg guardians were down, but most still fought, for it was harder to stab an eight-hundred-pound scaled monstrosity through the heart with a spear than some would assume. Minor injuries only pissed them off.

He spotted Tiny to the right, leaving a trail of destruction near the outer edges. The big man's weapon had an axe head backed by a wicked spike, but above it was a long spike that allowed him to use it as a stabbing weapon as well. Even the butt end was capped with a demon-steel spike, so he could reverse it and use the polearm as a spear when needed.

While the massive poleaxe had demon-steel for its axe and the spikes, the haft was made of simple wrought iron, two inches thick. It kept their use of the valuable driktenspal to a minimum, and the iron was strong enough to support Tiny's incredible swings. Will guessed they'd chosen plain iron for the haft rather than steel since it was less likely to shatter, but he thought spring-steel would have been a better choice. Even with a two-inch diameter, it would eventually get bent considering the force of Tiny's blows.

He marveled at his big friend's carnage. Selene had been right. The armored warrior shouldered dragonkin aside as if they were children. His poleaxe would sweep in and remove arms and legs, and when the swing was finished, he'd whip it back to bury the spike in another's face, or turn and drive the butt end completely through the ones behind him.

Claws, hammers, and two-handed great swords smashed into him, but it didn't faze the knight. The demon-steel robbed most of the attacks of their inertia, keeping him steady despite being hit by incredible blows. Both Tiny's armor and his weapon were burning with black flames, radiating deadly turyn that seared any enemies who came into contact with him.

That made Will concerned. *He should be dead already. That much void turyn would kill any normal person within seconds.* Tiny hacked down another of the dragonkin mages as he watched, then moved on. The black flames obviously weren't bothering him.

If Theravan and Mahak had been there, Will thought they could win, but without them, the vampires were slowly losing despite their numbers. It would take Tiny too long to circle the room, and in the meantime, the mages were turning an almost even fight into a massacre.

Will considered revealing himself, but he forced himself to wait instead, watching the lich. Grim Talek wasn't idle as he suppressed the magic users in the main portion of the room. Ebon blades of fel power spun around him, darting in and out to cut at the egg guardians nearby. Will didn't recognize the spell he was using, but it used the same type of turyn the lich had shared with him. It burned into the dragonkin, leaving painful wounds that hampered their movements.

At the same time, quite a few of them hurled stones, spears, and even vampires at him, anything that came to hand. The lich blocked them all with a rapid use of shields and fired back with a bewildering array of spells. As he watched, Will became convinced that at certain times the lich was casting more than one spell simultaneously.

Force spells were limited to one at a time, but theoretically other spells could be cast in multiples. Most people simply couldn't manage to do more than one thing at a time. Fog clouds appeared, obscuring vulnerable allies, while at the same time more black blades spun out to harry attackers, and the lich never missed a block to protect himself while doing those things.

They needed Will's help, but he could smell a plan in the works. The lich was holding his lieutenants in reserve, waiting for the dragon to appear and finish off the diminishing vampires. Will wondered what the two wizards could do that would save them once Lognion showed up, though. That part of the puzzle was still missing.

If things continued for too long, Grim Talek would have to face his nemesis without any soldiers at all, and from what Will could see, not a single egg had been damaged. Their shells seemed impervious. Numerous times they were struck by the combatants around them, but it didn't seem to matter. Whether it was a dragonkin thrown against them, a vampire's claws as it scrabbled for balance, or even a direct hit from a demon-steel weapon, the eggs were unmarked.

Will saw Tiny go down and started to intervene, but Laina warned him, *Don't do it. Wait for the dragon!*

He clenched his fists, but didn't move, hating himself even though he knew she was right. *I can't save everyone, and if the dragon doesn't die, I won't save anyone.* Bile rose in his throat as he imagined the egg guardians pulling Tiny out of his armor and tearing the flesh from the warrior's bones.

Impossibly, the black-clad knight rose from the cavern floor, throwing off enemies and reclaiming his fallen poleaxe. Blood and scales flew as he silently cut through his foes, stopping to drive the butt of his weapon through the heart of any dragonkin that fell in front of him. A juggernaut that wouldn't be stopped, John Shaw continued to fight, showing no signs of weariness or wounds.

Even the dragon-heart potions wouldn't let him do that, Will mused, wondering what trick they had used. He lost the thought then, for a jagged rip appeared on the far side of the cavern, a tear in reality. It widened, showing a sunlit field on the other side, but the view was quickly eclipsed as the dragon stepped through.

The battle was moving to its final stage.

CHAPTER 47

Without preamble or introduction, Lognion's vast jaws opened, and white-hot flames poured forth, bathing the world in fire. Will was on the farthest side of the area, but the dragon fire extended all the way from Lognion's position to the archway, and as it billowed forth it expanded to fill the place from top to bottom, leaving nowhere to hide. The nest had been purpose built with dragon's breath in mind.

The nest was still too wide, but the dragon's breath showed no signs of tapering off. Lognion began on one side and slowly swept the incinerating blaze across until the entire nest had been bathed in purifying fire. Will had several seconds before the cone of fire reached him, and he saw Tiny hit by the blast. The massive knight hit the ground and rolled behind one of the eggs, and then Will had to take care of himself.

He cast the cooling spell while simultaneously clapping his hands together, and the sonic barrier sprang up instantly. His practice hadn't been in vain, and Will's defense flawlessly diverted the flames. Despite his cooling spell, the air around him rose in temperature until it reached the point he thought his skin might begin to blister, before at last the flames passed on.

Will stared out at a room that was beyond anything he'd seen in Hell. Nothing had withstood the flames, except the dragon eggs, and even those showed the beginnings of cracks. A sense of horror washed over him then. The chamber had been made to allow a dragon to bathe the entire nest in dragon-fire for more than one reason. Defense was one purpose, but now that Will knew how impregnable the shells were, he understood why Lognion's eggs had remained dormant for uncounted centuries. The hatchlings needed dragon-fire to weaken the shells.

The vampires were gone, rendered to ash, and though the egg guardians resisted the flames, they had still succumbed. Their massive bodies lay scorched and still across the entire cavern. Some of them might still be alive, but they would need considerable time to recover, and Will had a sickening feeling he knew what their ultimate fate would be.

Once the hatchlings emerged, they would doubtless be hungry.

Tiny's armored form was still intact. While the demon-steel spearheads of the vampires had melted to slag, his armor had been sheltered enough by the lee of an egg to retain its shape. It glowed a dull orange from the heat while simultaneously blazing with ebon flames, trying to vent the excess turyn it had accumulated. Immune to the demonic turyn or not, if a man had been under that armor, his body would have been cooked to black char. Smoke was rising from every crevice.

If I'd been next to him, I could have saved him, thought Will sadly.

Lognion's voice echoed through the air. "For a moment I thought I was alone. That would have been a disappointing ending."

Will thought the dragon meant him, but a dark shadow rose from behind one of the eggs. Grim Talek had somehow survived unscathed. "I wouldn't dream of missing our reunion, old friend." The lich's body floated up from the ground to face his nemesis.

"Coming here was your last mistake," Lognion declared. "My children are beginning to hatch. The end you strove so impotently to prevent has come to pass anyway."

"You needn't have waited for me to release them."

The dragon showed its teeth. "I wanted you to see it, so you could taste your failure. Everything you've done has been a waste. If I can't kill you, I will instead savor your despair."

"Your brood may hatch, but I will at least see your ending, wyrm!" Another of his black, spinning spell-blades shot toward Lognion.

Will wondered why the lich bothered, for he'd seen what the spell did against the egg guardians, and he knew it would be less than an annoyance to a beast the size of Lognion. His eyes widened in surprise when the spinning turyn cut deeply into the dragon's chest, sinking in several feet before dissipating. Blood and bits of flesh were thrown out and fell to the floor, while the dragon screamed at the unexpected pain.

Grim Talek lifted his hands, and two more spinning blades appeared on either side, arcing out and sweeping toward his enemy from either side. A triumphant smile formed on his face. "You want to savor my despair? You cannot fathom it, but I will let you learn. Feel my pain first and eventually I'll teach you the final lesson, death itself!" Lognion tried to dodge, but he was struck by both blades, opening deep cuts on either side.

The power being drawn from the ley lines outside the nest was incredible, as much or more than Will had ever attempted to use himself, and considering the things he'd done, he found it almost unbelievable.

Grim Talek shouldn't have been able to manipulate that much power, yet he did it with ease, weaving spells and sending them at Lognion from every direction.

Roaring in fury, the dragon breathed out another blast of dragon-fire, forcing the lich to relocate. Grim Talek teleported to the opposite side of the dragon, but kept his attacks spiraling inward. Will noticed that this time they failed to do more than superficial damage. Something had changed.

Lognion turned, but not before the lich's newest attack cut deeply into one of his wings. He breathed again, and the lich teleported away. Again, the following attacks failed to draw blood.

The power being wielded by the lich made no sense either. From what Will could see, only half of the enormous flow was being used for the black blade spell. The rest was going…nowhere? Will shifted his vision. Even an artificial pocket dimension would have an ethereal counterpart, else the dragon and its children wouldn't be able to enter. A ghostly version of the room appeared, overlaying everything else. The eggs, the stone floor and walls, the dragon, and Grim Talek—existed in both. Tiny's body was the only exception, as an ordinary man made of ordinary matter, his body and the demon-steel covering it only existed on the normal plane. Will blinked. Grim Talek existed in both.

What?

As the battle continued, the lich teleported again, and Will saw the trick then. His ethereal self didn't teleport until a split second later, and when it did, it went elsewhere. The lich's ethereal counterpart had to teleport a second time to rejoin the spot Grim Talek had decided to move to.

The lich didn't exist on both planes. His lieutenant, Mahak, was in the ethereal, mimicking his master's moves. Somehow, the two of them were coordinating the black blade spell exactly, casting it in unison so that it struck the dragon in the same place and the same way on both planes. The result was that it did the sort of damage it would have done against a more ordinary target. The two wizards weren't able to time their teleports exactly, so with each escape, they were forced to match up again before they could successfully time their attacks.

The attack spell he's using must be designed in some way to let them work synchronously, but only while they're in the exact same place. Even knowing how it was done, Will felt considerable admiration for the lich's skill and planning. The attacks they were using might take a while, given the dragon's immense size, but eventually they would cut him down to size. Even a dragon couldn't lose blood forever.

Roaring and spinning in place, Lognion began sidestepping now and then, trying to dodge his attackers. The only thing he could do now was summon his elementals, at least in Will's opinion. If enough earth elementals started tossing boulders, they'd be able to disrupt the lich's tactics completely.

But Lognion didn't do so, though he seemed sure to lose if he didn't. Will had already taught him the folly of using elementals against a true wizard, when he'd stolen power from them and turned it against the king. Was that what the dragon feared? It hardly mattered with a ley-line nexus in the adjacent room. The wizards already had access to more power than they could use.

Stumbling to one side, the dragon seemed to trip, coming within reach of the archway, then he lashed out with his back leg, ripping away the edge of the arch. The access point to the nest collapsed, and the pocket dimension sealed itself. The archway vanished, and with it the power of the ley lines on the other side.

Lognion laughed, unleashing sporadic belches of flame. Grim Talek and Mahak continued attacking, but without access to the ley lines, their power was limited. Being undead, neither had a source, and once the turyn within the nest was exhausted, they would be powerless. The dragon had done something similar to what Will intended—he would starve them of magic. Lognion's wounds were ugly, but not enough to finish him, and the turyn left to them wouldn't last anywhere close to long enough to complete the job. "You think yourself clever?" screamed the dragon. "I have destroyed countless worlds, hatched many nests! This is only one of many battles I have fought. Before me, you are less than an insect."

Grim Talek snapped his fingers, and a bright light flashed, filling the cavern for a split second. It disappeared harmlessly, but as Will saw a moment later, it was only a signal. Tiny's still-cooling body lay close to Lognion's left front leg, and he suddenly surged up from the ground. His weapon wasn't in hand, but he held a black metal sphere in his fist. In spite of his size and the weight of his armor, he leapt seven feet from the ground and drove the metal ball into the cut Grim Talek's first spell had caused, right in the middle of Lognion's chest.

The dragon swatted him away, but it was too late. The metal sphere had ruptured, releasing a steady glow of turyn. Seconds later, a rock outcropping melted into the floor. It was close to where Will was hidden, and as the stone flowed away, he saw Theravan standing beside a massive ballista. During the early battle, they'd somehow gotten the weapon inside and hidden it with solid stone, along with its operator, who thankfully didn't need to breathe. The siege weapon was apparently enchanted, for when Theravan uttered a command word, the weapon fired, sending a demon-steel bolt into the air. Lognion turned, trying to avoid it, but the glow from his cut acted as a homing beacon for the runes engraved into the ballista bolt. It veered in mid-air and hit the mark. Eight solid feet of demon-steel, led by a massive, barbed head, buried itself into the dragon's chest.

Lognion screamed in pain, shaking the chamber, then collapsed to one side. Blood erupted from his jaws, and his body began to twitch.

Will stared in amazement. He hadn't been needed at all, and Grim Talek hadn't suffered even a scratch. He'd assumed he would have to help, and he'd intended to take the lich down afterward, assuming Grim Talek was vulnerable, but Mahak had emerged from the ethereal and Theravan was approaching. Guarded by the two vampire wizards, Will didn't face good odds.

I'll have to wait for another day. He started to step forward and congratulate them, but something clamped down on the chainmail behind one leg. Will almost jumped, then saw it was Evie. He tried to pull away, but she stubbornly held on, and since she was the size of a pony, she was hard to overcome. "What's wrong?"

Her appearance, along with his question, alerted the other wizards to his presence, so Will dropped his camouflage. As they turned to look in his direction the dragon's eye turned to focus on them, and then Lognion's jaws opened. Dragon-fire raged out, sweeping over all three and continuing on toward Will.

Everything happened in a split second. Theravan must have heard movement, and he reacted first, erecting a force-dome around them, but it failed without even slowing the onslaught. White-hot fire washed over them, and the two vampires became ash. The lich was smarter, and rather than raise a shield, he teleported, but his reflexes weren't quick enough. He reappeared a hundred feet away, blazing like a bonfire. He'd only received the slightest touch of dragon-fire, but it was enough to burn away his clothes and flesh, leaving only a loose pile of charred bones.

Will's sonic barrier snapped up to divert the flames as they reached him, and he made sure to include enough space for Evie as well. How she had survived the earlier blasts without him, he had no idea. When the fire vanished, Will stepped forward, sweating profusely, and started walking toward the lich's dwindling pyre. His two foes had done the work for him; he only had to finish the job. He needed to hurry before Grim Talek abandoned his body.

To his horror, Lognion's head lifted from the floor, and slowly, the dragon got back onto its feet. "I thought you were dead, William. What a pleasant surprise!"

A cracking noise echoed through the room, and Will saw claws pulling apart one of the eggs nearby. Turning his head, he saw similar movement in hundreds of other spots across the cavern. The repeated waves of dragon-fire had weakened the eggs even further, and the hatchlings were about to emerge.

It was time to run, but Will had already been to the deepest pit in Hell and returned. Something like this was what he'd been expecting from the beginning; he just hadn't known the exact form it would take. "Funny thing," he answered. "I could have sworn you were dead as well. What are the chances?"

Lognion was sitting on his hindquarters now, and he spit to clear the blood from his mouth. His spittle sizzled when it struck the ground. Reaching up with one foreleg, he clawed at the wound in his chest until he caught hold of the end of the bolt. Tugging, he tried to pull it free. The demon-steel emerged about two feet, bringing a gout of blood, before he stopped. "Damn it! Why the barbs? If they thought it would kill me, why make it so hard to extract?"

Will waved one hand. "Hello? I'm still here. You might want to wait and see if I finish you off before wasting time on such an unpleasant chore."

Lognion laughed, spitting blood and cursing as the wound caused him more pain. "William, I've missed your humor."

The dragon's head lashed forward suddenly, and Will reflexively teleported, placing himself twenty yards to the left. His eyes widened when he saw that the dragon's jaws held a struggling hatchling. They snapped several times, and Lognion swallowed the hapless whelp. His voice rang out again. "Now children, behave. Daddy's talking to a guest."

Will gaped at him, while taking a second to make sure the area around himself was still clear. "You just ate your own child!"

"Not the first, nor the last," said the dragon. "I think of you as a son as well. As you humans like to say, there's no meal as good as one filled with your mother's blood. The same holds true for other family members."

"Filled with a mother's *love*, you sick bastard!" swore Will. He was done talking, but he needed power to work. The turyn remaining in the chamber was too sparse for the magics he wanted to use. "Aislinn, Aislinn, Aislinn," he whispered under his breath.

"Same difference," replied Lognion, worrying at the ballista bolt again. "You should escape now if you have the power to do so. I prefer a chase." The dragon blew a quick blast of flame in Will's direction, and he created a barrier to deflect it. Lognion stared in wonder. "That's new. No magic or matter I've seen before could resist dragon-fire. How did you do that?"

"Tell me why you're alive and I'll tell you how it's done," snapped Will.

"Your idiot lich didn't know where my heart was. How many have seen the insides of a dragon?" Lognion chuckled. "The answer is no one. I planted the false information with the elves more than ten thousand years ago, and that crusty pile of bones believed what they told him."

"Why would they lie?"

"To save themselves, William. Everything in this universe quails before the presence of my kind. Now explain yourself!" Lognion had the ballista bolt halfway out now.

"I use sound. With focused vibrations, I can divert the flame. Your flames don't burn my barrier because there's nothing there to burn." Lognion sent another wave of flames at him, and Will diverted it again. "See?" Inside, he was beginning to worry, though. His sonic barrier used up almost as much turyn as teleporting, and he'd used up most of the energy he had.

Inside a pocket dimension, he would need a gate to exit, so he was both trapped and nearly out of power. *What's taking her so long?* Another blast of flame and his turyn dwindled even further.

"Waiting for something, William?" asked the dragon, still fussing with his chest. "Perhaps you have a secret plan as well? Maybe you think your so-called grandmother will open a gate from some other ley line nexus? That would be terribly convenient. With all that power at hand, you could fight—or flee if you've gained some wisdom."

Will's mouth went dry. Aislinn couldn't have betrayed him. It was impossible. The unbound favor guaranteed she would act as she'd promised. *Unless my favor conflicted with another, in which case she'd die, but she would have had to warn me before accepting.*

"Don't overheat that tiny piece of fat your kind use for a brain. Think! My nest is protected by a blood ward. Without the proper blood, no one can enter, except myself. Your surprise gate would have worked, while the way was open, but once it closed, the magic sealed this place again. You watched and waited, hoping your enemies would destroy one another, but you waited too long. Once I destroyed the arch, your fate was sealed."

Hissing sounds informed Will that the hatchlings were beginning to circle him, so he cast an elemental travel disk to gain some height. Again, he wished he knew the spell Grim Talek had used to hover and fly about. "You should summon some elementals," Will suggested. "It's lonely in here with just the two of us."

"So you can drain them? I think not." Another gout of flame filled the air.

Will canceled the travel disk. He couldn't afford the energy any longer. He barely had enough left in him for one more sound barrier, but one last idea had come to him. If it didn't work, he thought he might be happier letting the hatchling tear him apart rather than suffer Lognion's tender mercies. The ancient wyrm seemed to enjoy playing with his food.

Before he could do anything else, a light shone from behind him, and a rush of ambient turyn rolled in, like clouds on a breeze. Seizing the moment, Will created a sound barrier around himself and tuned it for flesh and bone. The dragonlings were all around him, and some of them had leapt for him. They regretted it.

A cloud of disintegrating flesh filled the air, coating both Will and everything else within ten feet of his barrier with a sticky layer of red ooze. The buzz in the air as the dragonlings half-destroyed themselves was a disturbing sound that vibrated in his jaw and made his tongue feel numb. Will barely saw the flames coming in the midst of the blood-bath, but he retuned the shield just in time.

Lognion's breath killed the wounded hatchlings and half-killed the ones that managed to get some cover behind the broken eggs. Dozens laid around Will now, smoking and dying. Hundreds more were still in the chamber, but he felt a small thrill of triumph. "Keep that up and you won't have any snacks left!"

The furious dragon switched tactics, bringing one of his huge claws down on Will's position. Not trusting his shield to stop it, Will retuned it for flesh again, teleporting just ten feet away at the last instant. He was rewarded with Lognion's pained scream as the shield destroyed some of the hide protecting the bottom of his clawed foot. The dragon swiped sideways, and Will repeated the trick. There was power aplenty now.

Glancing back, he saw why. The damaged archway was no longer there, but a gate had opened nonetheless, and it still opened into the same room. Selene stood over the circle, controlling the flows of power directly while blood drained steadily from her wrists. She stared at him through the burning gate with eyes that said she had nothing left to lose.

She was dying and there was no way to stop it, not without throwing away her sacrifice. Furious, Will turned back to the dragon and reached for the ley lines. The air was suddenly filled with lightning. It slammed into the dragon, and more branched out to find hatchlings around the room. Every living thing in the cavern was swept by the terrible incandescent power.

Moments later, it ended. The hatchlings still twitched, as did Lognion, and Will knew his lightning couldn't kill them. He did it again anyway, focusing the largest blasts on the demon-steel bolt sticking out of the dragon's chest, hoping it would overload.

The weapon was already burning with black flames, but his lightning didn't help. Driktenspal converted kinetic energy, not lightning or other magic. A sonic barrier might do the trick, however, given some time and effort. Will strode toward his foe with deliberate malice, his lightning filling the air to prevent the dragon or his children from recovering. If Selene was dying, at least she wouldn't die alone.

Even with the constant barrage, Lognion wouldn't stay down. Though his vast reptilian form refused to respond to his commands, his mind was somehow still clear enough to call on his elementals. Will felt a disturbance in the turyn behind him and turned, thinking he'd need to defend himself, but what he saw was worse. Three earth elementals surrounded Selene and though she saw them coming, she couldn't divert her attention from the task of keeping the gate open.

The Cath Bawlg appeared, leaping onto one and knocking it aside, but she couldn't stop them all. Before Will could waste breath yelling, their massive fists battered her into the floor, crushing her frail human body against the hard paving stones. Her improvised ritual failed, and the gate closed once more, leaving Will trapped with the monster she had once called 'father.'

Will turned back to face Selene's murderer, his heart filled with nothing but wrath. The power around him was rapidly failing, but he continued to focus it on the hateful beast that had taken his joy and smashed it forever. Incoherent rage twisted his face into a rictus grin, showing blood-stained teeth, and Will did his best to sunder the dragon into pieces with nothing but lightning.

His power failed briefly, but he remembered his idea from moments before—before Selene had given her life trying to save him. The pocket dimension might be sealed away, there might be no elementals for him to drain, ley lines to tap, but one incalculable source of power remained. The dragon himself.

In general, the first spell Will ever saw demonstrated, the source-link, was only used against weak foes. Arrogan had used it frequently against Will when he was an apprentice, and Will had used it often against normal people who weren't able to guard their own source. On occasion, he'd used it against sorcerers, especially those he knew lacked the strength to oppose him.

Between equals or near-equals it was unheard of. The will of the aggressor needed to be significantly stronger than the one he sought to dominate. Lognion was no wizard, but the dragon still possessed considerable inner strength to guard the vast power that fueled his terrible form.

Will didn't care.

He was within five feet of the twitching dragon, close enough to be crushed the moment the cursed fiend regained movement in its limbs, but he didn't wait. Reaching out with the simplest spell he knew, he drove his intent into Lognion's bloody flesh and sought the dragon's core. As a rule, a strong will made the source hard to find, but William found Lognion's in less than a second and seized hold of it.

The beast that claimed to be a part of the very pillars of creation lost after only the briefest of struggles, and Will began drawing on the dragon's source. Turyn flooded into him like a hot knife, and his rage turned it back against the dragon in the elemental fury of a lightning storm.

And still the dragon refused to die. Paralyzed and helpless, Lognion suffered intensely as the minutes ticked by, but his body refused to surrender. Unfortunately for him, the wizard tormenting him had no intention of giving up.

Over time, Will's brain began to offer suggestions that were able to cut through the rage and find a place in his actions. Moving even closer, Will created a sonic barrier tuned for flesh and pressed forward into the dragon's twitching body. The lightning never stopped, and the sonic barrier consumed incredible amounts of power as the reptilian flesh tried to dampen its insatiable appetite with sheer mass alone.

It resisted him like nothing else had, but with the endless resources of Lognion's source, Will kept inching forward, destroying everything his barrier touched. He intended to get to the demon-steel bolt still imbedded in the dragon's chest, for if he could overload that, it would blow them both straight to oblivion, but the damn thing was too high up.

Not caring to stop and try something else to reach it, Will let the lightning cease and focused everything he had into carving a bloody hole straight through the dragon. He was too far in to see anything now, aside from a dim light coming from behind. Rivers of blood and liquified flesh flowed around him, threatening his balance as he slogged onward.

Eventually, light appeared in front of him, and Will realized he'd gone completely through, yet Lognion's source was still in his grasp. Somehow, the dragon wasn't dead. "Why won't you die?" he screamed. Turning back, he prepared to do it again, but he saw something that made him stop.

Dozens of hatchlings had approached the meaty tunnel he had carved, and they began sniffing and tearing at the bloody flesh Will had exposed. Alive but paralyzed by the source-link, Lognion couldn't move to drive them away. Finally, Will found a reason to smile, and his white teeth appeared, centered in a face painted vividly red by dragon-gore.

Laughing, he created a travel disk and lifted himself up to avoid tempting the young whelps, but he needn't have worried. Lognion's children had found the tastiest meal in the nest, their father. More of them hatched with every minute, and invariably they found their way to the sanguineous feast in the center of the nest. Will watched delightedly as they slowly devoured the dragon, and thanks to the source-link, he knew that Lognion was awake and aware through it all.

The former king suffered unbelievable agony for nearly half an hour before his children found his heart and began to rip it apart. Will felt him die, as the dragon's source faded and slipped from his grasp.

Lognion, the tyrant of Hercynia and author of countless evils, finally passed into eternity. Will wished there was a real hell for the bastard to go to, but someone important had told him it didn't exist. He hoped they were wrong.

CHAPTER 48

Time passed while Lognion's carcass was gradually reduced to bones and tattered hide. Hundreds of hatchlings were swarming over the remains, and from what Will could see there were no unhatched eggs left. Given the size of the room, he couldn't be sure, though.

Some of the newborn dragons stared up at him curiously, and given that they were only ten feet beneath him, he felt understandably nervous. They seemed to have sated their appetites, but that was temporary. Eventually, they'd get hungry, and given that they were trapped within a very limited space, there weren't many options for food.

Cannibalism was a certainty, but Will would be the juiciest steak in the room once his turyn ran out. He wondered how long he could maintain the travel disk. There was no natural ambient turyn in the cavern, so the only energy available came from his source and the dragonlings. If he opened his source up to that of a normal person, he could potentially stay afloat for several hours, but the spell would gradually wear him down. The normal flow of turyn from a person's source was meant to sustain the body, not fuel external spells.

If he didn't decompress his source, he would run out of turyn much sooner, but he could surely do the same to the whelplings as he had done to their father. He imagined dropping to the floor and attaching to one of their sources. *If I create another sound barrier and use their strength to maintain it...*

It was a disgusting mental image, but he was already covered in blood and other foul substances. The jellied remains of Lognion were becoming dry and crusty on his skin and clothes. He'd literally taken a bath in liquified dragon flesh, and every part of him was soaked in gore. Beyond the biological obscenity of that idea, Will had a deeper, existential problem. Even if he managed to somehow slay every young dragon in the nest, he would still be trapped.

Maybe he could butcher and cook one of the hatchlings, but the rest would spoil soon after. Will had considerable amounts of food and water stored in his limnthal, but sooner or later he'd starve to death. "Assuming I don't kill myself to escape the stench of decaying dragons," he muttered.

The only way he could escape the pocket dimension was a gate, and no one could create a way in from the outside. Lognion's blood ward prevented that, otherwise Aislinn would have honored her debt to him already. Will wondered if the failure had killed her yet. He hadn't set a specific time frame, so she might potentially be forced to keep trying forever. He chuckled, thinking that she might somehow succeed years later, in the distant future, only to find him a pile of dried-up bones.

Looking down, he caught the eye of one of the hatchlings and told it, "This sucks." Its lips pulled back to expose needle-like fangs as it hissed back at him.

A final option would be to make his own gate. The blood ward probably wasn't designed to stop exits, but there were many problems with the idea. Finding the necessary power was the largest obstacle. Draining a large number of whelps might be enough, though he really didn't know how much turyn they could supply. The second issue would be trying to create a gate while his turyn sources were attempting to eat him.

Not to mention I've only done it once in practice, and that was using a ritual setup, he thought sourly. Even attempting what he'd imagined would require skill comparable to his grandmother's. Plus, there was a limit on how many sources he could connect to simultaneously, so unless a handful of the children were equivalent to their progenitor, he was still screwed.

With no way out, was there even a point to delaying the inevitable? Anguish pierced his heart when he thought about what awaited him outside. Selene was dead. She'd already bled herself dry for a second time before the elementals had pounded her into the ground. Will doubled over, fighting to control his grief as his stomach muscles contracted painfully.

He wasn't wounded—far from it. It was simple sorrow that assailed him so powerfully that even tears wouldn't come. His body twisted itself into a knot, and the travel disk began to waver in the air as his concentration started to fail.

This was worse than the pit in Hell. There, he'd expected a definite end, and he'd known that at least some of his family was safe. *They still are, idiot,* came Laina's voice in his mind.

"Sammy's lost her magic. She can't even talk or read," he whined angrily.

She's alive! So is your mother.

He couldn't deny that, but he refused to accept it either. His pain wouldn't allow for reason or rationalizations.

Tabitha will be shattered if you don't come back.

His eyes grew damp. "Shut up! Shut the fuck up!" he screamed, clutching his hair as though he could drive out the voice in his head.

Laina didn't respond, so he simply sat atop the disk, arms around his knees. Too tired to cry, he watched the milling dragonlings while he languished in dull despondency. The only excitement left to him was the occasional panic when he caught himself imagining what their teeth would feel like tearing through his muscle and bone. "An ironic end for the mighty dragon slayer," he mumbled quietly.

More time passed, and he found that the most miserable part of the present was the taste of Lognion on his lips. The crusted gore kept flaking away and would drift into his mouth and nose while he breathed, forcing him to spit as he tried to clear the salty sweet taste from his tongue. Casting Selene's Solution would have solved the problem, but he didn't have the turyn for that.

When light appeared and the gate opened, Will stared at it numbly, unable to accept what his senses presented. Through the ten-foot-wide opening, he saw Aislinn and the Cath Bawlg standing in the ritual chamber. Selene's crumpled form was in front of them. Fresh turyn drifted in, sending shivers across his skin. Unable to help himself, Will sent the travel disk closer, drawn by the inexorable pull of strange hope and the macabre sight of his wife's body.

The hatchlings followed, but he got there first, and after he passed through, a force-wall sprang up to block their passage. Will saw them scratching at it with sharp claws. Impressively, even the fresh dragonlings had the power to destroy it. Tears and rents began appearing in the magical barrier.

Aislinn urged him, "Name your second gate. Quickly." Her eyes had lit up expectantly. He'd planned it out before, but reluctance filled him now that the moment had come. Aislinn created a second force-wall as the first failed. "Hurry!"

"Hell," he whispered.

"I'm pledged to the Accord," she reminded him, as she had to. "Creating a gate from Hercynia to Hell will violate that. Is that still your wish?" There was hope in her voice.

"Yes," said Will softly. With two competing and incompatible compulsions, she would be forced to violate one, but it would be her choice as to which.

His grandmother smiled, then drew on additional power from the ley lines to create a second gate directly behind her now failing force-wall. When it opened, it was mere inches from the gate into the nest, and the hatchlings began to stream through to explore and conquer their new home.

The brute fact that Aislinn could create and control two such complex and demanding magics simultaneously, while also channeling the turyn needed to maintain them, was a testament to the legend of her skill and mastery. Those who understood nothing of the fae and their mortal origins had named her the Goddess of Magic, but they hadn't been far from the truth.

The unearthly vitality that had been ever-present in her form and features gradually faded as she maintained the two gates. Minutes passed and turned into a quarter of an hour, and after Will peered through the gap between the portals to confirm the young dragons were all gone, she let the second gate close. The one to the nest remained open.

Will's grandmother looked tired as she told him, "Do you remember our conversation about the lich?"

His mind was numb and mostly empty, but he nodded anyway.

When he failed to take the hint, she clarified, "Go through and collect Grim Talek's remains."

"Oh." That hadn't occurred to him. He'd assumed the lich was already elsewhere, making a new home for himself in a fresh body. The charred bones that remained didn't interest him, but he was too worn down to debate anything. Will went back in and studied the room, unsure how much time he had left.

He remembered where Grim Talek had died, but he went to Tiny's body first to confirm his suspicion. As he'd thought, the armor contained nothing but grey clay, which had dried and cracked from the heat. The demon-steel had melted in places. Some parts of the armor had been welded together from the heat, while others had fallen completely away after the dragon-fire destroyed the harness that held them on, exposing portions of the clay body.

Where the clay had crumbled, Will saw obsidian stones marked with runes hidden inside, control points that had transmitted the intent of the user and animated the body. It was with some interest that he noted the parts of the enchantment that acted as a transducer. The demonic turyn that the armor radiated had also served to power the golem's movement. Yet another example of Selene's cleverness. *Or Janice's,* he reminded himself. Either way, it was a brilliant solution to providing the necessary energy to keep the juggernaut moving. The blows of Tiny's enemies had served to keep the golem functioning.

The driktenspal had radiated most of its excess energy as black flames already, but through the haze of dark energy, Will saw something else that shone like a bright spark. It was located inside the helm, and after he pried the visor free, Will saw that it was a simple dagger, though it glowed with power.

There were no runes to explain its purpose. The iron blade was of a single piece with its twisted iron hilt. Will picked it up, but the residual heat burned his fingers, so he was forced to use Aislinn's cooling spell.

Carrying it with him, he found the lich's bones and summoned a sack from the limnthal to put them in before he carried them back to the ritual chamber. Aislinn was still waiting patiently, and when her eyes spied the dagger, she smiled. "You found it."

Will had no idea why it was important, but he held it out to her. "Want it?"

She shook her head. "I'm dying, William." Then she smiled. "Thank you."

"You were supposed to be in the mountains. Why did you come here, and how did you open the gate into the nest?" he asked.

"The beast that follows you came to find me." Pausing, she glanced at Selene's mutilated form, then said, "Blood is a formality, but flesh works just as well. I minced her organs and flesh until I had a pulp thin enough to use in its place."

As sickening as her explanation was, he had no room left for disgust. Tired and sad, he sank to his knees beside Selene, placing the bag of bones and the dagger to one side. When he felt Aislinn's arms around him, it was entirely unexpected. She had settled next to him, then leaned her head to rest on his shoulder. "I never thought this day would come."

"You really wanted this?"

"Every second of every minute of every day from the moment I sacrificed myself for him," she answered quietly. "It was the worst mistake of my life."

"But you saved him, and he saved many others afterward," Will argued.

"Saved him for what, to murder his friends and colleagues? Did I save him so he could spend the rest of his years hating himself? What he did tormented him continually, and what I did destroyed his heart. Was it love for me to suffer endlessly, or to remind him of it constantly? There are still souls enslaved as elementals. Wars are still fought, and evil persists no matter what we do. Neither of us deserved to pay the price we did, a price that made no difference in the grand scheme of things."

"You really believe that?"

A faint laugh shook her. "I could lie if I wanted, but the truth is a habit now. Cruel truth has been my only companion these many years."

"How long do you have?"

His grandmother slid one arm around his shoulders, then used the other to take his left hand and press it against her chest. "Do you feel anything there?" He didn't, but as a midwife's son, he knew it wasn't always easy to feel a heartbeat. He lifted his fingers to her throat. There was no pulse.

"I'm already dead," she confirmed. "My source disappeared long ago, when the last of my humanity vanished and my soul was replaced by the boundless, uncaring essence of my new home. My heart stopped shortly after you freed me. I can't shore up the walls keeping me here for much longer, nor would I wish to."

Will's grandfather had done the same, refusing to pass on for a short while after his life had technically ended. One of the gifts of third-order wizardry was the strength of will necessary to deny death itself, if only for a while. The lich's bones at his feet were a testimony to what could happen if a wizard decided to turn their talents to pushing the limit even further.

He didn't know what to say, so he said nothing. The desolate scene of Selene's death ate at him, but for the present, he was grateful for his grandmother's presence. She remained close, her unfamiliar hand stroking his head as if he were a child, but finally she broke the silence. "Before I leave you, I have a request."

Will nodded, squeezing his eyes painfully shut.

"Lay me beside my husband if you can."

After Arrogan had died, Will had given the body to Aislinn, and though she'd created the ring from it, he'd never known the fate of the rest of his grandfather's remains. "I don't—"

"I buried him in Branscombe, in a plot on the far side of the cemetery there, where the grass and trees have overgrown the graves. A small headstone will identify it if you search carefully, and at this time of year, you'll find the wildflowers grow thickest where his body rests. Put this beneath my head." She activated her limnthal, which he had never seen, and summoned the pillow Arrogan had made her, the one Will had given her after his grandfather's death.

The lump in his throat made it hard to ask, "What about the ring?"

"That was another evil I forced upon him," she replied. "He can decide for himself. I'm not worthy of forgiveness, so I won't ask it, but give him my love. I hated him and loved him in equal measure while I was trapped, but only regret remains in these final minutes." His grandmother's back, which had always been proud and straight, began to slump as her strength faded. She began to slide downward, so Will shifted to put her head on his lap.

Staring up at his face, she offered her final counsel to him. "Don't make the same mistake your grandfather did."

Blinking away confused tears, Will asked, "What mistake?"

"He was too softhearted to do what needed to be done. After I sold myself, he left me to suffer when he ought to have freed me. Remember that when you deal with your wife." Then her eyes turned toward the bag of bones. "I know your grief is overwhelming, but don't forget to finish Grim Talek while you have this chance."

"Isn't he gone?"

She shook her head faintly. "He's still there. I explained before." Aislinn's eyes started to close, while she lifted her fingers to her face and kissed them; her arm shook as she lifted it to press them against his lips. Then she was gone. Will caught her hand as it fell.

Remembering what she had said, he slipped out from beneath her head and placed it gently on the stone floor. He scooted over a little, then lifted the bag and placed it directly in front of where he sat. Now that he examined the bones, he could see a faint remnant of turyn lingering about them. Sitting down once more, he placed the bag in front of himself and took out the ward-cube he had made, then gave a warning to Evie. "I'm going to create a type of cage and it's rather big. Move over to the stair entrance so you don't get caught in it. This will only take a few minutes."

The large cat moved away without complaint, leaving him to his last task. Will hadn't thought it would be so easy. Without anyone to struggle or oppose him, he activated the ward-cube and used it to deploy his modified version of Erica's Abyssal Barrier. A rectangular boundary formed, similar to a force-cage, but with runes decorating it in long, swirling patterns that covered every square inch of the top, bottom, and all four sides. It stretched twenty feet in length and ten feet wide, and once he pressed his power into it, the world outside vanished, replaced by an endless darkness that devoured the light radiating from the runes around him.

The spell divided existence in two, separating them so thoroughly that neither had any relation to the other. Beyond the small space Will now occupied was nothing but an empty abyss defined only by nothingness. The only things that existed within his tiny reality were the lich's bones and the bodies of Selene and Aislinn.

Will addressed the bones. "I know you're there. Aislinn gave you away."

The lich's voice came as a whisper, for the turyn within the barrier was limited, and the ley lines that had been close by no longer existed within the small space. "This spell was a mistake."

"I had to be sure. Isn't this what you wanted?"

"You've broken off a piece of reality, but unlike our proper existence, this one has boundaries. Those edges expose us to the empty abyss," said the lich.

"There's nothing there," said Will. "And when you're gone, there will be even less."

"There *was* nothing there, fool. Now that it can see us, even the empty chaos becomes aware. It gains life as we observe it, and ancient things that never *were* begin to stir and gain substance. Once they look on you, they'll follow you to the ends of the universe. You need to dismiss the spell before it's too late."

"After you're gone," said Will, ignoring the threats. He began absorbing the turyn within the small area, denying Grim Talek anything to sustain his deathless existence. "You should have fled earlier, when you had the chance."

"I couldn't leave without seeing the dragon's end."

A flash of insight hit Will then. "No. You *couldn't* leave. You were trapped with me." The lich didn't answer, so he asked, "Why didn't you flee after I brought you out?"

"Your conversation with the fae queen was too interesting to miss."

Will's eyes narrowed. "Lies!" Aislinn had told him something before, and he hadn't thought it through fully. The lich couldn't pass through gates because it interrupted his astral link to his phylactery.

"She's dying, Will." Grim Talek's voice was almost too faint to hear. "She's still fresh and new—she can't survive the lack of turyn as long as I can."

"What are you talking about?" he demanded.

"Selene. She's like me now. She's still here with us."

"That's not true!" Will declared, but a sense of horror swept over him. The words she'd said earlier, his grandmother's warnings, and worst of all, the memory of that strange, cold turyn that had lingered around his wife when he had kissed her lips. He turned his eyes to the ruin of her body, but he couldn't see any trace of turyn there now.

"You know it's true. That's how she opened the gate the second time after you healed her. She bled herself to unlock the blood ward again, and after death took her, she rose to open the gate for you herself.

Lognion's elementals didn't kill her—she was already dead—they merely ruined her efforts."

"You made me swear to kill you, remember? Have you changed your mind?" Will demanded.

"Perhaps. There's never been another like me. I find myself wanting to see a little more. I won't punish you if you let me go. That was always a bluff, anyway."

"Nothing but lies from you," spat Will. "I know you were aware of what the dragon did to Spela. You wanted me dead."

"I wanted the metal I needed to kill the dragon, and I was willing to pay for it with your life. You'd have done the same."

"You're wrong there."

"She's almost gone, William. You have only seconds left to decide. She gave her life for you—twice. Do you intend to be her judge and executioner now?" As Grim Talek spoke, Will saw movement from the corner of his eye. A strange fleshy appendage caressed the outside of the barrier.

"Damn it and damn you!" he swore, then Will dismissed the spell.

Light flooded back in as they rejoined normal reality, and Will saw the traces of energy around the lich's bones vanish. Grim Talek had fled.

Returning to Selene's body, he couldn't see anything within or without, but he tried to straighten her limbs. Her head had caved in on one side and the front of her dress was gone, cut away so that Aislinn could get to the soft organs for her final grisly ritual. Beneath the open ribs, little remained. Her bare spine was all that connected the upper portion of her body to the legs and blood-soaked skirts.

If Will had still possessed any remnant of sanity or decency, he probably would have vomited at the sight, but he was long past that. He'd seen too many horrors, even before that awful day. Without the slightest degree of self-consciousness, he cradled Selene's gory head to his chest. His heart had clenched itself into a painful knot, but no more tears came. He couldn't even weep.

After a few minutes, he quietly rose and sought the stairs leading up to his city house in the central portion of Cerria. Evie followed on his heels, a silent shadow. As they walked she shifted into a humanoid form. "You won," she announced.

Will shook his head, and despite his internal desolation, he reminded himself he was speaking to a child, so he tempered his words. "I lost. Everyone loses in that kind of fight. Correction, everyone loses in every fight."

"Why fight?"

"It's a question of how much you're willing to lose. I thought that by fighting I would lose less than if I didn't fight. Now I'm not so sure." Pausing on the steps, he glanced at Evie, noting that her humanoid form had improved yet again. "How did you survive the dragon fire?"

"I hid outside."

Will nodded. The fire had scoured the cavern several times, so running had been the wisest choice. "Thank you for trying to save, Selene."

"It was all I could do."

The climb was slow, for there were many flights to be ascended before he exited into the closet under the home's main staircase. In the front parlor, Will grabbed a bottle of wine from the sideboard. His hands were shaking as he removed the cork, but he eventually worked it free, then he swallowed half the bottle, choking as he tried to gulp it all down at once. Putting the half-empty bottle aside, he left and went out into the street. Evie had returned to being a housecat and vanished soon after that.

Some children saw him and laughed, pointing and calling him a beggar, but when they got close enough to see what he was covered in, they screamed and fled. That was when he realized he'd have to clean himself before he could find help. No one would recognize him otherwise.

Using Selene's Solution, he cleaned himself and once it finished, no one would have guessed what he'd survived. Even the stench of his gambeson and mail had disappeared. He looked a little strange, wearing armor in the middle of the city. The guards rarely wore more than a gambeson, sometimes with a chain shirt, but Will even had mail covering his legs, and the black breastplate was definitely unusual.

Not caring, he walked to the half-repaired palace. Despite being clean, the guards there didn't recognize their prince at first. Grim Talek had earned him a reputation for elegant style and flawless grooming. Glaring at them, Will paused for his face to grant him passage, but it was the ominous thunder that broke from a clear sky that jolted the soldiers and brought recognition.

CHAPTER 49

Once inside, Will went to the bedroom. He needed time to collect himself before organizing some men to collect Selene's body. He told a guard at the end of the corridor he wanted privacy for at least an hour. Despite his instruction, a knock came at the door only minutes after he entered. "Not now!" he yelled.

"Milord, it's Janice."

Will hesitated, then opened the door. "Come in." She gave him an odd look, then entered nervously. Will waited, but she didn't speak. He ran out of patience after half a minute. "Are you going to start, or should I?"

Her head bobbed in a subservient gesture. "Forgive me, milord. I didn't expect your return so soon."

Will frowned. He'd never seen Janice so meek when they were together. With a sigh, he corrected her mistake. "Janice, it's me, Will. The one you're expecting probably won't show up for two or three days. It takes him a couple of days to replace his body and whatever else he does when he loses his old body."

She blinked, and he saw her taking in his attire. "Oh. Oh! I should have realized." Her mouth closed, and she looked around with some confusion on her face as her mind processed the information, then she gaped at him. "Will?" Her eyes were growing misty.

"Janice?" he replied, copying her tone mockingly.

Her expression became guarded. "Are you toying with me, milord?"

He threw up his hands. "For fuck's sake, Janice, it's me! Where's Tiny? He'll clear this up."

"He still hasn't woken up," she answered worriedly. "You're dead. How do I know it's really you?"

Worn and irritated, the last thing Will was in the mood for was convincing his friends he was who he said he was. "I'm not the lich. Tell you what, come back in the morning and check on me before I pee, will that convince you?" He was referencing an embarrassing moment from years before, and thankfully she made the connection immediately.

Janice's expression turned wistful a second later, then she hugged him. The breastplate made things awkward, so he pushed her away. "Help me get this off." A few minutes later, he stored the breastplate in his limnthal and gave her a better hug, though the mail and gambeson still weighed him down.

"Selene said you died, or worse. You went to Hell and didn't return. It's been a month! What's going on?" she demanded once the tidal wave of emotions receded.

"I escaped, Sammy was hurt, and I found out Grim Talek let me walk into the trap without warning me. I've been in hiding," he explained. "There's a lot more to tell, but first…"

"Why didn't you send a message? Something! Did you tell Selene?" She shook her head in response to her own question. "No, I've been watching her all this time—she was bereaved! What were you thinking?"

The words continued to spill out of her mouth until finally he interrupted, "I tried! Several times, in fact. Both of you were shielded."

Janice pointed her finger. "She tried to contact you. She told me. Why…"

He nodded. "I was shielded too, except for when I was trying to make contact. I couldn't risk him discovering I'd survived."

"Couldn't, or wouldn't?" she demanded.

He threw up his hands. "I don't know! Both? I gave up after a few weeks."

Tears were welling in her eyes. "You have no idea what it's been like, or what your wife's been through!"

Will's expression darkened. "I have an idea. Currently, I'm trying to decide what to tell people when I go to collect her body." Janice froze, and the two of them stared at one another for several seconds, before he added, "Can we just talk a little while before we start yelling? I've been to Hell and back, and that was easy compared to what happened today."

She began crying, which even given the circumstances was unusual. Janice was sometimes sentimental, and he'd seen her cry before, but she wasn't the type to dissolve into tears during an argument. Will's eyes took note of her swelling belly, and he reminded himself that he might need to be more empathetic. She pushed him away when he tried to hug her once more.

"Just give me a moment," she told him. Moving to the bed, she sat down and dabbed at her cheeks with one of her sleeves. After regaining her composure, she nodded. "Let's talk."

Will went to Selene's dressing table and claimed the chair she kept there, trying not to think about the last time he'd seen her in it, brushing out her hair. He dragged it across the room and put it a few feet in front of Janice, then sat down. "Want me to start?"

She did, so he spent the next twenty minutes explaining what had happened to him over the past weeks. They were old friends, so he told her everything, including his feelings at various points during the story. He did leave out his embarrassing near death while trying to feed Tailtiu, but that wasn't really important. He kept his trip through Hell brief and drastically abbreviated the weeks after, since not much had happened. Will spent most of his time describing what he had seen before, during, and after the death of Lognion. The ending was difficult as every word threatened to overwhelm him once more.

Janice listened patiently, only asking questions when he missed an important detail, or when she needed clarification. As he got to the end, her expression became sympathetic, but she didn't interrupt to comfort him. If his voice began to crack, she would wait quietly until he could continue.

Afterward, he could see her eyes had grown damp again, but she launched into her own story rather than make him wait. Will tried to get her to pause, but she refused. "No. You need to hear this. We can sort out our feelings after."

Her story made his chest ache. In the days after Grim Talek's announcement that he'd died in Hell, Selene had grown progressively more depressed. Having seen her just before the battle, Will had expected that, but what surprised him was the quiet dread in Janice's voice as she described her efforts to stop Selene's slide into despair. "She needed help, Will, but no matter what I tried, she wouldn't let me into her heart. It was as though her light went out and she couldn't see any more. She was walking blind in the darkness."

Will tried to emulate Janice's reserve while she'd listened to his tale, but it was difficult. He put his face in his hands and listened as calmly as he could, though yet more tears were making tracks down his cheeks.

Janice described their work on the golem that Tiny would use in the battle. She'd done quite a bit of the design herself, while Selene was the one who had performed the surgeries to implant enchanted gems into Tiny's body that would link up with similar items that were built into the golem itself. The puzzling potion use Will had previously observed had been part of his initial training. The golem's body was much stronger and faster, so until it was ready, Tiny had used the dragon-heart potions to polish his fighting skills under similar conditions.

Will asked her about the dagger he'd found inside the golem's helm, but she insisted there hadn't been one. "Whatever you found must have gotten in there during the fighting," she answered. "I checked everything before he left, and there was never a dagger in the design anyway."

He had trouble believing that one of the egg guardians or hatchlings had somehow cached a magical dagger on the fallen golem, but he urged Janice to continue her story.

"The last two weeks were the worst. Selene and I only talked when it concerned our work on the golem. She spent the rest of her time in Wurthaven, either at the Healing building or in your laboratory."

"Laboratory?"

"The workshop you built in the cellar," she clarified, referring to the addition Will had made to the house they had once lived in on the campus. "When she wasn't performing surgery or otherwise trying to help the children, she would spend her time there. She wouldn't let anyone near it."

He'd already told her about how Selene had died, then died again, so they both understood the implications. Janice went on, "Some of the children didn't make it."

"What does that mean?"

Her response was hesitant. "She was having a lot of success before, but over the last two weeks, her luck was bad. A lot of the patients, mostly children, died."

Will's heart dropped. "Do you think she…?"

"I don't know! I wouldn't have believed it." His old friend was as upset as he was, possibly more.

"Selene told me she'd figured out how the lich did it, but I never heard the details. Did she tell you anything?" asked Will.

Janice shook her head vigorously. "No, but Will, the ones who died—I don't think she returned the bodies. She told the families they weren't suitable for being seen. They were given sealed caskets to bury. It seemed odd to me when I heard, especially when I learned she was paying the families. Now I'm wondering if the bodies were really in the caskets."

Will's head hurt. "I think Grim Talek uses living adults when he needs a new body. As messed up as all this sounds, I can't imagine her hurting children." He got to his feet. "We should check the workshop and see what's there."

"Now?"

He nodded. "Grim Talek probably won't return for a few days, if he's planning to come back at all. Selene, I'm not sure. At the end, the lich kept telling me I was killing her. She may be gone for good. If not, she might be there."

Janice seemed reluctant. "John still hasn't woken. I need to stay with him. I rushed up here because I wanted to know what happened."

Will's eyes inadvertently went to her swelling belly, and he nodded. "You probably shouldn't be there, anyway. I have no idea what I might find."

"It isn't that," she argued. "I'm not ill. John will need me when he wakes up, and I want to be there. If you wait…"

Will shook his head. "You're right." Internally, he felt a fresh surge of guilt. *That's what I should have done.* His grandmother had warned him. *I wasn't there when Selene needed me, and now it's all gone to shit.*

Before he could step out of the room, Janice gave him another quick piece of information. "The staff all expect the queen to be gone for a week. She and the lich made a show of leaving for Rimberlin this morning. He wanted time in case he needed to find a new body after facing Lognion. That's the main reason everyone is surprised to see you back."

And she probably felt the same, thought Will. "I should be back before this evening. You said you were with Tiny. Where is he?"

"We share one of the guest bedrooms. He's laid out there. Just tell the servants you're looking for Dame Shaw. They'll know where to find me," she answered.

Will headed for Wurthaven, and after he left the palace, he smoothed out his turyn to make himself difficult to notice. He didn't bother with a camouflage spell as that sometimes made it more difficult to walk the streets. The combination often led strangers to bump into him, whereas just using Darla's technique alone meant they would just ignore him and step around.

He kept it up on campus since he knew most of the faculty. Today wasn't the day for small talk or questions. A short time later, he reached the house he had once shared with Selene while he'd been a student, before the war. It was empty now, and the doors were locked, though that wouldn't be an obstacle. Will walked around to the back where the cellar doors were located. Down there was his goal.

A chain and padlock held the doors shut. He'd had a similar arrangement before, but Will was pretty sure they'd been removed after they'd emptied everything out. The chain looked new, but what really drew his attention was the ward protecting the doors. *She really didn't want visitors,* he noted. The chain also told him the cellar was unoccupied, since it wouldn't have been possible to relock it after entering.

The ward would prevent most from entering, but Will wasn't most. He shifted his own turyn to match, then touched the lock and unlocked it with a bit of reflexive magic. He was irritated enough that he'd had the impulse to simply destroy both lock and ward, but it occurred to him he might want to keep his prying a secret, at least for now.

Down below, things had changed. Will had originally used the space to bleed pigs to feed his captive vampire, which he then bled in turn. The stone block for the pig was gone, as was the cage he'd used for the vampire. A long, wooden table now filled one wall, and in the corner was a stone box with an iron door and a chimney pipe that led up to the surface. Will thought it might be an oven at first, but when he opened the door, he realized that wasn't the case.

It was a cremation oven. He'd seen one at the Healing and Psyche building once. The top chamber was lined with bricks and large enough to fit a grown man. Beneath it was a smaller space with enchanted ceramic blocks spaced along the length of it. No fuel was required; a caster would simply apply the necessary turyn, and the enchantment would do the rest. The ceramic blocks would heat up to white-hot temperatures and raise the heat in the body chamber above. With the door closed, the top chamber was completely sealed, except for the vent that let gases escape through the chimney.

He was glad to find the oven clean and empty, but that meant little. Selene was an orderly person. Looking around, Will saw a long tool with a flat metal end used for scraping the ashes out afterward. Beside it was a stone box with a wooden lid. Inside, he found the ashes.

How many people's remains it held, he couldn't say without weighing the contents and accessing reference books to find out the dry weight of a human body. It depended greatly on the size of the people cremated as well. *It might be something else,* he told himself. *Just because it looks like a cremation oven doesn't mean these aren't wood ashes.*

Will couldn't think of a good reason to use an enchantment to heat wood to ash when one could simply burn it on its own, but he reminded himself that he didn't know everything. Reaching into the box, he sifted through the grey powder with his fingers. There was something solid within, so he lifted it carefully and saw it was a bone. It disintegrated when he applied a tiny bit of pressure, crumbling into dry dust. Exploring further, he found many more, though most were broken into small pieces.

He'd studied anatomy enough to know they weren't animal bones. They'd come from small humans—children. "Damn it, Selene! Why?" he swore.

The table was empty, but from the turyn traces, he could see she'd done considerable work there, though he had no idea precisely what she'd been doing. Unable to find further clues, Will closed the oven and ash box, taking care to hide signs of his search. Just as he was about to leave, he spotted a crumpled page in the corner behind one of the table legs. Bending down, he reclaimed it and spread it out on the table.

Selene had likely stored her journals and other work in her limnthal, but this page had been discarded, probably due to some mistake. It showed a rune construct and a ritual diagram. Both had been crossed out. Will didn't recognize either, though if it was an original design, that was to be expected. It was the notes at the bottom of the page that sent a chill up his spine:

> *Insufficient soul fragments leave the vessel unstable. Will redraw and balance for the next harmonic at nine since four was a failure. Don't know what material Grim used as base. Could make a significant difference. For now, carborundum seems sufficient.*

Soul fragment was an ominous term, and Will wondered how many could be gained from a single person. Was it one? Did it take four people to produce four? He wanted to burn the page, but he resisted the urge and stored it in his limnthal for future study. It wasn't her final solution, but studying the rune construct could teach him a lot about the technique she had tried to perfect.

"Did perfect," he corrected himself. He'd seen her open the second gate to try and save him, and though he hadn't realized it, she'd already been dead at that point. "The question," he asked the empty room, "is where is she now? Where did she put her phylactery and is she still in it, or has she taken a fresh body already?" He also didn't know what the requirements were for new host bodies. Did they have to meet certain criteria, and how did the transference happen? Will doubted they were volunteers.

Will left the cellar, replacing the chain and relocking it as he had found it. The ward showed no sign that he'd passed through it. He didn't have the emotional energy left to be disgusted. It was weariness and disappointment that defined him as he left Wurthaven. As he walked, he considered his next step, and his brain finally connected a few more of the dots.

Aislinn had reminded him twice to think about what she'd told him previously, and though he had, he hadn't fully processed it at the time. One line stood out now. *"His current body and the object that binds him here have to be on the same plane,"* she'd told him. Entering the pocket dimension would have required Grim Talek to take his phylactery with him, otherwise the gate would have disrupted his connection to his body and sent him back to the phylactery.

"It was the dagger." Will stopped in his tracks, then changed course. He needed to go back to the ley line chamber. He'd left the dagger there with the bodies. As he went his sense of urgency caused him to break into a run.

He felt like a fool. Recalling Aislinn's face when he offered her the weapon, he now understood. *She thought I was offering her the chance to decide his fate, but I was too dull to realize what she sent me to recover!* There had never been a reason for him to use Erica's Abyssal Barrier either. With the phylactery in hand, he could have simply destroyed it and ended Grim Talek then and there.

Ten minutes later, he was racing down the stairs to the chamber beneath the old Arenata house. At the bottom, he received a fresh surprise. Selene's body was gone, along with the dagger. Only Aislinn's remains were still there.

Will managed to find the energy to jump up and down while he practiced every foul phrase and vile swear he'd ever learned from his grandfather. Some of it he directed at himself, but most was aimed firmly at the lich.

Grim Talek had carried his phylactery with him, then hidden it in the golem's armor just before they crossed the gate into the nest. Will had found it and been completely oblivious. When he'd seen the lich flee, deserting his bones, the evil bastard had only gone a few feet away, returning to the iron dagger.

And now it was gone, and almost as bad, Will couldn't bury Selene now either. *Was it one of her people, or one of his that recovered the dagger and the remains?* It might not even matter, which bothered him more.

After he calmed down, he decided to store Aislinn's body in his limnthal. It felt somewhat disrespectful to the dead, but now that the others had gone missing, he worried someone else might steal his grandmother's remains. There was also the added bonus that it would keep her body from decomposing until he could bury her. *I should have done the same with Selene and the dagger before I left the first time.*

You were overwhelmed. You still are, suggested Laina's voice. *You need rest.*

Will's only reply was a growl as he left. Half an hour later, he was back at the palace, and after a few awkward questions, he found the room that Tiny and Janice shared. His overlarge friend was sitting up in the bed when Janice let him in.

"He just woke a few minutes ago and he's still groggy," warned Janice. "I just told him you're alive but that's all so far."

As Will stepped in, Tiny's eyes focused on him, showing shock for a moment before his expression went flat. "Where have you been?"

"A lot of places," said Will, trying to keep his tone light. "Hell and back, and today I saw the end of Lognion. That wouldn't have happened without your help."

Tiny lowered his brows. "Help? You're saying I helped? I marked him for the final blow."

"That definitely weakened him, but it didn't finish him off," said Will. "Not that it matters. I'm just glad you're doing well. Janice told me th—"

The big knight's face darkened. "Are you trying to claim credit for today?"

Will froze. "I don't really give a damn about credit. What are you so mad about? We haven't even talked about it yet."

"Screw talk! You weren't even there, Will! Now you're going to pat me on the back for being a good boy? Fuck you! You've apparently been playing dead somewhere all this time, and now you want to claim you did something?" Tiny's voice had risen to a thunderous volume, and his face had gone red. Will had never seen him so mad before.

Janice tried to intervene. "John, let him talk. You haven't heard about…"

"To hell with that, Jan!" yelled Tiny, causing Janice to blanch. "I was *there*! Not him! The damn place was swarming with lizards and vampires, not to mention that goddamned lich, but that was it. Even Selene stayed outside. I saw the dragon fall; I saw it *die*. Now this asshole wants to come in here and lie to both of us!"

Will closed his eyes and took a deep breath while his friend ranted, then tried to be reasonable. "I'm not trying to steal your glory. More happened after you fell."

"Aren't you supposed to be dead? I cried for you, not that we could have a funeral, but I felt terrible thinking you'd died," shot back Tiny.

"Sounds like you'd rather I was, since you won't listen," Will complained.

Tiny's voice was cold. "After I heard why you were dead, I realized it was probably for the best. I never thought you'd sell an entire city's worth of women and children to demons."

Will's mouth fell open. "That was the lich's plan, not mine!"

"But you agreed to it! It was only luck that the dragon killed them before you did. I was glad the demons didn't get those people, but you should have stayed in Hell. Selene said we should forgive, since it needed to be done, but I never agreed with that bullshit. It was pure evil."

Janice broke in again, "That's not what happened."

"That's exactly what happened," snapped Tiny. "The only reason I agreed to use the cursed weapons they made is because the dragon kept *him* from paying for it in souls." He glared at Janice then. "Why are you trying to defend him? You and Selene both keep apologizing for him, even though he's the one that left and put that damned monster in charge of things. I should feel *sorry* that he failed to be punished after trying to sell innocent people to demons? Or maybe I should feel sympathetic that he survived and was too ashamed to show up and help us today against the dragon?"

Janice's face crumpled as her husband directed his anger toward her, and once again her emotions got the better of her. She turned away, fighting against tears. The bedroom door slammed as she went into the hall.

Tiny realized what he'd done and stumbled out of the bed, struggling to maintain his balance as he went after his pregnant wife. "Jan, wait! I didn't mean to yell." As he passed Will, he turned furious eyes on his old friend. "You're not the man I thought you were, if you're a man at all." Then he was out the door, apologizing to Janice.

Angry and numb at the same time, Will left and went up to his bedroom. On the way, he spoke to the guards once more. "I'll take supper in my room. I don't want to be disturbed by anyone."

He's going to feel like an idiot after he cools off and she explains what really happened, said Laina consolingly.

Will didn't answer. All he wanted was sleep. Once the food arrived, he choked as much as he could down, though it was difficult with his stomach in a knot. Then he went to bed.

CHAPTER 50

Evie curled up next to him during the night at some point, and Will woke with her against his throat, while his nose was being tickled whenever he inhaled the bushy tail draped over his face. He sat up and regretted it. His body felt achy and feverish, and he wondered if it was because he'd overexerted himself the day before or whether it was a result of his emotional turmoil.

Either way, his body was fed up with the situation.

There were any number of things he needed to do, but he decided to stay in bed. For one, he didn't fancy what might await him beyond the bedroom door. The thought of facing more of Tiny's condemnation made him feel sicker, and none of his upcoming chores were pleasant.

Selene's pillow was there too, and he liked that, even though it made him want to curl into a ball. In the back of his mind was the idea that he could try and find her, but he kept that thought pressed fully into the shadows.

He rose from the bed and opened the door only long enough to give instructions to the servant who waited there. A mildly guilty sensation came over him as he returned to the bed, as though he was shirking some duty, but his dizziness argued that he might genuinely be sick.

Will climbed back in and pulled the covers over his head. When breakfast arrived, the servants had to knock for several minutes before he heard them. He ate what he could and went back to sleep.

In the late afternoon, he found himself awake, sweaty, and miserable. He'd filled the chamberpot, so he stuck it out in the hallway. Someone else could deal with it. Back in the bed, he was struck by the realization that he was paralyzed, not in the literal sense, but emotionally.

He was waiting for Selene.

Why? he wondered. *You know what she's become.* But he also knew she loved him, and he was haunted by her last words, begging for forgiveness. Now that he knew why, it made him want to vomit, but Tiny's anger had taught him a lesson. *I need to hear what she has to say,* he told himself.

There were other explanations for what he'd found. Perhaps the children had died naturally, and she needed the bodies for her research. Janice said that Selene had paid the families. He couldn't assume she'd murdered them, and the idea went completely against everything he knew about his wife. For years, Selene had championed mothers and orphans.

He had no doubt she was a lich, though, but was that necessarily an evil thing? What if she'd managed to create her phylactery without hurting anyone?

Whose body will she be wearing when she walks in? asked Laina's voice.

Will buried his head under Selene's pillow, inhaling her scent, but he knew the truth. At least one person had been murdered, and another would die each time Selene needed a new form. Grim Talek had lived for thousands of years already—how many bodies had he taken?

He spent the evening wallowing in self-pity and ate little of the food brought for him. Having slept so much during the day, he had trouble drifting off, so he spent much of the night staring at the ceiling. The empty place on his finger bothered him. He wanted to talk to his grandfather.

Some time close to dawn, he fell asleep, and he remained so until nearly noon, when a hiss brought him awake. Beside him, Evie was fluffed up, and Will saw a woman standing next to the bed, staring down at him.

Will jerked to full wakefulness and stared at the stranger. It was a woman bearing an uncanny likeness to his wife, but he knew better. Her hair wasn't quite as dark, the chin was too sharp, and the nose was perfectly straight.

"William?"

The voice wasn't right either. A male voice came from the doorway. "Is he here?"

She nodded, and the door clicked shut, giving them privacy. Will sat up, keeping the covers over his midsection. It wouldn't have mattered with Selene, but now, it didn't feel right. "Is that you?" he asked.

"You don't recognize me?" she asked.

"I know who you're supposed to be," he answered, staring at his feet. "The face is close, but…" He held his tongue. *It makes me nauseous.* "Did you do that?"

She nodded. "I'm learning. I thought I had it right."

"The nose, it had a slight bend. Your chin was rounder too," he offered, feeling strange.

"I never liked my nose," she agreed. "I couldn't resist the urge to fix it."

He met her gaze, and his voice broke. "I *loved* it."

Her eyes were wet, and she tried to embrace him. "I'm still the same inside. I'm still Selene."

For a moment, he almost melted, but the scent of her hair was that of another woman. Will flinched away, and she pulled back, instead sitting beside him. "Whose body was that?" he asked, hating the question.

"She worked at a dress shop in the market," said Selene.

Bitterness seeped into his voice. "She didn't have a name?"

"She did." A long pause ensued, but finally she continued, "I had to come back to you."

"Doesn't make it right to steal someone else's life."

"We saved the world, Will. We saved *everyone*. Don't we deserve to be happy? You've killed many times, and not always for the right reason. I still love you."

His heart ached when he looked into her eyes. They were blue as before, but too bright. The turyn around her was wrong as well. The warm human frequencies were gone, and a coldness had replaced them. Grim Talek usually imitated the turyn of the person he impersonated, but Selene hadn't bothered. "I went to my old workshop. I found the bones."

Selene's answer was immediate, and while frantic, it also sounded practiced. "They were already dying."

"Were they? I heard you were having a lot of success before the dying started. Were you still doing your best or did your needs change the equation?" he asked bitterly.

Her tone was firm. "Will. You know me. Those children were going to die. I couldn't have prevented it."

His eyes widened slightly. "You needed them alive?"

"It was painless."

Anger and an urge to violence nearly overtook his reason, but he simply stood and took a few steps to gain distance. "Does a painless death make it all right to steal their souls?"

"That wasn't necessary," she lied. "I only needed the special energies released at the moment of death. You have to believe me."

"I read some of your notes. Did I misunderstand?" He kept his tone level.

Selene's voice broke, and she began to weep. Will waited and watched, showing no sympathy. Instead, he began dressing. After a few minutes, she regained her composure enough to plead with him.

"Thirteen died so I could be here. Twelve to make the phylactery and one for this body. Is that too much to forgive?" He refused to answer, so she continued. "How many thousands died in Darrow during the war? Or what of the servants who perished when you destroyed the palace? You've killed innocents! Have I ever deserted you, blamed you?"

"We've both made mistakes," he agreed. "I've even killed a few in cold blood, but they weren't innocents. They weren't children!"

"I did it for you!" she screamed.

"You thought I was dead!" he yelled back.

"Fine! You're right! I wanted vengeance. I wanted the dragon dead even more after I thought he'd condemned you to a death in Hell."

"You were fine with selling the people in Shimera too," countered Will. "I *would* have died if I hadn't planned another way out, one that didn't involve sacrifices. The saddest thing to me is that your father may have killed those people anyway, but at least he gave them a clean death."

Selene shook her head. "He wasn't my father. He never was."

Will nodded, and they both fell silent while he finished dressing. His anger faded, replaced by empty despair. He started to leave, then asked, "Were you the one who took the body?"

She nodded. "One of my servants. I couldn't let it be found."

"You still plan to be queen."

Her face showed some confusion. "You think someone else should take the throne? Would you prefer it?"

"No!"

"Then no one else deserves my seat," she returned angrily.

Will's answer had a tone of finality. "I'm leaving."

"You're still my husband, Will. You're the prince consort. You can't just walk away."

"Until death do us part," he recited. "You aren't the woman I married, not anymore. If that's not good enough, get an annulment or divorce or whatever it needs to be called. You're the queen, you can do whatever the hell you want."

Selene's spine was rigid as she replied, "Queens don't get divorced, William."

He turned on her. "Are you threatening me?" The turyn in the room began to hum with the tension built between them.

She seemed hurt. "Of course not! I'm simply stating a fact. Monarchs don't divorce. At best, you get sent into exile; at worst, you have an accident. I don't want either of those things. You have to stay with me."

"Good luck," he told her. "I wouldn't advise trying either. I don't give a damn about being a noble either. You can stuff the land and titles, but if I hear that someone with my face is still walking around this city pretending to be me, the consequences will be dire."

"So you're threatening me instead?"

The look he gave her should have blistered her skin. "I *should* be out there right now telling everyone what you are. I *should* be giving you a true burial, but for some reason I can't do it. I have zero tolerance for the walking corpse who's been wearing my face, so I'm going to keep this simple. After I leave, I'm not coming back, *unless* I find out he's still wearing my face, and if that happens, I will be back, and you won't like the ending."

He started for the door, then stopped. "Where's my ring?" The look on her face as she summoned Arrogan's ring and handed it over nearly broke him. Only his anger kept his misguided sympathy from making him reverse course. Will slipped it onto his finger and left. The sound of her crying haunted him as he closed the door.

Out in the hall, the lich stood waiting. Their faces were mirror images, but Grim Talek lifted his hand and used a simple illusion to change his appearance to that of a nondescript man. "I'll make permanent changes tonight. Shaping the flesh takes patience and care."

"You heard us then," stated Will.

The lich nodded. "We'll have to tell the people something."

Will narrowed his eyes, noting the plural pronoun. "Tell them I'm dead then, I think that's what she really wants."

Grim Talek had centuries of dealing with every conceivable social situation, so he didn't press. "I'll remain as an advisor, but that's all."

"All I care to know is where my mother is."

"In the merchant's district," said the lich with a smile, then gave him the address.

That surprised him. "She was in Cerria all along?"

"Doesn't matter where, so long as you're sure the enemy doesn't know where to look. This made it easier for me to provide for her without giving it away."

"Lognion's agents had to be all over the capital," said Will.

The lich smiled. "Mine were always better. Go see her. The results speak for themselves. The dragon is dead. Your mother is safe." Will wanted to erase the smug expression from Grim Talek's face, and his features must have communicated as much. "Peace benefits us both, William," cautioned his enemy, leaving the threat unspoken.

Will turned away. He'd had enough. The lich called to his back as he walked, "She will be a good queen, William. You'll see. You're upset now, but she will bring in a golden age."

The words only increased his pent-up fury. Sparks raced up and down his arms, arcing to the rugs as he walked and leaving burn marks. Janice was waiting on him near the palace entrance, probably waiting for him, but she hesitated when she saw his face. Will met her eyes briefly, then gave her a single word. "Goodbye."

Standing outside the palace, he found himself unsure where to go. He slipped partway from his body, but most of the people he might have teleported to weren't good options. He settled on Sammy and vanished just as Janice came out and called his name.

EPILOGUE

Sammy was happy to see him return, so much so that she nearly squeezed him to death, but the happiest surprise was when she spoke haltingly. "M-missed you."

Will held his cousin out at arm's length. "You spoke!"

Emory was close by, standing beside the door to the house they'd claimed. "It started right after you left. She's drawing in turyn again too."

He was almost beside himself with joy. After so much gloom, his heart was leaping in the other direction. "Don't try any spells!" he warned. "Just leave your power alone for a month before you try anything."

Sammy's face was a picture of concentration as she listened, working to decipher his words. Will repeated the warning a few times, and eventually she nodded. "Don't."

He spent a quiet week there in Cotswold, though he did check on Tabitha a few times, watching her from the astral plane. It was obvious from what he saw that she didn't believe the story that the court circulated regarding his sudden death. She'd already been told about his trip to Hell, and had already thought he was gone. Tabitha played along with Selene's story that he'd taken a bad fall from his horse, but she was already grieving.

Will considered going to her and telling her he was alive, but his bitterness stopped him. *She's better off without me.* They all were.

He never should have left Barrowden, and if it hadn't been for the Prophet's invasion, he might still be there, living in happy ignorance. When the shield hiding his mother's location was removed, Will went and took her and Oliver away the same day. It took a lot of explaining before she understood everything that had happened, but he kept nothing from her.

They stayed together in Cotswold for another week, and Sammy's verbal skills improved rapidly. She still couldn't speak as easily as before, but he thought that with time she'd make a complete recovery.

To keep his mind off the might-have-beens and what-ifs, Will worked on a relatively simple artifice project. At some point during his recent life and death experiences he'd worried about what would happen to Tailtiu if there were no one to feed her and it occurred to him that one of the simplest enchanting techniques could solve her problem. In the years when true wizards weren't around, transducers had been devised to efficiently utilize turyn and reduce life span loss. They functioned as part of other enchantments for the sole purpose of converting one type of turyn to another.

So Will designed two devices using little more than short wooden rods and carved runes. One acted as a channel that could carry turyn from one person to another with a simple transducer that filtered but didn't alter the energy. The second was a transducer that would take the predominant turyn found in the ley line nexus at the mountain pass, and transform it to match Will's natural turyn. With the first item Tailtiu could receive energy from any willing volunteer, without direct contact, negating the pleasurable side effects of the process, and with the second she could draw directly from the ley line nexus and have the energy converted to a form she could use without needing to involve anyone else at all.

His aunt seemed happy with the gifts, for she was already beginning to suffer from several weeks of deprivation.

When the week was almost done, he had a more serious topic to broach. Will told Sammy he needed to move away from Terabinia, and she was supportive, but when Emory offered to join them, she politely declined. The young nobleman's heart was broken again, and although Will felt for the young man, it was ultimately Sammy's decision.

"Your family and your lands are here," she told the young wizard. Emory did his best to convince her, but she was adamant.

After Emory had left, Will brought it up once more. "You know he would do anything for you, right? He's head over heels."

"I know," she agreed. "It's just not what I want. Not today anyway."

They invited his Uncle Johnathan to come with them, but Sammy's father had fallen in love with a woman from Branscombe, and she was young enough to want children of her own. Sammy was a little sad leaving him behind, but she was young with a lot yet ahead of her. She had little fear of starting a new life.

Before leaving, Will took Aislinn's body to Branscombe, and with his uncle's help they found the small overgrown headstone marking Arrogan's resting place. Using the grave-digging spell, Will excavated the plot beside it and laid Aislinn's body there, putting the embroidered pillow beneath her head. Sammy and Erisa were also with him, but while Erisa shed tears, Sammy hadn't known Aislinn or the grumpy old hermit well enough to feel much other than a faint sadness.

Will lifted his hand and activated his limnthal so he could speak with his grandfather once more. They'd already had several lengthy conversations over the past week, but he wanted to be sure. "She's buried beside you. Do you want to see her?" He was offering to let the old wizard possess his body one last time.

"I don't think I could bear it, Will. Just set me free and leave the ring with her."

His eyes were filling with tears. "You don't think it will hurt?"

"I haven't been able to feel physical pain since she put me in this ring."

"Any regrets?" said Will, swallowing a lump the size of a frog.

"More than you want to hear, but I'm glad you gave her peace. I was never able to." There was a short pause, then he added, "I'm proud of you, William. I screwed up a lot while teaching you, but I loved you like a son, whether or not we shared any blood."

Will lost it then, crying and babbling in response, but finally Arrogan told him enough was enough. "Just do it, boy! Cry after!"

Somehow, he focused his attention long enough to set up a resonant vibration in the wisdom tooth that adorned the Ring of Vile and Unspeakable Knowledge. The tooth shattered a second later, and Arrogan's spirit was free at last. With shaking hands, Will put the ring on Aislinn's chest and they filled in the grave.

A few days later, they left for Trendham, the nation to the west of Terabinia. They left with few possessions other than what Will and Sammy had stored in their respective limnthals. Erisa's house had been razed by the dragon, and Will wanted to travel light. Though he'd been one of the wealthiest noblemen in Terabinia barely a week before, he took nothing from his former duchy. Technically, everything belonged to the queen, and he wanted nothing from her. *Owe no debts,* he reminded himself. He still had slightly over five hundred crowns saved, a fortune beyond what he'd ever expected to have before leaving Barrowden.

The trip took them close to Cerria, but Will insisted he didn't want to visit anyone, not even the sister who still thought he was dead. He would miss Tiny and Janice, but he doubted his large friend wanted to see him again. The big man had been very clear regarding his feelings. They followed the road north to Fernham and then beyond until they came to the northernmost city in Terabinia, the port town of Lindham. Janice had been from there, but Will did his best not to think about that.

From there, he bought passage for them on a trade ship bound for Lystal in Trendham. Sammy had been in favor of Bondgrad, the capital of the mercantile nation, but Will wanted to be as far as possible from Cerria. Traders from Terabinia visited Bondgrad frequently, and he wanted no chance of being recognized.

They spent a month in a boarding house in Lystal before Will succeeded in buying a small house on the outskirts of the city. From there, they began to settle in, getting to know the neighbors and trying to make a home for themselves in a strange land. The language in Trendham was different than the Darrowan they'd grown up with, but it was similar enough that they were soon able to manage.

Oliver began to make friends with the children nearby, and Sammy recovered her magic, seemingly without lasting damage. Her language skills were almost back to normal, and learning Trendish seemed to help with that somehow.

Although they didn't really need money, Will started thinking about jobs. People would talk if they didn't have an obvious source of support. He was discussing the idea with his mother when Oliver ran up panting and slapped his knee. "Hey!"

The boy had just turned four, and Will smiled at the interruption. "What?"

"Are you my dad?"

Erisa immediately intervened, "Olly, I told you already…"

Will held up a hand to stop her. Then he stared down at the little boy. "It was a secret before, but now that we're here, I can tell you the truth. I really am your dad."

Oliver grinned. "I knew it! They said I was lying!"

"Who said?" demanded Will, and then followed Oliver to reinforce what he'd said by repeating it loudly to the neighborhood kids.

His mother was frowning when he returned. "Did you mean that?"

"He needs a dad," said Will. "Who else is going to do it? I'm *not* going to tell him his father was a soldier that raped his mother."

"He already thinks I'm his mother. How will you reconcile that later? It won't make sense," she countered.

"We can explain you're really his grandmother, but then he'll probably ask about Annabelle. I don't know what to say in that regard."

"She died when Barrowden was invaded," improvised Erisa, before giving her son a serious look. "Are you sure about this? You can't change your mind later. This might be a lark for you, but it's everything for little Oliver."

"Mom," said Will, meeting her gaze. "You know me better than that. All we have now is family, and Oliver is family. I want to be his dad."

Sammy stepped out of the house, from where she'd been listening. "I'm already his auntie, so you're late to the party. I'll still have seniority, even if you call yourself 'dad.'" They laughed and then she added, "He's going to be shocked when he finds out his dad is the Stormking."

"Shhh!" snapped Erisa.

Will shook his head. "I'm no one now, and I prefer it that way. I just want to live like everyone else."

"You're crazy," replied his cousin. "Are you going to give up magic?"

He sighed. "I'll keep up my practice in secret, but that's it. I don't want anyone to know. Oliver can have a normal life. If word got out, who knows what sort of people would show up looking for me? That would defeat the purpose of moving all this way."

Oliver ran back to them, shouting as he came, "Dad, Dad!" Will thought he might have something to show them, but Oliver was just practicing the new word. He picked the boy up and put him on his shoulder, and the four of them watched the sun set over the mountains to the west.

The future might be ordinary, but at least it would be peaceful.

The story continues in the next series, Curse of Power. It begins with a new book titled:

A Wizard in Exile

Stay up to date with my release by signing up for my newsletter at:

Magebornbooks.com

Books by Michael G. Manning:

Mageborn:
The Blacksmith's Son
The Line of Illeniel
The Archmage Unbound
The God-Stone War
The Final Redemption

Embers of Illeniel (a prequel series):
The Mountains Rise
The Silent Tempest
Betrayer's Bane

Champions of the Dawning Dragons:
Thornbear
Centyr Dominance
Demonhome

The Riven Gates:
Mordecai
The Severed Realm
Transcendence and Rebellion

Standalone Novels:
Thomas

ABOUT THE AUTHOR

Michael Manning was born in Cleveland, Texas and spent his formative years there, reading fantasy and science fiction, concocting home grown experiments in his backyard, and generally avoiding schoolwork.

Eventually he went to college, starting at Sam Houston State University, where his love of beer blossomed and his obsession with playing role-playing games led him to what he calls 'his best year ever' and what most of his family calls 'the lost year'.

Several years and a few crappy jobs later, he decided to pursue college again and was somehow accepted into the University of Houston Honors program (we won't get into the particulars of that miracle). This led to a degree in pharmacy and it followed from there that he wound up with a license to practice said profession.

Unfortunately, Michael was not a very good pharmacist. Being relatively lawless and free spirited were not particularly good traits to possess in a career focused on perfection, patient safety, and the letter-of-the-law. Nevertheless, he persisted and after a stint as a hospital pharmacy manager wound up as a pharmacist working in correctional managed care for the State of Texas.

He gave drugs to prisoners.

After a year or two at UTMB he became bored and taught himself entirely too much about networking, programming, and database design and administration. At first his supervisors warned him (repeatedly) to do his assigned tasks and stop designing programs to help his coworkers do theirs, but eventually they gave up and just let him do whatever he liked since it seemed to be generally working out well for them.

Ten or eleven years later and he got bored with that too. So he wrote a book. We won't talk about where he was when he wrote 'The Blacksmith's Son', but let's just assume he was probably supposed to be doing something else at the time.

Some people liked the book and told other people. Now they won't leave him alone.

After another year or two, he decided to just give up and stop pretending to be a pharmacist/programmer, much to the chagrin of his mother (who had only ever wanted him to grow up to be a doctor and had finally become content with the fact that he had settled on pharmacy instead).

Michael's wife supported his decision, even as she stubbornly refused to believe he would make any money at it. It turned out later that she was just telling him this because she knew that nothing made Michael more contrary than his never ending desire to prove her wrong. Once he was able to prove said fact she promptly admitted her tricky ruse and he has since given up on trying to win.

Today he lives at home with his stubborn wife, teenage twins, a giant moose-poodle, two yorkies, a green-cheeked conure, a massive prehistoric tortoise, and a head full of imaginary people. There are also some fish, but he refuses to talk about them.